BIG BUCKS

P J KING

All characters in this book and events in this publication, other than those clearly in the public domain, are fictional and any resemblance to real persons living or dead, events or locales is purely co-incidental.

This book is sold subject to the condition that it shall not by way of trade or otherwise, be lent out, resold, hired out, stored in a retrieval system, or by any other means circulated without the publisher's prior written consent, or in any form of binding or cover than that in which it is published and without a similar condition being imposed on the subsequent purchaser.

Copyright © 2015 P J KING

All rights reserved.
ISBN: 10 151199603x
ISBN-13: 978-1511996037

DEDICATION

For Steve with love

ALSO BY THIS AUTHOR

Rough Ride © 2013

ACKNOWLEDGMENTS

I should like to thank my patient and tolerant family for putting up with me. Yes, I have an inordinately busy day job, and so, writing has to take second stage, and often the only available time I have, is during the unsociable small hours between midnight and the early morning. Thank goodness that I need little sleep - as equally, like **Rough Ride**, the sequel, **Big Bucks** is another lengthy tome.

My grateful thanks to my good friend Sam Lintott, for talking through the plot lines with me, (often during her lesson times) and agonising over the minutiae and the third book in the series, which is germinating as I write this acknowledgement.

To Sharon Smallridge, Christine Sparrowhawk, Rosie and Steve Andrews for proof reading the text - not my strongest point, as I write completely from the hip! The story line just explodes and I hammer it out on the keyboard!

For the technical stuff; to Mike Byers - the mega-vet extraordinaire. Jen Sadler, my great friend and patron for the racing information. Please don't ask me where I get the sex stuff from!

James Willis of Spiffing Covers for another great cover.

To all my fabulous friends (too many to mention and you know you are!) who've been loyal and spurred me on, and also to all those other Indie authors. I've loved the journey - enjoy yours!

Cast of Characters

Felix Stephenson — Event rider

Hattie Blake — Felix's groom

Alice Cavaghan — Vet and Felix's partner

Roxy Le Feuvre .... Bimbo, It Girl, Glamour Model

Aiden Hamilton .... Married to Roxy, celebrity chef

Stephanotis and Delphinium ..... Aiden and Roxy's children

Chrissie Keyes .... Aiden's P.A

Sebastian Locke .... Dressage rider stabled with Felix

Leo Cooper .... Seb's partner

Dougie Gilmour .... Commentator and old chum of Felix's

Roberto Bellomi .... Dougie's partner

Max Goldsmith .... London villain a close friend of Roxy's

Mr Sylvester .... Max's benefactor

Anna .... Max's Romanian muse

Jilly .... Max's first love

Margaret and Eric .... Jilly's parents

Sonia (deceased) .... Anna's friend

Sandy Maclean-Templeton .... Barrister

Mark Templeton......... Estate Manager at Fittlebury Hall

Lady Veronica Hartwell .... owns Fittlebury Hall

Will Fry .... the game keeper

Nina .... Lady Veronica's companion

Charles and Jennifer Parker-Smythe... main sponsors of Felix

Dulcie and Nancy .... Jennifer's grooms

Frankie .... Dulcie's sister

Colin Allington .... EstateAgent and part of syndicate

Grace Allington ....Colin's wife

Archie Allington ....Colin and Grace's son

George and Evelyn Bradford ....Grace's parents

Katherine and Jeremy Gordon ....part of the syndicate

Chloe and John .... friends and advisors of the syndicate

Ronnie French .... A villain

Sandra French ....Ronnie's wife

Tash .... Ronnie's tart

Frank ....A villain

Ernie .... A villain

Nigel Brown ....Private Detective

Andrew Napier.................Senior vet at Napier &Travers

Catilin Montague......................... Andrew's girlfriend

Julia Napier ....Andrew's ex wife

Oli Travers .... Vet and Partner atNapier &Travers

Theo Osborton .... Junior Assistant Vet

Paulene Godwin ....Practice Manage at Vets

Dick and Janice Macey .... run the local pub - the Fox

Dick Lewington/Frank Knap............old codgers in the pub

Fatima and Ravi Gupta ....Run and own the village shop

Kylie Simmons ....Part-time Groom and super-bitch

Ryan Clemence ....leading event rider

Brett ....Ryan's Groom

Lisa and Mike ....close friends of Roxy and Aiden

Simon and Ruth.................friends of Mark Templeton

Cheryl and Naomi ....identical twins employed by Max

Elizabeth Collins ....Branch manager at Estate Agents

Libby Newsome ....A floozy who rides with the hunt

Alan ....Aiden's Architect

Victor ....Maitre D at the Mill

Phillip ....Sommelier at the Mill

Kirstie ....Manageress at the Spa

Caleb Akkerman ....Max's Solicitor

Terry ....Max's right hand man

Sam .... Terry's second in command

BIG BUCKS

PROLOGUE

Roxy allowed the robe to slip seductively from her bare shoulders. Snakelike, it slithered onto the floor in a pool of shimmering iridescent silk. Stepping lightly onto the couch she rolled lazily onto her tummy, wriggling her lithe body comfortably into position. The masseur, who had kept his eyes cast discreetly down, picked up a small towel and laid it reverently over her pert buttocks before starting work on her taut neck muscles. As his strong hands worked their magic and the soft drift of hypnotic music played in the background, Roxy felt herself starting to relax and enjoy the release of the morning's tension. God knew it had been a bitch of a day already and it was only just after one o'clock.

Aiden was seriously beginning to annoy her. He had some hare-brained scheme about opening a trés chic restaurant in the country, as some kind of follow up to his latest green living push. Okay, she had to admit that the organic thing had been a great idea; everyone these days was conscious about what they ate, and yes, his restaurants in London had been doing well, but one in the country? How would he be able to keep his finger on the pulse down there? Moreover, how would she? It annoyed her just thinking about it.

"Just relax Madam, if you will," said the masseur quietly, as his slippery fingers continued their expert kneading along her toned backbone, "that's better. Just let all the tension fade away."

"Hmmm, yes, yes, that's very good Henry," Roxy purred, flexing her neck in a long arc, "Very good."

Willing herself to stay calm, she let his hypnotic hands take over and tried to lose herself in the restful music, but irritatingly her mind strayed back to the screaming row with Aiden earlier that day. He had been so damned pig-headed about it all. He didn't seem to have taken her into account at all. She was in the process of launching a new range of sexy lingerie; it was taking up a lot of her time, and time she needed to spend here in town, not down in the bloody country as a celebrity trophy to hang on his arm plugging his new venture. Still, she admitted grudgingly, Aiden was a celebrity in his own right, and together they did make a totally glamorous and steamingly hot couple. She supposed it wouldn't hurt, and it could be good for her own image, but if he thought she was going to bring out a range of wellies, he had another think coming.

"Ooooo Henry!" she squealed, as a delicious tingling shot across her buttocks and down into her groin, making her back arch sharply into the air.

"Does Madam enjoy that?" asked Henry innocently, his oily hands pushing down and sinking deeper exploring intensively between the cheeks of her bottom.

Roxy was fast forgetting all about Aiden and his organic greens. Lost in an overwhelming sense of lust, she rolled over, "Why not do the front now?" she suggested, parting her legs and licking her lips.

"My pleasure Madam," Henry acquiesced and, with a sly smile began work on her thighs.

CHAPTER 1

Despite his early start, the sun was already drilling a tattoo of strong rays along the rippling muscles of Felix's broad shoulders. His bronzed upper arms gleamed with sweat as he deftly worked the elegant horse through its paces in the arena, adroitly turning this way and that until he was satisfied with its performance. Gliding the powerful creature effortlessly into walk, he leant forward and patted the foaming chestnut neck. Flexing his own shoulders, he rolled his head back, and wiped his forehead, licking his dry lips - strange that he only ever felt hot when he stopped concentrating on the riding. He reached down, unlatched the school gate and slowly walked the horse back along the cinder track towards the stables.

It was a glorious June morning, the promise of a fine day ahead with a cloudless blue sky and not a hint of a breeze to tousle the leaves of the grand old oaks in the park. The Sussex downs rolled away in the distance, decorated with a patchwork of hillside farms, and swathes of burgeoning crops on their lower edges. Over the fields, work had already begun on the cross country course being built for next year's affiliated horse trials to be held here at the Hall and a bright yellow JCB and dumper stood idle waiting for the drivers to begin their day.

Felix was, without a doubt, one of the most gorgeous looking guys on the eventing circuit this season. He was tall and lean with messy white blond hair, a fine angular face, square cut jaw, and the biggest, bluest naughtiest eyes – in fact he wouldn't have looked out of place flexing his naked pecs and snogging a stunning girl for a perfume ad in Vogue. But Felix wasn't just a pretty face. As dazzling as he was to look at, he was also a beautiful and skilled rider. He'd ridden since he was a little boy and had a natural a graceful ease and elegance which many admired but few achieved. Brought up through the ranks of the pony club he'd tried all the equestrian disciplines but his favourite had always been eventing. He'd represented his school in the National Series, and then later ridden as an Under 18, right up until he left to go to study at Hartpury College for a Degree in Equine Studies, which he'd passed with honours. After keeping his head down in academia for those years, he dipped his toe into other equine establishments, and now at the grand old age of 25, he had finally decided that his equine career was to be in producing and riding eventers.

All in all, Felix was pleased with the way things had finally turned out for him. The previous summer he'd come to work for Charles and Jennifer Parker-Smythe for the hunting season - although ironically it was the season that was never to happen for Felix, after Jennifer's catastrophic first day out. Nonetheless, despite the initial disaster and his disappointment when he realised that his ambitions for a rollercoaster, hedge-hopping few months were not to be - he had, in the end, managed a few good days out with the local pack – the Fittlebury and Cosham. Despite all the initial dramas, there had been many upsides too, and over the last year he'd met a lot of people and made some great friends. Besides hooking up with the lovely Alice, the second best thing that had happened was that the Parker-Smythes had offered to sponsor him and formed a syndicate to buy a seriously talented event horse. Since then, spurred on by their support and his own enthusiasm, he'd found himself some more excellent patrons who were prepared to back him with other horses and the dream of having his own yard had become a reality. It had to be said, that a lot of the female clients, and several of the men too, were more than a little in love with him. Felix was a siren with his film-star looks and was a natural flirt - which was part of his charm - but he always went home to Alice.

The yard itself was ideal and perfectly situated just outside the village and rented from the Fittlebury Hall Estate. Although at first he had been a bit in awe of Lady Veronica, who not only owned the estate but lived in situ in the Hall, he soon discovered he actually got on well with the old girl. She was an aristo of the old class, well into her 70s now, and wore a curious mix of expensive Jaeger skirts and tatty Hunter wellies with quilted jackets, which more often than not were fastened up the wrong way. Her husband had died years before and she lived alone in the beautiful old Tudor house with only the enigmatic Nina as her live in companion. Outwardly she was totally eccentric and batty, but delightfully so, and she certainly had all her marbles and you didn't mess with her. In reality Felix didn't have a lot to do with her; occasionally she just popped her head around a stable door, with her pure white hair and periwinkle blue eyes twinkling at him, her dogs scooting about her legs, barking the odd vague remark and then wandering off. Other than that, he hardly saw her, which suited him just fine.

It was Mark Templeton who ran the show. He was the Estate Manager, and was a savvy and straight-talking guy who took no nonsense - but he was fair too. The old stable yard, still in its original state in many parts, had needed a lot of work. Lady V only had a few broodmares herself now, all of which were sent away to have their foals, returning a few months later to live out in the paddocks. As a consequence the stableyard itself was pretty obsolete as far as the estate was concerned and had become fairly run down. But it had a quaint charm with its weathered red brick walls and lofty vaulted roofs which were cool in the summer and snug in the colder weather. It made economic sense to let it out, but Mark was adamant that the day to day ambience of the estate, and indeed Lady V herself, were not to be disturbed by a lot of random people continually wandering about willy-nilly all over the place. That suited Felix just fine. He only wanted to produce serious competition horses, and didn't want happy hackers either. Mark had agreed that, as well as the repairs, the estate would fund the cost of an arena, working on the premise that this would add value to the property. So not only was the yard now looking damned smart with its traditional old stables all tarted up, but he had a huge all-weather surface discreetly placed well out of sight of the Hall, which was big enough to put up a course of show jumps as well as work the horses on the flat. As part of the diversification plans for the estate, and to bring in much needed revenue, next year Fittlebury Hall was to host its first affiliated British Eventing horse trials. Work was already well underway with the jumps, and the course designer was also putting in some smaller tracks to lure in clients for schooling, as another way of increasing the estate's return on their investment; although Mark would be strictly regulating these days, so as to have the least infringement on Lady V's privacy. For Felix it would mean he would have a cross country course on his doorstep, which couldn't have been more perfect.

The icing on the cake was when Mark had offered Felix and Alice his cottage on the estate, which he'd vacated the previous year. It was a lovely old place, a low-slung traditional tile-hung cottage, and a perfect stone's throw from the yard. Although Alice was probably just as busy in her job as he was in his, they had both tried to make time to do the place up and make it their own. They had spent their evenings with paintbrushes and bottles of wine, sloshing more paint on each other than they did on the walls, and then falling into bed laughing. Now they could both call it home, somewhere to hang their hats at the end of a long day and, although sadly neither of them had much time to do anything with the garden, other than to mow the grass, Felix felt at long last he knew which direction his life was going.

The sun was drenching the yard as Felix ambled back from the school, the gaudy hanging baskets hung limply from the walls, baking in the rising heat of the day. He clattered over the cobbles and slithered off, his long frame landing lightly, and he pulled the horse's ears fondly, scrabbling around in his pocket for a Polo. He had great hopes for this horse, which belonged to a lovely client called Sheena, whose daughter had given up riding and gone off travelling. So far they'd had a good season in the basic classes, and chalked up a modicum of success. Felix knew that there was so much more loitering under the bonnet. The horse was like a Ferrari to ride and just as sensitive - you just had to handle him with care.

"How was Woody?" called an enthusiastic voice, "he looks like he's worked hard."

Felix turned to see Hattie coming across the yard towards him, "Great, he gets better every day!" he grinned back at her, "He's gonna be a star!"

Hattie smiled dreamily into Felix's eyes, it was hard not to, "Well, he's not easy, but he's butter in your hands."

"Flatterer!" laughed Felix easily. He handed her the reins, "Take him for me would you sweetie, I need a pee!"

Hattie watched his departing back. She loved working here, just her and Felix and the horses. She'd dreamt all her life of having a job like this. She wasn't clever at school, but she was a grafter and she'd always loved horses. All through her school years she'd helped out in a yard in Cosham, the village next to Fittlebury, where she lived. Every night, every weekend and every school holiday she had doggedly pedalled on her ancient bike to muck out, clean tack and be a dogsbody, just so that she could be around the horses and be allowed to ride. She'd left school with no prospect of a job and gone on Job Seeker's Allowance, trailing from one dismal soul-destroying interview to another. Eventually she ended up working in an Irish dealing yard near Billingshurst, where the pay was rubbish and the hours longer than a decade. She was treated like total shit and had fallen off the barely broken horses more times than she could remember. Then she had seen this advert in the local paper for an eventing groom; she'd never thought she'd get it, but to her amazement she had, and she'd never looked back. Felix had been really patient with her, as these horses were totally different from the ones she was used to, but she was growing in confidence every day, and whilst she couldn't school them or do any of the technical work, she was ace at hacking out and pretty adept at the behind the scenes stuff.

Woody stomped crossly in the wash-down box, his hooves making a dull thud on the rubber mats as he waited for Hattie to turn on the shower. He laid his ears back crossly as the jets of water cascaded in rivulets over his sweaty body, whilst she gave him a thorough soaking, adeptly scraping off the excess water and then conscientiously checked his legs. She sponged his ginger face and ears tenderly before turning on the infra-red lamps to dry him off, although they were hardly needed in this heat. Hattie loved this part. To her the care of the horse was as important as the riding, and Woody was loving every nanosecond, even though he was pretending to hate it.

There was a crunch of gravel as car tyres crept down the drive and then swung onto the cobbles of the yard. A large 4x4 Toyota had stopped outside the tack room come tea room and a tall, slim young woman slipped out of the driver's seat. She had long fair hair, cascading out of a high pony tail, emphasising her high cheekbones and striking features. She stood for a moment in the yard looking about her, her hands shoved deep into her long shorts.

Felix, who'd obviously seen her arrive, noiselessly crept out from the tack room and tiptoed up behind her, throwing his arms around her and cupped both her breasts in his hands, burrowing his face into her neck and smothering it with kisses.

The girl leapt around "F'lix, you beast! You frightened the life out of me!"

"Doll, I just can't help myself!" he laughed, "Got time for a cuppa?"

"A quickie then, I've only hooked by to drop off that stuff you wanted," she grinned back at him, "and," she added kissing the top of his nose as she wheeled round, "by a quickie, I mean tea!"

Hattie squirmed in the wash down box - she always felt embarrassed when she watched Alice and Felix together. She persuaded herself that she wasn't jealous - not really anyway. Alice was lovely, and they were so nice to her, it just made her awkward, she never quite knew where to look, or what to say. In another way though it made her feel included, as they were never so open together around other people. It made her feel .... well... like family, she supposed. Alice was so beautiful, slim and clever; she and Felix made such a perfect couple together, and beside her, Hattie felt like Dumbo. When she looked in the mirror at herself, all she saw was a girl with reddish-brown hair and a square face which was smattered with freckles, with a nose that was too small and lips that were too fleshy and big. She had been verging on a size 14 when she came to work for Felix, and okay it was true, she had slimmed down with all the hard physical work, but compared to Alice who was a good two inches shorter, she would always feel like Godzilla.

"Hattie," shouted Felix, "Tea up."

"Coming," Hattie gave herself a mental slap and patted Woody's sleek neck, threw on a cotton cooler, narrowly avoiding his naughty nipping when she did up the front straps, and led him back to his box. At least she knew where she was with the horses.

Mark Templeton was happy; in fact he'd never been so content. Last year he'd been a single, albeit divorced man, living his footloose fancy free life. Now he was a married man, in love with a feisty dynamic woman, who had stormed into his life, and stayed there. He'd met Sandy by chance at a swanky party and they'd embarked on a fantastic sexual adventure, where they'd set the ground rules of *'no commitment*' from the start, and immediately begun to bonk each other's brains out. The surprise had been, that actually outside the bedroom, they'd really got a lot in common, and gradually the *'no commitment'* thing had been thrown out of the window. He'd moved in, and astonishing them both equally, at the beginning of this month they had been married in the quaint old village church. It was one of the biggest bashes Fittlebury had seen in many a year. The good thing about their life together was that they were great friends and lovers, but their professional lives were equally important to them both. Sandy was a successful barrister specialising in Family Law. She had a reputation for being ruthless and was a tenacious advocate in difficult circumstances, and was a favourite amongst solicitors in the South East. She'd been previously and disastrously married, discovering that her husband was in fact bi-sexual; a revelation that she had kept to herself and one that had made her very wary of men, hence her reticence when she'd met Mark. But that was all in the past - since they had met, neither of them had looked back. Living now in Sandy's Hansel and Gretel cottage just outside the village suited them both. He was in easy reach of the estate and she to her Chambers in Lewes.

Today Mark had a very clandestine appointment, and one he really couldn't discuss even with Sandy at this point. One of their friends, Colin Allingham, a local estate agent, had been in touch with him about a very delicate subject - The Old Mill. The very thought of the place made Mark feel uncomfortable. He'd been shelving the problem of what to do about it for months, and knew he must make some sort of decision as however much he put his head in the sand it wasn't going to go away.

The watermill itself was owned by the estate and was on the edge of its boundary with the hamlet of Priors Cross. Last year it had been the scene of an horrific kidnapping attempt, which was dramatically foiled by the local farrier, Patrick Hodges, who was quite the hero at the time. The incident however, was not without its awful casualties, when two men, albeit one being a psychopathic villain, and the other a mentally disturbed local man, had drowned in the mill pond. The drama did not stop with the tragic loss of life. The mill itself, the attached cottage, in which the hostages were held captive, and outbuildings had been partially burned down at the time. Luckily the fire had been contained and the sizeable barns adjacent to the mill were untouched, but since then, he and everyone else had felt disinclined to go anywhere near the place. For months its toothy blackened remains had stood like stumps of rotten teeth, and over the harsh winter, had rapidly fallen into further decay, and despite a minimal insurance pay out, there was no way the estate could renovate what had already been a dilapidated old building. In the normal run of things it would have just been demolished, but the mill was of historic interest and consequently the wrangle for what was to be done with it was a permanent headache. Now Colin had telephoned him and said that he had an anonymous celebrity looking for unusual premises in the area to convert into an upmarket restaurant, and did he think the Old Mill might fit the bill?

Mark's initial reaction was one of horror. Who on earth would want to go there, knowing of the history? But, upon reflection he supposed there may well be the ghoulish few, and perhaps it was what was needed to give the place a complete refurbishment. It was certainly beyond the means of the estate to do anything with it, the cost would be exorbitant. If this celebrity wanted to sink their money into a scheme like that, who was he to stop them? After all, they were only looking - it would probably come to nothing. He glanced at his watch. He'd better get a wiggle on. He was due to meet Colin and the client in 15 minutes.

CHAPTER 2

Roxy considered herself critically in the enormously ostentatious mirror, which took up almost the whole side of the room. She turned this way and that, her hands perched on her snaky hips, as she posed and pouted, the oil on her body still glistening from the work out by the masseur. Last year she had changed her whole image; the proxy-loxy blonde, dishevelled, *just got out of bed* hair had gone, along with the outrageously oversized melons that she'd originally loved when she'd had her boob job, which she now realised had been a disastrous and expensive mistake. It had taken a lot of pain with a sizeable reduction, coupled with some new lip implants, and now she had dark, sultry, deep brown glossy hair, verging on black, cut into a shaggy bob to give the image that now burned reflectively at her from the mirror. She twirled around, twisting her head back, watching her reflection and she felt immensely satisfied. Gone was the overt, seventeen year, old Page three glamour model, the immature raw girl she had been, the one that had raunchily removed her clothes at the drop of a hat, or a five pound note for the camera. She had been replaced by a sophisticated, or so she believed, "*it*" girl.

Roxy had always been shrewd. She was born poor, but with good assets in the looks department and it hadn't taken her long to realise that this was her best bet to make her way in life. Even from a young age she had been aware of the power she had over men, the way they had looked at her, lusted over her even, from the teachers at school to the bloke in the newsagents where she did a paper-round. They were all the same. She had been introduced to the glamour modelling scene whilst she was still at school by a letchy old photographer called Ron, whose breath stank of cigarettes. Ron had his own camera shop, and had offered her a few quid if she was prepared to get her kit off in his back room. Roxy hadn't hesitated, and soon Ron invited a few friends, and she'd made quite a little sideline out if it. It was all pretty soft core though, the old geezers just wanted a cheap thrill. They knew she was underage, and she had them by the short and curlies in the end. Roxy wasn't stupid by any stretch, but she wasn't academic either, and had left school at 16, dreaming of pursuing a career in modelling. What with the money from Ron and his cronies, and some pub work and waitressing, she saved enough to have a professional portfolio of photos which she'd sent to a variety of agencies, and it had been a lucky break when she'd been spotted by *The Sun* and offered a Page three slot. She hadn't looked back since then, and had taken her kit off more times than she could remember in those early days. *The Sun* job came to an end though when she'd had her tits done – they claimed they only featured models with natural breasts, but by this time Roxy was featuring in other men's magazines, and was beginning to make a name for herself, so to her it hardly mattered anymore.

It was at that time that Max came into her life. He was a name and owned a few smart clubs in the West End, up market places, but a facade for behind the scenes gambling, girls, and drugs. Roxy had been asked as a decoration to entertain some saddo clients from overseas at a private party one night and it was threatening to be a very dull evening indeed until he'd arrived. She saw him straight away, the moment he walked through the door, and was reminded of that Carly Simon song – *"You're so Vain"* – *"You walked in to the Party, like you were walking onto a yacht,"* and God did it sum him up. He was stunning to look at, tall and blond and mysterious, like Robert Redford when he played Jay in the Great Gatsby, even down to the clothes. She couldn't take her eyes off him and neither could anyone else in the room. It still gave her the shivers thinking of that night, how she'd tried to avoid staring at him, forcing herself to concentrate on the conversation in hand, yet continually finding her eyes drawn in his direction. Out of the corner of her eye, she'd watched him working the room, willing him to come over, but it was not until much later that the introductions were finally made. The frisson between them had been electric right from the start - well for her anyway. He'd eyed her with all the speculation of a prospective buyer choosing a bullock at an auction and she felt herself, not quite knowing how to meet his gaze. For Roxy, it was the first time in her life that any man had made her feel like that - wrong-footed and ill at ease. Normally she was the one who took control. It had made her cross and yet it excited her at the same time. She'd pushed up her tits in the low cut dress, and thrust out her hips just an inch further, daring him to be impressed. All he had done in response was to turn away and talk to some plebs on the other side of the room, and she'd felt herself simmering with anger at his lack of interest. The tedious hours had dribbled on, and the sweating Sheik who had latched himself onto her, no doubt in hope of a good finish to his night, was seriously beginning to piss her off. His pudgy hand grasped around her wrist, and he'd already signalled for his bodyguard that it was time for them to leave, when a fingertip traced along the side of her ear, sliding down the nape of her neck. Astonished, she'd turned around to find Max smiling down at her, much to the outrage of the flabbergasted Sheik and his entourage. Moments later, Max with his insouciant charm had confidently whisked her out of the door. They had laughed themselves silly that night, as they tumbled and romped in his oversized round bed, and she still smirked to herself when she thought about it. He had changed her life from then on and she'd never looked back.

She moved away from the mirror, pulling on her robe and tied it tight around her, and plonked herself down on the white leather sofa, and began leafing through the plethora of magazines and dailies her PA had left on the glass covered coffee table. It was her worst day of the week, scouring over these rags, but the power of press was never to be under estimated. Gulping down a bottle of Evian, she started the ghoulish business of sifting through the smut and detritus. She smiled when she saw that she and Aiden had made copy in most of them. There were some good shots, arm in arm arriving at a premiere last week, and another of them on their yacht with the children last month in a feature on glamorous destinations. Aiden featured talking about his restaurants, and there was a good article about her new and as yet unveiled range of lingerie. She threw the papers aside, cupping her hands around the back of her neck and sighing, it was damned hard work staying in the spotlight all the time. Roxy was a realist. Joe Public, would pretty soon get fed up with you if you were always the same. You had to keep reinventing yourself, doing something new, something fresh. She had no real specific talent, other than in marketing herself, and she was good at that. She'd been doing it for years, but you always had to be one step ahead of the game. Keep the punters interested, make headlines, that kind of thing. In a way, there may be a way to do that with this venture of Aiden's, but it would be up to her to exploit it to the max. Ah Max … Her beloved Max.

Colin and Mark had been waiting for about half an hour and were getting cheesed off. The sun seared down, and despite loitering under the shade of a lofty oak, both men had tiny beads of sweat appearing along their foreheads.

"Do you think this bloke'll turn up?" grumbled Mark, "Have you actually met him?"

"Nope, I got a call from one of the big London firms, asking me to keep an eye out for something that might do the job. I just rang them, and they organised it with his PA apparently."

"Oh well, it's in the lap of the Gods then" sighed Mark loosening his tie, "So, let me get this straight, we don't know who he is, and only that he wants it for a restaurant?"

"Yep, that's about the size of it, although he must have a shed load of money, 'cause when I said it was practically a shell, that didn't seem to matter. It was the location that was important – although frankly I can't see it as a goer myself."

"Me neither, but perhaps we're a bit biased eh?" Mark grinned, "Can you see any of us having a cosy dinner here – Christ!"

"No, but he doesn't know that does he?"

Colin took out a large spotted handkerchief and mopped his brow, shrugging his shoulders uncomfortably in the tweed jacket. The roar of a throaty engine resounded across the other side of the mill pond - a car was coming at a fast lick down the lane, and then slowing with a loud *putt putt* from the exhaust. Colin glanced at Mark as they heard the scrunch of tyres edging down the cinder drive.

Aiden Hamilton uncoiled like a sleeping cobra out of the

obligatory red Ferrari, pushed his Ray-Bans up onto his head, and looked momentarily dismayed as he stepped onto the dusty track in his £1000 Gucci loafers. He was taller than he looked on the TV, with ruffled iridescent dark hair and a rugged square jaw line. His eyes were of a deep chocolate brown and he had a strong tanned face with an easy charismatic smile, showing perfect veneers. His blue striped shirt collar was pulled up, and a long scarf was curled unnecessarily around his neck, a dark blue jumper thrown casually over his shoulders matching the carefully laundered chinos. In fact his image was just as it should have been for the dynamic celebrity chef he portrayed on the TV.

Wow! Aiden thought, this setting was sensational and was just what he'd been looking for - although the buildings were in a dreadful state by the look of things. He greedily scanned the site, hardly noticing the two men who had come forward to greet him. The mill itself had been ravaged by a fire, pretty recently too it seemed but had the bare bones of the framework still standing and the most fantastic old original water wheel which might still be salvageable. There must have been some other old buildings attached to it at some point, but it was tricky to see what they were now. On the opposite side of the mill, was a range of ancient barns, and they didn't look in bad shape. The situation was brilliant, less than an hour's drive from London, and set amidst some of the most awesome countryside, but still within easy access from the motorway. It was fantastically peaceful, set quite a bit off the road down the track - just the odd sound of a bird or two and the gurgle of the water from that old pond as it fed past the water wheel. Plenty of room for parking for the punters – yes it had definite possibilities. He tried not to look too gleeful, as he pulled his jumper around his shoulders, and walked over to meet the two country hicks who were waiting for him.

Colin appraised the languid newcomer with a practised eye, although naturally he'd recognised him immediately – how could he fail to? He held out his hand in greeting and fixed a smile on his face, inwardly disdainful – thinking how obvious he was, ostentatious wealth, image maker, and someone used to getting their own way. Still, he considered ruefully, it was business and good business too, if he were able to pull this deal off. Colin was one of the old school, he owned an old established firm of estate agents in the nearby market town of Horsham. He was well respected in the community, a member of the Rotary Club, hunted regularly with the Fittlebury and Cosham Hunt, and lived in a smart barn conversion in Fittlebury with the love of his life – Grace, who was six months pregnant. It had been a tough year financially, well it was for everyone, but his firm had made it through. With Colin's connections, and a lot of hard work, at long last he was beginning to breathe a bit more easily. When Gracie became pregnant he had worried himself sick. They had spent years trying for a baby and his heart had ached for her with the disappointment of every negative test. It was even more amazing if you considered all the drama of the previous year and the ghastly business at this damned place, during which he and Grace had been so shockingly involved. He shrugged his shoulders; the Old Mill with its blackened shell gave him the creeps, but he couldn't afford to let Aiden Hamilton see how much it affected him, - not if he wanted to sell him the place that was.

CHAPTER 3

Alice Cavaghan tipped back her head and slurped the dregs of her tea, smacking her lips together with satisfaction.

"Gotta go, otherwise Paulene'll be after me" she smiled disarmingly, crinkling her freckled nose at Felix and Hattie, "thanks for the char – just what I needed."

Felix grinned unable to resist twinkling his blue eyes at her, "We can't have that can we now? Any idea what time you'll finish tonight?"

"Nope," drawled Alice, her New Zealand twang evident, "Andrew's on call, so with any luck not too late."

"Okay, I'm meeting a client over at Pulborough, taking a horse cross country schooling at three, although, it's going to be bloody hot, and I don't fancy the ground much. Still I shouldn't be back too late." Felix grinned over at Hattie, "You okay to lunge a couple on the Pessoa while I'm gone?"

Hattie flushed, she loved the way Felix trusted her now to train the horses with the complexity of the Pessoa. "Yep, no problem, and I don't mind staying late to finish up if you want to get off."

"You make him do his share Hattie, otherwise he'll end up a spoiled brat" Alice winked at her, then turned to Felix "don't you dare take advantage!"

Felix pulled an *'as if I would'* face, and laughed "Bugger off Alice, see you later!"

Alice grinned at him and stuck out her tongue, marching out into the sun-soaked yard, leaving Felix and Hattie to finish their tea.

"You don't think I take advantage do you?" sighed Felix

"Of course not, and anyway I don't mind if you do." Hattie beamed at him, "I offered didn't I?"

"That's not quite the point though is it? Grooms shouldn't be taken advantage of Christ knows it goes on often enough, but I always swore I'd never be like that."

"Felix, for heaven's sake – Alice was winding you up – stop being so sensitive. Now I've got work to do!" She drained her tea, and wondered what have given her the courage to speak to him like that, normally she was the one who wouldn't say boo to a goose!

Felix watched her go and sat thinking for a while. She was turning into a bloody good groom was Hattie. She didn't mind doing all the shit jobs, or the shit money that went with them either. He would have paid her more if he could afford it. She had come on in leaps and bounds in these last three months, and she just soaked up every experience as though her life depended on it. Even her riding was different. To be fair, Hattie had never been nervous or afraid, but at first she was a bit in awe of the horses, never having sat on anything of their ability before. Now she confidently hacked them round the lanes with him, could ride them in the school, warming them up, or cooling them off if needed before he worked them, and had accompanied him on the gallop track. But, above all, she was always enthusiastic and good fun to have around. She didn't sulk and she didn't moan. In fact she was becoming indispensable and the last thing he would want to do was piss her off by being inconsiderate.

There was something else on Felix's mind too. This yard was fantastic; perfect in every way. The estate had been more than accommodating putting in the arena, then renting him the cottage an' all; what with the excitement of the cross country course being built for next year and everything - but … and there always had to be a but! Everything had its price, and the cost of running the place and the cottage was crippling. He never drew a penny piece for himself, everything he earned went into paying the expenses and he barely covered those. He had six good fee-paying horses, which between him and Hattie they managed well. He was planning to get some youngsters to bring on and sell – perhaps three, but the yard itself had eighteen stables. That left nine empty ones, on which he still had to pay rent. He needed to get them filled. If and when he did that, he would need more staff, and probably another rider – it was a *Catch 22* situation. At the moment, when he was away at events, they were either close enough that he could juggle the logistics of managing the yard and competing, or, he cajoled with his silver tongue, someone to cover for him on an ad-hoc basis. He knew though it couldn't go on like that. At some point in the near future he may have to be away for days at a time, and he would need to leave someone in charge in his absence. Was Hattie that person he pondered? Indeed, wouldn't he rather have her with him as a travelling groom? It was difficult. He must try and find time to talk it through with Alice, especially before his meeting with Charles Parker-Smythe next week. Alice was always the steadying hand that offered sound advice. He knew she wished she could offer more help financially, but an assistant veterinary surgeon's money was good but not the sort of bank rolling that was needed to fund an eventing habit – it was worse than cocaine he thought ruefully.

Mark could feel the sweat running down between his shoulder blades and his jacket felt cumbersome and uncomfortable. He loosened the knot a little more on his tie, adjusting his shirt collar. They had been at the mill now for well over an hour, far longer than he had anticipated and still Aiden Hamilton was not satisfied. His muddy brown eyes were everywhere, and his hands were busy on his phone taking pictures of everything, whilst he asked question after demanding question.

Mark envied Colin, his estate agent's brittle enthusiasm as he embellished each selling point to Aiden. Frankly Mark hated the place and couldn't wait to be gone, but he had to see this through, and he supposed if it were sold, then at least the place would no longer be his responsibility, or his headache. Even on this blistering day it had an eerie, haunted feel about it. The mill pond was seemingly absolutely still, with just the odd ripple of a water boatman making concentric circles on the water. Underneath that mirror sheen an unseen magnetic pull was drawing the water towards the rotting wheel and sucking it relentlessly downwards, as it came tumbling through the chute of the mill race, just as it had done when it drowned that man last year. Despite the heat, Mark felt himself shiver with the memory. He hurried to catch up with the others who were by now heading over towards the barns.

"These were untouched by the fire and are basically sound," Colin said, "lovely old tythes, with a lot of local history attached to them."

"Bollocks to the history," said Aiden, "what about planning?"

Colin winced, "Well of course you would have to make the necessary applications to the local authorities, and anything would have to be in keeping. What did you have in mind for these? That's if you decide to do up the mill as the restaurant."

"Dunno yet," Aiden said casually not looking at Colin, clicking away with his phone "They're a bonus, have to get the architect to come up with some ideas."

"Well as I said, they are pretty sound for their age and ripe for conversion."

Aiden hadn't heard him. He'd marched off inside the barns, exploring on his own, leaving Colin and Mark to hurry after him.

"He's an abrasive sod," mumbled Mark, "still, he does seem interested, have you thought of a price?"

Colin was panting, what with the heat and catching up with Aiden, who by now had disappeared up the stairs to the upper floor "No, I thought I'd gauge his reaction first, but he seems keen, and when he's gone, how about you and I have a pint at the Fox and we can talk money properly?"

"Perfect," muttered Mark quickly, as he heard the clatter of Aiden's feet coming back down the stairs. "Let's hope he buggers off quickly then!"

Alice had her hand up a horse's bum, probing about with a rectal scanner. There were better places she could be on such a hot day, she pondered. The beach, or the garden perhaps. She pushed her arm in further, gently exploring, her eyes intent on the monitor. Then she saw it on the screen - the tiny heartbeat of new life, and she knew that for her there was nothing better than this at all.

"Great, yep, she's in foal, look – there's the heartbeat." She inclined her head towards the screen and pointed with her free hand. "Good girl, good girl," she crooned to the mare as she eased her hand gently out, and ripped off the plastic glove. "Congratulations!"

"Oh Alice! Fantastic, I never believed we'd get her in foal, you're a genius!" spluttered Grace, "That makes the two of us then!"

Alice looked at Grace fondly, "It sure does Gracie! Except you'll be foaling down a bit earlier than this little darling", she slapped the horse's rump playfully "Now, come on, out of the way now, and let me get her out of this contraption."

"Oh, I'm alright, Colin makes such a fuss. He's treating me like I'm made of china. I can manage. Although I have to say his idea of rigging up these stocks for the examinations has made all the difference."

"Well, it makes my life a lot easier I can tell you – makes it much more efficient and safer for the mare and for everyone else too. It's only because he cares – you should be pleased."

Alice smiled to herself as she got the horse out of the stocks. Good old Colin, he had made a half decent job of them. It was true they did make a difference, if only more horse owners had them. Grace had waddled off to get them both a cold drink, and Alice turned the mare back out in the paddock and waited in the garden under a shady parasol for her to come back. She had become quite close to Grace since she started work for Napier and Travers last summer. At that time Grace had worked part-time for the Vets in the office, with Paulene as the Practice Manager, and she had not long been in the job when Alice arrived. They were the two new girls together and just hit it off. Now Grace had left, no hint of maternity leave for her, she'd made no pretence of coming back to her job.

Alice missed her a lot.

"Here we go, straight from the fridge." Grace plonked down a jug of lemonade and two glasses on the table. "How's life in the surgery?"

"Usual, busy, busy," said Alice, "although we're busting at the seams in that tiny office and still no sign of anywhere else on the horizon."

"Oh Alice, I don't know what you are all going to do. Empty property around here that would be suitable is so few and far between and would be astronomical. The mill would have been perfect, but of course it's out of the question now."

"Don't even go there Gracie, Andrew can't even bring himself to talk about it. It's not just the disappointment about losing the place, the fire and what happened, it's more about what happened to Caitlin you know?"

"Of course. How is she getting along? She's made marvellous progress all things considered." Grace sighed, "She's lucky to be alive after such a terrible head injury."

Alice smiled, "Well if you think Colin's over protective, you should take a look at Andrew. Now Caitlin is coming into the office part time to help out after you left, we see them first hand together. It's sickenly sweet to be frank. Her recovery's been slow, but she's pretty much back to normal, but I don't think she'll ever go back to being a groom again."

"How much does she remember of it all?"

"Not much, which is a blessing, but Andrew lived and still lives through every second. To him the mill is inextricably linked with what happened to her, even though of course she was just an incidental casualty in the grand scheme of things. She just happened to get in the way of those thugs when they tried to kidnap Jennifer and her step daughter." Alice sipped her drink, wincing at the tartness of the lemons, "Once the accident happened to Caitlin and the mill burned down, naturally any plans for the practice to expand, especially there, came to an abrupt halt. None of us have really had the gumption to mention them much since to be honest."

"Mmmm, well perhaps it's time someone did, after all Caitlin is well on the mend now, and life has to go on. Look at Jennifer, if anyone was a casualty she was, and she's picked herself up and got on with life." Grace muttered "Perhaps I should have a word with him?"

"Rather you than me!" grinned Alice, "He can be touchy around the subject you know."

"We'll see," said Grace darkly. "Anyway, how about Oli, what's he up to?"

"Apart from shagging anything that moves, he's fine." Alice laughed, "all except Libby Newsome, he does have some taste."

"Good for him, I hope he's having fun. You never met his wife, she was a first rate bitch."

"No, but I bet he wasn't an angel. When I was lodging at the cottage he could be a right slob."

"True, but a delicious slob nonetheless. You know for a long time, I thought he was having a thing with Caitlin."

"No!" Alice looked amazed, raising her eyebrows, inclining her head, "Go on?"

"Just the rumour mill, but it was Andrew all the time. That was the shock – mind you Andrew's wife Julia was a cow, always having affairs, eventually ran off with her tennis coach. Mum and I saw them one day in the garden centre together, he must have been 10 years younger than her!" Grace reminisced, "I'm glad Andrew is with Caitlin now, they make a lovely couple. Just shows you, you never know what people are up to do you? What secrets they have?"

Alice felt an uncomfortable flush creeping up her neck, and suddenly jumped up, leaving her drink half-finished and looked at her watch, "Nope, you never do that's for sure. Blimey, look at the time, I'd better run - catch up later". She plonked a kiss on Grace's cheek and was gone with more velocity than a popping cork.

CHAPTER 4

Aiden was lost in thought as he edged the Ferrari into the fast lane of the M23, overtaking the wankers in their BMWs and leaving them dreaming in his wake. With luck he'd make it into London by late afternoon, and Chrissie his PA would've had time to set up the meetings, and they may be able to get the ball rolling. He was smitten with the place, it had great potential. The mill would make a stunning location for a restaurant. He could see it now, the punters sitting looking out over the water, the wheel a feature, perhaps encompassed in the room itself. Upper floors too, either for dining or a bar, or maybe the other way round – the planning guys could come up with the ideas. The attached outbuildings could be extended and converted into kitchens and the accommodation restored. Fuck me, he thought, they could even grow their own organic veg! No shortage of labour either, people would be clamouring to work for him. Those old tythe barns were interesting too. Roxy could do something over there perhaps? He'd have to get her on side, pitch it just right. She was a greedy tart though and she'd see the potential. Meanwhile, he wanted this kept under wraps, otherwise the fucking price would go up. He'd let those two hicks sweat a bit, but set it all up behind the scenes for a quick sale, then blast the place.

He took his foot off the gas, slowing down gradually and pulling over into the middle lane, no point in getting another load of points. That was the trouble with having a car like this, never anywhere you could drive it to its max. The thought of Max made him clench his hands tightly on the wheel. He was an influence on Roxy's life he could well do without, although she flatly refused to relinquish any ties with him. He was a bad lot, into all sorts of scams, and okay Roxy may have needed him in the beginning but she didn't need him now. Somehow though she just couldn't cut herself free and Aiden didn't like it one bit.

The traffic was getting heavier as he approached the suburbs. He flicked on the hands free, barking down the phone at Chrissie. "It's me. I'll be with you in about 30 minutes if this fucking traffic doesn't get any worse. Have you got in touch with that fucking architect yet?"

Chrissie was used to being sworn at and ignored his foul language merely replying in her clipped tones, "Yes, he can't see you till tomorrow morning at the earliest and then he only has a 15 minute window. It was the best he could do at such short notice."

"Fucking hell, he charges enough," barked Aiden, "what about the solicitors?"

"They are on it now." Chrissie drawled. "Roxy called to remind you that you have a dinner engagement tonight with the Beckhams."

"Fuck, I'd forgotten!" snapped Aiden, "What's the plan?"

"You're to meet at their London home for pre-dinner drinks at 7pm, then after dinner on to a club I believe. The press have been alerted."

"Christ, that's all I can do with," snarled Aiden. "Okay, I'm gonna make a pitstop to the Fulham restaurant, that Ozzie chef needs a kick up the arse, then I'll go straight home. See you in the morning, I'll be there early."

He disconnected angrily. God help that fucking chef he thought sadistically.

Mark and Sandy sat at opposite ends of the pine table in the kitchen, the late evening sun was still strong and seeping through the huge open glass doors which took up most of one wall. The bees were busy making the most of the daylight hours, diving in and out of the clematis which was running riot over the loggia, its massive flower heads as big as saucepan lids. The smell of cooking laden with herbs and spices oozed out of the kitchen, and Sandy was twirling spaghetti onto her fork.

"God this is good, I'm starving, thanks for cooking."

Mark looked at his wife, admiring her pixie short cropped hair, and thought how much he loved her. "Pleasure darling, I knew you'd be hungry. How did the case go?"

"Bloody awful, and not over yet. Still, my turn to sum up tomorrow, then we'll see." She took a slug of wine, "Mmm, that's nice, how about you sweetie?"

"Well, you'd never believe it, but there's been a bit of a development with the Old Mill." He grimaced, "I would so love to get shot of that damned place."

Sandy put her fork down, "That was unexpected wasn't it? What happened?"

"Well nothing so far, but a glimmer of interest from an anonymous buyer," mumbled Mark through a mouthful of spaghetti, "Colin rang and asked me to meet them there today, swore me to secrecy!"

"Sounds a bit fishy to me," she leant forward with her elbows on the table, "who was it – anyone we know?"

"You'll never believe it!" Mark grinned, "Go on have a guess?" he teased, "Three guesses in fact!"

Sandy laughed, "could be anyone - okay though I'll play." She twirled her wine glass thoughtfully, "I'll aim high – Prince Charles?"

"No! Be serious!" laughed Mark "I'll give you a clue, they want to open a new business venture."

"Okay," She pealed into shrieks of laughter, "I know, Alan Sugar."

Mark grinned, "No you're way off. More celebrity status."

"Mmm, celebrity, man or woman?" Sandy tilted her head to one side quizzically inviting more clues.

"No, you've had enough clues – last chance," smiled Mark irritatingly, "or you'll have to pay a forfeit."

"Oh I like forfeits," smirked Sandy winking at him, "I'll just take a stab in the dark then – Mick Jagger?"

"Nope – prepare yourself for later," he laughed, "seriously, it was Aiden Hamilton, that celebrity chef, who's married to Roxy Le Feuvre – you know?"

"God yes, I know – he's an odious type. What on earth does he want it for?"

Mark muttered, "Wants to turn it into one of his organic restaurants if you please – all a bit pie in the sky, and of course we heard no more from him after he left. If he'd been really keen he'd have been on the blower. Anyway, Col and I had a pint in the Fox afterwards to discuss the finances, but to be honest, the estate would be well shot of it at any sensible price."

Sandy gave him a long look, "Business is business Hun, if this guy is keen, he'll pay. Just because you hate the place – he doesn't know that does he? Not unless you told him that is?"

"No, Col and I didn't mention a thing and he was too arrogant to listen to anything we said – the bloke was an arse. You're probably right darling, anyway, we'll have to wait and see if he comes back at all, but I'm not holding my breath." Mark scooped up another forkful of sauce and washed it down with a glug of wine. "Now let me think about that forfeit ..."

Sandy put down her fork and picked up her wine glass, refilling it up from the bottle. She slipped off her chair and sashayed over towards him taking his cutlery from his hand and laying it on the table. Bending over him, she dipped her fingertip in her wine and then lightly traced it over the edge of his mouth, leaning over she sucked and nibbled the wine from his lips.

The erotic gesture threw Mark. This was what he loved about Sandy, dynamic business woman one minute, sexy tigress the next. He put out his hands, dipping them inside her blouse, hooking out her small pointy breasts from her bra and gently rubbing her pert nipples between his fingers, feeling himself growing hard, his cock beginning to bulge in his trousers. Without taking her mouth from his, Sandy put down her wine, and started to unzip his flies, allowing her breasts to swing tantalisingly loose; he fondled them both in his hands. She dropped to her knees and took him in her mouth and he leant back in the chair, moaning quietly, until he could bear it no longer and pulled her upright, pulling off her panties and dragging her on top of him. All thoughts of Aiden Hamilton had disappeared for them both.

Roxy was taking off her make-up. She went through the same painstaking routine every night, cleanser, toner, moisturiser. A girl needed to take care of her skin, there was only so much Botox and Restalyne could do, you had to take some responsibility yourself. She flossed and brushed her teeth and was finally ready for bed. Yanking on a tee shirt, which, over her squashy breasts, barely covered her bottom, she sauntered into the bedroom. Aiden was already in bed. He'd put on the massive flat screen TV and was idly flicking through the channels. He gave her a half glance as she oozed in snuggling up beside him.

"Good evening baby wasn't it? Lots of press, should make *Hello* or *Heat* at least." Roxy purred, letting her hand stray over the top of his thighs, "You were a snipey fucker though – everything alright?"

"Yep," he answered her shortly, continuing his hunt through the programmes.

"Come on Aiden, you're not still uptight about this morning are ya? You never told me what happened down in the cow muck today – given up on the crazy idea?" Roxy gave a tinkly little laugh and sexily nuzzled into him, her hand straying to his cock.

"Pack it in Roxy. You piss me off sometimes. For someone who thinks she's so smart about reading the future, you can be so fucking dumb sometimes." He snarled removing her hand "this could be really big, you could be in it, but your vision is too narrow."

Roxy snatched her hand away, "What are you but a jumped up fucking cook. Who do you think you are speaking to me like that?" She leapt out of the bed, prowling over to the door, the cheeks of her bottom peeking out from beneath her tee shirt, "I'm gonna sleep in the guest room."

To her fury Aiden did not bother to acknowledge what she'd said, making her even madder. If there was one thing that Roxy hated, it was being ignored. She turned back, "You didn't make any effort with the Beckhams tonight, you're the loser!" she screamed.

Aiden turned to look at her freezing her with his contempt, "Actually David thought it was a brilliant idea, if you'd been bothering to listen, but as usual you were too busy trying to row your own boat – you're such a joke, a total bimbo, everyone thinks so." He turned away – she sickened him.

Roxy froze – he couldn't mean that could he? Suddenly, her self confidence in tatters, she crumpled onto the floor and started to cry, "Christ you can be vile, why are you being so nasty? Just 'cause I'm not interested in your fucking restaurants."

"Oh for fuck's sake Roxy, take a look at yourself. What is it you exactly do? Ask yourself that? Ponce off other people and their lives and reputations. When you're offered a chance to do something with yourself, you don't wanna fucking know." Aiden shouted, "You haven't even asked about this project, your idea of making money is to change your tits or your hair colour," he added spitefully, ignoring her shocked face, "go on then tell me what your next project is – new bras and thongs? How inspiring is that – it's all been done before and it's so tacky, just like you in fact."

Roxy's face hardened, "Okay what's your idea then Mr Big Shot?" she yelled, the tears of self-pity forgotten, her eyes flashing with anger.

Aiden's face changed, he smiled and his eyes softened, "Ah Roxy, I knew you'd see it my way, just listen my sweet, just listen!"

Felix rolled over, his hand flaying out across the cool pillow on his side of the bed. He let out a huge sigh, and felt his muscles relax, tired and satiated after a massive sexual marathon.

Alice murmured contentedly, her naked body glistened with pearls of perspiration. "Doll, you were awesome, no wonder you get those horses going so well, you never break rhythm."

"Flatterer," he mumbled, feeling an overwhelming desire to close his eyes and tumble into the chasm of sleep.

"Wake up, you slob," complained Alice, "don't you dare fall asleep on me!"

Felix struggled to stay awake, "Sorry baby, just been a long hard day." He forced himself up on his elbows and rolled over to look at her, running his fingertips down the length of her belly. "You're pretty fit yourself."

"Mmm, you said it too late."

"Aw Alice, sorry," he cocked his head on one side and winked at her "forgiven?"

"Alright. As long as you get me a glass of wine."

Felix heaved himself off the bed and stomped off down the little staircase, Alice admiring his firm arse and long legs as he disappeared. She ran her hands over her body, still tingling from a series of multiple orgasms, shuddering all over again as she played with herself. He was a good lover, and they were becoming more experimental in what they did, which she enjoyed, but lately he was tending to crash out afterwards, and that could be a bit of a turn off. She continued to caress herself until she heard the stairs creaking and he made his way back with the wine.

"Right – wow – what are you doing?" Felix's eyes widened in surprise as he walked in to find Alice sprawled out on the bed, her hands busy, "God you're so sexy!" He abandoned the wine, and threw himself down on top of her.

Half an hour later, the bed shipwrecked once again by their

mutual carnal cravings, they were sitting propped up against the bed head, gossiping about their day and drinking vast glasses of the now rather warm Pinot Grigio.

"Yeah, Gracie was delighted, it was a perfect time to put the horse into foal, and after all she won't be riding for a while, so it made sense." Alice smiled, "She's certainly blooming, you should see her."

"I'm really pleased for them both, they're such a lovely couple" agreed Felix, "it's fun for her too being part of the syndicate, even if they only have one leg of the horse."

"You're lucky with those two, they don't interfere at all do they?"

"Well it's early days of course, but no they don't. Charles though I think will want his pound of flesh. I'm a bit worried about this meeting with him next week," sighed Felix, "I don't quite know how I'm going to cope when I have to be away more, what with managing the yard and everything."

"Well it's obvious isn't it? You've got two options. You either take on more staff of your own and more liveries to pay for them, or you sub-let part of the yard to another rider with their own staff, and you can cover for each other when you each go away." Alice suggested, flicking off an imaginary piece of fluff from her nipple, "If you chose the second option, you could look for someone from a different discipline, say a dressage rider, or a show jumper, then you'd be unlikely to want to be away at the same time."

Felix gaped at her over the rim of his wine glass, his sapphire blues eyes appraising her, "Alice, how is it that you can see everything so clearly? I've been racking my brains about what to do." He put the glass down and grabbed her, almost knocking her own glass out of her hands, "You're a bloody life saver, of course that's a great idea!"

"Whoa, steady on lover!" Alice pushed him off lightly, "why didn't you talk to me about it before, you idiot?"

"I dunno really, stupid, I've been worried sick about it, how I was gonna manage on my own. The only thing is - can I sub-let? I'd have to run it past Mark."

"I don't see why not – after all, as long as the estate get their money, and you're still responsible for the tenure, I think he should be happy with that – you'd have to check, of course," she leant over and ruffled his hair, "you are daft, must be why I love you."

"Oh baby, I love you too," he sighed. "I know where I am with you."

Alice looked down and whispered, "You can always rely on me Felix my darling - always."

CHAPTER 5

The flags surrounding the dressage arenas at the Hickstead showground were dreamily floating in the gentle breeze sighing in from the downs as Felix and Hattie were queuing up on the concrete entrance drive. Even though they had left early to avoid the crowds, it seemed everyone had had the same idea, and the line of cars curled ahead of them taking what seemed an age to get through the pay booths. Felix had suggested they take a naughty and illicit day off, to go to the Derby meeting and Hattie was gabbling with excitement, as she had never been before.

"You'll love it Hattie, the fences are huge, much bigger than the eventing tracks" smiled Felix, "well the ones I normally do at the moment anyway."

"It's stupid really isn't it, living so close and never having been before," grinned Hattie back at him, "and I can't wait to see all those trade stands."

"Don't get carried away Hats!" laughed Felix, "not unless you've got shed loads of money to spend. It's bloody tempting, but we've got no spare cash at the moment – although we could do with some more hay nets and head collar ropes – but that's pretty dull stuff."

"Oh, I don't mind doing a bit of window shopping, and it's the horses I want to see more than anything else really." She smiled at him adoringly, "Do you think we'll have time to see any of the dressage?"

"I hope so, they've got the Premier League on and the finals of the Hickstead Dressage Masters League, so the competition will be hot and the horses will be amazing – some of the best in the country. Most of the big names will be there, other than those that are abroad competing – you'll love it. My old pal is doing the commentary – so I want to pop over and have a chat and a catch up with him if I can."

"Sounds as though we're going to have a busy day then, that's if we ever get out of this queue!" laughed Hattie, her cheeks getting quite pink as they sat in the stuffy car.

Felix turned to look at her, she was a good girl was Hattie and deserved a fun day out, she worked hard, well, they all did. "Won't be long, look we're nearly through now."

Finally the car was bumping across the field being ushered into place by a series of officious car parking bods in fluorescent jackets. There were already masses of people here. The sun shone down on the roofs of the cars, and everyone was decanting hurriedly, jamming on baseball caps, bum bags and trainers, anxious to get going for the relatively long walk across to the main ring.

As Felix was bending down to lock the car, he heard a commotion behind him. He glanced up to see a grotesque burly bloke, with bulging and heavily tattooed biceps oozing out of his singlet shouting back at a small dog, trapped in an old pick-up. As Felix watched, the man walked back opened the car door seized the little dog by its throat, shook it hard, cuffed it round the ear and threw it across the cab, and stomped off to join his girlfriend, who was waiting impatiently for him to join her.

"Hey buddy!" called Felix after the retreating monster, "You're not gonna leave that little fellah all day in the car are you? It's too hot – he'll die of the heat."

The huge guy turned round, glaring menacingly at Felix and marched back shouting, "And what the fuck's it got to do with you?"

"I was only saying it's gonna be a hot day to leave a dog in the car. Why not take him with you, or at least leave a window open?" Felix said patiently. He didn't want a fight, but someone had to stick up for the dog.

Hattie cringed, the bloke was enormous, "Felix ..." she began, "You can't reason ..."

She was cut short as, by this time, the girlfriend had tottered back, her peroxide hair dull in the sunshine, and was sizing up Hattie, "Hey spade face tell your bloke to mind his own fucking business. The mutt is staying in the car. It's not spoiling my day out with its whining."

Hattie was enraged, "Well you shouldn't have brought it then. People like you shouldn't have dogs if you can't look after them." She sized the girl up and down, defiantly eyeballing her, although inside she was terrified, her heart slamming against her ribcage like the chimes of Big Ben. As for calling her spade face, the barb had hurt, "You, you ... lowlife ..." she spluttered.

"Who you calling a low life!" balled the girl, taking a swing at Hattie, "I'll fucking kill you!"

Hattie, who was pretty nimble on her feet from avoiding the occasional lashing out of the horses, deftly moved to one side. The girl swayed for a moment and then crashed to the ground, landing heavily into a dog turd that someone hadn't bothered to pick up. "Shit to shit," sneered Hattie, her face contorted with anger.

Felix and monster man, who had halted their heated exchange to watch the cat fight, turned on each other. The giant yelled at Felix "Look what your tart has just done to my Shirley!"

"Looks like she fell over her own mouth to me," grimaced Felix. "Now what are you going to do about your dog?"

"Can die for all I care, but not before you do," growled the bloke, taking a lunge at Felix.

Felix sidestepped neatly and the man bulldozed his way to the ground, "Look if you don't want the dog, let me buy him off you?"

"Fuck off, it can die." He lumbered up, dragged his wailing girlfriend up from the ground and they stalked off towards the show jumping arena with Felix calling after them.

The incident was over in a matter of minutes. Hattie was shaking, and Felix had gone white, not with fear but desperation for the plight of the terrified little creature cowering in the battered old pick up. A few people had witnessed the incident, and suggested calling the RSPCA, and then wandered off, intent on enjoying their day out. Felix and Hattie sat on the grass, for them the day had been spoilt, but neither of them could leave the dog in the car either. To call the RSPCA was a long-winded affair - why not just take the dog anyway? Felix wandered over to the pick up, trying the door handles, it was firmly locked. He scrambled into the back. The rear window was broken and held together with duct tape. Gesturing for Hattie to give him a hand, they painstakingly peeled off the tape and managed to make a hole large enough for Felix to reach his long arm across to the passenger side and unhook the door latch. Holding his breath, he just hoped the damned old truck didn't have an alarm system. They carefully patched up the back window, and gingerly opened the door – phew – no alarms. The little dog huddled terrified in the corner, and Felix reached over and gently picked him up – expecting to be bitten at any moment, but he just whimpered pathetically, obviously thinking he was going to have another beating.

"There, there little fellah, you're safe now, you're coming home with me and Hattie." Felix crooned, stroking the little brown and white head, "No-one's ever gonna hurt you again."

He edged back out of the pick-up. Hattie was dancing about from one leg to the other, looking anxiously to the show jumping arenas, keeping lookout in case monster and the girlfriend came back. "Hurry up Felix, supposing he comes back!" she whispered urgently, her face even more flushed. "We're stealing his dog!"

"No we're not," said Felix firmly. "I'm going to leave him some money and a note to say that he was lucky that I and the other witnesses didn't report him to the RSPCA where he could be facing charges for cruelty and end up in court. Plus his girlfriend threw a punch at you and he did at me too – that's ABH you know!"

"But we didn't get the names and addresses of the other witnesses did we?"

"He doesn't know that does he?" Felix replied calmly, stroking the little dog, "Now, I'm going to leave him a £5 note – I can't afford any more. And he's lucky to get that!"

He walked back to his car, scribbled a note, wrapped up a fiver and shoved it on the driver's seat of the pick-up. Satisfied he relocked the car and marched back to Hattie, who was holding the trembling little dog, stroking and petting him. "He's very sweet Felix, what shall we call him?"

"Fiver," said Felix smiling, "after all that's what he cost us. Come on, now I'm gonna move the car, don't want old Monster Man bashing my car up when he finds his dog gone, and Hats, I think we'll avoid the show jumping. Sorry and all that, but don't want to bump into him – carrying his dog do I? We'll stick to the dressage today– I don't think that'll be his bag and the ladies who organise the dressage love their dogs – they'll be horrified when they hear what happened to this little chap – they'll make a big fuss of him."

"Suits me," sighed Hattie; she didn't mind where she went as long as she was with Felix.

After the stormy night of rows and screaming, Aiden and Roxy had made up their differences, finally culminating in the most spectacular and kinky sexual games. Now Aiden was in the shower, his sleeping beauty still in bed, and he was in a very good mood indeed. He knew that he could win her round. It was a question on knowing how to deal with Roxy. Fundamentally, despite her brash exterior, she had a few sensitive areas and he knew just where and how to play her. He had opened her up to some possibilities, in more ways than one he thought amusedly, thinking of her straddled out in the bondage equipment they had played with last night. Still he must get a shifty on, he had a lot to do. He wanted to get cracking on this new project. The Old Mill was a prime place, but needed so much work doing, and the summer was the time for renovation. He didn't want to delay, it would take twice as long once the weather changed.

He jumped out of the shower, vigorously towelling himself dry, and ruffled up his hair, its iridescent dark sheen catching the spotlights in the mirror. He shaved quickly, slapping on his favourite musky aftershave, brushed his teeth, and with once last glance at

Roxy, still sprawled in bed, he dashed out of the house to meet Chrissie for their meeting.

Roxy opened one eye lazily as she heard the gentle closing of the bedroom door and rolled over in the bed. She felt stiff and rubbed her ankles. They were sore, glancing down, red marks were quite vivid where he had strapped her up last night, she smiled to herself, for all her ballsy personality, she was a submissive in the bedroom stakes. He loved it. Not enough though, she thought, with mild reproach that he hadn't wanted her again this morning - no, he had been so full of this new idea that he rushed off without a backward glance at her. Nonetheless, she had to admit it was a good idea, the place, although it was right out in the sticks, could have a certain appeal, and if David was interested – well it had to be worth giving a second chance. Those extra buildings sounded interesting too, imagine if she were to have her very own spa and health centre – that would make headlines, especially if she could inveigle the likes of Victoria to pay a visit or two. Definitely worth her while thinking about it.

Aiden swooped into the office, chucking his briefcase down onto his desk with a crash, snapping at Chrissie, "What time's the first meeting?"

"Good morning to you too" said Chrissie, not bothering to look up at him, "Architect at 10.30. Solicitor at 12. Tea or coffee?"

"Sorry Chrissie. Coffee - double espresso purleeesee." Aiden sighed, "this is gonna be big, fucking big."

Chrissie gave him a cool look, "Everything's big, everything's important, but don't get so uptight, you'll have a heart attack." She stood up and went over to the coffee machine, her slim frame enhanced by a well cut navy skirt, with a blue and white striped shirt slightly turned up at the collar. The epitome of the Sloane Ranger with her short bob and translucent pearls. "You drink too much caffeine, sure you don't want a fruit tea?"

"Fuck the fruit tea." Aiden groaned, but he knew she was right, and Chrissie was probably the only person who could tell him. To the outside world he was Mr Organic, Mr Fresh and Wholesome. Behind the scenes, he was an uptight ball of anger. Chrissie knew him better than anyone, even better than Roxy, and she never rose to his temper tantrums. "I need it."

"Well, you'll be even more wired after this," remarked Chrissie, as she came back with the coffee "Now do you want to fill me on what happened yesterday – without any unnecessary expletives?"

Aiden took a slurp of his coffee, screwing up his face at the bitter taste, "Chrissie, it's the most amazing place – let me show you."

He pulled out his phone and started to download the photos he had taken yesterday. On the big screen, the photos made the mill look like something out of a Hammer House of Horror movie. Chrissie looked unimpressed, making clinical remarks about the state of it, and moreover the cost of the renovations. Aiden quelled each one with a *'but wait till you see it'* retort, and in the end she was quiet. She just hoped that Aiden wasn't making the biggest mistake of his life.

CHAPTER 6

The team of super-efficient ladies who ran Dressage at Hickstead, from the popular unaffiliated series for the amateur riders to the whopping great International Show every year, were a delightful and good natured crew. Housed in a Swiss Chalet style wooden building with veranda and decking, gaily adorned with riotous hanging baskets, there were always a throng of competitors and spectators milling around the score boards and a plentiful supply of jelly babies in glass bowls waiting to be consumed. Felix popped his head around the door of the main secretariat, putting on his most winning smile and twinkling his famous blue eyes. As usual they were rushed off their feet, scoring madly at the computers and dealing with competitor queries, but when Felix explained what had happened, and showed them the little dog, he was met with collective "*oohs*" and "*aahs*" and was generously invited to join the hospitality area, where Emily was on duty today and she would take care of them. Felix thanked them profusely, and he and Hattie made their way over to a roped off area reserved especially for the judges and VIPs.

"Blimey," whispered Hattie ,"Do you know anyone here?"

"Well, not sure yet," hissed Felix back at her, "but we soon will. Anyway I do know Emily, and so do you, she's often here when I've brought horses here competing."

"Is she that really lovely person, who always gives you a hug?" said Hattie, trying to keep the green-eye out of her voice, "the tall, slim one, with the long hair who always calls you 'Darling'?"

"Yes, she's a doll, really kind and loves her dogs, so she'll love this little fellah."

They tentatively walked into the echelons of hospitality, waiting outside on the grass area, where there were a few bench tables dotted about. Inside through the open doors they could see a number of people, cups clasped in their hands, eating sandwiches and Danish Pastries.

"Who are they?" said Hattie, nudging Felix so hard that he almost dropped Fiver, "They're pretty dressed up – look that bloke has got a suit on!"

"They're the dressage judges. At a show like this you have three judges for each class, and they're all pretty high powered – or at least some of them think they are." he laughed ruefully, "nowadays you have to have ridden at a certain level before you can take your judging exams, so they have a pretty good idea of what it is like to have ridden down the centre line, and the exams are really tough to get through. They have to know their stuff."

Felix was saved from further explanation of these paragons of knowledge, by their mass exodus from the chalet, followed by their writers who accompanied them across the grass to little wood and glass huts strategically placed around the dressage arena. The eyes of the spectators were all riveted on them as they settled themselves down. Hattie and Felix watched them go, and then almost immediately alongside them came the thud of footfalls as the first horse was ushered into the ring.

"That was quick," murmured Hattie, "they didn't waste any time."

"No, I bet it's a really long class, and they'll be pushing them through faster than the runway at Gatwick."

Suddenly, over the loud speaker, the deep brown chocolate voice of the commentator started.

"May I welcome you, ladies and gentlemen, once again to Dressage at Hickstead, on another fine and glorious morning. The next class this morning will be the FEI Intermediare II , kindly sponsored by ......"

Felix and Hattie were listening intently, hypnotised by the charismatic tone of the commentator, when a whispered husky drawl filtered over Felix's shoulder.

"Felix Darling! What are you doing here, and what's this about a dog?"

Felix spun round and stood up nearly dropping the sleepy dog, "Emily sweetie, how lovely to see you, I didn't like to come in with all the judges about."

"Oh don't mind them darling – they like dogs just like we all do. Now let's take a look at this little cutie." Felix held up Fiver carefully, the little dog was still trembling, and cowered back as Emily put her hand out to stroke him. "Poor little love, look bring him inside, let's see what we can find him to eat, and for you two as well."

"Thanks Emily – you're lovely." Felix said gratefully, "You remember Hattie don't you?"

"Sorry darling." Emily turned to Hattie, "Of course I do."

"By the way Emily, is that Dougie doing the commentating?" he nodded his head to the raised box high above their heads, "I'd really like to catch up with him. I haven't seen him for ages."

"Yes, he's such a love, why not have something to eat first, then pop up and have a word with him in the break?" Emily offered, "He's on terrific form and such a laugh, I've invited him to my wedding here in September – I hope you and Alice are going to come?"

"Yep, we're looking forward to it – gonna be a wedding to end all weddings" laughed Felix, "can't wait!"

"Well it's time we tied the knot isn't it?" grinned Emily "and all our friends to celebrate, what could be better?"

Alice pulled into Nantes Place, creeping along the impressive drive with its lofty horse chestnut trees and rhododendrons flanking either side, over the little humped back bridge and swung left into the stable yard. She pulled up the Toyota and sat for a moment admiring the immaculately kept yard. The Parker-Smythes sure did have some serious dosh to keep this little lot up to scratch, she thought derisively. She hated the way Felix doffed his cap to Charles. Although Felix always laughed it off and said it always paid to keep owners sweet, she couldn't see it herself. Charles ran the horse to indulge his wife Jennifer, who was smitten with the thrills of eventing and would never be good enough to do it herself, not in the big league anyway, having only started riding herself the year before. Jennifer also had a soft spot for Felix, not in *that* way, she adored her husband after all – everyone knew that - but it was after that nasty kidnap business. She sighed, she supposed she could see why Charles indulged Jennifer, but surely that made Felix even more on a safe wicket then? Of course Charles was a ruthless business man. He didn't keep up this country pile, and all the other properties otherwise, even though a lot of it had been handed down through generations, but the loathsome way Felix squirmed and jumped around Charles made her sick. Alice much preferred his other patrons.

There was a tap on the car window. Dulcie, one of the yard grooms, was obviously wondering what she was up to sitting here dreaming. She planted a false smile on her face and jumped out.

"Morning Dulcie, what have you got for me this morning?"

"Big leg – small cut, now infected I think. Needs a look, and whilst you're here, perhaps you can do a couple of vaccinations – they're not due till the end of the month, but you might as well do them now." Dulcie beamed at Alice, her round chubby face tanned from the sunshine. "Want a cuppa to be going on with?"

"No," Alice said tartly not sure why she was taking out her dislike of Charles on the buxom Dulcie, "Why did you leave the cut so long?"

Dulcie raised her eyebrows and ignored her - the gesture said more than any words could have done - "the horse is in the stable waiting for you."

That served me right, thought Alice, as she followed Dulcie through the yard and into one of the loose boxes. Bending down to take a look, it was clear that the cut was indeed fairly small and insignificant and was just one of the unfortunate ones that became infected, probably owing to the flies at this time of year.

"I'll just get my stuff from the wagon," Alice said stiffly, avoiding Dulcie's probing and scornful gaze, "back in a jiff"

Dulcie patted the horse's neck, and stood waiting patiently for her to come back, thinking what a snooty bitch Alice was, when she heard the clatter of hooves on the yard. It must be Jennifer back from her ride and she peered out over the top of the stable door, to see a pretty dapple grey prance over the cobbles. Abandoning the stable, she rushed out to greet her.

"Did you have a good ride Jen?" smiled Dulcie taking hold of the reins, whilst the rider dismounted, "you were lucky to get out before it gets too hot."

"Fantastic thanks Dulcie. Didn't do much cantering though, the ground is getting a bit hard." Jennifer enthused, groping in her pocket for a polo. She glanced through the clock tower arch towards the main drive "I came in the back way, - is that the vet's car for Scooter?"

"Yes, that cut is infected, just like we thought. She's just getting her stuff out now. Antibiotics and clean up I should think, but she's short on words this morning is our Alice." Dulcie grinned conspiratorially at Jennifer, "Asked why I had left the cut so long – bloomin' cheek!"

Jennifer laughed, "Take no notice, she's got a chip on her shoulder, actually two chips, and probably a large steak to go with them!"

Alice stomped back through the gate, kicking it shut behind her with undue venom, she scarcely acknowledged either Jennifer or Dulcie and marched off into the stable to see to Scooter.

Dulcie mouthed *PMT?* to Jennifer, grinning conspiratorially and then changing her expression, followed her into the loose box.

Jennifer sighed and took Polly into the wash down box, enjoying the cool water as much as the little mare did. She was surprised at Alice. She wasn't normally so tetchy, and Dulcie was a real of fuss pot when it came to the well-being of the horses, no-one could ever accuse her of being lax. They had been lucky to get her and Nancy - their other groom. When Caitlin had been so badly injured by those thugs last year, Jennifer had always known that she would never return to work at Nantes, despite how desperately Caitlin had wanted to come back. Felix himself, had never made any secret that he was only staying with them for one season, and both she and Charles had been delighted with the way things had turned out for him up at Fittlebury Hall, and he was making a real success of his career so far too. But it had left them high and dry as far as staffing here at Nantes was concerned. In the end they had to resort to advertising, which was never a good plan, it was always so much better to have a recommendation through word of mouth. They advertised the two positions together, one as Head Groom – responsible for more of the admin side of things, and one as the under groom, to do more of the shit shovelling – luckily there was separate accommodation for both, Felix's flat above the stable yard and Caitlin's cottage, which had been the old granary. Both she and Charles had been surprised by the number of applicants, and he had suggested asking their friend Chloe to help with the interviewing. Chloe had only been too happy to oblige. She ran a busy eventing come hunting yard – Mileoak Farm – which was just outside the village and was not only great pals with Jennifer but was also her trainer too. She had done a great job with her own staff, Bibi and Susie, who were fantastic fun, hard working and all of them had been instrumental in helping Jennifer during that first turbulent year when she was learning to ride at Chloe's place.

Jennifer smiled to herself, thinking back to those interviews, which had taken place in her study way back in early February. It had been as gloomy an experience as the downs on a rainy day, as one applicant after another trailed in, either boastfully spouting on about how good they were and they would soon lick the yard into shape, and when asked to demonstrate their riding ability had proceeded to beat the shit out of the horses in attempts to show how masterful they were; or alternatively never getting to the riding stage, falling at the first fence like novices in their first race when their inexperience was exposed. They had despondently begun to give up – staff for the yard here at Nantes had to be just right. Jennifer's own personal lack of experience didn't mean that she wasn't a hands-on owner. She wanted people whom she could look to for help, but also who were fun and that she could get along with on a daily basis and who were not going to make her feel stupid and inadequate as far as the horses were concerned. Charles also had to be figured into the equation; he loved his hunting, worked hard during the week, and certainly didn't suffer fools gladly. When his children, Jessica and Rupert came to stay, which they often did, they also rode, and the staff had to be good with the kids. It was a tall order and neither she nor Chloe wanted to make any mistakes – it was a minefield.

The last two to be interviewed had applied together, and Chloe and Jennifer had put them in as an afterthought, thinking that each applicant would be vying for the better job, and yard rivalry was never a good way to start. Mrs Fuller, the housekeeper at Nantes, who had been Jennifer's arch nemesis when she'd first married Charles, but who'd had a gradual renaissance over the last year, and now couldn't do enough for her, had bustled in with another cafetiere of coffee for the flagging troops.

"The last two are here," she'd announced loftily, "they're sitting in the hall – look nice enough. Doris had a gander though – she reckons they're queer – y'know, a couple like!"

Jennifer remembered all too well the look of astonished revelation on Mrs Fuller's face, and had laughed, "Better wheel them in then Mrs F – don't suppose you've got any cakes have you?" The best way of defusing Mrs Fuller, Jennifer had learned, was to ask for something to eat.

"I'll bring in some of my millionaire's shortbread and show those two in then." She whisked out of the door.

Chloe and Jennifer had had to stifle giggles when Mrs Fuller reappeared with the two girls. But it was luck indeed. Dulcie and Nancy were indeed a couple, neither wanted to be senior to the other and immediately said so. They would share the roles equally. They would only need one lot of accommodation too. They had lots of experience and both Jennifer and Chloe immediately warmed to them, even more so when they saw how well they both rode. The girls were home-makers, opting to live in the roomier Granary

Cottage. They were neither overt nor covert about their sexual preferences, and Jennifer couldn't have cared less anyway as long as they were good at the job.

Dulcie was the shorter of the two, verging a little on the plump side, with a round merry face, and riotous curly brown hair. She rode well and sensitively, with a whacky sense of humour she was rarely ever out of sorts or bad tempered. The other fabulous thing about Dulcie was she had an amazing voice and was always singing. It was infectious and the yard buzzed when she was around. The children adored her and she spent happy hours with them, never losing patience with Jessica and her incessant questions. Nancy was slightly older, taller and thinner, with short cropped dark hair, and although she was much quieter than Dulcie she was just as much of a laugh. Her humour was drier and more off beat, and she had an uncanny knack of making you feel everything and anything was always perfectly under control. She was incredibly strong too, more so than most men, her sinewy arms could lift any amount hay bales or shavings, and she drove the truck like she was born with a Yorkie bar in her mouth. Riding wise, she was tough, could ride all day if she had to, and never seemed afraid, even of Charles' mettlesome hunter Beano, who could be a total arse at times. She and Dulcie complimented each other perfectly, and for Nantes they had been an unexpected and perfect find.

The roar of an engine made Jennifer look up. It was the vet's car pulling away up the drive, and she saw Dulcie talking to Nancy over the loose box door. Both girls looked serious, then Dulcie stuck her tongue out after the retreating car, and Nancy gave her a friendly shove and they both started to laugh.

"What's up?" Jennifer called, leading Polly back out into the sunshine to dry off, "What's the verdict?"

Dulcie started to sing, her sweet voice rang out strangely menacingly as it reverberated around the old yard to the Michael Jackson song *"Beat It"*

"Just Beat it, beat it, beat it, no-one wants to be defeated, showin' how funky strong is your fight, it doesn't matter who's wrong or right, just beat it, beat it, beat it, beat it, just beat it!"

"Oh dear, I think Alice just got right up Dulcie's nose!" grinned Nancy to Jennifer, "The end result is that Scooter is fine, and Alice has kangarooed off in Ozzie mode, with an ego flying higher than a jumbo jet!"

Jennifer laughed, "She'll get over herself, she certainly needs too. I'm just going to chuck on Polly's fly rug and then we'll have a cuppa shall we?"

Dulcie and Nancy watched Jennifer ambling down towards the water meadow with Polly, admiring her long legs enhanced with tight breeches, her silvery hair catching the glints of sun and thought, not for the first time, what a great boss she was to work for, and what a lucky day it was when they had come to Nantes. Nancy slipped her hand into Dulcie's, and squeezed it in a rare and discreet display of affection.

Dulcie turned to look at her smiling "I know exactly what you're thinking doll, and you're right. Let's get that kettle on."

Alice drove erratically out of Nantes. She knew that she had behaved badly and irrationally. Dulcie was good at her job and there had been no need for her to be so high handed. It wasn't like her at all to be so carpy and unprofessional, and at the Parker-Smythes' gaff too. How could she be so stupid? They were probably taking the right piss out of her now. She just hoped that Jennifer, whom she hadn't even acknowledged, wasn't offended and wouldn't make a complaint about her attitude to Andrew or Oliver, who would take a seriously dim view of such stroppy behaviour. She pulled over for a moment before going onto the next call, composing herself. She'd been feeling uneasy ever since Grace had made that remark about secrets in people's lives. She had escaped from Oz to get away from all that. Surely it wasn't or couldn't be coming back to haunt her after all this time? She tried to think rationally. Was she just being silly? Over-wrought with too much work on, and not thinking clearly with paranoia seeped like a paralysing poison through every vessel? No, that was all long behind her. She was just over tired and sometimes living with Felix, however dynamic their relationship and however much she adored him, was like living with an over enthusiastic kid. She braced her shoulders, pretending to be talking into her mobile as a car swept past her on the road, and tried to calm herself down. She must banish these unwelcome thoughts. She was here in the UK now, it was a fresh start, and everything else was left far behind her. She was working in a well-respected equine practice and was well thought of, and if she played her cards right all would stay that way. She mentally decided that she would apologise to Dulcie at the first opportunity. The persona she was developing here for herself was one that she had earned by right. She was a good vet, skilled, efficient and kind, with a good client manner. I mustn't lose my head she thought determinedly.

CHAPTER 7

By 5.30pm that day Colin still had not heard anything from Aiden Hamilton. It was disappointing especially as he was like a man possessed yesterday, dashing around with his phone taking all those photos like a demented paparazzi. For once Colin thought ruefully, his estate agent's antennae had failed him dismally, and he had read the situation completely wrong – Aiden was just another time waster. He drummed his fingers in irritation on his desk as he watched the rest of his staff packing up their desks to go home, and realised gloomily that he could leave the dreaded call no longer. He picked up the phone and reluctantly dialled Mark's mobile number.

"Hi Mark, it's me Colin. I'm sorry to say that I've heard nothing back from that blighter about the mill. I really thought he'd taken the bait, but not a dicky bird. Guess it's a no-goer." Colin apologised, "I was so sure, just shows you how wrong you can be eh? Don't suppose you and Sandy fancied popping over for a drink later – to commiserate - or maybe in the Fox?"

Mark could barely hide his disappointment. He really thought this time he might be rid of the place, but it wasn't Colin's fault, after all he had lost a shed load of commission too. He always thought that bloke Hamilton was an arrogant tosser, even on the TV.

"What a bummer. Mind you, I thought he was too good to be true – didn't you?" Mark exploded, "Not your fault though Colin, you did your damndest. I think I'm stuck with the place, mill stone an' all." He laughed, "Just not meant to be – not sure about the drink – Sandy's right in the middle of a tough old case, although it should be wrapping up today – how about we make it tomorrow? Why don't you and Grace come to us? I'll cook."

Colin laughed, "Hmm, sounds risky – but we'll chance it!

Seriously, be nice for Grace, and we won't have much chance to get out once the baby comes." He added more seriously, "Do you mind if we make it early though, as she gets bushed now, lugging the bump about - the only consolation is that she always drives!"

"No, early suits us fine – Sandy's always starving when she gets in and otherwise picks on a load of rubbish if we eat late. See you about 7pm then?"

Mark ended the call. Bugger, even though he'd thought it was too good to be true at the time, there was a small glimmer of possibility that he might be rid of the mill once and for all. But it was not to be, by the looks of things he was going to be stuck with the bloody thing forever. Oh well, it had been in ruins for a long time now, let it decay even further and then he could knock it down without any more conscience.

Aiden, on the other hand, had been busy all day, with back to back meetings with architects and solicitors, and then architects again. In between times he had paid random visits to his restaurants, shaking up his chefs so that they quivered with nerves and made stupid mistakes, the small minions of the dogs' bodies in the kitchens scurrying for cover as he swooped in like a predatory bird of prey. His customers loved seeing him arriving out of the blue, as he stopped to chat at the tables to them, asking them about their food, buying them drinks, and making suggestions about what was exciting on the menu today. Behind the scenes though, all hell let loose, as he berated the staff, flooring them with caustic comments which stripped them of self-esteem as neatly as any industrial cleaner. He rubbished the vegetables which had been delivered insisting that they were not fresh enough, and made impossible demands of the chefs when they were at their most fraught. His eagle eye and acid tipped tongue did not miss a thing and he relished each moment of the staffs' discomfort when he ran riot in the kitchens. Then he would breeze out into the throng of the seated guests, charm oozing from every pore, and not one of them would realise the mayhem he had just caused behind the scenes. Despite his bully boy tactics and reputation for tongue lashing his workers, young hopefuls were desperate to be trained under his supervision, and no-one ever complained. Aiden adored this supreme feeling of power and control in the kitchen when the earth quaked as he walked in – almost as much as he fed upon the admiration of his diners, and patrons. To him it was a like riding the highest crest of a wave, you just couldn't wait for the next one. The press, of course, loved him not only was he extremely hunky and photogenic, but he made good copy with his emotional outbursts and extreme passion about food and his talent for creating gastronomic delights. His histrionics in the kitchen were no secret but everyone put it down to his food obsession rather than his innate need to control and bulldoze his way through life. Of course having successful and powerful friends helped and his dinner guests were often papped in *Hello* or *Okay* magazine – all the more grist to his peppery mill and for theirs too. So opening the Old Mill as a super duper new chic out of town restaurant appealed to him. There was a lot of money in that area, and if he could persuade a few of his mates to make a guest appearance or two, and get Roxy to play ball, it could be a seriously lucrative project.

The first meeting with the architects had not gone well. They'd been horrified by the initial photographs, being about as enthusiastic as a eunuch in a brothel. They could just not see any potential at all, and kept droning on about the outlay in terms of income. Aiden had bollocked them rigid in his usual way, and told them to get their arse into gear and come up with some goods by the afternoon, or he'd go to someone who could. He'd stalked out, saying he'd be back later. When Aiden Hamilton was in megalomaniac mood – you didn't argue, and by the time he'd returned, they'd put some ideas together and their enthusiasm matched a dog with two tails. Marginally mollified, he agreed to a site meeting the following week. The solicitors had none of the reservations of the architects, and confirmed that directly he gave the go-ahead they would be ready.

Chrissie was busy at her desk when he barged through the door after the last meeting. She looked up briefly, appraising his temper with a rapid glance. She had worked for him for a long time now, and she was probably the only person who was not afraid of him and his rapid mood swings.

"How did it go then?" she asked, her eyes returning to her computer screen, "What did they think?"

"Well I had to kick the fuckers into touch, but they saw my point of view in the end," Aiden snapped, spitting out his chewing gum, "They're a stuck up lot of wankers at times."

"Did they come up with any ideas about the conversion?" Chrissie said doubtfully, still not removing her eyes from the screen.

"Not to begin, but actually now I think they have come round a bit. I'm not gonna make any offers yet though, make those country bumpkins wait a few days, then once the price is fixed, we can really crack on." Aiden sighed "Fancy a drink – or a shag?" he asked hopefully.

"No thanks," replied Chrissie coolly, "Anyway, you've dinner out again tonight – Roxy's already rung twice here – your mobile's off."

"Christ!" moaned Aiden, "It's on silent. I suppose I'd better go then. I miss you Chrissie."

"Dream on Aiden," laughed Chrissie, "Enjoy your meal."

That night at the cottage Felix was attempting to explain to a bad tempered Alice how he'd come by Fiver. She was livid, and even more so that he'd invited Dougie, his old mate who was doing the commentating at Hickstead, to come over for supper.

"For fuck's sake Felix, you're like a child, you can't be left unsupervised for five minutes." she yelled, "you are telling me you stole a dog!"

"*Fiver* minutes actually and I didn't steal him, I paid for him sweet pea. If you'd been there you'd had been as mad as a wet hen – honest you would!" argued Felix, "as for Dougie, I haven't seen him for ages, why shouldn't I ask him over? What's got into you?"

"What's got into me?" screeched Alice "you are so bloody thoughtless that's what. You can barely afford to feed yourself, let alone a dog, and what happens when you go away – tell me that?"

"Well I'll take him with me of course, everyone else takes their dogs, why shouldn't I take mine? Don't be such a cow about him. He's such a cute little thing. You're a bloody vet, you should love dogs." Felix, who was normally affable and easy going was shouting back at her now, "I hate cruelty and this little chap was having a miserable time, I was hoping you'd check him over for me."

Alice glared at Felix and then at Fiver. They both looked pathetic, Felix's shaggy blond hair flopping over his eyes, badly in need of a cut, his long legs splayed out in front of him and Fiver angelically perched on his lap. "Oh let me have a look at him then," she said grudgingly, holding out her hands for the dog.

Fiver resisted with all his strength to go to Alice, and she took him by the scruff of the neck and quickly examined him, pulling up his lips and checking his teeth and gums, feeling his tummy and ribs.

"Well, he's not very old, probably about 6 months or so, and he almost certainly has worms, judging by his tummy."

"Oh, there was me, thinking he was just fat," sighed Felix, "I'll get some tablets for him."

"Don't be stupid, I'll get them, and a course of vaccinations too, as I doubt he's had them, and I'll check if he's been micro-chipped."

Felix smiled at her sweetly, "Oh Alice, would you? I'd be so grateful darling"

"Yes, all right no need to lay it on so thick – I get the message, he's here to stay. But get one thing straight, he's not sleeping in our bed - okay?

"Thanks Alice – don't worry I won't let him come between us – not in bed anyway." He grinned, "I'll throw some pasta and stuff together for Dougie, you'll love him, he's a real laugh and I haven't seen him since we worked together."

Alice was thawing now and stroking the puppy's ears, "Is he the one you worked with at that dressage yard?"

"Yep he's the one," said Felix, uncurling his long legs from the sofa to make his way into the kitchen to start the supper, "He's a bit older than me, beautiful rider on the flat, real poetry to watch, but he got the eventing bug and left. Been really successful too, but then had a bad accident, and was on the sidelines for a while."

"That's what freaks me out about this eventing," sighed Alice, "What happens if you have a bad accident like that?"

Felix laughed, "Well usually they are few and far between, but Dougie was lucky, and when you meet him you'll know why."

"Oh for fuck's sake Felix, don't be so irritating, tell me now," snapped Alice in exasperation, making the puppy jump up in alarm on her lap.

Felix glanced at her in concern, it was not like Alice to be so tetchy, but he turned back and carried on making the supper. "First, he's a great looking bloke, really tall, dark and handsome – James Bond sort – you know, but he has this amazing voice. It's got a real ring to it, sort of Prince Charles cross Charles Parker-Smythe – upper class drawl, but with a really dry sense of humour. You could listen to him all day. So he started doing a bit of commentating, just for fun to start and now he does all the big events – even Burghley. He'll be as famous as Raymond Brookes-Ward ever was one day."

"Well, I'll look forward to meeting him then," said Alice dryly, "I'm going to grab a shower." She turfed the little dog unceremoniously onto the floor and stomped up the rickety stair case.

Felix rushed back into the sitting room, automatically ducking his lanky frame under the low beam and scooped up Fiver and took him into the kitchen. What was the matter with Alice, she'd been funny all day? He tried to think if he had done something to upset her, but other than the dog and asking Dougie over, there was nothing he could remember. Surely it couldn't be Fiver, Alice was a vet after all, she wouldn't want to see animals suffering any more than the next person surely? As for Dougie, she hadn't even met him, so it couldn't be that – but something had upset her that was for sure. It was a side of her he hadn't seen before and he wasn't sure he liked it much.

CHAPTER 9

Max Goldsmith commanded the table, the affability on his face belying the tension in his powerful body. They were playing for high stakes and the atmosphere in the room was smouldering like the blue touch paper on a firework. The faces of the onlookers looked appalled and enthralled in equal parts, waiting for the explosion as the three men faced each other out, willing one or other to back down.

Max sighed, "I'll raise you £10k," he said quietly, smiling at the other men, one of whom now had tiny jewels of sweat beading on his upper lip, and pushed a pile of chips into the centre, to join the burgeoning pile already stacked there.

The little crowd gasped and waited expectantly for the response from the other players. The rotund sweating man took out a hanky, mopped his brow and threw his cards on the table. "I'm out," he moaned, and pushed his chair back.

Max raised his eyebrows slightly at the other man "Karl?" he questioned, "You still in?"

The other man glared at Max. He had small ferrety eyes, the whites were red rimmed and his face was flushed with drink. The comb-over covering his thinning hair was glistening under the centre table light, and Max could see a slight tremor in his hands – he knew he had him, but obviously the old bugger wouldn't give up as he shoved more chips into the pot to match the bet.

Max loved this part, the kill, the swoop, the delicious moment before he dealt the death blow. He took his time, smiling slightly before pushing another stack of chips forward. "I'll raise you another £20k."

It was too much for ferret man, who threw his hands down in molten fury, "Show me what you've got! I don't believe you!" He staggered up and lunged across the table at Max, who drew back in alarm, but not before two beefy hench men grabbed him and pushed the thrashing man back into his seat. "You fucker!" he yelled "You've cleaned me out!"

Max recovered his composure almost immediately, "I take it Karl, you are folding then?" he enquired quietly, he signalled to a man behind him, who collected the pot. "Thank you, it has been a pleasure to play with you." He nodded to the excited crowd which had tripled and were buzzing with the unexpected entertainment. "Good evening ladies and gentleman." He stood up, another one of his lackeys produced his cashmere coat and cane, and with all the elegance of a character from a 1920's movie, he elegantly made his departure. The throng of exotically dressed women in their sequined gowns and men, straining in over-tight tuxedos, parted deferentially as he swept through them, as easily as Moses had parted the Red Sea.

Max hardly noticed them as he made his way out of the club followed protectively by his minders, but stopped in his tracks when he heard a familiar provocative laugh. He turned his head momentarily, glancing to a corner table. Roxy Le Feuvre was sitting facing him, and in that instant, as she looked up and their eyes locked, all the old memories and passions came flooding back like an unwelcome rip tide heralding an approaching tsunami. He inclined his head slightly towards her, a hint of smile on his lips, and Roxy immediately stood up and beckoned him over. Max hesitated, but there was always something about her that made him do such stupid uncharacteristic things, he changed course and made his way over to her table.

"Max darling," Roxy screeched, "God, how wonderful to see you, it's been so long!" She leapt up and kissed him hard on the lips, the force almost making him take a step backwards.

Max could smell the alcohol on her breath, the faint tang of wine on her lips was sour on his, "Roxy my dear, how lovely to see you too." He disentangled himself, and leaned over to observe her companions. "Aiden, how are you dear fellow?"

Aiden stood up, clearly not as delighted as Roxy to see Max. He offered his hand nonetheless, "Max, good to see you, do you know Lisa and Mike?"

Max glanced at the famous couple, "Of course, not personally naturally," he reached over to shake their hands. "I was sorry to hear you had retired from International Football Mike, a great loss, I trust your injuries are recovering? And you my dear, I gather you are a rather wonderful horsewoman?" Max said smoothly, making Lisa flush with pleasure.

"I didn't know that Lisa," said Roxy surprised, "you never said."

"Yeah, my Lisa's into it big time, bought quite a few horses now aint ya Trace?" laughed Mike, "Cost me a bloody fortune!"

Aiden decided to take control, reluctantly asking, "Do you want to join us for a drink Max?" Mike and Lisa started to shift around the table to make room for him, clearly interested in this debonair man who knew so much more about their private lives than their supposed friends did.

"That's very kind Aiden, but I have a little further business this evening, so if you'll forgive me – perhaps another time. It's been a great pleasure to meet you both." Max inclined his head towards the others, kissed Roxy, on the cheek this time and made his stylish departure.

"Who is that guy?" hissed Lisa theatrically to Roxy, "he's seriously lush!"

"You don't want to know Lisa love," snapped Aiden, "he's trouble."

"Actually he's an old friend of mine," snapped Roxy, glaring at Aiden, "you can be bloody rude sometimes, he has been seriously good to me over the years."

"He's dangerous and you know it Roxy, don't pretend otherwise. He's into all sorts of stuff, you steer clear of him if you want my advice Lisa," snarled Aiden defensively. "Come on smile, the Paps are about."

Max curled back on the seat of the Mercedes, it was strange to see Roxy again after all this time. There was something about her that drew him in every time. He always felt like he was some kind of guardian angel when he saw her, with an overwhelming need to protect her. It had all been over a long time ago between them: she had been married twice since. The first marriage had been an unmitigated disaster, although it had been headline news at the time. *'Glamour Girl Weds Rock Star'* splashed all over the front pages of the tabloids, with the typical smutty copy beneath. *'Roxy gets her rocks off, when she marries her off-the-rails rock star, Peter Chambers in Las Vegas'*. Several grainy photos had accompanied the piece, one indecent shot of Roxy almost naked, and another with her wrapped around her new husband, clearly both of them out of their brains on dope. Of course, it had all been a cataclysmic failure. Pete continued his downhill spiral being blotto most of the time with alcohol and continuing to mainline on the hard stuff and attempting to take Roxy with him. As the months drifted by, so the days of lucidity became fewer and further between, but Roxy, in one rare moment of clarity, had rung Max in despair and desperation. Max hadn't thought twice, and ridden in once more like the knight in proverbial shining armour to salvage what remained of the once beautiful Roxy, promptly putting her into an exclusive and discreet rehab clinic. Max had been horrified by the state of her. She was always suggestible and crazy, but he was mortified when he realised how she had abused her body. The clinic were sworn to secrecy and to their credit, her whereabouts were never discovered by the media. Max visited her covertly, and when she was more coherent persuaded her to instruct solicitors for divorce proceedings, and a separation order was issued. Pete, meanwhile, shocked by Roxy's overnight departure and the nuclear bombshell of separation, was trying to make a bit of come back, and was actually writing a new album, the title song of which was making a bit of break in the charts. Although, Pete himself was still heavily tanked up with amphetamines and, privately, Max thought his renaissance would be short lived. Roxy began wavering about whether or not she should go back to him. Max was horrified, certain that it would be a colossal mistake and told her so in no uncertain terms. Roxy, it seemed, was determined that her life was on a collision course along with Pete's, and the stronger she became, the more she resisted his protection. In the end Max decided to pay Pete a little visit, to see for himself how the wild man of rock really was shaping up. Pete had laughed in Max's face, telling him to mind his own fucking business. It had been a serious mistake on Pete's part speaking to Max like that; and as a consequence and quite out of the blue, Pete had died four weeks later- seemingly from an apparent drug overdose. Although it had been sudden, given his life-style, no-one was particularly surprised - least of all Max, and the verdict at the inquest was put down to misadventure.

After Pete's death, a distraught Roxy, who blamed herself for his demise, lurched from one emotional crisis to another and came to rely upon Max's support all the more. Max, playing the role of noble hero, valiantly stayed around to pick up the pieces. It had taken Roxy months to crawl her way out of the gutter, let alone onto the pavement, and she made a lot of false starts, sliding hopelessly over and over again back into pits of black depression. To his credit, driven by his fatal attraction to her and also fuelled by a fleeting glimmer of responsibility for her grief over Pete's death, even if morally he would do the same again, he had supported her both emotionally and financially during this terrible time. As Pete's widow, she had eventually inherited a fair whack of money that had been left over from his estate, although how much he had snorted up his nose or injected into a vein was incalculable. Roxy slowly recovered, and once again rebuilt her persona in the public eye, carefully guided by Max, and her confidence grew in leaps and bounds. She became less and less dependent on him, and once again started to lead her own life, and he moved into her shadowy and unsavoury past.

Her second and current marriage was to Aiden Hamilton, the celebrity chef, and TV favourite. She met him on one of those frightful shows where members of the public were teamed up with second-rate celebrities on afternoon television, to cook up a meal between them, and the results were judged by a celebrity chef. Cheap daytime TV, with low budgets and saddos who had nothing better to do with their days but sit in all afternoon and watch rubbish entertainment. Roxy had been asked to do a stint. She had been excited at the time, she always glorified in any form of TV, whatever the genre, and had enthusiastically jumped at the chance, even though she was a lousy cook. Max had laughed and said why not, after all there was no such thing as bad publicity. It was before she'd had her tits reduced and she'd pitched up with a low cut T-shirt, her boobs hanging out the front, a miniscule pair of shorts, and her infamously dishevelled hair cascading out of an inadequate topknot. She looked every bit the glamour model, with her heavy make-up and pouting lips. The poor old boy who was to partner her in making the meal had nearly had a fatal coronary when he saw her. In the green room before the show, she'd met Aiden. They were all getting a bit tanked up on the free champagne and nibbles, and Roxy was flirting outrageously with Mr Flamminger her partner, when Aiden walked in, and characteristically made some snide remarks. Roxy laughed at him and told him to *'fuck off back to his cage'* hooting to Mr Flamminger that these hot chefs were nothing but bullies with small cocks. An enraged Aiden, who was used to people bowing and scraping when he walked into a room was enraged, but Roxy carried on laughing and joking with Mr Flamminger and ignored him.

From then on, it was a chase, not just from Aiden, but from a media frenzy. They both realised how good this was for both of their images, the public loved a love story, and they were certainly entertained by *'Rox-Aid'* as it was dubbed by the press. They were seen sneaking into restaurants, boarding aircraft, illicit holidays, dining with the greats. Roxy changed her image; the press went wild – headlining with *'Aiden tames Roxy'*. Speculation as to a pregnancy started when Roxy was seen wearing a floaty smock one day, and with advice from their publicists it seemed a good plan, and within a month she actually was pregnant.

The wedding was a circus, and read like a who's who of the celebrity greats. Anyone who was anyone was invited, and those who hadn't been asked were has-beens. *Okay* magazine offered a huge sum for the magazine rights and never one to miss a financial opportunity, Roxy had greedily accepted. Without any complaints, she'd changed outfits as many times as the stylist wanted in the shoot, although she was heartily sick of them by the time they'd finished. Max thought back gloomily to the day of the wedding. He had received an invite, not sanctioned from a snipey Aiden he was certain, but he knew that Roxy would never have left him off the guest list. It had been a blistering day in July, and the wedding was held in a stately home in Surrey which belonged to one of Aiden's chums. A colossal Georgian pile, which was normally open to the public, but had been closed for the day, and the whole place had been commandeered for the occasion. The house was splendid enough but the garden was spectacular, and from the balustraded terrace, a vast sweep of marble stone steps led down to an impressive symmetrical garden with small boxed borders enclosing water features, which later Max discovered had been designed by Capability Brown. Below the formal garden, rolling lawns with spreading cedar trees led down to a large lake. Bad tempered black swans clamoured around the edge, near a wooden boathouse, and within its centre was an island with an intriguing folly, shaped like a Grecian temple. Looking back, the sugar-white grandeur of the house stood proud and imperious, like a sentry keeping guard. It was certainly a fairytale setting, and Roxy and Aiden were in their element, laughing and talking to their guests; a never-ending flow of champagne, and of course the most delectable food. Guests were surreptitiously snapping away at any opportunity and far from shunning the publicity, the glamorous couple positively welcomed it – no-one could say that they were not a match made in heaven. They were as ambitious as each other. But love? No, Max thought sadly– the only love was for the camera and the money.

Since then, Roxy had had another child with Aiden, all much publicised of course, and naturally had a fleet of helpers ministering to their every need. Nonetheless Roxy publically claimed to *"adore her little babies"*, but these days Max was not close enough to her to know the truth. The little girls were beautiful, like perfect, artificial dolls. Roxy had maximised the business opportunity, bringing out a range of clothing for kids; published a few children's books, ghost written of course, and they were often photographed as a model family. Aiden too had cashed in, with a range of ready meals for kids, from babies upwards – extolling the virtue of his organic and welfare friendly ranges. Their daughters, Stephanotis and Delphinium, were angelic with cherubic faces resembling the Putti seen on fine Italian masterpieces. Behind the scenes, the little girls were brought up by a host of nannies and au-pairs and luckily for them were rarely involved in their parents' money making schemes, unless it involved some publicity stunt where they needed to be wheeled out for the cameras.

Max considered Roxy and her life with a weary resignation. There was, and always would be, a tangible thread that linked their lives, the old sultry magic always crackling in the air when they met like an electrical surge, their lives inextricably bound to each other. No matter what Aiden said or thought, Roxy would always have a place for him in her heart, and she in his, despite the years that had tumbled by since he had last seen her.

He tapped his driver on the shoulder, all this thinking of the past never did any good. He had a lot of business on tonight and this stupid reminiscing wouldn't help him get through it.

"Take me to Scotties," he ordered sharply, "and then wait. We've a long night ahead."

The chauffeur bobbed his head, touching his cap deferentially, "Yes sir." He answered quickly. He knew better than to make any further remarks. When Max said jump, his minions asked '*how high?*' and had learned not to ask any questions, and those that had, were no longer around to ask any more. Whatever Max wanted, Max got. He put his foot on the accelerator and started to drive.

CHAPTER 9

Dougie arrived late at Felix's, and rapped on the door with all the enthusiasm of a dawn raid, bursting in through the door with a flurry of apologies, clutching a bottle of Moet and a bunch of drooping flowers for Alice.

"Sorry I'm late mate, got held up in the prize giving, but managed to snaffle this baby!" He held the thick green bottle aloft, "let's chuck it in the freezer, it's had a right old shake-up, and we don't want to waste a drop." He turned to Alice, "and these are for you." He handed her the wilting flowers, obviously a hasty purchase from a garage on the way over.

Alice was frosty, "Thank you, they're ... very nice." She eyed him up and down, taking in the tall dark man. He was a cross between Pierce Brosnan and Clive Owen, dressed in pale chinos and a tweed jacket, which he was flinging nonchalantly over the arm of the sofa, as though he had lived there for years.

"Felix has told me all about you Alice," he drawled in his cut glass voice, which was like melted chocolate, "wasn't he a star rescuing that little dog? He was always such a hero."

"Damned stupid if you ask me - it's tantamount to stealing." snapped Alice, not liking how Dougie had made himself at home, and Felix had plied him with a cold lager, and was now lounging opposite him on the armchair. "You two obviously go back a long way."

Dougie decided to ignore the first remark. He'd never been fond of sniping women, "Oh yes, we worked together at a dressage yard in Chipping Norton way back," laughed Dougie, "We had some right laughs – didn't we?"

"Sure did," smiled Felix in his usual affable way, not rising to Alice either, if she wanted to be an uptight arse, then she could do it on her own he thought. "Do you remember when ..."

"I'm not going to sit and listen to you two all night reminiscing about old times am I?" Alice carped, "Tell me Dougie, what do you do with yourself these days?"

Dougie beamed at her, "I've got the most lovely yard in Gloucestershire, really quaint old Cotswold place, and do pretty much the same as Felix, ride and train eventers for clients and run a few of my own too. These days though I have a pretty big staff, as I'm away a lot." He took a slug of his beer, running the cool can against his face for a moment. "I had a bad accident a few years ago, broke my neck, luckily it wasn't too bad and I've made a good recovery, but since then I've been doing commentary for some of the horse trials and that's been going quite well - less risky too."

"You're too modest mate," grinned Felix, "You're doing some big events now, even Burghley this year, that's the big time."

"I'd rather be riding there" sighed Dougie, "but it's great fun, and I'm lucky to still be riding at all anyway. I've got some seriously decent horses, one just coming up to advanced, and a couple of intermediates, and a few promising youngsters cutting their teeth on the novices and BE100s. It's busy enough." He shifted his weight on the sofa, kicking off his loafers and swinging his feet onto the sofa, "you've got a nice set up here though Felix, posh old joint."

"Yeah I fell on my feet when I got this yard, I was really lucky. The people I worked for last season pulled a few strings for me to get it though, and have bought me a good horse. They've even sponsored my truck – so I mustn't complain, but it's always a juggle between finances and staff – you know what I mean."

"Same for us all, eventing's not a cheap sport these days. Still I'm lucky I've a great partner - Roberto. I don't know what I'd do without him. He kept the horses going for me when I was off, and the yard too. You need someone like that to back you up." Dougie looked pointedly at Alice, "And what do you do?"

"I'm a vet at a local equine practice, so I don't have time for any of the hands-on stuff," said Alice stiffly, "Felix has to manage that side of things himself. But I do my bit," she said defying either of them to say anything different.

"Lucky old you Felix!" laughed Dougie, "No vet's bills at least and you can get hold of any drugs you need anytime," he winked at Alice, "just what we could all do with!"

Alice was livid, "What are you insinuating by that remark? Absolutely not, I don't know what you think I am, but I would never do anything like that – ever! Felix is just like any other client, and it would be extremely unprofessional for me to behave any differently to him than to anyone else," she said hotly, "What's more all drugs are logged in and out and are strictly accounted for."

"Whoa calm down Alice, I think Dougie was joking," soothed Felix, alarmed at her volcanic reaction to what was obviously just a bit of a daft banter. "Of course you wouldn't do anything like that darling."

Dougie looked aghast at Alice, thinking how supremely touchy she was, but for the sake of harmony immediately apologised, "Sorry Alice, of course I was joking, I didn't mean to offend you." Although privately thinking, it didn't take much to offend her, and that her reaction had been a bit over the top if she was that squeaky clean. The lady doth protest too much he thought. Changing the subject quickly he turned to Felix, "Wanna show me around when you've finished your beer?"

"Great – love too, and if you wanna stay tonight Dougie and have a few beers, you'd be more than welcome, wouldn't he Alice?"

Felix stared hard at Alice willing her to agree, and she turned her head away and muttered, "Of course, there are clean sheets on the spare bed."

"Well that's great, if you're sure? Dougie locked his liquid eyes onto Alice and smiled, "thanks I'd love too, saves me going back to my hotel tonight, and I have to be back at Hickstead early in the morning so I won't outstay my welcome. We can have a good old catch up in the meantime mate." He leant over and clashed cans with Felix who grinned back at him, like two naughty school boys contemplating scrumping in an orchard full of juicy apples.

    The next morning Colin was sitting in his office contemplating the day ahead. He had a lot of work on, a couple of valuations to do of some sizeable properties which always took a long time and he was going to take one of his newer juniors along to give him a hand. The other staff in the office were busy, quite a lot of property in various stages of sale negotiation and the letting side of things was on the up, and recently he had taken on a new member of staff to help on that side. New smaller properties were being offered for sale on a regular basis and this was the bread and butter money, but Colin loved the big estates, they were so much more interesting, even if the market was not as good as it had been in that area. He still ran a weekly Friday auction in the old market hall, of old furniture, and bric a brac, and this was just as popular as ever, tempting punters of all shapes and sizes into the lofty old auction room. The dealers came as they always did to have their preview but Colin had strict codes of conduct about only selling at auction. If anything really interesting came in he might well ring one or two of them and ask if they wanted to have a look before the piece was catalogued, but once it was, it went under the hammer, just like everything else. Yes Allinghams was an old traditional firm, and there weren't many like them around anymore; lots of the local firms had been swallowed up by the big multi-national agencies and, as such, no longer offered the intimate personal service that his own firm provided. He had expanded, it was true, but only in a diminutive way, having a small office in Storrington; which was a tiny neighbouring town, hardly a town really, more like a large village. It was, however, a real tourist draw, with lots of quaint shops; upmarket boutique clothes shops, butchers, grocers, tea shops, that kind of thing and as such the office did well and had been a smart move for Allinghams. He had one other office which was in Cuckfield, an old toll town quite close to Horsham, and similar in size to Storrington, with the same type of clients and shopping demographic. For Colin it was enough, he didn't want to get any bigger. Bigger meant more staff and taking on a partner, and he didn't want to go down that road. He had good managers on decent salaries, with the usual perks and commission, with hand-picked staff to back them up. He ran good teams within each branch and once a week they all met together for team building and he prided himself on being a good manager of his three offices. Some years ago he'd met a woman at one of the Hunt Balls who specialised in this field. At first he had scoffed at the idea, thinking he could handle everything, but as he listened to the feisty, dynamic woman, he'd found himself agreeing to meet her. It had turned his work and staffing situation around, and now she was an important part of his team, and every six months she took integral members of staff for coaching and it had proved invaluable. Her book *"The Team Formula"* had become his bible and each member of his staff were provided with a copy directly they started working for him. Everyone felt part of the team at Allinghams and as such went the extra mile to provide the service for the client – it was a winning combination.

Colin gathered his paperwork together, picked up his trusty tape measure and Dictaphone, and was just preparing to leave the office en-route to the first valuation when Elizabeth his branch manager, popped her head around his door. "I've a caller on the line, only wants to speak to you Col, a woman, calling on behalf of a Mr Hamilton? Shall I put them through?"

"Well, well! Thanks Elizabeth." He sat back down in his chair, dragged out a pad and waited for the call. The phone on his desk buzzed and he picked it up "Colin Allingham speaking."

"Mr Allingham, it's Chrissie St John Stevens" came the brisk icy tones that Colin recognised straight away as belonging to Aiden Hamilton's PA. "Mr Hamilton wants a second viewing of the property next week. Tuesday would suit us. Say midday?"

Colin bristled at her, not a damned please or thank you. He stifled a rebuke, replying, "Hold on a moment, whilst I check my diary; we do have another viewing scheduled, but I believe that's for the Monday," he lied, thinking he should say *'no that's not possible'*, and then he thought of Mark and how much he wanted to get rid of the place and replied, "Yes that should be fine. Midday – Tuesday then."

"Excellent. Good day."

The call was ended and Colin was left with the receiver still glued to his ear and felt like a bloody fool. Who did she think she was, clearly as up her own arse as her boss. Honestly some people were so rude. How Aiden Hamilton thought he would make a go of it down here with that attitude would be a joke – still his was not to reason why. Mark would be delighted and he quickly dialled his number to tell him the good news.

CHAPTER 10

Felix looked bleary eyed this morning and wore a baseball cap pulled down low on his head, his blond hair sticking out at the sides like a gruesome clown. He could only grunt to Hattie's questions, and was drinking gallons of water.

"Heavy night?" she enquired, strapping one of the horses vigorously, "Did Dougie come back for supper?"

"Don't shout Hattie, I can't bear it," wailed Felix piteously, gulping down another pint of water, "yeah he did come back, we had a great night. He stayed actually, only left early this morning as he had to get back to Hickstead. Christ knows how he feels today, stuck up in that bloody commentary box, having to sound jolly."

"Ah well, I expect he'll manage, he seems the party type," laughed Hattie, "He's seriously good looking."

"Dream on Hats," Felix smiled, "he's seriously gay too."

"Shame, you must be the only straight one I know," she mused dreamily, wishing he was single too.

"Nah, there's loads of straight guys, but I'll grant you there are plenty that aren't, and some that swing both ways." He grimaced, "oh my bloody head."

"Zero sympathy I'm afraid," Hattie replied cheekily. She loved the easy banter that had sprung up between them of late, when there was just the two of them together in the yard, "anyway, you'd better get yourself sorted you've got Rackham tomorrow and two to ride in the Novice. What you doing with them today?"

"Don't bloody remind me, I think I'll puke over every fence the way I'm feeling" he groaned, "a quick half an hour in the school and then we can go for a quiet hack, you okay to help with that?"

Hattie preened with pleasure. "If you think I'm up to the school work," she asked excitedly, "of course the hack will be fine."

"They've only got to get round a novice test and they're both going great – you do Rambler, he's pretty straight forward, and I'll do Jacks, 'cause he can be a bastard sometimes, then we have a tootle round the park. One thing though doll, can you get them ready, I just don't think I can bend down to put their boots on!"

Hattie laughed, "You bloody skiver – okay." She bent down to stroke the little dog which was glued to Felix's side, he was still very shy and cowered behind Felix's boots, his little brown and white coat stiffening with distrust, and his tail jammed down between his legs. "Come on Fiver, you've got to get to know me, you're gonna see me every day."

"He's getting better, but I think at some point he's been given a right walloping. Every time you raise your hand he just shrinks back and hides. Poor little thing, still, he'll soon learn to love life again – won't you little chap." He leant down and stroked the dog, who rolled over on his back, his little white legs whirling like rotor blades when Felix rubbed his tummy.

"What are you going to do with him while we ride?" asked Hattie, "Seems mean to shut him in."

"No he can come with us, we're only going to be in the school and then going round the park, he can come along – he'll love it."

"You sure he won't run off? You've only had him five minutes." She looked at him doubtfully, "Well on your aching head be it."

Twenty minutes later they were clattering out of the yard towards the school, with Felix calling for the little dog to follow. At first Fiver just ran in circles, not sure where his new master was, and eventually ran and hid in the yard. Patiently Felix rode back on the frustrated Jacks, who just wanted to be off and was skittering about on the cobbles, his hooves striking sparks like Swan Vestas in his impatience to get going. Finally Hattie got off the more tolerant Rambler, and handed the shivering dog to Felix, who sat him on the front of the saddle crooning hypnotically to him like a baby, and they walked over to the school with Fiver riding up with Felix just like a figure head on a ship.

Felix was amazed at how well Hattie was riding Rambler. Guiltily he realised that he had not really taken on board how much she had progressed since she had joined him. Of course they hacked out together and he gave her the odd lesson when he had time, but she had certainly improved. It was more of a *feel* thing than anything else, and *feel* was something that you couldn't teach anyone. You either had it, or you didn't. Hattie had it in spades - that was for sure.

"Hats, you're really doing very well," he complimented, as he watched her execute a very decent set of canter, trot, walk transitions. "have you been having secret lessons?" he joked, but he meant what he said about her doing well.

Hattie smiled, "Don't take the piss Felix. I've just spent a lot of time watching you. You learn a lot by watching." She added more seriously, "I really want to improve."

"Well you certainly have, I'm impressed Hats, I truly am." Felix admired "I also feel a bit guilty, I should give you more help."

"I don't mind, I know you don't have enough time as it is," Hattie smiled understandingly her face aglow with his praise. "I love my job Felix, I wouldn't have it any other way."

Fiver shifted balancing awkwardly on the saddle and Felix adjusted his weight to stop him falling off, then groaning with the pain of his aching head. "It's no good, let's just go for a gentle hack, I'm wiped out. Anyway I want to talk to you."

Hattie brought Rambler down to a walk, patting the horse's bay neck gently, and reaching forward to open the school gate. "What about? Sounds serious."

"Well it is and it isn't," began Felix, hardly knowing where to start, "I'm going to have to make some serious decisions about the yard if I'm going to keep our heads above water. The bottom line is that I really want you to come to the events with me as a travelling groom – that's if you'd like to of course?"

Hattie flushed, to her it would be a dream come true, just her and Felix – it was her idea of heaven. So far she hadn't had much opportunity to go with him other than to the odd local event such as Rackham tomorrow, as there always had to be someone here at the yard. "You know I would Felix," she said quietly, "but I don't see how it's possible."

"Alice came up with some suggestions. Take on more horses, which would need more staff and probably a second rider to help out – which I'm reluctant to do because of the financial commitment." Felix hesitated before continuing, "Or sub-let a few of the boxes to another rider, who would bring his own staff, and we could cover for each other while either of us are away competing. I think that could work if I found the right person, and as it stands now seems the better option myself."

Hattie listened carefully. She hated the idea of sharing Felix with anyone, it was hard enough watching him and Alice together, but somehow that was bearable. But more staff and another rider, where she would become their skivvy too – the idea was horrific. It looked as though things were going to alter for her in a big way. Inevitably whatever choice he made and whoever joined them, they would almost certainly be more qualified than she was, and would she then be demoted in Felix's eyes? It was a gloomy prospect, and some of these grooms could be right bitches. Suddenly the day seemed very grey indeed. She turned away from Felix, so that he couldn't see the tears in her eyes, "Yes, I can see the problem," she muttered, "have you any ideas, about a suitable person to let to I mean?"

"Well, as it happens Dougie does know someone," Felix said, straining to catch what she had said, "A dressage rider, he's quite well known, up and coming, has half a dozen nice horses working at a pretty high level apparently. He's looking for a yard in this area, as he's losing the tenancy on the one he's in now. Dougie's going to have a word with him and give me a bell."

"Oh, okay," said Hattie so quietly that Felix could barely hear her. Suddenly her whole life had just fallen in around her ears. She could just imagine it, some poncey dressage rider with his grooms, making fun of her. All her lack of confidence came flooding back, how would she possibly cope? She glanced back at Felix, his eyes half closed in the sunshine as he cradled Fiver on the front of the saddle, he hadn't had any idea of what a nuclear bomb he had just dropped.

They ambled on in silence, the sound of the horses' hooves muffled in the grass, with not a hint of breeze stirring the bushes as they continued the ride, Felix harbouring his hangover, Hattie festering with visions of the misery that lay ahead of her.

Mark couldn't quite believe his luck when he received the phone call from Colin. Well, well, he thought to himself, so that arrogant prick was coming back for a second look – perhaps the estate might just get shot of the place after all. Colin had said he was coming back on Tuesday, but apparently the phone call from Aiden Hamilton's PA had been very short and sweet. Colin asked Mark if he wanted to be there on Tuesday, assuring him there was really no need, as he could handle things if he didn't want to be involved. Mark had considered for a moment, it would be tempting to cop out, but he was too professional and he owed it to the estate and Lady V to see the sale through, if indeed it was sold, and had firmly told Colin, that he would be there.

After he replaced the receiver, he sat back in his chair gazing out of the window to the rolling parkland with its spreading old oaks and ancient iron railings. Lady V's broodmares and foals had been brought up to the home paddocks and were sunning themselves end to end, lazily flicking flies with their tails as they dozed in the heat. In the distance Mark could see the yellow blur of the machines working hard on the cross country course and thought he must drive over and pay them a visit later to see how they were progressing. It would be exciting to have the affiliated Horse Trials here next year, and although there had been a myriad of hoops to jump through, it was at last taking shape, with the date firmly fixed in the BE calendar for next July. It wasn't a date he would have chosen himself, but he had no choice, as it had to be fitted in around the other existing local ones. The ground would be hard if they didn't have much rain, and moreover he wouldn't have got the harvest in either, which was a bugger, as it was being run around quite a bit of the arable before diving into woodland and then out onto the parkland. Still, it couldn't be avoided by all accounts, and he had made contingency plans with drilling the crops and would leave a good headland gap around the perimeter of the fields, so there should be plenty of room. Felix told him that most events rotavated the ground a day or two prior to an event if the ground was hard, and the estate had plenty of equipment, so that should be easy to arrange, even though BE had their own specialist equipment he could borrow if needs be. The organisational team was pretty tight. BE provided official people to work out and publish the running times, and also official stewards and delegates on the day. Mark had to form his own committee and needed to nominate a secretary to collate the entries and of course a treasurer; he had to organise all the sundries such as loos, booking the show jumps, catering, that kind of thing of thing and each member of his committee would take their share of the burden. He was lucky in that Simon Barford, who was an official cross country course designer and builder for BE, was an old friend and master of an adjacent hunt, and was building the fences for him. Mark had known Simon for years; he farmed over on the borders of Hampshire and Surrey and he and his wife, Ruth, had started running their own BE events ten years earlier. Simon and Ruth had been more than generous with their expertise and had helped Mark with all the red tape, giving out masses of advice. So whilst it seemed like a huge undertaking, he felt like he had things under control, and if it proved successful, would be a good and much needed income for the estate, especially if, once they had run a few, they could build up to running the more prestigious tracks. Luckily for him, Lady V, who definitely had a firm opinion about how the estate turned its hand to make money, was a complete supporter of eventing, ever since Princess Anne rode the famous Doublet in the seventies and relished the prospect of the forthcoming horse trials, and keenly followed the more contemporary royal - Zara Phillips. Since Felix had been rented the yard she had taken a keen interest in him and seemed very smitten, and ironically hadn't found him obtrusive at all, which had been a relief, as she could be a funny old stick when it came to privacy. She was now swept away in the excitement of it all, quizzing Mark regularly at their weekly meeting on its progress.

In the distance, heading towards the track machines, Mark noticed two horses plodding into view. He squinted to see, narrowing his eyes and bringing up his hand to shade his face against the sunshine which streamed through the latticed paned windows. He frowned, recognising Felix and Hattie. Renting the yard was working out well he thought, although he had received a mysterious text from Felix this morning, asking if he could find time to see him for a few minutes at some point very soon. He liked Felix, it was hard not to, with his boyish grin and easy smile. He liked Hattie, she'd fitted in easily, although it was perfectly obvious that she had a huge crush on Felix – poor kid, especially as Felix was so loved up with Alice. He wondered what Felix wanted – he wasn't in arrears with the rent, and the yard was pretty ship-shape, they all seemed to rub along well together, and actually Felix had been really helpful with some interesting suggestions about the Horse Trials. Well, Mark would just have to wait and find out what Felix wanted, he was sure it could not be that important.

As Mark was musing out of the window, Alice had also taken time-out to give herself a serious talking to. She knew that her behaviour over the last day or two had been totally crass. She had bitten poor Dulcie's head off, then gone home and been beastly to Felix and his old friend Dougie too. Seeing them together behaving like a couple of kids had made her blood boil – sometimes Felix could be so childish, and then Dougie's remark had really sent her into orbit. But it wasn't like her to behave quite so dramatically. Normally she would have just put it down to blokes being drunk, but the comment had hit home, more especially as she was feeling edgy about what Grace had said the other day. She tried to shake off the uneasy feeling. It was nonsense to be like this, she had a new life now, and a happy one. She wasn't going to fuck it up this time. She would stop in at the village shop and get something nice for their supper and make a real effort for Felix tonight. She thought of him and smiled, he was just a big kid really, he'd been so pleased with himself for rescuing that dog and she had been such a bitch about it, not even bothering to make a fuss of the mutt, which was not like her at all. This afternoon she had picked up some wormers from the drug cupboard in the office, and a vaccination to start him off on a course. Paulene their Practice Manager had rummaged around in their odds and sods box and found a collar and lead and she would take that home too. She was going to make a real effort and put that stupid nonsense behind her for good. Hattie and Felix had long since returned from the hack, washed the horses off and she was now cleaning the tack ready to stow it in the truck for an early departure in the morning. Felix was feeling a bit brighter and had gone off to exercise one of the youngsters and this time had left Fiver with Hattie and the little dog was curled up in the shade of the tack room gently snoring on the blanket. The air of despondency that had seeped into Hattie's normally ebullient soul was refusing to budge, despite the fact that nothing had been finalised by a long chalk, and she kept telling herself to not be silly. She had been so looking forward to going to Rackham tomorrow too, and now she felt the day was spoilt for her. She finished cleaning the last bridle, picked up the other three and trundled over to the lorry, carefully hanging them up in the tack locker. Fiver had wakened the moment she moved and was keeping close on her heels, fearful of being left behind. She bent down to stroke him, and smiled when for the first time he did not shrink away at her touch.

"We'll always be mates, eh Fiver?" she sighed, fondling the dogs ears, and as usual he fell submissively onto his back, legs akimbo, "you're like me in a lot of ways, so we'll stick together."

She went back to the tack room, stacking the trunks methodically. Conscientiously, she checked her lists to make sure that all the equipment was put in for the gruelling day ahead tomorrow, and then carted them all laboriously over to the lorry. It was essential and painstaking work, only to be repeated in reverse when they came home - and Hattie loved it. Normally she would pack the horsebox on the morning of show, but tomorrow Felix had been drawn to ride really early, so it meant leaving at sparrow's fart to get there in time, and she thought ruefully of how early she would have to get up and cycle over to get the other horses mucked out and done before they left. It was hard work, and looking at it like that she supposed she could see that they did need extra help, especially if the yard was full. She tried to look on the upside – she did love going to the events and being a travelling groom was exciting and a dream come true. She would have Felix all to herself then, but they weren't away that often were they? How would it pan out in the day to day work? She could only gloomily wait and see.

"Hey Hattie!"

Hattie spun round and in surprise saw the svelte figure of Alice coming across the yard in her khaki shorts and polo shirt. She looked her usual striking self, and for once her hair was down swinging around her shoulders which made her look younger and less severe somehow.

"Hi Alice, we don't normally see you at this time of day. Felix is out with Percy, you know that new youngster – he shouldn't be too long."

"That's okay, I've got the afternoon off and I thought I'd surprise him – got time for a cold drink?" Alice pushed her hair back from her face, "It's bloody humid."

"It must be then coming from you," laughed Hattie, "yes, I deserve a break; Felix was mighty hung over this morning I can tell you!"

"Serves him right – drinking with that Dougie till all hours and then crawling into bed snoring his head off!" sneered Alice. "Actually Hattie, I was evil to him last night, so I thought I'd try and make-up a bit, look I've brought Fiver a collar and lead." She bent down to grab the little terrier, and he shot off to the other side of the tack room in alarm. "Shit! He's nervous!"

"He just takes a bit of getting used to you," said Hattie quietly, squatting down and cajoling Fiver out of the corner, "I think he's had a rotten time. He adores Felix."

"Like everyone else," said Alice cattily, staring knowingly at Hattie, "Felix has the charm of the chosen few."

Hattie went red, and Alice felt a bitch – *stop it* she mentally chastised herself – don't take it out on her. "Sorry Hattie, Felix is lovely – until you have to live with him that is."

"Oh," said Hattie vaguely. She looked down at Fiver to hide her embarrassment, quite stung by Alice's snide comment. One thing was for sure she wasn't going to be drawn into a bitching session about Felix or Alice or their living arrangements. "Whatever."

Alice deftly changed the subject, "You seem a bit glum Hats, is everything okay?"

"Yeah, I suppose," Hattie kept her eyes on the floor, she wasn't good at lying and it wouldn't take much to make her cry. There was no way, she could look at Alice.

"Doesn't sound it," Alice persisted, "come on you can tell me. I know that Felix can be a bit insensitive sometimes, is it something he's said or done? Perhaps I can help?"

Hattie was immediately on the defensive. She loyally refused to criticise Felix, and she didn't like other people doing it either, however much Alice thought it was okay, "He doesn't mean to be insensitive, it's a bloke thing, he just doesn't think."

"You mean he doesn't engage his tiny brain before he opens his mouth," said Alice sarcastically looking hard at Hattie, "come on, what's he said?"

"Oh nothing much, he was just telling me about his plans for the yard," Hattie muttered feebly, her lower lip puckering, "I don't think he quite realised the implications for me that was all."

Alice moved over to Hattie and offered her hand pulling her up from the floor where she had been stroking Fiver. "Come on, buck yourself up," she said sharply, "let's talk this through."

CHAPTER 11

It had been a tedious, albeit successful night, and Max had not gotten in until the translucent pinks of the dawn were etching their way across the sky to herald the new morning. He had drifted into a sound, untroubled sleep the moment his head hit the Egyptian cotton sheets and there he had stayed until late morning. Only when the white rays of the sun had already climbed in the sky and were strobing in through the enormous windows and falling onto his face did he stir. He stretched luxuriously, like the predatory cat he was and star-fished his long limbs out across the bed, his hand straying down between his legs. It had been a long time since he had wanted to share his life with anyone. Of course he had women - he couldn't exist without them, wouldn't want to, but he didn't want to share himself or his home come to that with anyone.

He had lots of properties, but home for Max was now a smart flat in Docklands. He liked expensive things, and this place had been bloody expensive, with its balconies overlooking the Thames and vast expanses of glass, from the under floor heating to the ceiling. Spacious, airy rooms with concealed gadgets and sumptuous bathrooms. It was not huge, he didn't need huge, but it was very stylish, minimalist and chic. He never worked from home; he kept offices in all of his clubs and carried on his business affairs from those premises. He did have a study here, where he dealt with his personal stuff, and occasionally he would ask Sandra, his secretary, to do some work for him of a private nature, but never from here. This place was like a sanctuary, a haven and no-one was allowed in. If he wanted to entertain clients he would go to a restaurant or hotel, or even use one of the flats at the clubs and did the same if he picked up a woman.

He sighed, reached out for a tissue, and rolled out of bed, standing naked at the windows, flinging them open to study the scene beneath him and the flurry of activity on the river. Turning back he caught sight of himself in the mirror. He still had a good body and worked out in a private gym a couple of times a week to make up for all the good living. He flexed his shoulders, and bent his head. His blond hair, carefully touched up from any strands of white, had not thinned and he had a good thatch which pleased him enormously. The thought of going bald appalled him. Still he was not in bad shape considering that he would be 43 next birthday. He shrugged the unpleasant thought to the back of his mind and headed for the shower.

Ten minutes later he was feeling refreshed, wrapped in a snowy-white robe and sat sipping a vat of freshly squeezed orange juice on rocks of ice. Catching up with the news on the mammoth flat screened TV, which he had rolled out from its discreet hiding place in the wall. Suddenly feeling restless he threw down the remote, and wandered back into the kitchen.

The meeting with Roxy had unsettled him. What was it about her that always made him feel like that? How old must she be now he wondered – must be pushing 30 he supposed, it was difficult to tell with all the surgical enhancements. Perhaps he should give her a ring, suggest meeting for lunch and catching up? Yes he would do that, maybe later when he went back to work. There was another thing too that had been nagging him more constantly of late. It was as though getting older had made him face his responsibilities, making him feel the need to rectify the mistakes he had made in the past. He sighed, of course it could all come to nothing, probably would in fact. Nonetheless he was like a terrier with a rat and he was not going to let go until he had done his damndest to find out. Sighing he pulled his robe around him and walked through the light, airy atrium-roofed vestibule towards his study. Yanking open the door he sat down at the glass desk and opened the Apple Macbook. He drummed his fingers impatiently on the desk whilst he waited for it to load up, and stared again out of the window, his cold blue eyes scanning the buildings on the opposite side of the river bank. He wasn't quite sure what he was going to do, when and if, he had the information he wanted. He would think about that when the time came. He logged on to his personal pseudonym email account, which was uber confidential and was not stuffed up with the detritus of spam, and which had had little activity since he had last checked it. His eyes glistened - there had been a communication. His heart thudding, he opened the mail, not knowing what to expect. He scanned the document, quickly digesting its contents and disappointedly logged off, slamming the lap-top closed in frustration. In a moment of quick decision he reached into his robe pocket and dragged out his mobile, scrolling down for a number.

The phone rang a few times and went to voice mail, "You have reached the voice mail of Nigel Brown. Please leave a message and I'll get back to you as soon as I can. Thank you for calling."

Max's elegant face creased in exasperation as he prepared to leave a message, "Mr Brown, it's Mr. Cutter speaking" he rapped, disguising his voice into dull Cockney tones, "I want progress. I don't care how much it costs. Just find her. Report back to me by email, as usual, as soon as possible."

He turned his gaze back to the window and stared out, his eyes blank and hard. He didn't care how long it took – he would find her.

Felix was back on form this morning, having ridden a stonking dressage test on Rambler. He marvelled at how well the horse had gone, especially as it had been Hattie who had schooled him yesterday, he had half expected him to be a bit wooden. He was grinning from ear to ear, as he and Hattie were tacking him up for the show jumping.

"You did a really good job on Rambler yesterday Hats, he felt like silk" Felix enthused, "I'm gonna get you to ride him more often in the school."

Hattie was pleased but she still felt like she had a little storm cloud following her around, "Thanks, that'd be great," she said, "but when you have your new riders – they'll probably be better than me," she added bleakly, bending down and scooping up the brushing boots to camouflage her flat mood.

Felix stopped her, taking the boots from her hand. "Look Hats, sharing the yard is going to be better for you, not worse. Believe me, I don't want anyone else around much either, but I still have to pay for the boxes whether they're full or not, so it makes sense to have someone to share the financial load. I will still be in charge of it though and so will you. Anyway, a lot of the time you'll be away with me competing, especially in the season."

"But they'll be a lot more experienced than me, Felix," Hattie wailed, tears starting in her eyes, and her mouth trembling, "of course they will be, you won't want novices like me riding the horses."

"Stop putting yourself down all the time Hats," Felix said gently, "Look how well you've done with Rambler and I haven't helped you much with him have I? Imagine how good you'll be when I am able to give you more training, and I will, I promise. Do you honestly think I'd let anyone put you down?"

Hattie snivelled, "They can be really bitchy, and our yard is such a happy place."

Felix laughed, "We won't let them be bitches! Come on buck up, we'll have the owners here in a minute and you know what they can be like!"

Hattie gave a wobbly smile, knowing only too well how tricky owners could be, although Rambler's were really nice people and didn't give them grief on the whole. "Right, just the boots then and we're ready to go, then it's a quick change for Jacks to the dressage."

"Good girl!" smiled Felix, pleased with himself. Alice was right, he had been selfish, and had told him he'd better stir his stumps and explain things better to Hattie, otherwise he may find himself losing her. He hadn't thought about how Hattie had felt yesterday, he was too busy nursing that blinding hangover. Alice was back to her old self last night, They'd had stonking sex last night too and afterwards had twined around each other talking about his plans and Dougie's pal. She'd even made him supper, and was extra affectionate to Fiver, although strangely the little dog didn't warm to her much. He shook himself, better get on with the job in hand, and wagon this horse around the show jumping, which was never Rambler's forte.

It was packed at the arena when he rode down, with Hattie trailing behind him bucket in her hand full of bottles of water, brushes and other paraphernalia. He waved to a couple of people he knew, and searched the crowd for Peter and Abbey Marchant who owned Rambler. They rarely pitched up for the dressage, really only enjoying the jumping phases. He couldn't see them, but they were bound to be about somewhere. He glanced at his watch, he had about 15 minutes to warm up. Should be just about right, otherwise this chap got a bit over the top and peaked too soon. Hattie trundled into the middle of the practice arena, waiting to lower one of the fences to a cross pole when Felix gave the signal that he was ready. Hattie watched the other riders warming up. They were all riding well, but she only had eyes for Felix, and looking around so did most other people it seemed. He really was poetry on a horse, his skills fluent and deft. He gave her the nod and started to commence his jumping warm-up routine, the horse listening and waiting for his aids. Rambler was foot perfect.

"One to go before you Felix," Hattie called, watching the numbers on the bibs as they jumped in order in the ring, "Ready?"

"Yep! He's jumping super!" grinned Felix, enjoying himself hugely. "Bring it on!"

Felix steamed into the ring, halted before the judges and tipped his hat. He waited for the bell to start and calmly went from walk to canter in the most super transition, really sitting the horse on his hocks. Without breaking rhythm they bounded effortlessly around the first few fences, Felix never missing a stride or taking his eye off the game. The double was a big spread fence into an imposing upright. Rambler started to back off about five strides out, Felix pushed his bum down hard in the saddle, gave him a double kick, Rambler regained his confidence and flew over. Beside her, Abbey Marchant clutched Hattie's arm, and then released her, smiling weakly. Felix calmly sailed around the rest of the course without a problem as though the minor issue at the double had never happened.

He walked the horse out of the arena on a long rein, amidst the applause of the crowd and Abbey and Peter raced over to congratulate him. Smiling down at them Felix slithered off Rambler and handed him to the waiting Hattie, who the Marchants had then promptly ignored clamouring over Felix like flies on shit. Excusing herself, she raced back to the truck with Rambler to get Jacks ready for his dressage. As she walked away she could hear Felix chatting away to the excited owners and praising the horse roundly for his outstanding performance. Hattie knew it had been Felix that had got the horse round and now he was doing the other job he was good at - servicing the owners. She had better get on with her job and not let him down, she thought grimly.

CHAPTER 12

A whole gaggle of people had come to Rackham on that sunny Saturday; it was one of the local events as far as the folk of Fittlebury were concerned.

Mark's wife Sandy was riding in the Novice and had taken her spirited grey horse Seamus which she kept at Chloe Coombe's yard Mileoak. Although Sandy by admission rode purely for fun, she had been relatively successful on the hot headed Irish horse, thanks to a lot of help and training from Chloe and had actually been second here last year. Since they had got together Mark too had become quite an aficionado of eventing, supporting his new wife whenever he got the opportunity. Sandy's great friend, Katherine Gordon who had started affiliated horse trials only last year on her new horse Aramis aka Alfie, also kept her horse at Chloe's and was competing in the BE100 class. Katherine had sold her first horse Polly, to Jennifer Parker-Smythe and whilst Jennifer was not up to eventing herself, was a keen supporter of her friends and the sport generally, and had come along with Charles. Chloe had brought them in her truck and they made a jolly party parked close to Felix's lorry.

Eventing was one of those sports where all hands were on deck when they were needed, and Chloe nipped over to see if Hattie needed anything doing whilst she switched the horses over. Although she marvelled at how adept Hattie was - she was coping admirably on her own. Chloe was a fan of Felix, and thought he had a bright future. She just wished she'd had some spare cash to put into the syndicate which ran the horse that had started Felix off on his own adventure. She and her husband John had gone through a tricky time last year, with John leaving his steady job and starting up a business venture of his own, and they had needed every penny they had, especially with their three children to consider. So Chloe had reluctantly had to decline the invitation to join the syndicate, but she was still willing to give a hand when she could.

"Sure you're okay Hattie?" she asked, "Just give me a shout if you need an extra pair of hands. I know how fraught it can be when you have two to run."

"Thanks so much Chloe. You're really kind but I think I can manage, anyway Felix should stop gossiping in a minute," Hattie looked anxiously towards the show jumping arenas, "otherwise Jacks will have to ride round the dressage on his own!"

"He'll be here in good time I'm sure," laughed Chloe, "but I mean it, my truck's just over there, so let me know if we can help – there's loads of us over there."

Chloe made her way back to her lorry and the others who had settled themselves outside it with chairs and a table and rugs, and were now wolfing down the mammoth picnic that Katherine's husband Jeremy now ritually provided each time they went out. The only person abstaining was Sandy, who having done her dressage and show jumping was waiting for her own cross country round. Katherine herself had finished for the day.

Jennifer looked up, her mouth full of chicken drumstick, "Is Hattie okay?"

"Yes she's fine, although Felix should be back by now, he can talk the hind leg off a donkey!"

Charles piped up, "He rode a bloody good round on that horse of the Marchants'. It never used to jump like that before. Always took fright half way round and then had a cricket score."

"Yes he's certainly got talent" chimed in Jeremy, "let's hope he can do the same for our horse eh?"

They had all invested varying amounts of money into the syndicate horse, including Grace and Colin, with Charles and Jennifer owning the biggest share and the others putting in pro-rata. Although both Sandy and Katherine evented themselves, they were realistic enough to know that they would not be going to the likes of Badminton or Burghley or the other major events, but to be an owner was almost as thrilling. The route to competing at these big events was complicated. Most competitions, like Rackham, were run under national rules under the governing body for Great Britain – British Eventing - or usually abbreviated to BE. The classes fell into six different categories of difficulty, loosely defined from Pre-Intro or BE80, where the obstacles were 80cm high which was the easiest, to Advanced where the obstacles were 1.20m and obviously more difficult; with some of the categories having sub-sections in between. Each time a horse is placed, or completes a double clear in the show jumping and the cross country phase at a competition it gains points, which accrue and determines the horse's grade, thus they progress up to the next level of difficulty. The International events, were different, being run under FEI rules, and were either one day (CICs) or three day (CCIs) events, and were graded by a simple star system. The higher the star awarded, the more difficult the event – and there were only six events in the world that were awarded the prestigious 4*s, two of which were in Britain, being Badminton and Burghley. Despite the lack of 4* events, at the bottom of the International ladder there were quite a number of CICs and CCIs of varying stars which were held within easy travelling distance, but the rules were stringent about who could compete. A horse and rider had to have obtained a qualifying result at a number of the BE events at a certain level before being considered – these were called Minimum Eligibility Requirements – frequently abbreviated to MERs. The host nation for any such International event was responsible for checking the eligibility of the rider and horse and could impose their own stronger requirements for entries if they wished. All in all it was a minefield and the rule book was more complex than War and Peace, but it was for the protection of everyone – riders and horses, and there had been plenty of accidents in the past where gung-ho combinations had believed they were ready for the kudos of riding at International level, but had come unstuck - literally and often disastrously.

The aim of forming the syndicate had been to buy an already established horse which would help Felix wagon his way speedily to the ranks of stardom, and all of them could enjoy the ride alongside him. Of course it was a risk, Felix was hardly William Fox-Pitt after all, but after last year, they all seemed inextricably bound together and the horse if anything drew them closer. Jennifer, who after all had been the victim, had astonished everyone, including Charles, by recovering from her ordeal of the kidnap with all the tenacity of a pit-bull, and was determined to turn her negative experience into something positive. She declared that she'd made good friends, loved the eventing scene and was swept away on an exuberant tide for the new venture, and in admiration of her plucky recovery the others had agreed. Chloe had been put in charge of finding such a rare steed, and had initially baulked at the responsibility. It was a huge thing to ask, especially as she has been unable to be part of the syndicate, but out of loyalty to her friends, she had finally agreed. Buying any horse was a gamble and the last thing she wanted was for them to have been stitched-up with some no-hoper. So putting out feelers to her equine friends in as vast a net as she could find, and after viewing quite a number of unsuitables, she had been on the point of slashing her wrists. A phone call from a source way up country in Northumberland, had sounded promising and, in desperation one icy day last February, she and Felix had made the long trek up north to discover whether all that glitters really was gold.

The horse was called Picasso, which definitely suited him, as his coat was a startling black and white and was as irregular as a cubist painting, and whilst a lot of coloured horses could lack quality, this one was put together like the most perfect china ornament. Standing at 16.3 hh he was big enough to take up Felix's long legs and had a good deep body and sloping shoulders, with powerful quarters and hind legs. His head was fine with large intelligent, kind eyes, and he had a dopey way with him in the stable, patiently standing whilst Chloe and Felix poked and prodded him about, feeling down his legs, and pulling aside his tail to look at his hocks. Chloe had liked him immediately. Picasso's track record was good. At 8 years old, he was just the right age. Early last season he had sailed around the novice tracks with double clears and his last two events had been at Intermediate level – all with clear cross country rounds. As lovely as the horse was, Chloe and her suspicious mind wondered why they would want to sell this paragon of virtue. The woman who was selling him seemed honest enough – but the horse world was full of vipers. Apparently in this case, the rider who had taken the horse thus far, a keen semi-professional was having a baby, and giving up eventing. The owner wanted the horse to have a chance to go on, and no doubt cash in on its success Chloe thought pragmatically, so clearly now was the time to sell just before the season started. When a rotund, obviously pregnant girl ambled into the yard, bursting not just with the forthcoming infant but with clear dismay at the sale of the gentle giant, Chloe's fears were somewhat put to bed - the reason for sale did seem genuine enough. Even at 5 months pregnant she was quite prepared to ride the horse to demonstrate his flat work skills, even if she couldn't bend in the middle to jump him.

Felix had immediately gelled with the horse, and although it could do with some work on the flat, there was no doubt that it had a huge, scopey and bold jump. Felix, was never one to keep his powder dry, had jumped off with a huge grin on his face like he'd just won the lottery. Chloe had to admit she was impressed and they'd talked about it non-stop all the way home. Although when they excitedly showed the video of their day's exploits to the others, brimming with enthusiasm, Charles had immediately put a dampener on things by declaring that he couldn't abide coloured horses. Jennifer had been appalled - saying that he had left all that snobby behaviour behind him now, and to stop being so judgemental. Charles had looked rather abashed, and after sullenly watching the video even he had to admit that the horse did seem talented. So it was agreed to go ahead with the purchase subject to a vigorous 5* vetting with Andrew Napier, plus x-rays, endo-scoping and an embarrassment of other undignified examinations. Finally, one sharp day at the tail end of February Picasso was transported down to Fittlebury Hall and the syndicate was officially formed.

In the beginning Felix had started quietly – getting to know the horse, with plenty of cross country schooling and having decided to take full advantage of the sponsorship of the syndicate, had embarked on regular show jumping and dressage lessons too. Their partnership had blossomed, and their first events had proved spectacularly successful. Double clears in the cross country and show jumping phases, keeping them just inside the ribbons, but the erratic dressage scores not quite clinching the elusive wins. Picasso gave Felix endless pleasure and confidence, and also the experience of the bigger tracks and combinations that he ate up with gusto. They now had enough qualifications under their belt to enter their first seriously big event which was to be a held at Brightling Park in the second week of July. It was difficult to know who was the more excited, the rider or the syndicate.

Felix ambled back to the truck, leisurely avoiding the cow pats and waving to people he knew en-route. Hattie watched him, for once irritated at his indecent lack of urgency. His test was in 20 minutes and Jacks was never easy at the best of times.

"Sorry Hats," grinned Felix as he strolled over, "I got caught up with Pete and Abbey. They're such nice people and they were so pleased about Rambler – what a good old boy eh?"

"Felix, will you just get on!" Hattie snapped crossly, hanging onto the dancing Jacks who was narrowly avoiding her toes, "We haven't got much time!"

"Aw there's loads of time, stop panicking." Felix laughed "You'll only wind him up. I've probably got time for a roll up."

Hattie narrowed her eyes "No you haven't." She glared at him, "Now get on."

"Blimey you really are cross!" He stuffed his hat back on, and did up his jacket. "Okay, you win," and with one swift, fluid movement he vaulted on Jacks and, before Hattie could say another word, he was off across the field towards the dressage arenas.

Hattie swore under her breath, how could he be so… casual? She turned round and stomped back into the lorry to get the tack sorted out for Rambler's cross country round – he could jolly well sort himself out in the dressage.

The next day was Sunday, and whilst Hattie struggled with her conscience to lie in bed at home on a well-deserved and rare day off, Felix toiled away in the yard with the mucking out. Fiver was a great help; even after a few days the little chap had become like an appendage attached permanently to Felix's heel and although he still cowered when strangers went near him, Felix was his super-hero. Right now though he could have done without his assistance as it was taking twice as long to shovel the shit as it normally did. He bent down to retrieve another dropping from Fiver and put it in the barrow.

"Hello – anyone around?" called a voice from the yard, "are you about?"

"In here," Felix called back, as Fiver started to growl, and walked out of the stable to see Mark admiring the hanging baskets. "Morning Mark, you're early."

"Yeah sorry about that, thought it'd be the best time to catch you," laughed Mark, "Sandy and I are going out for the day and I'm pretty busy this coming week and I know you wanted a word with me, seemed as good a moment as any."

"Thanks, I really appreciate you coming over, 'cos I do need to have a word with you." Felix laid his broom against the wall, and cracked his famous smile at Mark, "Look shall we have a cuppa?"

"Well, I don't have a lot of time, but okay." Mark was no fool; he smiled back half-heartedly at Felix, his antennae bristling suspiciously, "What's it about?" he asked as he followed Felix into the tack room, "No problems I hope?"

"No, well I hope not either," began Felix, "I just need to run something past you." He flicked on the kettle, chucked some teabags into the mugs and sat down opposite Mark, "The thing is I need to talk through some ideas I've been thinking about."

"Go on then, I'm all ears" said Mark his eyes narrowing. He had a feeling he wasn't going to like what Felix had to say. Pity, as up until now it had been going well, but he couldn't let sentiment rule his business acumen, "Talk away."

Felix hadn't expected Mark to be so direct, and taken by surprise he found himself blathering away with all the clarity of a rap song, finally stammering away to the crux of the problem, and the possible solution. He tailed off ".... So that's about it then."

"I see," said Mark coldly, "In a nutshell, you are asking if you can sublet some of the boxes to another rider?"

"Yes," said Felix awkwardly, "I wasn't sure if I could, under the terms of the tenancy."

"Under the terms of your present tenancy you can't," said Mark his eyes thoughtful, "that doesn't mean to say that if it suited the estate we couldn't revise it, but I'd had to give it some thought. Sunday morning is not the time to be doing it though. I'll get back to you in a couple of days. Okay?"

"Oh Mark, would you? That'd be fantastic! Thank you so much!" enthused Felix, "I wouldn't ask but I can't see any other way forward at the moment."

"Well don't get your hopes up yet – but I can see the problem – look, don't be offended but forget the tea will you? Sandy 'll be furious if I'm too long." He stood up, dusting off his trousers, "I'll be in touch."

Felix watched him walk across the cobbles back towards his Landrover, and dropped back down on his chair, Fiver jumping lightly onto his lap. He ruffled the dog's ears absent-mindedly, "I just hope he agrees to amend the tenancy," he groaned, "otherwise we're fucking sunk."

CHAPTER 13

Tuesday blew in with a dramatic change in the weather. A rare old wind was gusting in from the east, and brought moody, grey clouds hurtling across the sky as the temperature plummeted. Roxy, cocooned in London over a baking hot weekend hadn't bothered to look at the weather forecast. She was now visibly shivering in a skimpy top as she picked her way around the ruins of the mill in her Louboutins trying to muster up some interest. Hiding her scowl behind her unnecessary, but ubiquitous dark glasses, she was inwardly fuming with Aiden, who was steaming ahead with the ever efficient Chrissie, who had naturally dressed far more sensibly in designer jeans and Dubarry boots. The boring guy walking beside her was enthusing about potential, and situation, and all she could see were some dilapidated old relics, which stunk of dirty smoke with about as much possibility as a dead polecat. To her there was no way it worth the enormous amount of money it would need to renovate, and who in their right fucking minds would want to come out here to this miserable Godforsaken place.

Aiden had stopped just up ahead, and he and the architect bloke were peering down into the pond, poking about at the rusty old wheel. God the place gave her the creeps! Chrissie was listening intently and making notes on a clipboard, and Aiden called her over.

"Hey Roxy, come and have a look at this, it's wicked! It's the original old wheel, and Alan here thinks we could make it a real feature." He yelled at Roxy, "Whatdya think?"

Roxy tottered over to the edge of the water, carefully wiping her muddy shoe on the grass, "I'm speechless," she drawled sarcastically, "Wow, how exciting will that be."

Either Aiden ignored her, or he missed the irony, "Yeah, it will be babe. Just wait till you take a gander upstairs."

Chrissie turned away, smirking slightly, if there wasn't going to be a nuclear explosion between them imminently, there would be pretty soon. But selfishly thinking of the dire journey home if the bomb went off now, decided she should diffuse the situation. "Roxy, why don't we take a look at the barns over here, they're not nearly so bad."

Roxy who could definitely have throttled Aiden, but equally didn't like Chrissie either, decided that Chrissie was the lesser of the two evils. She smiled at her sweetly "What a good idea darling," and then turning to Colin, who had turned quite pink as she flashed her smile at him, "Why don't you show them to us Clive?"

"Actually, it's Colin," stammered Colin, quite unable to stop his eyes straying to Roxy's nipples, which by this time were standing out like organ stops in the chilly breeze, "Yes, they're fine buildings, please come this way, I think you'll be jolly impressed."

Roxy put her arm through Colin's for support. "Excellent, thank you," she purred, and then called over her shoulder to Aiden, "Won't be long."

Aiden looked up, glanced at the architect and winked, "Good that'll keep her amused. Now seriously Alan, do you think this is a goer? I want vision here, something uber stylish, sympathetic but not chintzy. I want it light and airy, with space."

The architect smiled, "Oh I can design it Aiden, but can you afford it, that's the question? The place is wonderful, but it's going to take a hell of a lot of capital investment to restore it."

"I think I can get it pretty cheap. Something tells me they want rid of it. I'm gonna get them to come up with a price. I want you to do the same – can you get me outline ideas by next week, and some broad estimates – no hanging around."

"Aiden, this could take me weeks. I'd have to get a team down here, measuring up surveying – the whole shebang. Then there's planning, English Heritage – this place will be listed you know."

"Stop fucking whining – do your job Alan. That's what I pay you for."

Alan winced "I'll do my best, but I'm not promising, let's get that straight. When's the land agent coming? I thought he was supposed to be here to meet us. I could do with some plans of the area and the buildings, and I'll need to liaise with him if I'm to come down again."

"He'll be here, let me do the negotiating first. Then you can deal direct. Right let's move on before Roxy gets bored, she'll be a fucking nightmare otherwise."

Mark had been held up, and was cursing. He hated being late; but he had long ago understood the need to prioritise where the estate was concerned and today was just one of those days. Right up until he'd died, Lady V's husband had been a great supporter of field sports, and the estate had run its own private shoot for many years. Lady V had carried on the tradition in a small and exclusive way, and to her it was still very important. Will Fry was the gamekeeper, having taken over when his father died, and he lived in one of the cottages up on the north end of the estate. On the whole he did a good job, but he was still quite young, and Mark kept a keen eye on things, and he knew that Will got pissed off with him but the shoot was a big responsibility. Although it was a commonly held belief that it was a sport for the wealthy, and to an extent that was true, in reality it was this income that provided funding to manage and conserve woodland and wildlife, and gave private landowners a real incentive to improve habitats. Mark enjoyed this conservation side of managing the estate and at this time of year planning was crucial. Wild pheasants stocks were normally supplemented in the early summer by introducing hand-reared birds, although these days they bought in pheasant poults at six or seven weeks old, rather than raise their own as they had done in Will's father's day. The young birds were usually released into pens in early July, and the positioning of these pens was crucial, not just to the birds but this had a big bearing on conservation of ancient woodlands, fauna and other wildlife. Putting them in the wrong place could be really detrimental. So these plans had to be made carefully and not hurried. But as always – everything needed to be done at the same time, on the same day and now he was late for his meeting at the mill. He put his foot down on the accelerator, nodded to Will and headed off towards the Priors Cross road. He didn't hold out much hope for this meeting, but he supposed the fact that Aiden Hamilton had come back was encouraging. He slowed down as he approached the quaint hamlet of Priors Cross. It was just a few pretty traditional cottages dotted on either side of the road, their gardens a riot of colours in the obscurely grey day, but it was dominated by the ruins of the statuesque old Abbey up on the hillside. Today, the Abbey seemed even more forbidding than usual, the gothic glassless windows were strangled with ivy and looked like enormous sinister eyes glaring down from a frowning face. The ragged stumps of walls and fallen clumps of grey masonry a dismal reminder of its tragic past when it had been ransacked by looters after the decline of the monasteries in Henry VIII's day. Even last year it has been the scene of disaster, with the abduction of Jennifer Parker-Smythe and her step-daughter; and was where the kidnappers had hidden, waiting for them, before they had been secreted to the mill. Where poor Caitlin had lain so terribly injured for hours prior to being discovered. Yes, it was a place full of blood and history Mark thought grimly, fixing his eyes determinedly on the road ahead. Coming down the hillside on the bridleway adjacent to the Abbey he could just see two riders ambling along the track, making their way towards the road. He recognised them straight away – Felix and Hattie. Now there was another problem he had to deal with today – but one thing at a time he thought, and began to indicate left onto the cinder track towards the mill.

    Dulcie was singing at the top of her voice. She and Nancy were having a sweep-a-thon of the yard and her curly brown hair was rocking with energy, as she did a fair imitation of Shania Twain's *"You're still the one"* using the broomstick as a microphone.

    "You're still the one I run to, the one that I belong to, you're still the one I want for life. You're still the one. You're still the one that I love, the only one I dream of, you're still the one I kiss good night" she crooned, edging closer to Nancy, who'd abandoned her broom and was standing trying to look serious with her hand on her hip, "Aint nothin' better, we beat the odds together, I'm glad we didn't listen. Look at what we would be missin'." She stopped, planted a sloppy kiss on Nancy's mouth and fell about laughing.

"You know you're totally bonkers don't you?" grinned Nancy, pleased nonetheless and trying not to show it. "Come on, we'd better get this finished. This bloody wind has made a right mess of the yard."

"Lighten up cupcake, we're well on sched – what's to do later eh?" smiled Dulcie impishly, pushing back her curls, "Jennifer's ridden, Scooter's leg is done, the others don't need doing. Why don't we nip out this afternoon?"

"Nice idea – where'd you fancy – Brighton? Although this weather's shite."

"Where else is there? Who cares about the weather!" laughed Dulcie "Shall I nip over and clear it with the boss?"

"Okay, let's finish up here then; provided she says it's alright, we could be ready in less than an hour if we get a crack on." She picked up her broom and started sweeping demonically, the muscles in her arms whipping backwards and forwards like pistons on a V8 engine.

Alice pulled down the drive at Nantes, the steering wheel in a pincer grip and her jaw grinding like coffee machine. She was not good at apologising, and every word would stick in her craw; but good will was hard to gain and as fragile as an old twig, and she couldn't afford to lose the support of the Parker-Smythes either for the practice or for Felix. She just hoped that she had timed it right and that both Dulcie and Jennifer were in the yard.

Dulcie heard the engine stop outside and had already nudged Nancy in the ribs and they'd stopped sweeping and were leaning on their brooms when Alice opened the gate. Alice strode towards them confidently and then faltered almost imperceptibly when she took in their stony faces glaring at her with as much welcome as a dog with fleas.

"Ah, hello you two," she began hesitantly, "I was hoping to catch you, is Jennifer about?"

"Nope," said Dulcie curtly. "What can we do for you?" She was buggered if she was going to make polite small talk with this bad tempered bitch.

Alice produced a watery smile, "Well Dulcie, I just wanted to apologise to both you and Jennifer. I was rather abrupt the other day. I'm sorry; I had a lot on my mind. No excuse of course, but I just wanted to stop by and say sorry if I was a bit short with you."

Dulcie, always as squashy as a marshmallow, immediately softened, her naturally good temper content to take the apology on face value. "That's good of you Alice, it wasn't a problem, we all have off days." She accepted, "Scooter's fine now after the antibiotics."

"Well I'm glad to hear that, and pleased we're okay," said Alice relieved, her tone gaining ascendency once again, "Can you pass my apologies onto Jennifer?"

"Of course I will," smiled Dulcie, "As I said all forgotten about."

Nancy stiffened beside her, "It wouldn't do you any harm Alice, to remember that we are professionals too. We may only be grooms to you, but we know our job, just like you know yours - but we don't need to be rude and neither should you be. Dulcie's more forgiving than I might be."

Alice looked taken aback, "Nancy, as I said, I was just having a bad day, I've said I was sorry, I was really hoping we could forget it. I do see you as being professionals, I've never thought of you as anything different."

"Okay, we'll let it lie then," said Nancy, no chance of a thaw in her voice despite having said her piece, "and we'll tell Jennifer too. She'll be pleased to know you called, it was the right thing to do."

"Thank you," snapped Alice, her face ugly with anger at being spoken down to by a groom, "I'd better be getting on now. Have a good day."

"You too," called Dulcie, as they watched her disappear out of the yard. "Well, what do you think of that? Quite a big thing to do wasn't it?"

Nancy slipped her hand into Dulcie's, "My love, I think you're a bit bloody naïve. I've been around a bit longer than you and there's more to our Alice than meets the eye. She's not all sweetness and light - she's just making sure her own nest stays feathered, you mark my words!"

CHAPTER 14

Roxy was becoming increasingly bored with the cretinous Colin, or Clive, as she persisted in calling him. She and Chrissie had explored the undamaged barns, and she had to admit they were rather amazing in terms of space and potential. She could imagine opening up a really upmarket spa and gym here, with her own brand lines of glitzy sportswear festooned all over the beams. Coupled with Aiden's green restaurant it could be a real niche market. There were actually two cavernous barns, attached to one another, and a further smaller one, which could be for administration offices. She wondered if it would be possible to get an indoor pool in somewhere or even put one in a flashy glass extension. Having seen enough, she steered them outside and saw the old mill itself in a new light. Renovated it could be awesome and that miserable stinky pond could be made into quite a feature. Perhaps Aiden might have a point she conceded, although it would take a shed load of money, but she could just imagine her chic friends coming down here and the stunning feature of herself in *Okay* or *Hello*. It was just what she could do with in terms of image regeneration. Whilst it was being done up, she could leak little titbits to the press titillating their interest and if the builders got their arse into gear – it could be a grand Christmas opening – she pictured the snowy scene, pure white decorations, white twinkling lights and evergreens – very tasteful, even Suzanne would be impressed. The new gym and spa would be perfect for getting rid of all those extra pounds people gained over the holidays, and the healthy eating ethos was a brilliant way to start the New Year – good timing or what.

Chrissie knew Roxy well enough to know that glittering look in her eyes, she was hooked into the scheme alright, just as Aiden knew she would be. Chrissie herself was not so sure, it would be a damned gamble and a frigging huge amount of extra work for her too and no doubt she'd have to come down here quite a bit to make sure they were up to speed. She thought pessimistically of the drive down from her flat in London - what a chore. The countryside didn't worry her and certainly wasn't alien either. She had been brought up in Buckinghamshire, near Quainton and her parents had always preferred a rural lifestyle. Hence she could ride, albeit not brilliantly, and she'd even done a stint or two on the Hunt Ball circuit but finally escaped to live in London where she'd put down roots and stayed firmly entrenched in the smoke. Give her city life any day of the week. Now here she was again, contemplating making trips down to the green pastures of West Sussex. It was a ghastly prospect.

She caught up with Roxy, who was sycophantically chatting to Colin. He was enthusiastically pointing out more *enormous potential*, not realising that Roxy was playing him every step of the way. Chrissie had to give it to Roxy, she could turn the charm on when she needed to, and right now this goon was lapping it up, rambling on about ambience and serenity. She almost laughed out loud at his serious face and Roxy's overdone obsequious interest - it was like a comedy sketch. Suddenly she stopped herself - actually he really was quite a nice man. She'd spent too long with Roxy and Aiden and horrified herself when she realised that she was becoming as shallow and bitchy as they were.

Colin interrupted his spiel to Roxy at the sound of a vehicle coming up the drive and relief positively oozed out of his flushed face. "Ah, that's the Estate Manager, Mark Templeton, the chap I was telling you about. He was obviously delayed. Let's go over and meet him and he can tell you a lot more about the provenance of the mill and the land."

"Clive, what a good idea, I'd love to meet him," smiled Roxy, quickly taking Colin's arm, leaning on him exaggeratedly in her high heels, "although you have been such an excellent guide." Chrissie smirked down at her Dubarrys, realising that Roxy hadn't a clue what '*provenance*' meant.

Colin preened, "Thank you, but Mark knows a great deal more about the place than I do, and of course Lady Veronica who owns the mill and the Fittlebury Hall Estate will be your neighbour, should you decide to proceed."

"How interesting," Roxy's eyes flashing like jewels at the prospect of a titled neighbour, "although I imagine she's doesn't get involved that much – or does she?" she added hopefully.

"Well, she …ah here's Mark, let me introduce you."

Chrissie lingered behind appraising the newcomer, he was quite a looker in his own way. Not over tall, and had a good toned body – no trace of a beer belly to be seen, although there were some flecks of grey in his hair, which was the colour of soft brown sugar. He was older than he looked she mused. "Hi" she said, moving forward and holding out her hand, "I'm Chrissie, Aiden Hamilton's PA." She liked his hand shake, it was firm and warm, and his fingers were long and tapering; but straight away she spotted the wedding ring. Bugger, but it had never stopped her before, perhaps there would be compensations to this country malarkey after all.

Roxy immediately clocked Chrissie eyeing up Mark and pushed her way into the centre of attention, flicking her hair back seductively as the wind whipped it across her face. "Now Mark, I'm sure there's masses you want to tell me. Chrissie, be a dear, and find Aiden will you?" Dismissed Chrissie had no choice but to sulk her way back across towards the mill and leave Roxy to it, but once again she was bloody furious. That woman was heading for a fall and Chrissie was more than happy to give her a mighty push.

The blustering wind was strengthening: above them the whirling branches of the trees were performing like ecstasy-fuelled disco dancers. Roxy shivered, leaning closer to Colin, rubbing her body against his, and turned to Mark, "This is quite a spooky place," she whispered, gazing curiously at him, "I bet it has quite a horrible history…? What can you tell me about it darling?"

Mark looked at his shoes, "Well …" he began hesitating, "I …" and luckily was saved from comment by the rhythmical clacking of horses' hooves coming up the drive from the road, with the odd snatch of a voice before it was lost in a gust of wind. Two horses were marching up the track, their riders were gossiping and laughing, and were so engrossed they hadn't even noticed the cars and people up ahead.

Roxy was indignant, "Surely this isn't a public right of way is it?" she exclaimed angrily, "What the fuck are they doing here?"

"Oh that's just Felix and Hattie. He has a yard on the estate and uses this track as a cut through from the bridleway - saves them using the road. All the time the land belongs to the estate then that's fine," said Mark, breathing easily again. "If you buy the place then, of course, they'd have to go down the lane like everyone else."

"Well we certainly wouldn't let just anybody use it I can assure you," said Roxy testily, "it would be right select, no riff raff here."

Mark looked at her in astonishment, not sure if she was joking as he couldn't see her eyes through the huge glasses, thinking what a stupid remark and what a stuck up parvenu she was - why move to the country then? But he merely smiled and replied, "That, of course, would be your prerogative."

By this time, the riders were almost upon them and Colin tactfully disentangled himself moving over to greet the handsome pair. "Hi Felix, Hats – how are you, bloody windy old day to be riding."

"Hi Col, we're good ta! On the last two now, then Hats and I are going down the Fox for a pie and a pint as a treat – join us? Although you look like you're kinda busy – what's going on? That woman looks familiar, is it who I think it is?"

Colin put his finger to the side of his nose, "Can't say mate, not yet anyway, but fingers crossed eh."

Felix grinned, "Ah ha! Say no more - will we Hats?"

Hattie raised her eyebrows and rolled her eyes, "Felix you know who that is – perhaps you don't recognise her with her clothes on. Nothing stays secret for long around here Col, you should know that, but they won't hear anything from us." She turned to Felix for confirmation, but she was too late, he'd already fixed his eyes on Roxy and she was busy smouldering back at him. Hattie groaned inwardly as Roxy sashayed over. From that moment on, Hattie knew there was going to be trouble.

"Dougie! We're on! I've sorted out the tenancy with the estate." Felix gasped down the phone, "if your mate is still looking for a yard, perhaps we could meet up and have a chat?"

"Hey Felix that's great news – he'll be knocked out! You sure?" Dougie sounded dubious, "What's the score?"

"Well, long story but in a nutshell, Mark Templeton has drawn up a new agreement, allowing me to sublet boxes as I want. But I remain in charge of the yard and ultimately responsible for the monthly rent. There are a few other clauses, but that's the gist of it. So this fellah of yours has got to be kosher. He's a good payer – right?"

"Yeah, you can trust him. Actually you already know him anyway. "

"Do I?" said Felix suspiciously, "I hadn't heard of anyone looking. Who is it?"

"Sebastian Locke," Dougie said cautiously, "you know the fellah I mean?"

Felix whistled, "Yeah I do, he's bloody talented, and got some quality horses. I thought he had a good set up where he was?"

"Well he's fallen out of bed, literally and metaphorically with the owner of the yard where he is now, gotta be out by the end of the month. Quite a sad story really. He's lost two of his best horses as well, but the other owners are sticking by him I think, and a rider of his calibre will soon pick up any spare."

"Well he'd have to understand that I run the yard, and things have to be done my way, and as long as the rent is paid on time it should work. What about accommodation though, there's no house y'know." Felix thought and he's not bloody sharing with me and Alice, "the estate doesn't have anything either as far as I know."

"Well that's his problem isn't it, he'd have to sort out his staff too, so I imagine they'll all rent somewhere local. That's the least of his problems at the moment, he'll sleep in his truck if needs be. Look I'll give him your number and get him to call you. Then it's down to you both to work something out." Dougie sighed, "then don't blame me if it goes tits up!"

"I won't," laughed Felix, "anyway it might not even get that far – we'll see. Thanks though, I really appreciate the contact."

"You're welcome, keep in touch – let me know what happens."

Felix ended the call, and wandered back into the house. Alice was in the kitchen slicing runner beans at the table in an attempt to be a domestic goddess and cook something healthy for a change. "How'd it go?" she asked, "What'd he say?"

"Well you'll never believe who it is – Sebastian Locke. Had a row with his boyfriend who's chucked him out and taken away a couple of his best horses. Funny thing is I'd not heard a thing about it, although I suppose I might not on the eventing circuit, he's a dressage rider after all – but you'd have thought there'd be some gossip wouldn't you?" surmised Felix, snatching a raw bean and crunching it thoughtfully. "Dougie is gonna get him to call me. So I've just gotta be patient and wait – something I've never been very good at." He muttered sliding his arms around her waist and finding his hands straying upwards towards her breasts.

"Alice, why don't you stop doing healthy things and do some unhealthy things with me instead?" he muttered into her ear, his fingers now inching inside her bra and hooking out her tits. She resisted half-heartedly, but her nipples were starting to stand erect as he played with them and he could feel himself getting hard as he rubbed himself against her back. He allowed one hand to stray down the front of her belly, inching itself under the waistband of her shorts, deftly unhooking the fastening and pulling down the zip. Alice started to moan and squirm into him, arching her back into his, and he took her ear between his teeth and gently began nipping the lobe. Lazily, he eased his hand further down finding the edge of her panties, he could just feel the beginning of her pubic hair, a soft springy mass which he clasped between his fingers until he heard her gasp. Releasing the tension he explored his way downwards with his fingertips, parting her labia, finding her sweet pulsing clitoris sticky and wet with desire for him. He bit her ear a little harder, removed his hand from her breast, and pushed her forwards, splaying her out bum upwards across the kitchen table, the beans and bowl clattering to the floor. Keeping his hand firmly on her back, he pulled down her shorts and pants, exposing her bottom, and very slowly inserted his middle finger inside her, his forefinger working on her clitoris, stroking and wiggling, up and down and round and round, as she squirmed with desire underneath him. He pulled her further back towards him, her bottom virtually hanging off the table, and deftly with one hand pulled off his breeches. His cock sprang out, demanding to be serviced, and he plunged inside her, the force of it almost bringing the table down. As she gasped and he thrust backwards and forwards, grasping onto her shoulders for grip, he felt like a man possessed and in those moments before he exploded, he knew that it was not Alice he was thinking of.

CHAPTER 15

Max and Roxy had met for lunch at a smart Sushi restaurant designed for A-listers in Knightsbridge. Max detested the place, with its slithery bits of raw fish, wrapped with tricky-to-eat rice and sauce, inflated prices and the ingratiating staff. Roxy, on the other hand, loved it. Her publicist had previously tipped off the press that she would be going, and of course she'd discreetly hid her face when they hovered to take photographs when they'd made an appearance. Max knew the drill, and he'd expected nothing less, but it was tedious. A good old steak house wouldn't have enough street cred for Roxy but he would have it any day over this. He glanced around at the groups of sweaty, overloud bankers bawling to their mates and ogling at her surreptitiously, and wondered for the umpteenth time why he had rung her. Obviously for Roxy, everything these days was a marketing opportunity.

"It was good to see you the other night. Aiden looks well," he remarked, concentrating on the menu and ignoring the hovering waiters, "in fact, you look marvellous."

Roxy smiled at him, "Come on Max, stop making small talk, you hate Aiden."

Max didn't move his head but lifted his eyes to meet hers, smiling slightly, "As you say, just small talk Roxy, just small talk."

"It's good to see you though. I've missed you." Roxy put her hand out across the table and lightly skated her fingertips over his, "*really* missed you."

"Was that real or for the camera?" he said softly, acutely aware of the furtive looks from the other diners. "Don't make me your patsy Roxy, I'm not one of your publicity stooges."

"Max, as if I would," she said with a tinkly, little laugh and tossing her hair marginally nonplussed, "You know me better than that surely?"

"Yeah, you're right I do - don't forget it eh?" He pulled his hand back abruptly from hers, flicked his fingers and one of the waiters leapt to his side. "Whisky - on the rocks."

The waiter nodded obsequiously and turned to Roxy, "Madam?" he enquired, "for you?"

"Sparkling water," Roxy rapped out, "no lemon."

"Roxy, I asked you because I wanted to see you. It's been ages but I find this fucking charade unbearable. Your whole life has become a public performance even down to this," he nodded around the restaurant, "for God's sake!"

Roxy had the grace to look mildly discomfited; Max was probably the only person who knew the real woman underneath her carefully constructed patina. But this seriously fucked her off, the Godfather attitude he had with her - like he owned her. It was as though he had some inner power, a kind of personal in-depth knowledge that only he had a right to have and moreover to control. These days only she liked to call the shots, but neither could she afford to create a scene in a public place, where the press would be all over her salivating like wolves for the kill with every juicy heartbeat. No, she couldn't afford that.

"Max, I'm sorry, you know what it's like darling. You're right babe, this was the wrong choice. D'you wanna leave? We could go to a steak bar or summat?" Roxy looked apologetic even if she was thinking *fuck him*.

Max sat perfectly still, with not a flicker of expression, his eyes not moving from hers. It was one of the qualities she had normally admired, his ability for fathomless stillness when it mattered, and she'd seen it often, especially when he was dealing with his adversaries, just before he went in for the kill. But today, that awful calm veneer was calculatingly assessing her - it was un-nerving and damned irritating. After an ephemeral moment he replied. "Okay. I asked you to lunch so we could have a chat – a catch up. Absolutely no strings of course - just friends." He paused carefully, "So -that said - what've you been up to?" He put his head to one side, in a conciliatory gesture, "What's new?"

Roxy smiled back, relieved she was forgiven. Max was a great friend but she would definitely not want him as an enemy, "Oh baby, you just wouldn't believe it!" she said excitedly, her butterfly brain flitting instantly onto her latest venture, as the conversation settled perfectly back onto her. Her face lit up like a kid in a sweetshop, "you'll never guess where I went yesterday!"

Max threw his head back and laughed, making the other diners gawp at them, "Nope, no idea, you'd better tell me!"

Colin and Mark were having lunch too, but it was altogether a different affair, sitting quietly in the snug bar in the Fox at Fittlebury, with Dick Macy pulling pints behind the bar and a handful of locals exchanging gossip. They were waiting for Janice, Dick's wife, to bring their meal.

"Well, it's a waiting game now Mark, but I think he's on the hook" grinned Colin, as they clinked glasses, "Roxy seemed to love it didn't she?"

Mark took a slurp of his lager, "Yep, she did, not the only thing she took a shine too though. Poor old Alice, she'd better watch out if Roxy moves down to Fittlebury, she'll have her claws into Felix alright. Talk about man-eater! She wasn't doing too bad a job on you either mate!" laughed Mark, "She was all over you when I arrived."

Colin grimaced, "Totally," he said helplessly, "What Grace would have thought, I don't know, but luckily you came along. Damned woman couldn't even get my name right! Still, who cares if they make an offer."

"We won't count our chickens on that one. Aiden Hamilton – Mr Celebrity Greens - was playing things a bit differently – he's so damned rude."

"Yes he is, although the architect chappie wasn't too bad – at least he's civil. I warmed more to the PA too. She's always sounded a right snooty bitch on the phone, but was surprisingly rather pleasant, even if she is a bit Sloaney."

"I hardly had time to notice her, the divine Roxy despatched her pretty quickly when I arrived, but she seemed nice enough. I'll tell you what though Col, if that little menagerie comes to Fittlebury, it'll create some gossip." he laughed "Can you imagine!"

Janice had just arrived with the Fox's famous ploughman's lunch, plates teetering with chunks of seeded farmhouse bread and cheese. She plonked them down on the table "What gossip? Come on you two, you're plotting."

"Wow that looks great. I'm starving," drooled Colin, skilfully diverting the ferreting Janice "Got any Piccalilli?"

"Course – no problem. Mark you need anything else?" she asked disappointedly, and trooped off resignedly to fetch the sauce. She wasn't going to get anything out of these two.

"We'd better be careful Mark, we don't want this getting about, it was bad enough that Felix and Hattie came by. Do you think they'll say anything?"

"No, I don't. I've just done Felix a favour actually, to do with the tenancy on the yard, he won't let me down by blabbing. He might be young but he knows which side his bread is buttered and he won't jeopardise anything."

"Right then," Colin thought for a moment, as he balanced a slab of cheese onto a hunk of bread, "I reckon we'll hear by the end of next week, if not before."

Later that same afternoon Felix had arranged for Sebastian Locke to come over to the yard to see if they could come to an arrangement about renting some boxes. For the umpteenth time he wondered if he was doing the right thing. The thought of someone else being there filled him with dread in many ways. He had come to love the intimacy of the small number of horses they ran, and the closeness of his relationship with Hattie. Double the number of horses would mean sharing the school, the tack room, the wash down box, and all of the things that he just took for granted at the moment. He suddenly was overwhelmed with despondency. Was this just the slippery slope of failure? Alice had been brilliant, suggesting that a three month trial on either side would be a good idea - if it didn't work out, there would be no hard feelings on either side. At least this offered a window of escape if any shit hit the fan he supposed.

He didn't actually *know* Sebastian either, although Dougie said he was sound. He was one of the up and coming stars in the dressage world, and like Felix had some good horses, but relied on sponsors to run them. Sebastian's current odious predicament made Felix all the more aware of how tenuous his own situation could be. He felt sorry for him, but equally could he be a loose cannon if he came here? Who knew what had really happened and Felix couldn't afford to upset his own owners. He sighed gloomily, he was beginning to think this was a very bad idea, but it was too late - he could hear the throaty growl of a sporty engine coming along the drive towards the stables – it must be him.

Sebastian Locke was not the complete epitome of a dressage rider. He had the long legs and walked with the precision of a cat, but he was broad in the shoulders and had a hefty six pack. He had short, brown hair, a square face, and a crooked smile, and although he had definitely broken his nose at some point this only added to his irrationally attractive looks. At first glance he was probably about the same age as Felix, hitting somewhere in his mid-twenties, and was, without any doubt, as bent as a nine bob note. He bounded over enthusiastically with his lopsided smile and an outstretched hand. Felix who was not naturally a homophobe, was nonetheless relieved to find that his shake was as firm and hard as his own.

"Hi Felix, good to be here. Wow it's quite a place! I love it!" Sebastian gushed eagerly waving his arms around like a windmill.

"Yep, it is – let me show you around, and we can talk as we go" replied Felix cautiously, his warning antennae quivering on full alert. Fiver on the other hand had no such reservations, and unusually for him was busy rolling on his tummy enjoying a scratch from Sebastian.

"Darling little dog, such a sweetie. What's his name?" Sebastian admired "I love dogs and you are a simply divine little cutie." He dropped down even further and Fiver's head lolled back on the cobbles, wriggling in ecstasy.

"We call him Fiver, he must like you. He's normally shy with strangers, you've obviously made quite a hit."

Sebastian pulled himself up, brushed off his jeans and ran his hands through his short hair, "Well that's a good start. Let's have a look round then shall we?"

The tour took quite a while, with Felix, rather proudly showing him his horses and the set up. He briefly introduced Hattie, who was lunging a horse in the school, and she hardly even had time to even acknowledge him before they moved off again. As they walked and talked, Felix warmed to Sebastian. He was funny with a wickedly dry sense of humour but was also clearly knowledgeable and very ambitious. In fact in many ways he was a lot like Felix. They eventually made it back to the shade of the tack room and Felix made them both a brew. Despite his initial reservations, Felix liked the guy, but now the moment of truth had come - to thrash out the rules of the yard. He had to make it perfectly clear that it was his yard, and Sebastian would be his tenant – not the other way round. For once, his normal affable easy-going ways would have to be put aside, and he'd have to man up and just say what he meant, and mean what he said.

By the time Hattie came in, laden with the grubby tack, she found them both grinning stupidly and sprawled like a couple of kids on the scruffy old armchairs, their feet dangling over the arms and Fiver not much better, belly upwards on Sebastian's lap. Felix was beaming and jumped up to help her; the miserable troubled look which had clouded his face all morning had gone, and now he was full of glowing smiles.

"Hats, let me introduce you properly – this is Sebastian – he's going to rent six of the boxes."

Sebastian struggled to his feet, displacing a sleepy Fiver on the floor, "Please call me Seb darling – how simply lovely to meet you! I just know we're going to get on famously and have enormous fun!"

Hattie gave him a strangled smile; she just hoped he was right.

CHAPTER 16

The following weekend was Eridge Horse Trials in Kent. Felix was taking Picasso for an Intermediate run on the Sunday, and as the week wore on, the pressure of work resembled a steadily inflating balloon fit to burst. All the syndicate would be going, and probably a lot of the hangers-on too, as this year Eridge had gone up in the world and were hosting a Country Show, which included a dog show with terrier racing, and masses of stalls from shabby-chic to home produced pies and cheeses. They had even moved the siting of the main equine event, so that it was now at the front of the park, and had fantastic views over the cross country course.

Having run the novice horses the weekend before, they would not be competing this time, but Felix had entered Woody in the BE100 on the Saturday. Sheena, whilst being a great owner, was clucking like an alarming mother hen; it was the first time at this level for the horse and she was delighted and terrified in equal measure. Planning the event like the D-Day Landings Sheena decided to travel Woody in her own lorry and groom for Felix herself, which left Hattie at home to get everything ready for the following day with Picasso. Hattie was peeved at being left out, although she liked Sheena, and she did grudgingly have to admit that it made sense. Although another nagging worry was that it gave her the responsibility of exercising Picasso on the Saturday without the supervision of Felix, and that in itself, was daunting.

The atmosphere in the yard crackled like flames in a bush fire and was just as fierce. Felix hadn't had much time to talk to Hattie about Seb's impending arrival, and she had so many questions buzzing about in her head. She was seriously worried and her only answer was to work harder. She cycled furiously to and from the yard on her bike, and took out her frustration when she was mucking out, hurling the shavings against the wall with satisfying venom. Felix spent hours schooling the horses in the arena attempting to perfect his dressage, jumping down complicated grids with his trainer, and galloping along the downs. He would come back, his face animated and flushed with as much sweat dripping off him as the horses, laughing and calling for Hattie to give him a hand. The sweet irony was that the more he larked about swept away on the euphoria of horse therapy, the less he noticed how grumpy she was becoming.

Friday afternoon finally came, with Sheena festering around like a thing demented and driving Hattie crackers all day, getting under her feet packing the lorry for the early morning departure to Eridge with the irascible Woody. Hattie had already given him a bath, and he was standing in his stable glaring at her with indignation and refusing to touch his haynet. She'd decided to plait him later that evening when the yard was quieter and Sheena had finally gone home. Woody was as sensitive to tension as most people were to nettle stings, and it didn't take much to send him into a frenzy with him whizzing around the box in circles shitting everywhere. She didn't envy Felix taking him tomorrow with the excited Sheena - Woody needed calm not chaos. In a way, she was glad that she wasn't going to be there and tomorrow she would have the yard to herself and was looking forward to the peace and quiet.

At last, at five o'clock Sheena finally said she was off and would see them first thing, and Hattie slunk with relief into the tack room for a welcome cuppa before she started on the plaiting. She flung herself down on the armchair picking distractedly at the wadding vomiting out of the split seams, while she waited for the kettle to boil. She felt knackered and it was going to be a long weekend ahead. She knew she was being stupid, unreasonable even, but she was feeling desperately gloomy about the way things were bound to change in the future. The thought of sharing Felix was just too much to bear. The sensible thing to do was to cut loose and get another job; move on but to only have part of him was better than not having any of him, so for the time being she would just have to put up with it.

Felix, himself, was so preoccupied he didn't notice Hattie's glum mood. He himself worked as hard as she did - but for different reasons. The horses were all in fine fettle, fitter than they'd ever been, and jumping like rutting stags, but he still wasn't happy with the dressage. It was all very well jumping double clears – imperative, but without a good enough dressage score it just didn't cut the mustard and, above all, Felix wanted to win. It was the finer points that he needed to hone, and not for the first time, he wondered if Seb would help him. He ambled his way back to the curiously quiet stables with Picasso. It was getting late and he'd been riding all day, leaving Hattie to cope with the humdrum jobs in the yard. He put the horse away and strolled into the tack room, flinging himself down on the other armchair.

"Phew, I'm fucked. Got a brew on Hats?" he asked, "Looking forward to the weekend?"

Hattie struggled up from the arm chair, passing Fiver to him as she got up, "Yeah, I suppose."

Felix looked surprised, "I thought you'd be excited - I am. I know you're not coming tomorrow, but Sunday should be a great day. Eridge is a lovely course, really hilly, and it should be great now they've got all those stalls and stuff – they've even got terrier racing. Next year – you might even do it eh Fiver?" He crooned at the intelligent little dog, whose ears pricked up at the mention of his name.

Hattie's face softened, "Aw take no notice of me Felix, I'm just a bit tired. Sheena's been driving me nuts, and I've still got to plait Woody tonight, and then the whole lot to do on my own tomorrow; not to mention all the mucking and chucking before we go on Sunday."

Felix stood up and went and put his arm on her shoulders, "Ah Hats I know, it's a lot to ask, but that's why, when Seb comes, it'll be a whole lot easier for us all. I know you're dreading it, and in a way I am too, but I think in the long run it'll be a lot better for both of us."

Hattie bit her lip. She mustn't cry she thought. She felt herself quivering. "I hate change," she said, in a stifled little voice, "I like it when it's just the two of us."

Felix spun her round and folded his arms around her, "I know - me too. We get on so well together don't we, but we'll go under at this rate sweetie, and I don't want that for either of us, and just think, we'll have much more fun at the shows, knowing that we can come back and the work's been done." He gave her a kiss on the top of her head "come on, let's have that tea. I'll hold Woody while you plait the bugger, and we can talk about what you're gonna do with Picasso tomorrow – deal?"

Hattie hugged him back. "Deal," she smiled with happiness into his shoulder and just wished that she could stay there forever.

Max was intrigued. He'd been invited up to Wallingford by his old mate, Ronnie French, to see his latest acquisition – he'd bought a riverside manor house dating back to Henry VIII's time – for a snip or so he said. As Max's driver wearily struggled across London, leaving the city and picking up the A404 towards Henley on Thames the scenery began to become prettier. It was a lush part of the world, with plenty of money in evidence, and some quaint little villages along the route. Ronnie hadn't said much about the place, but he'd been excited all the same - Max could tell from his voice. He'd known him for more years than he cared to remember and they'd had some good old scams together, and Ronnie was someone he'd trust in a tight spot. A few years ago Max had saved Ronnie's arse when his freedom had been on the line - it had sealed their friendship for life. Max had never asked for any repayment but it was good to know that if he ever needed a favour it would be there. Just lately Ronnie had gotten into some big bucks, something to do with the racing scene. Once or twice he'd involved Max, but not often. He'd kept the con close to his chest, but it was obviously paying off as this place he'd bought wouldn't come cheap. If there was that kind of money to be made Max wanted to be part of the action and today he thought Ronnie may well let him in. Despite his curiosity, he felt himself nodding off as the countryside flashed by in a distortion of colours, the black Mercedes droning effortlessly along as it soporifically purred towards Wallingford.

He awoke with a jolt as the car negotiated a sharp bend and left the main road. Irritated, he leant forward tapping the chauffeur lightly on the shoulder "Where are we?"

"About five minutes from our destination, Sir," replied the chauffeur inclining his head, "should be along here on the right hand side. We've already crossed the river once."

Max looked out of the tinted windows. It was a private road with *nice* but fairly unremarkable houses on either side. He glanced at his watch, they'd been on the road for about two hours now – it had better be pretty special for him to have come all this bloody way. The Mercedes started to idle, the chauffeur trying to catch the names of the passing houses, although Max seriously doubted it could be one of these. They were too ordinary from what Ronnie had described. The river was coming up ahead of them, its dull broad width spanning out as the road curled alongside it, with a high beech hedge on one side. He could just make out towering red brick chimneys set at diagonals above the hedge; and then up ahead a gravel drive swept up behind shrubs and trees towards a house which flanked the river bank. Max whistled slightly under his breath, old Ronnie sure had come up in the world. He took in the old place – talk about private, it was wonderful; nobody would know it was here, but crumbling towers could also sum it up perfectly. The house was ancient, and Ronnie was probably right when he said it dated back to Henry VIII. The entrance was imposing, with a massive Tudor stone arch and a studded and planked front door, which was more than likely the original. For the most part, the walls were pargeted in a warm ochre colour, and the house had those leaded, stone-mullioned windows with tiny panes of glass, and, in others, the traditional red brick of the Tudors. It was a fabulous place, but it looked as though it needed a mint spent on it to bring it anywhere near up to scratch.

Ronnie's car was no-where to be seen. The chauffeur pulled up outside the main entrance, and got out looking about him before coming to open Max's door.

"Wait for me, will you. I'll see if anyone's at home." Max said curtly, cursing under his breath. He'd be bloody furious if he'd come all this way and Ronnie wasn't even here.

The front of the house looked deserted, so he walked around to the side. There were scruffy little box hedges, standing about two feet high enclosing weed encrusted flower beds, and the gardens sloped down and away to the river on one side and on the other, away to the back of the house. He took the route around towards the back, up a small flight of stone steps flanked with unkempt earthenware urns, and almost gasped in surprise as he took in the vastness of the house. Obviously added at a later date, although still clearly pretty old, was an enormous long stone addition to the main building, it could have been a barn, as it had some kind of red tiled oast house attached at the end. The potential of the place was seemingly endless, although it looked pretty shabby, even the gardens were run down.

The silvery tinkle of a giggle came from behind one of the low hedges further up the garden, followed by a shout of laughter. Max looked up and followed the sounds, picking his way along the little gravel path, neatly avoiding the encroaching cobwebs of brambles. There was another hoot of laughter, followed by some moaning.

"Hey Ronnie!" shouted Max, "Where are you?"

There was another shriek, and from behind the hedge, a pot-bellied man stood up. He was stripped to the waist, his flesh pale and pasty, the hairs on his chest once dark now curled and grey. "Hey Max brother, come on over, good to see ya!"

Max sighed. Obviously Sandra, Ronnie's missus, wasn't here and he had brought along a little amusement for himself. He trod wearily up the path, "Good to see you too – some kind of place you've got here."

Ronnie beckoned him over, "Great isn't it? Wait till I show you round." He motioned for Max to sit down, "Push off Tash baby – it's boys' talk." He leant down and upended the sun lounger and the near naked redhead tumbled off onto the grass "Go get some champagne."

"Oi Ronnie!" she muttered, "Don't be a pig!"

"Shut it and do as you're told sweetie," he said good-naturedly "We'll carry on where we left off later – alright?"

"Alright," she smiled lasciviously at him, "Promise?" She picked herself up from the grass, and brushed imaginary specks from her tits and flounced off towards the house.

"Christ Ronnie, you don't change do you mate – who's the scrubber?"

"Tash? She's a good girl, keeps me happy and stops me bothering Sandra. Best of both worlds. Nowt wrong with a nice bit of pussy – stop being stuffy. Anyway she's brought along a friend."

Max remembered all too well Ronnie's little private parties and mentally said a prayer of thanks that he hadn't sent his driver away. He changed the subject. "Some pile Ronnie, where'd you get the dosh for this then?" he laughed ironically, deciding to get right to the point. "What's the secret? Whatever it is, I want some of the action."

"Max brother, it's easy, so easy, and you want in, why not? I more than owe you."

Max smiled at him, "Go on then – I'm waiting."

Ronnie laughed, "Impatient!" He leant down and picked up his drink, taking a large noisy slurp, wiping his mouth with the back of his hand, "Racing. The sport of kings. Big bets, big bucks."

"It's a mug's game mate."

"It can be that's true, but it needn't be. Not with my contacts." Ronnie smirked, the bags under his eyes crinkling from too much drink. "Ever heard of lay bets?"

"You mean when someone bets on something not to win?"

"You got it. You back a favourite not to win. Based on insider information, or nobbling the nag. I've made a fucking fortune, not just here but abroad too."

"You've gotta have some pretty sound information if you're putting out big money or it could go seriously tits up," said Max thoughtfully. "Supposing they get it wrong?"

"Okay sometimes they do, but that's the skill, you regularise the betting, you lose the odd one, makes it look more kosher. And it's not just all about lay bets. I've got plenty of people in my pocket now. Bent jockeys are two-a-penny and the trainers aint much different if you know where to look."

"Why you gonna cut me in bro', not that I'm not interested," he waved his hand at the house, "this kind of money interests me, but why should you?"

"I pay my debts, you saved my skin and I was grateful. I owe you." Ronnie moved over and clapped Max on the shoulder, "Always will be Maxy, never forget a mate me. And you've got plenty of dosh to play with!"

Max laughed and shook his hand, "Well count me in, next time eh?"

"Definitely, we've something on for next week you'll be interested in I think, I'll call you with the details." Ronnie glanced up as Tash glided back with a bottle of chilled Cristal, four glasses and an ice bucket. Behind her, elegantly poised on a pair of high heels, a small thong and nothing else was a slim Latino girl, her dark curls as flamboyant as her bouncing tits. "Ah Max, meet Anna."

Max gawped, Anna was seriously attractive, not the normal tart Ronnie usually provided, this girl had class. Things had suddenly become more interesting. He smiled at the girl, "Nice to meet you Anna."

Anna smiled back at him, modestly, considering she was half naked, "Nice to meet you too Mr Goldsmith." She fluttered her eyelashes downwards, ironically in a way reminiscent of Princess Diana, and perched beside him on the grass.

"Now Tash, how many times have I told you the champagne should go in the ice bucket," laughed Ronnie, "That's what it's for y'know."

"Baby, I was thinking of a much nicer place you could put the ice cubes," laughed Tash delightedly, "And I wasn't thinking of me mouth!"

Ronnie grinned, "That's my girl, you'd better take off your panties then!"

Tash grinned and, obligingly and tantalisingly, did a striptease for them all, waving her thong around above her head and revealing a total Brazilian wax without a scrap of pubic hair to be seen. She spread her legs across Ronnie on the chair squealing, "come and get me, big boy!"

Ronnie reached over, plucking several ice cubes from the bucket and inserted them inside her one by one, watching the surprise and delight on Tash's face, conversationally remarking to the others "I can't abide pubic hair, always gets in my teeth."

Max looked at Anna, she really was quite delicious and, after all, why not? He reached down and stroked her little brown nipples and she obligingly pushed her chest out further, her hair falling backwards as she arched her back. She lifted her head towards him, but he avoided kissing her. He had his limits – and that was definitely one of them. He forgot all about the waiting driver, and slipped his hand down inside her thong.

CHAPTER 17

Saturday was a savagely blustery day for late June and, as Hattie was busy breaking her nails down at Fittlebury Hall, Roxy was having her nails manicured ready for the launch of her new underwear range later that afternoon. Her publicist Suzanne and stylist Rachael had been working flat out all week organising the show, and had past the point of the nervous breakdown stage and were into slashing their wrists at this point. Suzanne had tactfully tried to advise Roxy to go upmarket and introduce the range more traditionally, with catwalk models, a host, and a super selected and strictly invitation-only audience. Roxy, on the other hand, couldn't bear the thought of being out of the limelight and wanted to model the whole range herself and a right old rumpus had blown up. In the end a compromise had been reached. Roxy would present the show in a sexy number of her own design with the models coming on and off the catwalk, then a short champagne intermission with the scantily clad babes offering some freebies. The finale would be Roxy in the most sexy and outrageous of the lingerie, rolled along the stage in a huge bed with a couple of male models in bollock hugging boxers beside her for the press photos. It wasn't what Suzanne would have chosen but it was at least the lesser of the two evils.

The whole circus was taking place at *Gallomania*, an uber contemporary studio just off Covent Garden, ideally suited for location and they were wizards at creating the right ambience. An excess of press had been invited with the promise of Roxy's famous publicity tricks and the temptation of a celebrity guest list. As it was, not so many of the A-listers had actually accepted, but there were enough of the *also-rans*, and *almost-theres* to make their mouths' water. With an in-house kitchen more than able to provide the canapés and sweet treats, Suzanne was confident that she could leave the catering to the expert staff at *Gallomania*, even down to their guys engineering the enormous bed as the finale. All she had to do was keep Roxy and her histrionics under control. Looking at Roxy now, as she hurled a nail polish across the room having decided that she didn't like the colour, Suzanne was doubtful, and frankly she would be glad when the whole charade was over.

Down at *Gallomania* all was serene. The Head Chef was adding his final instructions to his Chef de Partie, and the bottles of Taittinger were slowly chilling to an icy bloom. The Studio Manager was ensuring that the chairs were set out to perfection, and the slinky silver and black catwalk drapes were swagged exactly as requested. The podium, from which Ms Le Feuvre would present her collection, was raised to ensure that everyone seated had an excellent view of her. He ran a sound check – levels were flawless. He sighed with satisfaction; they were all set front of house. He clambered down from the podium and made his way to the dressing room behind the catwalk. Large, floor length mirrors surrounded three sides of the room, with free standing clothes rails on one – they didn't need many for the flimsy morsels of material that made up Roxy's idea of underwear. Make-up chairs with unforgiving overhead lights were on the other side. The models, who would be arriving at any moment, would enter down the dais directly from this room, turn at the bottom of the stage, return up the catwalk and go out the other side, circumventing the huge round bed which was screened at the top end by rippling silver and black curtains and dive back into the dressing room again for a costume change. During the intermission, the models would carouse the guests in their underwear – showing their goods. Privately the manager thought this was rather tacky, but it was not his place to say so, especially as he thought the last part was even worse by comparison. He dived behind the illusive iridescent drapes disguising the bed. It was made up with stark white sheets, trimmed with black lace and once the audience were re-seated, the curtains would fall back and it was to roll down the dais to the front of the stage complete with Ms Le Feuvre. Gingerly he checked the mechanism which drew back the curtain - rather like at a crematorium, he thought grimly; and then flicked the switch to move the bed down the rollers – nothing happened. He tried again, this time it worked, whirring quietly towards the front. He sighed with satisfaction, returning the bed to its original position, and repositioning the curtains. The Stage Manager at *Gallomania* was concerned though? Supposing it went wrong during the show? No matter how ghastly the performance, he didn't want his Studio being bad-mouthed all over London. He would talk to the tech boys straight away.

Felix was in the throes of exhaustion as he slithered down on the springy parkland grass beside the lorry, whilst the exuberant Sheena walked Woody off. He'd been up since the crack of dawn, and had been worn out before he got to Eridge with Sheena's never ending, pent-up, nervous energy, and not for the first time he wished Hattie was here. Woody had picked up on the tension and travelled badly, stomping and stamping in the truck all the way, and then exploded down the ramp like he'd got a firework up his arse. It was all they could do to get the studs in. Luckily Felix had allowed plenty of time before the dressage, and he took him over to a quiet corner to work him in, trying desperately to compose the bunched up mass of solid muscle, but it was like riding an unexploded bomb with Woody leaping and plunging at every patch of grass which might hide a lurking monster. The test was terrible - talk about tense, nervous headache - take Anadin. Instead of trotting at the beginning, they had cantered sideways down the centre line with Woody stopping dead when he spotted the judge's car and rearing bolt upright. Felix, without the comfort of a martingale strap, had managed to cling on and encourage the horse forward again, gritting his teeth with determination and a plastered smile for the benefit of the judge and onlookers. Somehow he had managed to negotiate the movements and finish the test despite Woody's efforts to unseat him. The judge had smiled sympathetically to Felix as he nodded his head and dropped his hand at the salute, hastily grasping both reins again before Woody pissed off across the parkland. But sympathy didn't earn marks, as Felix knew only too well. In the show jumping phase they had fared little better. The fences were not big, but the horse was distracted by the crowds and a thumping great funfair which had been erected beside the collecting ring and, although they had jumped all the obstacles, Woody's inattention had earned them a fair old cricket score of knock downs. Luckily, not quite enough to have them compulsorily retired from going cross county, but definitely enough to be so far out of the running that they might just as well not bothered to have come at all. Despite this, Felix had been determined to finish the competition, and finish they had - with the duo storming round the hilly, old parkland in a magnificent round, to go clear but with time faults for going too fast. The horse was as bold and talented as any that Felix had ever ridden, but tricky didn't even come close to describing how difficult he was to ride. He slid off and handed him to Sheena to walk off and drained a bottle of water, slumping back against the truck, absolutely spent physically and closed his eyes mulling over the day's events. He was glad of the break from Sheena's incessant chattering, although he knew he was just being mean, it was her horse and she loved him. He wondered where on earth he went from here – there was no doubting the horse's ability, but did it have the brain to cope with the job and if it didn't, Felix didn't much fancy being upended underneath three quarters of a ton of horse meat.

Gallomania's white facaded and massive mirrored glass exterior was glacially imposing, and there was already a smattering of press loitering outside with their cameras sprouting enormous phalanx lenses. Roxy had arrived about an hour previously accompanied by her stylist. She'd stepped out of her personalised black Range Rover with its trademark silver lightening slash, wearing her customary bug eye dark glasses. She'd posed and pouted momentarily for the media as they frenzied around her like snapping piranhas clamouring for a quote.

"You'll have to wait fellahs," she giggled tantalisingly, "all will be revealed shortly," emphasising the double entendre seductively. A couple more poses and she was gone, with them rushing after her, entreating her to stay. She swished through the glass doors into the open spaced reception area, with Rachael following smartly behind, and they were immediately ushered through to the studio. Two burly bouncers dressed in black, folded their huge arms and stood menacingly astride and barred the way to the baying reporters, who turned back disappointedly. Once behind the security of the double doors, Roxy whipped her dark glasses onto the top of her head and glared around her, determined to find fault – her jangling nerves were making her seriously bad tempered.

Suzanne hurried over from behind the catwalk. "Hi Roxy, great, you made good time – what do you think – it looks sensational doesn't it?"

Roxy's eyes fixed on her, she said coolly, "It looks bloody boring to me Suzanne, not much glitz or glamour is there?"

Suzanne could have slapped her. The studio looked amazing. The black and silver theme – which was Roxy's emblem after all, was subtly woven throughout the décor. It was smart, chic and elegant. Perhaps on reflection, it was too upmarket for Roxy, not enough smut for her, she thought bitchily. She smiled sweetly, replying, "It looks really classy, just like you darling."

"Can't we add some fairy lights or summat, a few decent back drops?"

Suzanne knew all about Roxy's idea of backdrops – some tacky over-muscled blokes, or blow ups of her in next to nothing. "No, we don't need them darling, the collection is so fabulous, it is glamorous on its own, doesn't need anything else to enhance it."

Rachael interrupted "I think it looks marvellous Roxy, but we'd better get our skates on, and get your make-up sorted."

"Good idea," said Suzanne thankfully to Rachael, "The guests will be arriving soon, can't have you being seen without your face on Roxy, and I've got some last minute bits and pieces to sort out, so see you later." She turned away quickly to avoid Roxy's acerbic reply and went to find the Studio Manager who'd been trying to catch a word with her all morning.

Behind the scenes in the dressing room the other models all hushed reverently as Roxy strode in, but her mercurial mood had swung into beaming smiles and affected charm. She air-kissed them all ostentatiously on their cheeks, and thanked them for coming, and played at being *one of the girls*. Then she listened, in apparent raptures, to her production team as they checked over the running order, and finally she sat down, to let Rachael work her magic on her make-up, begging pathetically that someone *be a sweetie* and fetch her some water.

Outside in the studio space, a rainbow of guests was arriving and being greeted by Suzanne and her team, who were handing out programmes. Champagne sparkled in silver frosted, black flutes accompanied by black caviar on blinis, and the room was humming with voices against the discreet backdrop of classical music. Suzanne was pleased – it was going rather well, better than she could have hoped. The room was filling with beautiful people, who were lapping up the cameras and loving the ambience. She sighed with satisfaction. Most of the punters she knew by sight, if not to talk to, but one man stood out a little from the usual crowd. He was tall and blond, elegantly dressed in stone chinos and a stylish deep blue and chalk stripe Armani jacket. She was sure she had seen him somewhere before, but maybe it was his companion, a svelte, Latino girl with tumbling, glossy curls and smoky eyes. She didn't have time to ponder who they were as more guests were arriving and soon it would time to start ushering people to their seats. She nodded to her assistant to be ready to dim the lights and change the background music when she gave the signal.

Backstage, Roxy was ready. She brushed Rachael imperiously to one side and preened at herself in the full length mirrors. Her dress was outrageous – a thin sliver of black and silver forming a halter neck coming down the front to cover her nipples, each strap becoming wider at the base of her navel, to join the short, pleated, black and silver striped skirt. If she hadn't secured her tits securely with tape she would be completely naked on top. It was jaw droppingly risqué. She felt excited, and exhilarated. This was her show, her party and her press were waiting. Let the party begin! She gave a swift nod to her team when she heard the music cue and swept out of the dressing room and down the catwalk, her ears ringing with the sound of applause. She nodded, waved and curtseyed ostentatiously as the flash lights of the cameras exploded around her and she knew deep down that there was no other glory that she wanted in life other than this. She swaggered to the glass podium on her Jimmy Choos, the silver pleats of the skirt sparking in the spotlights as her hips swayed in time to the music. Taking her time, she glanced at her audience, but through the gleam of the lights it was impossible to pick out any faces; she threw out her arms and bade everyone welcome. There was a collective gasp from the audience as her buoyant breasts expanded in the dress but miraculously stayed put, and a further burst of applause exploded from the watchers. Roxy, oblivious to the joke, thanked everyone for coming and began the performance of her life.

Down in the Kent countryside, Felix and Sheena were rattling homebound in the lorry analysing the day's competition.

"He was amazing cross country- he went like a rocket," sighed Sheena, struggling with the steering wheel to negotiate the narrow roads, "just a bit too fast though."

"He's certainly keen, I was lucky not to get a reprimand for going too fast" said Felix tactfully, wondering how he was going to tell her that her nag was frankly dangerous jumping at that speed, "trouble is Sheena, he's also reckless, and we don't want him having an accident."

"No, nor you, of course dear." Sheena murmured, concentrating hard as she indicated to overtake a snake of cyclists riding four abreast, "These damn cyclists! Move over!" She yelled, then added as though nothing had happened "He moves beautifully too, but the dressage was a bit on the wild side."

Felix thought this was an understatement, "Yes it was, he just didn't settle. Of course there were a lot of distractions and there was a big atmosphere for him, but I wonder if he isn't just a bit too fit at the moment."

"What do you mean? He needs to be fit to cope with the jumping doesn't he?"

"Yes, of course he does, but he's on boiling point. I wonder if we shouldn't just let him down a bit, and perhaps consider a change of feed, maybe even a calmer in his grub. That might help him settle a bit more – at least until he's got a few more miles on the clock." Felix wriggled in the seat, it was never easy telling owners that their horse had issues. He knew only too well that when Sheena's only daughter had gone off travelling she'd felt bereft, and now, Woody and Felix had filled her empty void. Her daughter had previously never demanded much from the explosive Woody, other than to have fun, with the departure of her child, Sheena lived, breathed, and burned with ambition for the horse's future. How could he disillusion her? But it wasn't fair not to be honest. He stumbled on, with as much tact as he could muster, "we need to be patient and perhaps think of a different management programme." For the umpteenth time he wished Hattie was here, she was great with the owners, and more so with the horses – Woody would probably have been a lot better with her quiet influence. He suddenly longed for her to take over, so that he could close his eyes and go to sleep.

Sheena crunched down into second gear as they came up to a set of traffic lights. She glanced over at Felix, stretched out her hand towards him and smiled, "Look love, I'm not stupid, I know Woody has got his faults, but I love him. Let's just go with the flow shall we?" She pulled off jerkily, "it's just a bit of fun. Okay, so we'll let him down, so he's not quite so full of himself, and maybe you're right, we'll try one of those calmer thingies, after all, it can't do any harm."

Felix felt a huge surge of affection for this kind woman, "Thanks Sheena, I'm not saying he's not talented, he's got that in spades, and not that I don't like him either, because I really do, but he's such a sharp bugger and we've just gotta be cautious about how we bring him on."

"I know Felix, stop fretting, I understand completely. Perhaps next time, it'd be better if we brought Hattie too, he seems much more sensible when she's around."

"Funny isn't it, but you're right, she has great rapport with him doesn't she?" Felix laughed, "Do tell her that Sheena, she's been a bit down in the dumps lately."

"I'd noticed that too. Is she okay? The last thing you want to do is lose her Felix, she's a diamond. They don't come along like her every day of the week." Sheena paused thinking for a moment. "She's such a pretty girl too, does she have boyfriend trouble do you think?"

Felix snapped open his drooping eyelids and sat bolt upright with a jerk from where he'd been slouching in the passenger seat. "What? A bloke, are you joking!" His face clouded over, "You don't think she's going to leave do you?" he stammered "Has she said anything to you?"

"No, she hasn't, but don't sound so surprised, she's a lovely girl – why shouldn't she have someone? Anyway, she's not been her cheery self lately, has she? Haven't you noticed?"

"Well a bit I suppose, but …" Felix stopped himself, he hadn't told anyone yet about Seb, perhaps now was the time to come clean, "Actually Sheena …" he began, falteringly at first and then blurted out about the predicament in which he'd found himself and what he proposed to do about it.

Sheena listened, nodding her head, keeping her eyes on the road and letting him finish before she said anything. "Well Felix, I can see where you're coming from. On the whole, it's probably a good idea not to try and take on more horses yourself right now, and logically and financially sub-letting has to be an option." Just be careful this Seb is all he's cracked up to be."

"Oh Sheena, don't think I haven't agonised the whole thing through" grunted Felix, fiddling with his hands and glancing over to see her expression, "I'm fairly certain that he's pretty sound, and he's a really talented rider on the flat. In fact I'm hoping he'll give me a hand with my dressage and I can give his horses a jump for him – swap the work a bit. We could both win and the horses too."

"All sounds ideal on paper," Sheena remarked dubiously, "but these things often don't work out quite how you plan them. Just be careful – that's all."

"I think that's what Hattie is worried about; she thinks they'll all be better than she is, which of course they won't be, and that she'll be pushed out."

"Well it'll be up to you to make sure she isn't then. Her dedication and skills aren't in question are they, but she's got to believe in herself, and that'll be down to you." Sheena spoke emphatically, "Let her see how much you value her, and let the others know it too."

Felix brightened considerably, "You're right Sheena. I'd already planned to give her more lessons and stuff anyway, but there's loads more I can do." He thought for a moment, "Do you think she's got a boyfriend?"

The guests were mingling now during the intermission, tempted by complicated parcels of sushi, the most intricate, filo parcels drizzled with blackest balsamic, washed down by more chilled champagne. Roxy circulated amongst everyone, flirting outrageously with the tabloid press, all of whom were snapping away at her as she posed with various celebrities, who were either lapping up their moments of fame or shying away from the wrong kind of publicity. Suzanne discreetly watched the farce from behind the long swirling drapes; she couldn't wait for the afternoon to be over. Although, on the whole, she had to hand it to Roxy: so far so good, it had been as tasteful as it could have been bearing in mind that the range was bordering on tacky. Just the last finale and photo shoot to go and then they could pack up and go home; she was looking forward to putting her feet up with a cup of tea.

Roxy was in her element. By some miracle her virtually indecent dress had obediently stayed put and now everyone was congratulating her. She lapped up the admiration, her ego flying so high, as she basked in her success, that she missed all the misshapen faces from so many tongues in cheeks. She flitted airily from group to group, like some intoxicated bee, until she finally came to Max, who was standing quietly with Anna watching the charade with an impassive expression on his face.

"Max darling!" drawled Roxy, air-kissing him on both cheeks, "I'm so delighted that you came, I wasn't expecting you to make it."

Max smiled down at her, his eyes never leaving hers and said carefully, "Well done Roxy, quite a performance." He paused and turned to his companion, "Let me introduce you to Anna."

Roxy was fleetingly thrown by the first remark. Her face clouded over momentarily but she quickly recovered and, laughing, turned to appraise Anna. Max rarely, if ever, brought a companion with him, so her curiosity was aroused. "Well, well, nice to meet you Anna." She casually looked the girl up and down, and found herself feeling a flinty glint of jealousy: she was certainly a beauty.

Anna smiled shyly back, her soft sexy accent irritating Roxy all the more, "'Tis very nice to meet you too Roxy. Max 'as told me all about you."

"Mmm, I fucking bet he has doll. You and I will have to get together one day, and I'll tell you about him," Roxy sniped, her voice as crude as a sewer. She turned to Max smiling dangerously, "Eh baby?" She laughed, "Better push on, got the last extravaganza for the press, then how about we have a drink after?"

"Thanks sweetie, but we've got to push on too, haven't we Anna?" Max circled his arm around Anna's waist, "I just wanted to show my support, so we'll probably not wait – hope it goes well darling." He leant over and pecked her lightly on the cheek, took Anna's hand and they threaded their way through the crowds, leaving Roxy, for once in her life, lost for words.

Standing momentarily alone, Roxy was irrationally livid. How dare Max come here with another woman? Their swift exit reminded Roxy of that night long ago when he'd rescued her from the Sheik at the dreadful party; there'd always been something special between them and now she felt excluded, left out. She wasn't his special one anymore and she was fucking furious. Well no-one was going to have him but her, she would get him back, see if she wouldn't, but right now – her public were waiting. She could see Suzanne signally to her wildly from the rostrum and melodramatically pointing to her watch. Daubing a dazzling smile to any onlookers, she oozed python-like through the crowded room to get ready for her big scene.

The models were ready, barely dressed in miniscule triangles of lace and fluff. The male models were stripped bare; their rippling muscles were being oiled to sparkling perfection by the make-up girls before putting on their snowy white boxers. Roxy stripped off behind a screen, squidging her 34Es into a black and silver balconette bra which barely covered her nipples. Rachael hovered around her with the tit tape.

"Don't bother with that," snapped Roxy, "It'll be fine!" She pushed her out of the way and slithered into the lacy thong, pulled high at each side elongating the V towards her crutch to make her legs look longer. "Now get those muppets into the bed and we're ready!"

Suzanne stood on the podium, glancing confidently at the audience and introducing each model as she sashayed for the last time down the catwalk. Each girl was given a resounding round of applause. Suzanne waited and an expectant hush fell as the lights dimmed and a spotlight fell towards the back of the stage. "Ladies and Gentleman, the moment you have all been waiting for …please put your hands together for the designer of this wonderful new collection … I give you … Roxy Le Feuvre."

The audience started to clap; the curtains swished open to reveal Roxy displayed tantalisingly right at the back of the stage laying like Cleopatra on the big, round bed, propped high on snow white pillows and surrounded by the glamorous young men. The Stage Manager crossed his fingers, flicked the switch for the bed to roll its way down the dais …nothing happened. He flicked the switch a couple more times, feeling a hot flush creep over his face and the palms of his hands break into a damp sweat. He tried once more, but the bed remained firmly where it was. The audience started to murmur slightly as if sensing something was going wrong. It was an agonising moment that seemed to take years before the Stage Manager gave a desperate signal. Roxy continued to wave and pose, her smile freezing on her face, wondering what the fuck had gone wrong, when several brawny work men dressed in black leapt onto the stage. They couldn't have been less glamorous if they'd been selected for the *Mr Unappealing* competition. With their carpenters' aprons filled with tools around their pot-bellied waists, balding heads, wrinkled, unshaven faces and filthy hands, they got behind the bed and shoved it lustily down the catwalk where it juddered to a smacking halt. Roxy, taken completely by surprise, but ever the opportunist, leapt up at once, draped her arms around the necks of the work men, spread her legs around the hunks on the bed and laughed, "My collection folks – the good," she indicated herself, "the bad," she pointed to boys in the bed, "and the ugly," she threw her head back and laughed with the old geezers.

The audience went wild, laughing and applauding. The press were snapping away madly and screaming out, "Roxy, look this way", "Hey Roxy, give him kiss!" "Roxy, push ya tits up!"

Roxy smiled, and posed, and smiled again. Obligingly she kissed the work men, who blushed as one of her tits fell out. She helpfully straddled the boys on the bed, and answered the monotonous and stupid questions from the media. But underneath all the obliging façade of her plastered smile, she was seething. What the fuck had gone wrong? Heads would roll for this she thought bitterly.

CHAPTER 18

Sunday morning brought a blazing herald of smutty headlines in the newspapers. Aiden was tutting mockingly to Roxy as he scanned them over the breakfast table.

"Well you made the papers babe," he joked sarcastically, "Very tasteful."

"Don't take the piss Aiden," Roxy yelled, "those fucking wankers, I paid them a shed load of money and they couldn't even get that right!"

"Don't be stupid," he scoffed, "nobody in the audience knew it wasn't what you wanted, and let's face it, it would be just the kind of dumb stunt you'd usually pull – you like a bit of rough." He pulled open the paper to expose the grainy shot of Roxy standing astride on the bed, "it looks totally staged."

"Well it fucking wasn't," Roxy groaned, she could hardly bear to look at the photo, "it was lucky I was thinking on my feet."

"You were certainly doing that, from the looks on those guys' faces, they had a right good view of your bits." Aiden considered the shot, skewing the paper sideways to get a better angle, "not to mention that you can see your nipples, I bet those old farts couldn't believe their luck." He laughed out loud and threw the paper down. "Don't be fed up, it's good publicity and the line was catchy, the Good, the Bad and the Ugly – too true."

"Oh, just shut the fuck up Aiden," growled Roxy, "I'm not paying their bill, I can tell you, that *Gallomania* charge a fortune. It'll not be worth their reputation to argue. Not to mention Suzanne, she's for the chop."

"Don't be so fucking childish Roxy, it wasn't her fault, or theirs either come to that, it was just one of those things, and it turned out okay. Why not be a big girl and show how magnanimous you can be, instead of being such a prize bitch all the time? Anyway if it gets round that it was a fuck up – you'll be a laughing stock."

"I can just see you being magnanimous - you prick – you're a fine one to talk!" yelled Roxy, furious that he hadn't taken her side, "you'd have them minced up in your enchiladas!"

"Whatever," said Aiden calmly, bored with her, "I'm going to find the children, so quit the drama and pull yourself together." He got up from the table, neatly dodging the jug that Roxy hurled at him.

Roxy glared after him. If she'd been a cartoon character red steam would have been pluming out of her ears, but there was no doubt Aiden was right. She'd have to brazen it out, pretend it was what she'd organised all along. Okay, she could do magnanimous, but she'd get them back, and they weren't the only ones either.

Max was sitting in his Docklands flat. He, too, was perusing the morning papers and smiled wryly at the steamy photographs of Roxy. He might have guessed that she'd try some stunt to get the publicity which seemed to have taken her over these days as her chosen life-enhancing drug. He was glad that he'd not been there to witness the spectacle. He knew that he'd pissed her off when he'd arrived with Anna, of course - that had been his intention. The fact that he'd put Anna in a cab the moment they'd left the building was immaterial; he'd achieved what he had set out to do. He was tired of the way Roxy treated him, like some kind of adoring puppy to dangle along on a lead behind her, which on the odd occasion, when it suited her, she would turn around and fondle. She would find out that this puppy had teeth, he mused drolly, although naturally the nip would only be to give her a sharp reminder that he was no toy. The sad fact was that his life had been so intrinsically woven with hers now for so long, he could never quite let her go. He wished he could, and perhaps one day he would be able to walk away and not look back, but in some perverse way he enjoyed the bitter-sweet relationship they had. It suited him, and his perverse life style. Anna, in the meantime, was an entertaining diversion. After that first encounter at Ronnie's, he decided she was different from the usual run of the mill whore and he'd seen her a couple of times. Not too often, as it was never a good idea to get them too keen. She made a good companion when he needed one, like today, she was modest enough and she didn't talk much and he liked that. It had certainly irked Roxy, and for the next few days he wouldn't be answering any of her calls and he knew for certain she would be ringing. He gave a rueful smile and picked up the phone, there was a call though he had to make, and that was to the elusive Nigel Brown and woe betide him, if he was playing him for a mug.

Felix galloped with gusto towards the finishing line, the lathered up neck of Picasso straining forwards with his nostrils flaring red as they made the final turn of speed through the red and white flags.

"Just finishing with a seemingly stonking round is no 723, Felix Stephenson on Picasso," blared out the commentator over the loud speakers.

Hattie dashed over, and took the reins as Felix dismounted, his knees almost buckling underneath him. She loosened the girth, silently handed him a bottle of water and immediately began to walk the tired horse back to the truck, whilst Felix was mobbed by the syndicate, who'd swarmed over excitedly, prancing up and down like a fairground ride. Eridge was a notoriously hilly course, and the horse and rider had to be totally fit to sustain the energy to get round, let alone jump the obstacles but Felix and Picasso had been on wings, eating up the ground without faltering, jumping everything out of a good stride. Everyone was ecstatic and gabbling at once. Felix smiled at them all, but hardly took anything in, he felt exhausted. He just wanted to collapse and not say a word. He watched the retreating back of Hattie leading Picasso away; he knew she was quite capable of sorting him out, and he could see her patting him and making much of him and suddenly he felt desperate to be with them.

"Great round Felix, well done old man" enthused Colin, who

had the flourishingly pregnant Grace balanced on his arm, "He looked amazing."

"He jumped super, gave me a wonderful ride," smiled Felix, "didn't look at a thing."

"You may be in with a chance Felix," panted Grace, who was clearly feeling the heat, "I should think you were well within the time."

"Yep, pretty much I'd think," agreed Felix, "although it just depends on how the others go. Best not count our chickens – his dressage score was a bit disappointing."

"That'll improve with time," said Jennifer hopefully, "and even if there are better dressage scores, not all of them will go clear in the show jumping and the cross country like you, surely?"

"No darling, but some of them will, and Felix is right, the dressage does need to be better," remarked Charles and, as ever the pragmatist, added thoughtfully, "Any plans about that Felix?"

"Leave him alone Charles!" rebuked Jennifer crossly, "He's only just got off the cross country course for God's sake!"

Mark interrupted, "Well you've got that new lad joining you Felix, he's supposed to be a dressage wallah isn't he? Perhaps he can help?"

The others looked at Felix in surprise. They clearly hadn't heard the news about Sebastian, and so he wearily went through the whole diatribe of explanation again, watching their faces for adverse reactions.

"Well, as long as our horse doesn't suffer," said Charles blandly, "I suppose it'll be alright."

Mark came to the rescue, "It's only a trial, and Felix is still in charge. I think it could a very good move."

Felix smiled at him gratefully, "Don't worry, Picasso won't suffer at all and neither will any of my other horses," he affirmed confidently, but surreptitiously kept his fingers crossed behind his back.

Back at the truck Hattie had washed off Picasso, removed his studs and was walking him off when Felix returned. The big black and white horse was nibbling bits of grass and dragging her around on the end of the lead rope when he appeared.

"How is he – any lumps or bumps?" called Felix, anxiously biting his lip and shading his eyes against the sun.

"Nope, he's fine. I'll just give him a few more minutes then I'll put on those new cold leg wraps and put him on the truck. Why don't you go and get changed and have a rest, then we can go down and have a look at the scores?" She laughed, "You can buy me an ice cream and I wouldn't mind a look around those stalls."

"You're a star Hats! Okay – won't be a minute."

Hattie allowed the horse to dictate the pace, Picasso ambling from spot to spot picking at the odd tufts, and her eyes wandered over to the lorry. She could see Felix through the windows of the living area. He had stripped off and was standing flexing his aching shoulders, rubbing his hands around his neck. He looked gorgeous: his body rippling with toned muscle, not an ounce of fat on him, his blond hair damp from being under the crash hat was now drying and rumpled. She ached to touch him, but it was no good wishing, Felix didn't see her like that at all. He had the gorgeous Alice, why would he notice her? Picasso gave a sharp jerk on the lead rope, almost pulling her over as he yanked her towards a particularly juicy patch of grass, and she stumbled with him. At least she had him to bring her to her senses.

Fifteen minutes later they were heading towards the show jumping and main arena with Fiver trotting along jauntily alongside them on his lead. This year Eridge had blossomed from a run of the mill horse trial to a mini country show. Not only was there a Country Market, but a fun fair, and dog racing, which meant it was a fun day out for lots of people, and not just for those folk who were interested in horses and eventing. It was pretty crowded. Families with little kids in buggies, balloons hanging off the handles, toddlers whingeing for ice-creams, and plenty of other dogs straining to have a sniff at

Fiver, who immediately cowered away from them. Felix protectively picked him up, whilst he and Hattie, for once with no pressure on them, window-shopped along the stalls, rooting through the multitude of goodies on sale. Hattie bought herself some new lip salve made allegedly from the finest beeswax, and some all-singing and dancing cream for her roughened hands. Felix bought some for Alice and they then stopped at a stall selling home-made cheese. They both tried some samples, screwing their faces up at the stronger ones and offering them to Fiver, which he daintily declined. In the end Felix settled for some milder stuff, and Hattie bought the soft version. They moved onto a shabby-chic stall, and Felix deliberated about buying a little heart-shaped, woven, twig wreath, but then changed his mind. Normally Hattie loved these things, they were so pretty, but realistically she had no-where to put anything like them. She quickly moved on, avoiding the little twangs of pain that caught her breath as she watched Felix buying them for Alice. She called out that she was going to get them an ice cream and that she'd wait for him to join her.

There was a queue for ice creams, and Hattie swatted feebly at a persistent fly. Soon it would be the wasp season she thought gloomily, as she waited for her turn to be served. She had just ordered when Felix zoomed over.

"What did you get me?" he asked, gawping at the choices on offer. "They have such a fab selection."

"Mango and Peach – that okay?"

"Hats, you know me better than I know myself! It's just what I would have chosen." he laughed and gave her a hug, squashing an alarmed Fiver between them. "We should go on that TV programme, *Mr and Mrs*!"

Hattie snorted, "Never heard of it!" but she was delighted nonetheless and felt herself flushing with pleasure. She was just taking the cones when there was an announcement over the loudspeaker. *"Terrier racing will commence at 1pm. Entries have already opened, so any more competitors, please make their way over now please."*

"Wow, come on – let's go over there," grinned Felix, "although I don't think it's quite your thing, old mate, is it?" He pulled his ice cream away from Fiver who had decided he quite fancied a lick. "But they're great fun, have you ever seen it Hattie?"

"No, but please don't go getting any ideas about Fiver, he's too timid."

"Don't worry, I won't but it'll really make you laugh!" He darted off through the crowds with Hattie in quick pursuit desperately trying to lick her Toffee Crunch Crème before it melted all over her fingers.

The terrier ring was packed with people and wiry dogs of all shapes and sizes. The classes were divided into dogs of *'up to twelve inches'*, *'over twelve inches'* and then what was called the *'odds and sods'*, which apparently meant anything from a Pekinese to a Greyhound. The race track was, in fact, a thin stretch of grass about 50m long which had been cordoned off with plastic mesh on either side to form a barrier so that the terriers couldn't escape. At one end were a set of starting cages and at the other, after the finishing line, was a stack of straw bales with a little gap for a single dog to pass through into a holding area. The lure, a manky old piece of fur, was attached to nylon rope and dragged along the ground on a mechanical pulley from the starting box to the finishing line. The idea being that the terriers, suspecting it was a rodent would tear after it, chasing it to the finish. The first dog past the post won the heat. There were several heats and then a final.

The cacophony of noise was ear-splitting; with sharp little yaps and excited barks punctuating the air as the dogs revved up for the racing. Obviously quite a lot of them had been before and loved it, whilst others looked a bit bewildered and hadn't a clue what to do. When Hattie and Felix arrived, there was already quite a crowd alongside the track barrier, but they managed to find a tiny gap and wormed their way to the front so they had a good view. The first of the terriers were already in the starting boxes, their tails hammering backwards and forwards in frenzy, as they watched the lure dancing about tantalisingly on the end of the pulley. Suddenly they were off, the mesh fronts of the starting boxes were raised and several terriers hurtled out, tearing after the tatty bit of fluff flying ahead of them towards the finishing line. A couple ran confused to the side of the track looking for their owners, and one ran behind the start box. It was hilarious, as the spirited little dogs cavorted along the track. The crowd were yelling and screaming as they tore over the line and disappeared through the tunnel at the end, followed closely by the others who had, by now, cottoned on to the game. It was over in a matter of seconds, handlers were collecting up the stray dogs, and owners were being reunited with the winners and another lot of squealing and squirming bundles were being put into the starting boxes by their owners.

Hattie and Felix were holding onto each other and laughing. Fiver was really excited too, straining to get down and join in the fun. He seemed to have a new lease of life.

"I think he'd actually quite enjoy it!" giggled Hattie, "Look at his tail wagging it's going round like a food-mixer!"

"I knew you'd love it," laughed Felix, "but I didn't think he would get so keen – look at his little face – he can't wait to get stuck in! Shall we have a go?"

They were just debating whether they should or not, when Hattie noticed a peroxide blonde woman with bright red lipstick on the other side of the track. She was yelling at a gigantic man with tattoos all down his arms. Hattie clutched onto Felix's arm, "Oh God look who that is!"

Felix stared over at the woman. He recognised her from somewhere, then he followed her gaze over to the man, "Christ, it's that fucking thug who had Fiver!"

Hattie tugged at Felix "Come on - let's get outta here," she whispered, "before they see us."

Felix nodded his agreement, and they edged their way backwards, not taking their eyes from the pair, who luckily were too busy screaming to look their way. The crowd behind them surged forward to take their place at the front and Felix and Hattie melted away and, as soon as they could, took to their heels pelting back towards the safety of the Country Market. They ran through the people, brushing them aside as they raced, finally coming to a stop behind a marquee, gasping in great raspy breaths, and then looking at each other and falling about in peals of laughter.

"Christ, that was close, I thought he was sure to have seen us," spluttered Felix, "but there's no way he's having Fiver back now!" He cuddled the little dog protectively, and Fiver squirmed uncomfortably, wriggling in protest. Felix set him down carefully and looked at Hattie, "Well spotted though Hats."

"Be sure our sins will find us out," Hattie misquoted reaching down to stroke Fiver, "You're right though, those thugs definitely aren't having you, are they my little lovely."

"Right babes, let's have a quick gander at the scores and get back to the truck and go home. I don't know about you but I don't want to hang about here any longer than I have to."

"Too right!" laughed Hattie, "Why is it whenever we have a '*nice hour off*' we always get into so much trouble!"

CHAPTER 19

By the following Wednesday the success of Picasso's third place at Eridge had taken a back seat with the news that Sebastian and his entourage would be arriving at the weekend. He was bringing six horses, a groom, his dog and a smart truck, according to Felix, who was now dreading his arrival as much as Hattie was. The matter of where he was going to live still had not been decided, and Sebastian had airily said he would camp out in the lorry until he found something better – *camp* being the operative word. Still, there was no going back now, and they both tried to make the best of it as they sorted out some space for his kit in the tack room.

Mark had called by with a new tenancy agreement for Felix to sign, which had given the go-ahead for the sub-letting and stayed for a cup of tea. He was laid back enough but Felix always felt slightly uncomfortable when he was around, like he was a bug wriggling under the microscope. They chatted together whilst Hattie carried on with rolling and pairing up bandages and she was half-heartedly listening to their conversation. Her mind drifted back to seeing Roxy Le Feuvre that day at the mill, and without thinking, she spoke out loud.

"Mark, what happened about that woman who came to look at the mill, you know who I mean?"

Mark laughed sarcastically, "Her. Who knows? Haven't heard a dickey bird since and probably won't either. These people are all talk. I did see a rather tacky picture of her in one of the Sunday papers; she's obviously been too busy getting her clothes off. Remember though," he shot her a warning look, "don't mention it to anyone will you, just in case."

Hattie flushed, "Of course I won't – in fact I'd forgotten about it till just now anyway."

Mark smiled, "Sorry Hattie, of course you wouldn't. I'm just a bit over-sensitive about the place, y' know." He glanced over at Felix, but he seemed suddenly to be miles away, "I'd better be moving, hope it goes okay this weekend. I'll drop in sometime and introduce myself once he's settled."

"Sure. See you later," said Felix distractedly, thinking about Roxy. He'd seen the papers too. It was a tarty shot, but there was something about her that day when he'd seen her at the mill. The *come on* look she'd given him even behind the shades, he was sure he wasn't mistaken.

"You okay Felix?" asked Hattie, "You with us, or with the Woolwich?"

"Ha ha – don't be sarky" he put down his cup, "let's get cracking then."

By lunchtime they had made a good job of it, condensing as much of their own things as they could, and sweeping out the stables ready for Seb's horses to arrive. They were both filthy and exhausted. Hattie had a huge cobweb strewn over her hair and a large smut on her nose, and Felix didn't look much better.

"Let's get something to eat," Felix smiled at her, putting his broom to one side and brushing the cobweb off her hair, "I'm starving. Shall we go down to the Fox? My treat?"

"Aw Felix, look at the state of me, how can I go like this?" Hattie wailed, "I'm filthy!" She was delighted though, she loved these intimate times together when she had him all to herself. "Okay – why not – we've worked hard enough."

The Fox wasn't crowded that Wednesday lunchtime. The old regulars Dick Lewington and Frank Knapp were propping up the bar with their ubiquitous Jack Russell terriers snoozing at their feet, Angie, the voluptuous bar maid, was pulling the pints and cleaning the counter till it shone, and Janice Macey, the Landlady, was behind the bar slicing lemons and waiting for the food orders. Most of the customers who had been in so far had taken their drinks outside to enjoy the sunshine, and a few were in the snug perched around the twee little tables adorned with sweet peas in earthenware jugs.

Colin and Mark had chosen to sit in the garden away from Janice and her effervescent curiosity.

"You could have knocked me down with a feather!" Colin laughed, "Didn't even haggle, which surprised me even more!"

Mark was in shock. He couldn't believe it. Colin had rung asking to meet him for a quick lunch as he had some good news. He had just told him that Aiden Hamilton had offered the full asking price for the mill and wanted the sale to go ahead as fast as possible.

"I'm staggered Col, it was the last thing I expected," muttered Mark, "I was only saying to Felix and Hattie this morning that I doubted we'd ever hear from them again."

"Well, that must have been the exact moment when they were ringing me – kismet mate. Fate – whatever you want to call it. But we're on. Nice sale for you, fat commission for me." Colin raised his glass to Mark's, "Cheers!"

Mark picked up his own glass, "Cheers, but there's a long way to go yet." he added dubiously, "you know that better than anyone else."

"Of course, but I've just got a feeling about this one. They want the place all right and what our Aiden wants, he usually gets. Besides, unless the planning is tricky, which if it's done properly, I can't see it will be, then where's the problem?"

"Did he say what they were actually applying for?" asked Mark, "the Council can be sticklers, and what about English Heritage?"

"I didn't speak to him, it was Miss Cool - Chrissie who rang – she's thawed a bit too I can tell you." Colin grinned, "Quite a nice girl actually. Apparently, it is definitely going to be a restaurant, using the old mill wheel as a big feature – all done up in keeping. Renovating the whole thing outside, but state of the art kitchens and stuff inside. That architect chappie has been working round the clock on the ideas and spec and that won't have come cheap I can tell you."

"What about the barns on the other side?" asked Mark, "What are they going to do with them?"

"She didn't say much about that," Colin fiddled with his glass, "but from what I can gather that will be Roxy's little empire – spa, gym, that sort of thing. It's the mill that'll need the most work done, so I suppose that's where they'll have to focus first."

"So what's the state of play now then?"

"She's writing to me with a formal offer and giving the contact details for their legal team. We accept it in writing. The architect, as their agent, hasn't hung about apparently, he's already submitted outline plans to the Planning Officer and has arranged a meeting there with him for Friday, along with a bod from English Heritage. As you know, you don't have to actually own land to submit outline plans for something nor have firm specifications either – it's just the principle of the thing."

"Okay, so what then?"

"Well the planning is their problem not ours. You instruct the Estate's solicitors once we get the offer and it goes ahead like a normal conveyance; land searches, covenants that sort of malarkey. With any luck we could have it wrapped up in six weeks."

"Well I'll drink to that!" laughed Mark, "Although it's not over till the fat lady sings!"

"Nor the thin, sexy, big-boobed one in this case," chortled Colin, and raised his glass skyward.

They were both grinning at Colin's joke when Hattie and Felix walked into the garden looking like a pair of scarecrows, with bits of hay stuck in their hair, and their breeches filthy, their heads bent low in deep conversation.

"Now what have those two been up to? Looks like they've been having a romp in the hay."

"Now Col, I don't think there's anything like that between

them," said Mark quite surprised, "they've just been having a bit of tidy-up, ready for this new bloke coming. They're just friends, I think. Besides you're forgetting Felix has Alice."

"They look mighty close to me," smiled Colin knowingly, "Felix may well have Alice, but with a pretty, little thing like Hattie around him all day long … well I'm just saying."

"Hattie's not like that at all." spluttered Mark, almost choking on his beer "And neither's he come to that!"

"Keep your wig on Mark, I was only joking!" laughed Colin, "I couldn't blame him though, she's really come out of her shell since she came to Fittlebury Hall, hasn't she? Got a lovely body, especially in those tight breeches, and those eyes!"

"Aren't you getting enough Col? Never heard you like this before," laughed Mark, "although I agree, she has blossomed, but Hattie's really quite insecure I think. She's no idea how cute she is."

"Just as well probably! Alice had better watch out, that's all I'm saying."

"You're becoming a right old gossip mate – must be the onset of parenthood. How is Gracie? I thought she looked a bit tired on Sunday."

Colin scratched his chin and suddenly his eyes looked a little less bright, "Do you know, I worry myself daily about her. I try not to dwell on it too much. She did look tired didn't she? But she insisted she came to Eridge, wanted to see the horse run, but the struggle up that hill didn't do her much good." He paused for a moment, "I just wish she'd take it easy, it's not long now."

"Ah she's an independent soul is Grace, you won't change her and you wouldn't want to either. She'll be fine, she won't do anything she feels is too much for her. Exciting times ahead."

Colin brightened "I can't bloody wait!"

Felix and Hattie got their drinks and waved over to the two men chatting in the garden. Whatever they were talking about, it looked serious and they decided to sit at a little bench in the corner and leave them to it. They were starving – all that hard work had come on top of the mucking out and riding that they'd already done before they started on the grand tidy-up, and they'd been going like mad things since early on.

"Hattie," said Felix, his face suddenly serious "I need to talk to you about something important."

"Blimey," Hattie felt her heart sink to her boots and back into her mouth, "Go on then."

"Mmm, well I don't know quite how to begin really." He started, then took a swallow and looked her directly in the eye, "But I need to make a few things clear. When Seb comes, things are bound to change a bit. I want to try and have a proper lesson structure with you on the horses, so that you are involved with more of the technical stuff. You're a good rider and I should have done it before now." He paused, dropping his gaze and thinking for a moment. "Another thing, I know you have a lot to do, but I wondered if you would mind helping me out with the competition entries? They are a fucking nightmare what with all the closing dates and ballot dates. If we did the competition planning together, it would be easier for us to organise the horses' work regime. What do you think?"

Hattie's initial fear of what he had been going to say had been gradually replaced by a flood of glowing pleasure. She looked steadily at him, her grey eyes soft, "Sounds great Felix, I'd love it all."

"That's settled then Hats! Proper structured sessions, more hands on with the paperwork and planning – let's have a toast shall we? Fittlebury Hall Event Team – just the two of us!"

"Just the two of us!" Hattie chimed in enthusiastically, wishing in heart that it was really true.

Chrissie was on all fours on the bed. She dropped her upper torso and head onto the pillows bracing herself on her elbows, as she arched her bum upwards.

"Christ you've got a lovely arse," groaned Aiden lecherously, as he drizzled baby oil over her pert backside. "Don't move baby."

"Mmm, that feels good," she moaned, "don't worry I'm not moving anywhere."

Aiden continued his expert stroking, circling his fingers around the edges of her buttocks, every now and then dipping lightly and fleetingly between her legs and rapidly withdrawing as he teased her. Now he stroked between the cheeks of her bottom, smiling slightly as she obliging spread her legs apart for him and gently circled his fingertips deeper and further with more pressure than before.

"God Aiden, stop fucking about, I'm ready," gasped Chrissie, squirming underneath him, feeling the hot, beating pulse between her legs ready to explode at any second.

Aiden immediately stopped, "Be patient! You naughty, middle-class girls are all the same, you always want it your own way." He slapped her bottom playfully and she collapsed underneath him, rolling over onto her back.

"You fucking tease," she complained bitterly, as by now the insistent throbbing had started to subside, and she reached over and grabbed his cock, "Let me play with you, and see how you like it!"

"Go right ahead Chrissie, I'm all yours," he pushed himself down onto her face, ramming himself into her mouth, "Enjoy!"

Chrissie got to work. She was an expert at giving head; firstly taking the whole cock into her mouth, then carefully withdrawing backwards and forwards; licking along the shaft and around the tip with her tongue then plummeting down to encase it again – easy-peasy. All the while massaging his balls gently – he was putty in her hands. Aiden closed his eyes and relished every second, but he wasn't going to fall into his own trap. At the eleventh hour, he pulled her head back and pushed her back on the bed, kissing her hard on the lips, parting her mouth with his tongue, tasting his own saltiness on her lips. His hand strayed down to her breast, fondling the nipple and then further down to find her slippery wetness between her legs, and before she could object she found her hands pinioned by his above her head and, in one quick movement, he had pushed himself inside her and was gyrating backwards and forwards.

"Good?" he groaned, his eyes fixed on hers, "Want it harder?"

"Good," she panted, "but harder."

He rammed himself into her like he was riding a bucking bronco. As he felt her body twitching violently underneath his, and her eyes start to glaze over as she came, he let himself go into a glorious volcanic explosion of pure adulterous orgasm.

They lay afterwards propped up against the pillows, sweaty and satiated sharing a post-coital cigarette and a bottle of Dom Perignon.

"Here's to the new venture," Aiden toasted, "It's gonna be fucking awesome."

"New venture," agreed Chrissie, taking a slug of the champagne "It's a long haul yet Aiden," she reminded him, "plenty of hurdles to jump."

"Aw it'll be fine. I want it open for Christmas – that gives us five months."

"You're round the bend, it can't be done"

"Yes it can. You can project manage it Chrissie. Crack the fucking whip, grease palms, fuck who you have to – I want a grand Christmas opening. Christ knows I pay you enough."

She laughed at him. "You're nuts. I'm not promising you a thing, and you can shout as much as you like, it cuts no ice, you don't frighten me. I'm not Roxy y' know."

Aiden glared at her, and then laughed too, "Do your bloody best for me eh?"

Chrissie's face softened, "That's better. You know I will."

"What do you think of this latest stunt of Roxy's then – what a fucking farce."

"Aiden, you married her. You knew what she was like when you did, so how can you act surprised when she behaves like she does? It's your bed and you have to lie in it. Leopards don't change their spots."

"I know, she can be unbearable, but she is useful, and you're right, it is my bed." He grinned at her, "Meanwhile, this is your bed and I like laying you in it!"

"Oi! The deal was one celebratory fuck, chum!" Chrissie giggled as he leapt on top of her knocking the champagne out of her hand, "Oh alright then, one more then - for old time's sake."

CHAPTER 20

Max was flying up to Doncaster Races with Ronnie, that morning, in a private chopper they'd charted for the day. They were meeting some of Ronnie's cronies and Max had been invited to be part of their inner circle. So far the day had started well. He'd arrived at the small, private aerodrome just outside London in good time to meet Ronnie, and the pilot was ready and waiting for them. Max settled back in his seat, obsessively checking his seatbelt, and clapped on his earphones over the racket of the whirring motor blades whilst there seemed an interminable wait as the pilot did his pre-flight checks. As they hovered skywards, he felt elated. The flight proved spectacular; the chopper making good headway and the weather was ideal for viewing. He glanced at Ronnie, who smiled and gave him the thumbs up sign. Max felt the stirrings of real excitement in his belly, something that had been missing in his life for a long time. He could almost smell the money and couldn't wait to get started.

The helicopter had obtained special permission to land at the racecourse; rather than put down at the local Robin Hood Airport, which, although was only seven miles away from the track, was still inconvenient. They hovered over the area giving Max a bird's-eye view of the pear-shaped race track. The fancy, new grandstand, which had reputedly cost millions to construct, dwarfed the older, and Max thought, more aesthetically pleasing structures built in the 1880s. Now this massive ultra-modern building housed all the infrastructure necessary for the modern racing enthusiast; it loomed over the proceedings like some sinister creature, with its roof, like the beak of angry bird shrouding the grandstand seats. Max, whilst he was interested and excited at what lay ahead of him, scowled in distaste at the vagaries of modern architecture. Still he had better keep his opinions to himself, as Ronnie was clearly excessively proud of the new monstrosity.

BIG BUCKS

Once inside, they were quickly ushered into one of the private suites right at the top of the new building and were immediately offered a glass of champagne. They were one of the first to arrive, and they made their way out onto the balcony to survey the scene below. The view was, without doubt amazing, far down below them was the grandstand seating, where the main punters were, the parade ring, the bookies and all the melee of the crowds beginning to assemble for the afternoon's meeting.

"Fantastic view Ronnie," admired Max, "but hard to fathom you can make so much dough out of a race."

"Max 'ave some faith. Anyway, it's not just one race. It's races all over the world. The blokes you're gonna meet are big league players. Today, is just a little discreet social day out, but I just wanna introduce you. They're a close bunch, and they know I'm bringing you and they know why. It's a funny old business and we all have to work together. It's no good us all trying the same scam on the same day is it? It'd soon be rumbled, it has to clever, cleverer than the system."

Max was desperate to ask more but the sound of other voices coming into the room behind them halted their conversation, and Ronnie wheeled about abruptly and went back into the suite heartily greeting the newcomers. He followed him in frustration; there was so much more he needed to know.

At first it was just a lot of chit chat. To Max they were just a lot of ordinary blokes in smart suits, eating and drinking a lot and telling dirty jokes and tall stories. He listened with feigned interest and amusement, secretly sizing them all up, assessing each characteristic of their personalities, looking for their strengths and every sign of weakness. He had long ago learned how important this could be when the chips were down. He smiled inwardly at the pun. So far, little of the talk had been about gambling. As the new boy he let them take the lead: they would get around to the point of the meeting, and he would just have to be patient. Max was being careful about how much he drank, although the others were pretty pissed with all the free booze floating about, and he wondered who was footing the bill for the suite. By the time the runners had gone down to the paddock for the first race, most of the men were pissed, and as yet, no-one had placed more than token bets of a few hundred pounds with the hospitality runner who discreetly hovered in the background.

Max whispered to Ronnie, "Are they gonna back anything?"

"Nah, not here, it's all been done earlier. Relax, lighten up and enjoy yourself."

Max felt frustrated. He was no nearer finding out what was going on than he was when he'd got here, and these sweaty drunk buggers were not his idea of fun. He felt out of his depth, and he hated being out of control. He shrugged "Okay mate, your call."

The runners went down to the start and everyone craned dangerously out over the balcony to watch the race. Max, who'd placed £50 to win on the favourite, watched idly from the back and was bored with it all. The acrid smell of sweat from the bodies was making him feel sick, either that or those prawns had been dodgy. The crowd below were starting to get really worked up, screaming and shouting in response to the commentator's reports. Max started to become more interested, the favourite was in the lead, he could see in the distance the horses streaming in a long snake around the edge of the course, their colours flying in what seemed like one long rainbow of ribbon as they tore along the track.

"Come on, come on," Max found himself shouting, "come on Amber Light!"

"It won't win," whispered Ronnie quietly, and then laughed and shouted loudly, "come on Amber Light!"

"What…?" spluttered Max confused, "what do you mean? It's in the lead!"

"Watch," muttered Ronnie, "and learn."

"Amber Light being challenged by Mild September on the inside, only two furlongs to go," screamed the commentator.

The crowd were going wild, shouting and yelling. Max felt his palms growing clammy; the horse was going to lose. As he watched, the favourite faded further, finally crossing the finishing line into third place. The men in front of him clapped each other on the back and laughingly toasted each other. He was beginning to see what was going on.

Since the *Gallomania* disaster, Roxy had been in a foul temper, although she had heeded Aiden's warning and decided against sacking Suzanne. The girl knew too much for Roxy to risk her going to the media with any sensational leaks about her private life, and so she had been charmingly, but dangerously understanding. Suzanne, for her part, didn't know if she were relieved or dismayed by Roxy's attitude, especially when instructed to immediately pay *Gallomania*'s extortionate invoice, but that she, Suzanne, was to demand a considerable reduction for the faux pas. Roxy had Suzanne by the short and curlies, they both knew it. Had Roxy sacked her, Suzanne could have bad-mouthed her all over town, but if she walked out of the contract, the roles would be reversed and the likelihood was she'd never represent an A-lister again. After a tussle and the primeval fear of the bad publicity *Gallomania* had reduced the invoice substantially. Roxy had her, somewhat hollow, victory over them both, but ever the entrepreneur and attempting some form of damage limitation, she cracked the whip mercilessly at Suzanne. That week the fiasco had been turned into a triumph by a multitude of press interviews with Roxy gushing that her lingerie range *'was designed to make everyone beautiful'*.

One last score had to be settled, and Roxy had tried Max's private mobile a dozen times and each time he had ignored her. *Fuck him,* she thought, it had not even gone to a voice mail, so she couldn't leave him a shitty message either. Where was he when she needed him and moreover, she thought irrationally, who was he with? She was bloody determined to find out.

In irritation, she drummed her red talons on the desk, thinking hard and then scrolled through some numbers on her mobile and found the one she was looking for.

"Hey Lisa!" Roxy purred, "It's me, what are you doing? Fancy a little jaunt out later – undercover like?"

It was just past four o'clock in the afternoon when Roxy and Lisa were winging their way across town towards one of Max's clubs. Lisa had been riding her horses at the livery yard down in Sussex where she kept them when Roxy called, but intrigued she'd dashed back up to London to meet her.

"Where we going then mate?" she asked, checking her lip gloss, "I hope it's worth it, I had ta bribe the fucking Nanny ta do overtime."

"You remember that bloke Max, we met him the other night at the club?"

"Can't forget him can I?"

"Well he's up to something, and I want to find out what; turned up at my launch at the weekend with a tart on his arm and been AWOL ever since," grumbled Roxy.

"I knew you were having a thing with him," Lisa laughed, "you've kept that quiet!"

"No I'm not! He's just a friend, but a close friend and we go back years, he usually tells me everything and I want to find out what's going on, that's all." Roxy protested, and then as a quick diversion turned on Lisa, "Anyway, why didn't you come to the launch, you bloody turncoat."

Lisa blushed under her make-up. "Babes, I wanted ta, but Mike had an appearance to do, so I had ta go ta that, ya know I would have, honest…" she finished lamely.

"Never mind, forget that, I needed you now and you're here," Roxy smiled benignly at Lisa with her thick orange make up and common accent and was genuinely pleased, but secretly delighted that she'd herself had had those elocution lessons and changed her own image and didn't look or sound like her anymore either.

"What's the drill then babe?"

"We're going to one of his clubs where he usually hangs out at this time in the afternoon. Even if he isn't there, one of his lackeys will tell me where he is, they all know me well enough," smiled Roxy, "we'll use the back entrance, don't want to attract any attention, but if we are spotted, it'll be just two friends having a drink together."

"Whatever ya say – what happens if he's there? D'ya want me ta make myself scarce?"

"Let's play it by ear," Roxy laughed, "If he's there we don't know what he'll be up to - perhaps we'll catch him with his pants down."

They fell about laughing in the back of the cab, and the driver smirked to himself in the mirror, he'd been on the blower to one his pap contacts the moment he picked them up. Their tips were always fatter than the ones these silly cows gave him.

The taxi struggled irritatingly through the heavy traffic of Oxford Street, battling with the kamikaze cyclists, who were as dangerous as pedestrians these days for pulling out in front of vehicles. As it wormed its way along the busy road, Roxy suddenly tapped on the screen. She'd clocked this cabbie's number right from the moment they'd got in, she knew his type all right, "Driver, we've changed our minds, can you drop us here please."

"What lady!" moaned the cabbie, as he reluctantly pulled over. Roxy and Lisa leapt out and she tossed him a twenty pound note.

"Keep the change ducky, and next time be sensible – you didn't really think we'd give ya the real address," smiled Roxy, and they both disappeared into the crowds thronging towards Soho. "These idiots must think we're stupid," laughed Roxy, adjusting her sunglasses and pulling down her trilby hat. "Come on, we need to head for "Wardour Street."

The back entrance to the club was only known to the chosen few and rarely used. Most celebs wanted to announce their appearance as much as Max wanted to advertise it, but Roxy had snuck in here on plenty of occasions in times of crisis. A hefty, black guy stood guard as they approached. He looked fierce in his bouncer gear, radio set in his ear and bulging muscles straining under the uniform black shirt. Lisa clutched her arm in panic, but luckily Roxy knew him from old.

"Hi Amos," she called, "How are ya baby?"

"Afternoon Ms Le Feuvre. Haven't seen you in a while," he grinned at her, his white teeth sparkling, "club's pretty empty, we've only just opened."

"Good," smiled Roxy, edging past him "Mr Goldsmith in yet?"

"Haven't seen him Ma'am, but he's usually here around now."

"We'll go through to the cocktail bar and wait then, thanks Amos."

The bar was empty, which was hardly surprising and they ordered a couple of cocktails and sat in one of the discreet booths watching the door.

"What ya gonna do next babe?" sighed Lisa, swirling the little umbrella in her drink. "Ya gonna ask where he is?"

"No, let's just wait and see if he shows up," muttered Roxy, "he normally comes about this time."

They waited for about half an hour, by which time the bar was gradually filling with customers. The club was a popular meeting place for the chic and trendy wannabe crowd and a lot of them were in the media and fashion industry. Neither Roxy, nor Lisa, could afford to be spotted here without a legitimate excuse. Reluctantly, they decided they'd have to go before they created too much attention. They pushed down their glasses and sidled out, ostensibly to go to the loo, and then dived towards the back entrance, colliding heavily with Ricardo the manager.

"Ms Le Feuvre, I am so sorry," he gasped, "I had no idea you were in the club this afternoon. Mr Goldsmith will be disappointed he's missed you."

"No problem Ricardo, none at all," spluttered Roxy, adjusting her glasses which had toppled down her nose, "Where is Max by the way?"

"I haven't seen much of him all week, madam, to be honest, his driver seems to think he's gone racing today with a friend. He dropped him off at the airport this morning; they were taking a helicopter I believe, so I doubt he'll be back. Can I pass a message on to him?"

Roxy was astonished and seething but managed to spit out, "No thanks Ricardo, no message."

She grabbed Lisa by the arm, and they hurtled back out into the street and demanded that Amos call them a cab. She was going to find out what he was up to, if it was the last thing she did.

CHAPTER 21

Saturday saw even hotter weather with blistering sun and temperatures way up in the high 70s. Hattie was sweating already and it was only just past ten in the morning. She had arrived mega early, and she and Felix had been on the first horses by seven. Now the last of the bunch were finished and she was just washing Jacks down whilst Felix turned out Rambler, and they could have a well-deserved cuppa. She stuck the hose in her mouth and then trickled the cold water over her head and down the back of her neck. It felt amazing; so deliciously refreshing, and before she knew it, she was soaked all over. Jacks gave her a surprised look and she laughed and scraped him off, tossing on a fly rug and led him out to the paddock. She met Felix on his way back.

"Christ, what happened to you, Jacks play you up?"

"No!" she laughed, realising that she must look a right state, with her wet hair plastered around her head, and her face all red, "I was just hot!"

"Oh… okay, as long as you're alright," he looked down at the ground, "I'll get the kettle on, see you in a minute." He marched on back towards the yard not giving her another glance.

Hattie gazed after him forlornly, she obviously looked dreadful – otherwise why couldn't he meet her eye? She took Jacks out to the paddock, but the spring had suddenly gone out of her step. Leaning over the gate she put her face in her hands, why on earth had she made herself look so awful? She took out her scrunchie and tried to fluff up her hair, but it was still hanging in dripping tendrils, just like the rest of her, but at least her hair hid her sticky red face. She dragged herself despondently back to the stables.

Mayhem met her when she walked over the cobbles. A

flamboyant white lorry, with a daring gold and black decal of a dressage horse embellished on the side had drawn up and was parked right in the middle of the yard, horses stomping about inside. The cab was empty, but she could hear the sound of voices coming from the tack room, and suddenly out came Felix with two guys. She recognised Sebastian straight away, and the other chap must be his groom, she supposed. Self-consciously she walked over, fiddling with her hair and trying to cover up her face.

"Good morning Hattie, my little flower," grinned Sebastian, "If it is indeed you under all that hair!" he laughed effusively, "This is Leo, my number one man," he tittered, "my only man actually."

Leo laughed, "Nice to meet you Hattie," he smiled at her and held out his hand.

Hattie smiled, although no-one could see her face anyway, and self-consciously shook Leo's hand back. "Nice to meet you too Leo." She had never felt so embarrassed or felt so stupid. "I'll get the ramp down," she said, finding any excuse to get away from them.

"I'll give you a hand," said Leo, "or perhaps on second thoughts, you could show me the stables first and I'll get the beds down and I can put them straight in."

As they walked, away Sebastian winked at Felix, "What's going on here then – with the wet tee-shirt contest I mean? Hattie's tits look amazing - her nipples are sticking out like jumping studs."

"Don't," snapped Felix, "and don't let her hear you, she's very sensitive and I don't think she realises. She just doused herself with the hose because she was so hot – it didn't even occur to her. I didn't have the heart to tell her."

"You straight guys are all the same – poor girl. Good job we've arrived, she needs some girl power around here."

"For God's sake Seb – don't, she'll be terribly embarrassed."

"Lighten up Felix, you're not involved are you?"

"No, of course not, but we are good friends, I'm really fond of her."

"Right then, well she's just found two more, so quit worrying. Come on, we'd better give the children a hand."

Sebastian was like a nutty English Setter puppy with long legs. He cracked jokes the whole time, and dashed about organising the others with good humour, falling about laughing when things went wrong. He was incredibly strong, although he could mince along beautifully when he was camping it up, but he certainly didn't mind getting his hands dirty.

Leo clearly adored him. He was not much younger, or he could have even been the same age, it was difficult to tell. He was just as tall, but wiry and skinny, whereas Sebastian was broad. He had longish, dark hair, curling slightly at the nape of his polo shirt and he reminded Hattie slightly of Rufus Sewell in the film *The Holiday*, which she had seen countless times in the re-runs on ITV2. Why, oh why, were all the good looking guys gay, she thought desperately, Felix excepted of course, but he might just as well be for all the hope she had there.

Leo looked over at her, "Come on gorgeous, give me a hand to get the nags out."

Hattie went over willingly to the sparkling truck, ready to haul down the ramp. "Stand back sweetie," advised Seb, "it's got a power ramp." He flicked a switch and the ramp whirred down, coming to a clunk when it hit the cobbles. The horses inside all looked around interestedly, stamping impatiently and clamouring to see where they were.

Seb led each horse off and handed them to Leo. Hattie marvelled at the size of them; they were all huge and muscled up like body builders, quite the opposite from the whippet like fitness of their eventers. When the last horse was off, Hattie helped unload the saddles and bridles and lug them over to the tack room. Then came all the boots and bandages and a heavy trunk full of different bits. Hattie looked around doubtfully wondering if they would ever get it all in.

"Have you got much more stuff?" she asked.

"Fuck me - loads darling," smiled Seb casually, "we've only brought three horses so far, there's all the working tack for the other horses and we haven't even begun on their show stuff, plus all the rugs."

"Right," said Hattie, "I'd better try and make more space," looking around the over-stuffed room already spewing out with their paraphernalia, and wondering how on earth she could manage it.

Felix came in and looked shocked, "Bloody hell, we'll never fit it all in Seb."

"I've got an idea," Hattie said quietly, "Supposing we clear out one of the spare stables, and store the less important stuff in there – you know, the rugs, bandages – just till we can think of something better."

"This girl's got brains Felix," Seb looked at her appreciatively, "As well as being beautiful. Great idea Hattie!"

"Okay," muttered Felix, "Why don't you go back and get the last three horses and we'll decide which stable to use."

"Coolio. Come on Leo. Back soon then. Ciao dolls!"

Felix waited until he heard the lorry start up and looked at Hattie, "He's like a fucking whirlwind! I feel exhausted already."

Hattie laughed, "Don't be so grumpy. I think they're good fun. Come on let's make the best of it!"

Jennifer was delighted that the weather was so beautiful. She'd invited people over for a pool party that evening, and it was one of those functions that had just ballooned out of proportion. A couple of weeks ago when she'd suggested it to Charles, the numbers stood at about twelve, now it seemed about thirty or more guests were coming. Not that he cared at all – he was a great host, and the Parker-Smythes' parties were legendary.

Jennifer was ever mindful that Mrs Fuller was no spring chicken, and although she was in no way past organising things, for big dos they normally got outside caterers in. When she had tentatively mentioned it to Freda Fuller the previous week, tiptoeing around her impending umbrage of the insinuation that she was past coping, she was pleased to see that instead of ruffled outrage, there was nothing but extreme relief in her eyes.

"I think that'll be a champion idea," Mrs Fuller had sighed, "although who'd do it at this late stage I don't know?"

"Well, Chloe said she knew of a local pub that does a great hog roast. She went to a party where they did the catering and she said it was fab." Jennifer smiled, relieved that her idea had been received so well, "I'll give them a ring shall I? See if they can do it?"

"Well, I think you'll be lucky, if you don't mind my saying so, and it's a bit risky – as we don't know them either," Mrs Fuller had grumbled, "but I don't see you've got much choice."

"Leave it to me, Mrs F."

Luckily for Jennifer, The Lamb at Lambs Green obligingly came to her rescue, not only could they do the food, but would provide the waiting staff as well as a bar. She'd organised a Chinese hat marquee to be erected alongside the pool and the company would provide chairs, tables and interior lighting. The garden and pool itself had its own, and she didn't need to worry about loos, as with that small number, there were enough in the pool house, and, if needs be, they could use the house.

Music was a worry though, as no-one she tried seemed to be available at such short notice, and Charles did like live music. By Saturday, she still hadn't found anyone, so it looked as though it would have to be CDs playing in the background. Then she had a brainwave – what about Dulcie? She did have a lovely voice and played the guitar really well. After all, it was only a casual affair – what could be better? She'd ask her.

At first, Dulcie had been as reluctant as jumping into a wasps' nest, stuttering that she couldn't possibly; she wasn't good enough, she'd muck it up, and all sorts of excuses. But Nancy roared with laughter and exclaimed that it was nonsense and, of course, she'd do it for Jennifer, and what's more, she'd be brilliant. Dulcie looked desperately from one to the other sensing defeat and futilely decided to give in, smiling her agreement.

Jennifer threw her arms around her, spluttering, "Dulcie thank you so much. I am so grateful. I think it'll be really good fun – we can all have a great sing-song! Now do you need me to get anything – microphone, that sort of thing?"

"No!" grinned Nancy, "She's got it all, big old karaoke machine – plenty of amps, mike - the lot! Regular little x-factor devotee is Dulcie!"

"Fantastic!" laughed Jennifer, "I know, shall I invite some of the other grooms too? Susie, Beebs, and even Hattie up at the Hall, and they've got a new rider starting today I believe, I could ask him. There's going to be masses of food as I've ordered the hog roast for fifty people. Be much more fun for you both!"

"Aw that's great Jennifer," smiled Nancy, "I'd love it, a bit of company whilst Dulcie struts her stuff!"

"Don't take the piss now." warned Dulcie, but she was beaming, "Sounds lovely – what time do you want me?"

Just after lunch, Leo drove the flashy, white truck back into the yard with the last of Seb's horses. On the passenger seat beside him, sitting like a colossal, stone statue, was a gigantic Doberman with its head lolling out of the window. Seb was following behind in his car, although it was difficult to see him, crammed awkwardly in the driving seat; there was so much gear crammed inside it was stuffed fuller than a turkey at Christmas.

Felix groaned, "Christ look at the size of that fucking dog!"

"Look at all that stuff!" moaned Hattie, "Where's it all gonna go?"

"Now children, don't look so alarmed," soothed Seb slithering out, "There's only one more load to come. Heavens though, am I glad to get out of that damned car." He brushed down his jeans, and strolled over to the lorry, "Come and meet my Hero."

Felix and Hattie didn't know if he was talking about Leo, a horse or the dog, but as Seb was busy dragging the enormous brute out from the cab, they assumed it was the Doberman.

"Isn't he just the most gorgeous creature?" sighed Seb, air-kissing the dog's head, and embracing it like a long, lost lover. "Now come along, don't be worried, he's absolutely soppy, and a real coward at heart."

Hattie swallowed and, with about as much enthusiasm as eating a plate of cabbage, went over to stroke the dog. "Hi Hero, what a good boy, welcome to your new home."

Hero, who was quite the most enormous beast, standing at least thigh high to Hattie, looked at her disconcertingly with the palest of amber eyes, then promptly buried his nose in her crutch and had a good old sniff.

Seb shrieked with laughter, "Hattie doll, he loves you, he sniffs only the finest muffs!"

Despite her misgivings, Hattie had to laugh and fondled the dog's ears, to which Hero gave a throaty groan of delight, wagging his tail madly. "He's lovely Seb, you're right, he's a right old softie."

"He is, and a lazy dog too, can never get him out of bed in the morning." Leo laughed immoderately, joining them, "looks the part though."

"He certainly had me fooled," mumbled Felix doubtfully, "I just hope he doesn't have Fiver for lunch. You should have told me you had a Doberman."

"You didn't ask me, sweetie and of course he won't – they'll be great chums," placated Seb, "come on, let's get the nags off, and I'll do the last trip for the odds and sods."

Felix looked dubious, "By the way Seb, where are you going to live? Have you got anywhere fixed?"

"No doll, Leo and I'll kip in the truck for the time being and get somewhere local to rent. Shouldn't take us long to find something."

Felix looked unconvinced, "Well I suppose it's okay for now, especially at this time of the year, but obviously it can't be permanent."

"Too right it won't be," declared Seb, "Can you imagine – me camping out!"

Hattie and Leo fell about laughing, and Felix stood with his hands on his hips staring at them, and suddenly seeing the funny side of it, started to guffaw with them.

"And what is so funny?" affected Seb.

"Nothing at all Seb, forget it – come on, let's get these horses off," Leo said stifling a grin, "then we can make the truck nice an' cosy."

In the end, Seb and Felix disappeared in Felix's car to get the rest of the gear whilst Hattie and Leo toiled backwards and forwards with the horses. They unloaded the abundance of other paraphernalia, sweating and grunting with the weight of the trunks until, eventually, everything was out of the car and the truck.

Hattie felt exhausted; she was filthy and thirsty. "I've got to stop," she gasped, when they had lugged the last trunk of rugs into the makeshift tack room, "let's have a drink."

"Great idea," enthused Leo, "What've you got?"

"Ribena, Orange, tea or coffee," said Hattie stupidly, "or water?"

"Haven't you got any beer or wine in?" laughed Leo, "that'll have to change Hattie. Lucky I've got some in the fridge in the lorry. Hang on, I'll get something."

Hattie watched him go, sinking down on a bale of shavings. She had been right, life was certainly going to change, but smiling, she realised that it might be for the better.

When Felix and Seb returned, they found Leo and Hattie drinking slightly warm Cava out of plastic glasses, their backs to the warmth of the red brick stables. Fiver and Hero were curled up together on stable rug snoring gently in the shade of the tack room.

"Hey you two! Any for us?" called Seb "I hope it's chilled?"

"Dream on." shouted back Leo, "It was in the truck fridge and it wasn't switched on, but the bottle's in the tack room fridge now – so help yourself."

"These children," moaned Seb, "You just can't get the staff can you?"

Felix laughed, "I'll bring the bottle out, and we can toast to new good friends."

They lolled about in the yard, finishing the bottle between them, screaming with laughter like primary school kids at inane jokes as though they had been lifelong chums. None of them felt like doing anything else today, other than finishing up the yard later. Today was a day for chilling they decided, then tomorrow they would look at logistics.

The shrill, electronic ringtone of *"Simply the Best"* rang out in the harmony and Felix mumbled, "Christ – that's me," scrabbling for his phone, he put his finger to his lips, "it's Jennifer."

"Who's Jennifer?" giggled Leo, "the other woman? I thought his girlfriend was called Alice?"

"She is," whispered Hattie, "that's his main sponsor. Be quiet!"

The mention of a sponsor was enough to bring sobriety to the worst riding drunk and everyone immediately shut up to listen reverently to the call.

"Yes, yes, well that would be lovely." Felix made faces over the phone "Of course, yes, delightful." He raised his eyes to the sky, "Yes today and his groom, very pleasant, you'll like them." He paused again, "Yes, of course, if you'd like, about seven then – see you later, look forward to it. Bye."

"What did she want?" asked Hattie expectantly, "Everything okay?"

"Fine, she's asked us all, you as well," he indicated Seb and Leo, "to a pool party at her place tonight."

"How simply divine!" exclaimed Seb, "Very sweet of her."

"What me too?" spluttered Hattie, surprised, "What for? I mean, not that it's not lovely to be asked, but why?"

"Dunno? Just said she was having a casual pool party and wanted us all to come. Could hardly refuse could I? What Alice will say, Christ knows! She's working and she hates these things, I'd better ring her I suppose."

"Well, I think it'll be fun," reinforced Seb, "what nicer way to be welcomed to Fittlebury?"

"Who's driving more to the point?" laughed Leo, "shall we draw cards for it?"

"Good idea sweetie, get the pack from the truck, and nobody else touches a drop until we know," laughed Seb, "I assume you can drive, Hattie darling?"

"I can," giggled Hattie, "but you're out of luck, as I haven't got a car!"

"That old chestnut! You can drive mine," said Seb loftily, "Don't think you get out of being designated driver so easily."

Felix looked at them, suddenly feeling a stab of disquiet watching Hattie laugh and joke so openly with Seb whilst they waited for Leo to come back with the cards. He thought gloomily of having to pitch the idea of going to the party to Alice and wondered how she was likely to respond.

CHAPTER 22

Roxy was still irrationally obsessed with discovering about Max and his new woman. Ever since Thursday, and her disastrous visit to his club, he seemed to have fallen off the face of the earth. He was not picking up his mobile, and her anger was now subsiding into self-pity at his selfishness for abandoning her. Before, he had always been available whenever she made contact; she would only ever have had to ring or send him a message and he'd be there. She had no doubt that Ricardo would have told him she'd been in, and yet still he hadn't be in touch. She felt as bereft as if he had died.

Aiden was as much comfort as an ashtray on a motorbike. He'd spent all week festering on the mill project. He was rarely at home, either spending time at the restaurants or chasing up the bloody architect. Yesterday, she knew there had been a meeting with the planners and some stuffy old codgers about the designs, and that had gone well - at least she supposed it had, as he'd returned with a grin on his face the size of the Cheddar Gorge; but threatening she'd better come up with some ideas of her own before too long about what she wanted to do with those barns, or otherwise he'd do it himself. She'd glared him with contempt, and turned away. He sensed the fight oozing out of her and told her to get her finger out and stormed off. Once again she just wished she could talk to Max and dialled his number and once again he didn't pick up.

As Roxy was ruminating about Max, he was pre-occupied with a host of strategic plans. The day at Doncaster, which after the agonisingly meaningless start, had turned into a stonker of a day, and he'd come home with his mind whirling like the blades of the helicopter. When the first race had finished, and the victoriously pissed crew had stumbled dangerously off the balcony, demanding more champagne, and clapping each other on the backs like chimpanzees at a tea party, Max had been bewildered and angry.

Ronnie had taken him to one side and aggressively told him to cool it and be patient. It had been good advice; as the afternoon had progressed and he'd inveigled himself more into the group, pretending to be as sloshed as they were, they opened up to him. Now by Saturday, Ronnie had been on the blower and a scam had been set up for next week. Max couldn't wait to be in on the action, if the kind of money Ronnie was pulling was anything to go by.

Another interesting thing was that Nigel Brown, the illusive Private Detective, had sent an email asking him to call, intriguingly saying there had been some developments. Max had rung him immediately, to be told that he had traced the woman whom Max was seeking and he was now trying to locate her. Apparently, she had moved several times over the years, and was now living in the Oxford area, but he was making headway and would pursue the enquiries next week. Max mulled over the information. He was probably being irrational, trying to drag up demons from the past, but the need to know what had become of her still burned brutally in his brain and his culpability was something he had never been able to eradicate. Still, he was trying now and that was all he could do.

Roxy was another story. He smiled to himself as he considered what to do. He was all too well aware, just by looking at the embarrassment of missed calls on his private line, as to how many times she had called. It hadn't hurt her to be brought up short and consider her behaviour towards him, and taking Anna to that charade had done the trick, but, long term, he didn't want to fall out with her either. No, he would let her sweat for a day or two more, then ring her and ask her to lunch or something, but this time it would be a steak bar, none of that Japanese crap.

In the meantime, he was enjoying himself with Anna, playing Dr Doolittle to her Eliza. Despite the way they had met, she was a pathetically sweet girl really, one of the usual sad casualties of an East European trying to make a living and failing. Ending up having to sell her body to make ends meet, and with her looks, she'd been a goldmine for some of the pimps around here. Well, naturally he'd sort that out, nobody would fuck with him. He had no intentions of anything permanent with her, but for the time being she did have her uses. He sent her for a health check, and then moved her into a couple of rooms above one of his clubs, where she was given a proper job, not as a hostess or escort, but behind the scenes. He'd paid off the pimp and word was out that she was strictly off limits. He'd get her trained up as a croupier eventually, but in the meantime, she knew to keep her nose clean, and be available for him when he wanted her. It made him feel good, and she was a cute, little thing to dangle on his arm, as well as on the end of his dick. He was looking forward to this evening.

Leo had drawn the short straw as driver and was good naturedly moaning, "I knew it would be me."

"Stop it sweetie, it was a fair draw," laughed Seb, adjusting the rug straps on a particularly colossal horse, "anyway, it'll be nice for you to be sober for a change."

"Oi, you're a fine one to talk," grumbled Leo, "nice of this woman to ask us, it'll a good way to meet the locals."

"Yep, you're right there. So we'd better be on our best behaviour. At least we're going with Felix and Hattie, they can introduce us to people." Sebastian finished, straightening the rug and stepped out of the stable, "What do you think about this Alice then, not coming I mean?"

"Dunno. Felix didn't say much did he, other than that she was working late and might join us afterwards, but he did look a bit pissed off," observed Leo, "come on we'd better get changed. Hattie'll be back soon and we won't be anywhere near ready to go."

"Ah, the delightful Hattie, now she's a ripe bud for the plucking if you ask me."

"On the turn are you, sweetie?" laughed Leo, "But I agree, she's lovely but she doesn't know it. Methinks we'll have to take her in hand."

"I agree totally, darling. But I'll leave the hands on to you. I can be the brains behind your brawn." laughed Seb, winking at him, "What fun!"

"What are you two scheming about?"

Leo and Seb spun round to see Felix lounging against the doorway, his arms full of bottles, his face not visible as he stood in the shadows.

Seb recovered his sang-froid with lightning speed, cruising over to Felix and relieving him of the bottles, "Oh just gossiping, dear heart! Wow, all these bottles, how lovely, are we starting early?"

"Definitely," affirmed Felix, "I feel like getting pissed tonight."

"Trouble at mill?" asked Leo, checking all the stable doors before joining them, "I gather Alice isn't joining us."

"Don't ask," complained Felix, "Bloody women."

"Couldn't agree more with you. You should bat for the other side Felix, far less trouble," lamented Seb, thinking how gorgeous he was.

"Sorry mate, I've plenty of vices, but blokes aren't one of them," Felix sighed, "and Alice is great fun normally, she just doesn't appreciate having to hob nob with the sponsors."

"Silly girl, she should support you more. I expect you have to go to her work dos? It's the same thing isn't it?" said Leo sensibly, "You've gotta take care of your sponsors, look at the catastrophe we've just had. Still …"

"Hmmm, I think that's enough said about that," rapped Seb frostily, "That bloke's an arse!"

"Anyway, I don't want to talk about Alice, let's go and crack open a bottle and get wasted." Felix marched off towards the tack room to get some glasses.

Seb and Leo trailed behind him, with Seb hungrily assessing Felix's arse. "Poor old Felix," he remarked, "He should be with someone who understands him more."

"Like you, you mean!" laughed Leo, "dream on darling, you've no more chance of converting him than you have of that old hay loft!"

"I know," said Seb dreamily, "but it's fun thinking about it!"

The silvery tinkle of a bicycle bell made them look up to see Hattie swooping into the yard on her ancient bike; her bare legs splayed wide apart and her hair flying out behind like a demented Medusa, as she rattled over the cobbles. "Whooooo!" she yelled, "I'm not late am I?"

"Not a bit," laughed Seb, admiring her as she leant the bike against the wall. "I like your skirt."

"Christ, it's not too short is it?" said Hattie anxiously, tugging it down from where it had ridden up from the bike ride, "I haven't worn it for ages."

"No doll, you look lovely, you've got a smashing pair of pins!" laughed Leo, joining them and relieving Hattie of her rucksack. "This is heavy, what've you got in here?"

"Well thought I'd better bring a bikini and a towel, and a jacket," she smiled, embarrassed, "It is a pool party after all."

"Damn, thought you'd swim in the buff," laughed Seb, "More's the pity then! Felix has opened a bottle, let's get stuck in!"

"Before we do Hattie, just come in the truck with me a minute. I've got an idea," said Leo, winking at Seb, "You go on luvvie, we'll join you in a moment."

"Don't be naughty children will you?" said Seb mischievously, "See you in a bit, don't be long."

Seb sauntered over to the tack room to join Felix, who was splayed out on the armchair and was already half way down his first glass and looking miserable. "Where's the bottle?"

"In the fridge," said Felix gloomily, "Was that Hattie I heard?"

"Yep," replied Seb, ferreting for a glass, "she and Leo are just checking the horses."

"Oh, I thought you'd already done that?"

"Don't knock it sweetie, if the children want to be conscientious!" laughed Seb "Here, let me top you up, you look as though you could do with it."

"Oh I'm alright, just feeling sorry for myself, I got a right earful from Alice." grumbled Felix "You'd think it was the end of the world, instead of a party."

"She'll get over it, probably miffed because she's got to work and you haven't."

"Well it is work in a way. I mean, Charles and Jennifer are my main sponsors and most of the others are bound to be there as well. It just makes me wonder if there isn't more to it."

"Like what?" said Seb, his curiosity aroused, "You think she's got someone else?"

"No, nothing like that. She's just so aggressive lately especially around them, it's not like her at all."

"No? Well sometimes aggression can be a way of showing fear," Seb said thoughtfully, "You know how some riders can be like that with horses at times, beating them up, when really they're shit scared themselves."

"Hmm, that's true enough, but why would she be afraid or worried about what they might say or do?"

"Don't ask me sweetie, just a bit of amateur psychology on my part. She actually probably just thinks they're a load of stuck up wankers and she can't be bothered with them!" Seb roared with laughter at his joke, "Come on drink up, do you good to let your hair down."

"Why not – bring it on."

By the time Leo and Hattie crept out of the lorry 15 minutes later, Seb and Felix had finished the bottle and were just on the point of opening the next one. They crept up to the tack room clutching their sides with suppressed giggling. Felix hadn't moved and was still lounging in the old chair, with Seb sprawled like a spider opposite him.

"Ta dah!" announced Leo "Madam is ready for the ball!"

He ceremoniously ushered Hattie in through the door. She stood for a hesitant moment in her short skirt emphasising her Bambi legs, and a slinky tee shirt hugging her newly svelte figure, lithe and fit now from all the hard work and looked like a rabbit caught in the headlights; but it was her face that was different. Hattie, who'd never bothered with any sort of make-up before, was now looking like a girl out of a fashion magazine. Leo smirked by the door as he took in Felix's astonished face; he knew he had done a good job. He'd emphasised Hattie's eyes with smoky, grey shades and smudged kohl around the edges, lightly lashing on the mascara – she looked sensational. He'd left her skin tone natural, barely masking her freckles, with her lips the palest gloss, and cascading her hair into an unruly topknot, the whole effect was gloriously sexy.

"Darling!" exclaimed Seb, "You look simply divine – Leo has transformed you! Such a clever boy with the make-up! What do you think Felix?"

But Felix couldn't say a word, his jaw had dropped so far down onto his chest. He just gaped at Hattie as though he had never seen her before in his life.

CHAPTER 23

"Blimey!" exclaimed Mark, "Just take a look at Hattie, she looks so different!"

"Wow," said Sandy, "time she came out of her shell a bit and gave the boys a run for their money. She's been hiding her assets for too long if you ask me."

"Do you know I never noticed before the other day," laughed Mark ironically, "It must be married life! Colin was only saying to me in the week what a lovely looking girl she was."

"Glad to hear it," remarked Sandy, "who are those others she's with?"

"One of them must be the new chap who's renting some of the boxes from Felix, I suppose," observed Mark, "but no idea who the other one is. I should go over and introduce myself."

"Leave it for a bit darling, there's Katherine and Jeremy, with Grace and Colin, let's go and join them."

They wandered over to the others who were all gossiping about Hattie and her new image.

"Well good for her is what I say," laughed Grace, "She's a sweet girl, time she had some fun!"

"I don't see Alice anywhere – do you?" asked Chloe, who had joined them with her husband John, "She must be working I guess."

"Well, there's Andrew and Caitlin, and Oli is over there chatting to Jennifer, so perhaps she's on a call," said Sandy, "although she could make it later."

Colin nudged Mark, "She ought to make an appearance, keep an eye on Felix."

Grace smacked Colin playfully on the arm, "Stop making mischief!"

"He'd be a fool not to fancy her Gracie, she looks stunning tonight," laughed Colin, "and Alice can be a right grumpy old bag at times, even though I know you love her!"

"I do not," snapped Grace moodily, "Anyway, Hattie's hanging on the arm of that bloke!"

Hattie was indeed hanging onto Leo's arm like a blood starved leech, and not only as she'd had quite a lot to drink before she came, but because she needed a bit of the old Dutch courage. Felix's reaction had horrified her, and she had wanted to rush and wash the make-up off under the tap. Since she'd walked into the tack room, far from the look of admiration she had hoped for, he'd simply stared at her, and her self-confidence had crumpled like a dirty tissue. Now he could scarcely look at her and hadn't spoken a word since they'd piled haphazardly into the car. Leo and Seb seemed oblivious, but to Hattie, his disapproval was as unbelievably cruel as a dog abandoned on the motorway. But in another way, it made her all the more determined to have a bloody good time tonight – bugger him! The great thing about going out with gay guys was that she would be totally uncompromised and could flirt away to her heart's content, and the boys were more than happy to oblige.

She had never been past the stables at the Parker-Smythes' before and was over-awed by the opulence of the house and gardens. The perfectly striped lawns spread out at the back of the mellow old country house, with its rambling roses clustered over the walls, and the garden was festooned with gorgeous flower beds crammed with delphiniums, peonies, hollyhocks and herbaceous plants in a mutiny of colours. Enormous, ceramic urns were majestically arranged in strategic places alongside the terraces which flanked the back of the house. A jaunty marquee had been erected alongside the pool and, under a smaller, one a hog was slowly roasting on a rotating spit. Tables laden with salads and bread lay beside it and the wafting smell of roast pork was mouth-watering, and Hattie realised she was starving. From the pool a lot of shrieking and laughing was going on. Large splashes occasionally shot up like erupting geysers above the wooden terrace which discreetly screened the revellers from the garden. In the background, music was playing from a cd player and waitresses were circulating with canapés and champagne in long icy flutes.

Seb accosted a waitress, grabbing glasses and passing them to the others, "Now tell me Felix, who are all these people?"

Felix downed his drink in one and glanced around, then spluttered, "Right, that's our host and hostess over there, Jennifer and Charles Parker-Smythe," he pointed to a beautiful blonde woman, hand in hand with a tall Hugh Grant look alike, "He's a filthy rich, arrogant bloke, but dotes on his wife. Talking to them is Oliver Travers, he's one of the partners at the practice where Alice works and beside him is Libbie Newsome. Oli's okay, a Kiwi, wife left him last year, and he's foot-loose and fancy free, and Libbie's been trying to get in his boxers for ages. There again," he added ruefully, "she's after anything with a cock who earns enough!"

"Ooo, a right slag then!" squealed Seb, "but he's tasty. What about that lot over there?"

"That's the other lot from the syndicate. Mark Templeton, who's my landlord and the Estate Manager at the Hall, married to the tiny blonde woman, Sandy Maclean, she's a barrister. Then the pregnant lady next to her is Grace Allington and her husband Colin, he's an estate agent from Horsham, then Chloe and John Coombe, they've got a livery yard on the other side of the village – she's a good trainer and they're all lovely people."

"Who's that girl setting up with the mike under the marquee? Is she part of the entertainment or a guest?" asked Leo.

"Ah that's Dulcie," smiled Hattie, glad to have to something to say, "She's lovely, and that's her partner over there," she pointed to Nancy striding over with a couple of cans to the marquee, "You should have a lot in common, they're gay too."

"Velcro sisters! How delightful," cried Seb, "We'll definitely have to get to know them! But you didn't answer the question – who are they?"

"They're the grooms here, took over from me when I left, and after Caitlin had her accident" whispered Felix, conscious that people were looking at them, "that girl over there with the long dark hair is Caitlin, with that tall guy. He's Andrew Napier, the senior partner at the Vet's, they're together now."

"Blimey, what a den of iniquity!" grinned Leo, "We've a lot to learn Seb."

"Oh you'll pick it up soon enough."

"I'm sure we'll add to it too," Seb laughed wickedly, winking at Hattie. "What fun!"

Hattie strangled a smile, not able to look at Felix, "Do you fancy a swim?"

"Oh no you don't," said Leo, holding firmly onto her, "I've just spent ages on your make-up, it's not running all over your face now. Later on, when everyone's too pissed to care!"

"Oh look," squeaked Seb, "our hostess is coming over to greet us. I can't wait to meet her!"

Jennifer had moved away from Oli and Libbie and was moving with Charles towards them, her face smiling in welcome as she kissed Felix on both cheeks, exclaiming how lovely to see him and Hattie, asking to be introduced to the newcomers.

"How lovely to meet you both, I hope you'll be very happy at Fittlebury Hall" she smiled, "We have a horse with Felix don't we Charles?" She nodded to him for affirmation.

Charles, who had been busy gawping at the transformation in the hitherto mousey Hattie was wrong footed, "Yes, we do, sorry what're your names again?"

"I'm Sebastian Locke and this is Leo Cooper. We're dressage divas really, I gather eventing's more your bag?"

"Well," said Charles evenly, "flat work's never been my thing particularly, but I'm beginning to understand the importance of it more now – eh Felix?"

Felix, who knew where the conversation was heading, and looked as though he was about to jump out of a plane without a parachute, spluttered, "definitely Charles."

"Oh that's no problem luvvie," enthused Seb, "you've got the A team now!"

Charles remarked dryly, "I admire your confidence and look forward to the results."

"Oh you'll see a difference all right," smiled Leo, "just wait and see." He grinned and nudged Felix. "He won't know what's hit him."

Hattie smiled weakly, "Lovely party Jennifer. Is Dulcie going to sing?"

Jennifer beamed at her, "Yes, she is, although she was a bit reluctant," and then smiling at Charles, "I know it's not the kind of live entertainment we normally have darling, but I think everyone'll enjoy it."

"Hmm, you kept that under your hat," Charles grinned indulgently back at her, "Don't worry sweetie, I'm looking forward to it, and she does have a lovely voice."

"Look, excuse us, we've got to do the rounds, you know" smiled Jennifer, "very nice to have met you both, we hope you'll be very happy in Fittlebury, and enjoy the party."

"Thank you for asking us," acknowledged Seb, "don't worry we will enjoy it!"

Under the marquee, Dulcie was having a panic attack, and Nancy was trying to calm her down with a severe talking to and a bottle of Budweiser. She looked chalk white and her lips were dry and cracked from where she'd kept running her tongue over them.

"You'll be fine, just imagine you're sweeping up the yard and singing at the top of your stack, like you do every day," endorsed Nancy, "or getting up on the stage in a club in Brighton when you're off your tits!"

Dulcie snapped "It's not a bit like that though is it? I'm not in the slightest bit pissed or working off energy. This is much more cold-blooded."

"Aw stop it, find the red blood then." Nancy was starting to get annoyed, "Christ knows you've plenty of it."

"It's all right for you, you don't have to make a fool of yourself." hissed Dulcie crossly.

"Well you will make a bloody fool of yourself, if you don't show a bit of gumption. Now stop being such a weed and get up there and sock it to them."

Dulcie was so angry that she snatched up the microphone, picked up her guitar, and fiddled with the mixer on the karaoke machine. The music started to blare out, bouncing off the marquee and a sea of faces stopped what they were doing and turned around to look at her. Suddenly she was centre stage, all eyes were on her. She took a huge gulp and began to belt out the first song - Madonna's *'Material Girl'*. She mimed all the actions, threw her head around, gyrated her hips and finally flung her arms up in the arm. There was a collective cheer and a huge round of applause. She looked up astonished – she had been lost in the music, her anger at Nancy and in the moment had forgotten all about them. She blushed, stammered her thanks, and grinned at Nancy who gave her a thumbs up sign.

"Thank you, thank you everyone! Right, my next number is a good old favourite, and anyone who knows me, knows how much I love Shania! So here we go with *'That Don't Impress me Much'* – so let's get dancing!" She looked down, cued in the machine and the familiar twangs of the song sprang out.

At first, just a few people threaded onto the dance floor, self-consciously bopping to the music, but by the third and fourth numbers, quite a throng were thrashing around. Jennifer clutched Charles' arm, "Fancy a dance?"

"She's really good," he laughed, taking her hand, "Great idea of yours!"

The crowd from Fittlebury were busy stuffing themselves stupid on the hog roast trying to mop up the alcohol, and draped themselves languorously at a little table at the edge of the marquee watching the dancers. The music was dangerously infectious and, by now, lots of people were dancing, cavorting about madly, their arms and legs whirling; as others came back, sweating and exhausted to sit down wearily and knocking back the booze after their exertions. Nancy had come to join them and was clearly thrilled at the way Dulcie was performing.

"I knew she could do it. You should have heard her – she was a right wreck before she started. I had to get quite stroppy with her."

"She's bloody brilliant," slurred Hattie tipsily, "wait till I've finished eating, then, I'm gonna boogey!"

"I've gotta say Hattie, you look frigging awesome tonight," admired Nancy, "If I didn't have Dulcie, I'd make a play for you me self!"

Hattie blushed, "Not my bag Nancy, I'm afraid," she leant over exaggeratedly whispering in Nancy's ear, "Why is it that only the gay ones fancy me?"

Nancy smiled sympathetically, and stroked the underside of her arm, "Awe sweet, I know how you feel, but he's a fool frankly, he doesn't know what he's missing."

"Well he's got Alice, she is so lovely, how can I ever compare?" lamented Hattie quietly, "He doesn't even notice me. Oh God, what am I saying? I must be drunk - forget I said anything ... please?"

"He's a bloody fool. She's not all she's cracked up to be in my opinion" said Nancy tartly, "You make ten of her, let me tell you."

"Well that's lovely of you to say, but I can't change it, so I've just gotta live with it – meantime – come on – let's have a dance!"

Hattie gulped down the last dregs of her wine and grabbed Nancy by the hand, hauling her to her feet.

"Wait for me!" shrieked Seb, "I adore dancing!"

They wiggled on to the dance floor, their bodies gyrating with the contagious music, Dulcie's strong voice booming out around the marquee. Seb started flinging his arms around wildly, then seized hold of Hattie, twirling her around in exaggerated rock and roll moves, then moved onto Nancy, until they were all a mad jumble of arms and legs.

Felix and Leo were still sitting at their table watching from the edge of the marquee. Leo was tapping his foot in time to the music and shouting out encouragement to the dancers, but Felix was staring miserably down at his drink twirling a breadstick between his fingers.

"Cheer up mate," Leo laughed at him, "It might never happen."

"Oh I don't know what's the matter with me," grumbled Felix, "I just feel bloody fed-up. I hate it when Alice isn't here and she was right snipey with me when I told her about tonight."

"Well it strikes me you didn't have a lot of choice, did you? Could hardly say no could you? Anyway, I've not met Alice, but I'm sure she'd understand that, she's got clients too, she must know what it's like."

"I suppose, but I could just do without it. Sometimes she can fester on these things for days."

"Women eh? Mind you – your Hattie is gorgeous isn't she?"

"Hattie?"

"Come on don't tell me you didn't notice. Actually mate, you looked as though your nose was well out of joint. You don't fancy her do you?"

Felix spluttered angrily into his wine, "Me! No of course I don't. I live with Alice – if you hadn't noticed. Hattie is lovely, adorable, but we're just friends."

"Ah, the just good friends angle eh?" Leo threw his head back and laughed, "Well you looked like thunder when she walked into the tack room all glammed up earlier – thought you might have been a bit put out?"

"I was NOT, I'm pleased for her. I told you I'm just fed up about Alice." protested Felix vehemently, "I was a bit surprised though, I've never seen her dressed up before."

Leo grinned, "Well glad that's settled – I quite fancy her myself, and if it won't be stepping on your toes..." he added mischievously, "I'll see how it goes then."

"WHAT!" Felix hissed, "But you're gay!"

"Am I?" grinned Leo, and winked at him.

Jennifer was ecstatic; gasping and holding her sides with laughter as Charles twirled her into an elaborate finale as Dulcie ended her version of '*My Generation*'. "Darling, what a great party, I think it's going brilliantly – don't you?"

"I certainly do," Charles assured her, taking her hand and leading her off the dance floor to the bar, "I admit I had my doubts about Dulcie, but she's very talented."

"Well, it was rather last minute as you know, but she's been fantastic – everyone seems to be having a wonderful time."

They threaded their way out of the marquee, passing Felix on their way out, Jennifer leant down and whispered quietly, "No sign of Alice then?"

"No," muttered Felix, "she's working, although I would've

thought she'd have finished by now."

"Oh well, the night is young," murmured Jennifer sympathetically, privately thinking what a bitch Alice could be. "I'm sure she'll turn up later. Cheer up, have a dance. Hattie seems to be enjoying herself."

"Hmm, yes she does," grumbled Felix.

"Why not go and join them, cheer yourself up a bit," suggested Jennifer, "Do you good, blow away some cobwebs."

Felix glared over to where Hattie, Seb and Nancy had been joined by Leo. She was laughing and joking with them, her long Bambi legs whirling about in time to the new number and Leo prancing about beside her. "Good idea Jennifer, I think I will."

He lurched up unsteadily from the table almost knocking over his chair and stalked over to the dance floor to join the others.

Charles watched him go, "What's up with him?"

"Love sick," said Jennifer sadly, "but he doesn't know it."

"Really?" exclaimed Charles, "He and Alice are okay aren't they?"

"I wasn't talking about Alice, you idiot!"

"Oh, what do I know!" Charles laughed, and slipped his arm around Jennifer's waist, his thumb stroking against her breast, "What I do know - is that I love you".

Jennifer turned to him and brushed her lips gently against his, "and I love you too."

"Break it up you two!" called Sandy, "Get a room!"

"Don't worry, once we've got rid of you lot," laughed Charles "Now has everyone got a drink?"

"Blimey Charles, there's loads to drink – it's a free bar," exploded John, "Or didn't you know?"

On the dance floor, the Fittlebury Hall brigade had been joined by the grooms from Chloe Coombe's yard, Susie and Bibi along with Harry the whip from the local hunt and a couple of lads from the village. As Dulcie was getting more into her stride, so the dancing became wilder and more passionate, with the men pratting about like exotic peacocks to the girls' hysterical laughter. Seb and Leo were amazing dancers and knew all the club moves, their hands and fingers pointing skywards, toes circling exaggeratedly, and everyone was falling around laughing as they mimed a zealous tango. Suddenly mid-dance, Leo let go of Seb and dramatically put his hand under Hattie's chin, looking into her eyes like some crazed hypnotist and swept her into a theatrical embrace, swung her back, twirled her round and proceeded to continue the dance with her. The rest of the onlookers were in raptures, as Leo swept Hattie around the dance floor, his cheek histrionically laid against hers, his eyes fixed and glazed; no-one seeming to notice or care that Hattie was fluffing all the moves. The music finished, with Leo throwing Hattie back, balancing her over his outstretched leg like a rag doll as he leant over her and kissed her dramatically on the lips. The crowd went wild, cheering and applauding, as Leo pulled Hattie to her feet laughing.

"Darling you were awesome," he breathed in her ear, "simply divine!"

"Thank you," stammered Hattie, feeling green from all the twirling around, and struggling to rebalance herself. "Great fun."

Dulcie, who was delighted and now thoroughly enjoying herself, thought it was time for a change of pace. "Now for all those old romantics out there," she announced, "A good old favourite from the Corrs, '*Breathless*'"

The group stood around on the dance floor and suddenly Felix grabbed Hattie's hand. "My turn I think." He circled his hand around her waist, pulling her close to him and they started to sway to the music.

"'The daylight's fading slowly, but time for me is standing still, I'm waiting for you only, the slightest touch and I feel weak,'" sang Dulcie, mimicking the song perfectly.

"Felix I ..." Hattie muttered falteringly, trying to put some distance between them.

Dulcie was getting into her stride now, her voice was full of emotion," 'I cannot lie from you, I cannot hide, I'm losing the will to try it, can't hide it, can fight it'"

Hattie gave a low groan and suddenly caved in. As the alcohol wafted through her veins and she lilted along to the evocative music with Dulcie's sexy voice, she knew she was lost. All thoughts of how she should behave were gone, as she nuzzled into his shoulder and relaxed.

"'Tempt me, tease me, until I can't deny this loving feeling, make me long for your kiss'"

Hattie felt her hands stroke the strong muscles across his back and ease her fingertips up towards his hair. Was it her imagination or were they dancing closer now?

"'And if there's no tomorrow, and all we have is here and now, I'm happy just to have you, you're all the love I need somehow'"

Hattie was in a trance, and as though in some dream state, she felt his hands move from around her waist, up towards her shoulders, parting her hair, and his lips kissing along her neck. Her own fingertips wound themselves into his hair, and their bodies grew closer and more urgent.

"And I've lost my will to try it, can't hide it, can't fight, so come on leave me breathless,'" crooned Dulcie, revving up for the chorus, "'So go on, go on leave me breathless'"

The song ended to riotous applause, but Hattie and Felix were oblivious, still wrapped around each other, with his lips hungrily devouring hers. The others looked on astonished, nudging each other in the ribs, thinking that at any moment the pair would just laugh and part, but as the kiss went on longer and longer, their astonishment turned to toe-curling embarrassment.

"Hey Felix, put her down," Leo snapped, walking over and grabbing Hattie's hand, "Come on cupcake, let's get a drink." He dragged the astonished Hattie away across the marquee and left the others to an awkward silence.

"Blimey Felix, that was a bit strong," grumbled Nancy, "not very fair either, if you ask me."

Felix visibly drooped, "You're right Nancy, I was well out of order. I'm pissed but that's no excuse. I'll go and apologise."

"Not a good idea sweetie, let Leo sort her out, he's excellent at that sort of thing. She's pissed too, so probably won't remember much in the morning anyway." Seb laughed, "You certainly are a bit of a lad aren't you? And they say we dressage divas are a bad bunch, you eventers don't waste any time! No wonder Alice doesn't want to let you off the lead!"

Felix groaned, "Bloody hell Alice, I'd forgotten all about her, thank God she wasn't here."

"Just as well Felix, but actually I don't give a flying fuck about her," snapped Nancy, "It's Hattie I care about. You shouldn't lead her on like that. You're a shit."

"Please Nancy, I never behave like that normally, you know I don't, I don't know what came over me. I was fed up with Alice not being here, and I just had too much to drink – you know."

"Well you don't look very pissed now," fumed Nancy, "and whatever your relationship with Alice, don't fuck with Hattie's feelings. She's too decent – don't lead her on."

"Now let's all calm down a bit, shall we? We're making rather a spectacle of ourselves dears, and not the kind I usually enjoy," laughed Seb. "Felix, you were out of order, and of course you will apologise. We all know you are with Alice and no leading Hattie on in future – okay?"

"Okay," agreed Felix sulkily, looking at Nancy, "sorry – okay?"

"Alright," she said begrudgingly, "but don't do it again."

Seb watched Felix curiously. His face was flustered, his hair untidy, his eyes burning bright; it had been a stonker of an embrace, and Nancy was right, Felix wasn't that pissed and, until she was mentioned he'd forgotten all about Alice. Seb's antennae were bristling; there was a little bit more to this than met the eye.

CHAPTER 24

Alice had finished working ages ago and had been back in the cottage for a good couple of hours. It was strangely quiet without Felix; he was always so boisterous and enthusiastic about everything and she idly wondered what he had done with Fiver. She settled down with a cup to tea and flicked on the TV, casually skimming the channels with the remote. It was always such a load of rubbish on a Saturday night. She switched it off, and felt a pang of guilt, she should really have agreed to go with him tonight, but frankly she just couldn't be arsed. She hated the way he cow-towed to the Parker-Smythes and the syndicate, even though she was genuinely fond of Grace and Colin. At least she had the legitimate excuse of being on call and no doubt Andrew and Oli would be there to back up that truth, even if later, when they discovered that she hadn't been at all busy, they thought that it was strange she hadn't bothered to make an appearance.

She got up and looked out of the window over towards the yard which was sleeping in the last rays of the dying sunshine. Her eye was caught by a monster truck which she hadn't noticed earlier. She guessed it must belong to the infamous Sebastian Locke who Felix had been so busy festering about all week. She supposed he must have gone to the party with Felix and she wondered who else had gone. She knew that Sebastian was bringing a groom with him and that there would be a delectable feast of young women there, all looking for a good night out. For the first time she felt that she might just be missing out, after all, Felix was a good looking guy and she did often take his devotion to her for granted – perhaps she should go after all? Alice had made this kind of mistake before, back in Oz. She knew she could be totally self-obsessed and often didn't think through the consequences of how her behaviour would reflect on others, or indeed the repercussions it could bring. It had backfired drastically before – okay, not in her personal life, but professionally, but was there any difference when it came down to it – the emotional turmoil would be just the same. She turned away from the window and ran up the stairs, taking them two at a time, into their bedroom. She dragged open the wardrobe door, hurling clothes on the bed. She would surprise him.

At Nantes Place the party was roaring on, becoming more raucous as the daylight faded. The last of the stalwart swimmers had finally dragged themselves out of the pool and were huddled like drowned rats in the marquee, madly drying their hair and squeezing damp bodies into tight clothes. The sizzling hog roast was being carved into huge chunks to be kept warm, and piles of cheese and salads were heaped on the tables. The bar was busy with orders and the place was awash with booze. Dulcie was encouraging people onto the little makeshift stage to 'have a go' with the mike. Even Colin had been tempted and there was now quite a gaggle of people desperate to make their own guest appearance. It was Fittlebury's own answer to the X Factor.

Felix felt like he'd been plunged into an icy sea, his whole body felt cold and numb. His eyes roamed the marquee for sight of Hattie, but since she'd been shepherded off by Leo, he hadn't seen either of them again. His thoughts were percolating as madly as a coffee pot; he just couldn't understand what had come over him tonight, but it had just seemed so right at the time. He was frantic to talk to Hattie to try to explain, but explain what? He didn't know himself, but he didn't want to hurt her, or give her any false hopes either. It must have been the booze he thought anxiously. He'd switched onto water now, trying to soak up the alcohol but what a fucking mess.

Hattie was with Leo. They were both sitting perched on a sun lounger beside the pool, and she was obscenely drunk. As the turquoise water swayed gently, lapping at the edge of the tiles, it was making her feel sick. She closed her eyes and her head started to spin.

"Oh shit, I think I'm going to throw up," she gulped.

"Better out than in, luvvie," sighed Leo, holding her hair back and handing her a conveniently placed earthenware pot. "You carry on, I'm gonna get you some water."

Leo stalked back to the bar. He was furious, what did bloody Felix think he was playing at. He wasn't that drunk. He'd been like a miserable git all night about Alice, said he wasn't interested in Hattie and then pulls a stunt like that – anyone could see how fragile she was. He'd only met the pair of them this afternoon and it stuck out like the morning horn. Bloody idiot, he just hoped that Hattie was too far gone to remember much. He grabbed some bottles of water and marched back.

Hattie, having puked her guts up, only to find that the pot had a hole in the bottom, was weeping disconsolately and trying to clear up the mess.

"Here, drink some water," he said, "I'll sort it out."

"Thanks," she mumbled, unscrewing the bottle and taking a tentative sip, "I'm not normally like this y' know. I am so sorry. Whatever must you think of me?"

Leo stopped and looked at her, "You're a lovely girl Hattie, you've just had a bit too much to drink that's all – it's no drama babe. I've cleaned up a lot worse than this, let me tell you."

"I wasn't just talking about the sick. Although," she added, "that's a first for me too."

"Oh you mean the Felix thing – forget it – he was out of order."

"But I didn't stop him did I?"

"You're drunk Hattie, off your tits, everybody does crazy things when they've had too many."

"I just don't know how I'm gonna face him in the morning. I feel like running away."

"Don't be so fucking thick," Leo grabbed her hands, forcing her to look at him "You'll be fine. Treat it as a joke, or pretend you don't remember – that's what I always do when I've done something I regret."

Hattie stared at him blankly; the trouble was, she didn't regret it, not one little bit. Somehow though, she had to save face and mumbled, "You think?"

"Definitely, now drink that water, I'm gonna take you back to the yard, you can spend the night in the truck with us, there's loads of room."

Hattie blinked at him stupidly, "Is that a good idea, I could just cycle back from there."

"As if I'd let you do that eh? Now, let me finish clearing up here, and then I'll come back for the others."

By the time Leo had slunk away from the poolside, sneaking out by the kitchen garden to avoid everyone and supporting a wobbly white-faced Hattie, Alice was arriving at the front. The sound of pulsating music and voices drifted from the lawns behind the house and she followed them towards the brightly lit marquee. The smell of the hog roast was still lingering tantalisingly in the air, and she realised she hadn't eaten. She spotted Andrew and Caitlin chatting to Colin and Grace, and then Oli at the edge of the marquee with his arm around a pretty girl she didn't recognise. In fact there were a lot of people she didn't know, no doubt some of Jennifer and Charles' swanky cronies and she felt herself shrinking into the shadows to watch them. On the dance floor loads of people were shrieking with laughter and pointing, because the person singing was so appallingly terrible, sounding like an army of indignant cats, hitting all the wrong notes to *'Brown Sugar'*. To her astonishment she realised it was Mark Templeton. He was really hamming it up with his impersonation of Mick Jagger, waving his arms around, pointing his fingers skywards and stomping about like he was trying to stop a bad case of diarrhoea. Sandy was egging him on and taking pictures on her I-phone, and everyone was jeering and laughing. Finally, the song came to an end and Mark got down from the stage, red faced and hysterical. Alice couldn't believe her eyes, sensible old Mark – who'd have thought it. She scanned the revellers looking for Felix and then finally spotted him sitting on the far side of the marquee at a table on his own.

"Hi, everyone disowned you?" she remarked sarcastically,

plonking herself down beside him, "Drunk?"

Felix felt his face blanch, she couldn't have been nearer the truth, "Nope, just missing you. I'm drinking water now." He said glumly.

"Well cheer up – I'm here now. You can have a drink – I'll drive. How did you get down here then?"

"Seb's groom, Leo, brought us." Felix looked around furtively, "I don't know where he's gone."

"Oh well, I expect he'll pitch up in a while, you can introduce me then. Where's Hattie?"

"Dunno," said Felix quietly, "Was with Leo I think."

"Good for her, about time she found herself a bloke." Alice grunted, and glanced scornfully around the room at the other guests. "God, they are a stuck-up load of wankers aren't they?" She turned back to Felix, "Christ Felix, you look awful. Are you alright?"

"I'm fine, thank you Alice," he muttered defensively, knowing full well he was not fine at all, "and no, they are not all stuck-up wankers."

Hattie lay on the make-shift bed. She could hear the sounds of the early morning dimly in her subconscious but she couldn't bear the thought of opening her eyes. Her head felt as though someone was setting off explosives inside it, and her mouth was like the Sahara. Gradually, the soft whinnying of the horses and the sounds of buckets being crashed around outside made her take a tentative shot and she winced as the light hit her. It took some moments before she realised where she was and then the whole seedy events of last night came in like a rip tide. She buried her head under the duvet, which smelt strangely of cheese, and decided she never wanted to get up again.

"Wake up sleepy head, here's some water."

"Go away, I wanna die," she moaned, then poked her nose out from under the covers, "did you say water?"

"Come on, get this down you, you'll feel better."

It was Leo's voice, and Hattie felt her self-esteem crumble when she remembered how she'd sicked up over him last night, and he'd put her to bed when she'd hardly been able to stand. She fumbled over her body, realising that she was in her bra and knickers and she was reeking.

"I'm so sorry about last night. Was I sick all over you?"

"Yes, but don't be sorry. Come on sunshine, get this water down you and I'll get you some Alka Seltzer." Leo grinned at her, "don't worry, apart from the puke, your dignity's preserved."

"Where is everyone?"

"Well Seb is up, although fuck knows how he does it, he wants to ride first thing. No sign of Felix yet, but don't worry I've fed your lot and skipped them out."

"Thanks so much Leo, I seriously owe you."

"Yep you do, don't worry I won't forget!" Leo laughed, "You can do the same for me next time."

Hattie sat up in the bed, holding her head grimly, her eyes bloodshot and her hair wildly dishevelled. "Don't worry I will." She tried to grin, but it turned into a grimace, "What happened ... you know... about Felix."

"Alice pitched up and took him away. Remember what I said, just pretend nothing happened, treat it as a joke. You wait, he'll do the same, it'll be dandy."

Hattie pulled a face and drank down the water, "I was so obvious, wasn't I?"

"No you weren't. I'm not telling you again, you were drunk. Now get up princess, work to do." He grinned at her, and jumped down from the lorry, his head peeking back over the side, "You've got five minutes to be up and dressed."

"God," droned Hattie, "my head, I'll never do it."

Felix had hardly slept at all in the night. Alice had lain with her head on his chest, her arms and legs splayed across him. He felt like an insect in a Venus Fly trap, and if he fell asleep, would wake to find only a skeleton of himself was left. After he'd stopped boozing, he'd only drunk water and was feeling fine physically, but his head was reeling. He and Alice had not stayed long at the party; he had feigned being tired, and she was determined to find fault with it all anyway and he was glad to leave. After Hattie had fled with Leo, he hadn't seen her again and he wondered over and over what had happened. Restless and not wanting to disturb Alice, he peeled her arms away from him and slithered out of bed, snatching up some clothes to get dressed in the kitchen. He threw down some coffee and made his way out to the yard.

Seb was lumbering out of the tack room with a saddle and bridle slung over his arm, heading for the stables. "Morning Romeo," he called, "I'm gonna school one, that okay?"

"Sure," said Felix, deciding to ignore the Romeo remark, "I'll probably join you. Is Hattie in yet?" he asked tentatively.

"Still in bed in the truck, although Leo's just gone to wake her. Don't panic though, he's done your nags."

Felix hardly knew what to say, Hattie asleep in their truck? She'd obviously gone straight there with Leo after ...

"Morning Felix!" shouted Leo "how's the head?"

"Fine – thank you," snapped Felix irritably, not quite sure why he felt so angry. "How's Hattie this morning?"

"Hung over would be an understatement!" laughed Leo, "she was hammered! She's just getting dressed though, should be out in a minute."

"Oh well ... glad she had a good time."

"Oh, I don't think she remembers much – other than puking all over me." Leo looked at him carefully, "So best not mention anything eh?"

"No. Good idea. Thanks for taking care of her Leo."

"Pleasure was all mine, mate" said Leo sweetly.

CHAPTER 25

The sun filtered dazzling laser beams through the tightly entwined leaves in the loggia as Mark was laying the table for Sunday lunch. He was feeling decided groggy after the excesses of last night and he was glad of the shade. Sandy, who'd been driving and been stone cold sober, had little sympathy this morning, and had been ribbing him mercilessly about his Mick Jagger impression saying he would never live it down. He had a horrible feeling she was right, and no doubt he was in for more banter when Colin and Grace arrived, although, he smiled to himself, it had been a stonker of an evening.

"How you doing?" asked Sandy, coming out from the kitchen in her pinstriped apron, "How's the head?"

"It's not my head, it's my image that's taken a battering," he grumbled good-naturedly, "what a laugh though!"

"Yep it was," agreed Sandy, shoving some flowers in the centre of the table, "there that looks better. And you were brilliant on the karaoke – I never knew you had it in you!"

"Hmm – now I know you're taking the piss," Mark groaned, "hang on that's the door knocker, that'll be them. I'll get it."

"Go on then '*Jumping Jack Flash,*'" she laughed after him, as he disappeared back into the house.

Sandy surveyed the garden. It was looking gorgeous; she wished she had more time to enjoy it, but she was so busy at work these days. Their gardener was doing a stalwart job; the herbaceous borders were looking amazing, dancing with frothy colours of fat peony heads and rangy hollyhocks against the old stone wall. She loved this cottage, always had, and now she was so lucky to have

Mark to share it with too. At first she had been so afraid to commit to a relationship with him, now that initial angst all seemed so stupid; they were as compatible as two people could ever be. She had never felt so happy or content, and last night she had seen a side to Mark she had never knew existed – and it was one she loved. He'd discarded his serious side and really let his hair down – it had been a real laugh, and although she had taken the piss this morning, it had been a fabulous night.

Sandy spun round as she heard chattering voices coming through the kitchen and went in to join them. Grace was looking blooming, her belly round and swollen and her face aglow with the sort of benign *'lady in waiting'* look that so many pregnant women seemed to adopt.

"Hi Sandy," greeted Colin, "Lovely to see you – great bash last night eh?"

Sandy reached over and kissed him on both cheeks. "Indeed it was, made more special, of course, by my *'Little Red Rooster'* here," she laughed towards Mark. "Hi Grace, you okay after last night, it was quite a late night?"

"Yep, not quite past it," grinned Grace, "It's Col that worries more than me."

"Men! I must say, you are blossoming Grace – pregnancy suits you."

"It does," sighed Grace, "and, what's more, I'm making the most of it, I waited long enough."

"Now Col, what can I get you to drink?" asked Mark, "Obviously something non-alcoholic for you Grace?"

"Please," smiled Grace, "Just still water if you have it, anything fizzy makes this little one do somersaults," she patted her bump affectionately.

"I'll have a beer if you've got one Mark"

They gravitated outside with their drinks, Grace plonked herself down heavily and stretched out her legs, obviously dying to talk about the evening before.

"Well, what did you think about that young Hattie?" sighed Colin, "I was only saying to Mark the other day, she's a real looker."

"Keep your trousers zipped up Col," laughed Grace, "but you're right she is, but she'd obviously made a bit of an effort last night too."

"More to the point did you see her and Felix!" snorted Sandy, "What's going on there?"

"Absolutely nothing," said Mark, "Stop scandal mongering, they were both drunk."

"We all have hidden depths when we're drunk, and it looked pretty passionate to me," hooted Sandy. "Look at you *Mick*!"

"Well, I don't think there's anything in it. Felix adores Alice, and she adores him," said Grace loyally, "although I'm bloody glad she wasn't there to witness it."

"Well it wouldn't have happened would it, if she had been – why was she so late anyway?" Colin gossiped, "And do you know she didn't say a word to us when she did arrive, and she supposed to be your friend Gracie! She can be damned odd."

"She can be right up her own arse," agreed Sandy, "I much prefer to have Oli or Andrew out to the horse if I can."

"Oh don't be like that," Grace said surprised, "she's really okay once you get to know her."

"I thought Felix looked really fed up last night, and didn't look much better when she arrived either," laughed Mark, "the only time he seemed to be enjoying himself was when he was snogging Hattie."

"Mark! That's enough," grinned Sandy. "Let's change the subject. What did you think about your new tenants then?"

"Well, strictly speaking, they're Felix's tenants not mine, but a nice couple of ginger-ninjas. I'll reserve judgement till I know them better."

"Good-looking couple of lads," remarked Grace. "Where are they living?"

"Well, in their lorry I believe – for the time being at any rate," said Mark, "although that can't be permanent – Lady V would have a fit. Actually I haven't said anything yet to Felix but there's a possibility of something on the estate, but I need to have a bit of think and want to get to know them first."

"Well that'd be good – which cottage?" asked Sandy.

"There's a couple actually, one alongside the shoot which I'm not so keen on letting as it maybe that we expand in that direction and we may have to use it; but there's that old one down near the mill. It's been rented out until a few months ago."

"I know the place – you mean," said Col, "We did the initial letting I believe, to some chaps working on a project at Gatwick. Hasn't it been re-let then?"

Mark scratched his chin considering the question. "No I hadn't decided, to be honest. I was thinking that it could sold, but Lady V doesn't generally like selling stuff off, so to rent it out again pro temps would be a better solution, especially now we seem to have got rid of the mill itself. I'll have to run it by her though."

"Well if you decide to sell – I'm your man!" laughed Colin, clinking his bottle against Mark's.

Aiden was tired; his head was teeming with ideas which forced his body to behave like a kid with too many e-numbers. He felt like he was on the Tour de France, dashing from his restaurant to glittering socials with Roxy, to the bloody obstructive architect, and now he just wanted to laze about with a beer and chill. But his mind just wouldn't let him, he closed his eyes wearily, rubbing his forehead with his fingertips. The planner at the local council, although he had been a stuffy little bloke, couldn't see any fundamental objections provided they jumped through all the proper hoops; and the old girl at English Heritage had actually been quite enthusiastic, especially as it would mean saving the place. The ancient grinding wheels of bureaucracy were agonisingly sluggish, he ruminated wryly, and it seemed many palms would need to be greased to make sure they wound faster. He just needed to galvanise Roxy now. Those barns were easy to convert and he needed her to be more pro-active, because however successful his ideas were, as a team they were even better.

Roxy slumped down on the sofa beside him. The nanny had taken the children up to bed and she had poured herself a glass of Chardonnay.

"What's up babes?" she mumbled, reaching for a magazine from the table and flicking through it. "You look pissed off."

Aiden, never one to beat around the bush, especially Roxy's, came straight to the point, "You need to sort out what you want doing with the mill. Alan's got to have some ideas, or he'll just do it his way, and then I don't want any fucking histrionics 'cause you don't like it."

"Give it a rest will you, Aiden," Roxy moaned, "you're obsessed with that fucking place."

"We're sinking fucking piles into it, you silly tart, and it needs careful planning. I'd have thought you'd want to have you say."

"I do, but stop fucking pushing me every five minutes," Roxy complained, "If you haven't noticed, I've not had the easiest week myself."

"You!" Aiden snorted, "what with your bits of fluff and floss you call pants." He could feel his short fuse about to blow and forced himself to pause and take a slug of his beer. He needed her batting on his team, not a full scale war. "Sorry babes, I didn't mean that."

Roxy glared at him, "I should bloody think not. Actually it's going rather well, that debacle at *Gallomani* worked in my favour." She smiled smugly, "got punters from the rough side swarming in."

"Good for you." He forced a smile back, "I told you it would work out."

"Yeah you did, and you were right about not firing Suzanne either," she leant back against him, snuggling up against his chest, "she's worked her arse off this week."

"Ha! Great, never does them any harm to have a shake up."

"About the mill though, okay – you're right. Look, I'll take a mosey this week then." She stroked her hand down the length of his chest, fiddling with the buttons on his shirt and slipping her hand inside "I'll go down with Alan and work out what I want to do. Ask Chrissie to fix it will you?"

Aiden smiled down into her hair, perfect he thought. He slipped his hand up inside her velour top, circling her breast lightly and felt her responding against his touch "Wonderful babes, but why not go tomorrow? If you can manage it – the quicker we get it sorted the better really." His fingers started to rub the tips of her nipples and he moved his head down to nuzzle into the side of her neck.

Roxy sighed, she was now positively squirming. "Hmm, I suppose I could - okay get Chrissie to organise it."

For Felix and Hattie, the day had passed with them skilfully avoiding being alone together. It seemed that as soon as Hattie surfaced, Felix had saddled up Picasso and gone up to the school to join Seb, and when he returned, she and Leo had hacked out together. When their paths did cross later in the day, Hattie, who had by this time recovered from her hangover, although her normally sparking eyes still had the look of a pickled onion, giggled embarrassedly and muttered what a great night she'd had but couldn't remember a thing, she'd been so drunk. Felix, taking her cue, had laughed rather lamely and agreed he had been drunk too, and the uneasy question of what had happened was by-passed. After that, Seb and Felix had been closeted in the lorry discussing yard tactics, and Leo and Hattie were left to get on with their jobs.

"See, I told you it would be okay," grinned Leo knowingly, "all forgotten."

"Well, sort of," muttered Hattie, washing bits in the tack room sink. "I wonder what they're talking about?"

"Oh, who's doing what and when, I should think. Planning schedules, work load, that kind of thing."

"Oh," said Hattie slightly miffed, she was supposed to be planning schedules with Felix wasn't she? "Why do they have to discuss competitions then?"

"So we can cover for each other, dumbass," laughed Leo, "When you're away, we cover for you and vice versa. Wake up!"

"Oh right. I see. Do you stay away much?"

"Nah, not that often, but sometimes if we go to a Premier League or a Regionals, or the Nationals we do," advised Leo. "Although we chose to go to our local Regionals which this year is at Sparsholt in Hampshire at the end of the month. The Nationals – if we qualify – are at Stoneleigh in Warwickshire about the third week in September, and we usually stay away then."

"Will you be away for Sparsholt?"

"No, I don't think so, we can do it in a day, and Seb only has a couple qualified. The others, he had to leave behind when we left the last place, and the new rider picks up the qualification."

"He can't have been very pleased about that."

"No, he wasn't," agreed Leo, "But it wasn't his fault to be honest, the gay scene is pretty open minded, but there's a limit."

"What happened?" said Hattie, agog to hear what could have been so terrible that Seb was thrown out on his ear and lost some of his best horses, "Or aren't you allowed to say?"

"You might as well hear the real reason from me, as some trumped up rubbish from someone else," grumbled Leo. "One night we came home from a show and put the horses to bed. Juan, who was the guy who owned the place – Felix's main sponsor, decided he wanted a bit of a party."

"Go on, was he gay, this guy?"

"Behind the scenes, he swings both ways. He lives with a woman who, years ago, had a bit of success as a dressage diva, but is now a complete *'has been'*, and to boot a total fag-hag. Juan is constantly buying her horses, which she fucks up, but she gives him status and has a modicum of street cred in the dressage world. But he's a weird and dangerous bloke, getting on a bit age-wise and frankly he's a bit of a bloater now; likes the tight jeans and gold bracelets, you know the kind of stuff. He buys himself in with riders who are on the up and, in particular pretty boys, and I think that's why the dressage scene fascinates him – it's teeming with 'em. I think he's some kind of Arab, absolutely loaded, and has a really cruel streak, not just with the horses either. He has a hard core of mates about his own age and he was into a bit of S&M with them. I couldn't stand him and kept well clear. Seb was sort of obliged to go that night, but I didn't, said I had to finish off the tack and stuff."

"So Seb went on his own then?"

"Yep. About an hour later, he comes screaming back, and I mean screaming; stark bloody naked if you please, streaks right across the yard and locks himself in the tack room with me."

"Nooo! Why, what happened?"

"Well he was pretty incoherent, but from what I could gather, a whole bunch of them had more or less gang raped him, and were giving him what for, with whips and all sorts. You should have seen his arse - it was covered in red streaks. He managed to break away and tore off down to the tack room to lock himself in!"

"How awful," whimpered Hattie, "poor Seb, he must have been in a dreadful state."

"He was, I can tell you, and he's never let on exactly what happened either, but I'm pretty sure there was a lot more to it. Anyway the next thing, bloody Juan is banging on the door demanding that we let him in."

"Did you? Let him in, I mean?"

"Well we kinda had to, it was his yard," sighed Leo, "he tried to placate Seb, said it was all a misunderstanding, but Seb wasn't having any of it, said Juan was a sadist, a perv, all sorts. But you've gotta remember he was badly frightened."

"I don't blame him," said Hattie, "this Juan needs castrating. He should have reported it to the police."

"What good would it have done? Well, of course, that was the end. Seb wouldn't play ball. He lost the two top horses and we got chucked out with the rest. The only good thing was that the truck belongs to another sponsor, who knows what a cunt Juan is, and we managed to hang onto the ones we've got now."

"What a horrible story."

"Yes, it was and is. The wanker is putting it about that it was Seb who did the bed hopping and that was why we got chucked out, but it's not true. Juan is one of these treacherous blokes though; he's bought his way to the top. He sponsors so much that the powers that be brown-nose him all the time and, as such, it's best not to mess with him. So we moved out and moved on."

"Well let's hope what goes round, comes round, eh?"

CHAPTER 26

Roxy, having arranged to go to Fittlebury the next day and who could never do anything on her own, rang Lisa and asked her if she fancied a bit of an away-day. Lisa wasn't keen after their last disastrous sortie, and complained bitterly that it would mean missing out on riding her horse. Roxy was used to getting her own way, and threw a tantrum worthy of an Oscar, wheedling and pleading, and eventually persuaded her. The ever gullible Lisa reluctantly capitulated, but compromised saying she'd meet her in Fittlebury after she'd ridden. So Roxy was left to motor down with the boring Alan, who was blathering on about plans and permissions, and Lisa could give her a lift back to London.

It was a sparkling day, fine and bright, and the traffic was relatively light, which was lucky, as Roxy's mood when she arrived at the mill, much to Alan's relief, remained as sunny as the day outside. Alan had arranged with Colin that Mark would meet them and open up the barns and the mill if they needed access to it, but he would then just leave them to wander around on their own, and come back later and lock up.

For Roxy, the second look at the site was decidedly better than the first. The sun bathed the old tythe barns in mellow light and the unaccustomed ethereal serenity washed over her as hypnotically as Henry's slick fingers. It was a far-cry from the creepy, blustery weather when she'd first come. She thought back to that day and the hunky bloke on the horse and wondered if she might see him again, she rather hoped she would. There might be something in this horse riding lark, she mused, after all Lisa obviously got some kind of kick out of it. She tuned herself into Alan droning on about light and aura and tried to visualise what he was describing.

"I think we could do away with these doors," he said, "and replace them entirely with glass, so that the light streams in all day. It would be perfect as it faces South, and would maximise natural daylight all year round."

"Yeah, I'll go with that," murmured Roxy, "What about a pool?"

"Yes, you'd need a pool, although not a large one, and we could house that here. He indicated the smaller of the two barns, "again with glass sides, but emphasising the tythe supports. Of course, the natural mezzanine floor is a wonderful asset and gives good headroom, for massage and specialist areas," he gushed. "You'd need to decide a theme of course. You could do Roman, Grecian, or just good old Rustic – or shabby-chic French style. Whatever took your fancy?"

"I think it would have to be in keeping with what Aiden is proposing," said Roxy, surprisingly sensible for a change, "you know me, I like glitz and glamour, but that might be at odds here. Whatdya think?"

"As it happens, I agree. You're not in London, although you want chic, you don't want tacky," remarked Alan, unwisely not seeing the glint of anger in Roxy's eyes.

"Are you saying I do tacky," snapped Roxy, "fuck you!"

"No, no, not at all, I just agreed that glitz was not probably the right choice for this particular venture," said Alan diplomatically, trying to retrieve the situation.

"Good, otherwise you can shut the fuck up!"

"I wouldn't dream of saying such a thing," soothed Alan, thinking what a stupid cow she was and hating every second of being with her. "Why don't I run up some ideas and you see what you think?"

"Okay," Roxy glared at him triumphantly, "I want them by the day after tomorrow."

"Naturally. I'll do several themes for you to choose from," replied Alan - thinking *and you shall have them my dear and you will pay extortionately for them too.* "how does that sound?"

"It sounds like a car," Roxy shoved him aside, and dived outside into the sunshine to see Lisa's monster 4x4 pulling up the drive. "Ah, that's my lift. I'm just gonna show her round, you can stay if you like, then we're going to the local pub for lunch."

Alan was relieved to have the excuse to go. "No, if you don't mind, I'll head back and leave you girls to it. I've got all the measurements I need. I'll be back in touch the day after tomorrow. Can you lock up and leave the key under the churn when you go?"

"Fine," agreed Roxy, anxious to be rid of him and dash over to meet Lisa, who looked even more orange in the sunshine. "See you then."

Lisa, who having been lost several times and nearly smashed the screen of the sat nav on the dashboard in temper, stepped warily out of the car to be greeted by Roxy in her enormous glasses and stacked up heels. "Blimey love, what's this place? Took me fucking ages to find it!"

"Just wait till I show you," beamed Roxy, "you won't fucking believe it babe!"

Seb and Felix had decided to go down the pub for a quickie. Yesterday they'd gone over the finances and decided that they could find the money for another part-time groom to share the load to do the mucking out and *boring stuff* as Seb put it. Groom's wages were pretty much minimum wage and they could just about afford it. If they employed someone between them, then Hattie and Seb could do more exercising and schooling and they may even be able to take in more horses for training or for sale. It was exciting to be able to consider expanding, and both guys were very much up for the prospect. Even after a day together, they had both realised just how much they could both benefit from each other's expertise. Seb had ridden Picasso in the school and given Felix some tips, and Felix had jumped one of Seb's and it was surprising how much it had perked the horse up afterwards. Provided neither took each other for granted, it was seemingly a match made in heaven. Now heading down to the Fox, and leaving Leo and Hattie hacking, they were looking forward to finalising the plans.

The Fox was quiet although the weather was good, but there was no-one much in the garden. They'd taken their drinks outside to enjoy a bit of privacy from the nosey Janice, who was dying to engage Seb in conversation. Seb who had been pre-warned about her, was super camp and charming, but they departed without a backward glance, much to her disappointment.

"Right, so we'll advertise for a shit shoveller then," said Felix, "can we afford full time do you think?"

Seb was serious for a change, "Nope, let's go with part-time to start, or say hours negotiable, that way they could do mornings or evenings, whatever suits us. We could always change it later."

"Okay," Felix agreed, "We'll run it in the local paper, that's where I found Hattie after all, and she's been fantastic."

"Don't like to pry sweetie, but speaking of Hattie. Everything alright with you two?"

"Fine," said Felix, "don't you start, she was drunk, doesn't even remember anything, thank goodness."

"Just as well sweetie, that was some kiss – I was so jel!"

"Okay about the ad then," said Felix ignoring him, "I'll ring up later. Now I'm off early tomorrow to Tweseldown with two novices – are you okay to cover?"

"Yep. And I'm off on Wednesday to Hickstead with two, you okay to cover me?"

"Definitely," agreed Felix, "Great stuff - this is so going to work." He clanked his glass against Seb's

Janice came out of the snug with two plates balanced high with bread and cheese, just as a massive motor screeched over the gravel into the car park. Out plopped two women, both adorned with huge sun-glasses, skimpy tops and tottering on high heeled shoes. They beeped the car lock and picked their way into the garden.

Felix nudged Seb, "That's Roxy Le Feuvre," he whispered excitedly, "don't let on but she's interested in buying a place round here."

"Go on," gushed Seb, "where?"

"Right next door to us, as it happens, although I'm sworn to secrecy, but I bet she's come to have second look. I recognise that bint with her too – isn't that ..."

"Yeah, that's Lisa Bond, she's Mike Bond's wife - you know the footballer."

"Do you know her Seb?"

"Yeah, I know her," Seb replied dryly, "she keeps her horse with that cunt Juan. He loves sucking up to the nobs, in more ways than one."

"Just ignore them mate. Come on, here's Janice with our lunch."

Roxy had clocked Felix in the garden and nudged Lisa as they walked into the pub's snug bar. "Did ya get an eyeful of those two in the garden?"

"Nah?" said Lisa, turning round to gawp into the garden, "Where?"

"Don't be a twat Lisa – eyes to the front."

"Oh yeah, right okay."

"We'll take our lunch outside, babes, I think!" Roxy giggled, clutching Lisa's arm, "check out the locals at closer range."

Inside, they chatted nonchalantly to a fawning Janice, who had fairly run back in from the garden when she'd seen them arrive, and could hardly contain herself with excitement. Roxy switched on the baby-face charm whilst placing their orders and then they strolled outside. Felix cast a glance in their direction and nudged to Seb, who exaggeratedly tried to crawl under the table.

"Hi," called Roxy, "It's Felix isn't it? I think we met last time I came down?"

"Oh hi!" said Felix casually, "yes that's right we did, I was riding."

"Mind if we join you?" asked Roxy, "this is my friend Lisa, she's into horses."

"Please do, and er ... this is my friend, Seb," he pointed under the table, "he's just dropped his ....something."

Seb poked his head up, "Got it!" he laughed unconvincingly, "my fork ...dropped it," he finished lamely.

"Don't I know ya?" said Lisa, looking at Seb. "You know Juan don't ya?"

"Sadly I did, yes," lamented Seb, "but luckily, on the brighter side for me, no longer dear lady."

Lisa laughed. "He's a right slimy creep aint he? Such a brown noser! He's only nice to me 'cos of Mike and his money!"

Seb reached over and kissed her hand melodramatically. "A kindred spirit! How wonderful to meet someone who sees straight through him."

"Well he's useful, babe, but he is a tosser." laughed Lisa.

"Have you decided to buy the mill?" asked Felix conversationally "I assume that's why you're down in this neck of the woods again?"

"Ten points, gorgeous!" flirted Roxy "Yes, my husband has put in an offer, which has been accepted."

"Heavens darling, that's serious news!" shrieked Seb. "Famous neighbours! Do you ride, Ms Le Feuvre?" he added charmingly to Roxy.

"Looks as though I might have to take it up," purred Roxy, smiling at Felix, "perhaps you could teach me?"

"Or me?" demanded Seb, determined not to be left out. "I stable my horses with Felix too."

"Really? How interesting – but I don't know anything about horses to be honest, although, baby, I'm willing to learn," she smiled at Felix knowingly.

Felix felt himself blushing, something he hadn't done since he was a kid in shorts. "You must come and see the yard," he muttered, "once you've moved in."

"Or before ..." sighed Roxy, "I'll be down here quite a bit whilst the mill is being renovated."

"Anytime," smiled Felix.

"I'd like to come too," said Lisa determinedly, "You never know, I could move my horses to you? Especially if Roxy takes up riding."

"How divine would that be?" sighed Seb, thinking how he'd love to get one over on Juan. "Yes definitely come over."

"I think I'm gonna like Fittlebury," giggled Roxy, "Don't ya think Trace?"

Mark had spent his sunny morning closeted with the indomitable Lady V in her drawing room for their normal Monday meeting. Despite her dubious age, she was still super savvy and kept a keen eye on how the estate and Mark were performing. That particular morning, Mark had given her the low-down on Seb. As he blustered on, trying to paint as sympathetic picture as he could, she'd watched him carefully with her eagle sharp eyes, and he'd realised that he was telling her things she already knew. Once again, he wondered why he was surprised, there was very little she didn't know.

"Mark, dear chap, thank you," she murmured, glancing at him over the top of her specs which, as usual, were held together with a paperclip. "Excellent report, I've been watching and, of course, I do read Horse & Hound, not to mention hear the gossip." She tugged her ear playfully, her vivid eyes sparkling at him. "From what I understand from my dear friend, Marcia Hurlingham, who knows a great deal about that odious wog Juan, this young man has been much maligned and needs a port in a storm. I don't like parvenus either and, from what I gather, the other party involved is something of a ghastly social climber."

"Well, your Ladyship," replied Mark, trying to hide his shock not least at her racist remark "I …"

"Now," she added oblivious, looking down and picking up a sheath of papers from the table, "what do you think about renting them a cottage? I don't like the idea of them living in that …vehicle?" She looked back at him quizzically, "Do you?"

"No, certainly not, in fact I was coming to that."

"Good, I know we were considering putting Laundry Cottage on the market, but you know how I feel about that. What do you think about a short lease? Say three months to begin?"

"It could be a perfect solution, but do you think they could afford the rental? It's a large cottage after all?" sighed Mark

"I've been thinking about that too," remarked Lady V. "What about that sweet girl Harriet? Couldn't she share with them? That's the modern thing isn't it?"

"Well yes it is, but perhaps we should ask her first," muttered Mark, stifling his surprise, "She might not want to after all."

"Nonsense Mark, of course she will. Do you think a girl of her age wants to cycle every day from her parents' house?" laughed Lady V, "Do get with it!"

Mark looked at her and nodded his head slightly, concealing his amusement, Lady V never failed to astonish him, she was a game old thing. "I'll deal with it then."

"Yes, please do so and now, I think that's everything, don't you?" She waved her hand airily at him in dismissal. "Well done Mark, good job. Now I want to listen to *'You and Yours'* on Radio

Four - be a good chap and close the door on your way out."

CHAPTER 27

Brightling Park Horse Trials, held on the second blistering weekend of July, was a howling success for Felix and the jubilant and subsequently pissed syndicate. Seb, who had by this time been in situ at the Fittlebury yard for a mere ten days, despite feeling as though he'd been there for years, had drilled Felix with all the gusto of an over-exuberant dentist. He was a rigid task master, insisting that, in dressage every footfall counted, considering that Felix was as sloppy as a melting Mr Whippy when it came to preparation for the movements and needed to buck up if he wanted to win. Felix had, at first, been flabbergasted at the transformation of the normal easy going Seb to the obsessional perfectionist who now nit-picked at every opportunity, but resignedly he'd knuckled down. When it had come to the dressage phase at Brightling, their test had all the polish and precision of a Swiss time-piece and Seb, who'd come along to support, was gushing with anticipation for a good score. He was not disappointed and when Felix and Picasso went into the jumping phase, they were well ahead of the field. The jumping, which had never been a problem, went without a hitch, and now Seb was driving them home in the truck, with Felix collapsed in the passenger seat, cradling a bottle of champagne, a red rosette fluttering on the windscreen and £250 in prize money stashed in his pocket. He had a huge grin on his face - not only was it his first win on Picasso, but it was also a CIC* event. It was the first step on the road to heaven, he thought happily.

Hattie, daydreaming over his shoulder, was ecstatic. There was nothing like being part of the winning dream team. Since the Parker-Smythes' party, she and Felix had almost recovered their normal easy going banter, although admittedly for the first few days they'd been as stiff around each other as two dead cats. Gradually though things had returned to normal and now they were as good as they could be, despite Hattie fantasising nightly about *the kiss*. Leo had been a trooper, making her laugh, and keeping her busy and she wondered now why she'd worried so much about him and Seb coming to the yard. He'd not only been a physical life-saver but an emotional one too. If it hadn't been for him holding the fort at the yard, it would have been a real struggle for her to have come along today, and now the advert had come out for a part-time groom, life should be even better. She sighed; tomorrow she was going with Seb and Leo to check out a vacant cottage which Mark had miraculously come up with. It all just seemed too good to be true.

"He just ate the ground up," Felix reminisced deliriously, "took every fence like it was a twig!"

"Yeah right – you said about a million times," groaned Seb, yawning affectedly. "What you should be chuffed about is the dressage."

"Seb, don't think I'm not grateful, I am, but the cross country well … there's nothing like it."

"Sweetie, jumping anything without a six pack has always given me brown breeches," laughed Seb, "don't know what you see in it, myself, but if it rocks your boat."

"Oh it rocks, it rocks!" Felix burrowed down further into the seat and offered the bottle to Hattie, "Wanna slurp Hats? What a great team we make eh?"

Hattie leant over and took the bottle, her hair brushing his face as she reached over. Instinctively Felix put his hand out and stroked the strands, and she could feel the heat radiating between them, a heat that had nothing to do with the hot day. Her heart wanted to respond, to leap over onto the seat and curl up with him. To take his hair in her hands, put her lips on his and devour him; but her head told her that he was almost certainly drunk. With stomach lurching disappointment and a huge amount of dignity, she smiled, took the bottle and glugged down a massive slug of fizz which immediately shot up her nose making her sneeze violently.

"You okay doll? Take it steady!" said Seb, who was concentrating on the road "can't have anything happening to you."

Too late, thought Hattie, her mind turning somersaults, it already had.

Max had made Roxy sweat for a fortnight, doggedly ignoring her calls. Now, with a resigned sigh, he allowed himself to hit the green button on his mobile. The palpable surprise in her voice when he answered was obvious, and then her erupting anger followed like a tsunami. He held the phone away from his ear whilst she squawked at him with all the finesse of an irate parrot. Idly watching out of the window, as his car struggled through the choked streets threading out of London, the venom belching from the phone was almost as bad as the fumes of the traffic and finally when the tinny shrieking had subsided, he coolly asked her if she'd finished.

"Max baby, it's only 'cause I'm worried about you," she floundered. "I must have rung you a million fucking times, you must've seen the missed calls?"

"Roxy, my dear, calm yourself down. I'm fine; I've been busy. In fact I've been away for a few days - working," he lied, consoling himself that there was a morsel of truth in that he had been in France with Ronnie. "Big boy stuff."

"Well you could have texted me, you bastard!"

"Roxy, I didn't mean to worry you, as I said I'm fine." Max smiled to himself with satisfaction, enjoying himself, determined not to apologise. "Did you want me for something special?"

"No …well …I …just hadn't seen you since the launch, you know, and I wanted to make sure everything was okay between us."

Max hesitated briefly, "Of course it is love, why wouldn't it be? You're normally so busy, it's not like you to chase me – you sure everything's okay. Aiden alright is he? The kids?"

"Yeah they're fine; he's fine, very wrapped up in this mill project. And yes I am busy, but …" Roxy thought quickly, she was buggered if she was going to let him know how she really felt, "I wanted to run some ideas past you for my part of the conversion. It's a big deal, involves a lot of money, and you have such vision darling," she flattered outrageously, "I was hoping we could take a trip down there together."

"Oh right - I see," said Max, not fooled for a nanosecond. "Well I suppose we could, but surely you've had plans drawn up, can't you just show me those? I'm pretty tied up myself actually."

Roxy, who was used to getting her own way, was teetering on the edge of throwing a super-sulk. Irrational jealousy welled up inside her and it was all she could do to stop herself making a snide remark about Anna. Wrestling with her tongue, she managed to mutter, "Yeah, I've got plans, several designs, but not much cop unless you see the place, you need to soak up the vibes, but no sweat baby."

"I'd love to see them, but it's a bit of hike isn't it, can't we just meet for lunch?" he laughed, "I'll tell you what, we'll even go to that damned Sushi place."

Roxy was seething. What was going on? He had always been so pliable before. Well fuck him, she thought, but with a lightening change her anger had turned to calculating ice, she could play games too. "Lovely!" she simpered, "but I'm not going to show you the plans. I know, it can be wonderful surprise, for you when you come to the grand opening. You and Anna must come! By the way, how is Anna?"

It was Max's turn to be taken aback. He had expected her to stamp her feet and wheedle and plead with him, and now here she was asking about Anna. Perhaps he had gone too far? But no turning back now, "Great," he said, "can I be spared the Sushi then?"

"Of course!" she laughed, through gritted veneers, "you can choose the venue this time."

The conversation ping ponged dementedly between them for a few more stilted minutes and when Max finally ended the call, he felt vaguely uneasy and had no idea who'd scored the most points. They'd arranged to meet the following week and he wasn't looking forward to it. The Machiavellian Roxy was dangerous when she was in this mood. He sighed, anticipating trouble ahead. She was easier to deal with when she was outrageously angry, at least they were genuine reactions, straight from the heart, but this manipulative sweetness was something else entirely and he wasn't sure he could be bothered with it all right now.

More importantly, he was dreading the minefield of emotion which lay ahead of him today. Nigel Brown had come up trumps; he'd done the job he'd been paid to do. After all these years, he was going to find out what'd happened back then, and he wasn't sure how he was going to react. But he'd come this far and now he was like a dog festering with a rancid bone. Today, he might just take a gander at the house from the outside – there was no rush after all. The confrontation with Roxy had unsettled him, and he'd be stupid to explode another can of worms today when he didn't have to. Max turned the phone over in his hands and tried to relax, forcing his head back against the plush leather seats, but the demons were lurking in the depths of his subconscious desperately clawing to the surface of his thoughts. He knew that even if he walked away today, he would go back again – it would only be a matter of time. After he'd checked out what Nigel Brown had told him, he was going to motor on to Ronnie's gaff – but frankly he didn't want to go there much either. Ronnie's do's were always the same, nothing but boozing and tarts, but the last week had been enticingly lucrative and, so far, he'd only dipped his toe in the action. If there was one thing Max loved, it was the cut and thrust of making money, and he had no scruples about how he earned it.

The car swept on, out of London taking the M40 towards Oxford, swooping along the motorway in the fast lane. The countryside flashed past in a green and brown blur as the fields and hills melded into one, the chauffeur easing the powerful car past dawdling lorries and then dropped back to the speed limit. Max lolled his head back again, closing his eyes wearily, trying to blot out the unwelcome thoughts that persistently trickled into his mind. He drifted back to 20 years ago when he had been working in a club in the west end, in fact one of the clubs he now owned. Max had been an East End kid, brought up by his father, a shrewd Jewish man in the rag trade. His mother, a young Swedish model, hence Max's blond hair and good looks, had been the love of his father's life, but she was tragically killed in a hit and run when he was two. He had little memory of her, and his father had done his best but Max's childhood missed out on the warmth of a mother's love. He'd been a bright kid at school, but he'd learned to be streetwise and stick up for himself at an early age. He could remember as if it were yesterday; the day that he'd come home after knocking about with some mates from the estate, to discover two thugs demanding money from his father. He'd walked in quietly through the back door in his swanky new trainers, and for a moment no-body had noticed him. His father's face was drawn and white and suddenly he looked old and vulnerable. His back was shoved hard against the stove, the electric rings were glowing bright and menacingly red. Max replayed the scene in his head, as one brute held his father fast by the lapels of his jacket and the other was grabbing his hands, wrestling them onto the hot rings. Max didn't hesitate, he'd picked up a carving knife from the draining board and plunged it straight into the thigh of one man, viciously turning it round before yanking it out like lightning, and hammering it into the shoulder of the other. Looking back, he still didn't know who had been more surprised - the heavies or his father. The men, yelping in pain, as Max dived in for another attack, made a run for it, threatening that they'd be back, as Max helped his trembling father to a chair. It was an incident which proved to be the turning point of Max's life.

The East End was a den of iniquity, from small time cons running protection rackets, to the big firms with the knocking shops and drug rings, each taking a cut from someone further along the chain. Max's father was right at the bottom of the pile, paying for non-existent protection from a bunch of hoods. After the furore had died down, with the wounded men beating an embarrassing and unsuccessful exit, Max and his father waited for the inevitable reprisals. They came in a surprising way. Shortly afterwards, Max came home to find a black Mercedes outside, with a massive guy in a long, black coat and dark glasses leaning against the driver's door, smoking a cigarette. He nodded to Max but carried on smoking, and turned his back on him. Max remembered how hard his heart had slugged against his ribs as he steeled himself to go inside. Surprisingly, he could hear his father laughing and talking, and he'd followed the sound of the voices to the kitchen. His father was sitting at the table. Opposite him sat a man of about the same age and his dad smiled encouragingly when he saw Max and introduced him to Mr Sylvester.

Mr Sylvester was an elegant man in a camel, cashmere coat, clutching an ebony cane. He had a thatch of white hair with very black eyes; the lines on his face were deep and his lips were pale and thin. Over the years, Max was to come to know those features well. Mr Sylvester was intrigued by the story of young Max, which had been richly embellished by the small time cons in an effort to save face, and now he'd come to see for himself the youngster who'd stood up so loyally for his aging father. Far from retribution, this Godfather of the gangland Mafioso had singled him out as having special qualities – a cut above the others that were mere lackeys doing the donkey work. Max could still remember meeting him, eye for piercing eye, with a bitter determination not to be afraid, and that he would go down fighting, but with an icy dread inside which had made him feel sick. Heavy with suspicion, he'd listened to Mr Sylvester's low voice as he quietly outline his proposals, and when he'd left, an hour later, it had been agreed that Max would start working for him.

For the first six months it was just in one or other of the clubs as a bartender or waiting on the tables, then behind the scenes with the chefs and finally with the managers. He got to know how the clubs worked, what money they took, what punters they attracted, and what extras they offered. Everyone else knew he was Mr Sylvester's protégée and was being groomed for higher things, so despite the petty squabbles, the other staff pretty much left him alone. Max worked hard, kept his nose clean, and learned all that there was to know. Mr Sylvester kept a sharp eye on him and would often drop in unexpectedly to see how he was doing. Thinking back, it never really occurred to him, at the time, how everyone quaked when the boss came through the door, accompanied by his minders, or how they jumped to attention when he spoke. To Max, he was just Mr Sylvester and, apart from that first meeting, he had never really been afraid of him. As the months went on, Max was invited to his home for dinner to chat over the day's events, only to go back to work at the clubs for the night. He enjoyed the old man's company and they would talk about everything and nothing, and their indelible bond grew deeper.

    Jilly came into Max's life that same year, as the summer finally hit London with its long drawn-out days and sultry nights. He had been at Mr Sylvester's for supper and arrived at the Embargo Club at about ten that night, waltzing straight into the bar to check what was happening. She'd caught his eye straight away, whirling around in her short, black dress and white apron taking orders from the boozy Friday night crowd. He'd sat at the bar and watched her for a while, skimming about from table to table, delivering drinks, smiling and laughing with the punters. She was a pretty little thing, not the pan-sticked usual types they hired, but petite and bonny with naturally blonde hair tied back in an untidy high top-knot. Max sighed, the memory of Jilly still hurt him. He'd been able to shelve those feelings for so long, but every now and then, when he allowed himself the luxury of reminiscing, the ache was still as bad as if her loss had happened yesterday. Their affair had lasted only a few months, and he had fallen madly and hopelessly in love with her. He smiled sadly, twisting his hands in his lap, screwing his eyes tight, thinking of how it had ended. The tears, the recriminations, and the anguish; but he was given a choice and he'd made it. Jilly disappeared and, as promised Mr Sylvester swept him on to great wealth and bigger things, with Max finally taking over the firm when the old boy died. Now he had made up his mind he was going to find her.

CHAPTER 28

Mark picked up Hattie, Seb and Leo that morning in the Landrover and they were now steaming down the winding, concrete tracks which threaded over the estate heading towards the mill. Hattie was rocketing about in the back, pitching crazily from side to side like a white knuckle ride, and by the time Mark finally drew up outside the cottage, her hair looked like a haystack. The first glimpse of the cottage made her gasp. It was like something out of a kid's fairy-tale book, with its tiny lattice paned windows, crooked chimneys and slanted roof.

"Mark, it's gorgeous!" Hattie stuttered, excitedly jumping out of the Landrover "Really pretty. Like the Gingerbread House."

"Yes, it's a nice place and not too bad inside either. Hold on, I'll open up."

He fished around in his pocket for a key, whilst Seb and Leo craned through the windows. "Ooh! It's got an inglenook," exclaimed Seb, "How delightfully quaint."

"It's pretty old – several hundred years; no mains drainage or anything like that, but it does have water and electricity connected now, obviously," Mark said, opening the door and pushing it open.

The others followed him inside, itching to have a look around. The door opened straight onto an uneven flag-stoned hall with the stairs curling up on the right, low latched doors on either side, and a passage ahead, which presumably led to the kitchen. Seb darted off through one door and Leo through the other, whilst Hattie made her way through to the back followed by Mark. The original kitchen had been extended and was much larger than she expected. A sleeping Aga dozed in the corner set well back into an old range recess, with some gnarled wooden units on one side and deep set Belfast stone sink. At the other end of the room, the kitchen was dominated by a massive table which seemed to be made out of one huge slab of oak, planed smooth and varnished. Hattie clapped her hands together in delight and ran over, opening the cupboards and drawers, and then turned to Mark, her eyes gleaming.

"Mark, I love it," she gushed, "and much bigger than I thought."

Mark laughed, "Well, it was the laundry house of course, hence the name of the cottage. Have you seen this?" He walked past her to far end, and pushed open a door. "It's a utility room, and there's a little cloakroom too. Not very salubrious I'm afraid, but perfectly serviceable."

Hattie smiled, moving over to have a look. Mark was always so formal, everything looked fine to her. In fact, it was like a dream come true. She could never have afforded a place like this on her own, and the thought of sharing it with Seb and Leo was fantastic – they were such a great laugh.

"Outside, there're quite a few outbuildings too," said Mark, gazing out of the window, "but no garage, and you'd have to keep the garden tidy. There're some tools in the shed and a mower."

"Oh right," grimaced Hattie, who'd never done any gardening in her life, "I'm sure we'll manage. What about furnishings?

"It's only got the basics, I'm afraid. Anything else you'll have to get yourselves. I have an itinerary so you know what's included. Why don't you have a look around upstairs, but from the sounds of it, the lads have beaten us to it!"

The noise from above them was not much short of a motorway in the rush hour thundering over a bridge. They both looked up and grimaced. "Let's go up," said Hattie, "before they bag the best room."

Upstairs, the floor sloped at odd angles and the ceilings were low and crooked. Boisterous shrieks were coming from one of the rooms and Seb and Leo bounded out moments later, their faces flushed with laughter.

"Mark, this place is delicious! Absolutely thrilling – when can we move in?" enthused Seb. "Hattie, come and look at these darling rooms. There's plenty of room for us all."

Mark grinned. It was hard not to, Seb was like a kid in a toy shop, "Well, you must have done something very good in a former life, because Lady V is prepared to waive the references, so as soon as I've drawn up the tenancy, in theory by next week I should think."

Leo looked surprised. "Blimey, but why would she, she doesn't even know us?"

"No, but apparently she'd heard on the grapevine through a close friend of hers what'd happened in the place where you were before. Heartily disapproves of the man, was actually terribly rude about him – so you're to be given a break. Think yourselves lucky – she's a decent old bird."

"She is indeed," said Seb delightedly, "don't worry, we won't let her down, or you come to that."

"You'd better not," said Mark seriously, "but one thing I ought to mention to you guys, and Hattie already knows this already anyway, but the estate is in the final stages of selling the old mill to a couple of celebrities, which is adjacent to this cottage. I'd appreciate it, if you see them, not to go gossiping around the village until everything's signed and sealed." He looked serious for a moment, "just in case... you know."

"Oh mum's the word!" gushed Seb, feigning elaborate innocence. "Won't say a thing, but thrilling!"

"Hmm, depends on the celebrity. Frankly they're a bit *Essex* for me," mumbled Mark derisively, "Now Hattie, let me show you round the rest of the cottage."

Leo shot Seb a warning glint, and they dutifully followed Mark off on the guided tour. The cottage was truly delightful, with intriguing hidey holes and cobwebbed with irregular beams. Ducking their heads under the low supports, they explored the upstairs, discovering three fair sized bedrooms, and a decent sized bathroom. The low set windows at the back gave spectacular views over the downs, whilst from the front, the barn roofs at the mill poked out over the tree tops. Downstairs, apart from the kitchen, which spanned the whole of the back of the house, there was a sitting room with the inglenook and a tiny snug, and a dining room. Hattie was enchanted, the furnishings were sparse and utilitarian, but it would soon seem like home, and so close to the yard – she couldn't wait to move in.

Hattie was not the only one dreaming about moving to Fittlebury. Aiden was dreaming about his Christmas opening and, as a consequence was giving everyone a regular tongue lashing, although Chrissie, in contrast to the others, was finding hers rather stimulating. Aiden was a nightmare when he was in this mood, but there was no doubt that he could move mountains and the customary snail pace of the solicitors was whizzing along with all the urgency of a Wiggins Wannabe. He was expecting to exchange contracts on the mill within a couple of weeks, with completion immediately after. Outline plans had been rubber stamped by the Planning Officer and the detailed plans were ready and would go before the Planning Committee as soon as he had exchanged. There was no doubt that money talked. Alan the architect, despite garnering plenty of grey hairs, had done a good job. The restaurant plans were sensational and he'd cleverly retained all the special features of the mill. The rotten wheel was to be totally renovated and illuminated behind vast glass windows, taking up one whole side overlooking the mill pond, with the massive oak beams and joists in the centre of the main floor made into a feature. The ground floor would probably be a bar and seating area with doors at the back leading onto decking, reaching out over the pond, and the gardens were to be landscaped. The grain floor above, and the upper storey, would be identical to the ground floor but would be seating for the restaurant, featuring the same enormous glass side window. Behind the scenes, there was to be every modern essential for the kitchens and, next spring, the gardens at the back would be turned over to home produce. Outwardly, other than the glass wall overlooking the mill pond at the side, the structure would remain the same; wooden clad, with its traditionally, small, square paned windows, and the cottage and outhouses rebuilt and extended for the kitchens, storage and accommodation. The barns would follow the same theme; being fundamentally traditional, but with the huge floor to roof oak doors being replaced by sheeted glass windows. Alan had again placed emphasis on the beams and joists, and had made sure it was all in keeping with the environment, which had pleased the planning people and English Heritage. It hadn't, however, pleased Roxy, but she'd reluctantly agreed that if it was kept fairly plain and went through the red tape of planning quickly, she could glitz it up later with the décor. Actually, Roxy was beginning to change her mind about the venture in Fittlebury. Since meeting Felix and Seb at the pub with Lisa, life in the sticks seemed brighter and she was as keen as Aiden to get things moving.

Roxy considered her phone conversation with Max the previous day. She was buggered if she was going to give him any up-front information about the plans, but she was going to sew so many intriguing seeds he'd be able to open up a garden centre. He'd fucked her off big time, but she was damned if she was going to let him know it and would play him at his own game. She was meeting him later this week at some steak house, but in the meantime she had other plans. When she'd been down in Fittlebury last week with Lisa, she'd been astonished at her enthusiasm for this riding lark. She'd chatted glibly to those two young bucks, her big doe eyes hanging on their every word, talking about bridles and bridoons and fuck knew what. The only Weymouth Roxy had ever heard of was a place in the West Country, but there had to be something in it judging by the rapture on their faces. On the journey back to London, she'd given Lisa the third degree, but she hadn't needed much encouragement to talk and, ironically by the time they'd got home, she'd coerced Roxy into giving it a try. They were going out later that day to a discreet little place where Lisa had learned to ride, and Roxy was beginning to wonder what the hell she had gotten herself into.

Aiden, having kicked a few arses with the mill project, was hell bent on his next scheme, and was busy setting up a meeting with his mate Farouk at Channel 4. *Rox-Aid* was still a big pull on reality TV and, although the mill was still under wraps, once it was out in the open, it could make sensational viewing to watch the renovations with him and Roxy sparring together and making plans for the launch. A sort of diary of events – it was just the kind of thing the public loved, and he and Roxy were brilliant on these shows. She could be a right royal pain in the arse, but she knew how to pull the punters. He was pretty confident that Farouk would love the idea – it was cheap TV to produce and would get maximum viewings. What more could you asking for? he thought greedily.

Felix was having a lazy day, still reliving every heart-stopping fence on the cross country at Brightling Park, and dreaming about his next event with Picasso. The horse was showing fantastic promise, and with the help from Seb, there was no doubt that his dressage was improving, although he knew there was still more to come. He'd already entered the CIC1* at Chilham in Kent at the beginning of August, and now he was going to enter the CIC2* at Somerford Park. He was lucky to have the syndicate to back him with the exorbitant cost of the entries, let alone the cost of travelling and stabling.

He brought Rambler back to a walk, the horse stretching down to seek the rein as he finished the schooling session. Felix glanced at his wrist watch, the others seemed to have been gone for ages. He was mildly irritated, he missed Hattie when she wasn't with him, and he felt left out when she was larking around with Seb and Leo. It wasn't anything that they did, but he felt it just the same. He wandered back to the yard with Rambler just in time to see Mark's car leaving the yard, and Hattie dashing out of the tack room to help him.

"How'd it go?" he asked. "What's it like?"

"It's gorgeous," enthused Hattie, taking Rambler's reins from him and sneaking him a Polo, "Couldn't be nicer. Mark says we can probably move in by next week. Wait till I tell Mum and Dad, they'll be thrilled I've found somewhere."

"I'm pleased for you Hats, nice to have your own place, and easier for the yard too," said Felix, wishing he could sound happier about it, "How many bedrooms?"

"Three, quite big ones too, but only one bathroom. But it's got a huge kitchen and an Aga."

"Sounds lovely, you'll have to show me."

"Definitely – we're gonna have a house warming party," laughed Hattie. "Guess what too, it backs right onto the mill, so if '*you know who*' buys it, we can keep up with all the goss!"

"Great."

"You could sound a bit more enthusiastic Felix," Hattie complained, "I thought you'd be delighted that Leo and Seb have found somewhere to live - me too, come to that."

"Sorry, course I'm pleased," Felix said shortly, not quite meeting her eye, "Here, be a love and sort out Rambler can you? I need a pee."

Hattie watched him walk away, her insides lurching like a big dipper as he braced his broad shoulders under his tee shirt and twined his long fingers into the belt loops of his breeches, and she wondered why he seemed so fed up. After all, why should he care that they had found the cottage and were moving in. In her wildest of dreams, she'd like to think he was jealous, but rationally she knew that was a pile of poo. He wasn't, it must be something else. What though? -She had no idea. But what she did know was, she wasn't going to let Felix bugger it up and mess with her emotions. He'd been distracted ever since he and Seb had come back from the pub last week, sniggering like a couple of demented coke heads, but she'd been too busy to seriously wonder what had been going on. As she washed down Rambler, dodging his hooves as he stomped about to avoid the water, she thought about the advert that had gone in for the groom. Felix had promised that, this time, she would have an equal say in who they hired; along with Seb and Leo, it would be a real team decision. Whoever they hired would have to fit in and get along with all of them. She switched off the hose, feeling more optimistic than she had for a long time. She may not have Felix in the way she would like but, if she was honest, she knew she never had, and never would. But on the horizon was a new home, and exciting plans for the yard. She leant over and hugged a surprised Rambler. She felt things were definitely looking up.

Felix was slapping tack onto a bad tempered Woody, who was

busy trying to take a chunk out of his arm, when Seb popped his head over the stable door.

"Fancy a jump on one of mine, if I school this one for you?" he asked cheekily.

"Good luck to you then," grimaced Felix, neatly sidestepping as Woody lashed out with a back leg. "He can be a right arse, go steady though, tact and diplomacy is your best bet if you don't want to land on the deck."

Seb laughed, pushing back his hair and winking, "Don't go all tetchy and precious on me ducky - scared I might improve him?"

"Go right ahead, it was just a friendly bit of advice," Felix grinned back mischievously, "I'd rather jump any day of the week."

"It's a deal then …Leo!" Seb yelled, "Be a love and tack up Doris would you – Felix is gonna give her a pop!"

Felix fixed him with steely eyes, "What makes me think you're up to something?"

"Let's find out! The children can put the fences up while I start on this little gem."

"Right – you're on!" Felix coaxed Woody out of the stable and thrust the reins at Seb. "You'd better take Hattie with you, she can start getting the jumps out. But don't say I didn't warn you," he added and stomped off to find Leo.

Seb watched him go, stroking the jittering chestnut horse soothingly, whilst Woody rolled his eyes suspiciously. "There, there old mate, we're gonna get on just fine," he crooned. "Let's show Felix just how talented you are."

Ten minutes later Felix arrived in the school mounted on the big warmblood mare Doris, with Leo and the two dogs, who incongruously had now become firm friends, skittering around in front of them. Seb was cantering around the arena with a soft and relaxed Woody, who apart from a momentary glance at the approaching party, was stretching down happily, whilst Hattie was dragging out the jump wings. If Felix was surprised, he was buggered if he was going to say so, and made as much noise as he could to try and disturb the equilibrium. He chattered loudly to Leo as he altered his stirrups, yelled at the dogs to behave, and called out to Hattie about distances and combinations. Seb ignored him, concentrating on Woody, and astonishingly the beautiful horse was lithe and supple and seemed to be completely under his spell. Hattie was sweating buckets as she lugged out the jumps but couldn't stop staring at the normally testosterone fuelled Woody, who now was as obedient as a Stepford Wife. Every now and then Woody's ears would give a tell-tale twitch, or a swish of his tail, but there wasn't a hint of an explosion.

"Wow I'm impressed," called Hattie, as she paced out the distances between the jumps, "He's like treacle. What do you think Felix?"

"Okay – I give in – he looks great - you must have given him a calmer or summat!" laughed Felix, "Other than that you've got a bloody wand under your breeches!"

Seb brought Woody down to a walk and patted him, allowing him his head. "There's a good boy." He looked at the others, unusually serious "Do you know Felix, this is some horse, and no, I didn't give him a calmer. He's hot to ride, but he's amazing."

"Come on Seb – yes you did. He never goes like that for me."

"Hmm, he could, but you need to change your tactics a bit, I think. You need to be able to put your leg on. Just because he's so sensitive to the aids, it doesn't mean that he doesn't have to accept them and listen to you. That's the trouble with the feisty ones, once they learn that the seat and leg doesn't mean he has to piss off and go faster, he can use all that power and energy in a positive way."

"It didn't look like you were using much leg to me," exclaimed Hattie defensively, "hardly any actually."

"Ah, just because it didn't look like it, I was, but in a much more subtle way" grinned Seb thoughtfully. "Do you mind if I carry on for a bit, while you jump grumpy old Doris – see if you can sweeten her up? It'd be good to see how he behaves when there's more action going on?"

"Be my guest," said Felix, privately hoping that Woody was a total nightmare, even if it was to save face. "Right Doris old dear, let's see what you're made of. Hattie, be a love and just put out some trotting poles."

Leo and Hattie finished putting out the wings and setting up a grid, whilst the dogs tore round the school like a Scalextric track, narrowly missing the riders, before collapsing exhausted onto the grass outside the arena. Felix swore under his breath, but Seb didn't even appear to notice them and seemed to be in a serene trance as he worked. Woody, eyes rolling, had clocked the jumps going up and was immediately tense, but Seb's calm insistence that he pay attention to him despite the distractions eventually paid off, and once again the horse settled.

Doris, in total contrast to Woody's lean athletic frame, was like an elephant, with a massive body, although with a surprisingly attractive head. Doris lumbered lazily off, as Felix kicked her into a trot and was flabbergasted as he hurtled forward up her neck. Quickly adjusting himself, he realised what it was that made her special – she had the most gargantuan paces – even if she was the most slothful creature God had created. He sat deeper, wrapping his long legs around her and pushed with his seat, enjoying the surge of power, and the fabulous feeling of a horse truly going forward to meet his hand and loved it. Doris might look like a dinosaur, but she was a dream to ride.

"She's lovely," he called to Seb, as he pushed her into a canter that nearly sent him into orbit, "Idle, but lovely."

"She's a lazy old tart," shouted Leo, "Needs to be quicker behind for the more advanced work now. The jump'll do her good."

"Has she ever jumped?" shouted Felix back at him, coming across the diagonal and making a perfect flying change in the corner "Don't want to overface her."

"Not really, she's terribly clumsy, I've only done a couple of cross poles."

"Okay, I'll start with the trotting poles then, and we'll build up to a tiny grid. Bounces would be good probably, but she might not cope straight away – we'll see."

Doris, as it transpired, was not the most inspirational or talented jumper, but luckily Felix was, and by the end of the session she was enjoying popping down the lane of tiny jumps with all the exuberance of a mammoth on methadone.

Felix finally pulled her up, her grey neck dark with sweat and threw his arms around her. "You really enjoyed that didn't you old girl, although I don't think we'll hold our breath about the Hickstead Derby just yet."

Leo strode over to take the reins. "Brilliant mate, she loved it, just what she needed. Mind you, your nag's not doing too badly either."

Felix had forgotten about Woody in the twenty minutes or so that he'd been playing with Doris and glanced over to see Seb still concentrating and Woody astonishingly doing exactly the same. The horse looked wonderful, his iridescent coat was only just beginning to break with sweat as Seb came down the centre line and produced a respectable half pass. He had to hand it to him, it was more than he had ever been able to achieve, and it occurred to him, if he could crack the dressage, Woody could be another Picasso.

CHAPTER 29

Anna stretched across the whole bed, star-fishing her long legs wide apart, feeling the luxuriousness of the Egyptian cotton sheets. She flung her arm across her face to shield it from the morning sun filtering in through the window. She could hear Max in the shower, the noise of the jets pounding like heavy rain and, for the moment, she knew she could totally relax. He had been very good to her, had Max, and she was grateful, but of course everything had a price. True, he had rescued her, but, in reality, only to imprison her again. Neither her mind, nor her body was her own any longer. Before, she had been exclusive to no man, and her time after her job was hers. With Max, he owned her totally. Not only did he employ and house her but he chose the clothes she wore, what she ate, decided what she did and didn't do. And of course, he fucked her whenever, and however he liked.

The previous year, Anna and her friend Sonia had optimistically left their small village in Romania to come to England, lured by tales of friends who had already made the break. The attraction of the bright lights and good money was unbearably tempting compared to the dull greyness of their lives. Tasha, who was older than Anna, and had left two years before, persuaded her that she would have a ball and that she'd lend them the money for the airfare, explaining they wouldn't need a visa, and she could help them register with an agency to find hotel work. It had all seemed so easy, but three months down the line, they were working long hours for the minimum wage and still couldn't earn enough to pay the rent, let alone pay Tasha back. Looking back she now realised it was a setup, bringing over simple country girls, getting them in debt and forcing them on the game to pay it off. Tasha was complicit in the operation, but Anna could never truly blame her, she was as much a victim as they were – trapped in a life of prostitution. Anna and Tasha were lucky in a bizarre way, they were used at the private parties; rich city men wanting a bit on the side, who generally wanted someone classy for straight sex and paid good tips. Sonia, who was not so pretty, was less fortunate, channelled into the seedier side, working out of a cheap knocking shop just off Victoria, with rough clients who sported fetishes. The pimps worked them hard, especially Sonia, whose clients brought in less money, yet they never seemed to pay off their debt. After some weeks Anna knew that Sonia was using. She had always experimented with the odd spliff or pill, laughing at Anna's obstinate reticence, but now the track marks were obvious, as was her steady decline. She rarely came back to the rooms they shared, but on one night when she did, Anna confronted her. After a heated row, Sonia stormed out declaring she'd never come back and, to Anna's guilty sadness, she didn't. Two weeks later she was found dead in an alley way, having been badly beaten. Anna endured the horrific procedure of identifying the body, and gave details of her next of kin to the police who'd treated her like scum. It was not long afterwards, a desperate Anna, still mourning the death of her friend, had met Max and grabbed his offer of escape with both hands - despite the price tag.

She stretched in the bed again, arching her aching back upwards and pushed her head back against the pillow. He had put her though her paces last night, and she felt bruised and tired; he could be quite cruel sometimes. She wondered if she would ever see where he lived; he only ever took her to an hotel, albeit a swanky one. Only the best for Max, and he would never go to her rooms in the club. From the en-suite, the pulse of the shower jets stopped and she braced herself waiting for him to reappear and wondering what his plans were for today. With any luck, he would drop her back en-route to wherever he was going. She waited, her heart beating against her skinny frame.

"Anna, my dear, why not have a bath?" Max called from the bathroom, "I'm running it now."

Anna sighed, it was an order not a request. She slipped out from under the sheets and padded out into the bathroom.

Max was still wet from the shower and had a small towel around his waist. He appraised her as she stood before him. To Anna, she felt like an insect on a pin, her nakedness still felt awkward; it was the way he weighed her up that she hated, like he was assessing the goods. He put out his hand and touched the bruise on her wrist which was starting to show after last night. The touch was tender, "Come on, let's get you in – you'll feel better." He took her hand and helped her into the warm water and knelt down beside the bath passing her a sponge and shower gel. "Here you are, give yourself a really good wash for me."

Anna did as she was asked, liberally soaping her breasts so that her brown nipples poked out through the white suds. She moved further down with the sponge, over her belly, trying not to wince as the soap stung down between her legs from where he had been so rough with her.

Max, who had been watching her carefully, saw her discomfort. "Oh you're really sore my dear, such a shame, I was feeling rather horny this morning." His mouth drooped with disappointment, "I know, let's get you dry, and give you a break, I've got some Sudocreme in my bag"

Anna couldn't have been more relieved. She heaved herself out of the bath, and he wrapped her in a towel, and she followed him into the bedroom, sitting on the edge of the bed whilst he rummaged for the tube of crème.

"You put it on Anna, I'll just watch." Max purred, as he handed it to her and she obediently peeled off the towel and opened her legs. "Good girl, why not lay back on the bed and do it?"

Hesitantly Anna wriggled onto the bed, and opened her legs. Her pubic hair had been shaved to a mere goatee and she dipped her finger between her legs dabbing on tiny globules of the crème. Max watched her fascinated, his eyes glinting, and instructed her to open her legs a little farther, and she could see his cock growing harder with excitement underneath his towel.

"Of course, I could always fuck you up the arse Anna," he said smiling at her. "That's a good idea isn't it? Be a good girl and turn over."

Anna felt herself growing afraid, the crème was stinging and she hated anal, it felt like being split in two, and Max was a big man, with a large cock and last night had been rough enough. But she had no option and turned over pushing her bottom into the air.

"Spread your legs a little wider, my dear. Let the fox see the rabbit."

Anna pushed her legs as wide apart as she could without falling flat, her head drilled into the pillow, and she could feel the cold exposure as her bum cheeks drew apart. Max made no move to touch her and she could hear him moving around the room, unzipping his bag and taking things out and wondering what the hell was coming next. She angled her head so she could peep out from under the pillow and in the mirror she caught sight of him wrenching on a pair of latex gloves and next to him was a long flexible hose and some rubber sheeting. Despite herself, her clitoris was starting to throb, she was afraid, yet she was excited, it was the most bizarre sensation.

"Put the sheet underneath you my dear," Max said kindly, "We don't want to make too much mess."

Anna lifted her body up whilst Max placed the sheet over the counter pane, and once again she waited whilst he fiddled about in the room. The waiting seemed ghastly, embarrassingly sexy, and she felt violated before he had even begun.

"Now Anna, don't be alarmed, and you mustn't move, do you understand?"

"Yes," she whispered.

Max rubbed the ring of her anus with a circle of oil on his fingertip and gradually introduced the length of hose, feeding it right up inside her. To Anna it felt like having a poo, she wanted to wriggle, but as he pushed it in, he warned her to remain absolutely still. Suddenly she had the feeling that her insides were being filled with a warm flooding sensation, and she realised that he was pumping some sort of liquid into her.

"Hold it in Anna, I'm giving you an enema. I like my girls to be clean before I fuck them. When I say so, you go to the bath room and empty yourself, then you come straight back. Understand?"

"Yes. I understand," she whimpered pathetically. Anna had

never felt more humiliated. Mercilessly he pumped the liquid into her and she squirmed pitifully underneath him, feeling as though she would explode with the pressure, desperately clenching the cheeks of her bottom together and clutching the pillow frantically between her fingers. Her physical and emotional turmoil seemed to go on for aeons and she struggled to keep herself from collapsing. Gradually she realised that he had stopped filling her and was withdrawing the hose. He delivered a hard slap to her buttocks.

"Right, go and empty yourself."

Anna leapt obediently from the bed, her face sweating and flushed. She dashed off to the toilet, as the filthy liquid exploded out from her, and ran in greasy rivulets down the lavatory bowl. She cleaned herself and as instructed, returned, demeaned and embarrassed, clambering back onto the bed, her legs shaky; hardly able to look at him and glad to put her red face into the pillow, she offering her buttocks to a waiting Max.

Max heaved himself on top of her, shoving his cock inside her arse, without preamble and riding her like a bucking bronco as he pushed himself in further, savagely catching hold of her tumbling hair for support. Anna braced herself hard against the pillows, but the pain of her stretching sphincter to accommodate him was nothing compared to her debasement and humiliation. She longed for her family and to be back home in Romania.

Roxy had a sore bum, but for an entirely different reason than Anna. Roxy, by nature, was a competitive beast, and if there was one thing in life that seriously pissed her off it was someone like dimo Lisa being more successful at something than she was, and at this riding malarkey – Lisa left her standing. The bitch! In the grand scheme of things it wouldn't have mattered, she would have taken the piss out of Lisa and laughed it off, but it now occurred to her that if *Rox-Aid*'s latest venture was to bring home the big bucks, she'd better learn and learn fast.

Aiden had come back from his initial meeting with Farouk at Channel 4 pumped up with plans about the reality show. Farouk had loved the idea and was keen to get things moving. He and Aiden were going down to the mill to check out the site, and then it would be a series of bloody meetings and once it went into production the pressure would be on. Farouk wanted it to be a *'live and happening event'*. The series wouldn't actually go out live, but he wanted filming to take place two weeks before they rolled the national viewing, so it was broadcast continuously until the big launch. *Rox-Aid*, as the feisty dynamic duo, was primarily a delicious pull, and Aiden's restaurant conversion and culinary skills appealed to Farouk, but he was not so keen on the gym and spa idea as the focus for Roxy - it had been done to death. Life in the country was different and he'd suggested she should take up riding - it opened up all sorts of avenues -from altruistic opportunities for inner city kids, disabled riders to new ranges of riding wear, and the need for core fitness could then encompass the gym and spa angle. Roxy's interest in horses, spurred on by Aiden, had suddenly quadrupled overnight. The trip out with Lisa had been for a distraction primarily, but with the impending TV show, if she didn't up her game she was going to look like a total fucking retard.

To gain the maximum publicity and best outcome in front of the cameras, she needed to be a totally newbie novice when it came to sitting on a horse – which she was, but nonetheless a gifted one – which she wasn't. In her favour she was fit, and had good balance through all the gym sessions. On the downside, how could she practise without being found out? This was something she couldn't trust Lisa with, she had a mouth like a loud hailer and as far as she was concerned Roxy had given up. God she would love to wipe the smug smile off her face and it wouldn't do Aiden any harm to know how brilliant she was too, make him sit up and take notice of her for a change. Roxy sat at her desk, and surfed the internet for ideas. What a bleeding minefield. She had no fucking idea where to start. She Googled *'learn to ride in a day'* and found riding schools claiming all sorts of astonishing successes. Perfect, but not if you were in the public eye like she was – she'd be rumbled by some stalking pap and plastered all over the tabloids straight away. She scanned the screen, randomly clicking obscure links, when something caught her eye. Interested, she settled back to read more. Half an hour later she picked up the phone and rang Suzanne demanding she get her arse over to the house. Roxy leant back in her chair and sipped her water and waited.

"A what?" asked Suzanne, "I've never heard of one."

"Find out. I wanna buy one…yesterday. And remember, not a fucking word – right?"

"Look, just give me a clue, what's it about? Why do you need it so quickly?"

"Fuck me, you need to know the ins and outs of a duck's arse," snarled Roxy. "Anyway, I'm not sure I trust you."

Suzanne puffed herself up like a blue tit in a snow storm, "I can assure you of my discretion at all times," she rebuked frostily, "…and my loyalty."

"Well I'm telling you princess, if a word of this gets out you'll never work again – got it?"

"Absolutely understood, but unless I have the big picture how can I truly help?" simpered Suzanne, hating herself with every syllable, "what's going on?"

Roxy's botoxed face tried to frown, debating on how much to let on. "Okay I'll tell you. Listen."

Five minutes later, having fully appraised Suzanne of the problem, Roxy glared at her. "Now do you understand – I can't afford to make a total wanker of myself. So somehow I've got to have a head start."

Suzanne would like to have laughed, but managed to keep the right amount of concern in her voice, "Wouldn't Chrissie be better to help you out, she can ride can't she?"

"She's the last fucker I'd ask," spat Roxy, with enough venom to floor an elephant, "No, I want you to do it. Now either you can, or you can't, what's it to be?"

"Leave it with me," said Suzanne, with heavy resignation.

Mark had been busy and the lease for Laundry Cottage had been drawn up with a three month tenure to start, and a month's notice to be given on either side. Lady V had been too generous, in his opinion, about the rent, waiving away his objections in her usual airy fairy but stubborn way. She'd totally dismissed what he suggested, saying it could be reviewed at a later date. Privately, he thought she was crazy, it was worth twice the rental, but didn't argue, and in a perverse way he admired her fairness.

When Mark pitched up at the yard waving the paperwork for them to sign, Seb threw his arms round him and kissed him hard on the lips. Hattie had to hide behind the truck to stop laughing, the shock on Mark's face would have frozen a boiling kettle.

"Mark, I can't tell you how excited I am," shrieked an oblivious Seb, "It's marvellous news! When can we move in?"

"Well," spluttered Mark, struggling to recover his composure, "as soon as you've paid the rent – a month in advance I'm afraid. I'll need your bank details and we can set up a standing order."

"Oh sweetie no problem, pop in the tack room, and I'll fetch it from the truck. I won't be a jiffy."

Seb fairly skipped towards the lorry and Mark shook his head in bewilderment as he disappeared, shrugged his shoulders and marched over to the tack room where Leo was rolling up bandages.

"Hi Mark, lovely morning again – can I make you a cuppa?" asked Leo, struggling to untangle a basketful of jumbled white polo wraps. "To what do we owe this pleasure?"

Mark, quailing at the thought of another tactile embrace, hesitated, "Umm, I've brought the lease."

"Great, that's fantastic news," grinned Leo, tossing down the bandages. "What a relief – if I'd had to kip in that lorry for much longer I swear I'd have murdered Seb."

"I thought you were two were an item?" said Mark, surprised

"Did you?" laughed Leo, "You should smell his socks, let alone his farts!"

"Aren't you then …?"

"Mark! Have you got the agreement?" cried Hattie, from the doorway, "I'm so excited!"

"He has indeed – I'm saved – Praise the Lord!" laughed Leo, "I'm putting the kettle on to celebrate."

"Forget the tea lovelies – crack these open," boomed Seb, crashing through the doorway like an enthusiastic rhino, balancing two bottles of fizz, some plastic glasses and a wodge of buff folders under his arm. "Let's party!"

"It's a bit early in the day for me actually, tea will be fine, and we really do need to sort out the paperwork first," said Mark, stiffly.

"Tosh," laughed Seb, flinging down the files and putting bottles in the sink "Never too early."

"Mark's got a point Seb," said Hattie, "Let's get the formalities over and done with, and then we can toast our new home eh?"

Leo stooped down, collecting up the mass of bank statements spewing out of the folders, "Hattie's right Seb, calm down for Christ's sake. We all need to sign this lease and sort out paying."

"Spoilsports," sulked Seb, "Oh alright, let's do the boring stuff. I just can't wait to move in. I'm sick of using a bathroom at Felix's gaff, that Alice is such a bitch!"

"She's probably as fed up with arrangement as we are," said Leo reasonably, "It can't be easy sharing with us after all."

"No, but she could be more gracious, she's so spiteful all the time – there's no need to be so unpleasant," moaned Seb, "we bow and scrape to her the whole time, and keep the bath spotless."

"Oh come on, it can't be as bad as that!" laughed Hattie, intrigued nonetheless.

"You have absolutely no idea sweetie," complained Seb, affectedly flinging his arms about, "We tiptoe in, shower at the speed of light, creep out, apologising all the time, getting the evils at every turn. She's a witch!"

"Come on, it can't be easy for her either – she works terribly hard and probably just wants to come home and put her feet up," soothed Hattie.

"Humph, Felix works hard too, and he waits on her hand and foot believe me, I've seen him," grumbled Seb, "plus she's nasty to the dog! I hate going in there."

"Well not for much longer. Stop moaning and sign on the dotted line."

Mark coughed embarrassed, "There is the small matter of the money too."

"Oh that's no sweat." Seb pulled out a roll of notes from his pocket, "I'll pay cash this month and we can set up a standing order for the next lot." Casually he began counting out £50 notes onto the draining board, "there, that's right isn't it?" he said, thrusting the money at Mark, "Now where's this damned lease to sign?"

Mark couldn't have been more taken aback and looked as though the money might spontaneously combust in his hand, "Well …" he blustered, "Usually …well… I suppose it's alright, but of course I'll need to give you a receipt."

"Anytime," dismissed Seb. "Now Leo can do the red tape, whilst I open the fizz."

As the flustered Mark explained where they had to sign and Leo gave him the details of their business bank account, Seb festered about popping open the corks, only putting them down to come and scrawl his name when they called him over. Only when Mark finally squirrelled away the money and handed them their copy of the agreement did he accept the proffered celebratory glass.

"Cheers! Here's to our new home!" Leo, chorused, clinking their glasses together with gusto, the champagne splashing all over them, whereupon they fell giggling together in a group hug. Mark managed a superficial smile, but sincerely hoped that Lady V hadn't made a colossal mistake.

CHAPTER 30

By the end of the following week, Roxy's sleek, black Range Rover was weaving its way down the lanes towards Fittlebury. The countryside had never looked lovelier; little feathers of clouds wafted across a cornflower blue sky, the fields were a collage of different greens, the hedgerows tumbling with pink dog roses, wild honeysuckle and waving purple foxgloves. But their glorious display was lost to those in the car with its blacked-out windows clamped shut and the air-con going full blast. Roxy was driving. Beside her sat Aiden, with Farouk and Chrissie in the back, and the conversation was centred on the forthcoming show. Farouk, in the last week had moved more mountains than Mohammed, making a dynamic pitch to the schedulers at Channel 4 who'd enthusiastically agreed it would make prime time TV in the run up to Christmas. He'd provisionally organised his team, the main frame funding, and he'd got Basil Child to do the storyboard, which was a great result. Basil had worked on the *Rox-Aid* band wagon before and was used to the tantrums and mood swings of the main players and could always manipulate the histrionics to make lively viewing. Exchange of contracts was due any day and Farouk wanted to take a look at the mill and the village to get the ambience of the place - hence their trip today. A small advance film crew would be following them around from next week, capturing everything from snippets with the architects, planners and solicitors, which would make up the initial pilot show. Roxy had half an ear on their conversation, but was dreading the intrusion, she was already aching in parts of her body she didn't know she had, and now she would have to find the time to sneak out for more torture sessions without them knowing what she was up to – a nightmare scenario.

"Wake up Roxy – what do you think?" snapped Aiden.

"What do I think about what?" quipped back Roxy, startled, "Sorry I wasn't listening."

"For fuck's sake Roxy keep up. Farouk was asking if you've ever ridden before," snarled Aiden, turning round to the others in the back and throwing his hands in the air in exasperation.

Roxy caught Chrissie smirking sensually back at Aiden in the rear view mirror, and was livid. Conceited bitch, she'd bloody show her! She replied sweetly to Farouk, "No, well only once, and I was pretty hopeless to be honest, but I'm sure I'll cope." Too right I will, she thought grimly, even if it was just to wipe that smile of Chrissie's smug face. "Last time I came here, I met a couple of lads who run a horse riding yard on the estate, so I thought it'd be a good place to start."

Chrissie laughed spitefully "Really Roxy, if it's that chap that was riding through the mill the first time we came down, I think you'll be disappointed, they were hardly riding school nags, much too high quality. You'll want something that's brain dead to start with."

"Thank you for that Chrissie," spat Roxy, "Suzanne and I will sort something out I'm sure."

"I didn't know Suzanne knew anything about horses," said Chrissie innocently, "you don't want to make too much of a fool of yourself do you?"

"Chrissie's right," said Aiden, "Suzanne knows nothing about it, why not let Chrissie organise some riding lessons for you. She rides brilliantly - don't you Chrissie?"

Roxy sizzled with indignation, imagining the brilliant Chrissie riding Aiden armed with whips and spurs. "Thanks, but no thanks, I imagine you're busy enough keeping up with Aiden's demands aren't you dear?" she said, glancing knowingly at Chrissie in the mirror, "Suzanne and I can manage but I am sure I will need to talk to you about it again."

Chrissie felt herself blanch. The look that Roxy had given meant only one thing, she must know about her and Aiden. Not that she gave a shit about Roxy or about her feelings, but she did enjoy her job. If Aiden had to choose between her and Roxy, Roxy would win hands down every time. He was ruthless and Chrissie was dispensable. She knew how he worked; he would even capitalise on the publicity if it ever got out. The warning shot from Roxy hit her like an exocet missile and now she was trapped in the car with Roxy giving her the evils in the mirror. She peeked at Aiden, he hadn't noticed of course, he wouldn't, he was so wrapped up in himself and the new project. She looked out of the window, refusing to let her eyes be drawn to the mirror, and watched the countryside swishing past - God, she couldn't wait for them to arrive at the mill.

Roxy took her foot of the gas, luxuriating in every agonising minute that super-efficient Chrissie was compelled to sit in her car, and was, in all probability, now wetting her knickers wondering what Roxy might choose to do next. Roxy had enjoyed every nano-second of their little spat. She hadn't meant to let Chrissie know that she was aware of Aiden's little dalliance with her, but it was hugely satisfying to watch her smug jaw drop when she made it clear that she did. Poor stupid Chrissie, she must think she was born yesterday. What Chrissie did not know was that Roxy was not fazed. She was not the first, nor likely to be the last, in his little string of snooty tartlets in whom he chose to dip his wick when the fancy took him. Aiden was surprisingly discreet if nothing else, as was she, when it came to a little diversion, but they were both money minded enough to know that *Rox-Aid* was better together than apart, and if there was a little spice to pepper it up now and then – so much the better. Meanwhile, she relished the delicious power of the moment as once again she glanced at Chrissie and watched her squirm.

As the atmosphere washed blithely over Aiden, Farouk was soaking up the hostile vibes between the two women. On his radar, atmospheres meant either good or bad outcomes, and in the scheme of things Chrissie was totally replaceable, but it may be she could also add a touch of lustre to the story. He sighed, running his fingers through his hair, and stretched his long legs out as far as he could and wished Roxy would put her foot down, this journey was tedious and if there was one thing he hated, it was wasting time.

"Nearly there. This is Fittlebury, Farouk, that's the local

watering hole – The Fox, and we are just outside the village," remarked Aiden, "don't expect too much when you get there, you've got to envisage what it will be like when it's finished."

"We could do some footage in the pub maybe," said Farouk, leering out of the window "you know, a *'getting to know the locals'* shoot."

"I've already been in there actually," said Roxy, "they don't know we're buying it yet though – we can't do anything till it's signed and sealed."

"No, but once it is, would be good to get the local yokels on board," smiled Farouk, "gets people empathising with you as *'real'* people."

"Is that what you call them?" muttered Chrissie spitefully, under her breath.

"What did you say Chrissie dear?" shot Roxy dangerously, glaring at her in the mirror.

"I said *that's a good call then*," corrected Chrissie quickly, her eyes shooting down into her lap.

"Hmm, yes," purred Roxy, indicating to turn into the track to the mill, "here we are then everyone."

Laundry Cottage throbbed with music pulsating from the sitting room, percolating up the stairs, out of the open windows and doors, and drifting faintly out into the garden. Leo had set up the music system as his first priority and now, as they lugged their bits and pieces into the house, it already felt like home. They'd already had a pow-wow about who was having what bedroom, and agreed the fairest way was to draw lots. Hattie had been surprised that the chaps hadn't wanted to share the largest room and said so, only to be greeted by a naughty wink from Seb and they'd allocated rooms without further comment, although it had made her wonder about their relationship. She had drawn the bedroom which overlooked the front garden and the mill. It was a pretty room with sloping ceilings, the walls criss-crossed with beams, and two tiny square paned windows. The furnishings were sparse, a small double bed, a chest of drawers with a mirror and a wardrobe, a bedside light and oak floorboards with a single rug. After Hattie had paid her share of the rent, she'd gone to Horsham and chosen some bed linen and towels, and having put on the pretty duvet cover, adorned the walls with some posters, and put some clutter on top of the chest it felt infinitely more homely. She unpacked her clothes and shoved the suitcase under the bed and went to find the lads.

Downstairs in the kitchen, Hero, despite the heat outside, had made himself at home beside the slumbering Aga, curled Doberman fashion, into the smallest possible ball and was snoring gently on his bean bag. Hattie rummaged about exploring the contents of the drawers and cupboards, pulling out some mugs and finding teaspoons. Lugging the kettle from the back of the stove and filling it from the tap, she yelled that she was making tea in the kitchen if they wanted some. As she waited for the kettle to boil, she leant back against the Aga rail rubbing Hero's short haired body with her foot. She just knew she was going to be really happy here.

"Hey guess what?" Leo gasped, bounding into the kitchen and dragging her by the hand out to the front door.

"What?" yelped Hattie, rubbing her arm, "I was just gonna have a cup of tea!"

"Someone's over at the mill!"

"Oh, so what?" said Hattie exasperated, turning back into the kitchen, "if the sale goes through they'll be down there all the time, so it's no big deal."

"Oooo, do I get the impression that Roxy doesn't do it for you?" teased Leo.

"No, she doesn't," grumbled Hattie, irritated, "she's hardly talented is she?"

Leo laughed, "Depends on how you define talent I suppose."

"For God's sake – she's a bimbo with breast enhancements, not your bag surely?"

"Now, now Hattie, that's a really bitchy thing to say, and not like you is it? Let's have that cuppa and I'll give Seb a shout. He's probably folding his clothes in tissue paper – he's so obsessional."

"Who's being bitchy now?" Hattie countered, "Not like you either I suppose!"

Leo grinned, slapped her bum and made for the stairs. Hero rolled over and stuck all four paws in the air like he was giving a high five which made her laugh and she shoved the teabags in the cups.

Five minutes later, they both reappeared and plonked themselves down at the kitchen table and Hattie sat down with them for their first brew in their new home.

"I hate being heavy, but we need to sort out how we're going to manage things, you know – do we have a food kitty, or buy our own? Who does the cooking, or do we take turns each?" Hattie laughed, "And then there's the matter of the cleaning and the garden."

"Oh doll, how terribly organised," lamented Seb wearily, "can I bear it?"

"Yes you can Seb," said Hattie, "because if we don't do it now, it'll only lead to arguments later."

"She's right Seb," agreed Leo, "I think we should have a communal kitty for food. Rotas for cooking, cleaning, shopping and doing the garden – that way it works out fairly – no cop outs, and no excuses, Seb."

"You bloody bullies. Oh alright, you draw them up Hattie, and take charge of the kitty. Everyone happy now?"

"Perfectly," smiled Hattie, sipping her tea. "One thing though, we desperately need some biscuits!"

"Aiden man, this place has a serious aura," Farouk mused, "I mean it's wonderful, full of atmosphere. We should get some great footage here. Although you'll have to go some to get it ready by Christmas – the place is a shell."

"Chrissie has it all in hand, everyone is standing by, ready to start – that right Chrissie?" Aiden smirked confidently at her, "What would I do without you?"

"What indeed?" remarked Roxy sarcastically, "How are things going Chrissie?"

"Fine," grimaced Chrissie, who by now had recovered some of her composure, "just waiting for the off."

"I bet you are," Roxy smiled. "Tell me Farouk," she linked her arm through his, guiding him away from car, "what do you think of the gym area?"

"It'll be great when it's finished babe, and it shouldn't take much, but I'm more keen on this riding angle."

"I know darling, and believe me, I won't disappoint you. You'll love these two lads I've found, whatever she says," Roxy gesticulated at Chrissie, "they're terribly glamorous and so are the horses. It'll make great viewing."

"I can always rely on you darling, you're such a true professional."

Roxy stood on tiptoes and kissed Farouk's olive skinned cheek, "just leave it with me and Suzanne, I've never let you down yet."

"Farouk, come look at the mill and the plans mate," shouted Aiden, pinching Chrissie's bum when he thought that Roxy wasn't looking, "they're fucking amazing."

"Humour him," smiled Roxy, wanting to vomit at the mention of the precious plans, "although actually they are good, and it will make a spectacular restaurant."

Farouk walked over to Aiden and Roxy admired his skinny frame. He wasn't her type at all, although there was something rather feral about his lean, sinewy body, high cheekbones and long black hair, scraped back into a pony tail. Farouk had a fierce and demanding reputation; he wasn't into fine art, but he was into making fast turnaround telly, produced on a budget, delivered on time, for a maximum viewing audience. But it also meant he was ruthless, got what he wanted, and didn't mind who he walked over in the process – rather like Roxy herself.

Roxy watched them disappear towards the ruined mill and rapidly punched out Suzanne's number, snapping out instructions when she answered, and ended the call abruptly before joining the others. She smiled with satisfaction – fuck Aiden, she knew who was going to come out on top.

CHAPTER 31

As July tumbled into August, Felix clocked up some promising runs with the novices and, more remarkably, a 7th place in the BE100 with the irascible Woody at Iping, much to the elation of Sheena, who threw her arms around him and gave him a stonking kiss. Felix had been astounded, as they'd entered long before the disastrous round at Eridge, and only decided to take him on a wing and a promise. The dressage hadn't been mind blowing, but thanks to Seb's help the previous week, the horse was definitely accepting the aids better than before, although there was still plenty of room for improvement on the flat. It was the double clear that clinched the place, the horse was a jumping machine, and this time Felix did feel he had more control which was a bloody miracle. In return, Felix had sparked up dear Doris with the grid jumping. She'd really got the message and was skipping down the bounces, springing off her hocks like a fuel injected pogo-stick. Seb had engaged her fifth gear in the dressage arena and qualified her at the Regionals for a place in the Nationals along with one of his other horses.

The first weekend in August saw Felix take Picasso to a CIC1* at Chilham Castle in Kent. The dressage had been good, but it was a strong class and a silly break in the medium trot had cost them marks, coupled with a rolled pole in the show jumping had put them in 9th place. Not a disgrace by any means, but nonetheless Felix had been disappointed especially after the euphoria of Brightling. On the upside later in the month they were attempting their first CIC2* at Somerford Park in Cheshire and this was a long haul up country. It would mean a few days away, but at least now he didn't have to worry about leaving the yard, and his stomach fizzed like a super-charged energy drink every time he thought about it. He'd be returning the favour to Seb when he went away to the Nationals in September. The yard was running better than he could ever have hoped. The atmosphere was buoyant, the horses were happy and going well, and now Seb and Leo had found somewhere to live. He'd kept his promise to Hattie and she was blossoming with her riding skills and soaking up the extra responsibility of doing the entries and planning the work load. They'd found a new girl to come and help. She was starting tomorrow and he hoped that her arrival wouldn't upset the applecart. As it happened, they hadn't had an avalanche of replies from their advert. After sorting out the laughably ridiculous from the mildly unsuitable, they interviewed two; a precocious brat who was doing a gap year and wanted to bring her own horse, ride all day, and who it transpired felt that mucking out was beneath her. The other girl was in her mid-twenties; she'd been working in a riding school for a couple of years, and fancied a change and going free-lance. She emphasised that she knew what it was to get her hands dirty, and brought references which seemed kosher, so they took her on. Somehow Felix had reservations, nothing he could quantify about her, but he'd kept them to himself as the others hadn't said anything and he didn't want to appear to be an old woman. Christ knew he always seemed to the one to have reservations these days, and he was supposed to be the gung-ho eventer.

He was looking forward to his bed tonight as he ambled back towards the cottage, with Fiver sniffing around in the grass alongside the path deciding every spiky tuft was his own personal nirvana. It had been a hard day, but a good one and he was tired. Nonetheless, he had felt a stinging stab of envy as he watched the others finishing up and roaring off in the direction of Laundry Cottage, arguing and laughing about who was supposed to cooking that night. Kicking up the dust with his shoe, he thought of his own evening ahead of him, things between him and Alice had been more than tricky of late. He was trying hard, probably too hard, but she was as snappy as a bowl of cereal. He'd thought that once Seb and Leo weren't popping in every evening for a shower Alice'd be less stressed out, but it just hadn't happened - if anything, she was worse. He'd tried to talk to her, but she cuttingly dismissed him in that superior way she had sometimes. Okay she was a vet, bright, clever, and he was a rider, not academic, but he wasn't a bloody fool, and that was how she made him feel. Was the honeymoon period of their relationship over? When they'd first met, they could hardly keep their hands off each other, and now it was always him who seemed to make the advances, with Alice claiming she was tired. Her rejection stung, and when he'd backed off, she accused him of not finding her attractive. They didn't have much to say to each other anymore; Alice claiming he wouldn't understand her work, and she wasn't much interested in his, any common ground for laughter had disappeared down the plughole. He had a feeling that it ran much deeper though, but he was fucked if he knew what it could be.

Fiver ran ahead of him and then disappeared from view down into the back of the cottage garden and dived under the shed, ferreting into some intriguing holes that he was desperate to investigate. Alice's 4x4 was in the drive, so she must be home, Felix thought gloomily, pondering whether or not to call out as he approached the back door. Normally, Fiver galloped in ahead of him announcing their entrance with his new found gusto in life, and Alice would shout at him to be quiet, but today like Felix, he had other things on his mind. As he slipped in quietly through the back door he could hear Alice speaking urgently into her mobile phone from the sitting room. The tone of her voice was cold and icy, and he could tell she was agitated as he could hear her footsteps as she paced up and down on the oak floor. Felix waited in the kitchen and listened.

"I've told you before several times, I don't know what you are talking about. I don't know who you are, or who you think I am – but you've got the wrong person."

She paused and continued in a voice that would have frozen molten lead, "Well, you're mistaken. If you call again, I'll contact the police."

The footsteps stopped abruptly. Obviously she was listening to the reply and then screamed out in temper, "Try me! Now fuck off and leave me alone!"

Felix stood transfixed in the kitchen, wondering what the hell was going on, and undecided about what to do, when Fiver hurtled in from the garden, and, before Felix could catch him, he darted into the sitting room yapping for all he was worth, his little tail whirling around like a rattlesnake.

"FELIX!" shouted Alice, "Can't you control this fucking dog!"

Felix dashed in to find Fiver jumping up at Alice, clearly thrilled to see her, and Alice equally clearly, not at all thrilled to see him. It was more than that, her face looked ashen, drained of colour, her eyes wild and darting from side to side, and she was still holding the mobile.

"Fiver, down mate, get down, good boy," Felix coaxed gently, producing a dog chew from his pocket which Fiver greedily grabbed and scooted back to his basket in the kitchen. "Alice what's up, who was that on the phone?"

"No-one," snapped Alice, "Wrong number."

"Come on, it didn't sound like a wrong number, is someone harassing you? Is it a client?"

"Felix, I've just told you, it was a wrong number. Now can you just forget it please?"

"Well from the sounds of it, this isn't the first time they've called? Who does this person think you are then?"

"For FUCK'S sake Felix, I said leave it!" Alice screamed glaring at him "It's got nothing to do with you."

Felix gaped at her. She had really lost control, looking more like a snared animal than the sophisticated professional vet. "Alice," he said softly, "It's got everything to do with me. I'm your partner, your friend, we live together, if you have a problem, then I have a problem too. Come on, we can share anything."

"Don't be so fucking ridiculous Felix, you are not my intellectual equal and couldn't possibly understand - anyway, I've told you it was a wrong number." She changed tack, suddenly seeing the shock on Felix's face as he reeled back at the harsh words and rapidly managed to compose herself. "Really darling, just a wrong number. Nothing to worry about - the man was just rather insistent and rude that's all. Come on, I'm sorry, I shouldn't have shouted at you, or Fiver." She reached out with both hands and shrugged her shoulders. "Shall I run us a bath?"

Felix was sure there'd been more to the call than she was letting on, but short of saying she was a liar, what could he do? Worse still, the whole scene had highlighted the fraying holes in their relationship which were rapidly developing into sodding great chasms. He took her in his arms as gently as a fragile ornament, and her body felt more rigid than a statue under his touch. Things were going terribly wrong between them, tumbling out of his control and there seemed to be bugger all he could do about it.

Aiden was ecstatic, they had exchanged! In his usual ballsy fashion he rang Alan, bulldozing his instructions to submit the detailed plans and push the local council into action to make sure they would go before the next planning meeting; meanwhile they'd begin with the alterations on the barn conversions and demanding he get his arse into gear. He slammed down the phone, immediately redialled Farouk and left a message with his PA to say they were in business and asking him to call back, and then sprawled back in his chair with his feet on his desk, a self-satisfied expression plastered over his face. Chrissie defiantly ignored him, determinedly concentrating on her computer screen, tapping away furiously at the keyboard.

Aiden glanced over amused. She'd been tetchy for days, although he'd been the same, but now they'd exchanged, he felt fantastic and moreover, bloody horny. He flipped a rubber band in her direction, hitting his target bang on.

"Ouch! That hurt!" grumbled Chrissie, rubbing her cheek, "Grow up, can't you?"

Aiden laughed "Hey what's up with you sugar plum?"

"You know what's up," Chrissie snapped, "I'll have to watch my back more than ever now."

"Don't be stupid. Roxy doesn't *know* anything. She's just fishing, hoping you'll crack. Come on, let's celebrate. We've been waiting for this day for weeks." He strolled over to her desk, standing behind her, ostensibly to look at the screen and put his hands on her shoulders, kneading her tense neck muscles with his thumbs "Relax, Chrissie, over the next few months it's gonna be hard to find much time to enjoy ourselves, let's take the time when we can eh?"

Chrissie shook him off. "It's alright for you Aiden, she might not actually have any proof, but she suspects, and that's enough. You know and I know what that means. I just want to keep my head down - and keep my job. This project is going to take a lot of organising and neither of us can afford to fuck it up, especially with all the bloody camera crews sniffing around."

Aiden sighed, "You used to be such fun Chrissie, where's your sense of adventure?"

"Lining up in the job centre doesn't cut it for me Aiden," growled Chrissie, "and when the shit hits you smack in the face, that's where I'd be."

"She'll back off once the cameras start rolling sweetie," Aiden sneered, "you know she will."

"Whatever, right now I'm taking no chances."

"Sure I can't persuade you?" He leant down and ran his lips along the edge of her neck, running his tongue softly against her ear, "I know just how you like it."

Chrissie squirmed and sighed, enjoying the moment and then shrugged him off "No, behave Aiden, I mean it."

"Sure?" said Aiden softly into her ear, his hand straying down inside her blouse "Who's to know?"

As Chrissie turned her head to object, his lips moved from her ear to her mouth, kissing her deeply. His fingers stroking the tips of her nipples, he could feel her body melting into his and he knew he was winning. He swung the chair round and drew her towards him, unzipping her skirt so that it dropped to the floor.

"Suspenders and stockings so turn me on," he murmured appraising her, whilst he pulled off her blouse and unhooked her bra, "and you have such fine tits."

"You are so bad," gasped Chrissie, clearly gagging for him, "and I was trying to be so strong."

"Chrissie, darling stop panicking," smiled Aiden, "carpe diem doll."

Twenty minutes later, following a hot and sweaty session on the desk, Chrissie was getting dressed and feeling annoyed with herself. Against her better judgement she had once again allowed Aiden, of the multi-talented silver tongue, to coerce her into a shagathon, and what was worse, this time in the bloody office. That he was a sexual genius was in no doubt, as the throbbing between her legs was testament, but it had to stop. She glared at him from underneath her hair. Sexually satiated, he was slurping champagne and talking dramatically on the phone to Farouk, dreaming up schedules and storyboards and organising a camera crew to come over to mock up the '*exchange moment*'. So much for pillow talk, she thought angrily, if Farouk only knew. She had to get a hold of herself, she thought bitterly. At least with the mill project, she would have the chance to get away into the countryside and wouldn't be quite so much at his beck and call.

Whilst Aiden was treating himself to a canter on Chrissie, Roxy was struggling to come to grips with riding a bizarre mechanical horse. Suzanne had sourced the terrifying equine simulator which, whilst it might never turn Roxy into the next Olympian, she did believe it would give her a head start when it came to riding the real thing. Unbelievably, the erotically named *Equisator* was conveniently located in Watford at a private equestrian yard, and Suzanne had booked Roxy in for a gruelling groin busting course of 6 weeks, which included sessions with a decent trainer and, more importantly, a discreet one. They were more than accommodating to fit her in around her schedule and, whilst it wasn't cheap or easy, Roxy reasoned, it had to be worthwhile even if it was killing her. Driving away after a particularly gruelling two hours on Annie the Equine, feeling as though her thighs were about to spontaneously combust, Roxy headed towards Fittlebury in the nippy, little, black

Mini Cooper S she used to covertly avoid the Paparazzi. She dragged off the wig she adopted as part of her disguise, and shook out her hair, and edged out into the traffic-congested M25. It was the normal car park of choked vehicles and she had barely covered 100 yards before she slithered to a halt. Fuming, she tapped her red talons on the black leather steering wheel. *Fuck* she thought, and flexed her aching shoulders back in the cramped seat of the mini and resigned herself to a long wait. It had been a curious few weeks. In between her habitual manic diary, she'd finally managed to coerce Max into firming up a lunch date, and smarted at the stiff initial small talk when they'd met at the ghastly steak house. Several glasses of indifferent wine later on her part, she'd engineered the conversation around to herself, casting out intriguing little snippets about the mill project. To her frustration, he'd not even nibbled her provocative bait, and whereas he'd normally be probing keenly for more information, his glazed expression made her think he was scarcely listening let alone actually seeing her sitting across the table. At first, his lack of interest made her wonder if it had anything to do with Anna, but Roxy had never seen him like this. There'd always been this effervescent flash between them, each igniting the other's aura, but, that day, it'd felt like a sad deflated soufflé. He was being polite in the extreme but she knew him well enough to know that it was just lip service, and lurking beneath the patina he was bored and distracted. Roxy, irritated at not being the centre of his attention, but smart enough to know she was backing a loser, flirtingly steered him to talk about himself, delving into what he'd been up to and expecting to be bored shitless. At first it had been like drawing teeth, but Roxy was nothing if not tenacious, and when he said that he'd been going racing a lot and she clocked the gleam in his eye. *Bing* she knew - Max was savouring the smell of serious money. He'd always loved the cut and thrust of living on the edge and gambling was in his blood, but he'd finally admitted racing was something else. The sport of kings was aptly named, it seemed. As he talked and she heard the animation in his voice, she felt herself relaxing. The sparkle fizzed back between them like an opened bottle of champagne that turned out to be drinkable after all, and he hadn't mentioned Anna once. He'd even suggested she go with him to the races and fluttering her lashes at him, she'd agreed. Roxy smiled to herself as she sat in the traffic jam, Max was back on board, but she still had a sneaking feeling that there was something else on his mind but she'd find out what that was - she always did. Meanwhile, a day at the races was another great photo opportunity; but with the exchanging of contracts on the mill, the *Rox-Aid* TV show, and the organisation of the conversion and opening by Christmas, her life over the next few months was going to be frantic and above all lucrative. Still, she had a good team working for her now. Suzanne had pulled her finger out since the *Gallomania* cock up and Roxy had given her a hefty bonus for her effort with this mechanical horse. As for Aiden's mob, she smiled to herself as she remembered how Chrissie's superior face had blanched white that day at the mill. Smug fucking bitch. Still, she was useful to Aiden as a PA and would be more so until the conversion was over, then Roxy would deal with her, that's if Aiden hadn't tired of her - until then he could have his fun. She pondered her mission ahead as she sat in the slow moving traffic, her little adventure could prove rather delicious – dalliance wasn't exclusively Aiden's after all. With these steamy contemplations rocketing around in her brain, the tedium of queuing was to an extent alleviated and before she knew it, the blue motorway signs for Gatwick loomed ahead. Rapidly indicating and darting off, she took the road towards Horsham, finally threading down the country lanes towards Fittlebury.

CHAPTER 32

Hattie's morning had passed well so far. When she arrived back from an invigorating hack with the fit and sparky Rambler, she could see the new girl, Kylie, beavering away with the barrow and fork. She and Leo had agreed that, for the first few mornings, one or other of them would work side by side with her until she'd settled in, and Leo had agreed to do the first shift. It had been a real treat to leave the shit-shovelling to someone else and, for once, not be tearing around like a demented hamster on a wheel. She sponged off the barely sweating Rambler, threw on his fly sheet and dragged him out to the paddock. It was on her way back, that she noticed flames leaping from Felix's back garden. Great curls of black smoke and flakes of ash were floating towards the cottage. She knew that both Felix and Seb were out teaching clients and threw her hands up to her face in panic - not sure what she should do first. The whole place might go up at any moment and, dreading what she might find she careered over to the cottage. She drew up short by the garden fence gasping for breath, her hand on her mobile ready to ring for the fire brigade. The smoke was lessening but little bits of ash were still fluttering about in the air, catching on her hair and face, and she could make out a figure standing in the garden. Hattie's heart was thumping – who was it? As the smoke drifted further away, clearing her vision, to her immense relief she saw that it was Alice. She was standing with her back to the fence hurling reams of paperwork into a bonfire she'd made in a makeshift brazier.

"Thank God - it's you Alice," wheezed Hattie, bending over double, panting and clutching her sides, "I was just about to dial 999."

Alice whirled round angrily, her blonde hair whipping around her furious face "Is there no bloody privacy in this fucking place? What the hell do you want?"

Hattie straightened up surprised and not at all clear why Alice was so irate, "Sorry, I didn't mean to give you a fright. I thought there was a fire and I knew Felix was out, I just assumed you were too."

"Well now you know I'm not," snapped Alice, "I was just burning some old rubbish that's all. Or am I not allowed to do that without running it by you now? You know something Hattie, why can't you just butt out of our lives. Felix and I get sick of you."

"I'm sorry, I didn't mean to intrude," choked out Hattie, feeling like she'd been kicked in the guts, "it was a genuine mistake. I'll leave you to it then ..." she finished lamely.

Alice didn't bother to reply, and pointedly turned her back away to stoke the smouldering fire with a stick. Hattie gaped at her, wincing at Alice's cruel words and slunk pathetically like a whipped puppy back towards the stables feeling hurt and stupid. Did they really get sick of her? That was hardly fair she never went over to their cottage? Even more odd, was she was definitely sure she'd seen Alice driving out this morning, and she didn't normally come back home during the daytime, so how was she to know she's come home. Oh well, it was none of her business what she did, but there really was no need to be so bloody rude.

Back in the yard, Leo and Kylie had finished mucking out and were just brewing up when Hattie came back.

"You were a long time," said Leo concerned, "No problems were there?"

"Nope," Hattie replied, giving him a *'I'll tell you later'* look, "Just checking the troughs." She turned to Kylie, "How have you got on, not killed you off has he?" she laughed.

"Of course not, it'd take more than six boxes to do that," Kylie responded, a tad of Siberia in her tone, "leastways I'm quicker than you at turning horses out."

Ouch, thought Hattie, wondering what she had done to everyone this morning to make them so snappy. "Well there's a relief then," she smiled sweetly at Kylie, "at least we'll get our money's worth with you, especially as you're paid by the hour."

Kylie was just about to reply when Seb breezed in, pushing an indignant Fiver out of the armchair. "Morning all, make me a cuppa Kylie there's a duck – I'm bushed, that bloody Fiona Robinson is hell personified to teach."

Leo laughed, "Come on don't be a bitch, that's not like you to give up."

"I'm beginning to lose the will to live. She's got the loveliest horse, cost a small fortune, and she can't ride one side of it. I can cope with that, I try to teach her – I have inordinate patience, let me tell you." Seb moaned theatrically, flinging his arms out to his audience "then she bleats on about what she's read in this book and that, and promptly socks the horse in the gob, and kicks it in the ribs every five seconds. She just doesn't listen, it makes me cross – poor bloody thing."

Hattie turned away to stifle a giggle and caught sight of Kylie's gleeful face as she filled the kettle, she'd clearly been earwigging Seb's every rash syllable. She smiled kindly over at her. "Just to say Kylie that, of course, anything we talk about remains entre nous, eh boys?"

Seb looked up surprised, "Yes, naturally, I'm being totally indiscreet of course, and if I'm honest, unkind. We can't all be naturally gifted."

"I can assure you that I won't say a word," declared Kylie hotly, "Now Seb, do you take sugar in your tea?"

"Three please and not too strong. Tell me how's your first day been?"

"Fine thank you. Leo showed me the ropes and we mucked them all out, haynets, feeds, the works, whilst Hattie managed to ride one." Kylie glanced spitefully at Hattie, hoping to drop her in the shit for not pulling her weight.

"Excellent, well done, as you're so quick you won't be needing any help tomorrow then," said Seb, picking up the Horse & Hound and flicking through the pages, "Oh look! Here's a picture of me winning at the Regionals!"

Kylie glared across at Hattie as she craned over the magazine to look at the photo, "I thought Hattie was supposed to be mucking out tomorrow," she asked, "Leo said …"

Seb looked up, irritated at the interruption. "But you were so quick my dear, Leo and Hattie have horses to ride. I'm sure Hattie will give you a hand if you need it though - won't you Hats?"

"No problem at all," smiled Hattie. Seb was so clever in his airy, fairy way. He had Kylie's number straight away, and she was grateful to him. "I'm happy to help."

"Right, that's settled then, Kylie. If you need help whilst you're getting used to us either Leo or Hattie will oblige," he shifted his attention back to the magazine, "I think they could have got a better photo than this don't you? My leg position looks simply dreadful."

"It looks perfect as well you know Seb – you're just after compliments. I'm going to take Doris out for a hack. You coming with me Hattie?" asked Leo, straightening up "Who are you riding now Seb?"

"Be a doll and chuck some tack on Delaney for me will you, babycakes, and I'll be out in five."

"Okay but don't get your nose in the nag and dog and forget will you?" warned Leo, "You know what you're like."

"I won't - bugger off you two," laughed Seb, "I'll be out when I've finished my tea."

Once the other two had gone, Kylie sidled up to Seb, propping herself on the edge of the armchair. "I don't want to cause any trouble, but Hattie really didn't do much this morning you know. She only rode one horse and was gone for ages too when she turned it out. She left Leo and I pretty much to do everything."

Seb swivelled round in his chair and smiled at her, steepling his fingertips together and absorbing every minute part of her face. "Thank you so much for telling me Kylie," he said sincerely, "I really appreciate it. You never know what happens when your back's turned do you?"

Kylie's face glowed with pleasure. "Well" she smirked "I thought you ought to know, I'm so glad I told you now, she obviously doesn't pull her weight when you and Felix aren't about."

"Obviously not," said Seb intrigued, "Just keep an eye on things and keep me posted will you? One bad apple and all that …"

"Absolutely. I'll keep my eye on things." Kylie tapped the side of her nose "Don't worry nothing much gets past me."

"I'll bet it doesn't," said Seb, "Well I'd better go and ride Delaney and perhaps as the mucking out is finished you could clean some tack?"

"Delighted," simpered Kylie, watching him go and smiling to herself.

Leo and Hattie were striding out along the estate tracks, heading towards the mill. Doris loved hacking, it was something that they hadn't been able to enjoy at the previous yard owing to the traffic, but here, in Fittlebury, and on the estate, it was much safer, and all of Seb's horses were feeling the benefit. Hattie's day was not improving as the feisty Jacks was testing her sanity and patience as he spooked at imaginary dragons under every blade of grass.

"Stop grumbling Hats," Leo laughed. "He's just a bit fresh."

"It's alright for you on dozy Doris. He's being a right arse," Hattie complained, trying to shoulder in past a stack of fencing stakes, "it beats me how Felix ever gets him round the cross country."

"It's different then I suppose, his blood's up and he's galloping full pelt."

"Fancy a gallop do you?" Hattie tested, knowing full well Seb would have a nervous breakdown if Doris so much as trotted on the road "Come on, or are you a chicken?"

"I would if I could, but not on these precious legs," laughed Leo, "It always amazes me how much your eventers put up with."

"Oi cheeky - we're careful too – I wouldn't thrash around on the concrete either."

"Only teasing sweetie, I know how cautious you are. What's up? You're being uber sensitive?"

"Humph. That bloody Kylie pissed me off a bit. She tried to make out I hadn't done anything all morning."

"Oh take no notice, Hats, she obviously doesn't like women. Seb took no notice did he, and more to the point you don't work for Seb anyway do you?"

"No, I don't, which obviously the catty Kylie doesn't realise, but supposing she'd said it to Felix."

"Don't be stupid, Felix knows how hard you work. We all work hard come to that. We're a team – Kylie's just the hired help. Give her a bit of a chance, she was alright with me this morning."

"She would be. I don't think she plans on remaining the mucker outer, she's setting her sights higher than that. I think I need to watch my back."

"Don't be so melodramatic!" laughed Leo. "Honestly Hattie, you do make me laugh. Felix thinks the world of you, there's not any kind of comparison."

"Oh perhaps I am over reacting," Hattie sighed, "It's just the vibes I'm getting that's all. Anyway I've got to work with her tomorrow so I'd better pull myself together. She didn't like it when Seb suggested she mucked out on her own did she?"

"No!" Leo guffawed, making the usually placid Doris jump, "Seb is funny isn't he?"

"Yes, he makes out he's so camp and outrageous, but I think he knows exactly what's going on."

"You'd better believe it, he's nobody's fool."

They turned up the path towards the mill, intending to skirt alongside the ruins and nip in through the woodland behind their cottage and head back towards the yard along the concrete track. They reached the five bar gate behind the barns and ambled along the weed strewn drive towards the mill pond. The sombre ruins stood ahead like the set of a sinister horror movie, with the water lapping gently against the rotting mill wheel as a rat dived behind the reeds.

"This place gives me the creeps," said Hattie.

"Me too," agreed Leo, "rumour has it that two blokes died in that pond."

"It's true, they did - it was a terrible business. Happened last year. One was a nutty gardener who worked for the Parker-Smythes, but he died saving Jennifer and her step-daughter, who'd been kidnapped by the other guy. It was the talk of the county at the time."

"I remember reading about it in the papers," said Leo, "wasn't a girl murdered too?"

"Yes, by the kidnapper, but not here. She used to be the groom for the Parker-Smythes. She walked out, or got the sack or something, and helped the kidnapper with inside information about the family, and then he killed her. Used cocaine laced with strychnine."

"It's the kind of thing you'd only read about," sighed Leo, "it must have been planned well."

"It was - they reckon months in advance. Patrick, our farrier - he was quite the hero at the time you know, loves talking about it. He saw the kidnappers casing the village, so did Mrs Gupta in the shop and Chloe. But Patrick says the bloke always had an accomplice with him, a blonde haired girl. Very attractive; had a tattoo on her shoulder and called Laura that was all they knew about her. She completely disappeared when the police raided the kidnapper's flat and was never found apparently."

"Blimey! What a story."

"Well, as I said, talk to Patrick, he knows all about it. He was the one who rescued Jennifer and Jessica, and broke his leg in the process."

"I wondered why he always walked with a limp."

"Oh don't purleese – you'll never hear the last of it, he said it's ruined his dancing career!" laughed Hattie.

"I wonder what happened to the girl though," pondered Leo, "how come she was never caught?"

"Dunno. As far as I know she wasn't actually involved in the kidnapping, only in the planning and tricking the hunt sabs into creating a diversion. She was in London at the time, I think, and when the police found out where she was, she'd scarpered."

"Intriguing!"

"Horrible when you think about it, all the time skulking around here with a maniac and scheming. Mind you, I doubt she'd ever show her face around here again - she'd be long gone, probably abroad. The police looked for her for months."

"No, you're right there babe." Leo pulled a face, pulling up Doris and pointing "Hang on, what's that over there?"

"Oh for God's sake Leo, stop mucking about," laughed Hattie, then stopped grinning when she saw a dark shadow moving amongst the ruins at the back of the mill. "Christ! What is it?"

They both gawped open mouthed. The horses, sensing their agitation, started fidgeting. Jacks was fairly dancing on the spot, leaping and prancing. Doris picked up on the tension and started to emulate him. If the riders had not been so intent on watching the mysterious figure they would have realised they were performing the most perfect pas de deux. But they were oblivious, petrified by the moving shadow.

"Hi you two," called Mark from the ruins, "you look terrified – what's up?"

"Mark, you scared us half to death! We'd been talking of what happened here last year, spooked ourselves silly and then we saw this shadow in the ruins!" laughed Leo "Bloody hell, what a pair of idiots."

"Sorry to disappoint you, it was only me," grinned Mark, "another disappointment too, contracts were exchanged today, so no more riding through here now, I'm afraid."

"Crikey, does that mean *'those who cannot be mentioned'* have actually bought the place?" asked Hattie, "and… are we allowed to mention them now?"

"Yes to the first, Hattie, and I suppose no reason why it all has to be kept secret now it's all been finalised. I suspect the papers will be onto it soon anyway."

"We'll be under siege – Seb'll be in his element."

"Rather you than me," said Mark drolly, "Laundry Cottage will be under the spotlight, no doubt, as it's so close to the mill, but I expect you'll cope."

"Don't," groaned Hattie, "that woman's a nightmare by all accounts."

"Not counting the entourage she'll bring with her," agreed Mark, "but it was a good sale as far as the estate is concerned, and this place has a horrible history as you know, so good riddance. Let the others know will you - no more riding through here."

"We will Mark, we'd better move on, the horses are getting a bit restless."

"See you then," he called to their retreating backs, as they jogged past the ruins and away into the woodland beyond.

"Well things are going to hot up around here then!" exclaimed Leo, "It's finally happened. Celebrity neighbours, Seb'll wet himself when I tell him."

Hattie looked dubiously at the excited expression on his face and just hoped they didn't get too hot to handle.

CHAPTER 33

"**Hey, I thought** you were never coming back!" called Paulene, the Practice Manager, as Alice crashed through the surgery door like a tornado. "You've been out for ages, didn't you get my voice mails?"

"For Christ's sake Paulene, get off my case will you? No I didn't, I've had a terrible day," snapped Alice, shooting her a poisonous look. "What did you want?"

"Okay, okay - no need to bite my head off. What's rattled your cage? You're not the only one that's busy you know," grumbled Paulene. "Anyway Oli's gone on the call now."

"Well crisis over then," said Alice tartly stomping off into the back office and rattling the door on its hinges behind her, leaving Paulene and Caitlin exchanging horrified expressions.

"B'Jesus" murmured Caitlin in her soft husky Irish lilt, exaggeratedly raising her eyebrows and toying with her biro thoughtfully, "She's in a bait."

"Has been for ages," said Paulene irritated. "Bring back the sunny natured Alice from Oz of six months ago. She's been even more bad tempered over the last week."

"Things not good with her and Felix, d' you think now?" speculated Caitlin, "I've always thought they were so great together."

"No idea, but if she speaks to him like she speaks to us, I shouldn't think so," scoffed Paulene, "There's really no need for it, she's got right up her own arse, and she never used to be like that."

"Oh Paulene, she's just over tired I expect," said Caitlin, "You know how 'tis now."

Paulene grinned, "You're too nice Caitlin, but you could be right, we're all on top of each other in this little place which doesn't help. We need more space. If only we could find some bigger premises and set up the diagnostic centre like we planned last year. I know Andrew doesn't want to think about it anymore, but you know how excited he was when they were thinking of expanding and buying up the mill."

Caitlin pushed back her chair and sighed, "I know Paulene, he was full of plans so he was, but since my accident and the fire he's lost his mojo as far as that's concerned. But you're right, 'tis time to rekindle it."

"Well, if anyone can reawaken his ideas, you can," Paulene smiled, thinking back to last year when she had been half in love with Andrew herself, and he'd been married to his first bitch of a wife, Julia, and before anyone knew he'd got together with Caitlin. "Trouble is, where'd you start? The mill's out of the question and properties aren't easy to find around here."

"Hmm – where indeed? Have to get my thinking cap on, now my thinking cap works again that is," laughed Caitlin, who had virtually recovered since she'd been attacked. "There must be somewhere begging for conversion."

"Good luck with looking then, 'cos I'm buggered if I can think of anywhere."

"There's a gauntlet, if ever there was one, now," mused Caitlin, "but first I'll have to weave a little magic on Andrew."

Paulene leant both elbows on the desk and looked at Caitlin gently. "I think he's well and truly under your spell already and I think it's lovely."

"Aw thanks Paulene," said Caitlin coyly, "he's a wonderful man, and I'm lucky to have him, so I am."

"You're both lucky," grinned Paulene, "but that doesn't get us any nearer finding a new diagnostic centre."

Before Caitlin could answer, Alice stomped back out from her office, her face blacker than a double espresso and just as bitter.

"When you two have finished gossiping, do you know where the drugs requisition book is?"

"Where it normally is," said Paulene briskly, "have you looked properly?"

"Don't get smart with me Paulene. If I hadn't looked, I wouldn't be asking, would I?"

"Well, if it's not there you must have mislaid it Alice," said Paulene dismissively, "I have no idea where it is."

"Well Paulene, I suggest you get off your fat arse and look for it, that's what you're paid for after all," responded Alice hotly, "instead of talking about me behind my back."

Caitlin interrupted, "we weren't talking about you Alice, and I think you're being rather unfair."

Alice spun round to glare at Caitlin, "I'm going out on calls, just find the book."

She barged out the front door in fury, letting it crash shut behind her. Caitlin and Paulene sat gaping after her, as dazed by her outburst as though they had been zapped by a stun gun.

The black Mini Cooper S cruised along the lanes, finally slithering to a stop alongside two tall, stone pillars topped with moss covered, snarling lions. Roxy gazed between the ornate, iron gates which were fixed open, speedily reversed up a bit and crawled down the long drive towards the impressive Tudor house in the distance. She whistled under her breath at the huge, rambling place, with its myriads of ivy and creepers clinging to the walls and towering chimneys. The drive forked and she wound around to the back of the house and beyond to the right, where she could see the rooftops of the old stables in the distance. With one hand, she fluffed up her hair, and squirted on some perfume.

If Kylie inferred earlier that Hattie had been shirking in the morning she should've seen her now. She was sweeping the yard like a thing possessed, her hair piled high in a wild topknot twirled dizzily with the effort, whilst the sweat was running down her back soaking through her tee-shirt. A throaty *vroom* from a racy engine made her pause and she looked up curiously as a strange car rumbled towards her over the cobbles. Leaning her broom against the stable wall, she walked towards it enquiringly, trying to peer in through the tinted windows. As she approached the door swung open and Roxy stepped out. Hattie's mouth must have hung open like a car ferry ramp and all she could do was to gape like a half-wit.

Roxy, who was used to such slavish adoration, smiled sweetly, "Hi, we've met before, you were out riding with Felix. I'm Roxy Le Feuvre. I don't suppose he's about is he?"

Hattie, inordinately flattered that Roxy had remembered her, managed to stammer out that he was, and to follow her up to the arena where he was riding one of the young horses. She turned on her heel, supremely conscious of the sticky tee-shirt and her dishevelled appearance, and couldn't find a word to say as they walked up the dusty track to the school. Roxy was amused; these gawky dull girls were always so tongue tied around her, although she could be useful, so it might be worth making a little effort with some small talk.

"What's your name?"

"Umm, I'm called Hattie," said Hattie dimly, "I work for Felix, and he runs the yard and sublets a few boxes to a dressage rider called Seb, and his lad Leo. We share a mucker-outer called Kylie."

"Right. Yeah, I've met Seb," said Roxy, looking around at the set-up. "Nice place."

"It is," agreed Hattie, immediately falling into silence, not knowing what else to say, wondering what the hell she wanted, and wishing desperately that she didn't look quite so awful.

As they got nearer to the school Roxy suddenly clutched

Hattie's arm, "For fuck's sake, what's that?"

Hattie glanced ahead. Hero had lumbered upright from where he had been dozing, his massive bulk stood menacingly in the middle of the track, his pale unblinking eyes staring at them. Fiver joined him, the hackles on his back slicked up as though he'd been using some uber bizarre hair gel and he was growling like a demented lion. Hattie laughed "Oh that's only the dogs, they're cool, don't worry."

Roxy laughed nervously, "Little and large. Quite a team."

The noise had made the boys look up and Felix ingenuously came over to the gate calling out to Roxy, "Hey this is a surprise!"

Roxy batted her eyelashes, jutting out her hips like she was posing for a page three spread, "Just thought I'd drop by. We've exchanged contracts, we're gonna be neighbours."

"Congratulations," said Seb, mirroring Roxy's sexy posture, a twinkle in his eyes, "How long before you move in?"

"Oh ages yet, the whole place has to be gutted, and the renovations are gonna be part of a TV series, which is actually why I need to talk to you boys."

"Really? Why's that then?" asked Seb, flushing excitedly, relishing the thought of featuring on the box. "Of course anything we can do to help – eh Felix?"

Felix smiled, taking in her lithe snaky hips and full breasts "Naturally we'll do what we can, but what did you have in mind?"

Roxy looked up from under her lashes, licking her lips provocatively, "What I had in mind is one thing ..." she said softly "but first things first, how about a cup of tea?"

"Sure," replied Felix easily, "we can go back to the yard, we've more or less finished here." He nodded to Seb, but not before Hattie had clocked the electricity fizzing between him and Roxy.

Seb swung open the gate and they trooped indolently back to the yard with the dogs trotting behind them, their tongues lolling out like pink slippers dripping with jewelled saliva. Roxy talked enthusiastically about their plans for the renovations and the filming and said she wanted them to be part of it. Hattie, trailing a little behind the sycophantic boys, doubting that she'd be included in Roxy's schemes was curious to know what it was that she really wanted. Judging by the way she looked at Felix, his meat was to be on her plate as an entrée, but what was on offer for the main course? She felt a sting of jealousy and bitter anger as she watched him flirting like a moron with this silicone implanted bimbo and bent down to stroke the dogs in confusion.

"Hurry up Hats," called Seb, waiting for her. "Isn't it exciting?"

"I suppose so," mumbled Hattie, "Has she said what she wants?"

"No, not yet, but if you'll be a sweetie and take the horse, Felix and I can find out. Intriguing isn't it?"

"Definitely," said Hattie miserably, wondering how this day could get any worse "I'll make myself scarce then."

"Thanks doll, perfect" laughed Seb carelessly, dashing off to catch up with the others in case he missed anything.

Alice worked like a demented demon all day to catch up for her little detour that day. Since the phone calls had started, she'd felt so stressed she could hardly think straight. God, how had she gotten herself into this mess, and how had they found her? She pulled into the car park in High Ridge Woods and hid the car behind the trees, turning off the engine. She needed time to think. Shoving her head back against the seat, she stretched her body back, and then threw her face forward into her hands, clasping her cheeks between her hands. How had this happened? She had been so careful to cover her tracks, to leave Australia so that she could not be traced, and yet they had found her. Or had they? The phone calls were veiled, the man had been fishing for information and she had denied everything. Trust Felix to have come in when he did, he'd nearly caught her, but she had managed to brazen it out, and then today when Hattie had seen her with the bonfire. There was no evidence now, it was all gone. If it came to light, she would deny everything. But everyone seemed to be on her case, and she was so tense. If only she hadn't been so stupid, but she thought she was untouchable. No-one was immune she thought bitterly, there was always a payback day, but not for her, not if she could help it. So what if she'd been short with Hattie and those silly bitches in the office, they'd just have to get over themselves, and so would Felix for that matter. There was more than what they thought of her at stake here.

She thought back to the day it had all started. At the time, she'd been a junior vet at a smart equine hospital and, to her conceited annoyance, was given the mundane work. She was heavily in debt after vet school, especially having taken several extra-curricular courses; she worked long hours, had just come out of a failed relationship, and didn't have many friends. Life should have been good, but it wasn't. One day she was asked to take on the role of duty vet at the local race track. She had delightedly accepted, believing this to be a big accolade from the partners and a measure of their esteem. She soon realised that, far from being glamorous, it was dull work taking the blood and urine samples. The bloke who'd approached her had called himself Fred, a weasel of a man with the ubiquitous flat cap and corduroy trousers. He'd said she could earn herself a shed load of money if she was interested. She wasn't, she'd told him loftily and he'd drifted away, melting into the throngs of trainers and grooms who all looked pretty similar to her. Afterwards though, in her sad, lonely flat when she was dog tired, scooping up a bowl of tinned soup, she'd thought about what he'd said and wondered if she'd dismissed him too hastily. A few weeks later, he sidled up to her again, with a smirking smile and a nod in her direction, and it was tacitly agreed. It was so easy. Nothing to it really, just swapping the odd few samples and abruptly life at the track had taken on a different meaning. Within six months she had paid off her debts and then decided she'd had enough, saying she wasn't going to be a party to it anymore, but Fred was not so easily deterred. He delightedly played tape recordings of their conversations and showed her photographs of her handling the rigged samples. She'd had no alternative but to carry on, terrified that she'd be found out. She'd struggled through another few months and, to her enormous relief the veterinary partners had unexpectedly replaced her with another junior colleague and she was called back to base at the equine hospital. At first she'd thought they'd become suspicious of her, but it seemed they were promoting her and she was overwhelmed with pathetic relief. She ran her hands through her hair - how could she have been so stupid to have believed it would end there? As the weeks passed she relaxed and settled down to her work again, until one night she'd come home after a gruelling operation on a colic to find a dead cat on her doorstep. As she stooped down to pick it up, she remembered to her horror, to find its throat had been slashed, the blood still sticky and warm trickling onto the mat. There was no further contact until three weeks later when Fred was waiting for her. This time they wanted drugs, Ketamine in particular, and by this time she knew there was no way she could get out of their clutches. She began to make her plans for escape, supplying the drugs to keep them quiet and searching for jobs abroad. But the pressure was piling on with their demands becoming more insistent, she couldn't afford to wait any longer and making the urgent excuse of a sick relative in England to her colleagues, she jumped on a plane and left, finally taking the job in Fittlebury. Now it seemed her past had caught up with her. This morning she'd burned all past references of her work in the veterinary hospital, and any other incriminating things she had – but would it be enough? Fucking Hattie, she was so nosy, had she seen anything? As for Paulene, she wouldn't put it past her to go snooping. Meanwhile, every time her phone rang her body jerked like a puppet on a string and her mind wasn't in a much better place. What the hell was she going to do?

CHAPTER 34

Max had steeled himself to go in this time. His driver had cruised past the house at least five times and, by now, the ostentatious car was beginning to draw attention in the tedious street of identical houses lined row upon row on either side. Max tapped on the driver's shoulder and ordered him to stop and wait outside. The driver slid to a halt in the next available space between the parked cars and deferentially opened the rear door, wondering, once again, what the hell they were doing here. It was the third time Max had asked him to drive to this dump. Any thought of asking was immediately quelled as his governor strode back down the street without a backward glance. There was nothing he could do but wait – his whole life was spent waiting for him after all.

Max's emotions were in chaos. This was the moment he'd been anticipating for months, years even, and suddenly here he was, after all the angst, about to come face to face with her. Would she have changed? Would she remember him? Would she just shut the door in his face? It wasn't too late to run. But it was, he had to do this, for his own self, he had to know.

Number 43 was no different from the rest of the houses. A tiny front garden with some dusty shrubs, and a half-glazed front door which would need a lick of paint fairly soon. A bay window to one side had net curtains, and he half expected them to twitch with curiosity as he rapped on the door, but they didn't move. Whoever was inside obviously hadn't seen him arrive, although he was pretty sure there had been plenty of gleeful nosiness from others in the street. Now the moment had arrived he waited edgily on the doorstep. He would be inordinately frustrated to find there was nobody at home. He rapped again, his nerves overcoming his patience, and then he could hear shuffling from inside.

"Who is it?" A woman's voice called from behind the door, "We don't want to buy anything and we're not interested in any religious mumbo jumbo."

"I'm not selling anything," Max called back quietly, "and it's not about God, it's about Jilly."

There was no response to his answer, so he tried again, hissing through the door "Please, I'm not here to cause any trouble, I just need to talk to Jilly. I was a friend of hers from years ago, I'm just trying to find her."

Max heard the rattle of chain being pushed aside, and a lock being undone. The door eased open a little and a woman's face peeped around the edge, "Jilly you say? Who are you?"

"I was a friend of hers when she worked in London. I haven't seen her for years, and I just wanted to catch up with her, find out how she was ..." Max faltered. "We used to go out together for a while."

The woman sized Max up and down and reluctantly pulled back the door. "You'd better come in," she said, calling over her shoulder to someone behind her, "Eric, put the kettle on, we've got company."

Max stepped awkwardly into the immaculately tidy hallway and followed her retreating back down the passage towards the kitchen. A wiry, tall man, his grey hair thinning on top, was standing with his back to them, filling a kettle from the sink. He turned to stare at them as they came in, and Max felt a pang of hope as he caught a glimpse of Jilly in the man's eyes, but as he blinked it was gone.

"I'm sorry to disturb you" Max apologised, "I've been trying to trace Jilly. I knew her from London. We were close friends at one time and this was her last known address. Are you her parents?"

"Were her parents," corrected the man dryly, "she died near on 20 years ago."

Max clutched the back of the kitchen door. Whatever he was expecting, it wasn't this. He didn't know what to say, finally muttering, "I'm so sorry, I wouldn't have dreamt of coming and opening up old wounds like this. I had no idea."

"Margaret, get the lad a chair and sit yourself down while I make the tea, I can see it's been a shock. It were a long time ago," he mumbled, turning back to the sink.

The woman took off her apron and hung it on a hook behind the door. She smiled weakly at Max, "You weren't to know. We've no other children, you see, and we were devastated at the time, and it's not that we don't think of her every day, but there was the baby and we had to do our duty."

"The baby?" asked Max surprised, "I'd no idea there was a baby."

The woman looked surprised. "You said you knew our Jilly from London didn't you? She came home because she was pregnant. Didn't you know? She died a few weeks after giving birth, got septicaemia. There was nothing that could be done. She was dead within days, and we were left to bring up the child."

Max put his head in his hands, absorbing all the implications. There was a child. He mentally did the calculations, any child must have been his, it couldn't have been anyone else's. He looked at the weary couple setting out the tea things as though he was some revered guest, rather than some bastard who'd abandoned their only daughter to her fate. They'd struggled to bring up their only grandchild whilst he feathered his own nest, and he knew that this was not the time to making confessions. Inwardly, he fumed at the incompetence of the detective Nigel Brown, and his own stupidity of letting his only child disappear. But one thing he did know, this would not be the end of it as far as he was concerned, although right now a cup of tea and a rich tea biscuit would have to suffice.

That night in Laundry Cottage, Seb and Hattie were draped around the kitchen table glugging down large glasses of Pinot Grigio. It was Leo's turn to cook, and he was knocking up some culinary delight on the Aga, with Hero looking longingly at him, hoping for a windfall titbit.

"You're right out of luck, you old bugger," laughed Leo, "You're too fat as it is."

"Don't be unkind to him Leo, give him a scrap," pleaded Seb, "How can you resist his face?"

"Easily" grinned Leo, "pour me a glass will you, I'm the Cinders over here."

"Coming up," called Hattie. "What are we having?"

"Spag Bol, and don't complain, it's my best and only thing."

"No complaints luvvy, I'm starving," sighed Seb, "what a day we've had."

"It'll be great," assured Hattie, passing him a bucket of wine, and turning to Seb, "Now, come on, you said you'd tell us what Proxy Roxy Loxy wanted."

"Hardly Proxy darling, her hair's very dark."

"Whatever," said Hattie miffed, "what did she want?"

"Well," said Seb, pushing himself upright, "you'll never believe it!"

"We won't have a chance unless you tell us," laughed Leo, chucking in some basil to the mince, "you and Felix were closeted with her for ages."

"Whilst they're tarting up the mill, a film crew are going to be doing a reality TV show, and part of the remit is Roxy learning to ride. She wants us to teach her. She wants us to find her a suitable nag. It'll mean we're on camera – the whole works."

"Crikey," exclaimed Hattie, "that's a tall order, has she ever ridden before?"

"No apparently not. So it's got to be some kind of super-horse, good looking, but brain dead."

"Good luck with finding that then, they don't come many to the pound. And I bet she'll be a total nightmare to teach."

"Hmm, I know. I thought I'd give Dougie a ring, he's got fingers everywhere" he smirked at the joke. "He'll know of something, but it won't come cheap, but she said that money's no problem. Be nice little commission on it. Felix said he'd call Chloe."

"Oh God, we'll be inundated with press, let alone the camera crews" grumbled Hattie "hope they don't interfere too much with the yard. What did Felix think?"

"He's all for it – in fact, I think Alice needs to watch her step there," gossiped Seb, then quickly apologised when he saw the look on Hattie's face, "Sorry Hats, I know you fancy him yourself."

"I do NOT," said Hattie hotly. "You never know, there might be some dishy cameraman for me. Anyway, talking of Alice ..." She went on to regale how she had found Alice that morning burning a whole pile of stuff in the cottage garden, finishing crossly, "and when I saw her, she nearly bit my head off."

"Oh she's a right crosspatch that one," snarled Leo, "I don't know what Felix sees in her, but I'll tell you one thing, when Roxy comes on the scene she'd better pull her socks up if she wants to keep him interested."

"I wonder what she was doing though?" sighed Hattie, "She was livid when she saw me."

"Who cares?" Seb poured himself another glass of wine. "She's a law unto herself, I don't think she gives a toss about anyone or anything."

"By the way Seb, I just want to say that I wasn't shirking this morning, despite what Kylie might have inferred," said Hattie, "I'm not sure I trust her y' know."

"Ah, the delightful Kylie," laughed Seb, "such a sweet, innocuous girl. Can't imagine why you don't like her Hattie."

"Well ..." said Hattie, flustered. "I just ..."

"Oh Hats, don't panic, I can see straight through her. We'll have to be careful what we say around her I think, don't you?"

Hattie smiled in relief. She'd thought Seb was serious for a moment. "Have you said anything to Felix?"

"No, not had a chance, what with the Roxy business, but don't worry about it sweetie. Anyway, you and Felix go away in a couple of days to Somerford and you can forget all about it for a while."

Hattie smiled at him gratefully; she was looking forward to the Somerford trip. Felix had debated about taking one of the Novice horses too, to make the trip more worthwhile but in the end had decided that it would just be Picasso, as he wanted to concentrate all his efforts on him. So, with just one horse to do, it would a relatively easy few days away – she couldn't wait. "Thanks Seb," she mumbled, "hopefully with Kylie to do our mucking out, it shouldn't be too tricky."

"Nope, don't worry your pretty little head about it. Now Leo, how long is supper going to be, I'm getting pissed on this wine."

"Slave driver," grumbled Leo, chucking the spaghetti in a pan of boiling water "about five minutes."

There was a sudden, urgent rapping at the back door, which echoed ominously through the kitchen. They all sat petrified. Hero's hackles shot up and he lumbered his vast body up to the door and gave a booming bark. There was a sharp yap from the other side and Hero's tail started to wag.

"Christ – who can that be?" said Seb alarmed "what's the time?"

"Getting on for half past nine," whimpered Hattie, "it's bloody late."

"Oh for god's sake answer the sodding door," groaned Leo, marching over and yanking it open.

Felix stood outside, his shock of blond hair eerily translucent in the porch light. Fiver, delighted to see Hero, shot into the kitchen and leapt up on Hattie's lap. "Sorry, okay if I come in?"

"Felix, you old sod, you frightened the life out of me."

complained Seb "What do you want that can't wait?"

Felix slumped down in a chair, looking miserable "I've had a bloody awful row with Alice. I was telling her about Roxy, and she went ballistic. Shouting and screaming about the media swarming all over the place. You should have heard her – she was just totally irrational about it."

"Dear boy, have a drink," soothed Seb, "it's not as though you've got to drive on the public roads is it?"

"Thanks. You know, I thought she'd be interested. I didn't dream she'd react like this. You should've heard her. Called me all sorts."

Hattie handed him a glass of wine and he took it, smiling at her, "Thanks Hats, what would I do without you?"

Seb laughed, "Alice'll get over herself Felix. It'll be fine in the morning."

"You think? I'm not so sure."

"Of course, after all it hardly infringes on her life does it? All the filming will be done during the daytime, and she'll be working. She's just being a bitch, probably had a bad day."

Felix drooped. "Well there is some good news. I spoke to Chloe. She's got a very good horse called Ksar up at her yard on full livery. The girl who owns it is at Uni, goes back at the end of the month and hardly rides it at all the rest of the year. It's good looking, well trained and dead quiet. They wouldn't sell, but they may be prepared to lease it. Chloe says she'll have a word with them."

"Wouldn't that do Chloe out of a good earner?" asked Leo

"Well, we'd have to give her a finder's fee," said Felix, "or it may be that she keeps the horse at hers and boxes it down when Roxy wants to ride. Although that'd be a bit of a palaver, to be honest. I dunno, we'd have to work out the details, but I suppose, first things first; Chloe puts out the feelers, we try the horse and go from there."

"Well it sounds promising" agreed Seb "would save a lot of foot work if there was a nag on the doorstep. Now dear heart, do you want some supper, I'm sure Leo can make it stretch, and there's always a bed for the night here."

Felix sighed, and took a slug of wine, "Yes to supper, if there's enough, and probably no to a bed. I should go home."

"Suit yourself."

"I'll lay the table," said Hattie, depositing Fiver on the floor, secretly disappointed that he wasn't staying, and dismissing a fleeting image of him curled up in bed with her. "We need to talk about plans for Somerford anyway, Felix, so this is a good opportunity."

Less than a mile away as the crow flew, Alice was in a terrible state. Could her day get any worse? She had made an attempt at reconciliation with Paulene, only to get the cold shoulder, with her shoving the drugs requisition book under her nose and saying it had been on her desk the whole time. She'd had no opportunity to speak to Caitlin as she'd already gone home with Andrew, and was no doubt telling him what a cow she'd been. She'd driven herself back to the cottage full of good intentions to have a romantic evening with Felix and then totally lost it with him when he'd told her about this Roxy Le Feuvre business. How could he be such a fuckwit? To invite the attention of the international media would be catastrophic for her – what on earth was she going to do? She ran through a million different scenarios in her head. No-one had any tangible proof over here on her, other than the phone calls which were meant to scare her. She would have to stay out of the limelight, make it clear to Felix that she wanted no part of it. Thinking logically it could be done, she would be working, and there was no reason why the cameras would come to the cottage or involve her at all. The other alternative was to run away – but she just couldn't face it again. She thought of Felix and her life with him, and how happy she'd been at the beginning. He had never been her intellectual equal, but it had never truly mattered to her, he was intelligent in his own way; funny, happy and above all loved her. He enveloped her in a security blanket, gave her a sense of normality and stability, the first she had ever really known. But her fear of being discovered grew like a festering plague, insidiously destroying his sunny nature whilst she became more bad tempered and terse with him. She hated herself, and every day she tried to change, but the dread overwhelmed her, and then the phone calls had started. How long would it be before they starting making demands and then what would she do?

CHAPTER 35

As Hattie and Felix rumbled out of the yard in a laden truck carrying not only an excited Picasso, but more tack, food, and equipment than they would need for five horses, Kylie watched them go with a malicious smile. Over the past few days she had been enjoying putting the boot in about Hattie as much as she could to Seb, and had begun to work on Felix. To be fair, Felix hadn't even noticed. He was much too preoccupied with the forthcoming event, and much to Kylie's chagrin, he hadn't even acknowledged half she said, but Seb was thoroughly enjoying winding her up. He engaged her in covert little conversations, encouraging her to bitch as much as she could, and delightedly adding as much fuel to her fire as he was able. Leo had urged him to be cautious, as it was *'bound to end in tears'* but Seb had laughed and said he was having enormous fun and it added a little drama to the yard. Leo shook his head warning him to be careful, and was glad that Hattie and Felix were away for a few days even if it did mean they were going to have their hands full exercising their own nags as well as Felix's.

Roxy had been plaguing them twice a day about lessons, and before he left Felix had felt badgered enough to give Chloe another ring about Ksar. She'd been quite short with him, saying that these things couldn't be hurried, and in the end Seb had rung Dougie asking if he knew of anything suitable for a celebrity client who was looking. Dougie had been intrigued but couldn't winkle out any more information as, for once, Seb was discreet and said all would be revealed in due course. It was enough to send Dougie's whiskers buzzing into overdrive. Even so Seb wasn't to be persuaded, but hinted there would be a fat commission if he came up with anything. Dougie's fingers had immediately hit the phone keypad ringing around his contacts.

Farouk and his team had invaded Chrissie's space in the office.

She hated it. They filmed her every move; from going to the loo, to rousting up Alan, to instructing contractors to begin on the barn and clearing the drive. Aiden was in his element, feet akimbo on the desk hurling instructions at her in a lofty fashion, and making bullying phone calls to the solicitors and other officials. A crew were going down to the site tomorrow with him and Roxy to film the mill as it stood now, and although the actual footage would probably only be a few minutes, the shoot would take all day. Chrissie heaved a sigh of relief. She hoped they wouldn't need her, the thought of going made her feel sick. On top of all the extra work, there was the day to day running of the restaurants to oversee; she had no idea how she was going to manage it all.

Chrissie was re-checking a particularly gruelling set of spreadsheets for the Fulham restaurant, whilst Aiden was spouting a load of codswallop for the benefit of the lens when the door burst open to admit an ostentatiously attired Roxy. Chrissie could have vomited as she oozed into a seductive prattle about how excited she and Aiden were about their latest *Rox-Aid* project. She snapped her fingers at Chrissie demanding a mineral water and the cameras lapped up the action, swinging from Roxy to Chrissy, panning in for close ups of their faces as they glared at each other. Chrissie was just about to tell Roxy where to shove her mineral water when she managed a sweet smile, determined that to the public at least Roxy would come over as the spoiled bitch she was. Aiden watched on amused and Farouk clapped his hands with delight announcing that this would make great viewing.

The cameras were put down and they settled down to work out the filming schedule for the following day. It was agreed that Roxy and Aiden would drive down separately from the crew, so that they could film their arrival. Farouk and the team would go down earlier taking some recce shots beforehand. Aiden called over his shoulder off-handedly to Chrissie to organise it with Mark Templeton as they hadn't completed yet, although he confided to Farouk there shouldn't be a problem. Farouk said he wanted Alan the architect to be there with his plans, a couple of blokes with builders' hats, and if possible some footage of Mark and maybe some local people. This time it was Roxy who threw the instructions to Chrissie, and said she would need to be there to make sure it all ran smoothly. Chrissie was livid, but kept her face smeared with the placatory smile determined not to rise to the bait. But just who the hell did they think they were? The meeting broke up and Roxy swept out without a glance, along with the crew, leaving the two of them alone.

"I don't work for her you know," snarled Chrissie, "I work for you. I get fed up with the way she speaks to me."

"Oh just ignore her," said Aiden indifferently, "you know what she's like."

"That's so easy for you to say, not so easy for me though is it? She treats me like shit."

Aiden looked up, "I think you're seriously over-reacting, why not just chill out. This could be really fun over the next few weeks, why don't you stop moaning and try and embrace it?"

Chrissie glared at him stonily, "As long as when things go tits up you don't leave me in the proverbial."

"Chrissie, of course I won't. For fuck's sake!" Aiden suddenly laughed. "Talking of fucking … come and sit on my lap"

"What are you on?" grumbled Chrissie, but nonetheless smiling at him "Supposing Roxy comes back?"

"She won't, she's done her party piece for the day. We've got the place to ourselves, or we could go to yours?"

"No, we'd end up being there all afternoon, and surprisingly I've got a million things to do."

"Well come and sit on my lap then" Aiden grinned at her, opening his arms.

Chrissie shook her head in mock disbelief, gave him an exaggerated wink and sashayed over, levering herself astride him thrusting her tits in his face. "Just a quickie then," she whispered.

Felix and Hattie were well underway on the long journey up to Somerford. Luckily they'd had a clear run along the M25 and trundled along the other motorways relatively unscathed, stopping briefly at Warwick Services to grab a coffee, burger and to have a pee. The stretch between the M42 and the M6 seemed to go on for ever with Hattie constantly checking the map to see how much further they had to go. It transpired they had to go one junction further than they thought owing to the narrow lanes but, at long last, they were turning off and almost at the showground. The daunting journey had seemed never ending, especially as Hattie didn't have her HGV licence and Felix had to do all the driving. He looked exhausted and she'd tentatively suggested that, this winter, it might be a good idea for her to take her test so that they could share it in future. Felix had laughingly agreed and said why wait until the winter, and he'd see what he could do about raising the dosh for her to do it when they got back. Hattie gripped her knees in pleasure. As the showground came into view she could see all the impressive white marquees set well back, with their international flags wavering in the light breeze. A high brick wall encapsulated the beautiful undulating old parkland, its pastures lush and green as it spread out across the valley. Hattie felt her heart fluttering with excitement as they pulled in.

"Right, now we were lucky enough to get a box in the Monarch Stables, although Christ knows how we swung that, they're like gold dust," grinned Felix, as a steward in the fluorescent jacket came over to the lorry parking. "Otherwise I'm not sure where we'd be."

They inched further down the drive past a vast outdoor school, where several full size dressage arenas were set out. It all looked terribly smart, with posh wooden judges boxes shaped like ornate dove cotes and the arena letters festooned with gaudy flowers.

"Blimey, this looks pretty grown up stuff, you're playing in the big league here!" laughed Hattie delightedly, soaking up the atmosphere. "Look isn't that Bill Levett over there?"

"Yep. He's in my section, along with Bettina Hoy and some other top names."

"No pressure then," giggled Hattie, straining her eyes to see who else was wandering about, "at least we're here relatively early, enough time anyway to settle him down for the dressage tomorrow."

"I'm glad we gave ourselves plenty of time. He's not the only one who needs time to settle," agreed Felix. "Just look at all those kids – Christ those are smart ponies. Of course!" he exclaimed, "I think it's the final run for the Juniors before the Europeans, and they might even be running the Young Rider trial here this weekend."

"Wow! How fantastic!" cried Hattie, "I'd love to watch them."

"We should have plenty of time. My test is at 11.10 tomorrow, then Saturday is a rest day for us, and a frantic one on Sunday."

They followed the road round past the arenas and finally were guided into the lorry park by another man in a bright yellow tabard. Felix parked up, jumping out to stretch his cramped legs after the long drive. Hattie could hardly believe they were here at last, and they yanked down the ramp, and went off to find the stable manager.

By the time Picasso had been settled in the stables, and Hattie had strung up haynets, and filled water buckets, a good hour had passed. She'd told Felix to put his feet up in the lorry and have a snooze before she sorted the truck out, and when she tiptoed back, stepping quietly into the living area, he was sound asleep up on the Luton. It was all she could do to stop herself putting out her hand to stroke his face, he looked so peaceful. Rather than disturb him, she crept back out, wandering over to the stables and pensively took Picasso out for a hand graze marvelling at the awesome setting. There were other grooms doing just the same as her, wandering around with their precious charges snatching at the grass and she slipped into easy conversation with them, chatting about the course and the parties that had been arranged over the next few days. She felt the excitement welling up inside her – it was going to be fantastic fun. She'd never stayed away at an international before, and the atmosphere of camaraderie was incredible. Picasso seemed quite settled, tugging her from one patch of grass to another, more curious than hungry. Most of the other grooms were old hands at staying away at events and were only too happy to give Hattie tips and wrinkles about staying away and the accepted dos and don'ts. One of the don'ts was that you never allowed anyone to feed your horse –

you could never be too careful about nobbling, no matter how well-meaning someone might seem. An experienced groom would never offer they said, so anyone who did should be viewed with suspicion. But they all looked out for one another, and told her never to be afraid to challenge anyone she didn't recognise. Hattie listened to them and for a moment wondered if they were serious and then seeing their faces realised that this was no joke. She shuddered, it was hard to think that anyone could be so wicked. She rubbed Picasso's neck fondly, she'd never forgive herself if anything happened to this chap, and by default, Felix, either.

When she went back to the truck, Felix was still sleeping, but this time she wasn't quite so circumspect in being quiet. Reasoning, if he slept until late now, he wouldn't sleep tonight, and then he'd be tired for the morning. She rummaged about, hooking up the electrics, tidying up the living area, which looked as though a tornado had passed through and then put the kettle on the tiny gas stove to make a cup of tea. The gentle sounds of her bustling about caused Felix to stir and he lay with his eyes half open watching her before she realised he was awake.

"Thanks for letting me snooze, Hats"

She snapped her head up, "You startled me, I didn't know you were awake. I'm just making a cuppa, d'you want one?"

"Hmm lovely," he murmured, "it's really cosy up here."

"Good, you needed a sleep. It was a long drive. Picasso has settled in fine, and there's fab Pizza place, and the other grooms told me the showers are great too, so when we've had this we can freshen up and have something to eat."

"What would I do without you?"

"Smooth talker. You'd get on just fine" Hattie laughed "the kettle's boiling already, this little stove is really quick."

"You make me laugh. I never dreamt you'd be so organised."

Hattie smiled as she handed him his tea, "Well you do now. Enjoy."

"I intend to," he said. As Felix took the cup, he held her hand for a fraction of moment and looked at her, "thank you, I really mean it."

Hattie flushed and pulled her hand away quickly, "I enjoy it Felix, you know I do."

"Hattie …I …" Felix was flustered, "the pizza sounds good," he finished lamely.

If Hattie was disappointed she tried not to show it, "Yep, the other grooms are veritable gems for sharing their nuggets of comfort as well as other stuff," she laughed, "they've given me a crash course on being a proper international eventing groom."

"Good grooms are as valuable as diamonds," agreed Felix, "most top event riders wouldn't be where they are today without them."

"Nice to be appreciated," grinned Hattie, the awkward moment forgotten, "Come on drink up, I'm filthy and famished – in that order."

By the time they returned to the lorry a few hours later they both felt relaxed, clean and full up. The other grooms had been right – the showers were awesome and the pizzas pretty much the same. Hattie had enjoyed a few bevvies but Felix was on the wagon, deciding he wasn't going to touch a drop all weekend. Together they made up the beds. Felix offered to let Hattie sleep on the Luton, which spanned the whole cab, rather than on the bench sofa which pulled out to a double bed and was not so comfortable, but she said it was more important for him to have the best pitch, so he could have a good night's sleep ready for the dressage in the morning. She also knew how grubby Picasso's white bits could be in the morning and she wanted him all spick and span. She could slip out and get him ready long before Felix was up. They made some hot chocolate and ate malted milk biscuits going over the dressage test for the next day, working out tactics and finally ambled over to do late stables together. It was a comfortable lazy evening and finally they each fell exhausted into their respective beds, but ironically, neither one of them finding an elusive dreamless sleep.

CHAPTER 36

The following morning Hattie crept out of bed after a hopeless night of waking every few hours and glancing at her phone to check the time. Even though she felt as wrung out as a wet rag, it was a relief to get going. Slipping off the bench bed, she pulled on a pair of jeans, slithered into a sweat shirt and dropped out of the truck. Rummaging about in the lockers, she made up Picasso's feed and made her way over towards the stables and was mildly surprised to see they were already buzzing with activity, even at this early hour of the morning. She called out a greeting to a couple of people she'd met the day before, and dived into Picasso's box, where he greedily shoved his head into the bucket. She took one look at him and groaned in dismay. All the white bits displayed outside his rug were grimy with stable stains and nothing short of a full bath was going to clean him up. She left him to eat his grub, and donned some rubber gloves and started to skip out around him, feeling inordinately pleased that she had left oodles of time to get him ready. There was a gentle hub-bub of noise in the stables, grooms chatting to each other, and grumbling at stomping horses objecting to being groomed or plaited; the chomping of horses on their hay, and water being sluiced into buckets; riders calling in to see how their horses had fared overnight, and giving last minute instructions. Hattie felt happy; she could love this travelling lifestyle. She missed Fiver though; they'd left him behind with Hero, and the little dog's face when he watched her and Felix disappearing down the drive had tugged at her guilty heartstrings. Next time, perhaps they could bring him – all the others seemed to bring their dogs. It was just getting to know the ropes and, so far, everyone had been more than happy to share their knowledge – they were a nice welcoming crowd. They'd had fun last night in the bar, Felix chatting with a few of the other riders and talking about the cross country course, which none of them had walked yet. Somerford was renowned for being well up to height and needed big bold riding. They'd walk it later today after the dressage and again on Saturday. The grooms said this was one of the nicest and friendliest events, they provided buggies to take you everywhere even out to the furthest part of the course, and it was great for viewing. There were loads of trade stands, but she was not to worry, if there was any bit of kit they had forgotten, she only had to ask. Everyone would lend a hand if she needed help. Hattie had basked in the friendliness, especially having spent the last few days with the waspy Kylie who stabbed her in the back every five minutes. Picasso was, luckily for Hattie, one of those horses who loved being bathed. He relished all the attention, enjoying all the massaging and even tolerated her sponging his face clean. She supposed, being black and white, he'd been used to it since he was a youngster, but nonetheless it did make it so much easier than some nutter who lashed out at every opportunity. She took him out without his rug onto the grass to have a nibble in the sunshine, hoping he might dry off, and, to her satisfaction, his coat was sparkling.

"You've made a good job of him," called a voice, coming from a guy who was holding another horse a few metres away. "He's gleaming."

Hattie laughed. "Thanks. I guess I drew the short straw having a coloured – still better than a grey I guess."

The bloke edged nearer with his horse, "he doesn't kick does he?"

"No, he's the kindest chap – yours?"

"No, sorry to ask but you know how it is, you can't be too careful. I'm Brett by the way."

"Hi, nice to meet you," said Hattie flushing a little, this bloke was drop dead gorgeous with his unruly blond hair, "I'm Hattie."

"Well Hattie, nice to meet you too. I haven't seen you before have I?"

"No, this is my first proper International. Well my boss and I did Chilham, but nothing like this before. So I'm a real gringo! What about you?"

"Oh, I've done quite a few, but I love the life. You have to, to put up with being on the road constantly."

"Hmm," said Hattie deflated, "I don't think we're quite in your league then."

"Don't be daft, everyone's the same. Eventing's the best leveller there is, one day you can be right at the top, the next down at the bottom. But it's the ones that strive to get back up that make it."

"Wow, arcane philosophy for this time in the morning." laughed Hattie. "As long as they both come back home safely, that's all I care about."

Brett laughed, "That too of course! What's your rider's name?"

"Felix Stephenson, this is Picasso, but as I said this is our first 2*."

"I'd like to say I've heard of him, but I haven't, but that doesn't mean a thing," he joked. "This lovely boy" he patted his horse fondly, "is Winter Clover and he's in the 2* as well, so I'll probably be seeing a bit of you."

Hattie gaped, how could she not have recognised the horse? Although naturally they all looked different without their tack and riders, Winter Clover was a real rising star and had been in the Horse and Hound only a couple of issues ago. His rider, Ryan Clemence, rode for New Zealand and was based over here this year with his horses and had taken the season by storm. She felt embarrassed and stupid for not realising, "God Brett, I had no idea, he's a fantastic horse."

"No reason you should know," laughed Brett easily, "Ryan's had a good season on him and the others and, hopefully with the wind blowing our way, we should have a good competition. He's certainly fit enough."

"Well I wish you good luck," Hattie grinned, "He's certainly a fine stamp."

"Thanks and you too," smiled Brett. "Look I'll be in the bar later, fancy meeting up for a drink?"

Hattie flushed, "I'd love too, provided Felix doesn't need me."

"You're not involved are you?" asked Brett

Hattie laughed ,"No, not at all, but just in case you know."

"That's good – I'll see you later then. Good luck today."

Hattie watched as he strolled back towards the stable block with the elegant grey horse, admiring his pert bum in his jeans. He had an ace body, long legs, lean frame with broad shoulders, his tangle of blond hair ruffling in the breeze. He was certainly good looking, but there again he knew it. The guy was obviously a player, probably had a new girl at every event. Still it couldn't hurt and it might do her good to have a bit of fun.

To say that Mark Templeton was irritated at being summoned by Chrissie for this damned photo shoot was putting it mildly. He was pretty certain that Lady V would not be happy, but as the contracts had only been exchanged and completion not yet taken place, he felt he had to oblige. Once it was done and dusted he could tell them to piss off. He'd grumbled to Sandy about it this morning over breakfast, but she'd laughed her head off, saying she'd couldn't wait to see him on the telly and perhaps he could do his '*Mick*' impersonation. In the end he'd laughed with her, there was a funny side to it, he just hoped that he would still be laughing this evening when he came home and hadn't committed mass murder and been banged up in Haywards Heath police station.

He'd been waiting at the mill since nine o'clock, initially ferreting distractedly around in the ruins killing time, and finally sitting in his car growing more frustrated and bad tempered at being kept hanging about. It was after ten o'clock when an Audi A5 appeared, hurtling down the drive and shuddering to abrupt halt casting a hail of stones to cascade across the pond, triggering mayhem amidst the terrified wildlife. The driver, was a sallow faced bloke with a pony tail whom he didn't recognise, and was ignorantly oblivious of the chaos he'd caused, clearly, being far too busy on his mobile. Chrissie was sitting in the passenger seat. She gave him a royal wave and a little shrug, and Mark reluctantly swung out of the Landrover and went over to meet them.

Chrissie made the introductions, and Mark with his normal civility shook Farouk's hand, asking if they'd had a good journey down. Farouk hardly acknowledged him. His eyes were roaming everywhere. Mark took an immediate dislike to him and was half tempted to get in his vehicle and beat a hasty retreat when Chrissie put her arm through his and began to explain what they hoped to achieve today. Marginally mollified, Mark thawed and decided to stay, leaving Farouk to stalk around the ruins on his own. The roar of a white van with *Sunrise Productions* emblazoned on the side, rumbled down the drive making them both look up in surprise.

"That's the crew," explained Chrissie

"I thought there'd be more people than that," said Mark doubtfully, looking at the van.

"We not filming *Far from the Madding Crowd* you tosser," snarled Farouk from behind him, "we only need a camera man, someone to do sound and lights and a few extra bods."

"However many people you need, is neither here nor there to me frankly, they shouldn't be driving so fast on these country lanes, they're not built for speed" snapped Mark angrily, marching off to berate the driver, "you'd do well to remember that if you want to keep in with the locals."

"Bad tempered fucker," remarked Farouk.

"I think you need to remember we're not in London now Farouk, and if you want co-operation from the locals probably best to be pleasant," smiled Chrissie condescendingly, "a lot of these people are old school and don't appreciate being called a tosser."

"Whatever," dismissed Farouk, "let's get started, I want some footage done before the dynamic duo get here. I'll leave *Mr Stuffed*

Shirt to you then Chrissie."

Chrissie sighed, sometimes she wondered why she did her job. It was like someone throwing a whole set of crystal glasses in the air, and she had to make sure not one of them got broken. She walked over to try and appease Mark who was jabbing his finger angrily at the van driver.

By eleven o'clock filming had started. Mark had been placated and primed for his small part in the proceedings and was now sitting drinking lukewarm coffee from a thermos, with Chrissie watching Farouk whipping the crew into shape. They were taking random scenes of the mill, the pond, the barns and in the ruins. They wandered down the drive, moving all of the vehicles out of shot and filmed the whole length of the approach. Chrissie explained that most of this would be discarded in the editing suite, but it was important to get as much footage as they could before work on the renovations began in earnest. Today's schedule would involve a scene with Roxy and Aiden '*being delighted*' with the new purchase and shaking hands with Mark, and them talking about their plans. Chrissie had rung the Landlady of the Fox where they would go for a late lunch and they would do a few short takes there, canvassing opinions from the locals in the bar. If they were lucky, they would get through it all today and go home, if not, they might have to come back tomorrow. Mark listened, he had no idea they would be going to the pub and he had a nasty feeling that the likes of the old codgers who propped up the bar most days, would be only too happy to regale the horrible history associated with the place. On balance though, that wasn't his problem, and there could be no backing out now on their part. After all, Mark had told no lies about the place, but he had been somewhat economical with the truth about the history of the mill – he wondered uneasily what would happen when they found out.

By midday, the coffee in the thermos was finished, and Chrissie suggested they take a stroll around the site. He had to admit that she was entertaining company, and the hour had passed swiftly as she rather indiscreetly told him what a nightmare Roxy was, and amused him with funny stories including how Roxy was intending to take up riding. Mark, who was not a rider himself, but knew enough about horses through Sandy and the boys at the yard knew that this would be no mean feat. He privately thought she must be a pretty gutsy woman, especially if she was prepared to let her efforts be filmed. Chrissie, rather carelessly said she was particularly looking forward to that part, she hoped she'd make a right arse of herself and thanked God that she worked for Aiden and not Roxy so she couldn't be blamed when it went belly up. Mark glanced at her speculatively, clearly there was no love lost between the two of them and he wondered why she stayed in her job.

Roxy and Aiden had left London late and were now sitting in sultry silence after a full scale atomic row. Roxy had plugged in her earphones and Aiden had wound up the CD as loud as he could and they were both studiously trying to ignore each other. As the urban streets turned into motorway and then into the frilly cow parsley-decked lanes surrounding Fittlebury, Roxy pulled down the vanity mirror and checked her make-up. Her long fronded falsies were perfectly in place, with a smoky line of grey kohl emphasising her eyes. She smacked her lips together and applied more gloss, raking her nails through her hair. She looked fine. Her stylist had done well with the togs too. Today she had on a snaky pair of jeans, with a chunky belt, tucked into knee high boots which really highlighted her long legs, and a simple polo shirt with a small crystal *R* on the breast. A bit plain for her but she'd go along with it, especially as she had to mingle with the plebs in the pub later. She didn't want them to clam up and say nothing.

Aiden was thinking about the planning and how he could push it through any faster. It was mid-August now, and he was bloody determined to have his Christmas opening if it was the last thing he did. He was even planning the menus for Christ's sake, and to keep in with the locals, was going to be sourcing everything from the area. The TV show would be a great publicity stunt, and he would get Chrissie to get some top marketing people on board. They would need to be taking Christmas and New Year bookings pretty soon and if he could persuade someone like David and Victoria to come down, think how people would clamour to book. There was nothing like a few A listers to draw the crowds.

"You fucking idiot," snapped Roxy, "You've driven straight

past."

Aiden looked up, he'd been miles away. He ignored her, did a swift three point turn in a gateway and roared back down the road and up the driveway, scattering cinders and twigs as he arrived.

Mark looked up angrily, "Jesus!"

"The circus is in town," remarked Chrissie dryly, "I wouldn't bother Mark, they're such a pair of drama queens, if you say anything, we'll never get finished today."

Aiden stepped out of the car, shouting out to Farouk, "Sorry we're late, Roxy took fucking ages to get ready."

Farouk stalked over, "You're always late. Let's just get on with it shall we?"

"Right. Where do you want us?"

"Happy and smiling would be a good start," suggested Farouk, "we can have the histrionics later," he said, glancing at Roxy, who so far had not deigned to get out of the car. "As Roxy seems glued to the passenger seat, can you just make your entrance from the drive again, not so fast this time and we'll just shoot you arriving."

Aiden got back in the car, turned it round and drove back down the track. As they disappeared Chrissie and Mark could see Roxy slapping Aiden over the head with the back of her hand. "The fireworks are just beginning; hold tight for a fun day." Chrissie laughed bitterly, "Don't worry, once she has to do her bit and is centre stage she'll change, just watch."

"I'll have to rely on your judgement, Chrissie, but right now it's hard to credit."

Chrissie proved to be totally correct. When Mark's big moment came, he was to shake hands with the happy new purchasers, hand over the keys and congratulate them. The cameras panned in on the scene, the ruined mill and pond as the back drop. Roxy, her face beaming with smiles hugged him hard, kissing him on both cheeks as a delighted Aiden then pumped his hand and accepted the keys. They all turned to smile at the camera and say their final piece, when a shrill '*beep beep beep*' rang out.

"Cut," screamed Farouk, "Whose fucking phone is that?"

"Err, it's mine," admitted Aiden, "Sorry."

"You fucking moron Aiden, you're a total wanker." screamed Roxy, "Chrissie get me some water."

"Okay, let's go again," grumbled Farouk, "you'll have to wait a minute Roxy."

Roxy was immediately all sweetness and light, and after three agonising takes, Farouk was satisfied. "Right, thanks Mark, that's all we need from you. Now Roxy baby, some shots of you in the ruins, and outside the barn. Nearly done sweetie."

"Just get me the fucking water," snapped Roxy to Chrissie, who was loitering on the periphery, "do your fucking job."

Mark, who could have slapped Roxy, went over to join Chrissie, "Is she always like this?"

"Pretty much," sighed Chrissie, "you get used to it."

"She's a harridan, a total nightmare. I don't know how you put up with it."

"I don't have much to do with her normally, but she's gonna be pretty involved with this project which is a gloomy prospect."

"Rather you than me," Mark said sympathetically, "I'm going to push off now, if you don't need me anymore. I expect I'll see you soon."

Chrissie unexpectedly kissed him on the cheek, "You've been a real support Mark, thanks. See you next time I'm down."

Mark pulled himself into the Landrover, careful not to start the engine if they were filming and touched his face. She was a nice girl, what on earth was she doing working for this bunch.

Picasso looked amazing, his neat plaits were totally uniform and his coat was gleaming. Hattie had put on white bandages and put leg wraps over the top, so he didn't shit all over them before they got to the working in. She'd already been back to the truck to make sure Felix had eaten some breakfast and laid out his breeches and tailcoat, telling him not to worry about the horse, she was well under control. They'd laughed about him remembering his dressage test and she'd put a copy on the table for him to go through once more. They decided what spurs he should wear, and worked out exactly what time he should be on the horse, to factor in how long it would take to ride down to the warm up. Hattie had made up a 'groom's bag' complete with Picasso's passport, bottled water, spare spurs, a copy of the test, and some brushes, that she could take down with her, not forgetting to put in her camera. Now it was just the waiting for the off. Picasso was really calm, not at all anxious like a lot of the other horses in the block and she prayed that he would stay that way. Although sometimes they needed to be a little hyper to give them the '*wow*' factor, it was a fine balance. She glanced at her watch, it was time to take him over to the truck for Felix to get on. She felt nervous enough herself, she couldn't imagine how he was feeling.

When Hattie saw Felix, she could have cried. He looked so amazing in his kit. She brushed away a tear and smiled bravely. It was no good, you could have all the Bretts and Leos in the world but no-one ever made her soul sing like Felix.

"He looks fantastic. You've done a brilliant job. Thanks so much," Felix grinned, "Just hope he feels like playing the game today."

"Just try and think of all the stuff you've been doing with Seb," advised Hattie, "he's a master at test riding, so don't throw away a mark."

"You sound just like him," laughed Felix, "Don't worry I won't."

Hattie whipped off the leg wraps whilst Picasso obligingly stood, tied up to the truck, snooping in her pockets for a treat, and then helped Felix to mount without getting slobber on his breeches. She watched them proudly as they strode off towards the warm up –

the huge black and white horse and the handsome rider – they were a striking combination and one nobody would forget in a hurry. She so desperately hoped it went well today, but it was down to them now, she'd done her bit and all she could was pray for some decent dressage judges. She grabbed her bag and dashed after them.

Picasso worked in well, and he certainly did catch everyone's attention in the warm up. Who couldn't spot him after all, the hulking great black and white horse that moved like a ballerina. Felix was concentrating hard, oblivious to anyone else around him, but Hattie could see that he wasn't satisfied with the way he was going. She caught his eye and pointed to her watch and flashed both hands, indicating he had ten minutes. He trotted over and she began to take off the bandages.

"How's he going?" she asked "he looks great."

"He's a bit dead off my leg to be honest," said Felix worried, "I wonder if I should have put on those other spurs?"

"Hmm, no, I don't think so, they just make him really tense in his body, lay back his ears and swish his tail."

"Maybe. He feels like he's had a day out hunting to be honest – quite tired."

"Perhaps the journey yesterday took more out of him than we thought. But look there's nothing you can do about it now, more sense to have him quiet than tense – you'll get better marks."

"I suppose"

"Felix, will you just pull yourself together," snapped Hattie, quite unlike herself, "get a fucking grip and go and ride for your life, surely you can wagon him round in walk trot and canter for five minutes and make it look easy. Man up for Christ's sake!"

Felix looked really shocked and then laughed, "Of course I can Hats, you're quite right."

The steward shouted over that they had five minutes, and Felix gave Picasso a couple of sharp raps with his legs, and made some short rapid transitions. Picasso reacted with surprise and seemed to wake up a bit. They did a couple of half steps in the Piaffe and then moved off in collected trot. The steps seemed perkier and more elastic but all too soon it was their turn to enter the arena and all Hattie could do was bite her nails and watch.

Felix trotted grandly around the edge of the arena, smiling and nodding to the judges in their boxes, waiting for the signal to start. Picasso, however, had other ideas; he didn't like the look of the flower planters at all. Felix felt the horse shortening in his body and his steps grow higher and more elastic as he passed the markers, and suddenly thought '*whoopee*' this was the energy that had been missing outside in the warm up. If he could just harness it to his advantage then they could do an awesome test. The bell rang signalling for the test to begin. For Hattie, every step was a nightmare of worry, for Felix it was a joy. He rode the test with exquisite confidence executing each movement with as much poise and precision as he could, whilst capturing the verve created by the spooky flowers. At the final salute he raised his hat with great aplomb and a huge grin on his face for the judges, throwing both hands over Picasso's sweaty neck in grateful thanks.

Hattie couldn't believe it, it was a clear round as far as dressage was concerned. Of course, the marks were another matter, but there were no glaring mistakes and where Picasso had found his fifth gear, she had no idea, but find it he had.

She raced over to them as they came out, loosening off the girths and hugging the horse, sneaking him a dozen Polos. "Well done, it looked great, really great, you must be thrilled."

"He was marvellous wasn't he? Gave me a super ride. But you gave me the kick up the arse I needed Hattie, just at the right time. We make a great team."

"It takes team work to make the dream work." Hattie quoted their favourite saying, "come on let me deal with this chap and then we can go and have a well-deserved ice-cream. You go and get changed."

CHAPTER 37

By half past two there was no sign of the film crew at the Fox, and Janice had just about given up on them. She'd promised old Dick Lewington and Frank Knapp, who were regulars in the bar every lunch time that they were in for a surprise and had bribed them to stay with a free pint. Most of the other locals had been and gone, but in the garden Katherine Gordon and her husband Jeremy were just finishing off lunch with their children Susannah and Marcus. Janice was really made up at the thought of the filming, although she had no idea what it was all about and couldn't believe it when Chrissie had rung her yesterday, organising refreshments and saying that they would want to get some footage of the pub and maybe do some interviews although she had been irritatingly elusive about the subject matter. She sighed, looking at the trays of curling sandwiches she'd prepared, and wished they'd hurry up otherwise there'd be no-one left in the pub at all. Frank and Dick were definitely getting more cantankerous and restless with or without the promise of another free pint.

The menagerie of *Rox-Aid* arrived at about quarter to three. Two vehicles and a van swooped into the car park, making the Gordons look up with surprise from the garden. An olive-skinned man with a pony tail was shouting instructions to what appeared to be a film crew, who were unloading equipment from the van. A flaxen haired woman approached them quietly saying that they were filming for a new TV series and hoped they didn't mind. Katherine's first instinct was to say that, actually they did, but the excited look on the children's faces made her stop. It might be fun for them she thought, and looked at Jeremy for his approval. He just shrugged his shoulders and smiled, and so they stayed. Katherine and Jeremy both watched open-mouthed as they realised just who was featuring in the shoot. Jeremy, who like most men, had a covert hankering for Roxy was intrigued to see her in the flesh and Katherine watched equally entranced, as her favourite celebrity chef and his infamous wife strutted before the camera. They nudged each other and smiled when Janice came over to the table bearing drinks, saying they were with the compliments of the film crew. The blonde haired woman reappeared and asked if they would agree to being filmed having a drink with Roxy and Aiden in the garden. Jeremy laughed his approval and Chrissie whipped out a form explaining that she just needed agreement in writing before they could continue. Jeremy signed with a flourish, and Chrissie brought over the famous couple who introduced themselves whilst Janice replenished the drinks. Katherine felt self-conscious at first with the cameras rolling, but Jeremy didn't seem to mind and the children were in their element. Roxy and Aiden chatted encouragingly, asking where they lived, and where the children went to school. When Katherine asked what had brought them down to the Fox, it was the million dollar question Farouk had been angling for, and he gestured to the camera man to pan onto Roxy's face, capturing her explanation of them buying the mill and their plans for it. A secondary camera was homing in on Katherine's reaction. He was not disappointed, she could not have been more flabbergasted and, if he wasn't mistaken apprehensive. Jeremy covered for Katherine quickly, blustering enthusiastic congratulations and the camera swung round to focus on him. Luckily, Katherine's uneasy initial reaction was glossed over. Aiden finished off by eagerly inviting them to be his guests at the opening night. When the little scene had been played out, Roxy and Aiden thanked the Gordons charmingly and moved off to do a similar take with Dick and Frank in the pub, whilst Chrissie took their names and address and assured them she would be in touch about tickets.

"Well," said Katherine, not quite having recovered from the surprise, "What do you make of that? Do you think they have any idea about what happened there?"

"No, I don't," said Jeremy, "and we aren't going to be the ones to tell them either. But whether Frank and Dick do is another matter. I'm going to nip in and pay the bill and let's go quickly before they come back out."

As it transpired the interview with the old boys passed favourably enough. Having propped up the bar since midday they were both vaguely addled from the drink, and were too busy being goggle eyed at the cameras to take in what was going on. There was one awkward moment when Dick piped up about the place probably being haunted, which fortunately was obliterated with a loud belch. Janice too, kept her mouth shut, reckoning they would find out before long anyway, and the restaurant and spa was hardly likely to be in competition with her pub, and might even bring in more trade for her, what with some celebs hanging about. She was rather frustrated that Aiden hadn't handed out any more free tickets to his opening night – trust the Gordons, who had loads of money, to get in first. She gave the blonde girl, Chrissie, the bill for the sarnies and couldn't wait for her husband to come back from the cash and carry so she could tell him all the gossip.

Felix was on the phone to Jennifer reporting back on how Picasso had gone, what score he'd got, what it was like at Somerford, and filling her in on the minutiae of the competition so far. Hattie was standing at the little sink in the truck whilst Felix lounged on the bench seat, twiddling a schooling whip in the air. She glanced over at him, rattling the kettle, and he nodded back. Hattie listened whilst he patiently explained every footfall of the dressage and what the cross country course was like, and how much he was looking forward to them coming up to watch on the Sunday. Finally the call ended and she plonked the now made cup of tea in front of him.

"All right?"

"She's such a nice woman, you couldn't want for a better," Felix enthused, "They're all coming up on Sunday now, except Grace and Colin, she's just too pregnant."

"Blimey they'll have to leave early then," exclaimed Hattie, "They do know your times do they?"

"Yeah, but I think the plan is to drive up on Saturday night, stay in a local hotel, so they can get here early the following morning. Although she did mention something about a helicopter and, frankly, nothing would surprise me with Charles."

"What did she say about your dressage score – was she pleased?"

Felix grinned, "What's not to like? A 45.6 is a pretty decent score, equates to 69.63% in dressage terms and puts me in with a chance. Although when you see Bettina Hoy getting a 34.7 it makes you realise I've still got homework to do."

"A vast improvement though," sighed Hattie loyally, "You've done wonders really."

"Yes, I'm pleased, but I'm shit scared of that cross country, the track is big and there are some tough questions. The first water is easy enough but the one before home is quite hard. My bogey fence are those skinnies right over in the far edge, it needs really strong but totally accurate riding."

Hattie thought back to the jumps when they'd walked them earlier that day and recalled how relieved she was not to be riding them. A host of riders were congregating there, discussing the turns and angles and worrying about the situation of the rope which segregated spectators from riders, and made the turn so much more difficult.

"Oh you'll be fine – he loves the cross country – it's his best phase." She said confidently, "when we go over to the bar tonight you can talk to the others about it, and don't forget we have another opportunity to walk it tomorrow - it'll seem easier."

"I bloody hope so," lamented Felix miserably, "I'm no chicken, but it'll take every ounce of courage on his part and he's got to be listening to my aids."

"Drink your tea," soothed Hattie pushing the cup towards him.

Just as he put the drink to his lips there was a sharp rap on the outside door and Felix jumped so violently he spilt the full boiling cup all over the bench seat. "Bugger, bugger, bugger!" he screamed. trying to leap up, but his long legs were trapped behind the table.

"God Felix are you okay?" cried Hattie. dashing over with kitchen roll and shouting at the door. "Hang on a minute."

"I'm fine, it only got the top of my jeans, but your bed's soaked." groaned Felix. "It's gone right through."

"Forget that for a minute, let me see who that is." Hattie dashed over to the door and was startled to see Brett standing on the steps. She looked at him dumbly for a moment, glancing over her shoulder before inviting him in. "You're a surprise" she spluttered stupidly.

"Sorry, bad time?" asked Brett, looking at Felix, who had wriggled out from behind the table, yanked his trousers down around his ankles, and was now standing in his pants and looked ridiculous.

"No of course not, we've just spilt a boiling drink that's all" laughed Hattie "No damage to anyone, other than my bed that is. Let me introduce you to Felix."

"Hi mate," greeted Brett, "Well done on your dressage score, you did really well."

"Thanks," muttered Felix, pulling up his jeans nonchalantly, as though greeting someone in his pants was something he did every day. "Hattie tells me you work for Ryan Clemence."

"That's right, I just popped in to make sure you were okay for tonight Hattie? You too, Felix. Ryan'll be there and we usually have a good laugh, and a heavy debate about the course."

"We'd love to," Hattie answered for them both, "what time?"

"See you about eight-ish? I'll leave you in peace, looks like you've got your hands full here," Brett laughed, as Felix was levering the mattress off the bench. "You might need to find another bed for the night Hattie!"

"See you later," called Hattie, as he left and turned to Felix, "Did you have to be quite so rude?"

"Hattie, I've kinda got my hands full here, or haven't you noticed?"

"Okay fine, well perhaps you'll be a bit more civil tonight?"

That night, the bar was really crowded. It seemed the whole

showground had congregated intent on having a wicked time in one way or another. Music was pumping out and people were jigging about whilst they talked. Sitting at tables around the room were groups of serious riders nursing soft drinks, looking thoughtful, and drawing diagrams of jumping lines on serviettes. Girl grooms dolled up in skimpy tops and short skirts, with full on make-up, were drinking hideously coloured alcopops and getting outrageously drunk. There were some older, very stylish women sitting in cloistered groups with almost identical clothing, chic bobs, immaculate make-up and cut glass voices - the mums of the junior riders. They had their eyes glued on their kids, obviously policing them and checking they weren't getting up to no good, but who were clearly not averse to being chatted up either, judging by the fawning and simpering smiles they were flashing to some of the good looking young guys.

Hattie had taken care with her appearance tonight. Since living with Seb and, more especially Leo, she was now adept at putting on her make-up and although she didn't wear it often, when she did she looked sensational. Just the right amount to enhance her best features, but not too much to make her look tarty as Leo had laughingly instructed. She hadn't brought any smart clothes, probably because she didn't own any, the skirt was the same one she'd worn the night of Jennifer's pool party and she shoved on a clean tee-shirt and some converse trainers. It was not as upbeat as some of the others but she felt good. Felix didn't say anything about how she looked, and she felt slightly miffed with him, but didn't make any comment, making a bee line for Brett as they walked in. Brett whistled exaggeratedly under his breath and introduced them both to Ryan, who was dispiritedly propping up the bar nursing a bottle of Budweiser. Felix looked disapproving but shook his hand nonetheless, ordering a diet coke when Brett asked him what he wanted to drink. Hattie, on the other hand, asked for a large white wine, determined that she was going to have a good time and that included plenty of alcohol. Pretty soon Ryan and Felix were animatedly discussing their horses' performance that day and the cross country course yet to be tackled on the Sunday. Brett and Hattie left them to it and were soon yapping and laughing as their talk became more flirty and their body language more intimate.

Snapping up a vacated table, they all took their drinks over and sat down. They were joined by a couple of other worried riders and they began loudly discussing tactics for riding the tricky combination of skinnies. Brett raised his eyebrows to Hattie and held out his hand and they shuffled out between the throngs of people to dance. Hattie was feeling pissed and light headed, and enjoying Brett's attention. It was heavenly for once to feel that someone wanted to be with her, she felt his hand slip around her waist and she leant her head against his shoulder as they swayed to the music. His lips strayed to her neck and began to nuzzle against her neck, his tongue licking her ear lobe.

"You're very sexy Hattie," he murmured, "I fancied you from the moment I saw you this morning."

"Really?" countered Hattie, not believing him for a second, but enjoying it nonetheless, "You're a player Brett, and I'm not stupid."

"I mean it Hattie," his embrace becoming more insistent, "You are so beautiful, and you're so unlike the other run of the mill girls."

"Hmm Brett, and you are so beautiful and quite unlike anyone else I've met too," giggled Hattie.

Brett feeling encouraged, moved his hand to cup her breast, but Hattie wriggled away smiling sweetly, "Brett, I really like you, but I'm no easy lay okay, that's exactly why I'm not like the others. Let's get that straight from the start. So we can have a laugh, a good time, but I'm not sleeping with you, so don't think I am."

Brett pushed her away and staring at her face said, "You really mean it don't you?"

Hattie smiled, "Yeah, I do. Now we're clear about that, do you want to dance, or shall we sit down?"

Brett had to laugh, "Fair play Hattie let's dance – you're right, you're not like the others!"

He wrapped his arms around her and they twirled exaggeratedly around the dance floor, swooping and laughing to the astonished stares of the other dancers. Brett was great company, and once the ground rules had been established Hattie could relax and enjoy the fun. They had a wonderful evening, getting more and more tipsy between them, finally throwing themselves down at the table exhausted and laughing.

Felix and the other riders were looking less serious having decided to walk the course again together tomorrow, and had now turned their conversation to gossip, predominantly about who was shagging who. The hottest topic was that Elise Humphries one of the leading riders in the country had come home to find her husband in bed with her groom, who just happened to be an 18 year old lad. Ryan then revealed that one of the New Zealand riders had been bi-sexual for years but he was naming no names. Curiosity aroused, they all threw into the hat a number of candidates, both likely and unlikely provoking huge hilarity and even madder suggestions. The talk became lewder and balder as the evening drew on and what gossip they didn't know they made up. Eventually by midnight Hattie felt her eyelids drooping and said she was knackered and going to bed. Brett said he'd walk her back to the lorry, but Felix leapt up and said there was no need he was going back too, and the rest of the group winked lasciviously and took the piss. But he ignored them with good nature and wrapped his arm around Hattie's shoulders and supported her as she staggered back to the lorry. She stumbled up the steps, tripping over the top one and fell flat on her face, sprawling like Bambi on her long legs. Felix jumped up after her pulling her up and dragging her into the living, remembering that she had nowhere to sleep. She protested drunkenly as he yanked off her clothes and hoisted her up onto the Luton, quickly undressing himself and clambering up beside her. Hattie wrapped her arms around him, and he responded holding her close, stroking her arm and pressing his lips into her hair. She smelt of apples and lemons, and he closed his eyes pulling her tighter towards him, drinking her in, and feeling her skin on his skin. Overwhelmed he found his lips straying down her neck with a flutter of tiny kisses.

"I love you Felix," she whispered, snuggling into his shoulder and letting her body relax into a hazy numbing sleep.

"I love you too Hattie," he mumbled, as he struggled to pull himself together.

CHAPTER 38

Alice, with a gargantuan effort, had succeeded in calming herself down over the last few days and even managed to regain something of her old self in the office. She'd mustered an apology to Paulene and Caitlin, excusing her rudeness by saying she'd had a devastating row with Felix, but they were okay now, and she was sorry for biting their heads off. Paulene, with a beady eye, had accepted the apology but only for the sake of peace, she had a multitude of misapprehensions about Alice's sincerity and wouldn't trust her an inch. Caitlin accepted the excuse with an easy good grace, the quixotic notion of Alice and Felix's stormy and passionate love appealing to her romantic side. It was true that Alice had made up with Felix before he left for Somerford, but he was not easily fooled. In fact, she didn't think he was fooled at all when she claimed she was under a lot of pressure at work and wondered if she'd done irreparable damage to their relationship with her irascible behaviour. Nonetheless, Felix had taken her in his arms and comforted her, but worryingly they hadn't made love, and now he had gone she realised just how much she missed him. She hadn't even got his bloody dog to keep her company as Seb had taken charge of it, claiming it was better off with him. She thought back to her behaviour towards Seb and Leo. She'd been pretty hostile, but that was when the phone calls had started and, irrationally, she believed it might have had something to do with them, but of course it couldn't have. Mysteriously she hadn't had one for a week now, and she desperately hoped that the matter was finished; she had been pretty firm last time he called. Now her plan was to throw herself back into her work. She was good at it and, deep down, she loved her job, even if it had gotten her into the most unholy mess. She was going to make a real effort with Felix and everyone else too and try and build some bridges and get back to normal.

Caitlin had been pre-occupied thinking about what Paulene said about finding new premises and expanding the business. After all, this time last year Andrew had been all fired up with plans and ideas of buying the mill and setting it up as a diagnostic centre. Then after the horrifying ordeal of the kidnapping, when she was so badly injured, he had been focussed purely on her recovery. Caitlin herself could remember nothing about what happened. The doctors called it 'retrograde amnesia' and said she would probably never recall that dreadful day, which was just fine with her. But poor Andrew had kept vigil by her bedside for days and weeks afterwards; he couldn't have cared less about the destruction of the mill or his own plans, his only concern was for her to get well. Even when his wife had flounced off with her lover, Lance the tennis coach, everyone said he showed no emotion at all. In fact if it hadn't been for Sandy Maclean, Mark Templeton's wife, he would have given away everything he had, but she'd made sure that the odious Julia only came away with her rightful entitlement and not a penny more. Now though with the practice growing steadily, the premises bulging at the seams and the other vets chomping to do more exciting and demanding work – a new diagnostic centre would definitely be the way forward. The business plan had been put before the bank last year and approved, and they were more financially stable now than they had ever been, so it really was the right time.

Caitlin had come up with a brainwave, but before she was going to say anything to Andrew she wanted to see if it was going to be viable. So when she finished her stint at the surgery that afternoon, she got into her car and drove up to pay a visit to Grace Allington. Caitlin had always got on well with Grace; in fact it was through her that Grace had once worked at the surgery. At that time, Caitlin had worked as a head groom for Jennifer and Charles, with Felix as second groom, and against all her catholic upbringing, was having an illicit love affair with Andrew, who was then still a married man. Andrew had confided in Caitlin that he was looking for an office assistant to help Paulene in the surgery and she had tipped off Grace, who'd applied for and got the job. Grace had loved working with the vets and then to everyone's surprise a remarkable thing happened. Despite believing she couldn't have children, to her and everyone's amazement, she fell pregnant, and having waited for so many years to have a baby, decided she would leave the job. Following Caitlin's accident, it was obvious that she would never go back to working as a groom and once she had recovered enough, Caitlin had taken over Grace's job at the surgery. During the handover period the two had become close and had remained good friends ever since. Grace and Colin lived just the other side of the village in a converted Sussex barn, which was surrounded by its own land. But more importantly, it was adjacent to Grace's parents' farm, which at one time was a big thriving dairy unit. Now long since abandoned and turned to arable, thanks to the BSE crisis, even though they'd had no infected cattle themselves. Caitlin knew that Colin had tried to persuade Grace's parents to consider using the plethora of under-utilised farm buildings for industrial units, but they would not hear of it, and the matter had been dropped and not discussed again. Caitlin wondered if, just maybe, they might consider a veterinary practice there. It was certainly worth tapping up Grace to see what she thought.

Caitlin swung the car into the drive and parked alongside the barn. She walked around the edge of the garden, admiring the pots and hanging baskets planted out gaily with petunias, geraniums and lobelia, their frails petals bobbing as she swished past. The conservatory doors at the side of the barn were clamped open and she could see Grace inside reading a book and laying on one of the steamer chairs, her swollen belly looking fit to pop at any moment.

"Hey Gracie!" Caitlin called softly, "Can I come in now?"

Grace looked up surprised, "Caitlin how lovely to see you, of course, I'd love some company, come and sit yourself down."

Caitlin reached over, gave Grace a kiss on the cheek and patted her bump, "Holy mother, you're enormous so you are."

"Don't I know it, and I've got another three weeks to go too," grumbled Grace, "I'm getting really fed up now."

"You make the most of it, you'll be rushed off your feet when the little one comes." grinned Caitlin, "Do you know what you're having?"

"Nope, and we don't want to, we want a surprise. After all this waiting as long as it's healthy that's all I care about."

"What about names, have you decided on anything?"

"Don't start me off purleeese! Col and I have this every night. You'll never guess what he came up with last night! Alistair – said it could be shortened to Alex – all well and good, until you put it with Allington – I ask you Alistair Allington! Poor little chap!" Grace roared with laughter "I'm hoping something will just pop into our heads and we'll look at each other and scream – yes that's it! Some hope."

"Rosie is a pretty name for a girl, or Posy, or Poppy?"

"Hmm, I like Rosie, that goes well with Allington" murmured Grace "and we could have Roland if it's a boy – shortened to Roly?"

"Or Rory?" added Caitlin.

"No, Chloe's got a Rory hasn't she?"

"Oh yes, how about Ryan?"

"I can't stand it anymore Caitlin – it's driving me nuts," implored Grace "Tell me some gossip."

"Right! What can I tell you? Oh I know, the old mill's been sold."

"Well I'll have to confess I did know about it. Col's been handling the sale, but I was sworn to secrecy."

"Oh," said Caitlin disappointed, "So you know who's bought it then?"

"'Fraid so, and good luck to them, that's all I can say. It'll be a flash in old Aiden's pan I think."

"They were down at the Fox yesterday with a film crew apparently, doing some tacky TV show about it. They inveigled an interview with Katherine and Jeremy who were having lunch in the garden with the kids, and then collared old Dick and Frank in the bar."

"I don't think Col knew about that! Oh well, I don't suppose it matters now."

"No, I don't suppose it does. Actually Grace, there's something else I wanted to talk to you about, and of course, it's only an idea on my part you know now, so you can shoot me down if you think I'm out of order."

"Sounds serious Caitlin, are you okay?"

"I'm fine to be sure, but it is serious," said Caitlin, her husky voice quavering slightly, "it's about your parents' farm."

"Crikey! Sounds like we might need a cuppa. Come on, let's go into the kitchen and you can tell me. Give me a hand to pull me up will you?" Grace laughed struggling like an overturned beetle to get up. "Now, I'm all ears Caitlin. what is it you want to talk about?"

Half an hour and two cups of tea later, they were back in the conservatory. Grace had listened to Caitlin without saying a word whilst she made the tea, allowing herself plenty of time to consider what she was saying. The irony was that, she herself, had remarked to Alice only a few weeks ago that Andrew should investigate ideas for new premises – but she hadn't given her parents' place a thought. It was in principle, a brilliant idea - there were loads of redundant buildings which would be perfect and ripe for conversion. The nuisance factor for her parents would be minimal and it would be in keeping with a countryside ethic. She didn't think her parents could be persuaded to sell, but they might consider a long term rental. She knew that Colin would approve, but would her mum and dad?

Grace turned to Caitlin, "I'll be honest, I've no idea what my parents would say, but it's definitely worth thinking about Caitlin, and I'd want to talk it through with Col before I mention anything to them. He's so much better at this sort of thing than I am. You say you've not broached it with Andrew?"

Caitlin looked guilty, "No I haven't yet, I hate to be keeping things from him, but I wanted to know if it was a possibility first. He's got his head in the sand about it, you know."

"I know, but you're right, it is time to move on from what happened, especially now the mill's been sold. Leave it with me – okay?"

The weather was lovely at Somerford, although Hattie had nursed the most blistering hangover for most of it, drinking bottled water by the litre and overdosing on Paracetamol. She'd woken to find herself in her bra and pants, snuggled under a duvet on the Luton and the rest of the living area totally deserted. Her eyes felt as though they were glued together with grains of sand, and when she moved, a bolt of piercing pain shot across her forehead. Struggling to come round, and groping out to find her phone, she tumbled out of the high bed with a crash and was promptly sick all over the floor. It wasn't the best start to the day she'd ever had. Felix was nowhere to be seen, and with Herculean effort she'd managed to clear up the mess before he'd boisterously leapt up the steps and into the living.

"Blimey Hats, you look terrible!" he laughed, "don't worry I've been up and mucked out. Let me make you some tea."

Hattie just groaned. She huddled like an ignominious little gnome on the damp bench seat, still in her underwear from the night before, her hair like a bird's nest and felt wretched. "Did I make a total fool of myself last night?"

Felix whistled as he filled the kettle. "Nope, you were hopelessly drunk of course, and that striptease on the table maybe was taking things a bit too far, but I managed to get you home in one piece."

"Please tell me that's not true." mumbled Hattie. "and remind me I am never going to drink again."

"Okay. It's not true, and you'll feel better after a cup of tea and some scrambled eggs."

"Oh God, I just couldn't Felix" cried Hattie, gulping "I think I'm gonna be sick."

"Be sick after you've had something to eat – at least you'll have something to bring up," he laughed, handing her a pair of sunglasses, "come on, buck up and get over to the showers while I do the cooking."

Felix had been right. She did feel a tad better after a shower and managed to keep down the food, but still needed to gulp down water like some dehydrated camel. Donning the dark glasses, she'd then endured the lusty jeers of Ryan and Brett when they saw them later on the cross country course. Hattie glanced sideways at Felix and wondered what it was they weren't telling her, but he seemed blissfully chilled out laughing with the others. In the afternoon, he and Ryan took the horses for a gentle hack around the myriads of wood chip tracks weaving through the park and, before he'd disappeared, he'd tucked her up in the truck with the Horse & Hound and a carton of orange juice and suggested she have a rest. Hattie could hardly believe it - she'd expected him to be annoyed after she'd got so pissed last night but he couldn't have been sweeter. She hugged herself, perhaps she hadn't made too much of a fool of herself after all. The thought of him riding round that huge course tomorrow terrified her, although today when they'd looked at the jumps, for what was now the third time, the questions didn't look quite so daunting. Still, she'd feel a lot happier when he was coming over the finishing line. Thank God they'd got an early time. The show jumping was at 8.40 am with a quick turnaround for the cross country at 9.40 am. It would mean an early start but she would rather that, than hanging around all day getting more nervous and jittery as the time ticked on. With any luck, by ten they would be celebrating. Hattie tried to remember each one of the fences in order, the exact stride, distance and angle that needed to be taken, just as Felix would have to do tomorrow, and by fence five her head lolled onto the cushion and she fell fast asleep, and that was just how Felix found her when he came back from his ride. He watched her for a moment or two, standing in the doorway to the living area. She was deeply asleep, her breathing rhythmical and peaceful, with a strand of hair falling over her face. One arm had fallen slightly to one side and the orange juice was untouched on the table. He leant over, gently brushing away her hair and tucking the blanket around her. Her eyelashes twitched and she murmured in her sleep. He turned away and quickly left before she woke.

Felix was absurdly restless. He'd wanted Hattie to wake up, but, in another way, he didn't. In fact he didn't know how he felt, but one thing he did know was that he had six missed calls from Alice and that he really must ring her back. The awful thing was, he had absolutely no burning desire to talk to her. He strolled towards the show jumping arena trying to rationalise his emotions and, reluctantly decided he couldn't put off returning her calls, He punched out the number. Alice answered on the second ring, which was unusual for her, and equally unusual she seemed pleased to hear from him, chatting easily. It was almost like she used to be in the old days, but oddly, he found he had to make an effort to talk to her. She seemed not to notice and he was relieved, saying he'd be home as soon as he could tomorrow and that he was planning to leave as soon as he'd gone cross country. He eked the conversation out for a few more minutes and then made a feeble excuse and said he'd see her tomorrow and guiltily ended the call. He cradled the phone in his hands and tried to reason why he felt like he did, and then decided to ring Seb. Leo answered curtly, and said he was riding so couldn't be a minute as he had his hands full, but assured him all was well with the yard. Seb was schooling Woody, and Kylie was a pain in the arse. Fiver was missing him but loved living with Hero and good luck for tomorrow; abruptly Felix heard a torrent of expletives and realised Leo had rapidly disconnected. He smiled to himself, it was great to know that everything back home was in safe hands, although he wished he'd had more time to find out what the problem was with Kylie – she was only a mucker-outer after all. The nagging doubt he'd had about her from the off crept back. He'd talk to Seb about it when he got home and see if he could he persuade Hattie to open up about her on the long drive back tomorrow.

Hattie woke up to find the sun streaming through the lorry windows and amazingly, as though something had finally snapped the crippling elastic band that had been attached to her head all day, she felt great. She yawned, and stretching, caught sight of herself in the mirror. Christ, she might feel good, but she looked a wreck. Her hair stuck up at right angles with static, like some wacky lunatic and her eyes like jewelled pinpoints didn't help the demonic look either. She rummaged about in her bag, found the baby wipes and her hair brush and tried to repair the damage before she made any more of a fool of herself than she had already. Looking in the mirror as she cleansed her face, she forced herself back to the events of the night before, and dimly remembered being in bed with someone. But who was it and what had she done? Her body went hot and cold at the thought of what might have happened, moreover that she had been too sloshed to even remember. She'd just have to brazen it out. Felix after all had been so sweet this morning, so he obviously wasn't mad with her, or mad for her either, she thought sadly. Her face in the mirror was beginning to resume some of its healthy glow and she lashed on a bit of mascara and decided she'd have to do. There was loads to do before tomorrow morning's frazzled activities so she'd go and get a head start on herself and try and find Felix later. No doubt he was out with Ryan and his crew and, right now, they were the last lot she fancied meeting up with. She dropped out of the lorry and made her way over to the stables, guiltily realising she'd pretty much neglected Picasso all day.

Picasso, on the other hand, clearly didn't feel neglected. He had a decent hay net, fresh water and his bed had recently been skipped out. All the sweat marks from the hack had been brushed off and he was happily dozing in the corner basking in the sunshine streaming in through the window. Even outside the stable looked shipshape, his headcollar and rope all neatly coiled up outside, the grooming kit tidily lodged on the top of the haylage bale, the bandages rolled together and the rug folded over the rack. Somebody had gone to a lot of trouble.

"How's the head?" a voice from behind her called, "I see you've taken off the dark glasses."

Hattie spun round, Brett, shadowed in the sunlight cascading through the open barn doors looked like the gunfighter from the *O.K Corral* and just as romantic. "Hi" she stammered, "thanks for doing Picasso."

Brett laughed, "Wish I could take the credit, but it wasn't me babe, Felix did him." He came closer, his eyes dancing with mischief, "You're looking one whole lot better. You looked terrible this morning."

"Well thanks for that," mumbled Hattie, bending down quickly to examine the grooming kit and wishing she hadn't. "I had way too much to drink last night. Never again."

"I thought you said there was nothing going on between you and your boss?" asked Brett lazily, pulling her upright, "didn't look like it to me, the way he whisked you back to your truck last night."

"Actually, I know this sounds corny, but there really isn't, and I don't remember much about last night either, other than dancing with you and getting hammered."

"Well you were hammered that's true, but the way Felix looked at you when you were dancing with me, I wouldn't bank on there being nothing between you," he grinned, "and don't give me a load of bollocks that you don't fancy him – 'cos it just won't wash."

Hattie stared down at her feet miserably, "Am I that transparent?"

Brett gave her a friendly push, making her look up at him, "Look doll, you were right about me – I am a player, and when a girl turns me down, which is rare let me tell you," he winked at her, "it's either 'cos they're gay or they've got someone else! It's not rocket science."

"But he lives with a really nice girl and they're very much in love."

"You are so naïve! Remember I'm an expert. He looked like a dopey puppy, not like some bloke who was on a diet and fancied straying off the menu. He's just in the wrong relationship, but can't admit it. Like a fellah who's really gay but can't come out."

"Do you think?" whispered Hattie, desperate to clasp any glimmer of hope, "He's never made a move on me – well only the once and then he backed off like he'd been burned with a red hot poker."

"That proves it then," said Brett triumphantly, "he's secretly gagging for you."

Hattie slumped down on the haylage bale and put her head in her hands, "I don't know what to do."

"Nothing you can do, he's got to make the moves hasn't he, but in the meantime you can make a strategy."

"God you sound like Seb and Leo," grinned Hattie, thinking of the help and support they'd been to her over the weeks, "they're a couple of gay friends who share the yard back home."

"Well it sounds as though you've got a couple of allies then, and one in me too. You're sweet Hattie, but don't be too sweet to be wholesome! Come on, let's go and find him, he's with Ryan watching the show jumping and you're gonna be the beautiful life and soul of the party, and I'm gonna mildly flirt with you and just make him a teensy-weensy bit green eyed. Not enough to take his eye of the game for tomorrow, but enough to make him think twice about you."

Hattie stood up and linked her arm through his, "Don't overdo it though will you? I don't want him to think I'm a tart."

Brett turned her round to look at him "Now you're just being thick – you a tart – I don't think so!"

CHAPTER 39

That night Caitlin lay with her long legs wrapped around Andrew's, her body curled into his, and her head snuggled onto his chest. His hand stroked her hair and for the millionth time he thanked God for bringing her back to him. How he could have lived for all those empty years with Julia was now an impenetrable mystery to him. Her cruel daily verbal lashings of his inadequacies were a thing of the past, as were the ceaseless demands on his bank balance. Caitlin was like a breath of spring air and he just couldn't gulp down enough of her.

"Andrew?"

"Hmm?" he said sleepily, tiredness ebbing over him like a warm wave as he nestled in closer to her.

"I've been thinking?"

"What about darling?"

"Expanding the practice," said Caitlin cautiously, circling her hand over his belly and wrapping her legs a little tighter around him as she felt his body stiffen at the mention of the forbidden subject.

"Oh Caitlin, I've forgotten all about those stupid ideas. When you had your accident, it taught me what's important in life."

Caitlin struggled up in the bed and switched on the lamp, forcing him to look at her "I know darling, it taught us all a lot, and we are so lucky to have each other to be sure, but that doesn't mean that you can't carry on with the expansion ideas now."

"I just don't have the energy for it any more darling. I just want to be at home with you."

Caitlin laughed, "And I want to be at home with you too, but does that mean the practice can't have bigger premises? We're all so on top of one another in the surgery now, it drives everyone nuts so it does, and they're all frightened to death to talk to you about it."

Andrew smiled at her benignly, "Really? Well, you've obviously given this some thought, so, come on, tell me what no-one else can."

"Awe Andrew, don't get all huffy with me now will you?" Caitlin pleaded "But the atmosphere in the office is hell on earth at times so it is, you must have noticed? Alice is like a bear with a sore head, and if Paulene'd the opportunity she kill her, so she would. We need more space from each other."

"You're right about Alice. I'd noticed she was tense and spoke to Oli about it. He's too busy shagging his new bird to notice much and said she was probably having an off-day, but didn't know it extended to you lot in the office."

"Well tense is an understatement to be honest, she's a bitch. You should be a fly on the wall the way she speaks sometimes, especially to Paulene. She's more careful with me, probably because of us, and for fear I'd say something to you."

"Well she was right wasn't she," laughed Andrew, "but I'm glad you did, she's out of order. I'll keep an eye on things."

"I think you ought to, but please don't say I said anything will you now?" begged Caitlin, "and I do think more space would help, even if you can't get your head around the diagnostics centre yet."

"You're probably right, but finding somewhere is not going to be easy, and I'd never consider the barns at the mill. Can you imagine looking at those ruins every day and that fucking pond."

"Holy Mother!" laughed Caitlin "I forgot to tell you - the mill's been sold, barns and all, to that page three girl Roxy Le Feuvre. They were filming there yesterday."

"You are joking!" Andrew's horrified face clouded with angry, painful associations, "It's hard to believe anyone would want it."

"I don't suppose they know," said Caitlin sensibly, "but Andrew, forget that, I've got another and much better idea."

Andrew's eyes refocused on her, "Okay come on then, you've obviously been busting to tell me something, I know when I've been set up."

Laughing, Caitlin leapt astride him, straddling her legs around his cock, putting her face into his and planting a smacking kiss on his lips. "You're gonna love my idea."

Andrew grinned, "Hmm, well it's got off to a flying start so far," he said feeling his cock start to stiffen, "But I'll need you to outline the whole plan – nice and slowly…"

Since Max's disturbing visit to Jilly's parents, he'd scarcely been able to string two civil words together. Fuelled by suffocating guilt, he'd mercilessly barked out orders to his lackeys, callously ignored Anna completely, and made cruel and ruthless business decisions. Torturing himself with the bald fact that, throughout his money laden years, he'd had a kid, which had been brought up by two old codgers who hadn't got a pot to piss in between the pair of them. He'd irrationally hungered for Jilly, but more than that, he now yearned for all those missed opportunities with his child. He had given away those milestone years, the first birthdays, the Christmases, the first day at school. But how could he have said all those things in that sad kitchen pretending to be a mere friend of Jilly's? The gloomy old pair had welcomed him into their home, given him tea and narrated how their beloved daughter had returned from London pregnant. Jilly had stubbornly refused to talk about the father of the child, but they'd made the best of it and they had six joyful months together as they prepared for the baby. Max had squirmed as Eric recalled his pride and unconditional love for his daughter, and how strong she'd been during that time; and even when the baby was born by caesarean, she'd been really stoic and brave. After the birth, Jilly was weak, but they'd rallied round and done the night stints with her expressing the milk; after the second night she'd become listless and started a fever. Eric explained that they hadn't liked to call the doctor, but in the end they'd had no choice. The doctor had given her some pills to start but they hadn't helped, and finally Jilly'd been admitted to hospital, leaving the little one with them. They'd trooped backwards and forwards every day, hoping taking the baby would cheer her up, and expecting positive news, but if anything, each time she seemed a little worse. Their old fashioned notion of *not wanting to trouble the doctors* with their worries left them in a hazy cloud of fear and despair but by the tenth day, when Jilly had slipped into unconsciousness Eric finally asked to see the ward sister. At this point in the story Eric paused with tears in his eyes and squeezed Margaret's hand. The ward sister, who must have been the bitch from hell, callously said she thought she was probably dying, and they should see the social worker to decide what to do about the kid. Max could hardly believe what Eric was saying, struggling to take in the next part. Jilly had died the next day and the post mortem declared the cause of death to be septicaemia. After that, what else was there to do but for Eric and Margaret to bring up their grandchild – adoption was out of the question. Eric said they had tried to do their best, but it had been a struggle at times as money was short. Max didn't know what to say to them. The telling of the story had visibly upset them both, and the tears rolled freely down their faces. He so desperately wanted to open up to them and tell them that he was the father, but hadn't known about the baby, and that even though he wasn't around to help then - he was now. But how could he own up to the child being his? He'd shrunk away from admitting the truth, and there was only so far he could probe as to where the child was now without giving the game away. He garnered as much information as he could store in his reeling brain, and left them to their grief, pathetically promising to keep in touch. He'd been a coward all those years ago, and he was no better that day in the kitchen with Eric and Margaret.

Max disconnected the call to Nigel Brown. He'd never felt so angry, the bloke was a fucking imbecile. Brown made a feeble attempt to defend his position blustering he'd only been hired to find out the address of where Jilly had gone, nothing else, and that was exactly what he'd done. The fact that he'd employed zero initiative seemed to totally escape him and he whinged that, just because she was dead, it was hardly his fault. Max's enraged response rocked the building like a nuclear explosion, issuing him with further instructions spelt out in words of one syllable and with life-threatening recriminations should he fuck up this time. The only other thing he could do now was to alleviate some of the financial pressure from Jilly's parents. Money was not a problem but his instinct told him, that for the time being at least, this should be carefully orchestrated. If he suddenly gave them a shed load of the stuff, they'd want to know the reason why. Well, their luck was about to change, he would talk to his money men to see the best way to go about it. He could do with laundering some dosh anyway and what better cause. What would happen when Nigel Brown came back to him was a different matter and Max knew that anonymous money would not be enough for him.

He pushed back his chair irritably from his desk and wandered over to look out of the window. The Thames, with its oily steely water glided silently past, erratically glinting as the sun made an appearance from behind the clouds. On the other side of the river, little dots of people were walking along the embankment, and cars, like toys, moved slowly along between the wharf buildings. The skyline was jagged with bizarrely shaped buildings and, for the hundredth time he wondered where in this great metropolis his child could be, if in London at all, and he clenched his fists in rage and despair for all his past failings and mistakes.

Anna was enjoying the respite from Max's increasingly demanding carnal attentions. She enjoyed working in the club, even if the other staff were a bit wary of her at first. Ricardo, the manager, had menacingly told them she was the Boss's property, and out of bounds, and nobody in their right mind would fuck Max off, not if they wanted to keep their kneecaps that was. To start with they'd skirted round her, kept her at a distance, but soon discovered that she was alright, worked hard and wasn't sly. She was trying to make a living just like they were. Some of the girls even asked her if she fancied going out with them one evening, but every time she'd reluctantly declined. Anna considered her position; Max only wanted her as a presentable and useful escort and for sex on demand. He didn't seek her company, or her mind. In return Anna gave up her freedom, but gained a proper job, had her debts cleared, had money of her own, beautiful clothes and was occasionally taken to some nice functions. More often than not she was alone and alienated by the strange and controlled curfew which surrounded her. In the beginning it had been enough, but now she was hankering for more freedom. She wanted to be like the other girls, to be able to out and enjoy herself, meet a man who cared about her for who she was, not how pliable she was in bed, or presentable in public.

"Hey Anna – wake up!" shouted Ricardo, "my office."

Anna glanced at the other girl serving behind the bar with her and shrugged her apologies, slipped off her apron and with a sinking feeling, walked away from the smiling faces, the happy, laughing groups of punters and normal people with normal lives. She knew only too well what this summons meant. She slipped away behind the glitzy façade of the bar into the gloomy depths of the club behind, and knocked timidly on Ricardo's door.

"Anna," Ricardo barely looked at her, "Phone call from the boss, he's picking you up in 45 minutes. Says to wear something for a cocktail party and pack an overnight bag. Get your skinny butt up the stairs and don't keep him waiting."

Anna glared at him, but he didn't even notice "Right," she mumbled, and blundered out of the office and up to her room, hurling herself on the bed in despair.

An hour later, she had showered, washed her hair, shaved her pubes, put her face on and was still waiting to be picked up. She'd chosen a simple figure hugging ruby red dress, which accentuated her dark glossy hair, and a black clutch bag and matching shoes. She twirled in front of the mirror; she looked good, sultry and sexy, just how Max liked her, but she just wished it was for a proper date. There was a shout from downstairs and checking herself once again, she picked up her overnight bag, engraved a smile on her face and willed herself to get on with it.

Max was waiting in the car. His mood hadn't improved since the afternoon, and he wasn't looking forward to a fucking cocktail party of all things. Trust Ronnie, but apparently it was essential that he go, and so go he would. Anna was useful for this sort of do, she scrubbed up well and knew not to say much. When he saw her stepping out of the club, with Amos the doorman, deferentially opening the car door for her, he smiled, she looked good. Cinderella good and was pleased that he'd been able to rescue her from those low-life pimps. He wondered how old she was. He'd never bothered to ask her, and thinking about it he actually he'd didn't know anything much about her. Perhaps that was just as well - best to keep her at a distance. After all he ran a lot of girls himself in plenty of establishments all over London, but he made sure they were treated fairly - provided they towed the line and did as they were told. Anna suited him just as she was right now, and when he grew tired of her, she'd do all right out of him, he'd make sure of it.

"Anna my dear, good evening, you look lovely," he smiled at her, "I hope you won't be horribly bored tonight. I fear I will be."

Anna looked up at him through her lashes, "Thank you Max. Can I ask where we're going?"

Max yawned and looked out of the window, "One of Ronnie's racing friends is hosting a drinks party. It's a girlfriends rather than wives affair, so Tasha will probably be there."

Anna didn't know whether to be pleased or disappointed. If Tash was there with Ronnie, it would turn into a drunken debauched evening, although to be fair, Max didn't usually indulge in sharing and at least she'd have someone to talk to before things got too hot. Some of the places he took her she scarcely uttered a word to anyone and it was hard to know what was worse. She forced a smile on her face as she looked at him "Ah," was all she could muster.

"Something wrong?" he asked sharply, turning to look at her, his eyes narrowing dangerously. "We won't stay long, I've some business to talk through, and then we'll go. I'm not into their games."

"Fine" she murmured, so softly that it was difficult to hear "Naturally I'll do whatever you want Max."

Max didn't reply and turned his head away distractedly. Anna fell silent and stared down at her shoes as though they held some magical secret, and felt her red fingernails digging into her palms like martyr's spikes biting into the flesh and wondered what he had planned for the remainder of the night.

As they left the depressing bustle of London behind the roads grew quieter and eventually became silent, narrow lanes. It was not quite dark, the sun was dropping fast and was a red orb just visible dipping over the horizon, blushing the green stain of the countryside a dazzling crimson. The car started to slow and turned down a long concrete driveway, cruising to its end and pulling up in front of an old farmhouse. Anna was surprised, looking around as she climbed out of the car. She could make out horses in stables, barns stacked with hay, horseboxes and there was a distinct smell in the air. It was the last thing she'd expected. She glanced at Max. He offered her his arm and they walked over the uneven flagstones to the front door.

Inside there was a babbling hubbub of voices, the chink of glasses, and light background music. It was a small gathering and it was not difficult to clock Ronnie, surrounded by half a dozen men, all dressed in dinner jackets, and knocking back the booze. They beckoned Max over, and he picked up two glasses of champagne, handed her one, and then left her on her own. She looked around for Tash, but she was no-where to be seen, but there were a few other bits of fluff loitering by the fireplace looking like the tarts they were with their tits hanging out. She moved over to the opposite side of the room to study the bookcase, taking down a volume, every now and then peeking over the top of the page to watch Max. He didn't glance her way and seemed engrossed by what the others were saying, his eyes alight with interest, his head nodding intermittently and then laughing. The man who was doing most of the talking was like a small wizened monkey, tiny in stature with deep facial crevices, pointy ears and would have looked more comfortable in tweed jacket than a bow tie. Anna was intrigued, what could such an incongruous little man have to say that was so important to a man like Max?

"Hello puss," a husky voice purred in her ear, "how's tricks?"

Anna dropped the book flustered and, bending it down to pick it up came face to face with Tash's endless fake tanned legs. "Fuck, you gave me a shock Tash, where've you been?"

Tash wiped her nose, brushing away any residue, "Just a quickie before the action starts, it's the only way I cope babe," she laughed, "you should try it, might make you less uptight."

"No thanks," Anna responded coldly, "you wanna be careful Tash, that stuff's no good for you."

"Give it rest will ya. You don't know what side your bread's buttered. That Max's a hefty catch and to think I gave him to you on a plate." Tash giggled, "still what are mates for eh?"

"For Christ's sake, you're stoned Tash," muttered Anna, "I hate what I've become."

"Oh for fuck's sake, don't go getting all pious on me petal, you don't do so bad."

"You don't know the half of it," said Anna grimly "he's got quite a few fetishes."

"So what, they all have. Just pop a bit of amyl if you don't want to do coke, relaxes you all over, makes it a lot easier, let me tell you."

"I can't believe you sometimes!"

"Oh for fuck's sake Anna, grow up. So they like it warped, it's what they pay for – grin and bear it baby and enjoy the spoils."

"But I'm a virtual bloody prisoner most of the time," Anna complained, "I can't even go out."

"Well ask him for more free time, and stop fucking whinging!" Tash laughed, "You're becoming a right moaner! Don't look now but here come the boys."

Ronnie reeled over, leering at Tash, drunkenly attempting to claw one of her tits out of the low cut dress. "Anna little sweetie, fancy playing games tonight?"

Anna's face looked stricken; whilst Max seemed amused "You don't fancy it then Anna" he asked, "you never know you might enjoy yourself for a change."

Tash giggled stupidly, stretching out her hand and stroking Anna's cheek, "it could be fun."

Anna panicking backed away slightly, and found Ronnie pushing her towards Tash, "Go on Anna."

"Max?" asked Anna, her eyes pleading, "I thought you wanted to go?"

"Well we could stay a while, why not?" his eyes were gleaming, the pent up anger of the last few days spewing spitefully out of him, "go upstairs with Tash and Ronnie. I'll join you shortly."

"What fun!" squealed Tash, seizing Anna's hand. Ronnie winked at Max and they dragged the unwilling Anna towards the stairs. Max watched them go impassively and, grabbed another glass of champagne from a passing waitress tossing it down in one gulp.

By the time Max slipped into the room, Anna was laying whimpering on the bed with her hands tied to the posts. They had stripped her naked and Tash was on all fours busy prising her legs apart, whilst Ronnie was laughingly untying his belt. Tash dived down and began to lick and suck between Anna's legs. Anna's face was a mixture of shock and surprise as she shot Max a beseeching look, her back arching upwards as she wriggled to free herself. Tash was unrelenting, pushing down hard on Anna's belly with her hand. Anna was gasping, begging for Tash to stop, when Ronnie towered over her grabbing her hair, forcing her head back and shoving his cock into her mouth making her gag, squashing her nose between his fingers so that she could hardly breathe. Anna's eyes were wild as Ronnie's cock thrust harder into her mouth, and Tash's teeth sank into her thigh. Suddenly Ronnie withdrew and laughed and the ordeal stopped momentarily, whilst they changed places. Tash levered herself over Anna's face, rubbing her shaven genitals over her mouth and nose, commanding that she lick her, and pinched her nipples hard until she obeyed. Ronnie levered Anna's body up and glided his cock inside her slippery wetness, simultaneously inserting his finger into Tash as the pair of them rocked rhythmically until they cascaded into orgasm.

When the sweaty bodies collapsed on top of her, Anna felt as though she would die from suffocation and claustrophobia. Her face was sticky and wet, her arms were sore from struggling. Perhaps she should have taken Tash up on her offer of the Amyl, it might have made it easier in the long run. From where Tash had fallen on top of her she couldn't see if Max was in the room any longer, and she wondered if he had just left her there. Once again she felt desperate and hopeless and humiliated. She felt Tash's body shift, and roll away to the other side of the bed. Ronnie was still inside her and felt heavy on her legs, but at least she could see. Max was sitting in a chair on the other side of the room, a bottle of champagne beside him, and he was staring at her with a vacant expression in his eyes. She stared back at him with hatred and this time she didn't care what he thought of her.

CHAPTER 40

The morning of the jumping phase at Somerford dawned bright and Hattie was up with the dawn. She'd kipped well on the bench bed, which had dried out in yesterday's sunshine, after a fun afternoon with Felix and the other riders and grooms. They'd opted for an early dry night and she'd imagined it would be difficult to get to sleep with all the hype, but the minute her head hit the pillow she'd fallen into a wonderful dreamless and deep sleep. How Felix had managed she had no idea, but as she left the truck that morning he was sparko and she left him to slumber on whilst she got Picasso ready for his big moment. As usual the stables were buzzing. The 2* was running first, so the big guns were getting ready, and Brett met her with a warm hug and lots of advice. Jennifer and Charles were arriving at about eight along with the others. They'd motored up the previous evening and stayed in a local hotel and had telephoned to say they had arrived and would see them in the morning. Hattie felt she had everything under control, even down to Picasso's white bits which miraculously he'd managed to keep relatively clean in the night. The tack was all spotless, the plaits were done, and she'd got all the stuff ready for the quick change over for the cross country phase. Now it was all down to Felix and Picasso. There was still plenty of time and she wandered over to the show jumping to check the course. It was big but fair, and as long as they didn't let nerves get to them they should be fine. It was just the bloody cross country that held so many questions.

Felix groped for his phone to check the time. The bed below was empty. Hattie had obviously gone over to the stables. He hugged himself with delight, he felt happy and excited. He couldn't wait to get on board Picasso, today was the fun part. Jumping was his forte, and he'd made up his mind to go for a steady round on the cross country, even if it meant time faults. He couldn't afford to take risks with speed yet and as long as they came home safely, that was all that mattered to him. He just hoped that Jennifer and the rest of the syndicate would agree. He knew that Charles wanted the results but Picasso was still a relatively young horse and miles on the clock were more important than money at the moment. He thought back to last night. Neither he nor Hattie had drunk a drop of alcohol, both for different reasons, but they'd still had a fantastic evening. The camaraderie within the eventing circuit was amazing, all the riders exchanging tips about the fences, ideas for riding lines and angles. The grooms were the same, each looking out for the other, happy to help. Yet there was, within the camaraderie, a definite competitive edge which kept them all on their toes. Talk last night had been gossipy, funny and zany, and when he and Hattie had walked back to do late stables together they'd felt as light-hearted as though they'd drunk ten bottles of wine. He'd taken a while to get to sleep, rather hoping that Hattie might have suggested they bunk up together but she'd said nothing, and he'd lain awake listening to her breathing and finally realised that she was fast asleep and that he should be too. But sleep had been as elusive as a shooting star, seemingly only catching minute snatches and then jolting awake again with each stirring of the night, eventually drifting off in the early hours. He woke with a start - a flash of excitement like a 240v charge shot through him and he felt incredible, even more so as he heard Hattie calling for him to get up. To Felix his day could not have started more perfectly.

The syndicate members had arrived and were all in fine fettle despite the early hour. Charles looked marginally bored as usual, whilst the ladies, Jennifer, Katherine and Sandy were excited at the size and capacity of the event. Jeremy was interested in the trade stands, although they were barely open, and Mark, in the estate itself, especially curious about its management and the administration and running of the horse trials. They hooked up with Felix and Hattie in the warm up arena for the show jumping. Picasso was so easy to spot with his unusual markings, and they were leaning against the railings holding their breath as Felix put him through his paces over the practice fences.

"He looks fit enough," said Katherine, "his muscles are rippling."

"Do y' mean Felix or Picasso?" laughed Sandy, "they both look pretty fit to me."

"Now ladies," grinned Mark, catching hold of Sandy's arm "if you weren't a happily married woman Mrs Maclean-Templeton …"

"Oi! Just because I invested my money in you, a little speculation never did anyone any harm, keeps you on your toes," she laughed, reaching up to kiss him "you know I don't mean it."

"You'd better not, you'd break my heart and my bank balance."

"How many to go before Felix?" asked Jennifer, deftly changing the subject. This kind of talk reminded her of the bitter times when Charles divorced his first wife, "He looks so laid back doesn't he?"

"Hmm, I bet he's bricking it," remarked Jeremy, "there's a lot of pressure on the lad, big competition like this, especially with us all having trekked up here to watch."

"It'll be good to see how he handles the stress, there are some top names here" agreed Charles, "if he wants to go to the top, there'll be plenty more of this ahead."

"Charles, you are just so unkind," scolded Jennifer crossly, "this is about us all having a bit of fun. Fantastic if it goes further, but have some empathy please!"

"Darling, don't be such an old softie. Of course we're having fun, but we've invested quite a bit of dosh too, no good having some wimp on board who can't deliver the goods is it?"

"Actually Charles, I happen to agree with you there," said Sandy, "but this is quite a step up for Felix, and for the horse too, so let's try and proceed with positive and dynamic thoughts, rather than wondering if he'll fall at the first metaphorical fence."

Charles roared with laughter, "Spoken like a true advocate Sandy, and I take your point, lots of encouragement then. Sorry Jen darling, I didn't mean to sound so ruthless, I've had a long and difficult week at work – it's hard to switch off I guess."

Jennifer looked at him sideways, "The only thing I can say Charles, is that I am truly glad I don't work for you anymore." She grinned, her eyes twinkling, "Okay you're forgiven, now shut up and stop condemning poor Felix before he's had a chance to show you what he's made of."

"I hate to interrupt but I think Felix is just going into the arena and if we don't hurry over we're going to miss the round," said Katherine, picking up her bag and dashing off, towing Jeremy along behind her. "Darling have you got the video set up?"

They tore across towards the main arena, where Felix was already cantering around the edge, and the last disappointed competitor was leaving, having had a fence down. They were just in time to hear the start bell, as Jeremy fumbled with the camera, and Jennifer, Sandy and Katherine clutched on to each other for dear life. Mark watched the slick organisation of the camouflage clad arena party and was impressed, hoping his own event at Fittlebury Hall next year would run as smoothly. Charles for all his sang froid found his heart beating just a tad faster than normal as the great black and white horse flew over the first fence.

For Felix in the practice arena, he couldn't have said who was there, such was the unadulterated bliss of riding this wonderful jumping machine. The horse felt as though it had wings, he'd never felt so good. The sky seemed to be the bluest it had ever been as they soared into the air to join the cosmos and the pure power and exhilaration made Felix feel as though he would never land again. He hardly noticed the fluttering international flags, the trade stands opening the flaps of their marquees ready for a day's trading, any of the other riders, and certainly didn't give a second glance to members of the syndicate. His focus was entirely on his horse and now and then on Hattie as she altered the practice jumps and finally when she beckoned him over, to check the girth before it was his turn. He leant down and kissed her lightly on the lips before bounding into the ring.

With the early draw and riding on such an impeccably groomed and huge arena the going was perfect. The fences were big but inviting and dressed with gaudy flowers, some spookily underneath the jumps and others on either side cascading out of tall urns. Felix heard the start bell and took an invigorating breath. This time Picasso didn't notice the flowers. He pricked up his ears, and Felix felt an enormous surge of controlled power underneath him as they locked onto the first fence. Soaring over, they were already sizing up the next one, the big horse coming back onto his hocks with ease into a perfect balance. It was a copybook round, jump, balance, jump and rebalance and as they cantered through the finish it was hard to believe that they'd achieved a clear in their first 2*.

Hattie was weeping and whooping alternately as Felix trotted back out, his eyes burning like blue sapphires, his face flushed with glorious elation. Hattie flung her arms around Picasso's sweaty black neck sobbing with relief, and Felix slid off the saddle and turned her round and took her in his arms. She fell against him "You did it!" she whispered "you were brilliant."

"We make a good team Hats. Two phases down one to go," he said grimly, releasing her abruptly. "We'd better get cracking. You take him back to the stables and I'll go and get changed at the truck."

Hattie grimaced, "Too right. Before the others get over here, you'll never get a moment to concentrate else."

"I bloody need it. There are some tough old questions on that cross country, the last thing I want is them blathering on to me when I need to focus."

"Go on then, get going quick, I'll field them off."

"You're a star Hats, I be back at the stables by quarter past," he grinned, as he turned on his tail and strode off over the grass.

Hattie groped in her pocket for a Polo and began to lead Picasso away, trying to ignore the shouts from behind her. "Hattie, wait a minute!" Reluctantly, she paused, "Where's Felix dashed off to?"

"He's gone to get changed, it's a tight turn around now for the cross country. Why don't you follow me back towards the stables, then you can head off on the course to get a good view?"

"I definitely think we should go and congratulate him!" enthused Jennifer, "He rode a marvellous round."

"Weren't they super," agreed Hattie, "but honestly Jennifer, I think he needs a bit of space and time to focus on the course."

"Oh, do you think so, I was hoping to wish him good luck," said Jennifer disappointedly, "surely he'd want to see us?"

"Jennifer," said Sandy kindly, "really when you're absorbed on how to ride a tricky course you can't be doing with small talk, let's leave him alone, we can chat afterwards after all can't we?"

"Sandy's right darling, leave him be. Thank you Hattie, we'll leave the horse with you, and see you all when he's safely over the finish line," smiled Charles, "Right, I know just the place we can stand to have a good view."

"Good idea Charles," agreed Katherine, slipping her arm through Jennifer's, "I know you're busting to talk to him, but truly they are right. I know how nervous I get just before I go cross country, and I'm only doing small stuff compared to this." She laughed, "We could grab a coffee before we go – come on."

The others mumbled their agreement and the little party walked away in the opposite direction. Hattie sighed, hoping she hadn't upset them.

Back at the stables the peaceful atmosphere was punctuated by a series of moaning and grumbling about how tough the cross country course was riding. So far only Olly Townend had come home clear in the time, and even though it was early in the day there had been several eliminations, and plenty clocking up time faults. Hattie tried to blot out what she was hearing. Felix had walked the course enough times, had made his plan and, if all went well would ride it, but the level of skill required was enormous. She washed off the sweat from Picasso's noble head, and whispered in his ear to take care of Felix and himself; to come home safe was all that mattered to her. On automatic pilot she screwed in the studs, changed the boots, and swapped over to the cross country bridle and sat down to wait for Felix to come back.

Felix was on automatic pilot too. He oozed into his lucky breeches, which in truth were long past their sell by date, tugged on his cross country shirt, and zipped up his boots. He took a long cool look at himself as he buckled on his crash hat, relishing the confident embalming feeling that seemed to be enveloping him. He had never felt more alive or focussed. Snapping on his back protector and air jacket, he snatched up his whip, number bib and spurs and jumped out of the truck, striding over to the stables with more tenacity than he'd ever felt before.

As the sun was climbing higher in the sky, way over on the course the members of the syndicate where watching the downfall of the numerous riders who had so far attempted to get round. Fence four had been causing a lot of trouble, some imposing wide tables which needed strong confident riding, as well as the set of three skinny corners much further on, which if you rode the direct route were really tricky.

By now, Felix had already joined Hattie at the stables, leaping up onto the waiting Picasso, and they were heading off down to the start box with Hattie running behind desperately trying to keep up. Felix had hardly spoken a word to her when he arrived and she'd kept quiet, figuring the last thing he needed was her gabbling away to him. But her breath was coming in short rasps and not just because she was running. As Felix got to the warm-up for the cross country, a few other riders were patiently waiting for their turn to go and were popping the odd fence, or walking quietly in circles. They all looked the same, tense and anxious, their brows furrowed and with faces like statues; those that had returned looked flushed and relieved and few of them looked elated. Hattie's sense of doom deepened and she could hardly bear to even glance at any of them. Felix popped a couple of fences whilst she went over to check they were running on time and came back giving him the signal that there were three to go before him. For her this was the worst part, the waiting for the off. All too soon, she was tightening the girth, offering him a glug of water and Picasso was dancing over to the start box, his ears pricked liked sharp thorns.

They were a well organised and friendly bunch at the start and the steward explained they were just waiting for an overdue finisher before Felix could be counted down and set off. The delay seemed interminable and Picasso's eyes were like lasers as he skipped and pranced waiting for his turn. Felix tried to calm him by walking circles, but Hattie could see the horse's black and white coat was trembling with excitement. Finally a flagging grey horse came into view, Picasso's head shot up with a jerk; the rider's legs were kicking like a beating drum and Hattie watched them lurch over the last fence with a heave and laboriously canter over the finish line. The starter, trying to catch up on time gave Felix the countdown signal and immediately he galvanised himself into action, sharpening Picasso into a small canter circles and before Hattie could start to panic any further it seemed they were off, and she didn't even have time to wish him good luck. As the black and white flash flew off towards the first fence and the commentator was announcing the next starter Hattie felt her heart beating a tattoo against her ribs and the desperate need to pee, as she tore up to view as much of the course as she could, but not daring to stray too far from the finish line.

Felix could feel the wind rush against his skin as he tore over the first few fences. Picasso was eating up the ground like a thing possessed. He'd never felt him fitter or more full of running. He just needed him to keep listening and not take matters into his own hands into the trickier fences. The next fence was the table conundrum, and it needed serious handling; he steadied and, miraculously, Picasso checked too. Felix found his line and they sailed over and were galloping off looking for fence five. The exhilaration between man and horse was infinite. At the far edge of the course was the bogey fence, a left hand turn committing into a corner of three strong curving strides to a skinny brush, with an identical skinny brush one stride after but on another hooked left hand turn. The problem being, you couldn't mark the line easily as the distances were so forward, and it needed absolute accuracy and there was not a hope to loop out to the right as the marker string was in the way. Felix was approaching at a fair old lick, the massive horse eating up the ground. He could see the jump judge's car ahead but other than that, being so early in the day, thankfully no other spectators to take Picasso's eye off the game. He hauled him round to eyeball the fence and locked on, focussing onto the second part, counting the strides in this head. For such a huge horse the twist was a big ask, but with superhuman effort and a turn that a London taxi would have been proud of, they were over in three perfect strides and onto the next fence. Felix gasped as the breath pumped out of him and he rasped in another lungful of wonderful air and galloped on.

The watchers on the course clutched themselves with joy and

amazement as the black and white blur streaked past them, hardly taking a break in their stride.

"My God, what a round, they're fucking awesome," breathed Sandy, "that boy's got style."

"It's not over till it's over," remarked Charles sarcastically, "quite a few more to go yet."

"Charles you old cynic. They're doing bloody well, you know they are," said Jennifer delightedly, punching him lightly on the arm, "Stop playing the grump."

"You've got to hand it to him Charles he was a real pro' over those skinnies," enthused Katherine, "still as you say, still quite a few more questions to go."

Charles grabbed Jennifer's hand, and the others followed and they raced back towards the finish, keeping Felix and Picasso within their sight, stopping each time to watch as they soared over another fence. They hesitated as they saw Felix check for the last water, a tricky combination and a lethal line out. Sandy gasped and bunched her fists to her mouth in anxiety as Picasso gave a colossal leap into the murky water. Felix was unseated, his hands flying around the sweaty black and white neck, as he struggled to remain on top. The great horse dithered for an agonising moment, waited for his rider to rebalance himself and plunged on out of the water to leap out with gusto and gallop on towards home.

Hattie who'd seen the faux pas was screaming inside. She shut her eyes, praying desperately – *please God not now, let them come home safely*! She could hardly bring herself to look and when she did snap her eyes open they were already on to the next fence with Felix clinging on for all he was worth. Picasso was hugely enjoying himself but starting to look tired. Hattie bit her lip and felt the salty tang of blood in her mouth, if he could maintain his stamina they'd be home and dry. As she watched, she saw the horse's pace start to flag, his big loping stride wilting with effort. Felix was spurring him on, but although Picasso had a big heart and was trying for all he was worth, he looked spent. There was still one fence to go. Picasso lumbered over the rise, his pricked ears now flaccid and floppy. Felix drove him on, his face set in a hard line and, brave horse that he was, Picasso took up the challenge and miraculously they rumbled over the last fence and over the finish line.

Hattie tore over to them, taking the sticky reins, as Felix slithered off gasping, bending over double to catch his breath. She handed him a bottle of water and promptly loosened the girths, undid the noseband and began to walk Picasso back to the stable, praising him madly as she went. The horse's flanks were heaving wildly and she looked anxiously at him, leaving Felix to follow in their wake. To her relief within a few minutes he had recovered his normal breathing rate and seemed no worse the wear for the tough old round but it had certainly taken its toll on her. She must have bitten her nails down to the quick and the inside of her lip was still sore. Of Felix there was no sight, but for once she didn't care. Picasso was her priority and she was relieved to see Brett when she got back to the stables. He was a mine of information, and helped her cool the big horse off. Together they checked him for injuries, put cooling gel on his legs, and settled him back in his stable once they were satisfied he was okay. Hattie hugged Brett gratefully, throwing her arms around him and plonking a smacker of a kiss on his cheek.

"Steady on Hattie!" He laughed, pushing her back and staring at her. "A fellah can only take so much you know."

"I was worried sick. He looked so tired, I thought he'd never recover," she smiled, grinning stupidly at him "thanks for helping."

"You'll get used to it. He's a grand horse and a brave one, but it takes it out of them at the end of a long old course. We'll keep an eye on him now, and that's where you come in. The riders get all the glory, but it's us grooms that keep the horses going and make sure they stay well. He'll be fine for an hour or so, let him rest. Come on I'll buy you a coffee." He took her hand and led her outside into the sunshine and ran slap bang into Felix who was still in his breeches and cross country shirt, his crash hat dangling off his arm.

"Oh Hats, I was just wondering where you'd got to," Felix grinned, rushing over to her, his face still flushed, "I couldn't get away. How's Picasso?"

"He's fine, no damage – thank goodness. Nibbling some hay now." Hattie surreptitiously dropped Brett's hand, and stared down at her feet, "Brett's been marvellous and helping me with him."

"That's good of you mate," Felix inclined his head towards him, but quickly turned his attention back to Hattie, "I was just coming to find you though Hats, Jennifer and the others wondered if you wanted to join them?"

"Well, er …" stuttered Hattie, "I was just going for a coffee …with Brett."

"You go with Felix," smiled Brett knowingly, "I'll stay here and keep an eye on Picasso. Keep the owners happy. It's fine honestly."

Hattie looked awkward, "Well if you're sure? I mean …"

"Go on, enjoy really I mean it. I've got stuff to do anyway."

Hattie was torn. She felt incredibly mean leaving him, he'd been so brilliant helping her with Picasso - to just ceremoniously dump him didn't seem fair at all. Felix was on a real high and didn't seem to notice any awkwardness, blathering for her to hurry up and not keeping the sponsors waiting. In the end, she turned away half-heartedly to join him, guiltily leaving Brett behind, who grinned knowingly and gave her the ghost of a wink, to go back to the stables and the horses.

CHAPTER 41

Three and half hours later they were on the road home for Fittlebury. If Hattie was disappointed at not staying longer to mooch around the trade stands, she didn't say anything. She had never been more emotionally confused either. Felix had been agitated to get on the road despite being exhausted after the morning's exertions and, in a way, she could see his point - even leaving just after lunch, they still would not be home until late afternoon at the earliest. She said her reluctant goodbyes to Brett and Ryan, who had done their bit by then, and had achieved a double clear too, but been faster on the cross country than Felix; who had racked up a few time faults and ended up 13th in the end. It was an amazing achievement for him in such strong company, but Hattie knew that he had a pang of frustration that he hadn't just pushed on a bit faster. The odd hesitation, especially in the water, had cost him dear. For her, she was just relieved that they were both back in one piece. The syndicate were busy whooping it up and celebrating with champagne, deciding to stay on for a while and watch the 1* cross country, which was just getting underway.

The truck rattled along the motorway, with Felix reliving every passionate step of the course to a good natured Hattie. She listened patiently, letting him prattle on, and feeding him chocolate and biscuits to keep up his sugar levels and suggested they pull over at the services on regular intervals as he must be tired. He leant over and stroked her knee fondly, but said he felt great, never better or more fired up. Gradually as the miles rolled by in a blur of green and grey, she struggled to concentrate on what he was saying, fighting to focus as her eyelids continually drooped. Felix smiled when he caught the odd glance of her nodding off and said he'd listen to a CD whilst she dozed. Hattie didn't argue and gratefully wriggled down in her seat, allowing the delicious numbness of sleep to creep over her.

As he concentrated on the road ahead, buzzing along to an old favourite of the *Black Eyed Peas* he'd never felt more hyped up or exhilarated in his life. He'd let Picasso down a couple of times today, but next time he'd be better, and next time he'd be in the money – he just knew it. He mentally tuned into the electronic ring of his phone from the back of the lorry and glanced over to Hattie. She was out for the count, and there was no way he was going to rouse her. Whoever it was would just have to wait, there was no way he could pull over. The way he was feeling, he would definitely drive all the way back with no stops.

Seb and Leo looked at each other ashen faced. News like this was what every rider dreaded to hear. They knew Felix was okay, he'd rung them to say he was on his way back before he'd started the long drive home, but Seb had gotten the update via Twitter, although there were no details yet. Mark had then rung him from Somerford to say that the 1* had been abandoned and he'd tried to get in touch with Felix, guessing he would want to know, but he'd not answered his phone, and could Seb try?

"I think you should leave it," said Leo. "It'd be so much better for him to hear when he gets home. He'll be upset, and shouldn't be driving that big old bus if he's in a state."

"You're probably right duckie," agreed Seb, "we'll wait for them to get back. They'll need a hand unloading anyway."

"Poor Felix, it'll be such a shock."

"Don't forget Hattie too. Bloody tragic waste of life, eventing's a dangerous old game."

"Well don't go on too much about that, it won't help will it?"

They both looked at each other helplessly. "Let's have a cup of tea, I always feel better after a cuppa."

Felix pulled into the yard just on half past five. He was knackered. Hattie had woken as they were pulling onto the M23. She was full of apologies when she realised how close to home they were, guiltily promising she'd deal with everything when they got back and he should leave everything to her. She couldn't believe she'd slept for so long, and had woken feeling refreshed but nevertheless with an uneasy feeling of anti-climax as they approached Fittlebury. They'd had such a great time away. Mixed emotions swirled around inside her and she glanced over at Felix. His fizzy mood had popped and now he just looked weary, rubbing his eyes and yawning. She felt a huge surge of love for him. Now he was returning to Alice and the intimacy they had shared over the past few days would be over and she would go back alone to Laundry Cottage. Being away was like living life in a bubble, but she was sure that they had grown closer and was positive she hadn't imagined those reciprocated glances. Brett had said he thought Felix felt the same, but Felix hadn't made any overtures to her, and after all, there was Alice. How could she, Hattie, be so duplicitous wishing for more? As the driveway into Fittlebury Hall loomed into view and the lorry swept down the track, in the distance she could see the stable yard. Home at last and she needed to get her metaphorical house in order. Picasso knew he was home too, stamping from the back, and whickering gently to the broodmares in the meadows as they rumbled down the drive and Felix swung into the yard.

Leo and Seb were waiting for them. Hattie waved out of the window, and as they rolled to a stop, she threw herself out of the cab and gave them a hug, pulling back with a jolt when she registered their frozen responses.

"We've got something to tell you both" said Leo, his features wooden and strained as he waited for Felix, who was clambering out of the driving seat and stretching his aching arms high above his head.

"Christ, what a great time we've had! The horse was bloody awesome!" Felix yawned noisily. "But what a drive, I'm bushed!"

"Felix, Hi," called Seb, moving towards him, his hands outstretched. "Look mate, I'm not going to beat about the bush and there's no easy way to say this, we've got some shocking news I'm afraid."

Felix stopped short and stared at him. Suddenly he looked

terribly afraid; his face blanched, "What? What is it?"

"A rider - in the 1* at Somerford died. Just after you left there was an accident at fence four. They've abandoned the event. I don't know any more, but they think it was a rotational fall."

Hattie whimpered, her hands flying to her face, "Oh my God how dreadful, who was it?"

"I don't know sweetie. The details are so sketchy at the moment. Mark tried to call you, but you didn't answer," said Seb, "so we thought we'd wait till you got home."

"Look, I'll get Picasso off," said Leo practically, "Come on Hattie love."

"Are you okay Felix?" asked Hattie, her face creased with worry and tears in her eyes. She reached out to touch his arm.

He stroked her hand, but he looked like a corpse, his face white and pinched, his lips blue. "I'm fine," he croaked. "If you don't mind, I think I need to be on my own for a bit." He smiled weakly at her, "Sorry Hats, can you cover for me for a bit."

Hattie could have wept, for the awful loss of life, but also the realisation that it could so easily have been Felix lying dead, but fate interceded, it wasn't his turn, not his time. She watched his shoulders droop like a shrunken old man as he stumbled back home towards his cottage. She wrapped her arms around her body, hugging the turmoil of emotion inside her, all she wanted to do was comfort him and all he wanted to do was go home to Alice.

"Hattie," Seb's gentle voice was etched with concern. He wrapped his arm around her shoulders, "come on lovie, he's in shock, let him go, and I'll take you home. Leo'll see to 'Casso for you and anything that's not done can be sorted in the morning."

Hattie crumpled against his broad shoulders, "Oh Seb," she wailed, "Why? Life's so bloody cruel."

Seb stroked her hair as she sobbed against him. "I know petal, I know." Over her shoulder he watched Felix disappearing as those legendary twin vultures rattled bitterly in his brain, "Come on baby, let's get you home."

Felix stumbled up the path in a stupor. The tiredness spread through his body like a canker as his mind reeled, ricocheting from one reaction to another. As he reached the cottage he was glad to see that Alice wasn't home yet, he just wanted to be on his own, to sink down in a chair, shut his eyes and try and make sense of it all. He looked around for Fiver, but realised, of course, that he was with Seb and Leo, and felt another huge pang of misery assail him. Dragging a bottle of Jack Daniels and a glass out of the cupboard, he slumped off to the sitting room and poured himself a slug, sinking it in one. Gasping and wincing as his throat caught fire, he fell into the armchair, poured another measure, and tossed it back. Nothing was making any sense to him but at least the hit of alcohol was numbing out the emotions ferreting around in his exhausted brain.

Roxy was sick of the cameras already. Aiden had been like a dog with two dicks. He was full of posturing and posing, whilst Chrissie skulked in the background hiding behind her clipboard. Roxy thrived on her discomfort every time she glanced in her direction. At least her escapades with Annie the Equine were getting easier and, by some miracle, no-one had the least suspicion, but she badly needed to find a real horse now. Farouk was starting to pile on the pressure about the riding scene, which scored several smirking points when it was mentioned in front of the detestable Chrissie, and she was going to have to come up with some results soon. She hadn't heard anything from the elusive Seb or Felix despite badgering them, and was beginning to wonder if she'd backed some losers. She dare not speak to Lisa, and Suzanne knew fuck all about riding. She'd give the boys another week and, if they still hadn't come up with anything then she'd have to look elsewhere. In the meantime, completion was in two days and contractors were all standing-by, ready to start work. They didn't need planning to tidy the site and start the ground work, or begin on the barns either, so for the time being, Farouk's team would be preoccupied with them, which would give her a little bit of lee-way. She tapped her red nails on her desk, considering the best way to deal with the no-nag problem and decided to ring.

"Hi, Seb?" she drawled sweetly, "How's tricks? It's Roxy."

"Roxy – hi!" answered Seb flustered, "I'm fine and you?"

Roxy bit back her natural lambasting response, managing to sound pathetically desperate. "Darling, I'm in despair, I was so hoping you'd have found me a horse by now. I'm really keen and these TV guys want to get started as soon as possible. I was kinda relying on you sweetie."

"I've been trying honestly, but it's got to be the right one. The quiet horses are often not terribly glamorous to look at and you don't want some old dog, do you?" Seb explained, grimacing to Hattie who was earwigging the conversation, "Equally, you don't want something fabulous looking that's going to chuck you off at every opportunity."

Roxy felt her hands clenching, surely it couldn't be so bloody difficult could it? But there again what did she know? She'd have to trust him. "Okay, well look do your best. We have a time frame here, a week at the most, otherwise I'll have to go somewhere else. I don't mind how much it costs – just get on the case. I'll ring you later."

"Right," said Seb, "I'll get on the blower and see if any of my contacts have come up with anything."

Roxy hit the red button and threw the phone on the desk. She wasn't used to not getting her own way, or not being able to buy what she wanted, when she wanted it. What did occur to her was, what kit she would need for her new hobby? So far she'd only used basic stuff on the *Equisator,* but if she was going to be on camera, she wanted to look stunning – not for her what that awful girl, Hattie, was wearing when she went down to the boys yard in Fittlebury. She picked up the phone again and rang Suzanne, barking out instructions to research what she'd need and where they'd get it and to bring the information round that afternoon. She took a gulp of water, and smoothed her hair back from her face. At least she was doing something proactive, and, anyway if she decided to have her own range of riding stuff, then she'd want to blow the opposition out of the water with her designs.

Seb was tearing his hair out. He'd been on the phone to Dougie directly Roxy had rung, telling him this was bloody urgent and they had to find this wretched horse, and fast. Dougie, who could smell the commission winging his way, said he'd call him back, but, so far, Seb's phone had remained obstinately silent. Felix had rung Chloe about Ksar, and got short change from her, saying the owners were still considering a lease. Hattie had even spoken to the old Irish dealer she worked for prior to coming to Felix, but he was a dodgy as a forged fifty pound note, and according to him every horse he had would fit the bill and could read, write and tell the time. Leo was keeping Kylie occupied in the yard. The last thing they needed was her getting wind of the crisis, but she wasn't stupid and she kept making excuses to go into the tack room where the others were huddled making their desperate phone calls.

"Aren't you feeling well today Hattie?" Kylie asked sweetly, "You look a bit pasty."

"No, I'm fine thanks Kylie," Hattie replied quickly, wanting to smack her in the face, "Just a bit tired after our few days away."

"Oh, I was just wondering if you weren't well enough to do any work today?"

Hattie gaped at her and was just about to reply when Felix jumped in, "Hattie is working, and I suggest you get on with what you are supposed to be doing Kylie, which is mucking out and not loitering about in here every few minutes."

Kylie looked furious, "I came in for a drink of water actually. I was only concerned about Hattie - if she's not well that is, perhaps I could ride some of the horses."

"Well she's fine, and it's very good of you to be concerned," said Seb seriously, "but we're really busy now, so off you pop sweetie and we'll see you later – okay?"

"Right – so you don't want me to ride then," said Kylie crossly, "I was only trying to help."

"I am sure you were, but there's no need, but thank you anyway," Seb smiled at her emphasising, "see you later then."

Kylie turned on her heel and stomped out leaving the others in horrified silence.

"That girl is the bloody limit," moaned Hattie, "she's angling after doing my job, I knew it."

"Take no notice, she was taken on as a free-lance shit shoveller, she knows that, she's just testing the water. Don't rise to it Hattie – we can deal with her, can't we Felix?"

Felix reached over and took Hattie's hand. "Don't give it another thought, nobody could replace you, you know that. If it comes to it and she causes a bad atmosphere, she'll have to go."

Hattie smiled at them both, loving the feel of Felix's hand in hers, "Do you mean it? We really do need someone else to help."

"Of course, we'd never upset you doll," laughed Seb, "but right now we're up shit creek without a paddle and I've got to go and teach that Fiona Robinson in a minute. You two keep ringing anyone you can think of and I'll be back as soon as."

Kylie watched Seb drive away from her vantage point in the stable. She was livid, stabbing the shavings viscously and muttering to herself. She'd had high hopes for this job when she came for the interview, thinking that the doe-eyed Hattie was a simpleton, and she'd have no trouble pushing her out. Now here she was closeted with the bosses, and Kylie would love to know what was going on and she was definitely going to find out.

Grace had spoken to Colin the same evening that Caitlin had called round with her idea to expand the veterinary practice to her parents' farm. She'd been taken aback by his response as he thumped the table with excitement, the cutlery leaping of his plate like spawning salmon. Grace hadn't been quite as keen. Her parents were getting on, and had resisted all attempts so far at a change of use, and why would this be any different for them? Colin, ever the eager entrepreneur, argued that this presented an entirely different proposition. It was a perfect solution, and he was pretty certain that the local authority would grant any necessary permission – sensible, sympathetic diversification was being encouraged these days, he expounded, and if those upstarts who'd just bought the mill could get planning, no reason her folks wouldn't. It wasn't as if her parents didn't know the practice partners well either. There would be little daily intrusion to them, the nature of the business was sensitive to a rural lifestyle, and, on the plus side, he was fairly sure the staff would keep a discreetly watchful eye on her mum and dad, alleviating a bit of the worry from Grace, especially with the baby due at any time. Grace had to admit she could see the advantages. Sinking into a chair after dinner and rubbing her somersaulting bump, and uncomfortably dealing with the indigestion she invariably got after eating these days, they decided to pop up and see them together the following day. Unsurprisingly, her parents had not been as enthusiastic as Colin, but weren't refusing at the first fence either. Her father, a quiet, undemonstrative man, polished his glasses thoughtfully, whilst her mother blustered that they didn't like strangers about the place, turning to her husband for his agreement. Before he could reply, Colin had interrupted sensibly suggesting that they at least sleep on things before dismissing the idea out of hand, pointing out that it wouldn't be outsiders, plus it was a good way to make sure that the buildings didn't fall into needless disrepair and they'd get an income from them at the same time. Her father had always admired Colin and his business acumen, and said they'd think about it. Yesterday, he'd telephoned and proposed they meet Andrew but emphasised they were not committing themselves yet. Colin had been boyishly elated, but a weary Grace, merely daunted she just hoped it wasn't asking too much of her mum and dad.

Andrew was not nervous or even worried. There was none of the excitement racing around his brain like before when he was planning the expansion and he'd almost gotten on his knees to Lady V about buying the mill. This time around he felt dull, he couldn't have cared less if it came off or not. He was only going through the motions to placate Caitlin and because he said he would. Last year's events were still so raw, like a festering wound, the very word expansion chilled him to the bone. Colin wrung his hand with enormous bon homie when he arrived and Grace's father looked as pleased to see him as the bubonic plague. The farm was as neat and tidy as any which had suffered the forlorn loss of its herd as its life blood. Gone was the slurry and mud, and weeds had sprang up in the cattle yard. The parlour was sadly empty, its milking machines long since sold off, with the white tiled walls of the once clinical and sterile adjacent dairy, now mildewed and long since redundant with a large empty space where the bulk tanks had been. There were a myriad of rearing and beef barns, cattle yards and small loose boxes, all unused and in danger of falling into a pitiful disrepair. Only a few tractors remained in an implement shed, and Andrew felt a well of pity for the plight of the old man, who had worked the land hard all his life and for what? That the place could be rejuvenated was not in doubt, but whether either of them have the heart for it, remained to be seen.

Seb returned to the yard in a hurry, just managing to contain himself enough to walk from the car to the tack room to avoid the inquisitive and prying eyes of Kylie, who was watching him with suspicion, menacing and hawk like with a fork in her hand. Felix and Hattie were still where he had left them, their phones glued to their ears like bizarre attachments; they looked gloomy and Felix rolled his eyes in dismay as Seb raced in, a huge maniacal grin distorting his face.

Hattie disconnected her call. "That's another one, a no-go" she said miserably, "I've run out of ideas."

"Hattie my dear, the problem is solved," grinned Seb, "we have lift-off."

"What! How? Who?"

Felix, who'd caught the gist of what they were saying, hastily finished his call, spinning round to face him. "What d'ya mean Seb?"

"Fiona Robinson," he laughed gleefully, clapping his hands together, "she's decided she wants to sell that lovely horse. It'll be perfect for our Roxy – impeccable result all round I'd say."

"Nooooo! I don't believe it. What happened?"

Seb sank down like a deflated balloon into the armchair, "I didn't push her honestly I didn't, before either of you say it," he said dramatically, throwing his hands out, "I didn't even think of it, to be truthful."

"Come on Seb, we not as green as we're cabbage looking." Felix raised his eyebrows in disbelief, "what brought about this sudden change of heart then?"

"Kismet," sighed Seb, affectedly rolling his eyes, "the Gods of luck are shining on us dear boy. Her husband is buying himself a lumbering Irish hunter and she's decided to give up on the dressage game and is going hunting with him. Can you believe it? More than likely to keep an eye on him mind you, you know what Michael Robinson's like with the ladies. That's why they have that rather delicious young lad working for them; our Michael could never be trusted with a girl groom."

"Blimey," said Hattie, "You're right about fate, but will the horse do for Roxy? It won't be too much for her will it? It's gotta be brain dead with satellite delay reactions."

"Yep, it's a total saint. Would have to be to put up with Fiona, she's got hands like meat cleavers. You can almost hear it groan with relief when she gets off."

"What's the score then?" asked Felix, "I mean how soon can we have it?"

"Our Fiona just wants it gone, so she and Michael can go over to Ireland and buy a couple of nags to start cubbing on straight away, so whenever really. Her mind is made up, and what our Fiona wants our Fiona gets, and of course I was only too delighted to be able to help."

"Does Roxy need to see the horse do you think? She might like to try it" said Hattie "and what about the price, and we'd need to get it vetted."

"No point in Roxy trying it, she can't even ride," laughed Seb, "and as for the price, we could be onto a good commission as Fiona just wants it gone, more money than sense that one. I think the best thing to do is, I ring Roxy, provided she agrees, we allegedly get the horse vetted and bring it here *tout de suite* so that we're ready for when Roxy tips us the wink."

"Right," said Felix, "ring her straight away Seb, but we must keep totally schtum about who actually owns the horse, except for

Leo of course, after all, Roxy's supposed to be just coming up to learn to ride isn't she? No-body's supposed to know she's bought a horse."

"Good point," agreed Seb, "I'll pretend it's a new dressage horse for me, she can always claim to buy it later. I'd better prime her on that. If anyone found out she contrived it beforehand, she'd look a bloody fool, so it's in her interests to keep quiet."

"Oh God" wailed Hattie "it's bound to bloody go wrong."

CHAPTER 42

The following week tumbled past with all the furore of a Boxing Day sale. After Roxy had agreed for Seb to go ahead with the purchase, a speedy vetting was arranged with Andrew. But Felix's nose was well out of joint, feeling that Alice as his partner has been usurped. Seb, who frankly wouldn't have given Alice the drippings off his nose, had shrewdly declared that it was best there appeared to be no veterinary bias in any way that could come back later and bite them in the bum. Hattie shrivelled miserably in the background as she listened to Felix hotly defending Alice's integrity, but said nothing, and was mightily relieved when he backed down and stomped off. As it was, the horse was examined and passed by Andrew, with Leo picking him up from Fiona's yard the same day.

Galaxy was a fine 16.2 dark brown warmblood, his coat the colour of the glossiest melted chocolate and a small white star nestled between his gentle eyes. He had a sweet nature to match, and settled down happily in the loose box accepting as much fuss as Hattie was prepared to give him that afternoon.

Felix leant on his elbows over the stable door, his chin resting on his hands looking thoughtful. "He's a good stamp, let's hope he performs as well when he's ridden."

"Hmm, he's kind enough in the stable, but you can never tell. Is Seb going to sit on him in the morning?"

"No, I think the plan is to give him a quick ride tonight. Leo's checking out the tack now. We're going to have to be pretty careful with Kylie in the morning when she comes in. I don't trust her an inch."

"Thank God for that, I thought I was the only one with any sense about the conniving bitch." Hattie grimaced, "she's been stabbing me in the back and drawing blood ever since she arrived."

"Try and ignore her Hats, it cuts no ice with me, and you've got to admit that it does make a difference having someone to take the strain."

"It does, and I think if she wasn't quite so damned pushy I'd have been happy to share the more interesting work, but she's just so unbelievable devious."

"Well as I said, try and ignore her for the time being. Once these camera crews start rolling in, she'll lap up the limelight and leave you alone."

"Pigs might fly," Hattie grumbled, "let's hope Roxy doesn't have any purlers and that Galaxy is as smooth to ride as the chocolate. Christ knows how you'll get on though if she's never sat on a horse before."

"Don't - it doesn't bear thinking about does it? But if the wind's blowing the right way and she's a natural it could be a good move for us. Think of the publicity."

"And if it's an east wind blowing and she makes a complete arse of herself, then you'll ruin your reputation in a heartbeat, and it'll all be recorded on national TV," Hattie reminded him, "there's a lot riding on this Felix, and I don't mean fucking Roxy either."

Ronnie was entertaining in the Wallingford house. It had been a great week, Sandra, his missus, had gone with her sister to their place in Spain, and he'd had a free rein to dip his wick all week. Tonight he was having a few racing mates over. He was looking forward to it, a bit of business first and then a bit of the other after. He thought back to the last time they'd met and the little game he and Tash had played with Anna, she'd been like fucking a statue. Uptight bitch, Max could do so much better for himself; Tash was much more fun. He should dump Anna and find himself a better tart. He relit his cigar and sat back in his chair to concentrate on the race. He felt his heart begin its customary thump as he watched the runners cantering down to the start, the polished coats of the sleek horses iridescent like quick-silver fish in shallow green pools mingling with the rainbow colours of their jockeys straining in the stirrups. Ronnie had a lot of money riding on this race, and even though it was a pretty sure thing, it still got the old blood pumping. He watched the starter send them off and the thrust and push of the race as the runners jostled for position and then his horse making a break and streaking ahead of the field with a few others galloping pell-mell after him. They were a couple of furlongs from home and then the leader started to falter, the rider whipping the flagging horse half-heartedly as the other sprinted past him. Ronnie crushed the end of the cigar between his thumb and forefinger, the shreds falling onto the floor, and leant back in his chair. He smirked to himself, it was as easy as pissing. There'd be big bucks to celebrate later.

Max was on his way up to Wallingford. Anna was with him but she was as jittery as a rat in a trap. Max regretted what'd happened before, and although he wasn't going to admit it to her, he wasn't going to let it happen again. The girl was pitiful and vulnerable and it was a shit thing to have done, but making small talk was beyond him. Anna was wired, terrified of the evening ahead and what might happen. If only she could talk to him, but she was just his commodity, nothing more. She sat stiff and miserable beside him, her head turned towards the window and vowed that one day her life would change.

When their car drew up into the driveway, there were already a fair number of top-end motors strewn over the gravel - Mercedes, Porsches, and even a red Ferrari. The party was obviously already in full swing, the music was pulsing out from the garden, and Max made his way around to the back of the house taking the scenic route with Anna following reluctantly behind him. The place had certainly changed since he was last here, the weeds had gone and the whole place had been vamped up. Ronnie was holding court on the terrace, wielding a bottle of champagne in one hand and Tash in the other. Max winced as he yelled lustily at him, and he reached back and clutched Anna by the hand, feeling her stiffen as he dragged her over.

"Max! You've arrived, and Anna too my vestal virgin." He laughed, chucking Anna under the chin. She wrenched herself away and Ronnie clutched her face between his stubby fingers, "don't be like that Anna."

"Hi Ronnie," said Max coolly, casually glancing around, clocking who else was there, "good result today, made a packet."

Ronnie laughed gleefully, "So sweet Max!"

Max had to laugh, "Right, too sweet! I backed the winner on your suggestion."

"I backed it too – nice little earner. Put a grand on the favourite each way, and it came in third, but I also backed it not to win and made fifty times more," grinned Ronnie, "Funny that eh?"

Max examined his fingernails carefully, "I am getting into this racing lark."

"I knew you would," Ronnie sneered, "It's addictive and for the chosen few, of course. Now, a little business before pleasure," he glanced at Anna, "us boys need to talk tactics for next week. Go an' amuse yourself baby - get a little tanked up. Loosen up for later."

"Anna, just give me an hour – okay?" said Max, pushing her off lightly in the direction of the other tarts and joined Ronnie as he walked towards the house "I won't be long."

Anna quailed, tottering away on her stilettos. Her legs felt weak and if she had the strength or indeed anywhere to go, she would have run away. Tash was beckoning to her with a bottle in her hand and she smiled faintly, thoughts of that awful night flooding back and she thought she might be sick. She watched Max's retreating back and realised that there was no way out.

Max helped himself to a soft drink and sank down on the leather sofa as Ronnie welcomed each member of the gambling ring as they drifted into the study. He shifted along on the couch to make room until they were all present with drinks in their hands to discuss the day's takings and the proposals for the weeks ahead. For Max, a lot of the goings on still remained a mystery, but, by now, he'd twigged that Ronnie had not brought him in for purely altruistic reasons. They needed someone like him to make big genuine bets on horses that were not expected to win, so the odds were good. Max was not involved with racing in any of his business ventures, so he had no insider knowledge and he was considered just a lucky punter. The outsider horse would come in, whilst the ring nobbled the favourite and had placed a lot of money out on lay bets. Max's part gave legitimacy to the operation. He won big bucks and so did they. How the actual rigging of the race took place Max had no idea and he didn't care. He just put the money on when he was told, and reaped the benefits. But they must be making a shed load of money judging by the wheels on the drive. Tonight he was in for a surprise. A wizened old con called Ernie, of the Ronnie ilk, with hair oiled back slickly to match the sweat beading on his forehead piped up with something that made Max sit up a lot straighter. Ernie was giving it large, waving his hands about, the ghastly gold rings dripping off his fingers, flashing like beacons in the fading sun.

"Yeah, it's a result all right," he laughed, "she's on the hook, got her running scared." He took a large swig of his whisky, "nice bit of skirt too."

"Working on the tracks is she?"

"Nah, she used to in Oz. Was as bent as then, taking regular happy backhanders. Decided she wanted out and did a fast runner, just upped and fucked off – disappeared off the face of the earth. Spotted her name in the paper last year over here when some psycho kicked off and run amok. Right old fucking hoo-ha it was." He paused and took a swig of his whisky, "happened in a little place called Fittlebury in Sussex and she was the vet that got involved in resuscitating some horses – that's how her name got in the rags. I've been keeping a good old eye on her, and now I've started putting a bit of gentle pressure on." He laughed, his gold crowns flashing, "She's scared alright; won't be long before we have another dodge-pot in our pocket."

"I like it, in fact I love it," laughed Ronnie. "The more the merrier. You sure she'll play ball?"

"Yeah, she's got the wind up, give it a few weeks and she'll be coughing up whatever we want."

Max stored away the information, what a coincidence. The very village where Roxy was doing up her old mill and there was a bent vet in residence. Now that was interesting and who knew when *that* sort of dirt would come in useful. He considered telling them about Roxy moving there, and decided against it, they'd know soon enough when the tabloids got hold of the story. He'd keep his powder dry for the time being.

Anna was nervous and could feel the cold sweat of fear prickling through her clothes. Tash was well coked up, a small residue of white powder clinging to her nose. She was taking the piss out of Anna, chiding her for being frigid and telling her she needed to lighten up if she wanted to keep Max and not find herself working back on the street. Right now, Anna felt she was caught between a rock and a hard place, and however much she fought her principles, a hefty snort of drug induced oblivion was tempting.

"Anna," Max growled, coming up quietly behind her, "We've got to go."

Anna jumped, shaking visibly, "Now?"

"Yes, now. I've got an appointment back in town. Sorry Tash, fun's over."

"Oh Max, don't be such a spoilsport," whined Tash, her pupils the size of ten pence pieces, "I'm thirsty and the party's just starting. You enjoyed watching last time."

"Not for us I'm afraid," replied Max tartly, grabbing Anna's hand. "Night night you all. Speak to you in the week Ronnie." He turned on his heel and picked his way back across the grass tugging Anna unsteadily behind him.

"Well" laughed Tash to Ronnie as they watched them go, "Max is a strange one isn't he?"

"Strange but definitely sound, now forget him and let's get our kit off eh?" leered Ronnie, "I fancy a bit of bondage tonight."

Kylie was pissed off to find that there was another horse to be mucked out the following morning. Those smug bastards hadn't mentioned a word to her about it, and yet she was the muggings who was doing the extra shit shovelling whilst that lazy Hattie got all the plum riding work. Her day had started badly enough as it was, with her car coughing and spluttering all the way over here, and looked as though it was on its last legs. She pushed the new horse irritably out of the way, stabbing it viciously on the ribs with the shavings fork.

"Hey, no need for that," growled Felix, who'd strolled over and caught her unawares "bloody unnecessary."

"Oh Felix," spun round Kylie startled, but recovering herself quickly smiled meekly up at him from under her eyelashes, "he just tried to bite me. He needs to be told off."

"Hmm, right, yeah – well he was as sweet as a nut yesterday – what did you do to upset him?" snarled Felix, marching into the box and trying to calm down the skittish horse, "Are you frightened of him – is that it?"

"No I'm not!" said Kylie her eyes welling up with tears. "He's a brute, he went to bite me and needed a slap, and that's what he got."

Felix looked at her suspiciously, "okay forget it for now, try and be a bit quieter around the horses, especially the ones you don't know."

"Of course," Kylie whispered sweetly, unable to resist adding with a sly touch of malice, "although of I wouldn't be in such a rush if Hattie pulled her weight more and gave me a hand."

Felix glared at her with dislike, "Let's get one thing straight shall we? Your job is to muck out. Hattie works for me and is here to ride the horses unless I say otherwise. And, for your information, she didn't have any trouble handling Galaxy yesterday, so perhaps you should take a leaf out of her book."

Kylie's eyes flashed furiously into steely sharp points, "Right," she muttered through clenched teeth.

"Everything okay darlings?" called Seb brightly, "What do you think of my new horse Kylie? Handsome isn't he?"

"Damned thing just tried to take a chunk out of me," Kylie appealed pathetically to Seb, "Turned on me and when I protected myself Felix had a right go at me – it's not fair!"

"Poppet, are you sure you're not over-reacting, just a teensy-weensy little bit?" laughed Seb, ruffling her hair, "Felix was only saying to me how wonderful he thought you were and what an asset to the yard you've been – what would we do without you? Dear Galaxy is such a sweetie he probably just thought you had a titbit or something."

Kylie gave a loud sniff and cleared her throat importantly. "I do try and do my best, I know I've not been here long, but I work hard."

"You do indeed my dear, now come on, let's get on shall we? I'll take this chap out and tack him up and leave you to muck out then – coming Felix?"

Felix was already out of the stable; he couldn't stand the thought of being in the company of the waspy Kylie a moment longer. He knew exactly how Hattie felt now – she was a witch and a dangerous one. The sooner they replaced her the better, but the problem was, even after this short period of time, they'd come to rely the extra pair of hands and now with another horse in the yard they needed help all the more. Seb was about as good as a chocolate teapot, he almost enjoyed the little spats she created. He huffed with exasperation and strode over to Picasso's stable where Hattie was finishing tacking up and waiting to hack out with him on Casey.

"You alright?" she asked looking at his cross face, "what's the matter?"

"Bloody Kylie – you're right about her, she's a total bitch. She just walloped the new horse for no reason at all."

Hattie couldn't resist a feeling of *I told you so*, and then immediately regretted it when she thought of poor Galaxy. "What a cow, I hope you gave her what for."

"I did, but I don't think it had any effect at all. She's fucking sly, tried to make out the horse had bitten her, then Seb came along. He seems to delight in stirring it up – she'll have to go, but we'll have to try and find someone to replace her first."

"Christ – what a bitch. He's the sweetest horse, wouldn't hurt a fly. I'm so glad you saw her, I was beginning to think you all were on her side."

"Don't be stupid Hats," sighed Felix, "Of course I wouldn't be, I couldn't bear to lose you – but her …"

"Felix, that's a nice thing to say," Hattie smiled like all her birthdays had come at once, "don't worry it'd take more than that bitch to get rid of me."

"Trouble is, with Roxy and her circus coming up here, that means Seb and I are going to be pretty pre-occupied, so we can't spare you and Leo to do the mucking out when our own horses need working. We'll have to put up with her unless someone else springs out of the woodwork."

"We'll have to start putting feelers out for someone else then. Are you going to let Kylie in on the TV crews filming here?"

"Nope, Seb and I thought it best to keep schtum – the least intrusion into the yard the better, otherwise we'll be besieged with poxy paparazzi and when I mentioned it to Alice, she went totally ballistic – although Christ knows why it would affect her, but there was no reasoning with her."

"Blimey it's going to be hard to keep it quiet once word gets about – you know what this village is like for gossip."

"Don't I know it," groaned Felix, "it's as inevitable as rain on a bank holiday, but I grovelled around Alice whilst she was hurling things at me, pleading pathetically we'd do our best, so at least I've gotta do just that, otherwise my life won't be worth living."

"Poor old Felix," sympathised Hattie, guiltily hiding a perverse delight that things weren't going too well between them. "Why's she so uptight about it – any idea?"

"No, there's no reasoning with her sometimes, especially lately. I don't know what's up with her - she's milk on the boil."

"Well, she's got a stressful job. Come on, let's get the nags worked. When's Roxy coming down?"

"If she can arrange it, tomorrow afternoon for a secret shufti at the horse, then probably a week or so later with the crew."

"Right, then the fun begins I suppose," laughed Hattie, "I'll be keeping my head down."

"Hmm, I wish I could," grumbled Felix, "I've a feeling things are going to get a lot hotter before they cool down."

CHAPTER 43

Roxy was champing at the metaphorical bit. She'd been playing happy families with Aiden and the children over the weekend, all on film of course, and was at snapping point. The girls were bored and restless and playing up at every opportunity; batting one parent off against the other with all the skill of two Wimbledon finalists, much to the relish of Farouk and the crew. She couldn't wait for tomorrow when she would escape to Fittlebury and see her new purchase. But in the meantime, she kept her cards close to her chest – just in case things went tits up and this all singing and dancing dressage supernova turned out to be a damp squib. It wasn't so easy these days to sneak away but she'd invented a meeting which she could eke out all afternoon if necessary and, with any luck, hoped to get down just after lunch. Exasperatedly, Roxy handed five year old Delphinium over to the nanny, whilst Sam the cameraman panned in on seven year old Stephanotis scrawling on the wall with a green felt tipped pen. Roxy yelled at the golden child whilst Aiden humoured her indulgently and then cajoled the pen out of her hands, playing good cop to Roxy's bad cop to perfection.

"Cut," screamed Farouk. "Fantastic, I don't know how you two do it."

"Easy. Roxy's just being herself," smiled Aiden, his voice dripping with sarcasm. "Off you go now sweetie." He laughed, benignly patting the blonde curls of the demonic Stephanotis as she poked her tongue out at him. He sighed resignedly and handed her over to the long suffering nanny.

Roxy glared at Aiden and Farouk, and took a swig from her Evian. "I've had enough for today. I need a bath, unless you're planning to film that?"

"Don't tempt me darling," laughed Farouk, "the punters would love it."

"Fuck off," snarled Roxy, "You've seen enough of me this weekend."

"Don't be like that Roxy dear – think of the money," grinned Aiden aggravatingly, "and you're usually all too eager to show off your bits."

"Not this time, I'll leave you to it …dear. Perhaps Farouk would like to film your bits instead?" retorted Roxy, her eyes flashing with confrontation, "Bye Farouk."

"Oh Roxy, before you go, I just wondered if you'd made any headway on the riding angle. I want to start getting something in the can within the next fortnight – don't sit on your laurels darling," called Farouk, "you know dangerously how time ticks by."

Roxy turned round slowly, flicking on the full beam switch, "Darling, don't worry, I have it all in hand."

Aiden almost spat out his beer. "Come on Roxy, you've done fuck all and you know it, why not swallow your pride and get Chrissie to sort it out for you."

Roxy shot him a look that would have sent a deep freeze into spontaneous combustion, "Really no need, As I said I have it all in hand," she said sweetly to Farouk, "goodnight."

Aiden watched her leave with haughty dignity and, once she'd disappeared, started to titter like a two year old. "Like I believe that," he laughed, "She's got no fucking idea, it's gonna be a balls up."

Farouk smiled, his thin lips twitching with mild amusement, "Make all the better TV then won't it?"

Andrew was hosting an impromptu, private meeting with Oli down at the surgery, following on from his visit to Grace's parents' farm. He'd thought long and hard since his desultory visit, but egged on by a persuasive Caitlin, had begun to see that it could be a goer, and in truth he did acknowledge they did need to expand. He'd had his head in the sand for long enough, and now she was so much better, it was time to put the past behind him and move on. He'd noticed too how edgy Alice had been lately, and although she'd been careful around him, he knew Caitlin hadn't been stirring the shit when he was told how the others felt. He could only think it was because she was disappointed that the promise of the larger premises and expanding practice when they'd hired her last year had not come off, and with the disillusionment came her disgruntlement and dissatisfaction. He didn't want to lose her, she was a damned good vet; even if her client skills were not always up to the mark, so it really was time he did something about it.

"What's it all about then mate?" asked Oli good naturedly, throwing his long legs on a spare chair, "must be important to meet down here on a Sunday evening."

"Well I think it is, and I think you'll be pleased when I tell you too – here fancy a beer?"

"Why not - Alice is on call, but better make it just the one, as I'm on second take."

"Right," Andrew chucked him a can from the fridge, and settled down, spreading his big hands out like two Geisha fans on the desk in front of him, not knowing quite how to begin. "Okay, I've been hesitating about expansion from the last year, and I don't have to explain why to you, but I reckon it's time we dragged the plans back out again and had a rethink."

Oli swung his legs down and sat up, a huge grin on his face. "That's a fantastic idea buddy, it's just what we need, we're all on top of each other in here, and I'm desperate to get my hands on some more diagnostic stuff." The excitement in his voice made his New Zealand twang all the more pronounced, "the practice is growing all the time but the million dollar question is, where the hell could we go? Premises that'd be suitable don't grow on trees around here."

"Well, the truth is I've had a look at somewhere, and sorry if you think I jumped the gun here, but I needed to get my head around the idea first, but I think it'd be perfect."

"Bloody hell Andrew, you kept that quiet mate," gasped Oli, "I'd no idea."

Andrew laughed ruefully, his eyes twinkling, "Well let's just say Caitlin convinced me."

"She's a beaut! If anyone could persuade you, she could. So go on then, spill the beans."

Twenty minutes later Andrew had outlined the idea to Oli, who was, for once, listening carefully without interrupting. When he had finished, he sat back in his chair. "So what do you think?"

Oli nodded his head, "Well the location is perfect, couldn't be better and, from what you say it'd take far less money to renovate than the mill project would've done. But on the downside, we can't buy it, so we might shell out a load of money and then lose the lot if anything happens to the farm or to Grace's parents."

"To be honest, I hadn't thought about the legal aspects too much, but I suppose we'd have to have a water-tight lease of some kind – or they may even be persuaded to sell at the right price, I suppose. All I did was take a look at the place. Obviously you'd have to have a gander too before we went any further. Colin didn't seem to think there'd be any problems with planning permission for the change of use on the buildings and, in theory, we could be up and going pretty fast, I should imagine."

"Well you know me, I'm definitely on. Can we go this week and have a look together d' ya think?"

"I can ring Colin, I think he's the best one to organise it, what with Grace's baby due any minute. Meanwhile, I think we'll keep it between ourselves for the time being – don't go getting any hopes up – just in case it doesn't come off"

"Do you think we should tell Alice?"

"No, not yet – just between us partners for the time being. We can tell the rest of the staff when we have some concrete news. Talking of Alice, have you noticed she's been a bit tetchy lately?"

Oli considered, "Well she's not the ray of sunshine she was when she first came here, that's for sure. But she does her job well enough. She's been alright with me, but I don't know about the others. Why?"

"Oh just something Caitlin mentioned the other day that's all, probably nothing."

"Pillow talk?" laughed Oli, "Nah, she's okay as far as I can tell."

Alice had been called out and was heading back to the surgery to replenish her drug stocks and was, in fact, very far from okay. Ever since Felix had gleefully told her about that trollop Roxy Le Feuvre and her proposal, she'd been in a state of intolerable agitation. She could hardly believe that Felix had been stupid enough to agree, and to say that she had hit the roof was an understatement. They'd had a row of Vesuvius proportions and now he was tip-toeing around her, which made her even more irritable and angry. He had assured her that the riding would be a secret and that only the film crew of a couple of blokes would be coming down. But surely he wasn't naive enough to believe that was he? When she'd hurled another plate at him, he'd even had the gall to say what did it matter anyway? Christ he was stupid. The only thing she could do was to make sure that she didn't go down to the yard when the crews were about, and to use the back entrance to the estate when she was going home to the cottage. But it could only take a few pictures in the tabloids and she was scared enough after those phone calls - even though she hadn't had one for a while. She just had to keep her head down. She'd destroyed as much as she could about her past life, and now just as she was finding a niche with her new one this happened. She considered how she could alter her appearance – dye her hair perhaps, start to wear glasses, that sort of thing – God what a palaver and would it work anyway? She was considering that it was certainly worth a try and thinking when she could nip into the chemist for a kit, when she pulled the 4x4 into the surgery and was surprised to see both Andrew and Oli's identical Toyotas parked side by side. Her heart started thumping against her ribs, why would they be here on a Sunday? She was the one on call – had they found out about her? Were they waiting in there to confront her? She took a lungful of air and walked purposefully into the surgery, determined to brazen it out, swinging open the front door with a crash and barging into the back office.

"Hi Alice. You gave us a start," said Andrew, "Been called out?"

Alice glared at him with suspicion, "What are you two doing here on a Sunday afternoon – got nothing better to do?"

Oli looked surprised, the unnecessary hostility in her tone taking him aback and making him think twice about what he'd just been saying, "Just talking – finance stuff, you look worried, got something to hide?"

"Don't be daft," Alice faltered, her bravado evaporating, and she nippily turned away into the drugs room, but not before Andrew had seen her neck start to flush an angry red, "glad I'm not involved, I'm not good with figures," she called over her shoulder.

Andrew glanced at Oli and put a finger to his lips, mouthing '*Later*'. Out loud he said, "Right, I think that just about wraps up the paperwork don't you, I'm for going home."

Oli shrugged and took a slug of his beer. "Dead right bud, I'm bushed I had a heavy night last night."

Andrew laughed, "Another Fittlebury femme falls for the fatal charm then?"

"Nah, Cosham cutie this time. Actually I was rather smitten."

"Put the bloody flags out – it's about time," snorted Andrew, "She'd have to be some woman to tame you."

"Hmm, well don't let Caitlin go buy a hat yet!" He levered himself up, and tossed the empty can in the bin, shouting out, "Night Alice, see you tomorrow."

"Yeah night Alice, hope it's a quiet one," called Andrew, "make sure you lock up after you."

A muffled response came back from the other room; Oli and Andrew nudged each other and made their way outside. "Blimey, she was hostile wasn't she?" said Andrew, pausing beside the vehicles. "I thought she was going to give us the third degree. I can see what Caitlin means now, she could cut paper with her tongue."

"Backed right down when I asked if she'd got something to hide though didn't she?" mused Oli, "I thought that was odd, didn't you?"

"She definitely showed a different side that's true, and not a very pleasant one either, but we're probably reading too much into it mate. Caitlin said she's having aggro with Felix"

Oli scratched his head, "I think she looked bloody shifty. Perhaps she's got another bloke on the go."

"Possibly, but when would she have the time? Anyway, in this village, everyone would know about it?"

"That's rich coming from the bloke who was having an affair right under everyone's noses for months and nobody had a clue, including Paulene who's the world's biggest busybody!" laughed Oli, "Anyway, I'm buggering off, we could speculate all night. Let me know what you fix up with Colin."

"That's rich coming from the bloke who can't keep his cock in his trousers!" countered Andrew "I'll let you know about Colin - see ya."

Andrew sat in his car for a moment and watched Oli roar off down the lane and thought about Alice. Caitlin had been right. In that moment in the office she had momentarily let her guard down and nearly bitten their heads off. The guilty flush on her face when Oli confronted her was proof enough for him that something was going on – but what it was, he had no idea.

That night at Laundry Cottage, Seb, Leo and Hattie were having a pow-wow around the kitchen table. They were expecting Felix to arrive after he'd done late stables, but in the meantime, they'd got well stuck into the plonk. A large bottle of Chardonnay was already upended in the recycling, along with the empty cartons of the Tesco Ready Meal that had been Seb's efforts at cooking their supper, and they were now half-way down another bottle and hypothesising about the dramas that were almost certainly to be unleashed with the arrival of Roxy the following day.

"What time's she pitching up?" asked Hattie rubbing Hero's ear, as he lay his enormous head on her lap, "We'll have to make sure that we're shot of dear Kylie before Roxy arrives."

"Hattie my dear, your paranoia about that girl beggar's belief sometimes," drawled Seb, helping himself to some more wine, "she doesn't suspect a thing."

"SEB!" shouted Leo, leaping up from his chair and thumping his wine glass on the table making them all jump, and Hero disappear as fast as if it was Guy Fawkes night into his bed by the Aga, "I've had enough of this shit! Will you stop fucking about and playing games! She *is* trouble and you know it. Hattie's right. She's as treacherous as a black widow spider and it'll only take one phone call to the sewer press and we're totally fucked! So will you please be serious just for a minute?"

Seb shot them both a rebellious look and tossed his head in defiance, "I think you're being a tad theatrical Leo, and what do y' mean I'm playing games?"

"You know perfectly well what I mean. You drama queen. So far I've kept quiet, but enough is enough. Stop being such a fucking screamer and behave yourself. She's got to go, if not this week, then pretty soon – none of us can stand her."

Hattie's eyes were super-glued to the table; she couldn't bear to watch. Leo and Seb never argued. Leo was glaring at Seb, and Seb was staring right back at him. It was a standoff and neither was prepared to back down. The anger ricocheted with a fierce electricity crackling between them like the machine gun fire in a comic strip, broken only with Hero's whining from his bed. Hattie felt like whining herself, cringing in her chair, her fingers gripping her wineglass like a time bomb.

As abruptly as it had begun, Seb suddenly shifted into a

mercurial U-turn, guffawing with laughter, and throwing his hands up in pseudo surrender, "You're right darlings – of course she has to go. But what a pity! I've had such entertainment while it lasted. She's a ghastly girl, but terribly useful – after all, who else have we got to dish the dirt so amusingly?"

"Seb you really are the bloody limit." moaned Leo, sinking down like a deflated balloon, "One day you'll get us all into serious trouble."

"Stop fretting dear Leo," beamed Seb infuriatingly. "No harm done, top up your glass and chill out."

Hattie stifled a muted laugh and handed Leo the depleted bottle, rolling her eyes in exasperation. Hero slunk out of his bed and sloped over pathetically and shoved his head under her elbow, gazing at her with adoring, woebegone eyes. "Okay, back to the original question, what time is Roxy arriving?" she asked, trying to get back to the point, "and moreover, is *she* going to ride?"

"After lunch, whatever time that means, and no, she says she's not going to try riding. I'm going to put Galaxy through his paces so she can have a gander," said Seb smugly, "I can show her how it's done."

"Hope he doesn't buck you off then," Leo snorted derisively, "pride comes before a fall they say."

"Don't be such a mega-bitch darling – it really doesn't suit you," Seb responded, casting him an offended smile, "anyway, you know she can't ride yet, can she?"

"Boys – stop squabbling purleeese!" pleaded Hattie, looking desperately at them, "we're arguing and she hasn't even arrived yet."

"Hattie's right," said Leo, attempting to be reasonable, "okay so she's coming in the afternoon, that's good, means we'll have plenty of time to get rid of Kylie before Roxy arrives and Hattie and I can make ourselves scarce too – what d' ya say Hats?"

"Sounds perfect to me," agreed Hattie eagerly, "she won't want an audience, not when she has you and Felix to dance attendance."

"What's perfect and who am I going to dance attendance on?"

Seb spun round to see Felix standing in the door way. He leant against the door frame, his lean angular body etched against the dying rays of the sun. "Come in, come in, join the party," he waved the bottle expansively at Felix and motioned for him to sit down. "Just talking about our troublesome ladies."

"Not talking about Hattie and Leo are you?" Felix asked, his eyes crinkling with amusement, and grabbing a glass from the cupboard before plonking himself down on a chair. "Phew, fill me up, I'm knackered."

"We were just saying we need to get Kylie out of the way tomorrow," explained Hattie, "and Leo and I plan to go out hacking when Roxy comes down."

Felix took a gulp of wine, "Christ this stuff is like rocket fuel," he gasped, his aquiline nose wrinkling in distaste. "We need to do something about that snipey Kylie first."

"Oh for the love of God, don't you start. I've just had an earbashing from Leo," grumbled Seb, "I surrender, I agree, whatever …she's got to go. We know."

"I was only saying," spluttered Felix, "No need to bite my head off mate."

"Sorry," said Seb, recovering his sang froid, "trouble is although she's only been here a few weeks, it has been bloody useful having someone to do the dirty work."

"She's been dishing the dirt alright," said Leo, rolling his eyes with irritation, "aided and abetted by you! Anyway, we are agreed she's got to go, but for the time being, we'll have to put up with her until we find someone new."

"That's settled, but meantime we've got to keep her out of the way of Roxy tomorrow. Once the news is common knowledge it won't matter, but we don't want the leak to come from our yard do we?" Hattie appealed to them, her eyes troubled and biting her lip in anxiety, "So if Leo and I keep out of the way and leave you two to deal with Roxy?"

"That suits me fine, I think the quieter we keep the whole thing, for as long as possible, the better for everyone – I've had enough earache from Alice as it is," mumbled Felix. "Seb and I will take care of Roxy. You two give Kylie a hand in the morning and pack her off early."

"Okay," said Leo, "but how are we going to replace her – the sooner the better, especially after the incident with Galaxy."

"I've got a feeling she could turn nasty when she gets the old heave ho. I wouldn't put it past her to creep back and do some serious damage," said Hattie anxiously, "she's spiteful enough."

"I think we should tell her tomorrow," confirmed Felix, "as Leo says, she needs to be gone. I don't think she'll come back Hats, she's all puff and wind."

"No, not tomorrow, we can't afford to risk any scenes with Roxy likely to come into the yard at any time. Let's leave it until later in the week." Seb waved his glass airily to them all, "Let's keep her on side till then."

"Seb, okay, but don't go stirring the shit will you?" said Leo sternly, "What'll we do? Re-advertise?"

"I don't think we can – not if we don't want to wind her up, and the last lot of replies to the ads were pretty bleak weren't they? No, we'll have to invent an excuse to get rid of her, you know, like we can't afford her – something like that, then struggle on for a bit on our own and see who else we can come up with."

"Well I'm willing to put in more hours Felix, if it means getting rid of her," smiled Hattie, her face relieved that, at last, her nemesis was leaving. "I can always get in earlier."

"Me too," agreed Leo, reaching over and squeezing Hattie's hand, "she's a fucking witch."

"Okay children, that's sorted," Seb grinned, "she goes at the end of the week."

CHAPTER 44

Alice slammed the door shut and buckled up her seat belt. She bumped down the farm drive towards the lane and turned left at the end towards Fittlebury. The positive and constant thing in her life was that she loved her job, and that last visit had been really satisfying. Suturing had always been her forte, relishing the concentration required to perform the most intricate and methodical work, keeping the wound as aseptic as possible, and sometimes, like today, in the dirtiest of conditions. She hummed to herself as the car sped along the road, the overgrown grass on the verges whirling madly in her wake. Apart from her one outburst with Felix over that stupid tart Roxy, she had forced herself to be calmer since he got back from Somerford. The shock of that young rider dying had really upset him, and she determined that she was just being stupid and she needed to take stock of what she had here with him and her life in Fittlebury and to stop being so unreasonable and protect what she had, not destroy it with her paranoia. She thought back to yesterday when she'd interrupted Andrew and Oli in the surgery, she knew she'd nearly lost it then. Luckily neither of them had noticed; they were pretty thick as far as picking up on emotions were concerned. She smiled to herself – they were blokes after all – nice blokes though. Heading out onto the road towards Priors Cross, she passed the old Abbey looming up on the hillside, its lofty walls craggy against the skyline. Two riders were ambling alongside the ruins, and she recognised Jennifer Parker-Smythe's horses – ridden in all probability by those two dumb dyke grooms - hardly likely to be Jennifer after the aggro there last year. She slowed down on a blind corner and swore under her breath, nearly ramming into a huge low-loader laden with a digger, attempting to negotiate the tight turn down the drive to the old mill. Alice tooted her horn furiously, throwing her hands up in pointless despair at the driver who was ignoring her. Drumming her fingers on the steering wheel in irritation, with her short temper beginning to simmer she was just about to leap out of the car ready for a row when her phone rang and impatiently she clicked on the hands free.

"Alice Cavaghan," she barked at the caller, all good intentions of being calm and pleasant to the clients gone, "What can I do for you?"

"Ah Alice my dear," said an oily dangerous voice, "there's a great deal you can do for me."

Alice felt numb; her voice quavered slightly, "Who is this?"

"Alice, you don't need to know about me, but I know all about you," the voice at the other end sneered, "and the point is, what I want from you."

"I've told you before, I don't know what you're talking about, and if you don't stop pestering me I'll go to the police!" Alice shouted down the phone, "I mean it, leave me alone!"

"No you won't Alice, because if you don't want your partners and the police to know all about your shady dealings, you are going to do exactly what I say."

Alice's heart was slugging against her ribs, her hands felt clammy but she managed to keep her voice steady, "I don't know what you're talking about."

"Yes you do, and I've got proof. So if you want to keep yourself out of trouble you'll meet me and we can discuss how you can keep me quiet."

"I won't," said Alice hotly, "I won't meet you."

"I think you will Alice, and you know you will. Remember what happened to that cat on your doorstep? Did you think you could run away? Now don't be a silly girl. Meet me tonight – at the Bolney Stage at 6pm. Don't be late. If you don't show, the evidence will be with the press and your partners in the morning."

"How will I know you?" Alice whispered, "that's if I decide to come?"

"I'll know you, I've been watching you," the voice laughed spitefully, "And believe me Alice, you'll be there."

Alice heard herself whimpering like a trapped animal and realised that not only had the phone disconnected, but that the lorry had moved and the road was clear. The nightmare had begun again; she pulled away in the car, her vision clouded with tears as fat as raindrops and knew that she would be at the Bolney Stage that night.

"Blimey, have you seen the diggers are at the mill already?" said Leo, "They haven't wasted any time have they?"

"No, it's going to be a right mess for a while, but I suppose it'll be worth it when it's finished" said Felix thoughtfully, loosening Picasso's girth and pulling off his saddle. He glanced over Leo's shoulder into the yard, "How's the calculating Kylie this morning?"

"Moaning about her car – apparently it's on its last legs. Needs to get it repaired but doesn't have the money, she was saying she could do with some more hours here," sighed Leo, "in her dreams methinks."

"Too bloody right, she's in for a shock then," snapped Felix, "How much more has she got to do before she finishes?"

"She's on the last loose box, so another half hour should do it. Hattie's doing the tack, and we've left Rambler and Doris to hack out later."

"Good, get her out of the way as fast you can, I can hardly bring myself to look at her."

"Don't let her wind you up Felix. She might be a bitch but she's a good shit shoveller."

"She's a good shit stirrer," grumbled Felix. "I won't have her upsetting Hattie like she has. If I'd had my eye on the ball in the first place – she'd have been out before now."

"Well you have now," Leo smiled sympathetically, "Don't worry I've been looking out for Hattie."

"Thanks Leo, I know you have. Seb can be a tosser sometimes though."

"Oh take no notice," laughed Leo, "he knows more than he lets on. He just likes to have a bit of amusement usually at everyone else's expense – although this time he went a step too far. We nearly came to blows before you arrived last night."

"Christ! Did you?" Felix spun round, bridle in hand, "I had no idea."

"Well he's all mouth and trousers. He soon backed down, but he behaves like a prick sometimes."

"Good on you, he was a bit outnumbered last night then."

"Oh don't get me wrong, he knows what sort of girl Kylie is, all yards come across them at some time or another. Seb's just playing gay games and went a bit overboard."

Felix tossed a rug over Picasso, "Thank the Lord we're all agreed now. Come on, let's get our heads together for the onslaught of what is Roxy."

Leo grabbed the saddle Felix had slung over the stable door and they stalked off to the tack room to join Hattie, who glanced up from soaping a bridle as they walked in.

"Okay," she queried, "has she gone?"

"Not yet," said Leo, dumping the saddle on a rack to be cleaned, "I'm going to hurry her along now, you two stay where you are."

Felix moved over to the sink and filled the kettle, "Want a cup?" he asked, picking up a cup and waving it at her, "I'm gasping."

"Please."

"I'll be glad when this afternoon is over."

"Me too. Leo and I are going to head out directly Roxy pitches up. Galaxy is sparkling, all you'll have to do is shove the tack on."

"Fine," said Felix, chucking teabags into mugs, "I'm dreading it, I just hope things don't go tits up and Roxy likes the bloody horse."

"Of course she will, what's not to like? He's good looking, quiet enough for her, unless she's a complete dork and he does all the tricks for Seb to show off."

"Let's hope you're right," said Felix, pouring in boiling water to mugs, "you know that feeling when you wish you'd never agreed to something?"

"Yeah I do, but what's done is done, and think of the commission!" laughed Hattie, "buck up Felix, this isn't like you."

"You're right," agreed Felix, "I'm just being stupid." He handed her the tea and picked up a cloth to help with the tack.

Twenty minutes later they heard Kylie's car splutter out of the yard and Leo stomped back in looking frustrated. "Right, I'm nipping down to the Gupta's shop in the village for some sarnies, what d' ya want?"

"I'll have a steak bake, if they've got any left, or if not - you choose – anything but cheese – I seem to have lived on it lately," said Felix, starting on the next saddle, "and some Red Bull."

"Crikey – Red Bull – what d' ya think ya gonna need all that energy for?" laughed Leo. "How about you Hats?"

"Oh, I'll have a baguette – anything, I don't mind, and a diet coke," Hattie reached into her bag to fish out her purse.

"I'll get it Hats," said Felix, handing him a couple of tenners, "yours too Leo, I owe you both big time."

"Right on," laughed Leo, taking the money, "shan't be long then. Seb'll be back in about 20 minutes."

Roxy was wending her way towards Fittlebury. She was a whole lot earlier than she'd planned. The racy, black Cooper S hurtled along the lanes, its throaty engine accompanied with Michael Jackson . Her brain was fizzing as much as her stomach with an irrational mix of emotions. Fear, excitement and dread churned together in a huge adrenalin rush, coupled with a touch of sexual frisson. It was going to be an interesting experience if nothing else. She just hoped she'd impressed upon the boys how important secrecy was and that they didn't screw up by opening their mouths in the pub or somewhere equally stupid. Dropping the revs on the mini to change gear and swing into the drive to the Hall, she almost wrote off an old banger of a car stalling in the entrance. Swearing, she edged past it and swept on, not looking back, glad for the millionth time for the blacked out windows.

Kylie, whose car had finally faltered with all the grace of tug boat battling against a force 11 gale, was sure that the mini was going to hit her. She braced herself open-mouthed in astonishment for the inevitable impact, but the driver scooted up on the verge like a pro skateboarder, narrowly missing the stone pillars by a whisker, and drove on without even stopping to see if she was okay. *Fucking Hell*! It nearly took her out it was going so fast. Shaking with anger and relief, she tried the ignition again, the car spluttered pathetically for a second, wheezed, and then faded miserably. There was nothing for it, she'd have to walk back to the yard and get help, or she supposed she could ring them - perhaps they'd come out and rescue her. Grumbling, she levered herself out of the car and picked up her rucksack, deciding she'd start walking back and ring Leo on the way. Fuming with angry frustration, she realised her phone had no signal and tossed it back in the bag. If the driver in that fucking mini had been more considerate and stopped, they might have been able to help, or at least given her a lift. Stalking towards the stables, she wondered who it could have been. Not a car she recognised, and hardly one that would be visiting Lady V, so it was more than likely heading for the yard – but who was it? Leo hadn't said a word to her about a client coming, she thought savagely, neither had that skanky bitch Hattie, and Felix was so far up his own arse he didn't even notice her half the time. Curiosity made her climb up on the park railings and crane to get a better look, but she couldn't see a thing. Well she'd surprise them and creep back, she had perfect justification after all, and there was definitely something going on, she'd been feeling it for days – bugger ringing.

Leo had just jumped into Felix's VW Golf and was toddling off to the shop with his sandwich order, when a black Mini skated across the cobbles, executing a perfect handbrake turn spinning through 90º and narrowly missing his own car by inches. Enraged as a speared bull and intent on murder, for once the pupils of his sleepy green eyes were so dilated they looked almost black and were flashing with rage, he leapt out of the car and hurtled towards the Mini and yanked open the door.

"What the fuck do you think you're doing driving like that!" he yelled, his dark Mediterranean skin flushed an angry red, "this is a bloody yard, not a race track!"

Roxy looked him up and down carefully, assessing every fine quality of his physique. "Hello, I'm Roxy," she said sweetly, "I don't believe we met last time, you must be Leo?"

Leo was flustered; he stood back assessing her, balancing his battle of natural animosity against a nutcase driver with the need to humour an important client. The humour won. "No you're quite right, I don't think we've met Ms Le Feuvre, I'm Leo. Sorry - but horses are fragile creatures and …"

"No need to explain Leo, my fault entirely," Roxy sighed, stepping seductively out of the car, her long legs encased enticingly in tight breeches and boots. "I have so much to learn, I hope you'll be able to show me the ropes?"

"It'll be my pleasure Ma'am," smiled Leo deferentially, "if you could just drive a bit slower next time."

Roxy put out her hand and touched him briefly on the arm, "Of course I will, let's take that as read, it was stupid of me not to have realised. And please call me Roxy." She cast her gaze around her, "Now I know I'm terribly early but I was supposed to be meeting

Seb and Felix. I gather they've been out shopping."

Leo laughed in spite of himself, "Yes they certainly have, Galaxy's a fine horse. I think you'll be delighted."

"God, I hope so, he cost enough. Can you show him to me?" purred Roxy, clutching Leo's arm again, "Oh, you were just going out though?

"Hi Roxy, you're early," called Felix, who'd heard the commotion and come out from the tack room, "we weren't expecting you till after lunch."

"Sorry darling, my sched is tight – and I knew you wouldn't mind," she paraded over to Felix and kissed him on both cheeks, "I'm terribly excited."

"I'll show you the horse for now. Seb'll be back soon and he'll ride him for you. Leo was just off on a food run, do you want anything – sandwich, baguette?"

"I wish," sighed Roxy, patting her concave tummy, "maybe some fruit?"

Leo clearly starstruck, was reluctant to leave, "I won't be long" he said, and spun round to his car and whizzed off down the drive.

"Hmm, he's a bit of boy racer, and he's just told me off for driving too fast," remarked Roxy, amused and enthralled at Leo's reaction, "charming, young man though."

"Very charming," agreed Felix. "Let me show you your new horse, he's just over here. Hats?" he called over his shoulder, "Grab a head collar can you, and then put the kettle on?"

Hattie hurried over, she'd been watching from the tack room door as the men melted and fawned over the starlet. She gave a beaming, welcoming smile but, this time, she was virtually ignored as Roxy clung like a limpet to Felix's arm and gazed into his eyes, and Felix was lapping up every moment.

Leo crashed the gears of the VW down the drive in his anxiety to get to the shop and back in record time, so as not to miss a moment with Roxy, all thoughts of a hack with Hattie evaporating like a puddle on a hot day. Roxy was so different in the flesh – quite … mesmerising. He squinted up the drive with the sun in his eyes. There was someone walking towards the yard. To his horror he realised it was Kylie. *Fucking hell*!

"You okay hun?" he called over-brightly, as he pulled the car to a stop. "What's up?"

"My sodding car's conked out – up at the gates," grumbled Kylie, looking over his shoulder, "whose car was that just now, it nearly ran me over."

"What car?" smiled Leo innocently, getting out and taking her bag and putting it pointedly in the back of the car, "Let's take a look at yours."

"A black mini, going like shit off a shovel. You must have seen it," sniped Kylie nastily, "It pulled into the yard."

"Oh yeah – driver's lost," said Leo casually, "Look, I'm going to the Gupta's shop in the village, I'll take a look at your car on the way, jump in."

Kylie hesitated, she didn't believe him but she didn't have a choice, other than call him a liar. Furious, she stomped over to the front passenger seat and plonked herself down "Come on then, stop dawdling about" she muttered with all the graciousness of a toad in the hole.

CHAPTER 45

Situated high above the manic melee of the A23, on what was the old Brighton Road, the Bolney Stage was a legendary old coaching inn; roofed with heavy hand cut stone tiles, its brick and daub walls were painted a traditionally, startling white and, threaded with sooty blackened beams. Inside two massive, stone fireplaces divided the inner bar from the dining areas and, the low ceiling gave a dark clandestine intimacy with its tiny seating areas. By contrast, the main restaurant was lighter and airier leading onto a small terrace and garden. It was the epitome of a traditional English pub and was popular with both the locals and passing trade. Alice drove in at 5.50pm. She was ten minutes early and in the hiatus of trade between lunch and supper had no trouble finding a place to park amongst the few vehicles in the car park. She edged the 4x4 hard against the leafy hedge in a far corner hoping that the conspicuous Toyota would be less visible to the odd passer-by, especially the horsey brigade who might know the car. Huddling in her seat, she surreptitiously glanced in her rear view mirror at the other vehicles, trying to work out which one would be his, or was he even here yet? The minutes ticked past like a death knell whilst she steeled herself to walk in – should she go to the garden or into the bar? She'd been for a meal here with Felix a few times and there was a chance she might see someone she knew; she wrung her hands in despair and felt her body sweating through her clothes as she pondered what to do. Gritting her teeth, she reached over for her shoulder bag and gasped out in fright to see a face leering at her through the passenger window.

The man was not tall, but looked broad and sturdy in his checked jacket and open-necked shirt. His face was pudgy with heavy jowls, strands of oily, dark hair slicked in strands across his balding pate. The flushed cheeks, threaded with red spider veins betrayed he was a heavy drinker, and dark pouches of skin puckered under his bloodshot eyes. He beckoned at her to get out of the car, with a fat, square hand; large gold rings, like knuckle dusters encrusted on his fingers.

Alice felt sick, but took a lungful of air, squared her shoulders and got out, beeping the car shut behind her.

"Alice my dear, we meet at last, although your reputation quite precedes you," the man said smoothly and, had by this time, come around behind the car and trapped her alongside the hedge. He put his hand out to shake hers, and when she tossed her head in defiance, he merely laughed. "Suit yourself darling. Let's go inside and talk business."

"I've nothing to say to you. Whatever you have to say to me, you can say it here."

The smile on the man's face switched to an ugly frown as fast as if someone had turned out the lights. He grabbed her arm viciously, "Now get off your high horse you silly tart," he growled, "you're gonna do exactly what I say, or otherwise I'm gonna ruin you – got it?"

Alice tried to wrench herself back, but the man spun her round by the wrist forcing her arm up hard behind her back, with his other hand slamming her face against the car window. The pain in her arm was excruciating, shooting like sparking electric shocks through her whole body as he jerked it harder up between her shoulder blades. Her knees were crumpling with the agony. "Stop, please, stop," she whimpered, her words barely intelligible, "I beg you, stop."

"That's better Alice," he chided, dropping his grip from her arm and releasing her head as she slumped against the car, "next time I won't be so gentle."

Alice snivelled pathetically, righting herself and rubbing her arm, "What do you want?"

"Well for starters …" The man began licking his lips, but suddenly he stopped talking, tensing visibly as a Vauxhall Corsa drew into the car park. A couple of women were in the car and took their time getting out, fiddling about with cardigans and handbags and then finally, as they began walking towards the pub, they nudged each other and glanced over towards the hedge, laden with curiosity at the incongruous couple. The man grabbed Alice in a tight embrace and snogged her hard on the lips, his tongue drilling between her clenched teeth. The two women looked away quickly in disgust and hurried on into the pub. As soon as they'd disappeared the man shoved Alice roughly into the side of the Toyota, "right you stuck up bitch, where was I? Oh yes, What do I want?" He sneered menacingly, "Not *that*, well not today anyway." He chucked her under the chin, "Next time eh? Today a bit of Ketamine will do nicely."

Alice winced. She did have some Ketamine on board, and she could give it to him, but once she did, she'd be back to where she started. And she knew it wouldn't end there. She was weighing up all this up in her mind, the man's malodorous sweaty body so close to hers, and thought she just couldn't do it. She couldn't live like it again – she'd rather go to prison.

As he waited, almost as though he was reading her mind, he said, "Of course Alice, it's not just you in the equation now – you've got a pretty boyfriend and a cute little dog, not to mention all those horses of his. He wouldn't be so pretty once we'd finished with him – probably wouldn't walk again, let alone ride, and remember that sweet, little cat …" he smiled pleasantly, "you know it makes sense, now hand over the gear like a good girl."

"Well that went well," Seb enthused, "She adored the horse."

"She was so much nicer than I thought she'd be," Leo drooled, almost salivating at the memory of Roxy in her tight breeches, "and she was very game."

"You're not on the turn luvvie are you?" winked Seb at the others, "I always knew you batted for both sides."

"I never thought she'd have a sit on him, did you?" said Felix ignoring him, his mouth full of crisps, "she didn't do badly considering."

"He's a bloody good horse to tolerate such a beginner though," said Hattie, "they don't come many to the pound like him."

"No cupcake, you're right there," agreed Seb, "we were lucky to find him – let's have a celebratory toast." He lobbed his mug skywards, slopping the contents onto the floor, "Here's to Galaxy – what a star."

"I'll drink to that," giggled Leo, "although that was close run thing with Kylie this morning. I nearly wet myself when I saw her coming down the drive – I thought I'd never get rid of her."

"God, what a stroke of luck you went on a food run when you did. D' you think she saw anything?"

"No I don't think so, but she was bloody curious. She saw the Mini, but she couldn't have seen who it was. I managed to get that old banger of hers going and she toddled off. I half expected her to turn round and go back, but I was following her as far as the village shop, so she didn't have much option but to carry on driving. I wouldn't have put it past her to have come back."

"We'll have to be careful."

"When's Roxy coming back again?" asked Hattie, "I mean she's gonna be a pretty regular fixture isn't she?"

"Hmm, yep, she is, tomorrow," agreed Seb, and for once thinking rationally, "but I've gotta sneaking suspicion that if we dump Kylie now, she'll sneak back and blow the whistle."

"For fuck's sake Seb! You're not saying what I think you saying," snarled Felix, amazed. "Absolutely no back tracking – she's got to go!"

"I know what we said, but just think about it for a minute without getting on your high horse," sighed Seb, "she's a spiteful creature, imagine if we had the tabloids on our doorstep before we're ready. Roxy would string us up by our balls."

"No," said Felix flatly, "they'll get hold of the story anyway, if it's not this week, it'll be next."

"Hold on," said Leo rationally, "let's think about this carefully. As much as I want her to go more than any of us, I think Seb has a point. We could stomach another week with her if push came to shove, and it would be better to know where she is, than not."

Hattie put down her cup, and ran her fingers through her hair, suddenly she felt gloomy. Kylie was a loose cannon in so many ways, and no-one wanted rid of the cow more than she did, but they did need to keep her and Roxy's good will if they weren't to be exposed, along with her, as a public laughing stock in what would amount to a TV scam. What a nightmare. She wished they'd never got involved.

"Plus," emphasised Seb, "Alice was pretty anti, wasn't she Felix? Let's err on the cautious and keep the unpleasant little Kylie on our side. I know it's a pain in the proverbial, darlings, but you know what they say *'keep your friends close, but your enemies closer'*."

"I just can't believe we can make such an about turn like this," grumbled Felix, "she's poisonous. I don't trust her an inch."

"And that's the exact reason why we've got to keep her close, don't you see?"

"Oh alright," agreed Felix moodily, chucking his crisp bag in the bin and missing by a country mile, "but only for as long as it takes for it to become public, and then she's out the door."

"Cheer up, it'll only be for a week or so, then you can have the pleasure of giving her the old heave-ho."

"And a pleasure it will be too," Felix said grimly, "then we'll have to think what we're going to do to replace her. It's going to be a busy few months ahead. You've got the Nationals in September, that'll mean you being away for a few days, and if we've got Roxy to contend with too."

"We're gonna be flat out," said Leo, "but we'll manage somehow."

"I'm sorry you couldn't enter Gatcombe International Felix"

apologised Seb "I know you wanted to go."

"Actually, I wasn't that fussed. It was the syndicate who thought it would be a good idea – purely for the kudos of the HRH venue, I expect. Anyway, that was our agreement, and it coincides with your Nationals, so it's not up for discussion as far as I'm concerned."

Seb reached out and fondled his knee, "Well darling, I really appreciate it."

"Hey don't go getting carried away mate," grinned Felix, "otherwise I might change my mind."

"Too late sweetie, entries closed ages ago."

"I was joking, Hattie does the entries these days, don't you hun?"

Hattie laughed, "Sure do, they have to be in weeks in advance. Picasso is entered in the Intermediate at Goring Heath on 8th September, and then later in the month at the CIC2* at South of England on 29th. Although you said you might not do Goring didn't you Felix?"

"I'll see how he is, I want to make sure he peaking for the final run at Weston Park in a CCI** in mid-October."

"Fuck me, that's a big event," exclaimed Leo, "a three day isn't it?"

"Yes it is – exciting huh?" laughed Hattie, "and in between times there's all novices to do. It's a busy time. We're aiming to take Rambler, and possibly Woody to Aldon International at the end of October to do their first CIC*."

"My dears - makes our little dressage outings look positively humdrum," sighed Seb dramatically. "What dreadfully exciting lives you lead. All I do is enter at A, twiddle about pathetically for a mere five minutes, then for a finale - make a skulking exit on a long rein stage A." He quoted morosely, "That's the way the world ends, my dears, not with a bang but a whimper."

Felix howled with laughter, "Go on, you're a right old

professional and you know it, and I wish I could ride a test like you."

"If only you meant it dear Felix, if only …" Seb cast him a doleful look, "but at least you've agreed to hang on to the odious Kylie for the time being. That is such a help to those of us left behind."

Felix shook his head in disbelief. He had been well and truly '*Sebbed*', and unless he came up with an alternative solution there wasn't much else he could do about getting rid of Kylie.

Roxy was buzzing. She drove back towards London on a rollercoaster of a high that would have made *Kingda Ka* look tame. The boys had come up trumps with the nag, it reminded her of one of those china ornaments her mum had lovingly dusted on the mantelpiece when she was a kid. She hadn't intended to ride it either, but when she saw Seb making it perform ballet like Mikhail Baryshnikov it had all seemed so easy, she was sure she could do it. She laughed to herself – thank the fuck for *Annie the Equisator,* at least she hadn't felt a total pleb when she'd clambered on with Seb holding her leg on one side and Felix clutching onto the other and that rather gorgeous Leo holding the front end of the thing. They'd been more nervous than she had. Unsurprisingly, she decided not let on about *Annie*, so they just thought she was a natural, and lapped up their attention and she'd loved every minute. But what was unbelievable was that she got a real kick out it, the whole shebang – not just the attention thing, but from perching high up on a living, breathing creature and having the power and skill to control it. For her, there was going to be a lot more to this riding malarkey than a marketing opportunity, although of course it would be a great one; she was actually going to relish the challenge. It opened up so many new horizons and, for the first time, she could see exactly where dear old bimbo Lisa got her kicks when Mikey was up to no good getting his. If she could become accomplished at this, produce her own lines of equestrian gear and market them, she could be on a winner. Judging by the cost of these fucking breeches, not to mention how much she'd had to pay for the horse, there would be money to be made in the process. She licked her lips, pleasure and profit – the perfect combination in Roxy's opinion.

When her car phone rang she was irritated. She was enjoying her musings, lost in the daydream of buying more horses, designer label breeches and accompanying the boys to competitions. She contemplated ignoring it, but knew she wouldn't, she never could.

"Hi!" she shouted unnecessarily into the loudspeaker, "I'm driving – who is it?"

"Hi baby, it's me."

Roxy recognised Max's voice straight away, but she was still miffed with him, and even more miffed that she'd answered, "Who?"

"Roxy, it's me – Max."

Roxy smiled wickedly at the exasperation in his voice, thinking *you can fuck off Max*, "Oh hello stranger. How's the king of the sport of kings?"

"Ha ha. Very funny. Thought I'd try and catch up – haven't seen you for a while. Fancy meeting for lunch sometime this week?"

Roxy thought quickly, she was desperate to prattle on about her new ideas and before, Max would have been the perfect sounding board, but now … "Oh babe, I'd love to, but I'm seriously tied up this week. I've got so much on with this mill project thingy. Aiden's giving me such ear-ache about it all."

"Oh Roxy, for Christ's sake it can't be that important can it?" complained Max "I hardly ever see you."

No, thought Roxy, you're too busy with that tart Anna and going fucking racing to bother with me, and I'm not some toy you just pick up when you fancy lunch "Darling I know, Aiden's got that Farouk from Channel 4 doing this TV show, I'm sure you remember me telling you. It's a bleeding pain, but they're following me around like a fucking shadow, I can't even poo in peace!"

"I'll call you next week, shall I then?"

"Great idea sweetie. Look I'd better go, there's a policeman. I don't wanna get pinched for being on the phone. Call me next week, Ciao."

Roxy sighed in satisfaction, her day just got even better. Irrationally she was pleased he'd called; made her feel she had the upper hand in this bizarre game they seemed to be playing just lately. When she'd seen him dangling Anna on his arm and he'd ignored her; if she was totally truthful, it had hurt - she had always been the special one. Now she was going to fling herself into this new project and was glad she'd resisted the temptation to talk to Max. In the old days she would have blurted out all her plans to him, but something made her hesitate now. This wasn't the old days, he'd changed.

Max disconnected the call and bounced his phone across the desk. His whole life seemed to be a frenzy of never-ending frustrating calls and this was just another one. He got up and went over to the massive floor to ceiling windows which led out onto the balcony. Yanking them open, he stepped out. The Thames, its huge, grey expanse far below, rolled unhurriedly along and Max leant alongside the Perspex and tubular steel railing and peered sullenly into the river, pondering its timeless journey into the great metropolis. Roxy must think he was stupid. She was on her hands free, she didn't need to hang up. The plain fact was, she didn't *want* to talk to him, and didn't *want* to meet him for lunch either. He felt annoyed with her, and then sad, perhaps he had played the Anna card too strong. He'd wanted to teach her a lesson, but he didn't want to lose her in his life. Then there was Anna, far from being her Dr Dolittle, he'd become little more than her tormentor. She was terrified of him – poor cow. Last time he'd seen her after Ronnie's party, he'd taken her out to dinner and tried to talk to her, find out more about her, but every question he'd asked she reacted like he'd stuck her with an electric cattle prod. He couldn't blame her really, he'd treated her badly. That was after he found about his kid though, he'd been shell-shocked. Nigel Brown was slow, but he now knew the baby had been a little girl and even knew her name. Max had given him instructions not to harass the grandparents, so it was a tedious business but Brown was thorough, even if Max had to spell out the instructions in words of one syllable. He was arranging for Jilly's parents to have a little windfall soon. He knew they were too proud to accept hand-outs, but were too naïve to question something so random. It was, to Max's mind, numbingly slow, but he'd waited years to find Jilly, he could wait a few months to find his child.

He turned abruptly, dodged around the table and chairs and paced along the balcony, which ran the whole length of the apartment. He bypassed the kitchen and ducked into his bedroom, heading for the shower. It was getting on for four, time to start his working day. The clubs would just be opening, although the massage parlours ran a brisk daytime trade and he left that to his team to organise. Business was good, brisk and on the up. He was coining in a fair old wedge on the racing but he knew there was so much more to come. Ronnie was only throwing him the crumbs, but for the time being he was content to peck at the table. He thought about the bent vet they'd talked about, and decided it was even more reason to make sure he kept in touch with Roxy. He liked to be ahead of the game and she just might be able to open a little window of opportunity – after all, Max only needed a small break, it could make all the difference. He began to hum quietly, suddenly his day had gotten a whole lot brighter.

CHAPTER 46

"**Alice, have** you got a spare moment later? Oli and I were hoping to have a chat," asked Andrew, "say about six-ish?"

Alice's stomach lurched like she'd jumped off a cliff and her heart started to race. "Sure" she answered quickly, "What's it about?"

"Oh, I'd rather talk when I've got more time. I'm dashing off on a call and Oli's down at the racing stables this morning, so he'll be a while – I'll see you later." He picked up his phone and shot out to the front office, dropping a kiss on Caitlin's dark head as he passed.

Alice clutched the side of the desk and watched him. Had he somehow found out? What could he want to talk about? She glanced furtively at Caitlin and Paulene, who were busy at the computers, and edged her way into the drug's cupboard. Stuffing what she could into a spare cardboard box, and signing out just the minimum, she shuffled back into the office and dumped it on the desk.

Paulene was watching her closely from behind her screen, clocking the box and Alice's shifty expression. She would dearly love to know what she was up to. She was definitely behaving oddly, furtively even, and had been ever since the beginning of the week. She didn't know what was worse, her previously irascible bad temper or this secretive cloak and dagger stuff. On the up-side, she had been sickly sweet to them, even down to bringing in a box of chocolates yesterday. Paulene didn't trust her an inch, but perhaps she was just being paranoid; Caitlin hadn't mentioned anything and Andrew and Oli were on good form. Whatever, she was going to keep a careful eye on her.

Alice blustered out of the back office, clutching her box tightly, the lid firmly taped down, "I'm off girls, see you later. Anything you need brought back?"

"Not for me," smiled Caitlin, "Have a good day now."

"Me neither, thanks," said Paulene. "By the way Alice, you have signed out those drugs haven't you?"

"Of course, more than my life's worth to forget," joked Alice, breezing out of the door quickly before Paulene could see the tell-tale flush of the lie creeping up her neck.

Outside, Alice threw the box into the back of the Toyota. Her legs were shaking and she stumbled into the driver's seat, hardly pausing before roaring off down the lane and unaware of Paulene watching her from the surgery window.

"I'm sure she's up to something," observed Paulene, "she looked shifty."

"Oh don't be exaggerating now Paulene," laughed Caitlin, "she had a bit of a bollocking from Andrew, probably a bit wary of us that's all."

"Hmm, that's as maybe, but I've got an instinct for someone up to no good," Paulene tapped the side of her nose, "and she *is,* let me tell you."

"Well, I've got a bit of news to tell you," Caitlin giggled, mirroring Paulene and tapping the side of her nose back, "but you'd better keep it under your wig."

Paulene's face brightened, "Go on? What?"

"We're moving!"

"Who is? What you and Andrew?" gasped Paulene, "Not leaving us?"

Caitlin pushed back her chair, "Nooo! Don't be daft, the practice. Remember I told you, I was going to look for new premises - well I did." Her voice bubbling with excitement, she relayed her visit to Grace and what had happened since. "So Andrew has spoken to Oli, and it's all been settled with Grace's folks."

Paulene plonked herself down on her chair, pushing her hair back from her face. "Well blow me down, you don't hang around do you?" But it's fantastic news, Caitlin. I thought Andrew had a spring in his step, and Oli too. Does Alice know?"

"No, they're going to tell her tonight. Andrew said I could tell you today but don't blurt anything out until they've spoken to Alice, and he'll give you the full low down later. Isn't it exciting?"

"I should say. It's just what we need!" exclaimed Paulene, glancing around the cramped office, "I'm going to make us a brew to celebrate."

Alice was far from celebrating. She was sweating and frightened. After the terrifying ordeal at the Bolney Stage she quaked every time her phone rang. She was constantly looking over her shoulder. The man, whoever he was, had been watching her. He knew all about Felix, what he did, where she lived, the horses, even down to Fiver. How could she have believed that running away from Oz would have been enough, stupid to think that burning the stuff in the garden would have solved everything and they would just go away. They were never going to go away. She should have 'fessed up when she had the opportunity before she came to England. Now, here she was, being sucked into the spiral again, and she couldn't see a way out. So far the demands had just been minor, but she knew it wouldn't end there, just like it hadn't before. She wrung her hands in despair. What the hell could she do?

For Roxy, the subterfuge involved in fooling Aiden and the smug Chrissie when she was sneaking out to Fittlebury, became a scintillating and delicious game. Their own sordid and grubby, little affair had reached the point when they could scarcely keep their hands to themselves. Roxy had, jubilantly been on the point of catching them *in flagrante delicto* on several occasions when she'd deliberately breezed into Aiden's office unexpectedly, to see Chrissie smoothing down her skirt, and Aiden looking guilty. If Roxy hadn't been cooking her own particular gourmet meal of deceit, she might have been annoyed; as it was, it suited her perfectly and for Aiden and Chrissie, they were always relieved when she disappeared under the guise of invented appointments with dentists, doctors and stylists, and never questioned or noticed how long she was gone. Roxy had been able to make the tedious journey to Fittlebury on a fair few occasions, and each time she went to the yard the more hooked she became - riding, and moreover Felix, had gotten under her skin. But for all that Roxy flaunted the persona of a bimbo, she was no fool about her career and was uber-paranoid about being seen in the locality, especially as work on the mill was well underway. The charred ruins, whilst not having the go-ahead for restoration yet, were being cleared ready for the work to start as soon as they were tipped the wink. The barns though had been cleared and carpenters and workmen were manically busy working under the close eye of Alan and the chosen builders - Bryce Brothers, and David Bryce was there most days checking on the proceedings with him. Once Aiden and Farouk had made an appearance for the sake of the cameras, but they were just snapshots until there was something fancier to film, so Roxy only had to do a cameo attendance, and luckily she'd had plenty of notice. But she still had to be careful, just in case Alan should inadvertently spot her. But considering he'd never seen her Mini before, unless someone let the cat out of the bag, she was relatively safe. On the whole, the barns were shaping up just fine under Alan's eagle eye. She would put her personal stamp on them later, but for now her passion definitely lay elsewhere - in more ways than one and her fascination for the horse game was not just for the four legged variety. She'd flirted outrageously with all of the lads, but she'd centred her attention on the seriously fuckable Felix, who'd been nothing other than charm personified, but nonetheless hadn't once given her any hint of a come on. Roxy was mildly irked, she was used to men dropping their boxers at the merest hint, but Felix seemed oblivious. Undeterred, it made him all the more fascinating, and there was nothing Roxy enjoyed more than a good chase, and after all she had plenty of time. She licked her collagen, inflated lips in anticipation and scooted down the drive to the stables.

All the previous week, the gang at the Fittlebury Hall yard had been juggling timetables. Falling midway between *Sliding Doors* and an *Alan Ayckbourn* farce, the strain was crippling and, to an outsider, would have been hilarious, but they were all at breaking point.

"I can't keep this up much longer," moaned Hattie, flumping down on the armchair in the tack room her legs akimbo. "I'm gonna go mad."

"Just hold it together, Hats purleese," smiled Felix sympathetically, tousling her hair and putting on the kettle. "As soon as Roxy gives the go-ahead and we go public, we can get rid of Kylie."

"Felix, get real for Christ's sake. We're stuck with her and Roxy – aren't we?"

"No, we're not, don't you see? Once the cameras are here, the game's over. We can ditch Kylie and Roxy can bask in the glory – we can go back to normal."

"Huh! Normal what's that then?" grumbled Hattie despondently, twiddling her hair around her thumb and finger desperately. "Have you seen the way Roxy looks at you?"

"Don't be dumb Hattie, now you really are being stupid."

"Whatever." dismissed Hattie, "you think I'm dumb. You need to wake up, Felix, and smell the coffee."

"Well, here's your own coffee. Shut up and drink it, before Roxy arrives," Felix smiled supportively, as he handed her a scalding cup. "It won't be long now."

Hattie took the mug, wincing with the heat of it, but couldn't return the smile. She felt really pissed off. She couldn't decide who was the most unbearable of the pair, poxy Roxy or catty Kylie. Last weekend, Felix had taken some horses to Firle Place Horse Trials and they'd spent a great weekend together, albeit with Sheena in tow. Woody was continuing to show improving form with a 9th place in the BE100 on the Saturday and Felix was beginning to have high hopes for him. On the Sunday, Jacks had clocked up quite a few faults with an erratic show jumping, not enough to stop him going cross country, where luckily he'd redeemed himself with a stonking round. Rambler performed as his average self, but Abbey and Peter Marchant played the delighted owners and mobbed Felix with enthusiasm as they bounded over the finish line. Topped off with a mega ice cream and watching the CIC1* which was running on the same day, it was a great weekend. Now the week stretched out like the bloody Nile with the ceaseless manipulating of the obnoxious Kyle and Roxy, let alone the sponsors and other clients. It was all becoming a frigging nightmare. This coming week was an important one for Seb when Wellington Riding were running the Area Festivals. He was entered on several days in the Freestyle classes, with the biggy on Wednesday where he'd qualified for the championship and the prize money was £250 – a pot of unheard of in dressage classes. If they didn't have Kylie, it would be almost impossible to get everything done and keep their own horses, and the ones Seb had left at home, exercised and then be dripping with enthusiasm should Roxy pitch up.

The sound of a car pulling up into the yard had Felix rushing through the door like his dick was on fire. Hattie laid aside her coffee resignedly, struggled out of the armchair and followed him with all the enthusiasm of a dog going to the vet's. To her surprise, and obviously Felix's, it wasn't Roxy, but Alice's car outside and, judging from the look on Felix's face, he wasn't too pleased to see her. Hattie, sensing a row, sidled off to Galaxy's box where Leo was strapping his smooth, chocolate coat to a glossy sheen and nipped in the stable door crouching like a sniper behind the wall.

Leo looked on in amusement, "What on earth are you doing?"

"Shhhushhh! Come and look," Hattie hissed, her eyes riveted on the yard outside. "Alice has just arrived, they don't look very pleased to see each other."

Leo crept behind the good-natured Galaxy, who, unperturbed, was still pulling at his hay net, and putting his hands on Hattie's shoulders craned round the door. "No, you're right they don't – Alice is waving her arms around."

"Don't let them see you for Christ's sake," spluttered Hattie, pushing him back. "Felix was looking daggers when she arrived."

Alice's voice resonated around the yard, clearly becoming raised and agitated. Leo and Hattie nudged each other but could only catch the odd word. "*I need*" "*now Felix*" and then "*I mean it now*", "*trouble*", "*dangerous*" "*finished*". The words seemed meaningless, and they couldn't hear Felix's response. Hattie peeped through the doorway. Felix looked calm but anxious, and he was holding Alice by her shoulders looking at her seriously, talking quietly, and trying to calm her down. Alice shoved him away in anger, her face ugly and red with rage. Slapping his face as hard as she could, she turned and ran over to her car and jumped in, driving full throttle out of the yard, narrowly avoiding Seb who was coming back from the school with Doris.

"Fuck me!" said Leo, "What was that all about?"

"No idea?" said Hattie, "Poor Felix, she can be such a bitch, it's not as if he's not got enough on his plate."

"We all have, she's a selfish cow that one, gives no thought for anyone but herself. look at poor dear Doris, she's really upset." Leo pushed past Hattie out of the stable and went to rescue Seb, who was white faced on the skittering horse dancing all over Lady V's rose bed.

Hattie didn't quite know what to do, finish off Galaxy who was still contentedly eating, or go and find Felix? In the end, her curiosity got the better of her. She padded over to the tack room to find him huddled on the armchair she'd vacated not ten minutes earlier, cradling the coffee she'd reluctantly abandoned.

"You okay?"

"It's at times like this I wish I smoked, or drank during the day, or both," mumbled Felix, his eyes dull "Alice just thinks I can drop everything and go off and have a '*serious talk*' with her. I don't know what she thinks I do all day, I really don't. I've got Roxy coming any minute, been flat sticks all morning. I've been telling her all week how stressed I am."

Hattie perched on the arm of the chair and patted his back, "Come on, it's only a lover's tiff, she'll get over it and understand when you explain tonight."

Felix sniffed, and put his arm on Hattie's leg, "Thanks Hats, you're such a rock, I know she's busy too, but I don't know if my arse is bored or reamed these days with her – she's all over me one minute, shouting at me the next."

Hattie's heart was pumping like a V8 engine, no matter how hard she tried it was almost impossible not react when he touched her. Alice didn't know how lucky she was, but now was not the time to be telling him. "You'll sort it Felix. Once she's had time to calm down."

"What the fuck was all that about?" blustered Seb, thundering into the tack room, his face ashen and his normal bonhomie slipping into his boots. "She nearly bloody killed me, and as for poor Doris! She should know better, Felix, being a vet an' all."

Hattie exaggeratedly raised her eyebrows to Seb, who to his credit when he saw Felix slumped in the armchair like a someone who'd just been told he'd got a month to live backed right off, "You alright cupcake?"

"Yeah, but you're right Seb, I'm sorry," said Felix dejectedly, levering himself up "I'll go get Galaxy tacked up, Roxy'll be here any minute – the show must go on."

When he had gone Seb demanded a full post mortem of what had happened, although Hattie was pretty sure that Leo had given him the low down. Seb stood with his back to the sink, cradling his chin in his hand "Poor old Felix, and you're certain you couldn't make out any more than what you've told me?"

"Nope," said Hattie frowning, "I wouldn't go reading too much into it, you know how demanding Alice is."

"Hmm, that's as maybe, but you didn't see the desperate look on her face when she nearly took me out," remarked Seb thoughtfully, "I think there might be more to it than meets the eye."

Alice was distraught as she sped out of the yard, tears blurred her eyes and she was only dimly aware of the terrified grey horse and rider spooking into the rose bushes as she hurtled off. Wiping her hand across her face, mascara streaking across her cheek, she groaned in despair. She'd hoped, that by talking to Felix, somehow she could make it alright, they could even disappear together, anything, something. But he'd had no time to talk, didn't seem to grasp her urgency, how important it was that she speak to him. She pulled the car over into a lay-by, the sweat beading on her upper lip, her palms damp and the tears rolling uncontrolled down her cheeks – how had things become so bad? Felix was so stupid, but how was he to know? She mustn't blame him. All she could do was to keep quiet and see how bad the demands became. She rubbed her eyes and attempted to pull herself together. She must face this alone, not involve him, she was crazy to try. Her phone beeped a message and her heart started racing. She glanced at the screen, but it was only the surgery asking her to make a call to a client. Picking up the phone, she tapped out an affirming reply. She needed to get a grip, muster some fighting spirit, and that's just what she'd do, fight for her life.

As the afternoon crawled past and the sun began to cast longer shadows across the downs, Kylie was limping her way back from her afternoon job in her tired, old motor towards her home in nearby Cosham. As she came nearer to Fittlebury Hall, she stuck two fingers up in defiance at the grand old house across the park. She was sick of mucking and chucking out, and was beginning to regret giving up her job in the riding school – at least there had been more variety in what she did then. Now, her life consisted of looking at the inside of stinking wheelbarrows and dragging nags out to paddocks or bringing them in and spending the day smelling like a muck heap. The thought of doing it in the winter; her hands frozen with the chilly rain or even worse, bloody snow, filled her with deep gloom. She'd hoped that the job at Fittlebury Hall would come to more, and she'd soon oust that dimmo Hattie, but it didn't seem to be working out that way. Even Seb, who she'd thought was on her side, had been strangely elusive over the last few days. Still she'd work on him, he was a push over, but Felix must have the hots for Hattie, which was a pity as she wouldn't have minded have a crack at him herself, but why else would he defend her like he did. Leo was okay, kept a low profile, and Hattie was just plain stupid. Kylie laughed to herself, Hattie dropped herself in it every time, and Kylie loved sticking the knife in. With any luck, if she kept the pressure up, it wouldn't be long before Hattie chucked it in, and Kylie took over. She'd be the one going out on the jollies with Felix and they'd find some other mug to do the mucking out. She ran her rapacious, pink tongue over her lips, gleefully enjoying the thought. Hattie's days were numbered.

The car chugged fitfully along the winding lane towards the Hall. Kylie flipped down the visor, squinting through the changing, shifting light as the sun dropped and big, fat, cumulus clouds rolled across the sky. She groped in her pocket for her fags and, scrabbled to find a lighter from the dashboard; she looked down for a split second, the car wandering onto the other side of the road. A ferocious blaring horn made her gasp and look up; a black Mini hurtled out of from Fittlebury Hall accelerating straight towards her. Frantically she wrenched at the steering wheel, and amazingly pulled over to a shuddering halt with her heart palpitating like a bat's wings. By the time she'd recovered and looked in her mirror, the Mini had disappeared from sight. The aftermath of fear prickled all over her angry body as though she'd been stung by a hundred nettles, and her panic gave way to fury. That fucking Mini again! That was the second time it had nearly written her off. There was no way she could follow it, but she had no doubt now that it had come from the yard, she was certain. Something was going on. Her first inclination was to dash in and confront them, but sitting back and lighting up her fag, she thought again. She'd catch them unawares and it might just be the lever she needed.

CHAPTER 47

Roxy sped back to the smoke. For once, the M25 was not strangled with vehicles belching pollution like Chernobyl, and the Mini ate up the miles like a voracious, jet-propelled bug. Roxy was totally oblivious to the whirling chaos she was leaving in her wake. As far as she was concerned, today was the day - it had been spectacularly successful. Okay, she was no Olympian, but she wasn't going to look a complete tit when the cameras were rolling, and now she would positively welcome them. She would be a triumph; natural, talented and accomplished; she'd show them she had a bit of class – that would wipe the smile of their fucking faces. Taking her foot of the gas she slowed the car and dropped down into the underground car park flashing the remote control to open the gates. It was action time.

Aiden was not at home, but she'd hardly expected him to be. Probably out shagging the delectable Chrissie, after all, he'd upgraded her from casual pussy to the full Billy Ocean. *Whatever* she thought, snatching out a bottle of Evian from the fridge and picking up her mobile, punching out a number and listening impatiently to the ring tone.

"Hey Farouk baby, it's Roxy. I've got good news and better news," she purred, "what d' ya wanna hear first?"

"Roxy… doll!" exclaimed Farouk cautiously, toppling off the nubile brunette perched on his knee, "great to hear from you, sounds good - what's up?"

"I've found the perfect place to do the riding scenes. As it happens just around the corner from the mill. It's all organised - they can start whenever and they have a horse which will be fine for me. And even better, the two lads that run the place are perfect eye candy, it'll be sensational babe."

Farouk hauled himself back to *Rox-Aid* with all the emotional enthusiasm of returning to work after a holiday as he watched the brunette hoist her tits back inside her bra, "that's awesome baby," he scrambled his thoughts half-heartedly, "how quickly can we begin?"

"As soon as you like," Roxy took a slug of her water, "obviously you'll want to get the first visit on film."

"Definitely. You've not been there yet then? It's all a bit sudden isn't it?" Farouk said suspiciously, "How'd you find out about it?"

"I'd met one of the lads when I first went down and then, by chance, met them in the pub again when I went down with Lisa. I asked them to have a look out for something and they made a few calls and discovered a suitable nag." Roxy lied economically, "but the sooner we get started the better – don't ya think?"

"Yeah," croaked Farouk, marshalling himself into action. "Look I'll call you first thing and sort out a time – ya?"

Roxy smiled to herself, *Bingo* she thought. "Do that baby," she said dangerously ,"don't wanna let the grass grow or are you smoking it as we speak?" she laughed, "you sound half asleep."

"No, no you just caught me at a bad time."

"Got your trousers down?" sneered Roxy accurately. "Okay call me tomorrow – make it early." She tossed the phone down on the work top, and snapped on the TV, flicking through the channels impatiently and, just as rapidly, switched it off. She prowled around the kitchen like a panther, wrenching open the fridge and picked at some prawns, distractedly gazing out of the window watching the last fingers of the sun streaking the skyline in a blaze of colour. She could hear the children chattering from upstairs and the nanny organising them for bed. Guiltily, she couldn't be bothered to make an appearance, she felt restless and distracted and their incessant prattling would set her nerves jangling. She needed to think and they would irritate the crap out of her. She had to get this just right. So far it had gone as slick as a tube of lube, but one false move now and she could still look a right tit. A cold chill of fear swept over her, if anyone found out – she needed to cover all her bases. Stalking back to pick up her phone, she punched out Seb's number.

"Babes, it's me," she purred, "sorry, to be such a pain, but I've had a thought and I need to run it past you."

"What did she want?" asked Leo, pitching balsamic dressing onto the salad and tossing the bowl onto the table, "everything okay?"

"Yeah, she's spoken to that Farouk character like she said she would, but I've a feeling she's got cold feet. Says she's not coming down again, unless it's with him and the entourage."

"God help us, the Queen has spoken," groaned Hattie, pulling a face at Hero and tugging at his ears, "life will never be the same."

"Come on misery guts," guffawed Seb, giving her a playful slap "You never know you might meet the man of your dreams behind the lens, or ..." he hesitated and gave Leo a meaningful look, "I might."

Leo plonked down the plates in front of them and ruffled first Seb's hair then Hattie's, "Eat," he commanded, "and Seb ... for once stop manipulating."

"I don't know what you mean!"

"Yes you do, eat your jacket potato, drink your drink and tell us what the plan is – we've got a really busy week ahead if you haven't forgotten."

"Don't remind me luvvie," gasped Seb, "I'm bricking it, and I could so do with that prize money on Wednesday – the only good thing about the Freestyle is that if you make a fuck-up nobody really notices."

"The music is sensational," smiled Hattie, forking up some chicken, "so dramatic."

"Yep, it really suits him alright, but there are some big names entered – after the pot of course." For once, Seb's normal ebullient façade seemed to have slipped as he spun his wine glass between his fingers.

"You're as good as any of them," grinned Leo, reaching out to touch his arm "have faith."

"Course you are," agreed Hattie. "I wish I could come and watch."

"I suppose in theory you could come later, the class isn't until the evening" hypothesised Leo. "You could drive down."

"It's a lovely idea, but there's late stables, the dogs, and I can get supper ready for you and be there for when you get back – you can video it for me."

"Up to you, it would be lovely to see you but there *is* a lot to do here, and it will depend a bit on how quickly Roxy gets this Farouk bloke down here."

"Right, now we've all got a glass of wine in front of us, start telling us what she said."

Seb took a huge glug of wine and leant forward in his chair, "Well, she sounded quite agitated, as I said, like she was getting cold feet."

"I don't know why - she did fantastically today," interrupted Leo "she's come on really well, you'd never believe she'd not ridden before."

"No indeed," said Hattie sarcastically, who secretly didn't believe Roxy was quite the natural she made herself out to be, "quite astonishing really."

"No, I think it's more that she doesn't want to be found out. She says she's not coming down again unless it's with this Farouk, and we've all got to remember that she's never been here before."

"What about Galaxy? How is she going to explain away the horse then?" asked Hattie "Surely she paid for it, there must be some sort of paper trace?"

"Nope, she gave me cash, and I haven't registered the horse yet. I'll do that in a few weeks when she *officially* buys him. It'll all be above board, just a few weeks later than when she actually did."

"So, as long as we keep our gobs shut, she's safe you mean? No wonder she's so jittery! There's a lot riding, if you'll forgive the pun, on our integrity isn't there?" grumbled Hattie who was getting pretty fed up with the way Roxy fawned over Felix and batted her eyelashes at the boys, yet flicked her fingers for attention when she wanted something from her.

"Don't be spiteful Hattie That's not like you – you sound like Kylie! And you'll get your whack out of the commission when the time comes, I promise." said Seb crossly "This could mean a lot to us all."

"I am not being spiteful, I don't like the woman much, and she doesn't treat *you* the way she treats me. I just get a bit fed up with it Seb – good old Hattie, she won't mind. Well actually I do mind being asked to keep quiet about her scam. The woman is a shabby fraud with an over-inflated ego and tits to match."

"Darling Hattie purleese! I had absolutely no idea," Seb threw his hands up in mock horror, knocking over Leo's glass, "I'm so abjectly sorry."

Hattie, emotionally deflated after her outburst, had to laugh at his histrionics "Oh take no notice, she just pisses me off that's all. You need to take a step back and watch her working you guys over – she's a genius, and you fall for it every time."

Leo, mopping up the spilt wine with the sleeve of his sweatshirt, chimed in, "the only good thing is that we don't have to worry now about Kylie finding out and we can get rid of her PDQ."

"One step at a time," said Seb, holding up his finger, "Let's see what the plan is with Roxy first and get this week over, we need the help with us being away so much."

Hattie groaned in true *Victor Meldrew* fashion ,"I don't believe it!"

Leo laughed, "For Christ's sake will you eat your bloody dinner – I've spent hours slaving over that Aga."

"Changing the subject, what about that scene with Alice today?"

said Hattie "Is she getting worse or is she getting worse?"

"She's always been a bitch," denounced Seb, "total fucking cow. Nothing she does surprises me."

"Do you know Seb, she didn't used to be like this. When I first came here, she was really quite nice to me. They were pretty loved up," said Hattie, "I don't know what's happened to them."

"Hattie, despite your outburst of a moment ago, you really do see the best in everyone my dear. That woman is a spiteful witch, who is rude, demanding and arrogant. Felix needs to ditch her," declared Seb, "and the way that Roxy is making eyes at him, I think Alice needs to watch her step, frankly."

Leo, seeing Hattie's face wince with pain, countered, "I don't think Felix even notices Roxy to be honest. He's too wrapped up in his horses."

Hattie smiled at Leo gratefully "I wonder what the big bust up was all about though?"

"Who knows, and who cares? I wish he'd wake up and smell the roses. She might be a smart arse vet, but she's the nastiest bit of work. She didn't give a thought to me and Doris today."

"We know Seb, we know, but get back to Roxy can we? So, we don't know when she's coming again, only that, when she does, it'll be with a camera crew and we've got to act like we've never met her before?" said Leo, "And that Galaxy isn't her horse – I think Hats and I just need to get it straight."

"Yes, that's right. Although I've no idea when she'll be coming down next, or how much notice she'll give us – it's in the lap of the gods, my children," sighed Seb, pushing away his plate, "do you know I'm absolutely knackered?"

"Don't get too comfy, you're on washing up," laughed Hattie, "and no excuses!"

"Noooo! Surely not," grumbled Seb, looking pleadingly at the other two, "Didn't I do it last night?"

"Nope you didn't, and nope you're not getting away with it," said Leo, "I cooked tonight, and it's your turn – no arguments."

"You're beasts the pair of you and after all I do for you," Seb looked at them imploringly, as they pushed back their chairs and plonked their plates in the sink, "and bastards!" he hissed resignedly after their retreating backs.

ı Alice lay wrapped around Felix, trapping him like a spider with her long legs entwined around his, and her cheek forced against his chest, listening to the rhythmic *lub-lub* of his heart beating in what, she suspected, was a post coital sleep. It had been a frantic, desperate coupling on her part. At first, she had wanted tenderness, a demonstrative apology for the way she had behaved that afternoon, a declaration of their mutual love. Felix, who was always usually the bridge builder, had been stony and tense with her, responding to her in a desultory fashion. The more she tried to coax him, the less interested he seemed, and the more fraught she became. It almost seemed to suit him to ejaculate with lightning speed and turn over and feign sleep, but she'd snared him with her body, snuggling up to him like a whipped dog. She knew that he wasn't really asleep, but short of shaking him and demanding he speak to her there was little she could do, other than force herself into his unwelcoming arms. His rejection worried her; up till now his undying devotion to her had always been a given, that his slavish adoration would be there for her constantly. The cold rejection tonight was new and she didn't like it. She had always pulled his strings, called the shots, worn the trousers in the relationship; basked in his admiration of her and normally, when they quarrelled, he was only too happy to make up. But not this time it seemed. She stroked the side of his arm, but he didn't stir or move. She loved the feel of his powerful arms, his rounded biceps; the way his stomach muscles rippled and the feel of his strong legs. Her hand itched to trace the shape of his beautiful mouth. She loved the softness of lips when he kissed her and she could still taste him in her mouth. The way he moved and the way he spoke. Above all, she loved the way he loved her; he never glanced at anyone else, although Christ knew, he must have had offers; you only had to look at the way the girls drooled over him, but she trusted him completely, and now suddenly he had turned away from her. She plucked at the hairs on his chest anxiously – if she wasn't careful she would lose him too, the one thing that had been a constant in her life. She felt stronger and more resolved about everything now. The man – Ernie – could only make small demands - after all what was a bit of Ketamine. She never worked the tracks – Oli did the racing yards, so she couldn't be involved in any other scams. Andrew had told her tonight he was pleased with her work; they were moving to new premises and, if all went to plan, the possibility of the equine diagnostic centre would come to fruition and she would spend more time on site. But what would it all be for if she lost Felix? Her erratic, spiky behaviour over the last few months had pushed him away. She had been so wrapped up in her own problems she hadn't given him a thought. She snuggled up closer, he wasn't going anywhere, she'd see to that.

Felix was making a bad job of trying to control his breathing. He was so tense and Alice's grasp felt like he was being suffocated. He barely managed to stop himself from taking great gasps of air and throwing her off him. His mind urged his body to stay relaxed, so that she would think he was asleep, the thought of another debacle with her was just too much to contemplate. When he'd finally dragged himself into the cottage that evening, she had been waiting for him; a look of total contrition on her face, the smell of supper wafting from the kitchen and a cold beer in her hand by way of apology. She'd said she was really sorry for the row, that she hadn't known what had come over her, and had kissed him with great tenderness, easing her hands inside his breeches and rubbing herself against him. Normally he would have melted in response, and kissed her back, made love with abandonment; but lying there now in the semi-darkness he tried to reason why he'd held back. There was just a lot more to it than she was telling him, and even when he'd quizzed her, she'd laughed her behaviour off, doubling her sexual advances and although he had gone along with it, he didn't believe that she wasn't hiding something and worse still, for the first time, he actually didn't enjoy the sex that much. Her touch almost nauseated him. Now with her clinging around him like a limpet, he felt trapped and choked and wished she would roll over and leave him alone so he could get some sleep.

CHAPTER 48

"She'll never cope," Chrissie sneered nastily, the next morning when Farouk was updating her on Roxy's call of the previous evening. "If it's the place I think it is, we saw the calibre of those horses when we were down at the mill one day, they're real competition animals."

Farouk yawned, lazily swinging his legs off the desk and sat up to face her, "She says she met the chaps who run the yard down at the pub, and they've found a horse that's perfect. More to the point, we can start filming whenever."

"This I have to see," laughed Chrissie, "she's kept it mighty quiet. Aiden doesn't have a clue."

"Really" drawled Farouk, "that's interesting." He fixed her with a shrewd eye, "how do you know - you two are pretty close are you?"

"Of course we are," snapped Chrissie aggressively, as furious as her rapidly flushing face "I am his PA for Christ's sake."

"Right, course you are," Farouk grinned, "what time's he coming in then?"

"He should be here by now," mumbled Chrissie defensively, "and anyway why are you here? I didn't think you were doing any filming today."

"Keep your drawers on. Nope we're not. I just wanted to talk through this latest story line with him, and see if he wanted any part in it - before I get the cameras organised. He'd be pissed if I left him out – Roxy says these guys are hot."

"Humph – well he'll get the right arse if you don't talk to him about it first. He won't like being upstaged by some interlopers in bollock-crushing breeches."

"My thoughts exactly, although it'd make for some interesting spats between them eh?" He stood up and walked over to the window, watching the traffic crawling along the road below. "How do you think Roxy'll cope with the riding, Chrissie? You're a rider – how difficult is it?"

"Bloody hard – it looks easy, but just try it and you'll find out how tricky it is. I think she's in for a tough time, if you want my honest opinion." Chrissie could hardly contain the glee in her voice, "and she's hardly a spring chicken is she?"

Farouk traced imaginary scores on the window pane, "Should prove entertaining then. Do I detect that you wouldn't mind being a fly on the wall for the first shoot?"

Chrissie clasped her hands together, "I simply cannot imagine anything more hilarious. Too right I'd love to be there, watch her fall off on her skinny arse."

"We'll have to see if we can sort it then," said Farouk, spinning round to fix her with a naughty glint in his eye. "Add another angle to the story. Love triangle, jealous PA."

"Don't you bloody dare Farouk – I skate on enough thin ice where Roxy's concerned," Chrissie grimaced, "count me out."

"Count you out of what?"

Farouk and Chrissie spun round to find Aiden lurking in the doorway, his face stormy with irritation. He glared at the pair of them and stomped over to his desk, tossing his jacket over the arm, "Get me a coffee doll. What are you both talking about?"

"Roxy's found a horse to ride and someone to teach her," said Farouk, picking at his nails. "I wanna go down pronto to get something in the can."

"First I've heard about it," Aiden nodded at Chrissie, "What about you?"

"No, she's not said a word to me, but she wouldn't would she?"

Aiden laughed, "No probably not. When do you want to start? I'm pretty hectic this week, and I definitely want to be there."

"I definitely want you there – it's *Rox-Aid* that gets the viewers. I can do the fly on the wall prelims with Roxy at home beforehand – the 'buying the kit' with her, and that stuff and I'm gonna want to go down and do a recce of the place and do the same with them – so next week should be fine."

"How's it shaping up?" asked Aiden, "making good footage so far?"

"Yeah not bad – early days," said Farouk evasively, "it'll be all right on the night as they say."

"You don't sound very enthusiastic."

"It needs spice, that's what makes the ratings. You and Roxy – now next week bring Chrissie here along – give Roxy a bit of the green eye – nothing like a bit of a cat fight."

Aiden looked thoughtful, "Hmm, yeah, I can see that would work. Good idea."

"Oh for God's sake," drawled Chrissie, her cut glass voice as cold as crystal meth, "I am not some kind of entertainment."

"Of course you aren't, my dear – it's Roxy who'll provide that," sneered Farouk, "and she will do it beautifully."

Alice was in the surgery early, long before Paulene and the others and was busy doing an investigation of stock in the drugs cupboard. There was only so much that they kept in and to over-order would make the partners suspicious; more to the point - Paulene, whom she already knew smelt a rat, and would be like a terrier with a bone. No, she would have to think of a way of ordering things for herself and getting them delivered without the others knowing. On the other hand, she could always just give Ernie a prescription on headed notepaper and they could get it filled themselves; there were plenty of places on the internet that would do it. That might be the way forward. She slumped down in a chair. So far the demands had been small, but she wondered where it was all going to end. Luckily for her, she was not involved in any of the racing yards, that was primarily Oli's domain, thank God; but how long before they put the screws on some more. She constantly admonished herself to say she could deal with it all, but sometimes, especially in the dead of the night, she would wake sweating and shaking feeling hopeless and defeated. She knew too, that she was losing Felix. The last few days he had not been the same towards her, almost impatient, although he would never be unkind, not like she had been towards him. Christ, what a fool she had been. Now with this move to the new premises who knew what that would bring. She dreaded to think.

The door pushed open and Oli walked in – obviously surprised to see her so early and looking pretty much the worse for wear himself. His eyes red, the capillaries spun like fine spider webs and underneath, deep, dark pouches hung like crevasses through lack of sleep. His face looked haggard and he smelt as though he had slept in his clothes.

"Blimey! You look a sight," exclaimed Alice, "Good night?"

"Don't ask?"

"Coffee?"

"You're a lifesaver. What are you doing here so early?" Oli grimaced flushing out some Paracetemol from his desk drawer. "Nothing better to do?

"Eh – don't be sarky. Otherwise you'll get your coffee over your head," snarled Alice, "Just want to get ahead of myself, busy day and all that. More to the point, what are you doing here?"

"I've not gone to bed yet Figured I'd be better just carrying on, "moaned Oli, clutching his head in his hands, "mistake I think."

"You tosser – go home," laughed Alice, "I'll cover for you this morning."

"Oh baby," sighed Oli, in true *Austen Powers* style, "would you?"

"Of course I will, you can cover my on-call till 11pm in return – how about it?"

"Absolute deal," grinned Oli, "bloody amazing I can go back to bed."

"Bugger off then and I'll tell Andrew. What have you got on this morning?"

"Routines – praise the Lord," said Oli, whose face was turning a delicate shade of green, "just the racing yards "easy-peasy."

Alice didn't know if her jaw dropped, or her head drooped, "fine," she stammered, "just fine."

"You okay Alice?" asked Oli, "you look like I'm feeling."

"Nope, I'm fine," stammered Alice, desperately wishing she hadn't opened her mouth.

Down at Fittlebury Hall Stables, the yard was humming with all the tension of a battalion before it goes into combat. Seb was theatrically strutting around, panicking and commanding in equal measure. Leo was his usual calm self, ignoring Seb and doing his own thing. Kylie was sticking the knife in, and Felix was exasperated. Hattie was trying to keep her head down and please everyone. The lorry was packed with every conceivable bit, rug, saddle and piece of equipment. Immaculate, white breeches and shirts were lovingly stowed into the lockers, and Seb's jacket hung reverently in the wardrobe. His patent boots shone like mirrors and his spurs were polished to perfection. The music CDs were checked and rechecked, and two copies of each packed to go. The horses were plaited, and their coats gleamed iridescent as their fleece rugs were flung over them. They were loaded on the truck and, at last, the lorry rumbled down the drive with Hattie and Felix waving goodbye enthusiastically from the yard.

"Blimey what a bloody palaver," grumbled Felix, "All for five minutes in the ring. You'd think it was the end of the world."

"Well he is very good at what he does. It's his attention to detail that's got him where he is, after all. Anyway you can't moan, he's turned your dressage scores round," grinned Hattie, "I know he is a tad theatrical but he is a real showman."

"Poser you mean," agreed Felix, "You're right of course. But Christ when I think of what we have to take for a competition, it does make me laugh."

"I know. Leo is funny with him though isn't he?"

"Yep, he's got him taped, never gets wound up does he? Now here's something I've been meaning to ask you Hats – what gives between those two?"

"What do you mean?" Hattie looked guilty, kicking up the gravel with her shoe. "They're great friends."

"You know what I mean Hats – whenever I've tried to pin Leo down he's always been evasive. Are they are a couple or aren't they? I mean do they sleep in the same bed?"

"I've always assumed they are," said Hattie defensively, "as to where they sleep – not my business, nor yours either Felix. They've been lovely to me."

"But Hats, they have separate rooms!"

"We all have our own room Felix, but it doesn't mean they stay in theirs, does it?"

"You know perfectly well what I mean Hattie!"

"If you're that interested, why don't you ask them yourself?" said Hattie crossly, "I'm not going to gossip about them – just like I wouldn't gossip about you and Alice."

The mention of Alice sobered Felix, "Fair play. I was just

curious that's all. I admire your loyalty."

"Put it this way Leo is a good shag!" laughed Hattie, "and Seb's not bad either!"

"Bloody hell Hattie!"

Hattie doubled over laughing, holding her sides, "Oh God, the look on your face Felix. Priceless!"

Felix roared with laughter, and threw his arms round Hattie's shoulders "Come on, let's get some horses ridden."

Kylie was glaring at them both from the stable. What were they both laughing at? She was sure something was going on. She would like to wipe the smile of that smug cow's face. She'd love to be the one going out for a ride, instead of being knee deep in the acrid smell of horse piss. Still, if she played her cards right, she may well be.

Felix's phone rang when they were half way round the park. Hattie watched him struggling to hold Woody whilst juggling with the mobile. The look on his face varied from horrified to resigned to petrified.

"Who was it?"

"Roxy. She couldn't get hold of Seb. An advance mob is coming down to do some filming at the end of the week. It'll just be with us, not her. Asking how we feel about teaching her – that sort of thing. What our set up is."

"Christ, and we've got to lie and say she's never been here or sat on a horse before. Bloody hell – I don't like it Felix."

"No, me neither."

"Any idea when they're coming? With any luck we could be at a competition."

"No she didn't say. Some bloke is going call and let us know when he's coming down apparently. Foreign sounding name – can't remember Mamouk or something."

"Well, it's obviously the tip of the iceberg isn't it? They're gonna be following her progress all the time – so we'll just have to get used to it."

"Focus on the money and the good publicity – you never know, she may even sponsor a horse."

"God, I'm not sure I'd want to be beholden to her whims and fancies. It's blatantly obvious she's got the hots for you as it is."

"Don't be daft Hats," defended Felix hotly, "of course she hasn't."

"Felix, you must be the most naïve person I know. But don't take my word for it – ask the others and see what they say!" laughed Hattie. "We all know you've only got eyes for Alice though – so you obviously don't see it."

Felix stuck out his tongue, kicked his horse into a fast canter, and left Hattie with long reins floundering aboard Rambler, who was hell bent on catching up with Woody. The horses galloped along, straining to gain ascendancy. Felix's eyes were running as the wind stung his face, and he thought about what Hattie had said and for the first time admitted to himself that Alice was no longer the centre of his universe.

CHAPTER 49

By the end of the week the yard had undergone a makeover worthy of any TV show. There was not a weed in sight, the hanging baskets were deadheaded and jaunty, the arena was harrowed and not a dirty bridle or unruly bandage could be seen in the tack room. Even the mugs had undergone a thorough bleaching. Because of all the sprucing up, they'd reluctantly had to bring Kylie in on the fact that a TV crew were coming down – although she still didn't know the whole truth, believing they were just doing a small piece about Felix and Seb for a documentary. The others were not going to tell her until the 11th hour if they could help it. Hattie was dubious, she didn't like to think of the fallout once she found out the real truth and although she was an ace bitch, she'd feel pretty pissed off too if she was the one being kept in the dark. So come Friday lunchtime, they were all sitting on tenterhooks waiting for the crew to arrive, no-one knowing quite what to expect. For September, it was a lovely day. The air as crisp as a new season's apple and just as sweet. The leaves were well on the turn now and soon they would be a riot of glorious colours, and the view across the park would be even more fabulous. The posse from *Sunrise Productions* were due to arrive at 12.30 and it was now well after 1pm. Obsessively, Felix looked repeatedly at his watch, and Seb was strutting up and down the yard like a demented rooster. Kylie must have checked her make-up a thousand times, and Hattie had long since disappeared and was busy grooming Galaxy like a thing possessed. The only one that was calm and eating a massive baguette, whilst reading the *Nag and Dog,* was Leo.

"If they don't get here soon," wailed Kylie, "I'll have to go. I've got to be at my other job. I said I'd be late today but I don't want to push it."

"That'd be a pity," said Leo sweetly, "You look lovely today."

Kylie visibly preened, "Thanks Leo, you are lovely. I've tried to make an effort."

"Don't go getting your hopes up," said Felix, "they may not want to interview you – it's only a small piece."

"Well even if I'm only in the background, I want to look nice"

"None of us have any idea what they'll want really."

Seb strutted back over, glancing at his watch. "Bloody hell, this waiting around is killing me. Do you think I ought to give them a ring?"

"No, they've probably been caught in traffic," said Felix, "you just have to be patient."

"I wish I'd had something to eat now," grumbled Seb, "I'm bloody starving."

"You are a tosser," laughed Leo, "I told you to eat something! Here finish the end of this baguette."

"You are such a doll," grinned Seb, "I should listen to you more often."

Half an hour crawled past with tensions and frustrations smouldering like a bonfire about to erupt into flames. Seb had resumed his pacing, Hattie had returned from her grooming, Leo had finished eating and Felix said he was going for a ride and was fed up with wasting time. Kylie was seething and, with a face like a slapped arse, reluctantly said she would have to go, and even if they turned up now, she wouldn't be able to stay. The others said a silent *thank you* prayer as they watched her get in her old car and chug up the drive.

"Right, I'm gonna start packing the truck for the event tomorrow" said Hattie, "I'm fed up with all this hanging around."

"I'll give you a hand," offered Leo, "I owe you big time after helping me all the week."

"You don't owe me you silly arse," grinned Hattie, "glad to

help, but be nice to have some company – this tension is killing me."

"It's all right for you two," moaned Seb, "It's me and Felix that'll be the ones making tits of ourselves."

"That's right lover," laughed Leo, "Enjoy!"

Max was in his element. He and Ronnie had been invited by some cronies to watch some horses training that morning. It had been a struggle getting up early to watch them breezing over the downs in what, seemed to him, to be middle of the night. Afterwards, the trainer had laid on a breakfast and it had all been lots of clapping on the back and bonhomie. Max didn't really know what they were talking about half of the time, but he went along with it all, nodding his head in the right places, or so he hoped. On the gallops that morning, there was one horse that they were all raving about, it had left the others standing – even to Max, who admitted he knew nothing it was a clear winner. The horse had not been raced, apparently, in over two years, and had been kept under wraps. It was to be run next week, and the syndicate were going to have a big bet. The odds would be good as it had no recent form, and they were going to put big bucks onto a three horse accumulator. The last bet to be on the good horse. Max listened to the talk bubbling around him, and kept quiet, absorbing what was being said. The problem, it seemed, was who would take a bet of that proportion, and they would need to spread the bets. When Max and Ronnie went outside for a smoke, Max asked what sort of stake they were talking about. Ronnie quelled him with a look – and, glancing furtively around him, whispered back, at least a million. Max could hardly believe his ears, if they got the odds they were hoping, the last horse at 20-1 – it could mean a fucking fortune! This was how Ronnie had been making all that dough, and now he was in on it too. He couldn't believe his luck. He just had to keep his nerve.

Alice knew it was him before she answered the phone. She was tempted to ignore it, but he would only call again, and there was always the remote possibility that it might be a client. She dare not leave it.

"Alice Cavaghan," she answered, "How can I help?"

"Good afternoon Alice, my dear," Ernie's oily voice oozed down the line at her. "How's your day been?"

"What do you want?" Alice rasped back at him, "there's only so much stuff I can get you."

"Now that's not very friendly is it Alice?" wheezed Ernie, "A little bird told me you were at Pitt's racing yard this week. I thought you said you didn't do the racing stables?"

"I don't normally," Alice spat down the phone, "I was covering for my colleague. Anyway how did you know?"

Ernie laughed, "I know everything Alice. You might be going there again I'm thinking."

"No I won't, it was a one off I told you."

"Ah that's what you think. Some of the owners might be putting in a request for you in the future."

"That's not very ethical and would look extremely odd. You wouldn't want to draw attention to yourself would you?"

Ernie sneered nastily, "leave that side of things to me, you just go and do what you're told. I'll be in touch."

Alice looked down and realised that he had disconnected. She pulled out into the lane with a doom-laden heart. *Just go with the flow* Alice, she thought, *just go with the flow*. She made her way up towards Grace and Colin Allington's place to do the routine vaccinations and teeth for their horses. Grace's baby was due any day now, and she was getting mightily fed-up and frustrated with the waiting, her belly stretched like a balloon about to pop. She was really pleased for Grace – she was so excited, not to mention Colin, who was like a dog with two tails, and it would be all she could do to stop Grace trying to help with the horses today and the last thing that Alice wanted was Grace to have the baby in the stable. Delivering foals she could cope with, but babies – not a hope. She swung the Toyota up alongside Grace's car, surprised that the dogs were not lazing about in the garden and thumping their fat Labrador tails in greeting. Scrabbling about in the back of the car, she loaded up the vaccine in syringes and grabbed the bag with all the paraphernalia for rasping the teeth. Andrew had ordered a new Power Float for doing the teeth and she couldn't wait for it to arrive, doing teeth killed her arms. Once they moved to the new premises they could offer more comprehensive services with x-rays and a diagnostic centre. It was what she had always wanted, and if she didn't have the bloody threat of this man Ernie over her, her future would be perfect. She sighed. Her new way of dealing with him was to just take one day and one request at a time. Cover her tracks as best she could and be ready to deny everything. She shouldered the heavy bag like it had all her worries in it, as well as the kit, and stomped off in search of Grace.

She walked over to the stables. It was eerily quiet; the horses were out in the paddock, and the little yard was strangely empty, with only the swallows diving in and out of rafters agitatedly preparing for their long migration. Alice glanced around debating whether to just get on with the job and bring the horses in herself, or go and find Grace. She picked up the headcollars and started to open the field gate, and then paused. It was just not like Grace, she would have been looking out for her to arrive, even if she wasn't able to have got the horses in herself. Alice tossed the headcollars down and stalked back across the garden towards the house. There was no movement from the windows, no cheery wave from Grace from the kitchen, only the distant mournful bellow of a cow, and the drone of late bees in the flowers. Pausing at the back door she called out, then when there was no reply she turned the handle and walked in.

"Grace, Grace," Alice called, quietly at firstly and then much louder. From behind the closed kitchen door the dogs barked. She tentatively drew the door open, crooning to the dogs that it was only her. Despite their size and the velocity of their grumbling, the dogs were soft old things, and knew Alice well. She knelt down and gave their ears a rub. "Where's your mistress then eh?" Calling out all the time, she tentatively moved beyond the kitchen, but the dogs were before her, positively leading the way to cavernous beamed sitting room. At the foot of the stairs from the galleried floor above, lay the inert shape of Grace, her body large and ungainly, not just from pregnancy, but from where she had obviously fallen. Alice dashed over to her, her head scrambling together the ABC of first-aid training, which when Andrew had made her go on the course, had all seemed a bit tedious and beneath her skills, but now she was so glad she had gone.

Grace had fallen awkwardly, one of her legs was at an odd angle, and she looked very pale and clammy to the touch; that she was unconscious there was no doubt. *Think, think* Alice urged herself, *what to do first*! She pulled out her mobile and dialled the emergency services putting them on loud speaker, whilst they talked her through what she knew she had to do. The wait and the questions seemed interminable and Alice found her temper rising with all the inanity of it, but she managed to keep her head together. Everything looked so easy on "*Casualty*" and if it had been an animal she'd be fine, she reasoned. But this was Grace, who was probably her only real friend. It made everything so different. The hardest part was ringing Colin, who went into a dithering, frenzy of shock, stammering that he was on his way home now; Alice could only urge him to drive carefully. She knelt beside Grace from where she'd rolled her into the recovery position and stroked her hair, talking to her all the time, and waited for the ambulance to arrive. The wait seemed to go on forever. Grace's eyelids began to flutter erratically, and eventually she opened her eyes and began muttering incoherently, trying to move and then crying out with pain. Alice had never been more relieved, or pathetic as she felt fat tears rolling down her cheeks; she cradled Grace soothingly in her arms, urging her to be still, and wait for Colin and the ambulance. The delay was probably only about 20 minutes, but to Alice it felt like days, as she held the whimpering Grace, with the dogs looking on with their pathetic eyes looking as stricken as she felt herself.

The ambulance arrived 10 minutes before Colin and a hearty, competent pair of paramedics took over from an exhausted Alice, who hovered anxiously in the background whilst they made their examination. Grace, who was in shock and had possibly fractured her leg in the fall, was given gas and air, and was being strapped like an upturned beetle onto a stretcher when a white-faced Colin arrived.

"Mother and baby are fine," reassured the female paramedic, "just a bit shaken up, but I think your wife may have fractured her leg, and she was unconscious for a bit, so probably has a concussion."

"Oh my God!" wailed Colin, losing control, "Grace darling, what happened?" Grace, who by this time was conscious but in a lot of pain, just grimaced through the gas and air mask. "No darling, don't try and talk. As long as you're okay and the baby too."

"Now Sir, we're going to be taking your wife to hospital, she'll be kept in of course, so do you want to get some things together for her and follow us in?" asked the other paramedic, who was busy monitoring Grace's blood pressure.

"Can't I come in the ambulance with you?" asked Colin, "I don't want to leave my wife, it's our first baby you see …"

"Colin, why don't you go with Grace. I'll put some things together now and come over to the hospital later with anything else you need" offered Alice, "and if you leave me your keys, I'll bring your car, and get Felix to pick me up."

"Oh Alice, would you? I'd be so grateful; I really don't want to leave Grace."

"No, of course you don't" smiled Alice, "No, you go, and ring me later and let me know how she is."

"You're a bloody life saver Alice. Thank you."

A small whimper came from the stretcher, "Can you tell my parents," gasped Grace, "they'll be upset if no-one lets them know."

"Darling, I'll call them," reassured Colin, "of course we'll let them know."

Alice leant over Grace and stroked her face, "Don't worry about a thing, I'll see to the dogs and the horses, and pop up and see your mum and dad too. Just you get better."

The ambulance sped through the village with its blue lights flashing. Kylie pulled over in her old car to let it pass, wondering who was inside and what on earth had happened. It was unusual to see an ambulance and her curiosity was aroused. She stopped at the shop, and Mrs Gupta, the shopkeeper, who'd also seen the ambulance roar past, was agog with who it could have been inside.

The white van from *Sunrise Productions* was just dithering about in the middle of the lane contemplating the entrance into Fittlebury Hall, when the ambulance approached, putting on the blues and twos for the van to move. The ambulance shot past and in haste the van skuttled down the drive and into the yard.

Felix and Hattie looked up as they heard the siren, "Is that an ambulance?" asked Hattie, "God, I hope it's no-one we know."

"I hate the sound of the things," agreed Felix "Always gives me the willies."

"Look lively!" shrieked Seb, tossing his head back and running his fingers exaggeratedly through his hair, "They're here!"

"About bloody time too," grumbled Felix, as he watched the van pull into the yard, followed by an Audi, driven by a bloke with a pony tail, sporting Ray Bans and who looked more like something from the Mafia than a film set. "These jokers think we've got all day to hang about waiting for them."

"Chill," admonished Hattie, "don't get wound up before you start."

"Too late, I already am," spat Felix peevishly, "it's a fucking joke."

Farouk oozed, cobra-like, out of the Audi and was busy having his hand pumped by a melodramatically gushing Seb, who was more camp than Graham Norton in full flow. Farouk swiftly withdrew his hand distastefully, pushed his sunglasses to the top of his head, threw a fleeting and imperious glance towards Felix and Hattie, and allowed his hawk-like eyes to swoop around the yard.

Felix could feel his temper rising, and Hattie put her hand on his arm and shot him a warning look. She could feel the tension radiating off him like electric charge. "Wanker" he hissed under his breath.

"Farouk, come and meet Felix and Hattie," simpered Seb, "and somewhere around is my right hand man Leo."

"Hi," drawled Farouk, holding out his hand to Felix, "good to meet you." He turned to Hattie, almost undressing her with his eyes and held her hand for a moment longer than necessary. "And you Hattie."

Hattie felt herself flushing to her scalp, looked down at her feet as she shook his hand. "Errr hello," she stammered, "we thought you'd never get here."

"Sorry," lied Farouk, "the traffic was bad on the M25. How about you show me the set up and we can get started?"

"Sure," jumped in Seb enthusiastically, "you put the kettle on Hattie, we'll all join you in a minute."

Farouk shouted over his shoulder to the two blokes loitering by the van "Start getting yourselves organised – ready in about 10 minutes."

"Right, I can show you around, and you tell me what sort of thing you want" sighed Seb happily, "we'll do our best to accommodate you."

"Just a simple piece with all of you talking together, and some shots of yard life, the horses that kind of thing. A sort of preamble before Roxy comes down. We'll carve these takes in with footage of when she's having her lessons. It'll cut together well."

"Sounds simply fascinating," said Seb clapping his hands together in delight, "do we have a script?"

Farouk shot him a withering look, "No, it's all just off the cuff mate. The more spontaneous the better."

Hattie watched them walk off, stifling a giggle. Seb was just soooo funny! Leo came up behind her, cupping his hands over her eyes, "God, he's dreadful isn't he?" he laughed, "still I love him."

"We all do," gasped Hattie, as she leapt round in surprise, "I'm gonna fill the kettle and keep my mouth shut as much as I can."

"Good plan," agreed Leo, "I think I'll join you. Although that bloke with the camera is giving you the glad eye Hats. Perhaps you should offer him more than a cuppa?"

Hattie blushed but couldn't help staring over towards the van. A tall, tanned guy, in a white tee-shirt and shorts, with short dark hair and a day's growth of beard was quite blatantly ogling her. "Bloody cheek," she muttered, "talk about obvious."

"Hmm, he might be obvious but he's cute," said Leo, "nice body too."

"Leo! For Christ's sake!"

"Come on darling don't tell me you hadn't noticed," laughed Leo, "Go on, get him to show you his equipment!"

"You are incorrigible Leo. If you're so bloody keen you ask him."

"I would, but judging by the way he's staring at your tits Hats, I don't think he bats on my team." Leo said sadly, "Still might be worth a try."

By this time the guy was sauntering over towards them. Hattie had to admit he was cute. He was lean but with broad shoulders, strong, she supposed, from having to haul that weighty bit of video kit around. Despite the growth of beard, he had a roundish baby face, with soft blue eyes fringed with dark lashes, full, fleshy lips showing very even, white teeth. Hattie guessed he was probably in his late twenties.

"Hi, I'm Sam," he said not taking his eyes off Hattie and holding out his hand, "nice to meet you."

"You too," spluttered Hattie, making introductions and offering to make tea, "do your mates want a cup? Are there just the three of you?"

"Yep, for today, we're just the advance party." Sam shouted over to the van, "Gary, Luke – tea?"

Hattie gaped as two big guys appeared from behind the open doors at the back of the van, one holding a furry boom and the other a tripod. They rested them against the side and sauntered over – if this was the calibre of the camera crew, then things were definitely looking up, and perhaps it wasn't going to be such a pain in the proverbial having them around after all. Judging by the grin on Leo's face he agreed with her, as there was little doubt that Gary was giving him the once over.

The tack room suddenly seemed tiny, filled with these hulking great guys lounging on the chairs, and Hattie was all fingers and thumbs as she made the tea.

"Will you be the regular crew who come down?" she asked "or will it be different people each time?"

"Nope, it's usually us. You haven't met Roxy yet, but she can be a bit tricky to work with sometimes, so she likes a crew she's familiar with and we've done most of her reality shows. There'll be a few more though when we next come. I'm in charge of the camera, and I usually have an assistant or two, then Luke here is what we call the Gaffer, he looks after the lighting with the best boy, and Gary is the sound man. Depending on how much we plan to shoot and where will depend on who else comes, but generally they'll be hair and make-up people, mobile food supplies, and of course all the production assistants."

"Crikey!" exclaimed Hattie, "will we ever get any work done?"

"There's a lot of hanging around to be honest, especially when Roxy's on set, but I imagine you'll be okay," said Sam ,slurping his tea, "just don't get in the way of the director and don't make a noise when the cameras are rolling."

"I'll try to remember," laughed Hattie nervously, "I think I'll steer well clear."

"Not too clear" smiled Sam "you'll look great on camera."

There was a sudden yelling from the yard – Fiver ran outside yapping, followed by a lumbering Hero. "That's our cue," grumbled Gary, "his master's voice."

"See you later, thanks for the tea," grinned Sam, and levered himself up and ambled out to join the others.

"Well they were nice," said Hattie to Leo, "although that Farouk bloke sounds like a right git."

"I think they're used to him," observed Leo, "they didn't seem that bothered did they? Let's go and see what's happening."

"Oh do we have to, can't we just stay in here?"

"Nope, out you come Cinders, no hiding your light under a bushel, as Sam said you'll look great on camera."

Reluctantly, Hattie dragged herself out after Leo to find a little conclave going on in the yard. Farouk was talking, waving his arms around and Felix and Seb were looking serious. The other lads had gone back to the van and were assembling their kit. Hattie and Leo came in on the tail-end of the conversation.

"Right, now I think we'll shoot this scene out here in the yard, as the light is good, and the stable yard is a nice back drop. I just want you to talk naturally together, all four of you. Imagine you've just heard that Roxy is coming to learn to ride here and your first feelings. Discuss it naturally amongst yourselves, forget we are here. Got that? Whilst we're setting up the scene - you have a little practice." Farouk smiled patronisingly at them and spun on his heel and stomped off to the van.

"Well, I thought he'd ask us questions, that'd be so much easier" grumbled Felix "we'd better each think of one to ask each other I suppose."

"Good idea," agreed Leo, "Seb you could kick it off by telling us that Roxy had called and you'd agreed to train her."

"Then I could chime in – with what horse we could use I suppose?"

"Yes, then we'll just take it from there, ad libbing as we go. Farouk said it only has to be a few minutes at most."

"Then he's going to do a scene where we show him Galaxy" said Felix "and they're going to do some general filming of the yard. The drive, the school, that sort of stuff."

"Holy-moly," said Hattie, "I just hope none of us slip up and let the cat out of the bag."

"Don't even think about it," squeaked Seb, "Can you imagine…"

CHAPTER 50

The following day the village was humming with the news about Grace's accident and Alice's heroic rescue. Grace, it transpired, had broken her ankle in the fall. Luckily the baby was unharmed, but to be on the safe side, as Grace had lost consciousness and was mildly concussed, and especially as she was so near to her due date, the doctors decided to deliver the baby by caesarean section, setting the fracture at the same time. Now mother and the new baby, Archie, were doing well in the Princess Royal Hospital in Haywards Heath. Colin was beside himself. The initial anxiety had turned into euphoria at the birth of his son and now he was more excited than a big lottery winner. Everyone had wet the baby's head in the Fox and set up an unofficial tab to celebrate - much to Colin's astonishment when he and Mark dropped in later the next day for a lunch time pint and Dick Macey presented him with the bill. But nothing could dim his mounting exhilaration at the thought of his new born son and Grace coming home.

"How long will she be in hospital?" asked Mark, slurping his pint, "I expect she'll want to be out yesterday if I know Grace."

"She's being pretty stoic at the moment, thank goodness," smiled Colin, popping open a bag of crisps," I think the fall shook her up more than she'll admit and the operation has taken a lot out of her. She'd be in for a couple of days with the caesarean, but it'll be a bit longer with the fracture too."

"How will she manage at home with the baby and all?" said Mark "after all, she won't be able to go up and down the stairs will she?"

"No, definitely not for a while anyway. But we've got plenty of space downstairs. We've got the annexe – okay, not quite what we planned, but it'll be fine for a bit."

"Will you need to get some help in though Col? It's gonna be tough."

"Well, Grace's mum says she can cope, and I have to say I think it's what Grace wants. She wouldn't want a stranger."

"You're lucky to have her," said Mark, "she's a real diamond."

"Yep, she is. Mind you, so is Alice – what would have happened without her? I just can't imagine. I've a lot to thank her for. Right now though, I just can't wait to have them back home."

"Well, just make sure she's well enough first, and take the chance to enjoy a bit of peace and quiet, the lull before the storm," laughed Mark. "On a sensible note, do you need a hand shifting any furniture around downstairs or anything before they get back?"

"That'd be great. Do you mind?"

"No, of course not, just don't ask me to change any nappies!" laughed Mark, "I'll pop over in the morning shall I?"

"Thanks pal," grinned Colin, clunking his glass against Mark's, "about 10 am?"

"That's fine. Sandy asked is there anything you need doing?"

"No, I think Grace's mum's got all the domestic stuff organised. I'm taking time off work when they come home."

"How are you managing with the horses and the dogs?"

"People are incredibly kind. Jennifer rang this morning and said her girls, Nancy and Dulcie, would do them until we got ourselves sorted out. It's not too much of a problem, Grace's mare's in foal so roughed off and my chap can have a bit of a holiday. I can't see me doing much hunting with the new baby this autumn."

"Nope, you've got other fish to fry. It'll be all pushing buggies for you now!" laughed Mark.

"I know," sighed Colin dreamily, "I know."

"Changing the subject – have you seen the work they're doing up at the mill?"

"No, not given it much thought since the sale went through, to be honest," said Colin stifling a yawn. "Sorry mate, seems like I've been up half the night."

"Get used to it Col," grinned Mark. "Seriously though, you should take a gander if you get a chance, you wouldn't recognise the place. The barns are looking amazing already and the mill has been cleared up ready for rebuilding. It must be costing a fortune. He got the planning permission you know?"

"I heard," said Colin distractedly, "no stopping them now then."

"No indeed, will life ever be the same in Fittlebury one asks oneself?"

"Exciting times ahead for us all," laughed Colin, "shall we have another half?"

If looks could have frozen boiling water, the glare on Kylie's face that morning would have taken a prize. The talk in the yard was all about Grace and Alice and the accident, and the others were skimming over the TV crew's visit as best they could. Kylie wasn't fooled; a cow she was, but stupid she wasn't. She hurled a pile of shit into the barrow with enough force that it bounced out; they had clammed up tighter than a duck's arse and she just knew there was more to it than they were letting on, but short of calling them all liars, there was little else she could do but fume on her own.

Hattie was keeping her head down. So far she'd hacked out Rambler and Woody and was now putting travelling boots onto Picasso and Jacks; she and Felix were going out in the truck to the gallops at Coombelands. She'd never felt more relieved to get away from the malevolent blasts that Kylie was shooting in her direction. Last night they'd all decided that it was still best to keep her in the dark until the day foxy Roxy actually made an appearance with the cameras. After all, as she wasn't coming down on her own again, there was no danger that Kylie would see her, so what she didn't know now, she wouldn't find out. The risk that the tabloids would mob the yard was too much to contemplate, and none of them thought Kylie was above tipping off the paps for the big bucks they'd be prepared to pay for that sort of juicy titbit. But Kylie, clearly, was about as satisfied with their vague descriptions of yesterday's antics as a slimmer with a carrot stick. Hattie felt as tense as a racehorse in the starting stalls. She hated lying, and although strictly speaking they weren't, they were definitely being economic with the truth. She was torn between being glad when it was all out in the open and dreading the invasion of the yard with Roxy and all her hangers on. Although, meeting Sam had been a bonus, and she'd been surprisingly relaxed in front of the camera. They'd done pretty well, all things considered and Farouk had seemed pleased. They'd taken a lot of footage of the yard, the horses, the boys riding and even her cleaning tack. Sam said that only a small amount would probably be used in the final edit, but Farouk was a genius at hashing it all together. Hattie considered he was being optimistic about her role in the proceedings but was flattered nonetheless. He was rather gorgeous and she couldn't go on mooning over Felix all her life.

Felix had picked Alice up from the hospital last evening after she'd dropped off Colin's car and, by the time they reached home, he was already fed up with hearing how marvellous she'd been in her heroic rescue of Grace. He'd glanced at her sideways as he was driving and thought he actually quite disliked her. She'd reached over and put her hand on his leg and he'd almost shuddered at her touch. His feelings changed so much, and the awful part was, he couldn't pinpoint when it had happened either. One day he was in love and the next day he wasn't – it was bizarre. He needed to sort things out with her, but she seemed so fragile and he just didn't know how to begin to tell her. He was frightened that if he came clean, she would go over the edge, her emotions were so up and down. That morning when she'd gone off to work, her mood was almost manic, laughing and garrulous; she'd driven off with gusto, plumes of dust in her wake, and Felix watched her go with gloomy despondency, wondering which he preferred, the miserable bad tempered Alice, or the chatty over the top, all over him one. He was dreading the next few weeks ahead with Roxy and all he could think was, thank Christ for Hattie. He glanced over at her as she was loading the horses onto the truck, laughing and joking with Leo, who was helping her hoist up the ramp, and hurried over to give her a hand.

"Ready boss," Hattie joked, "Let's hit those gallops."

"Can't wait, I could do with shifting some cobwebs."

"You two speed freaks," said Leo, "although I wouldn't mind coming one of these days."

"Nothing like it," laughed Hattie, "you should come, we'll give you a run for your money!"

"Not sure I could trust you!"

"Sensible move," advised Felix dangerously, "we'll show you stuffy dressage riders how to open up!"

"That sounds like a challenge to me!" roared Leo, "you're on!"

"Hold your horses," said an icy voice from behind them, "not with my horses you don't."

"You spoilsport Seb," laughed Leo, "might do them good!"

"I'm all for a gentle canter, but not a mad free for all," warned Seb, "their legs are too valuable."

"And my horses' legs aren't?" chided Felix, "you're just chicken!"

"Your horses' legs are hardened to it, and you know and I know it's a different kind of fitness," grumbled Seb, "and … you're right I probably am chicken!"

"Seb you are a little love," sighed Hattie "Come on Felix, let's get cracking and hit the track."

"See you later sweeties!" grinned Felix, blowing them both a kiss and jumping in the truck, where Fiver had taken up his post in the passenger seat. "Be good!"

"Cheeky sod," shouted Seb, as they pulled out.

None of them saw the filthy looks darting out from the stable, as

Kylie watched them larking about together. The hate emanating from her was palpable. She threw down the shavings fork in temper determined to get them all back for excluding her.

Max had made a fucking fortune. He still couldn't believe it. The horses had come in on the accumulator and, although the pot had been split several ways and he was only a minor player pro rata, it was more money than he could possibly have imagined in a month of Sundays. He was starting to get the hang of the way things worked now. It had paid off keeping his mouth shut and just listening on the periphery. These big accumulator bets, although they seemed risky, actually weren't at all. They were all rigged. The horses either nobbled to win or lose. They had people in their pockets all over the country and abroad it seemed, and his role was to help spread the bets. No wonder Ronnie had been coining it in. Of course they had the odd loss, but it had to look kosher. Max, who was well satisfied with his cut, wondered just how much the boys at the top had actually made, a shed load more than he had, that was for sure. He wouldn't mind more of that action, but for now he'd be patient and bide his time. He'd make his move - but not yet awhile. As it was, the afternoon stretched out before him. The car pulled up outside the Fifty Club and the driver got out and opened the door for him. Max stepped out into the autumn sunshine and made his way through the back entrance to the office he kept in the gloomy labyrinths of basements below. His crew were already assembled waiting for him, the weekly meetings were tense affairs of reporting back, explanations given and received and often hard decisions made. None of the people who worked for Max were under any illusion that they could pull the wool over his eyes. He had spies everywhere; knew everything that was going on in his empire. He was generous to his loyal supporters, but ruthless to those who crossed him. No-one could claim to be close enough to him to be immune from reprisals if they fucked up, and they were all willing to drop each other in it, to save their own skins. The *respect* as Max called it, was in reality an overt fear.

The room was a dingy place with no natural daylight and the

only illumination was provided by wall lights shaped liked candles, which were dull and brown with age. A large, mahogany desk faced the room and was bare apart from a desk lamp on the leather top. To the right of the desk was a drinks cupboard, stacked full of bottles, glasses, and incongruously, an ice machine. Around the room were an assortment of cupboards, chairs and small tables, and ominously at the far end on a small plinth one chair stood alone, immovably fastened to the floor, with straps attached to the arms and legs. The contingent who had gathered there were a curious bunch varying between men in sharp suits, to lads in jeans, and a woman dressed in Armani. As diverse as they were, they all had one thing in common, they were all nervous and visibly jumped when the green, baize sound-proofed door swung open to reveal Max.

"Good afternoon everyone," he said smoothly, "I trust I've not kept you waiting?" He walked round to sit behind the desk, tossing his briefcase onto the top and sliding out his macbook and voice recorder. "Can someone pour me a drink please, and can you all make sure you have one yourself before we start."

There was a flurry as the woman rushed forward to pour Max a drink and chairs scraped as they were drawn forward around his desk. An expectant hush fell over everyone, while they waited for him to begin.

"Isobel my dear – perhaps you'd like to start?" Max fixed her with a steely glare "How's the world of escorts, tarts and toms?"

"Right now," smiled Isobel, "Business is good. Following the internet ads the escort services are on the up. Clients have increased this week and we've taken on two new girls. Both high class and British, would you believe. We're charging a lot, and they are taking their cut for the usual extras. I've got the figures here for you." She handed Max a sheet of paper. "The houses are busy, we could almost open up another we've got so many clients and there's no shortage of girls wanting jobs either. The saunas and massage parlours are holding their own well too. Plenty of punters, especially lunch times and the usual after-work trade. Only one isn't performing so well, that's the one down near Victoria, but I'm investigating that."

"Ah yes I was going to talk to you about it," said Max,

consulting a notebook "that's run by Ruby McHenry isn't it?"

Isobel gasped, "How did you know Max?"

"I make it my business to know Isobel," replied Max dangerously, "I think our Ruby has her hands in the till, what do you think?"

"Well I think it is a distinct possibility, but I've no proof as yet."

"Do we need actual proof then? Suffice to say I know. We'll have to deal with her of course; do you have anyone you can put in there instead? What about the girl …" again he consulted his notebook, "Irene … I believe she works there and has been reliable for a while?"

Isobel blanched, it was obvious what had happened. Irene had grassed Ruby up and was now setting herself up for the plum job. "She is certainly ... loyal," said Isobel carefully, "What will you do about Ruby?"

"I think you can leave that to me my dear," said Max calmly, "Don't worry about it any more. You've done well. Now Terry, what have you to tell me about the world of gambling?"

CHAPTER 51

Roxy oozed herself into her tight-fitting breeches and smoothed down her polo shirt, zipping up the killing boots and flopped down into the make-up chair. Rachel was fussing around her, brushing on powder and lashing on mascara.

"God. do I have to wear this fucking helmet," shrieked Roxy, playing her part for an Oscar winning performance, as she was perfectly used to wearing it by now. "My hair will look a friggin' scarecrow poking out underneath!"

"Don't be such a diva," complained Aiden, "Come on calm down, I know it's only because you're so nervous."

"No I fucking am not!" snarled Roxy furiously, desperately wanting to spill the beans that she was more than capable of riding Galaxy but knowing she daren't. "It makes me look a complete dork and I am not wearing a fucking hair net!"

Sam, behind the camera, was panning in and out from Roxy to Aiden capturing the sparks flying between them with satisfaction.

"Can you just fuck off!" yelled Roxy, screaming at him.

Farouk was loving every glorious temper tantrum. Chrissie was smugly playing his assistant and just couldn't wait to see Roxy launched on board the rather lovely looking horse that had been selected for her. She glanced around the yard; the lads were certainly worth putting on celluloid, especially the blond one. The gay guys were gorgeous but pretty overt in their sexual preferences although they were getting plenty of looks from the crew. The girl, Hattie, was stunning in her own way with those long legs and huge eyes, but she'd made no effort to tart herself up for the camera at all, whereas the other girl had so much make-up on you could scrape it off with a knife and was busy getting in everyone's way, making a bloody nuisance of herself. There always had to be one, mused Chrissie.

Kylie was lapping up every second. After her initial fury at being kept in the dark she had eventually come round to the fact that she would be on national TV and that had to be a good thing. Seb explained that they'd had to keep absolutely schtum about the programme and emphasised this was really important for fear of the press finding out, and he knew that he could rely on Kylie's discretion. Flattering her ego perfectly, she assured him that she could be trusted completely, and was now telling the sound man just what an important and integral part of the team she was. Hattie watched with amusement and was glad to let her take centre stage, whilst she took a backseat.

Roxy was ready and stumped out in her boots, all kitted out for the part of novice rider. Felix and Seb were showing her how to hold the reins prior to her getting on the horse, and demonstrating how to mount. The plan for this first session, was for Seb to lead Galaxy around the arena, whilst Felix held onto Roxy to stabilise her. If all went well then they would put her on the lunge. Of course, the key players knew that it would be fine, but the audience didn't and the oohs and ahs were gratifying. Only Kylie and Chrissie weren't taken in. To both of them, it was obvious that this wasn't the first time that Roxy had sat on a horse.

By the end of the session, Roxy slipped off, feigning exhaustion. Aiden rushed over to her, throwing his arms around her, "Darling you were simply marvellous, I had no idea you'd be such a natural!"

"Am I? said Roxy feigning modesty, "I've no idea, it just seemed to come so easily – extraordinary really." She turned her smile up full beam to gaze into Aiden's eyes.

Farouk raced over, "Well done Roxy, some great shots – you were fab!"

"Yeah, well done," caroused Chrissie, "No-one would believe you hadn't done it before."

"Well I can assure you I haven't," said Roxy crossly, "Other than one terrible attempt with Lisa and you can ask her about that!"

"Don't be spiteful Chrissie," rebuked Aiden, "I think you've done really well Roxy, I'm proud of you!"

Kylie glanced sideways at them all. Roxy had been brilliant for a beginner. Quite unbelievable really. She had to agree with that Chrissie, she'd bet that Roxy had ridden before and it was all a set up. Still why should she care? They filmed a bit of her leading the horse out, she'd made sure Hattie didn't get in the frame, and if they were coming down regularly then she'd make sure she featured some more. Who gave a stuff whether Roxy Le Feuvre was lying or not.

Alice had been on call last night and was starting work later this morning. She decided it was high time she stopped in to see Grace – who'd been home from hospital for a week now and, whilst loving being a mum to the cute little Archie, was pretty fed up with the restrictions of a broken ankle. Her mum, of course, was being brilliant, but Grace was not a good patient and hated being incapacitated – it meant she couldn't even carry the baby without help, and although the break in itself was not complicated she was likely to be in plaster for at least six weeks. Colin was still on leave and ushered Alice into the conservatory where Grace had her leg up on a stool and baby Archie was sound asleep in a Moses basket.

"Alice how great to see you," whispered Grace quietly, struggling to reach up to kiss her "Archie's just gone off, so I don't want to wake him."

"I'll be as quiet as ..." whispered Alice back at her, "how you doing?"

"If it hadn't been for you, I'd have been a lot worse," said Grace, "I'm okay, just frustrated and cross with myself."

"Well it was lucky I came when I did," said Alice smugly, enjoying the praise "and how's the baby?"

"Oh he's grand, gaining weight well, demanding to be fed every four hours – just like his father," laughed Grace, "gorgeous!"

Alice stood up and craned into the basket, "He's very cute," she said, not knowing what else to say. She really could never see why people raved about babies, "Looks like Colin," she lied.

"Do you think so?" gushed Grace, "I think he has his nose, but my eyes probably."

"Definitely," agreed Alice, thinking what a load of baloney, they all looked the same.

Colin bustled back in with the tea. "Here we are, pot of Earl Grey and home-made cookies for my two favourite ladies."

"Thanks love," said Grace, "I'm guessing my mum made these though, not you."

"Caught out!" Colin laughed, leaning over and pecking Grace on the cheek "Whilst his lordship is sleeping, I'm gonna read the paper - so don't mind me Alice."

"You go ahead Colin, make the most of the peace and quiet," laughed Alice, "Thanks for the tea."

Colin flumped down in his chair and shook out the newspaper. No more than a minute had passed before he was muttering, "God above, makes you glad we live in the country."

"What?" said Grace, irritated at him interrupting, "Something in the paper?"

"That woman they fished out of the Thames a couple of days ago - the prostitute who they thought was drunk and drowned. Turns out, the bruises weren't from the fall, she was brutally murdered. Just shows you eh?"

"How horrible," shuddered Grace, pulling a face "there are some nasty people about."

"Police seem to think it's some kind of retribution thing," said Colin, "all seems a bit gangland."

"Thank God we don't live up there."

A shrill beep pierced through their conversation. Alice felt her heart skip a customary beat as she realised it was her mobile. Glancing down and, recognising it was Andrew, she answered with relief, but felt her face blanch when she heard his news.

"I'll come in right away," she choked, her voice husky with emotion, "I'll be about twenty minutes."

Grace looked at her, "Everything okay?"

"It's Oli," whispered Alice, "he was involved in an accident last night, Andrew wants me back straight away." She jumped up and picked up her car keys. "Sorry I have to go."

"Of course you do. Oh God what's happened?"

"He didn't say, only that he was in hospital."

"You go, but just let us know how he is please?" begged Grace, "And if there is anything that we can do of course."

Colin ushered Alice to her car, hardly knowing what to say as she stumbled into the driver's seat and tore off down the drive. He gazed, watching her car disappearing for a while and wondered what the hell had happened to Oli.

Alice's mind was racing. Andrew hadn't said much on the phone, just to get back PDQ, and he'd explain when she got back. As she negotiated the narrow lanes, her mobile went again, she answered unhesitatingly on the hands free, "Andrew, how is he?"

"Hello Alice," said a familiar, oily voice, "I see you've heard the news. Don't worry your vet friend will be okay, just a little incapacitated for a while. Lucky he has you to cover for him at the racing yard my dear."

Alice found herself spluttering, "YOU! You bastard, what have you done? Why did you have to hurt him?"

"There, there my dear, calm yourself; no permanent damage done. Do as you are told and all will be well. You wouldn't want anything to happen to that pretty boyfriend of yours would you?"

"No," whispered Alice. "Don't hurt him"

"Just do as we ask. I'll be in touch."

The line went dead and Alice felt sick. She floored the Toyota down the lane towards the surgery, terrified of finding out what had happened to Oli and knowing that it had been all her fault.

CHAPTER 52

The news of Oli's accident ricocheted around the village faster than a Von Trapp yodel and became the talking point in the shop and the pub for several days to come. He was still in hospital and likely to be until the end of the week having been knocked flying by a hit and run driver. Amazingly there was no lasting damage, but he'd been badly shaken up, with a broken jaw and arm, together with a positive feast of cuts and bruises. Painfully, through a wired-up jaw bone, he'd struggled to recount to the police that he'd been ambling up the road for a pint at the Fox, leaving the cottage to meet Patrick and the others for their regular game of darts. He wasn't on call so he could have a drink and, as usual, had decided to walk. He'd heard the car, rather than seen it, as it roared up behind him and, the next thing he knew, he was hurtled into the hedge by the glancing blow off the wing of the vehicle. The police officer who had taken the details said it was probably a stolen car full of joyriders who'd scarpered once they knew what they'd done, but that Oli was lucky as it could have been much worse. Oli was in too much pain with his jaw to attempt to mumble that he didn't feel particularly lucky, when an attractive, young nurse came along with a pain killing injection and he decided he couldn't be bothered with it all and fell back against the pillows. The police officer packed away his notebook and gave a sad shake of his head gloomily conceding that it was unlikely that they would find the culprits.

Back at the surgery, Alice, riddled with guilt, listened to Andrew marshalling his troops and informing they were all going to have to do more hours to cover for Oli, and he wanted her to take on the racing yard work. Naturally, she could do nothing but acquiesce, and the relief on Andrew's face was evident - even if he didn't see the dread on hers. She was pushed into a corner and she knew it. Ernie and his mates had ensured that she would be working the racing yards and they hadn't cared who had gotten in the way. It was bollocks that it was joyriders, despite what the police thought. Alice knew different and she was scared. Oli could have been killed, these people were ruthless. For the millionth time she wondered if it was time to come clean about it all, but the coward in her shrank away from facing the truth and the inevitable furore it would cause. She kept her head down, cringing inwardly and said nothing while Andrew rambled on about shared responsibilities and whether or not they should employ a locum whilst Oli was off. Their workload, since Alice had joined the practice had more than doubled and it was hard to see how they would manage if he was off for any length of time. In the end it was agreed to wait a week or so and see how they coped, and that Paulene would put out feelers for any students who had graduated and were looking for work. The practice carried insurance cover if any of them were injured, so hopefully it would cover the expense, but again all this would need to be investigated. Andrew pushed his hands through his thick black hair, greying slightly now, but still as handsome as ever, and asked them all to bear up under the crisis and do their best. Everyone nodded their heads, indicating that of course they would and Alice looked at her hands glumly – for her, the nightmare was just beginning.

The first shoot had gone so well that everyone was celebrating. Seb was crowing like a cock rooster reliving every take, whilst Felix crashed out in the armchair saying it was a '*bloody miracle*'. Hattie was making tea and smiling to herself as Kylie preened in front of the mirror, smacking her lips together and saying that Farouk had remarked how photogenic she was.

"I told him I'd always wanted to be an actress," Kylie simpered, tossing her hair back, "You never know, I might get talented-spotted."

"You may well indeed," agreed Seb, playing up to her outrageously, "you could tell he was definitely interested in you."

"Did you really think so?" said Kylie, clearly delighted and her eyes shining, not realising that Seb was taking the piss, "I knew I wasn't mistaken, he really did single me out." She gave a little tinkly laugh, "well I expect he'll want me around a lot more next time."

"Absolutely. Helping Roxy, palling up with her, that sort of thing. It'd be right up your street."

"She's not the bitch everyone makes her out to be is she? I thought that Chrissie was a mean cow, but I'm sure Roxy and I will get on brilliantly."

"I think so too," said Seb, "it'll be huge fun, but just remember, mum's the word, we don't want the papers getting hold of the story just yet, not until it makes the airwaves, or we could get into trouble."

"They won't hear it from me, but I can't vouch for everyone," said Kylie spitefully, looking at Hattie vindictively. "I'm no gossip, but others are."

"That's enough," spat Felix, tired of Seb and Kylie and their stupid games, "not one of us would be irresponsible enough. Isn't it time you were getting on to your next job Kylie?"

Kylie glared at him, "I'm freelance, I can go when I like," she countered, "but as it happens, I do have to get a shifty on."

"Well enjoy the rest of your day," said Felix sweetly, "thanks for your help."

Kylie didn't know whether he was being sarcastic or not but gave him the benefit of the doubt, smiled resignedly to Seb, ignored Hattie and flounced out almost knocking over Leo who was just coming in.

"Are you off?"

"Yes, some of us have to work for a living," she complained, "see you tomorrow."

"Blimey, what's up with her?" asked Leo. "What did I say?"

"Nothing, she's just a stupid tart, who thinks she's God's gift and Seb has been winding her up," grumbled Felix, "makes me cross."

"Calm down and see the funny side!" laughed Seb. "Chill out

for a change Felix, you're bloody uptight these days."

"You are actually mate," agreed Leo. "What's up?"

"Nothing," snapped Felix, "Just a bit tense with all this Roxy business I suppose, and I'd dearly like to get rid of Kylie."

"We've talked it to death. We can't if we don't want her to bubble us. So we've got to put up and shut up."

Hattie handed him a cup of tea. "Cheer up Felix – it won't be for long. Do you know what I think?"

"Well I'm sure you're going to enlighten us," grumbled Felix, "What?"

"I think we should have a party – a house warming party and a celebration party – after all, we're all going to make big bucks out of this Roxy affair, and it's time we all let our hair down."

"Hattie that's a splendid idea!" roared Seb, "I simply love it, and I love parties!"

"Fantastic plan Hats!" chorused Leo, "trouble is when? How long is it going to be before we can come clean about Roxy? Also too, it would have to fit in around your competing schedule wouldn't it?"

"Well, let's sit down and work out a date. How exciting!" shrieked Seb, "Something to really look forward to – I know, we could have a theme, fancy dress, or a masked party!"

"Steady on Seb, don't get carried away," laughed Leo, "they always end up in tears!"

"Not necessarily," said Seb, feigning hurt, "just the odd mistaken identity once or twice."

"I think it should be an end of season party," said Felix, "that would be October time. Otherwise I'm going to be flat out, what with Weston Park and then I can really enjoy it."

"Oh that's ages away – at least 6 weeks," moaned Seb, "But I suppose we have the Nationals coming up next week too."

"Also too, it'll give us plenty of time to plan, and Roxy will be more of a fixture here then too, and we won't have to worry about any adverse publicity."

"I know - it could be a Halloween party!" cried Seb. "How perfect would that be!"

"Ghosts and ghouls, bats and broomsticks, murder and mayhem – why not?" laughed Hattie, "Good idea, that's settled then. All Hallows Eve it is!"

Max rolled over in bed and opened one eye. The midday sunlight, streaming in through the window, drilled into his brain and he wrapped the pillow over his head and groaned. He rarely drank as much as he had last night when he'd got so pissed he could hardly remember how he'd gotten home; only how Terry and his driver had manhandled him up to the flat and thrown him into bed. He was still in his shirt and trousers and they hadn't bothered to close the blinds. He had that sour smell of booze seeping out of him that made him want to throw up. In fact he probably would at any minute. He rolled out of bed, making it to the bathroom in the nick of time, and heaved his guts up into the lavatory pan. He leant back against the wall wiping his mouth. He disgusted himself in more ways than one. Perhaps he was going soft in his old age, but no, Ruby had got what she deserved. The old tom had been on the take, cheating him for months, probably years, and had just got too greedy. He'd had a soft spot for her though, known her for what seemed like a lifetime, but he could no longer overlook what was happening under his nose. She had to be made an example of, make the others realise they couldn't take the piss. He hadn't liked it when she begged though, said she was sorry, it wouldn't happen again, clung to his shirt pleading with him when the boys took her away, knowing what was going to happen to her. He'd surprised himself by being so affected. Normally when someone crossed him he was as hard as nails, but for some extraordinary reason this time it seemed different. He pulled himself upright, gulping down a glass of water, trying to rehydrate himself, and leaned over and switched on the shower. He wanted to feel good, he was having lunch with Roxy today and bloodshot eyes, stinking of stale booze was not a great look. Flinging off his reeking clothes, the freezing jets blasted down on him as he stepped under the water. Feeling the million laser-like rays hitting him at once, he almost reeled from the shock, gasping and throwing his head up to absorb the full impact. He began to purge himself of the dreadful memory of Ruby's pleading face and desperately tried to replace it with Roxy's foxy one.

Roxy arrived twenty minutes late. Max was already seated in a discreet corner table when he saw her breeze in, hidden under the ubiquitous, dark glasses and a Glynis Barber blonde wig. There was not a camera lens in sight and, for Roxy, she was very under-dressed in a pair of black jeans and an old sweater. Used to her being late, but not to her being incognito, Max was taken aback, this was not the Roxy he knew of late, when any opportunity was a possible photo opportunity.

"Sorry I'm late," she gushed breathily, leaning over to kiss him, "I've got these bloody camera bods following my every move. Took me ages to shake them off. I can't even piss in peace!"

"It's fine," said Max cautiously, scanning the pub, expecting a photographer to pop up from behind a plant pot. "Doll, you'll have to fill me in on it all, I'm behind with what you've been up to." He leant over and poured her a glass of Evian. "Do you want to order first?"

"Good idea, what're you having?" Roxy glanced down at the menu, "It's pretty basic but I quite fancy the scampi and chips."

"I was just going to have a sandwich, I'm not that hungry."

Roxy pushed up her sunglasses and looked at him properly, "You look fucking terrible Max! You been out on the lash?"

"Hmm, a bit of a heavy night you could say," said Max evasively, "Just taking it easy today."

Roxy's eyes flashed dangerously, "Who were you with –

Anna?"

"Nope, out with the lads as it happens. I'm well into my racing now y'know."

"Roxy relaxed, "Yeah, you did say – celebrating a good win, were ya?"

"You might say that," grinned Max, "but tell me what you've been up to? Why the disguise?"

"Just fancied a lunch with an old friend without everything I do or say being recorded or filmed, plus I've got something to tell you." Roxy tapped her nose, "you'll never believe what I've been doing!"

"Well I reckon you're gonna tell me," laughed Max, "and it's good to see you looking more like the real Roxy too, not some jumped up Barbie doll!"

"Thanks for that."

"You know what I mean."

Roxy sighed, "Yeah right I do. Let me order first darling and we can have a good old gossip."

Max went over to the bar, organised the food, replenished their drinks and sat down. "Now tell me everything."

An hour later Roxy had told him all about progress on the mill and how Farouk wanted her to learn to ride. She explained about finding the yard and how she had surprisingly been a natural – leaving out all the salient parts of her previous secret visits and her torture sessions on the Equisator; but adding that she was really hooked and was planning to buy this horse, Galaxy, that she'd been riding. Roxy smiled excitedly up at Max, not letting on for a moment that she had bought the horse weeks before.

"Wow Roxy that's amazing," laughed Max. "You're a dark horse, if you'll forgive the pun! I'd love to come and watch one day."

"Would ya?" asked Roxy surprised, "I'd fucking love it!"

"You keep it in Fittlebury you say," said Max, thinking immediately of Ernie's bent vet "I think one of my pals knows some chick, who's a vet there."

"Really?" said Roxy surprised. "One of the lads who've been teaching me to ride – his girlfriend is a vet – it could be her, there can't be too many girl vets in a village can there?"

"Shouldn't think so," sighed Max, "small world eh?"

"Deffo," grinned Roxy, "why don't you come down with me one day next week, when they're not filming?"

"Love to – can't wait to see you in action babes," agreed Max, thinking it might also be a perfect opportunity for a little action of his own.

CHAPTER 53

For Alice the action was hotting up. Forced into the racing yards following Oli's misadventure and, having been given strict instructions by Ernie, she was feeling worse than ever, knowing she was getting deeper and deeper into the quagmire of horse shit. She shut out her feelings and ignored the trusting eyes of the horses as she pumped them full of all sorts, and ran false bloods, under the appraising eyes of dubious owners. Even worse was when she came back to the surgery to find Oli struggling to eat and talk, his face looking as though he gone ten rounds with Mike Tyson, and swearing incoherently as he tried to manage one handed with his busted arm. The police, predictably, were no nearer finding out who had hit him, or the car involved and all had gone quiet on that front, but luckily the insurance company had agreed to finance a locum and a young, newly qualified vet was starting next week, and he would chauffeur Oli around, and work under his instruction. But to Alice's chagrin, it would not include the racing yards, and would be the routine stuff, vaccinations and the like. The more complicated lameness diagnosis with the nerve blocking and intricate work would be done by her and Andrew. She had been hoping that she might get off the hook, but if anything she seemed doomed to carry on even longer. She had begun to resign herself to her fate, and even the arrival of the film crews at the yard had not worried her, after all – what did it matter now, she had been rumbled big time. She and Felix were settling down, she was really trying hard, but he seemed so distant at times. Alice was sure she could win him round and was going to make a real effort to be more involved in his work and take an interest in the yard, even if it meant getting involved in this filming lark now, as much as the thought of sucking up to those idiots stuck in her craw. Seb was away competing this week at the National Dressage Championships, which meant that it would just be Felix and Hattie holding the fort and the part timer, Kylie. So far

Alice had avoided all contact with her, but had gathered that Felix was singularly unimpressed, although getting him to talk about anything, let alone some staff minion, wasn't easy at the moment. He just seemed to bottle everything up and shut her out. Once this new locum started, she'd have time to pop into the yard more and see how he was during the day; try and rekindle a bit of the old spark they had. She sighed happily at her plan, it was the only bright thing on her horizon right now. You never know, she thought positively, she might even be able to build some bridges between Kylie and Felix – she was good at that sort of thing. She would even make an effort with that stupid bimbo, Roxy, if it helped Felix. Thickos like her were always impressed and slightly over-awed when surrounded by intelligence, fawning over doctors and probably vets too. She would run rings round her intellectually but make her feel special all the same, she could just picture the scenario. She'd show Felix just what an asset she'd be with Roxy and Kylie.

Max had invited his new cronies up to one of his more infamous clubs in the West End. Scantily clad babes waltzed around with drinks and appetizers on trays, whilst porn played on screens. The air in the private room was feathered with smoke, whirling in curling blue trails through the subtle lighting. Draped on leather sofas Max and Ronnie were discussing the forthcoming week and Ernie was holding court with them all about the latest bent vet, who was now well in his pockets and performing like a circus seal. The others were laughing at his stories and Max joined in but stored every syllable. A big race was coming up, they were spreading bets and laying bets. It was a big operation, but if it came off it would make them extremely big bucks. Max was now too savvy to ask what sort of money they were talking about – he knew already. The new vet was to be critical in the operation and Ernie planned to give her a little frightener to make sure she played ball.

"Can't be too careful where the big dosh's involved," he grinned, his bulbous red-veined eyes gleaming in his sweaty face, "just a little reminder not to mess us about."

"You're a bastard," laughed Ronnie, "pretty is she?"

"Yeah, but frigid," laughed Ernie, "could do with a good shagging if you ask me, perhaps she's not getting enough from her nancy boy."

"Go careful my son," said Frank, a hard-nosed villain, with a blonde on his knee, her tits in his hand, "don't fuck it up for a bit of fanny."

"Nah, I won't – don't worry. I was thinking something a little more subtle."

"Such as?" asked Max, signalling to Anna, who was in charge of organising the girls, that they needed more drinks.

"Well, they've got a cute little dog …" said Ernie, leaving the sentence unfinished

"I hate that kind of thing," growled Ronnie, "poor fucking dog what did that ever do?"

"Needs must mate," laughed Ernie, "don't go getting soft in your old age!"

Ronnie's face went puce, "I mean it, I don't like it."

"Ronnie, have a drink pal," soothed Max, as a blonde with nipples the size of dustbin lids leant over him with a tray. He turned to Ernie, "Ronnie loves his dogs y'know."

"I can see that," grinned Ernie. "Don't fret Ron, don't fret. We can't afford for anything to go wrong and I'm telling you it always works – leave it to me eh?"

"Alright, I suppose so," grumbled Ronnie, "Just don't tell me."

"Right," said Max, attempting to diffuse the situation, "have we decided then what we've all got to do? If so … shall we party gentleman?"

Murmurs of contented assent rumbled around the group, most of whom were unaware of what had happened anyway, and were already well into the booze and had several lines under their noses. Max grinned and flicked his fingers, "Anna my dear, can you organise your ladies for my friends please?"

Anna sashayed politely over towards him in a cherry red dress, her dark curls tumbling over her breasts. "Of course Max," she said sweetly, "the girls are at your guests' disposal, private rooms are available and naturally any extras."

"Good girl," admired Max, smiling at her. She had been the perfect hostess "good job, thank you." He watched as his cronies lapped up the attention from the pretty babes in their miniscule outfits and felt very satisfied. Anna had come a long way, and was proving invaluable in organising these select little parties – he was pleased with her.

Anna smiled back at Max, thinking thank God she was no longer one these bimbos summoned to entertain these tossers, but it was only a tenuous thread from where she now found herself and deep down, she hated and resented this tawdry and distasteful lifestyle and would do anything to crawl out of it. She loathed these men and their disregard for the law, women and the depths they sank to get what they wanted. Every time she was privy to their conversations she found herself sickened even more and, what they didn't realise, was that the quiet and beautiful Anna knew more about them than anyone and one day she would use that information to her own advantage.

The vets' move up to Grace's parents' place was happening quicker than anyone could have thought possible. Permission to change the use of the buildings had gone through without a hitch; the local authorities, being keen on sympathetic diversification plans, meant they had brooked no objection and already the builders were busy erecting walls and putting in windows. A lease had been agreed, with an option to either renew or possibly buy, which had suited all parties. The facilities were excellent, with good and spacious offices; an x-ray facility, dispensary, small treatment room and diagnostic centre, plus stabling. Later, hopefully, they would put in a full operating facility and an arena. Although David Bryce from Bryce Bros was working flat out on the mill project, he had taken on the job and brought in extra men to do the work for Andrew. He estimated it shouldn't take longer than four weeks. Andrew couldn't have been more delighted. That Oli was still out of action was a blow, but that the locum was starting next week was a bonus. They'd been lucky in that an old vet chum of his knew of a graduate who'd worked with him on a placement and came thoroughly recommended. Andrew hadn't interviewed the lad, just gone on what his mate had told him, and the arrangements had been made via email for Theo to start on the Monday. Andrew was delighted – and excited – the new surgery at Coombers Farm was now starting to become a reality and things were on the up. The only one who seemed mildly stressed was Alice, but Andrew just assumed it was the additional workload that they had all had to take on for the time being, and that she would lighten up after next week. He voiced his concerns to Caitlin one night in bed, and she had agreed with him. Alice was highly strung and it was just her nature, she never seemed to lighten up – some people were just like that. And when Caitlin had gone down on him, taking his erect cock between her lips, he had forgotten all about Alice and her problems.

CHAPTER 54

The larger of the two blokes slid the noose over the little dog's head as it bounded up to them wagging its tail with pleasure. Before it could begin to bark in surprise, he yanked the rope as hard as he could until Fiver began to choke, saliva and spittle coming out of his mouth in shock. Fiver pulled back spluttering and flaying like a salmon on the end of a line. The man laughed maliciously and pulled harder and the dog gasped, dropping onto his belly in submission. The other man kicked him hard and, tugging him up from the floor chucked him into a sack. Fiver thrashed and struggled as they tied the top tight and they slid off surreptitiously into the gloom of the evening. They would chuck him into the river on their way home.

The outside lights of the cottage blazed on, and a tall, blond, lanky man came into the garden, calling out for his dog. His hair stood out like a surreal white halo in the eerie light as he shouted. The two men flattened instinctively against a shrub and oozed carefully into the shadows, moving quietly towards their van. As the silver-haired guy called out more frenziedly, a torch beam slid across the garden, prising into the corners of the shrubs, seeking out the crevices as his voice became more frantic, and then was joined by a woman's voice. The two men slid into the van, chucking the whimpering bag into the back; quietly they drove away, without putting on the lights and, the voices from the garden faded behind them.

"Where can he have got to?" said Felix exasperated, "he never runs off."

"No idea," replied Alice. "Bloody thing, he's a pain in the arse Felix."

"Don't be like that Alice, perhaps he's gone after a rabbit or something. Did you just hear a car?"

"Possibly, but I'm bushed. I've had a horribly long day, you'll have to look for him yourself."

Felix looked annoyed but said nothing. "That's your phone ringing I think?"

"Yep, you're right, I'd better get it. It might be a client. You keep looking."

Felix watched her disappear and he carried on shouting, but it was no good, Fiver had disappeared.

Seb and Leo were coming down the drive in the truck. They were knackered. It had been a great Nationals. Seb had pulled out all the stops with Doris and come 3rd in one class and won another, albeit only the medium but it was a real accolade. They couldn't be more ecstatic – moreover it had given that bastard Juan something to think about. But, right now their eyelids were drooping and Seb was dozing in the passenger seat with Leo driving. Hattie, bless her, was waiting for them in the yard – and they had texted her to say they were nearly home.

They had just turned down the drive when a vehicle appeared in the gloom – its headlights were off and it hurtled up the drive towards them at break neck speed, but unable to pass the huge lorry, it straddled the path, shot over the verge and headed off over the parkland like a meteoric blur.

"Blimey did you see that?" spluttered Leo, "what the fuck?"

"What?" exploded Seb, waking up with an effort, "I didn't see anything."

"A bloody van, nearly hit us, driving like a frigging lunatic with no lights on, coming from the yard!"

"Where?"

"It's disappeared over towards the parkland!" exclaimed Leo, "driving like a total nutter!"

"Sure you didn't imagine it?"

"No I fucking didn't!"

"Right, well, not much we can do about it in the truck is there?" said Seb sensibly, "Perhaps Hattie knows about it?"

"We'll see," said Leo darkly, "I think it was up to no good."

The van hurtled wildly across the grass like a heat-seeking missile, the men hitting their heads on the roof with aplomb as it careened over the bumps.

"Fucking hell," exploded the one driving, "where did that lorry come from?"

It had been a close run thing – they had nearly been annihilated. The terrified dog was whimpering in the bag and the stench of its pathetic dog shit pervaded the small space. He stopped and picked up the bag, leapt out of the van and, with gusto, hurled the sack around his head and let go – and it flew off into the air, landing against a large, yellow digger with a sickening thud. The driver jumped back into the van and beat a hasty retreat, glad to get out of the countryside and make his way back to the smoke – they'd done the job - what happened to the mutt now was immaterial.

Alice felt sicker than a teenage mother in her first trimester. Ever since she'd ended the call she'd been shaking. Tearing outside and screaming for Fiver, she ran around the garden like a demented thing possessed, eventually falling to the ground and shrieking irrationally, much to Felix's total amazement. Eventually sobbing, she pulled herself together and they continued searching for the dog. Although Alice remained frenzied and illogically distressed. Felix looked up as he saw the headlights of the truck coming down the drive in the approaching gloom but took no notice, and carried on calling hopelessly. But there was nothing, not a whimper, not a bark, not a sniff of Fiver. He had disappeared without trace.

Distracted, and wondering if Fiver had disappeared to the yard to wait with Hero for the boys' return, he went down to the yard and Alice scuttled back into the house – almost inconsolable, although for the life of him Felix couldn't understand why, as she had been so blasé earlier and had never really liked Fiver. He strode towards the stables, urgently calling out into the gloom, desperately hoping to see his little dog pop up from the undergrowth. By the time he arrived the lorry ramp was down and the horses were clattering into their boxes, weary after the long drive. The yard was ablaze with lights and humming with activity as Hattie and Seb were unloading the truck and Leo was occupied in taking off the horses' travelling gear.

"Hiya," called Hattie, "What are you doing here?"

"I can't find Fiver, I thought he might have come here?" said Felix, "You seen him?"

"No I haven't," said Hattie looking worried. "When did you last see him?"

"I let him out about half an hour ago and he didn't come back," grumbled Felix, "surely he can't have gone far?"

"He's probably after rabbits," said Hattie reassuringly.

"He normally comes back within a while though, there's no sign of him at all. I'm really worried."

"Look, let me just finish up here and I'll give you a hand looking for him."

"Thanks Hattie," sighed Felix, "I know you probably think I'm just being stupid, but I've got a funny feeling something has happened to him."

"We'll take Hero – he's a big coward but he does love Fiver," soothed Hattie. "Where is Alice, is she looking?"

"Dunno, she's in a terrible state, I can't make head nor tail of her these days, she's all over the place."

Seb was coming back from lugging the saddles back to the tack room. "We nearly had a nasty accident coming down the drive."

"Really?" said Hattie, not particularly interested, "What happened?"

"Some bloody idiot in a van driving with no lights on, tearing up the drive from the stables towards the road – who was it?"

"No idea," said Hattie, "they must have come from the house. I've been waiting in the yard for you and no-one was here. Probably some batty friend of Lady V's. You know how eccentric some of them can be."

"Odd though," said Leo, coming up behind them, "drove like a bloody maniac up over the parkland to avoid us."

"Must have been something to do with Lady V," said Felix, "Why else would they go up over there?"

"Yeah – you're probably right," agreed Seb, "I heard what you said about Fiver, once we've finished here, we'll all look."

"Thanks mate," said Felix, gratefully.

But they searched for hours and there was no trace of Fiver. Reluctantly in the end they had to abandon and agree they would start again first thing in the morning. Felix's heart was heavy as he traipsed back to the cottage. Alice was waiting for him and she looked up when he crept in. The look on his face quelled any questions and she stood up and took him in her arms whilst he cried like a baby.

Bright and breezy the next morning, Dulcie and Nancy were setting off for an early morning hack. Autumn hunting had started a couple of weeks earlier and the horses were pretty fit, and needed to stay that way for the season ahead. The weather was chilly with a heavy jewelled dew, and a sinister mist had tumbled into the valley from the downs and lay like a steaming witches' cauldron waiting for the sun's cleansing, evaporating rays. The girls did not have to use the foggy roads initially and could set off across the fields belonging to Nantes Place, which joined the southern tip of Fittlebury Hall's estate, and from there they could hack around the park, then up to the old Abbey. By the time they had to hit the road they should be safe and clear of the mist. Jennifer was going to join them, as Charles was away on business, and she enjoyed their company. The girls, far from being miffed, were pleased. Jen was good fun and they knew that once they were finished with exercising, she was decent enough to let them have the rest of the day as their own. They set off just after eight; the still air carrying their voices as they walked across the relatively hard ground of Nantes before emerging onto the Fittlebury Hall Estate. They made their way around the newly harvested fields, the stubble which would soon be ploughed and re-sown was spiky and stiff with hard, upright stalks. The horses stamped eagerly on the ground, but the ladies still walked carefully around the headland, until they reached the green stretches of the parkland. Ahead of them the grand Tudor house lay snuggled in the distance, with the yard nestled to the right and the cottages just beyond. The lofty oak trees, their leaves, always the last to turn, were still green and the grass looked lush and dramatic as it swept away towards the house and the driveway. Away to far side the yellow diggers ,for once, were idle, halted by a problem with the water complex they were struggling to complete for next year's horse trials.

"Shall we mosey over and take a look?" suggested Dulcie, "might be interesting to see what they're doing."

"Definitely, if you don't think we'd get into trouble," said Nancy, "I'd love to see."

"I'm sure it'll be fine," laughed Jennifer, "you can blame me if you like!"

"Right boss – we will," agreed Dulcie, her eyes sparkling, "I can't wait to have a gander!"

They kicked the horses into a canter across the stretch of grassland, pulling up beside the yellow digger. There were great mounds of earth piled up on one side and a big excavation was going on, with pipes and drains stacked in piles. A big stretch had been hollowed out and was being lined with scalpings and a thick membrane. It was going to be a massive complex. The mounds of earth were being fashioned into a square bank of different levels, presumably for jumps into and out of what would be the water jump. They circled around the quarry on horseback, chattering and gesticulating, guessing and conjecturing about the end result, eventually kicking on towards the stables. Jennifer was laughing about her own ineptitude and that she would never have to worry about jumping such obstacles. Dulcie and Nancy were giggling and they kicked the horses on into a canter. None of them noticed the hessian sack, tied at the top, laying alongside the digger, and why would they? There was no movement from inside and it was covered in mud where it had rolled after last night's impact.

The girls clattered into the yard and were surprised to find the others absent and only Kylie mucking out. She was ungracious, sweating and angry.

"They're looking for Felix's fucking dog," Kylie snarled, "like that matters - just left me with the shit as usual."

"Poor Felix, I had no idea he had lost his dog," said Jennifer sadly, "when did he go missing?"

"No idea," muttered Kylie, "and frankly I don't care, fucking little mutt."

Jennifer looked aghast. Nancy interceded, "no need to be nasty – tough mucking out on your own, but tough losing your dog too. Anything we can do to help?"

"Muck out this lot duckie," sneered Kylie, "that'd be a start."

"Forgive me," said Dulcie sweetly, "but that *is* your job isn't it?"

Kylie threw down her fork and glared at Dulcie, "Why don't you just fuck off."

Dulcie threw her hands in the air laughing. "Whatever, you are a sour bitch aren't you?"

Nancy threw her a warning look and then smiled at Jennifer. "Come on, we'd better get going."

"What a horrible girl," exploded Jennifer, as they left the yard, "I had no idea she was so unpleasant."

"I think that was quite mild for her, to be honest," said Nancy, "she has quite a reputation that one, but luckily not our problem."

"We'd better keep our eyes peeled for that little dog," pleaded Dulcie. "How dreadful."

"Definitely," agreed Jennifer, kicking her horse into a smart trot up the drive, "there have been a lot of dogs stolen recently I believe."

"Yes, it's been all over Facebook," said Nancy, "I hope they find him. Felix thinks the world of that dog, and so does Hattie."

Alice winced every time she heard Felix calling out Fiver's name. She'd known ever since Ernie's call it was pointless. He was dead and, just like Oli's injuries, it was all her fault. Just another turn of the screw to ensure she did as she was told. They had a big race coming up this week and Ernie had made sure that she would play ball. She wanted to have the strength to tell him to piss off, but it was all too late for that – she'd never be able to hold her head up again if anyone ever found out about what she'd done and what she was responsible for. She would do as she was told every time, and they knew it. Every now and then there would be a small reminder she guessed, and Fiver was a victim just like Oli had been. She left the others searching on the pretence of being called out to work, but, in truth, she could bear it no longer, this fruitless searching. Felix's white pinched face, Hattie's tear streaked cheeks and red rimmed eyes. It was all too much to bear. Even the gays, who usually irritated the hell out of her with their sanguine humour, were subdued and sombre this misty morning. She spun on her heel and left them to it, stomping back to the cottage in irritation.

Felix and the others were searching in the woods behind the cottage. The fog hung like ethereal grey veils strewn across the trees making the echo of their voices calling seem sinister and unreal. These woods were a favourite haunt of Fiver's, littered with rabbits and a positive paradise for dogs. Hero was with them this morning, bounding like the spectre of the hound of the Baskervilles from one burrow to the next, but no trace of Fiver could be found. They poked long sticks down holes thinking he may be stuck, but nothing, not a squeak, and their voices were hoarse from calling. The search continued with everyone expecting the jaunty little chap to come bounding up wondering what all the fuss was about, but as an hour passed and the mist began to lift, it became increasingly obvious that Fiver wasn't there. Felix looked around bleakly, and held out his arms to Hattie who fell weeping into them, and they stood rocking together for some minutes. The boys came and joined in a group hug and Hero started to howl pitifully for his missing friend.

The sun was making its slow ascent up the sky, spreading mellow rays over the park casting long shadows from the majestic oaks. The grand Tudor house stood proud and lofty surveying the scene, with the park railings flanking either side of the drive. Roxy was making an unscheduled visit to the yard accompanied by Max who was, for once, driving himself today.

"Impressive place," he whistled, "must be worth a bob or two."

"Yeah, the stables are at the back. The house is owned by a Lady Veronica, game old girl by all accounts, I haven't met her though."

"Is that who you bought the mill off?"

"Yeah, but we dealt with the Estate Manager."

"Do they know you're coming down?"

"Nope, thought I'd give 'em a bit of a surprise," grinned Roxy, smacking her lips together and checking her lip gloss in the mirror, "keep 'em on their toes."

"Never does any harm," laughed Max, "after all you are paying their wages."

"Well not all of them," advised Roxy, snapping the mirror shut, "they have other liveries too."

"None as high class as you babe I bet," laughed Max, "Nor as high maintenance." He swung the Aston, a new acquisition, into the yard and pulled up cutting the engine. "Hmm very quaint."

Kylie chucked down her fork and strode out from the stable into the courtyard her face black with bad temper. She clocked the posh car and then spotted Roxy in the passenger seat and plastered a smile on her face. *How perfect, no-one else was here, she had her all to herself* she thought gleefully.

Roxy slithered out of the car, followed closely by Max who was eyeing up Kylie with interest. "Hi babes," smiled Roxy, "where is everyone?"

Kylie smiled back. "They're all out looking for Felix's dog, it's gone missing, but I'm in charge – did you want to ride?"

Roxy looked a bit uncertain, she didn't know this girl, in fact had only met her when they'd come down for the filming. She wasn't sure how much she knew or conversely didn't know. "How long will they be, do you think?" she asked, "I know I'm early and haven't made an appointment, but thought I'd get a bit of extra practice in."

"It's absolutely no problem Roxy, I can teach you," said Kylie, "in fact I am probably better qualified than the others anyway – I used to work in a riding school."

"Really?" said Roxy doubtfully. The girl obviously thought she was shit-hot and Roxy didn't like the way she'd automatically used her first name either. A bit up herself. "How long will the boys be?"

"No idea, to be honest, but, as I said I can teach you," enforced Kylie, "I'll make you a coffee and then I'll get the horse ready."

"Coffee would be nice," agreed Roxy, turning to Max, "it's a nice yard isn't it?"

"Lovely," said Max, greedily soaking up the scene, "do they live on the premises then?"

"Felix - that's the one whose girlfriend is a vet, lives in a cottage just towards those woods, and the others live in a cottage just behind the old mill we're buying."

"Nice," mumbled Max again, glancing over towards the woods, "handy for the yard then – pity they're not here."

"Hmm," whispered Roxy. "Not sure about this little madam, she's a bit cocky."

"Not like you to be affected by a silly tart like her – you could cut her up for arse paper!"

"True, but if I fuck her off, I could also fall off big time, and I don't fancy that either. So – I'm at her mercy a bit."

"Let's have that coffee, I'm parched."

"I just hope the boys get back soon," grumbled Roxy, "Somehow I've got a nasty feeling about this."

"Chill out baby – what could go wrong?" grinned Max, enjoying Roxy's discomfort "I quite fancy taking up this riding game myself."

"Reeeallly?" gasped Roxy, "You don't mean it?"

"I might," said Max, "I can see myself as a country gent, especially now I'm into this racing malarkey. Don't you think I'd cut it as a huntin' fishin' and shootin' bloke then?"

Roxy gave him a long look. "Actually I do, and if I'm gonna do my riding and country range you might just be the model I'm looking for."

"And you my dear can piss orf!" laughed Max, "where's that bloody coffee?"

Over on the parkland, the digger driver had just arrived for the day. Old Mark the Estate Manager was giving them a hard time about this water complex and wanted them to get a move on. It had to be finished before the weather set in for the winter, so that it had time to settle and bed in ready for the horse trials next year. Everybody wanted everything done yesterday, he grumbled, as he revved up his machine and rumbled over onto the man-made bank to tamp down the loose soil that had been dumped from the excavations of the lake. Jumps were going to be erected on top of the bank next spring, so the footings had to be firm, and then other jumps around the complex to make a variety of combinations in and out of the water. Small conifers were being planted at strategic places, along with carved lengths of oak, shaped like crocodiles – it was going to look spectacular once it was finished. But it was boring work going over and over the same heap of soil burying all the rubbish and levelling it nonetheless. The driver plugged in his iPod and started work, not noticing the hessian sack lying inert at the side of the pile of mud.

Kylie was ecstatic, now was her chance to shine and befriend Roxy while the others were out of the way looking for that stupid dog. She'd tacked Galaxy up in double quick time, only having given him a cursory brush, and now she was leading him up to the arena with Roxy traipsing after her with about as much enthusiasm as a trip to the dentist. The bloke, who was actually rather gorgeous looking if you liked older guys, was following with an amused grin on his face.

"Now I know you've only been on a horse once or twice before, but just relax. I'm a good teacher, much more experienced than Felix or Seb actually, and can really help you, if you'll let me," soothed Kylie, edging Galaxy up to the mounting block and pulling down the stirrups. "Here, I'm going to balance the saddle this side and you just swing on – like you did before."

Roxy could have hit her, but without blowing her cover, as clearly this girl was not party to her having been here before, and, realising she had to play the true novice, did as she was told. Swinging her leg easily over the horse and settling into the saddle.

"Marvellous," said Kylie, "Really good."

Max leant against the fence watching in admiration – he had to admit Roxy did look good, her lean frame suited breeches and long boots, her voluptuous tits moulded like sumptuous blancmange into the polo shirt. It was just such a shame she had to wear that stupid crash hat, so much nicer if her hair was whipping around her face. But it was a good look, and he could see that a range of riding wear would sell well – she had a good head and body for business did our Roxy. She oozed sex appeal, demonstrating perfectly that you didn't have to dress like a horse to be good on one.

The lesson progressed. The bint Kylie was a sycophant, and Roxy was licking up the praise all the way. That Roxy was a natural, Max had no doubt, as natural as her tits that was … something didn't ring true here. He knew her better than anyone and this was a steaming pile of horseshit – she must have been learning somewhere else. This was more stage managed than *Strictly Come Dancing*.

Mark Templeton was not in a good mood. Sandy and he had rowed this morning, which although was not the end of the world, had made him cross. She was a feisty woman was Sandy and he loved her for it, but sometimes, just sometimes, it would be nice to have a more docile woman he thought. It was all over a holiday. He wanted to go away, she didn't. She wanted to ride her horse and chill and he said he was around here every day and wanted a break. Sandy had stormed off to work, slamming the door behind her. He had let her go, drinking his coffee and forcing himself to eat toast and Marmite, even though he felt it would choke him. He knew she worked hard, he knew she loved her horse and the solace that brought, but he worked hard too, and he needed a break from the estate. It had been a stressful year, what with selling the mill and building the new course for the horse trials next year. He fancied getting away, she didn't. They had to reach a compromise, but right now that didn't seem a possibility. Knowing Sandy and himself, they would sort it, but it was infuriating and he had a busy day ahead. He was going to have to chivvy up those buggers building the course and, luckily, Ruth and Simon were coming over this morning to meet him to give him some advice. He glanced at his watch, shoved down the last of his toast and swilled it down with the coffee, he'd better get a shove on he was meeting them at the estate office in 15 minutes.

Simon and Ruth were the nicest couple, and were waiting for Mark when he arrived.

"Sorry," laughed Simon, "I know we're early but we've got loads on, our own event's only a couple of weeks away."

"I'm bloody grateful to you for coming," said Mark apologetically, "I know how awkward it can be at this time of year."

"No trouble," laughed Ruth, swishing her blonde hair behind her ear, "but let's crack on shall we?"

They jumped in Mark's Landrover and sped across the park towards the lake complex where the digger was working doggedly backwards and forwards, tamping down the bank. Mark slewed the vehicle alongside the dugout and they piled out to inspect the work. The digger stopped and the driver clambered out and they huddled together talking about the project. Simon paced the length of what would be the water jump, carefully looking at the distance between it and the position of the jumps and Ruth walked up onto the bank striding out the distances. All the time the sun was climbing higher in the sky – it was going to be a lovely day. Ruth stood with her hands on her hips surveying the beautiful parkland, but she didn't notice the hessian sack which was now almost obliterated by the soil below. Scrabbling down to join the others Simon was suggesting a few amendments and a special sort of membrane for the water complex. They were all nodding in agreement, walking around the perimeter and then shaking hands and moving off. The digger driver scrambled back into the JCB and fired up the engine.

Felix, Hattie and the boys had admitted defeat. They'd called until their throats hurt, shouted until they could hardly speak, looked in every rabbit hole and place that Fiver had frequented. It was hopeless. They had given up the ghost and were walking back as frustrated as a eunuch in a brothel to the yard. Hattie was still sobbing miserably, and Felix had his arm around her shoulders in an attempt to console her. Seb and Leo were trying to make helpful suggestions, but were speedily running out of ideas. Felix looked dreadful, having been up half the night and none of them noticed until they were nearly back that Roxy was riding around the arena on Galaxy with Kylie giving her a lesson. Seb clicked his tongue in exasperation and Hattie stopped her whimpering as she watched, astonished, as Kylie assumed control of Roxy's lessons. Felix's face had gone whiter, if that were possible, and then his eyes had glinted dangerously – he was seriously angry. As they came down the track toward the school a blond man was leaning over the fence watching, absorbed in the proceedings, and Kylie was so engrossed as to be totally oblivious to their returning. Moments before they arrived at the school, a Landrover hurtled across the park, tooting its horn and flashing its lights coming to a violent and abrupt halt just outside the arena. Galaxy, unsurprisingly, spooked and jinked to one side, depositing an unbalanced Roxy with aplomb on her skinny arse. Kylie was outraged, shouting and swearing at the driver, waving her lunge whip in anger, causing a terrified Galaxy to panic all the more and gallop off around the school. Roxy lay like a floppy rag doll in a heap, not moving a muscle. Hattie tore into the arena towards her, ignoring the shrieking Kylie and knelt down beside Roxy dredging up every vestige of her first aid training. Mark leapt out of the Landrover – his normal calm composure nowhere to be seen – he was yelling something at Felix. Bedlam broke loose with Max screaming at Kylie, and Seb running into the school to catch the petrified Galaxy and Leo trying to placate Max. Mark was ushering Felix to the back of the Landrover, and before anyone could say anything, they had both jumped in and floored it up the drive with all the compulsion of a getaway car in a bank raid.

CHAPTER 55

To Hattie's immense relief, although Roxy lay crumpled in the school, she was moaning, which meant she wasn't unconscious, and she'd had a relatively soft landing. With any luck, she was just being a drama queen and it was just a sore bum and wounded pride. Hattie went through all the rigmarole of checking, astonishing herself that she remembered all the '*Annie can you hear me*' stuff she'd learned on the course and was bloody glad that she had. Eventually Roxy sat up, spitting bits of arena and sand out of her mouth and looking furiously at her assembled audience. Max was crowding over her looking concerned, and Seb was standing to one side biting his nails in anxiety. Kylie was holding Galaxy by the gate with Leo.

"That stupid fucking girl, I knew she was an idiot," yelled Roxy, "I should never have trusted her. Oh God my back is sore."

"You're bound to feel a bit shaken up," soothed Hattie, "let me get you a drink of water. I think you're gonna be fine, it's just a shock."

Roxy put out a claw-like hand, clutching at Hattie's, "You've been absolutely wonderful doll, not like that stupid imbecile."

"I hate to say this Roxy, but you need to get back on, it's the only way forward," mumbled Seb, "otherwise you may never ride again."

"You are fucking joking right?" snapped Roxy, "I will not!"

"There's no way she's getting back on that dangerous beast," snarled Max, "This place is a fucking charade."

"Listen," soothed Hattie, smiling at Roxy, "I know this has been a terrible shock, but it really wasn't the horse's fault, nor yours. He was frightened by the Landrover, it was stupid of Mark and Kylie, but they didn't think. But we are here now, trust us, you'll be so pleased you did – I promise." She looked hypnotically into Roxy's eyes, "Come on, give it a try – please?"

Roxy looked mutinous, and then relented, "Okay, but get that fucking girl out of here. I never want to see her again, and I want you to be here – what's your name?"

"Hattie – it's Hattie, and, of course, I'll be here."

"Okay, and you too Seb, just get that fucking half-wit out of my sight. I never, *ever* want her around me again – got it?"

"Absolutely, got it Roxy," agreed Seb, "I'll go over and sort it, and get Leo to bring you out some water too."

Max looked at Roxy, "I think you're completely nuts babes. Why do it? What does it matter?"

"Actually it's a real challenge Max, and I'm gonna fucking do it – that girl's a tosser. But this girl …" she glanced over at Hattie, "is going be my guiding light, right Hattie?"

"Whatever you say, Ms Le Feuvre," agreed Hattie, "whatever I can do to help."

"Hattie, sweetie, you call me Roxy. You and I are gonna be great friends, I don't forget my friends – do I Maxie?"

Max allowed his gaze to flick idly over Hattie appraising her for the first time. "No Hattie, neither Roxy nor I, forget our friends, nor our enemies either."

Felix and Mark sped off like nutters in the Landrover, lurching towards Horsham. .It had been a pure fluke that Mark had spotted the hessian sack when he did before it was ploughed into the fabric of the bank. As he had curiously peered inside and seen its grisly contents he had totally abandoned Ruth and Simon with hardly an explanation, speeding over to the yard like a total maniac to find Felix. Fiver was barely alive, he was in a great deal of pain and severely dehydrated. When he heard Felix's voice he gave a pathetic and desultory wag of his stumpy tail and then rolled his eyes and fell still again. Felix had acted quickly, there was no point in ringing Alice – she was an equine vet - and on the way had telephoned ahead to a friend of his, Emma, who had just set up her own small animal practice and was a wizard with dogs. She assured him that she and her staff were on stand-by to receive them and Felix knew he couldn't be in more caring hands. As they made the mercy dash over the country miles, the questions kept churning round and round in his brain – who had put Fiver in the sack and who had tried to steal him? Thank God Mark had been over at the new water complex that morning otherwise who knows what might have happened – he might never have been discovered. Felix gulped and choked back the emotions. He knew he should have told Hattie, but the vision of Roxy flying off Galaxy was sketched in his mind and she was rushing to deal with that emergency – he would call her directly he had news – whatever that news might be. Fiver had been missing since the previous evening that meant that he had been injured and without water since then – he glanced at his watch – it was well past midday. He took a deep breath – if the little dog got through this it would be a bloody miracle.

Emma was waiting for them in her smart, mauve overalls along with her veterinary nurses. She was the epitome of efficiency and far removed from the Emma Felix knew from the hunting field.

"Is he going to be okay?" he whispered, "I can't bear it, do anything you have to do."

"Just take it easy," said Emma, "We'll do all we can. This little fellah has had a shock and that's often the worst of it. I'll make a thorough examination and we'll do some x-rays, but if you could just stay as calm as you can, it would help him … okay?

"Sorry," mumbled Felix, "I'm being a whimp."

"It's okay," smiled Emma, "you're allowed, just let me do my job eh?"

Half an hour later, the x-rays and the examination completed, Fiver was sleeping more comfortably with a painkiller and a drip which had been set up.

"Right," said Emma, handing Felix a cup of coffee and smiling at him, "you're lucky. At the moment there doesn't appear to be any significant internal injury, his gums and his vital signs seem satisfactory. There are no bone breaks, but the big danger here is that he could be bleeding internally, as I think he took a good old bashing, and he's in shock which can be as dangerous as anything else. So we're going to keep him here making sure he's hydrated. We'll be reviewing him constantly, watching for any changes and, if he remains stable over the next 24 hours, you can take him home – so the next few hours are crucial really."

"Oh God," gasped Felix, "Can I stay with him?"

"Do you really want to?" asked Emma, "It's a hard floor."

"I don't care," emphasised Felix, "I think he'll be better if he knows I'm there."

"Your choice, but not something that I'd let everyone do, let me tell you!" grinned Emma. "Why don't you go home and come back later? He's sleeping now, and you can do the night-time vigil."

"Thanks Emma, I owe you."

"You do," laughed Emma. "Hopefully it'll be okay though Felix, he's a grand little chap and a fighter too."

Roxy had clambered tentatively back on Galaxy, but good horse that he was, he stood like a statue, patiently and calmly for her. Seb at his head and Hattie at her side they moved off around the arena. Roxy's face looked pinched and strained. Hattie crooned inanities to her all the while that it would be fine and not to worry; Seb kept his head down and didn't say a word. Leo had dealt with Kylie, shooing her out of the yard with as much diplomacy as he could muster under the circumstances. Max was observing, sullen faced and taking photographs, and Seb felt they were all under the microscope. Galaxy walked initially, rather gingerly, around the arena until Roxy started to relax, listening intently to Hattie chattering to her. The horse visibly relaxed too and amazingly Roxy started to trot and they seemed to have bonded and made a partnership again. Max watched from the side lines and was impressed. Hattie loped around the arena beside Roxy, her tits swinging from side to side, her long legs taking the increased pace well in her stride and he was impressed. This fresh-faced, beautiful girl was a natural. If she didn't have a career in horses, she certainly had one in modelling or in being a hostess. Max was intrigued – this country life had a lot to offer. Seb let Hattie take the lead, keeping quiet. After a quarter of an hour, they pulled up Roxy looked flushed and triumphant and Hattie was laughing with pleasure.

"I knew you could do it!"

Roxy smiled down at her. "Seriously chick, this is down to you, I wouldn't have got on the fucking thing again. You're magic. I owe ya!"

"It's nothing honestly." grinned Hattie. "just pleased it all worked out well. We all have the odd fall – just have to get on with it."

"But I wouldn't if it hadn't been for you. I won't forget," said Roxy. "But you," she gesticulated at Seb, "get rid of that other tart – she's a waster."

"She had no right to put you on the horse," simpered Seb apologetically, "no right at all. I am sure she was only trying to be helpful, but she's only a mucker outer that's all."

"Shit to shit – how appropriate," flounced Roxy, "don't let her near me again."

"You're lucky Roxy wasn't injured," said Max menacingly, "you could have ended up in court."

"Leave it Max. I wasn't and I've had a great ride thanks to Hattie." Roxy smiled, probably the first genuine smile Hattie had ever seen her give, "Let's get back home."

"Actually," said Max, "despite the debacle, I wouldn't mind giving this a go." He laughed and looked at Roxy. "We could ride together doll," and turning to Seb asked, "Do you have anything you could teach me on?"

"Well," stuttered Seb, for once lost for words and not sure that he liked this sinister pal of Roxy's, "have you ridden before?"

"Nope, but I am fearless," laughed Max, "and I am loaded."

Roxy cackled with laughter. "True on both counts, go on Seb, see if you could find him something it would be such a craic," she looked coyly at him under lashes, "and I'd be eternally grateful."

"I'm sure we could find something," Seb said, forced into a compromise, and wondering what the hell he could put him on. "I'll see what I can do, but you'll have to give me a bit of notice before you come down next time, Roxy – so that I can make sure we are around and available. I don't want another fiasco like this afternoon."

"Deal," laughed Roxy triumphantly, "get something sorted by next week Seb – I know you can do it. And make sure that Hattie is around – no more hiding your talents Hattie, you are fab!"

"Hmm, of course," smiled Hattie uncertainly, not sure how this would go down with Seb, and more especially Felix, but how could she argue. "Happy to be here to help."

"You'll look great on camera, won't she Max, with those long legs and huge eyes. I can't imagine why Farouk didn't notice you when he was down last time," squeaked Roxy "where were you hiding?"

Hiding actually, thought Hattie, but that would be no longer an option, it would appear and Christ knew how Kylie was going to react after today – it didn't bear thinking about. She smiled at Roxy and Max, and grabbed Galaxy, excusing herself, took him back to his stable and left Seb to it.

Kylie was lurking in the yard as she walked back from the school and followed her into Galaxy's stable, wrenching the door closed behind them. She'd picked up a pitch fork and was waving it menacingly at Hattie, whilst Galaxy snorted and cowered in the corner.

"You fucking bitch Hattie, you did that just to make me look a fool," Kylie hissed, making stabbing gestures with the fork, "it was all going brilliantly until you pitched up."

"Calm down Kylie," soothed Hattie, holding out her hand and trying to placate her, "you know it wasn't like that. Galaxy was spooked by the Landrover, it could have happened to any of us at any time."

"You made me look a fool, rushing over to her Ladyship and administering First Aid."

"What else was I supposed to do?" snapped Hattie, anger overcoming her fear. "Shout like you were doing and lose control, or behave rationally?"

Kylie stabbed at Hattie again with the fork, and Hattie, used to dodging Woody's kicks, neatly side stepped her, but Galaxy gave a whinny of alarm. "You bitch – well I've had enough of you," and she jerked the fork again, this time narrowly missing the terrified horse.

"ENOUGH!" yelled a voice from the door. Felix had returned and witnessed the whole scene. "Kylie, I don't know what's gone on here, but get out of that stable right now."

"She started it," whimpered Kylie, "she provoked me."

"Get out," snarled Felix, "and get into the tack room – NOW. Hattie deal with Galaxy."

He waited for Kylie to vacate the stable, and marched her off towards the tack room with her bellyaching loudly all the way. Seb having just waved off Roxy and Max, looked over annoyed, and stomped towards them demanding to know what was going on. He followed Kylie and Felix into the tack room and closed the door firmly behind them.

Leo came over to Hattie, "You all right luvvie?"

"Blimey, she's nuts!" exclaimed Hattie, "she went for me with a pitch fork!"

"Let them deal with her, and we'll sort out the nags. I don't think Seb can turn a blind eye to her antics any longer, do you?"

"God I hope not – but more importantly – what about Felix, what's happened?"

"No idea – we'll have to wait and see."

They took Galaxy over to the wash down box and could hear raised voices from the tack room and then, a lot of screaming and yelling, obviously coming from Kylie as moments later she stormed out her hair flying behind her and looking like some kind of demonic witch.

"You'll all fucking pay for this – I promise!" she shouted, "I'm not finished with you lot yet. You owe me – you promised me great things and let me down."

Seb and Felix followed her out of the tack room. Felix was trembling with anger, and Seb was shaking his head in disbelief, as they watched Kylie storming around the yard hurling barrows, forks, brooms and shovels into disarray and screaming at the top of her voice. Finally she got into her car and chugged off down the drive in a huge anti-climax and Seb leant against the wall in relief.

"Thank God for that – good riddance I say."

"I hope it's as easy as that," said Felix gloomily. "I've a shitty feeling that this isn't the least we've seen of her."

"Don't, don't, don't," moaned Seb, throwing his hands up in despair, "and there's more bad news – we'll need to find another school master and, this time, a big horse for Roxy's pal."

"I don't give a flying fuck," spat Felix, "I'm going back to the vet's to be with Fiver. I've only come back to get Hattie – you'll have to sort it yourself Seb."

Seb looked bereft. "Sweetie, I am so sorry, I had forgotten, of course you two go, leave it to Leo and me – we'll come up with something … somehow."

CHAPTER 56

If Kylie's car could have roared up the drive, burning the rubber off her tyres, she would have been delighted, but sadly, the best it could manage was a pathetic rumble and splutter, belching black fumes as it went. She felt like screaming. Reaching onto the dashboard for her fags and careering over to the wrong side of the road as she lit up, she was so consumed with rage that she could have spontaneously combusted. *How fucking dare they* she fumed, she was better than any of them put together. How unlucky that stupid arse Mark had come over when he had and frightened the fucking horse, it was all going so well till then. She was so totally impressing Roxy with her teaching skills - she could tell. Then that cunt, Hattie, had stolen her limelight – on purpose, of course. Kylie'd had everything under control. Roxy was just being a drama queen, she wasn't really hurt at all and Hattie had steamed in with her Florence Nightingale act. Then to top it all, when she'd tried to have it out with Hattie, Felix had come along and got the wrong end of the stick – it should have been Hattie that was fired, not her. Well they would pay, she'd make them pay. She pulled the car up alongside the village shop, taking long tokes on the cigarette to steady herself and wondered what she could do next. She looked at the inviting display of fruit, flowers and vegetables under the gaily striped awning and felt like smashing the lot to shreds. Then the stack of newspapers on their racks outside caught her eye and it came to her. The tabloids – they would pay well for her story. It would be a great compensation for losing her job and a form of divine retribution too. Kylie took another long drag on her fag and felt a glow all over – that's exactly what she would do – sell her story to the highest bidder.

Hattie drove back to Horsham, resisting the urge to race along the roads with Felix fidgeting in the passenger seat and telling each other that if there was bad news Emma would have rung by now. They were both shell-shocked – neither wanting to think who could have done such a thing to Fiver, but moreover, was their beloved little dog going to come through the ordeal?

"Do you think he'll be okay?" whispered Hattie, "I mean he must have been in that sack for over 12 hours."

"Emma said they needed to monitor him for signs of internal bleeding, and that he was in shock."

"Shock can be serious can't it?"

"Yep," admitted Felix, "but he's comfortable, and he looked okay when I last saw him, but I just have this feeling I need to be there."

"Of course you do, we both do. After all, we rescued the little blighter from that over-sized ape all those months ago, didn't we – not to get duffed up later by some other nutter."

Felix reached out and grabbed Hattie's hand, "It's so great that you understand Hats."

"Of course I do, you daft sod," squeezing his hand right back, "have you told Alice – she must be frantic."

Felix felt his skin crawl, "No I haven't – what with the day we've had. And she's never really liked Fiver anyway."

"Aw Felix don't say that, of course she has."

"No she hasn't," mumbled Felix. "I don't think she gives a fuck actually."

"I think you're being a bit harsh – go on, give her a ring," urged Hattie. "It's not fair *not* to tell her, is it?"

"Oh okay – I suppose you're right."

Felix pulled out his mobile and dialled Alice's number – her voice mail cut in. "She must be with a client," he hissed. "I'll leave her a message."

"Well at least you've called her," smiled Hattie, as she pulled into the surgery car park and reversed into a space. "Let's hope all's well with his Lordship now we're here."

Alice picked up the voice mail and couldn't believe her ears. It seemed that Fiver had been reprieved – although why that would be, she wasn't sure. From the brief conversation with Ernie last night, she had assumed they would never see him again, but somehow they had changed their minds or, and more likely, something had gone wrong. Whatever, he was safe and she had never felt more relieved; although he was far from out of the woods yet. Professionally, she knew that Emma was good, but she also knew only too well that, if the dog had been beaten, he could be bleeding internally and shock was the least of the problems. Alice was glad that she didn't have to be with Felix holding his hand. It would be difficult to remain sympathetic when she'd want to be brutally objective about the possible outcome. In the meantime, she was going to have play ball with Ernie and his demands of her this week, and fuck knew what would happen if she made a mistake. There was obviously a lot riding on it and, any more than that she didn't want to know. Okay, it may be an ostrich attitude but it was the way she got through. She didn't ask any more questions than she had to, and right now, she was heading up to the racing stables perfectly prepared to carry out their plans.

Kylie was on the phone to the news desk, her eyes were gleaming. She had arranged to meet a reporter in Horsham later. She wanted to tie up the loose ends first, make sure she cut a good deal and then they could do what they liked with the story. How much to ask though? She decided she'd wait for them to make her an offer and then double it. She smiled to herself and lit another fag. This would be worth a lot more than a crummy groom's pay.

As Hattie and Felix walked into the surgery they knew from the look on Lynne, the receptionist's face, that things were not looking good. She blustered that they had been trying to get in touch with Felix but hadn't been able to get through, but she'd fetch Emma straight away. Felix clutched the side of the desk. He had gone quite white and looked sick. Hattie rubbed his shoulder whilst they waited for Emma to come through into the reception area. She felt sick herself, but knew that she had to be strong, although one puff of wind, and she thought, she'd fall over. Emma marched towards them, her kind face was serious.

"I think he's may have a slow, internal bleed. His tummy is distended, and his gums are paler. I'm just about to do another x-ray and take a little bit of fluid from his tummy to see if there is any blood in the sample. If there is he will need surgery."

"Oh God," whimpered Felix, "just do whatever you need to do Emma, I beg you, just save him."

"I'll do everything I can I promise. I think he's had a kicking or a big trauma – it could be a rupture of the spleen. We're on top of it Felix, and we can remove the spleen if necessary, but he's weak and dehydrated, so he's in ITU and we'll be making decisions moment by moment."

"Oh Felix," snivelled Hattie, "I'm sure they're doing everything they can, he's in good hands and we just have to trust them."

"Oh Hattie I can't bear it, who could have done this?"

"I don't know love, but right now all I care about is him getting through it."

Max and Roxy were heading back up to London. Max was handling the Aston with all the sensitivity of a brain surgeon.

"Wow, this baby rocks," he purred, as he accelerated past a Porsche with ease. "I just love the power." He took his foot off the gas and the car responded smoothly and he pulled over into the middle lane of the motorway.

"You're being a pussy," grumbled Roxy, "either drive the thing or don't, make ya mind up."

"It's all right for you kitten," admonished Max. "You forget I don't get to drive too often – I've normally got a bloke to chauffeur me about."

"Well, you're making a right pig's ear out of it if you ask me."

"Actually I didn't ask you, and actually I don't care what you think either," laughed Max accelerating again.

"Why did ya buy it in the first place, beats me? You don't really need it do ya?"

"I fancied it, that's why, and I can afford it so why not?" argued Max, pulling over again. "I can do what I like with my money. After seeing you ride – and fall off …"

"Don't take the piss!"

"And fall off, I think I could even be tempted to buy a horse."

"For fuck's sake Max, you haven't even tried it yet!"

"Do I have to? If I want to have a go and try it – why shouldn't I?"

Roxy purred with giggles. "There never was any stopping you when you're mind's set on summat; it'll be fun to do it together."

"Yeah great idea," said Max, and thinking to himself, that it would also be a good opportunity to get nearer to the vet he wanted to meet. "That Hattie's a sweet kid."

"Yeah isn't she?" said Roxy, looking at him sideways, "got the hots for her have ya?"

"Nope, but she's wasted shovelling shit – she could earn a fortune as a model or an escort. Perhaps you could get her to model your new riding range?"

"Now that is a good idea," agreed Roxy, perking up, "she'd be perfect for the job with the length of her legs. But don't you go fucking about with her – you hear me?"

Max gave her a mock salute. "No Ma'am- understood." He laughed, "Let's stop of for a drink, I'm gasping."

"Okay, just make it somewhere quiet, with no hint of a bleedin' camera."

"What do you take me for? You're with me not Aiden," snapped Max nastily, "I can't abide the fuckers."

Roxy put her hand on his knee and smiled gratefully. "Thanks hun."

Whilst Max and Roxy were having a quiet drink on their way home, Kylie was ringing yet another national paper. Although she'd set up one meeting already, she was still casting out feelers with other papers. They were prepared to pay big bucks for the story – anything exclusive to do with Roxy was worth money, and if Kylie had information, they were willing to pay. Kylie just needed to weed out who would pay the most and that they didn't shaft her when it came down to the nitty gritty. She wasn't going to be treated like an idiot.

Finally, she thrashed out a deal and agreed to meet their reporter, instructing him to bring the cash with him. She rang the original paper cancelling the meeting with their reporter and they immediately doubled their offer. *Wow* thought Kylie, this was fabulous. She loved being the centre of attention, and being able to command such figures was to her … like … unbelievable. Rubbing her hands with glee, she played one against the other and, finally, a meeting was arranged for later in the day. Kylie couldn't believe her luck – if it all came off, she'd earn today what it'd take her a couple of years to pull, plus the payback would be extremely sweet. She'd just like to be a fly on the wall when they opened the paper!

Felix and Hattie sat miserably in the waiting area, neither one speaking, just gloomily reading the posters on the walls or distractedly leafing through the magazines. Lynne kept glancing at them sympathetically from over her keyboard and asking them if they wanted tea or coffee, to which they both just shook their heads. Each time the inner door to the surgery and treatment room opened they jumped up, only to sit down again heavily when it was just another patient. The agonising minutes ticked past. Felix got up and paced backwards and forwards, his face etched with worry until he suddenly flumped down with a huge sigh and Hattie reached over and held his hand, her eyes moist with fat tears.

"Poor little Fiver," she whispered, "what did he ever do to deserve this?"

"I dunno," said Felix, "but if I ever find the sod, I swear I'll do the same to him."

"Have you noticed any one strange hanging around?" asked Hattie. "When was the last time you saw him?"

"When I let him out for a pee last night, about nine it was. I called and called and went in the cottage to fetch a torch. Thinking back though when I came out, I might have heard a car drive away, but I didn't see any head lights. I didn't think about it till just now."

"I heard a car too, when I was waiting in the yard for the boys to come back in the truck," said Hattie, "but it didn't come through the yard. It must have gone along the back drive from your place around the stables."

"That must have been who the boys nearly collided with then, when they were coming down the drive," reasoned Felix, "it's starting to make sense now. That van careered off across the park, and Mark said that's where they found Fiver."

"By the sounds of it, if they hadn't met the boys coming home, they would have been away with him and we'd probably never have got him back," whimpered Hattie. "God, it doesn't bear thinking about does it?"

"But who were they? And moreover – why?"

"Oh I don't know Felix, I really don't, but I hate the thought of someone lurking around in the dark."

"There have been a lot of dog thefts in the area."

"Yeah, but not at night, and he hardly merits targeting does he? I mean, a little Jack Russell Terrier. A lot of those thefts are just opportunists," said Hattie thoughtfully, and then she went pale. "You don't think it's his previous owner come to get him back do you?"

"No, I don't, that bloke wouldn't do anything quietly, he'd have made a song and dance about it. Try to duff me up, I shouldn't wonder. No it's bloody odd, but I don't suppose we'll ever get to the bottom of it."

Talking had alleviated the gloom and taken their minds off Fiver's struggle for life in those moments, but as the surgery door opened and Emma walked out in her operating gear with a serious look on her face, the horror of the situation flooded back hitting them both like a hurricane. Hattie felt herself go numb, and gripped Felix's hand tightly, she could hardly bear to look and listen as Emma sat down beside them and pulled off her cap.

CHAPTER 57

Kylie was sitting in the Bear in Horsham, nursing half a lager and waiting for the reporter. In agitation she tapped her lighter on the table, wishing desperately she could smoke, bloody stupid ban – these non-smokers pissed her off big time, it ruined going to the pub these days. She felt her chest quicken as the door swung open and a group of lads sauntered in, she turned disappointedly back to her drink and waited. She wasn't sure what the drill was – what he would do, how he would proceed with the story. She'd just have to play it cool and let him take the lead. She continued her tapping with the lighter and waited.

The reporter, who had been watching her covertly from the other side of the dingy bar, guessed he'd left it long enough. This one was as jumpy as a bag of fleas, and sure looked as though one spark and she'd explode. He grinned to himself and sauntered over.

"Kylie?"

Kylie jumped as the shadow passed over the table. "Yeah," she spluttered, "that's me."

"Hi, I'm Steve, you've got something for me I think?"

Kylie looked up into the face of the stranger. He was not at all what she had been expecting, not the older, weasel-faced reporter in a sports jacket or the trench-coated snoop type either. Much younger, late twenties at a guess, with brown hair cut short. Just a pretty standard bloke in skinny jeans and a leather jacket – you would have passed him in the street and had no idea what he did for a living. She smiled nervously at him as he pulled out the chair opposite her and sat down.

"Okay what's the story?"

If Kylie was surprised by his abruptness she recovered her composure remarkably. "Not so fast buster, how do I know you're gonna pay me? I wasn't born yesterday."

"Yeah right," grinned Steve, reaching into his pocket and pulling out a fat envelope, "but first I want the story."

"Show me the colour of your money," said Kylie, her greedy eyes locking onto the packet, "then we'll start talking."

Steve flashed the contents tantalisingly at her, revealing a wodge of notes, the unique smell of the money wafting under her nostrils. "Satisfied?"

"Definitely," said Kylie, the glee lighting up her face. "Just wait till you hear what I've got to tell you."

Steve inclined his head slightly towards her, carefully stowed the money back in his pocket and took out a small digital recorder placing it pointedly on the table between them "start singing baby and the money is all yours."

Some fifteen minutes later Kylie came to a breathless conclusion, "Well that's about it really." She looked up expectantly at Steve, who'd only interrupted her once or twice during the diatribe.

"And when you say you're pretty certain that she'd ridden before, what makes you think that?" Steve asked, jotting down some notes in his pad, "I mean, I'm not horsey, how can you tell that sort of thing?"

"She just wasn't a beginner, it was her posture, her balance, that kind of shit. Also too, I've never known a total novice be able to rise to the trot first time on board. No, she'd ridden before, but was giving it a lot of bollocks about being her first time an all."

"Perhaps she is just a natural?" said Steve. "We have to be really careful about what we print; she could sue the arse off us."

"There's another thing I've just thought of. Over the previous few weeks, before the filming, the other lot at the stables had been acting strange – they were definitely up to something. She could have been coming up secretly to the yard before. The horse she was riding Seb had bought quite randomly a few weeks before."

"It's not proof though is it, just a feeling you had and we can't run with hearsay. We have to know that she was going there before."

"Wait a minute!" Kylie clutched the sides of her chair excitedly, "I've just remembered! This happened twice, I didn't think much about it at the time, but I was bit curious, I'd forgotten until now. I saw a black Mini Cooper S driving in and out of the yard a couple of times, like a nutter, nearly mowed me over – that could have been her!"

"Got a registration number?" Steve drawled, making notes on his pad, "did you see who was driving?"

"No, the windows were tinted, but I bet it was her," said Kylie, "In fact I'm sure of it – it all makes sense now. Why they were acting so strangely, why they wanted me out of the yard in the afternoons, and why Seb bought such a random horse. Then when the filming started - hoping they'd get me on side and I'd keep quiet. Fucking hell, I've been a right mug!"

"Possibly, and it will make a great story, but I'll have to do a bit of background first and get a discreet shutterbug out there with uber long lenses. Now you've gotta keep schtum – you understand. Not a fucking word to anyone. No other rags involved. I'm gonna give you half the money now and half when we print. Got it."

Kylie gulped. He certainly wasn't one for small talk, and she could only hope that he came across with the other half of the money, but she had a feeling he would, and she could see why he had to build the story. "Okay, don't fuck me over though."

"As if I would," said Steve, smiling at her sideways and, taking out the money envelope, counted out the notes with aplomb.

"God we were so lucky," sighed Hattie, sprawling in an armchair in Laundry Cottage, her long legs dangling over the edge of the arms, a wine glass in her hand. "Emma was bloody fantastic, wasn't she Felix?"

"I don't think I've ever been in such a state," Felix admitted, running his fingers through his hair, "we were lucky on all counts. If Mark hadn't decided to go up to the water complex this morning, Fiver would have died in that sack."

"I'm surprised Jennifer and the girls didn't see him when they hacked past," said Leo, "they went that way and must have gone right by him."

"Mark said, by all accounts, he was half hidden under the bucket of the digger – unless they were looking, or right up by the JCB they wouldn't have noticed. It was just pure chance he saw him."

"It must have been that van that night mustn't it?" said Leo. "Fucking bastards! It shot off in that direction and it had no lights on, they were obviously up to no good."

"But why?" said Felix, "I mean, why Fiver, it's not exactly as though he's worth a lot is it, and then just to chuck him out and leave him to die?"

"Look lovelies," soothed Seb, "I think we should try and forget about it, it's not going to do any good is it. The amazing part is that Fiver is going to be okay, thanks to a lot of luck, quick thinking by Mark and skill on Emma's part. So let's crack open another bottle and celebrate."

"I'm just going to say one more thing Seb," said Felix, "I think we should all be more vigilant about strangers around the place. We don't know why Fiver was taken, but they might come back. Also we've got Roxy coming down a lot more, and we need to preserve her privacy, and ours come to that. Now Kylie's been given the boot, I wouldn't put it past her to be very vindictive – come and cut the horses' tails off, that sort of shit. We should be careful."

"Well I agree about Kylie," said Hattie, swirling the wine around in her glass "she's vicious that one, she nearly had me with that pitchfork – bitch!"

"You're right of course, I should have listened to you all and gotten rid of her ages ago," sighed Seb, "but hey ho, we didn't, but I don't think she'll do us any harm."

"Dream on lover," grimaced Leo, "she'll be as bitter as bag of lemons. No you're right, we should be on our guard. When's Fiver coming home then Felix?"

"Not for a day or two, but we can go and see him whenever," smiled Hattie, "poor little love, he was very woebegone, but managed to thump his tail at me."

"Ah bless," crooned Seb, "What a little darling, we'll have to take great care of him when he comes home. No rough and tumble with Hero, eh old man?" he fumbled the huge dog's ears affectionately. "He misses him terribly y' know."

Felix looked at him sideways and pulled a face, "You're nuts, you know Seb?"

"Doll, you shock me sometimes, of course Hero misses his little buddy, and it's been a frightful ordeal for him."

Hattie laughed, shrugging her shoulders helplessly, "Whatever you say Seb!"

Seb turned to her smiling lazily, "If you weren't so much in my good books young Hattie, I would have to scold you," he scratched his nose thoughtfully, "you did a seriously good job with Roxy."

"Bollocks," hooted Hattie, "You know and I know that there was nothing hurt other than her pride, massage that and you're in."

"It matters not, dear heart," placated Seb, "she has taken to you and you are her new best friend. The one that she relies on it seems."

"Lucky you," countered Leo, "you'll be having your tits done next!"

"Shut up you lot," muttered Felix, "Hattie saved the day from that poisonous cow Kylie, and salvaged our reputation with Roxy."

"Calm down dear," goaded Seb sarcastically, "keep your pants on, Hattie knows we're joking!"

"It's okay Felix," grinned Hattie, "actually I rather enjoyed it – she was okay. It was Kylie who was nearly killed me!"

"You can forget about her now"

"Thank Christ!" Hattie turned to Seb, "did Roxy say when she's down next?"

"She rang me whilst you two were at the vet's – she wants to come down in a couple of days, and guess what - that chap she brought with her definitely wants to ride too."

"You are not serious," choked Felix spluttering on his beer, "we can't cope with another bloody beginner, what the fuck can he ride?"

"It'll be a flash in the pan," said Leo, "stick him on Doris – she's a lazy old trollop and won't deck him, and he's hardly likely to spoil her is he?"

"I'd be surprised if he can get her to move," laughed Seb, "she's so idle."

"Perfect then, and now the nationals are over the pressure is off, she can doss about with a novice on her. It won't kill her."

"No, I suppose you're right."

Hattie grimaced, "Poor old Doris."

"I doubt it'll ever come to anything," argued Seb, "and if he is serious, we can look out for something for him. It could mean a big old commission."

"Well, I could do with the money," grinned Felix, "Fiver's vet bill is gonna be pretty expensive."

"I don't mind chipping in with it," offered Hattie, "I've got quite a bit saved up."

"I wouldn't dream of it Hats," said Felix, "but thanks for the offer. Right you lot, I'd better get off home."

"Not staying for supper then?"

"Nope, although I am tempted – it smells great."

"One of Hattie's nights to cook, so it's not out of a can or a packet," enthused Seb. "She spoils us – don't you darling."

"You sure Felix, it's cottage pie," asked Hattie, tilting her head to one side and raising her eyes, "your favourite."

"Better not, much as I'd like to, I should get back."

"Your loss," laughed Leo, "and all the more for us."

Felix hesitated but dragged himself off the sofa, with as much enthusiasm as a dog on firework night, ruffled Hattie's hair as he passed and bade them all good night. The others waited till they heard the back door slam before shooting each other knowing looks.

"I don't know why he goes back to her – she's hardly been supportive has she?" snarled Leo, "he deserves so much better."

"Did you hear her on the phone when he rang her?" grumbled Seb, "she couldn't have given a shit about Fiver."

"Come on lads, don't be too harsh," said Hattie, trying hard not to be bitchy, "she just shows her emotions in a different way."

"Bollocks," snapped Seb, "she's a witch."

"Come on Hattie, stop being so fucking *nice* – she's bloody horrible most of the time. I don't know why he stays with her."

"Okay, I know," Hattie sighed, "she can be difficult, but you know until he wakes up and smells the roses I have to be supportive, even if it sticks in my craw."

"You're too fucking noble girl, or too much in love."

"Oi – that was a bit below the belt Seb," Leo defended Hattie ferociously, "no need eh?"

"Sorry Hats," said Seb waving his hand in the air, "love you doll, you know that."

"I know," groaned Hattie dramatically, desperately blinking back the tears, "and of course you're right, I just wish I could get over him."

Leo moved over and sat on the side of the armchair and folded his arms around her, kissing the top of her head. "Darling so do we, or rather we wish he'd stop being so daft and see what he was missing. Come on sweetie, I'll give you a hand in the kitchen."

When Felix got home the house seemed as eerily cold and quiet as an ancient mausoleum. There were no warm, welcoming lights and no lingering smells of a supper on the go. No Fiver bounding around the house like a demon on speed and, as he closed the back door after him, he felt a cloud of loneliness and despondency wrap around him like some sinister cloak. He suddenly missed the warmth and happy chaos of Laundry Cottage with its easy camaraderie, and felt a gloom descend on him which had his mood sinking into his boots faster than a parachute jump. Alice had said she wouldn't be too late, but of course she was, and in a way he didn't care either, he couldn't bother to pretend any more with her and, if he was strictly honest with himself, it was only a matter of time as to *when*, and not *if* they parted. He sat down with a large whisky, hoping to inebriate himself before she came home, to avoid the inevitable questions and probing. He put his hand down to stroke Fiver, feeling his stomach knot in anguish when he remembered he wasn't there and thought again about who could possibly have wanted to harm him and why.

CHAPTER 58

The following week marched on as ferociously as ants invading a picnic. Roxy and Max came down several times, with Hattie taking as much part in their education as the boys. Max, surprisingly, was an able pupil and Doris tolerated him with a shrug of the withers and a dogged reluctance to go forward. But nonetheless, with some coaxing from Seb, they'd managed to muster a trot, albeit rather unbalanced and wobbly on Max's part; Doris delightedly grinding to a lumbering stop without much invitation. Roxy, on the other hand, was blooming like a florist's window and lapping up every second. Her enthusiasm was as infectious as a dose of clap and she just couldn't get enough. She had forged a good bond with Hattie since the debacle with Kylie and was picking her brains about fashionable riding togs. With the departure of Kylie, Hattie and Leo had been working their butts off, getting up early to manage all the chores before the celebrities arrived and they still had to make sure that the eventers were getting enough work to keep them fit enough and up to their game on the flat too. It was exhausting but the yard was a much cheerier place since the pernicious influence of Kylie had gone.

The good news was that Fiver had come home and had made a remarkable recovery. He was ensconced in the tack room with Hero standing guard over his pal and seemed none the worse for his adventure, and it was all Felix could do to keep him still. His dapper, little tail was working overtime and he seemed quite restored to good health, although Emma had warned not to let him jump about too much and to keep him as quiet as possible. The little bugger had shredded everything in sight when Felix had left him in the cottage, howling with anxiety at being left alone. The lesser of the two evils seemed to be the yard, but everyone was fighting a losing battle at keeping him from being his usual ebullient self. In the end they had penned him and the lazy Hero in the corner in a makeshift cage and a positive butchery of bones, which seemed to be doing the trick. The prognosis from Emma was good – provided he didn't overdo things in the short term, he should heal and recover completely to live a perfectly normal life. In the meantime, the little dog had never been more spoiled and he was relishing every moment.

To everyone's relief, they had seen nothing of Alice. She was too busy covering for Oli and, although the newly qualified locum had started, the more difficult cases were being dealt with by her and Andrew. Oli was mending and his initial incomprehensible mumblings were now making more sense as his jaw became more comfortable. The girls in the surgery had been apprehensive about the new addition to the team but Theo was the most delightful young man with charming manners. Not only was he grateful to be given such a plum locum post straight after qualifying, but he knew exactly how to behave with clients and his colleagues and had an extraordinary knack of saying the right thing at the right time. Paulene, despite the fact that he was almost twenty years her junior, had developed a real soft spot for him, and rushed to make his coffee in the morning, smothering him with attention. Caitlin smiled to herself, after all why not, the lad was certainly good looking with his sandy, blond hair and cheeky, brown eyes, and, my goodness he knew how to lay the butter on with a trowel. It was certainly a change from the prickly monster that Alice had become – no wonder Paulene was smitten – they all were – it was such a change to have a smiling face around the place. Caitlin said as much to Andrew and he had patted her hand indulgently, which had infuriated her at the time, but she knew that he didn't quite know how to handle Alice either. She was certainly becoming a loose cannon especially with the clients and, no matter how good a diagnostician you were, theirs was a service industry and if you fucked off the clients, then you might as well give up.

Alice, herself, was in denial. She blocked out what had happened to Fiver and was just relieved that he was okay. Ernie never mentioned anything about his reprieve and neither did she. But she had no qualms about doing whatever he asked and kept her head down and shut out any reservations she had about right or wrong. Whatever Felix thought about her, she was pleased that Fiver was okay. She just found it harder and harder to show her emotions for fear of giving herself away. She was planning to go down to

Fittlebury Hall stables this very afternoon to see him and make a fuss of the little dog. She'd bought some chews from the village shop and was determined the visit would go well. She knew that Kylie had left under a rather large cloud and reasoned that it was just as well – she had been irritating Felix beyond belief and Alice was rather hoping that, now she was gone, he may well relax a bit more. This visit of hers was destined to be a step in bringing them closer together. It was a lovely, early autumn afternoon, a sigh of a breeze coming off the downs and the sun casting long shadows despite the warmth. The hint of the season changing was in the air, with the crackle of leaves turning golden on the horse chestnut trees. She pulled the Toyota down the long drive and, as she looked across the park, she noticed a flash from just behind the trees. Slowing down and staring she looked again, but could see nothing and, thinking she must have imagined it, she moved on towards the yard.

Roxy was in seventh heaven. Her lesson had been spectacular today with her body performing perfectly in tune with Galaxy – it was an awesome feeling. Max, sadly, had not fared so well, the lumbering Doris kept grinding to a halt and scratching her knee, with him lurching forward onto her shoulders and him getting angry as his balls hit the pommel with aplomb. Doris, ever the piss taker was thoroughly enjoying Max's chagrin and became lazier as the lesson progressed. His humiliation complete, Max slithered off, hot in the face and indecently angry, fuelled further by Roxy laughing her head off at the side of the arena.

"This bloody horse is hopeless," said Max dangerously, "get me another."

"It's not as easy as that," explained Felix. "You can't just magic them up from nowhere. In fact you're lucky we've got Doris."

"I don't care how much it costs," snapped Max, "just get me a decent horse, one that goes when I ask it, not a dobbin like this."

"Right," said Seb, "we are on the case but it takes time to find the right one."

"Don't give me that bollocks – do your job. What about a race horse?"

"Er – not quite right for you I think," stuttered Seb, "they can be a bit temperamental and quirky."

"Better than this old cart horse," said Max dismissively, slapping Doris on the rump. "I want something with a bit of quality."

"You do make me laugh," tinkled Roxy, "she is quality, you just can't ride her. Seb did really well on her at the nationals, you're lucky to be riding her."

"Whatever, find me a horse."

"Oh shut up Max," said Roxy exasperated, "you're starting to piss me off with all this macho crap – come on I've gotta get back – let's get moving. Thanks Felix darling."

She moved over and kissed Felix exaggeratedly on both cheeks, squeezing his bum at the same time. Max glared at him, and they walked over to the mini. None of them noticed the flash of the camera lens behind the trees.

The Toyota breezed into the yard and Alice jumped out, the bundle of dog chews clasped in her hand. Max, who hadn't yet climbed into the Mini, looked at her in appreciation and expectation as Felix was forced to make introductions. The glint in Max's eye was missed by Roxy as she got out of the car to meet Felix's girlfriend. For once, to Felix's relief, Alice managed to be civil as they made inane small talk for a moment or two. Max, in an attempt to prolong the conversation, said he was thirsty and asked for a drink of water and Roxy, despite being exasperated, agreed to go into the tack room. They trooped in to be heralded by a series of barks and yelps from an over-excited Fiver, delighted to see Felix. Alice bent down to stroke him absent-mindedly and he licked her hand thoroughly attempting to ingratiate himself and grab the chews, although Hero was having none of it, and curled his lip in distaste.

"That big dog doesn't seem to like you," said Roxy nastily, "he's growling."

"That's because I'm a vet," replied Alice in a condescending voice, looking down her nose at Roxy, "dogs are always a bit wary – but of course Fiver knows me well."

"Really – a vet," said Max sycophantically, "how marvellous."

Alice cast him a long withering look. "I rarely deal with small animals," she declared patronisingly, "I work for a strictly equine practice."

"Really?" said Max, "how very interesting. You must be a great asset to Felix and the yard here."

"I don't know why everyone just assumes that," replied Alice. "I do have a life outside this place."

"I've only just started riding with Roxy down here," smiled Max disarmingly, "but I confess I am inordinately fond of racing. Are you much involved on the track?"

A wave of sick dread swept through Alice; she turned to glare at Max searching his face for guile and certain she'd flushed guiltily but he merely continued to smile and she visibly pulled herself together before replying. "Sorry, what did you say?"

"The race tracks – do you get much involved?"

"No, not much, although I do go to quite a few trainers' yards, but I'm only covering whilst one of my colleagues is unwell."

"Ah, I've become quite keen over the last six months," enthused Max obsequiously, "although I'm a complete amateur you understand."

"Really," answered Alice unpleasantly, clearly bored with him now, "a gambler are you?"

"We all take a gamble now and then dearie," remarked Roxy cutting Alice down to size. "even smart arses like you and it pays your wages eh?"

Alice began to splutter a sarcastic reply when Felix jumped in. "Well they call it the sport of kings don't they? Now Max, we do need to find you a horse, Seb was telling me he had one in mind for you."

"Did he?" said Roxy surprised. "That's news to me doll, he

didn't say anything earlier."

"No he said something just as you were leaving," improvised Felix, "let's go find him. See you later Alice." He waved a hand at her and ushered Roxy outside into the pale sunshine.

"Bye Alice, very nice to have met you," said Max shaking her hand before turning to join the others. "I hope we meet again soon."

Alice didn't return the smile but was forced to shake his hand, watching him go with dislike. She hated common people and common they certainly were. The chap had given her a bit of a fright talking about racing, but he was just an idiot and, as for that bimbo, she was all tits and teeth. She felt sorry for Felix having to toady up to the likes of her. She bent down to stroke Fiver, who cowered away from her whilst Hero raised his top lip in a snarl. Alice retrieved her hand sharply and beat a hasty retreat – she had never liked Dobermans.

Outside, Max joined Roxy who was talking to Seb and Felix. Seb, clocking Felix's difficulty straight away, was coming up with some tale about a horse and she was listening intently.

"Get on the case then babes, you should've said before – hey Max you're keen aren't ya?"

"Yeah – for sure. I've got the bug alright but I want something more quality – like I said."

"I'd only just thought of it - so leave it with me then," said Seb. "I'll get on the case."

They stood in their little group deep in conversation, Max waving his arms in the air, Roxy pushing her tits together, and the boys lying creatively. None of them noticed the camera lens trained on them in the copse behind the stables.

Steve and his lensman had been in the woodland since early that morning, crouching behind the trees. It was a risky business, especially out in the country where normally a rogue dog would have sniffed them out by now. Kylie had warned him of a large bloody Doberman but, thank fuck, he hadn't seen hide nor hair of it. Today had been a real hit. They'd got a bundle of shots of Roxy and the blond giant with her, and it was the third time – so it was more than just a one off co-incidence. He could run with this now and they'd hurry back to the smoke and tomorrow it would hit the headlines. He felt excited – it was a really great story, the lovely Roxy always made headline news. They would love this one with her skin-tight breeches, a long black whip and big tits bouncing like enormous, rubber balls. Her snaky thighs wrapped around a horse and her arse grinding into the saddle, her head thrown back with a look of ecstasy on her face, it was almost indecent – simply perfect for publication.

Chrissie had her juicy thighs wrapped around Aiden with her head thrown back in ecstasy as she writhed and jerked around on top of him. His hands clasped around her waist, hoisted her skywards, then rammed her back down on top of his erect, dancing cock, whilst she gasped and clawed at her hair, her back arched, her breasts thrust perkily in front of her.

"Don't stop," she gasped, "harder, harder."

"You're such a bad girl," panted Aiden, "so naughty, you know that?"

"Ram yourself inside me," wheezed Chrissie, puffing like a pair of old bellows. "I love it."

"So do I," huffed Aiden, "you're fucking horny." Expertly and without his cock slipping out for a stroke, he flipped her over onto her back, her legs automatically wrapped themselves like cling-film around his neck and he carried on pumping.

"Yes, yes, yes," she yelped, "don't stop."

Aiden kept up the pounding rhythm, and then slipped his hand under her backside, pulling her up under him for a deeper penetration. As Chrissie gasped, Aiden pushed his finger up inside her anus and wiggled it back and forwards as hard as he could. He felt her stiffen under him and shake as she reached orgasm in a series of shuddering jerks, her body convulsing and stiffening into a livid arc. He pulled out his finger holding onto her hips with both hands and, gyrating his pelvis like a demented mixer, finished himself off with gusto, collapsing heavily onto her breasts, panting like slavering dog.

"Baby – you are brilliant," drawled Chrissie in post coital bliss, "fucking awesome."

Aiden tried to speak but couldn't catch his breath and nestled into Chrissie, enjoying the softness of her breasts as opposed to Roxy's pert silicone monsters. For some obscure reason he could have stayed here for hours, he felt so content. He reached up and stroked her arm. "I love you Chrissie."

"Don't be daft Aiden, no you don't," Chrissie giggled. "You're just enjoying a bit of nooky – I'm not glamorous enough for you."

"I mean it you know," said Aiden, "I'm fed up with pandering to Roxy, I feel great with you and we make a good team."

"We do my darling, but we don't make the big bucks like *Rox-Aid* does, and all the time that show's on the road that's where your allegiance lies."

"Oh ye of little faith Chrissie," sighed Aiden sadly, struggling up to look at her, "do you really think that?"

"Strangely I do," laughed Chrissie ruefully, "I'd like to think it wouldn't be the case, but you and I both know you'd be out of that door like a cat with its tail on fire."

"Oh Chrissie, I'm sorry," said Aiden. "Are you screwed up about it?"

"Nope, I'm not, but I'm enjoying being screwed by you all the same, and if anything changes it'll be a nice bonus."

"You are so stoic darling, and so good for me," grinned Aiden, "so totally non-demanding, well emotionally anyway."

Chrissie pushed him off and engineered herself carefully out from underneath him, sitting on the side of the bed stroking his belly. She levered herself up and sashayed over to the kitchen, the cheeks of her bottom full and ripe as she walked. "Coffee or something harder?" she called over her shoulder. "I've got some prawns and avocado in the fridge if you're hungry."

Aiden staring up at the ceiling, his naked body splayed out across the bed. Chrissie was right of course – *Rox-Aid* was something he couldn't afford to relinquish in the matter of a heartbeat, no matter how fed up he was. It was just too lucrative, but he was mighty sick of Roxy and her tantrums. Surprisingly though, she had come up trumps with this riding lark and was a total natural – of that he was quite proud and mightily relieved. Even Farouk had been impressed. Chrissie had been scathing but he had to hand it to Roxy, she was gutsy and talented – together they were a visibly golden couple, and Chrissie was right, she wouldn't have the same charisma. As a mistress she was remarkable, fucking horny and amazing in bed, and she put absolutely no pressure on him. He idly played with his cock whilst he mused on their relationship. It was perfect, but some small part of him hankered for more.

Chrissie, in the kitchen, was deep in her own thoughts. Chopping the avocado with vigour she imagined it to be Roxy, the stone rolling onto the board like a head from a guillotine. *I wish* thought Chrissie vindictively. As the weeks had rolled past, her liaison with Aiden intensifying daily, she desperately clawed onto lucidity and the desperate sanity of keeping her feet on the ground. Determined not to cling onto him and keep her head held high, Chrissie was determined not to go the way of so many before her. She played him like a fish on a reel; teasing him, coming on to him, fucking him, and then being indifferent and a tad illusive. So far it had worked perfectly, but she had a funny feeling that Roxy was up to something which had left the way clear for Chrissie. There was no way she hadn't ridden before that first film shoot. Chrissie wasn't stupid, she knew a beginner when she saw one, and Roxy certainly wasn't. Was she having an affair herself? What could she be up to? Whatever - Chrissie didn't trust Roxy an inch. But she was more concerned about her relationship with Aiden. He was so close to being hooked but she dare not make a false move – it was just so frustrating. She'd keep her powder dry and play the long game. No pressure – but it was a hard act to keep up.

"This looks great," expounded Aiden, as he took the tray

Chrissie brought back into the bedroom. "I'm starving."

Chrissie climbed back into the bed, snuggling under the duvet. "Hmm, sex always makes us hungry."

"Don't you just love avocado?"

"Yep I do. You know it's supposed to be an aphrodisiac?"

"Really – well it's working on me sweetie"

"Seriously, it used to be called the testicle tree, because the fruit hangs in pairs on the tree - like testicles!"

"You've gotta be joking!"

"Nope, why do you think I eat it all the time, lover?"

"Now I know why you're so good at giving head!" Aiden laughed, scooping up more prawns, "and let me tell you, I'm not complaining."

"I should think not," smiled Chrissie, a naughty glint in her eye, her hand reaching down to stroke his cock, "you like receiving as much as I like giving."

"You my dear," said Aiden putting the tray on the floor, "are a bad girl and I may need to spank you."

"Surely not," squeaked Chrissie excitedly, as he grabbed both of her hands and forced them over her head. "I promise to be good."

"No, you need to be spanked and to take your punishment. I shall have to tie you up."

Chrissie dropped back onto the pillows in surprised delight as Aiden straddled over the top of her. "Are you serious?"

"Deadly," smiled Aiden dangerously, "turn over and hands out."

Chrissie looked at him uncertainly but nonetheless wriggled onto her tummy putting her hands out to the bedposts on either side. Aiden produced a length of cord and leant over, rapidly securing her first hand and, as she started to squirm, leaning on her shoulder and secured the other.

"Where did the rope come from?" said Chrissie, her voice muffled in the pillow "I had no idea you had it."

"Just a little something I prepared earlier," he laughed, "don't tell me you won't enjoy it. Now you've been a naughty girl Chrissie. I'm going to oil your bottom and then we'll begin."

Despite her acquiescence, Chrissie began to have reservations and wriggled underneath him. "Look Aiden I'm not sure about this."

"Relax you'll enjoy it, you can tell me to stop if you don't like it – okay?"

"Okay," said Chrissie her voice wobbling. "Promise?"

"Promise – but I also promise you'll like it. Roxy does."

The bald statement inflamed Chrissie. "She would," she snapped, "doesn't mean I will."

A sudden, sharp whack on her bottom caused her to recoil dramatically "Naughty, naughty," said Aiden, "don't be rude." His fingers rubbed and massaged tenderly to take the sting out of the blow. He crooned to her sweetly, stroking her, until the cheeks of her bottom relaxed visibly and, just as unexpectedly, he delivered another vicious wallop with great aplomb. Chrissie flinched again and gasped as Aiden followed this with another loving caress. Despite herself, the punishment and pain and subsequent stroking were the most erotic thing she had ever experienced and she found that she became more and more aroused as he repeated this over and over. The more the cheeks of her bottom became inflamed, the more she throbbed between her legs and longed for him to sink his cock inside her. Moaning and writhing on the bed in an exquisite mix of pain, pleasure and expectation she reached a superlatively hungry orgasm pushing her bottom enticingly in the air like a dog on heat.

"You're a dirty bitch Chrissie," laughed Aiden, "you know that?"

"I am," gasped Chrissie. "I so am."

Excited more than he would admit, he pushed open the cheeks of her bottom and eased himself inside her, holding onto her shoulders and working himself backwards and forwards in a smooth rocking rhythm until he felt himself explode. He fell on top of her, their sweaty bodies welded together in a satiation of mutual desire and they lay locked in their clammy embrace lost in the moment and drifted off to sleep.

An hour later, Aiden awoke with a start. He was cold and stiff and levered himself off from Chrissie. She was fast asleep underneath him, although how she could possibly be sleeping under his weight and with her arms straddled out like a starfish beat him. He reached out and unleashed her, and she began to stir, turning and wrapping herself around him with all the tenacity of an octopus. Carefully, dis-entangling himself, he eased onto the edge of the bed swinging his legs over the side and crept into the bathroom. He pulled up the lid from the bog and sighed heavily as he relieved himself, feeling lazy and contented with sleep. Shaking his cock, he moved over to the wash basin and looked at himself in the mirror. His chocolate brown eyes glazed with lethargy. There was just something about Chrissie that he loved, she was so undemanding, so in tune with him, so refreshingly different from the histrionic raucous demands of Roxy. He never felt relaxed like this with her. It was a knife-edge, roller coaster ride from one screaming drama to another, and, in truth, he was sick of it, however much it pulled in the punters and the money. Not for the first time he wondered how much longer he could stand the pace of their life together. Perhaps, once the mill restaurant was up and running and the TV programme was over, it would be the time to move on.

CHAPTER 59

The same September day that the tackiest of the tabloids led with scintillating photographs exposing Roxy bouncy aloft Galaxy, the flags at the Hickstead Showground were flying high for the marriage of Emily to Roland. The Fittlebury Hall gang had all been invited to the marriage celebrations. Seb, Leo and Hattie were hoping to get to the ceremony and wedding breakfast, with Felix and Alice joining them for the knees up later in the evening. Felix was competing in the CIC2* at the South of England and his dressage was on the Saturday, but he'd assured Hattie that he could manage to do dressage without her and she should go and enjoy herself and not worry about him, he'd finish up the yard and hook up with them in the evening. She had reluctantly agreed, as the wedding was going to be a seriously amazing bash and they'd all been on the go since first light, whirling around like dervishes, with no-one talking much, keeping their heads down and getting on with their work so as to finish in record time. No-one had seen the paper or heard the news. Their leap of fame onto the front page of the nation's smuttiest rag went unnoticed and they soldiered doggedly on in supreme obliviousness so that the Laundry Cottage mob could make the Hickstead showground clean and spruced up in time for the wedding.

Leo and Hattie were out hacking when the black mini screamed down the drive and into the yard. Roxy was at the wheel, disguised in her Blondie wig and huge dark glasses, with Max sitting next to her rigid in the passenger seat. She leapt out into the yard bawling out for Seb and Felix, who were schooling horses in the arena. She hurtled up the track, a thousand expletives tumbling out of her mouth with all the rapacity of a machine gun, the air electric and crackling with venom as she strode towards the dumbfounded lads whose mouths were hanging open wide enough to admit three juggernauts side by side.

"What the fuck are you playing at? One of you has leaked to the fucking tabloids about me!"

Felix felt his insides tingling with panic, *it couldn't be true, they'd been so careful. None of them would have been so stupid ... unless ...*

BIG BUCKS

Seb immediately took control. "What do you mean luvvy? Don't be ridiculous. Of course we wouldn't do anything like that, it would drop us in it as much as you."

Roxy, her face puce with indignation and anger, stood on the bottom rail of the fence, pointing her finger menacingly. "Of course it's you, who else could it be?"

"Keep calm and stop over reacting," said Seb calmly. "It is not us or from here, why would it be? Calm down and think clearly, of course we wouldn't. Now what are you talking about?"

Max touched Roxy on the shoulder and whispered in her ear and she almost visibly deflated. "Alright, I can see that," she agreed, "have you seen the papers?"

"Nope we haven't," said Felix, "why not tell us."

"Headlines, front page. Pictures, the works. Claiming all sorts. Fucks up the TV programme and me," lamented Roxy. "Aiden is livid, Farouk is worse."

"Don't they say any publicity is good publicity?" asked Seb. "Surely it's gotta be of public interest?"

"Well I suppose," admitted Roxy, "But it's a bit of fuck up as far as the programme is concerned."

"Why?" Felix laughed nonplussed. "After all, you don't claim much do you, and a few photos of you riding don't make you out to be a liar do they? You didn't ride before did you? Just been doing a bit extra since you first came down – hardly a hanging offence is it?"

"Maybe?" sighed Roxy, "but they will make more of it. You don't know what they're like once they've got hold of sniff of a story."

"So what?" said Seb. "What does that matter, no proof is there? Galaxy is still registered in my name after all. And those papers will be in the bin tomorrow."

"That's true," agreed Roxy, "a few photos don't prove anything do they? But who could have bubbled me?"

"Not us, I can assure you," said Seb, privately thinking he knew exactly who it was. "Let's have a coffee, the others will be back any minute."

"God," wailed Roxy despairingly, "How could this have happened?"

Max stood beside her impotent and implicated. "Come on baby – it really isn't the end of the world."

Roxy rounded on him. "It's all right for you. They don't know who you are do they?" she shouted. "I'm sick of all the negative publicity. Just for once I didn't deserve this!"

Not much you bitch, thought Felix spitefully, but instead said encouragingly, "Try and make a positive out of a negative," smiling sympathetically at her, he slipped off Casey and put his arm around her. "Come on, you need a drink."

Roxy leant against him, melodramatically tossing her hair back. "You are just so sweet darling, of course I didn't really think it was you."

"I know," said Felix soothingly. "It must have been such a horrid shock."

Seb wanted to vomit as he got off his own horse and wandered up behind them, glancing at Max, whose face was as black as a bruise, shooting Felix the evils as he supported a pathetic Roxy by the waist. "Have you brought a copy of the paper Max?" he asked. "Was it just the one, what did it say?"

"As far as I know," snarled Max, "but the others will be onto it like an epidemic. Roxy rang me directly she found out this morning and we came straight down. The pictures are obviously photo-shopped but they do link me too. Aiden is livid. It screws up the notion of the dynamic duo."

"Did you bring the paper then?" asked Seb again, intrigued. "When were they taken? It must have been recently if you're in them."

"The paper's in the car," snapped Max irritated. "I can't bear to look at it. I'm telling you that fucking journalist will be sorry he lived, and if I ever find out who grassed they'll never walk again."

Seb's face blanched. "Well I can assure you it wasn't any of us – why would we? Hardly going to bite the hand that feeds us are we. We come out of it as badly as Roxy."

"No," said Max thoughtfully, "but who hurts Roxy, hurts me, and I'm not to be fucked about with," he added dangerously.

"I'm sure not," replied Seb, his voice shaky, "but I seriously have no idea who it could have been."

"Whatever," snapped Max dismissively. "One thing's for sure, Roxy and I are keeping our heads down and staying out of London this weekend."

"Good Lord!" exclaimed Seb. "Where are you going to stay?"

"A hotel's out of the question," grumbled Max, his eyes narrowing, "but I'm sure you'll think of something - let's find that coffee. The last thing I needed this morning was this charade, let me tell you."

"I'm sure," gasped Seb, thinking exactly the same thing. All he wanted to do was go to Emily and Roland's wedding and have a blast. Now it looked like he was going to be lumbered with Roxy and Max. The very thought was not only daunting but as depressing as losing a winning lottery ticket.

"Max darling, hurry up please," called Roxy affectedly, leaning heavily against Felix, "I feel totally exhausted, and we need to make plans."

Max glared at Seb and hurried after Roxy with all the obsequiousness of a waiter hoping for a big tip. Seb smiled ruefully, this was going to end in tears, he just knew it – but whose tears remained to be seen and, meanwhile, with Felix disappearing to do his dressage at the South of England, he knew exactly who was going to be lumbered with these two.

Everyone who was anyone had been invited to see Emily and Roland tie the knot at Hickstead that Saturday and more besides to the evening extravaganza. Guests were clamouring outside the members' enclosure chattering and gossiping; the ladies all looking like fabulous exotic birds with a spectrum of colours and extraordinary fascinators and hats in a concoction of feathers and bows. The men were posing equally alongside their partners of either gender in stunning ensembles with much posturing and excitement. The air hummed with the thrill of a brilliant celebration to come – the joy where all of the guests knew each other and were serious party animals, many of whom had already had one or two snifters to see the revelries off to a good start and were delighted that, at last, Emily and Roland had decided to make it legal. The early autumn weather that afternoon was perfect; balmy and warm with a little hint of a breeze as the guests filed into the reception area to be seated for the ceremony. Roland looking a little nervous as he waited inside twiddling with his cravat. Seb,

Hattie and Leo slipped into the very back seats at the last minute with two others, who were curiously under-dressed, yet vaguely familiar, the woman in large, dark glasses. The bride arrived outside in her open carriage pulled by perfectly matched black horses. A murmuring ripple ran through the crowded reception area, and as she stepped into the suite and Roland stood up to meet his bride, the music started with the evocative beat of Chanson d'Amour and everyone reached for their tissues. Emily looked amazing, with her tall, reed-like figure and trestles of long hair; she had chosen a stunning strapless fitted dress of pearlescent silver with a long train and banded with pearls and diamante which shimmered and changed its luminosity as she moved. Unsurprisingly her dogs, two enormous standard Poodles, were with her wearing matching diamante studded collars. There were collective oohs and ahs as the bride and groom made their vows. After the service, a proud and handsome Roland took his bride on his arm out onto the hallowed turf of the main Hickstead arena to pose for photographs, to the shrieks and whoops of applause from the congregation – the party had begun. There had never been a more smiley bride or elated groom.

Emily and Roland paraded like triumphant gladiators around the main arena in the horse and carriage, surrounded by their euphoric family and friends hurling confetti. From behind a floral festooned pillar, a beady-eyed Roxy ogled the proceedings with unaccustomed restraint, jealous at taking second best in the limelight, whilst Max skulked loyally behind her; Seb, Leo and Hattie hooted and cheered with the crowd on the sacred turf, the lurking photographers urging everyone into poses for posterity. It was a totally magnificent spectacle as the much loved couple lapped up their moments of glory, parading around the ring with their friends toasting and celebrating their union. Roxy and Max, the interlopers hanging back furtively from their hiding place, felt a creeping and melancholy envy as the lap of honour drew to a close and the happy couple alighted from the carriage. Their own world suddenly seemed false and closed amidst the genuinely open warmth and love enveloping the newlyweds. Roxy felt an irrational and absurd anger at being compelled to linger behind the scenes; conversely Max was content at being side-lined – he hated the publicity and the charades she played.

"Fuck me, how long is this gonna take?" moaned Roxy. "I'm starving."

"No idea."

"Christ, look they're only doing a load of group shots now."

"What did you expect? It is a wedding after all," said Max laconically, "have some empathy."

"Hmm, I'm surprised you know what the word means," said Roxy nastily, "anyway it's just so boring. I don't know why we came."

"In the scheme of things, it was the better of the options don't you think? What did you want to do – skulk around at home, hang out in a hotel somewhere, or stay at the yard – either place you'd have been papped. No-one here is likely to spot you and if they do, it adds credence to your new found hobby. You were lucky that Seb got us an invite."

"Oh Max, I know, you're right. Sorry. I'm a bitch sometimes."

"Yep, you are, most of the time in fact, but that's why I love you," grinned Max, over her shoulder, "now just shut up, be patient and try and be charming."

"I will, I will," grumbled Roxy, more to herself than to him, "charming, I'll try, but if I find out who dobbed me in, I'll kill 'em."

"You and me both, but right now – nothing much other than you bouncing around on a horse with me has hit the press. It's not so bad - they have nothing else on you – do they?"

"What else could there be?" asked Roxy innocently, "All I've done is learn to ride."

"Yes, but the crux of it is, *when* did you learn my little cream puff? Are you trying to pull a fast one and if you are, is there any way it can be leaked or proven?"

"Oh Max," Roxy sighed, "I've a feeling this could get rather embarrassing."

"Now why doesn't that surprise me?" Max looked at her sideways, his eyes crinkling up in disbelief. "Roxy will you never bloody learn?"

"Oh babe," Roxy whined, "what am I gonna do?"

"Fuck knows how you get yourself into this shit. You'll have to brazen it out," shrugged Max, "like you always do; turn on the old charm to full beam. I'll be beside you, never let you down yet have I?"

Roxy squeezed his arm gratefully, threw back her head and, running her hand through her hair, took off her sunglasses. Creaming her pearly lip gloss to a sultry sheen, she stuck out her tits, plastered a smile on her face and, totally oblivious of upstaging the bride, sashayed out from behind the pillar like she was accepting a BAFTA from an adoring audience. At first no-one noticed, but gradually as she moved like a royal on a walk-about, people began nudging each other in the ribs and surreptitiously nodding heads in her direction. Roxy slid the glasses back over her pert little nose and oozed, with all the discretion of a police vehicle howling with blues and twos over towards Seb, Leo and Hattie who, bless them, hadn't noticed a thing. A hum of gossip followed in her wake and seeped into her aura as she surreptitiously slithered in between them. Mutterings clammered like the drum of a heartbeat and Roxy, in her element, lowered her head and cast her eyes low like a latter day Lady Diana as she played her audience as exquisitely as a fine instrument. All eyes were now diverted from the bride to astonished acknowledgement as she sank into ostentatious oblivion and basked in the admiration of the gaping onlookers. Max had to hand it to her, she was a master of hypnotic art – her audience were now agog with curiosity, and yet allegedly she had done nothing to alert them. Ever the poser, Roxy chatted exaggeratedly to Hattie as though totally unaware of the waves ricocheting around her, and Hattie, ever ingenuous didn't notice anything untoward either.

Emily and Roland, homing in on the murmurings, had halted the carriage up alongside and Emily, as charming and graceful as ever stepped out towards Roxy.

"Well, this is a total surprise! When Seb asked if he could bring a couple of friends along unexpectedly, I simply had no idea," she laughed delightedly, turning to Roland. "Did we darling?"

"I'm so sorry sweeties. Let me make the introductions," grinned Seb, "I didn't have time before."

"No indeed we didn't," replied a reddening Roland. "No introductions necessary Seb - pleased to meet you Roxy - I'm Roland and this is my beautiful wife Emily."

Roxy gave them a dazzling smile. "Congratulations and very nice to meet you both. I hope you didn't mind us gate crashing and I must apologise for being somewhat under-dressed," she threw open her arms indicating the clothes she'd borrowed from Hattie, "it was all very last minute."

"Not a bit darling," giggled Emily, "you look gorgeous and, the more the merrier, as they say, and who is the dazzling man with you?"

"Ah, meet Max," explained Roxy, "an old friend."

"Enough of the *old* my dear," smiled Max, taking Emily's hand exaggeratedly and kissing each of her fingertips in turn. "Congratulations to you both and thank you for putting up with us."

"Our pleasure - have fun darlings," laughed Emily, flirting outrageously. "Now forgive me if I leave you for a while - my husband needs me."

Emily and Roland were ushered away to be posed for pictures with the dogs, the photographer arranging them in a variety of stances. But more cameras were surreptitiously scanned on Roxy than on the happy couple - and some of the photos, no doubt, would feature on Facebook tomorrow, if not sooner. This time, at her own behest and design and, notwithstanding, carefully posed and orchestrated, Roxy was turning the negative publicity into positive publicity and was determined to be everyone's golden girl here today.

By the time Felix and Alice arrived, the party was in full swing. The twinkling lights sparkled across the main arena and those who weren't boogying to the band were outside smoking and propped against each other, or drunkenly chucking up in the bushes. Inside, Emily and Roland were fishtailing like spiders on methadone, as they whirled around the dance floor. Emily's long hair in total disarray as Roland whisked her from one reverse turn to another, flinging her like a floppy puppet to the hoots of approval from the onlookers. Their dogs were going mad, snapping at Emily's dress and hanging onto the silken train as she dragged them, obliviously, along behind her. On a side table sat the abused cake, a huge confection of an ornate chocolate masterpiece which could have passed as an entry for the Turner Prize, but had now been sadly depleted and looked woebegone, leaning dangerously and suspiciously reminiscent of a famous Italian tower. From the spectators' point of view it had been a fabulous wedding without exception. What a wedding! A celebrity guest, who was willing to chat to them all and pose for ridiculous selfies, copious amounts of booze, great food, good company with old friends and a plethora of remarkable gossip - what more frankly could you ask for?

"God, what a shambles," remarked Alice. "How tacky is this? What terrible music."

"Emily looks lovely, really the radiant bride," smiled Felix, waving over to her excitedly as she and Roland quick-stepped past with aplomb.

"She looks pissed," said Alice, "and her hair is all over the place."

"Christ Alice, don't be so nasty, it's her wedding day - she's entitled to have fun and let her hair down isn't she?"

"Literally and metaphorically in this case - she looks a right state," sneered Alice. "And tell me Felix, just why is that stupid bimbo Roxy Le Feuvre here? That is her over there isn't it?"

"Yep. Well spotted. Nothing wrong with your eye sight is there?"

"Don't be facetious dear, it really doesn't suit you," Alice glared at Felix. She felt so tense she could explode. "Why is she here?"

"Long story and it really doesn't concern you," dismissed Felix, suddenly tired of Alice and her sniping. "Just fucking stop being a bitch and get on with it will you?"

Alice snapped her head back, like he'd slapped her. "Don't speak to me like that," she snapped, "who do you think you are?"

Felix glared at her coldly. "Do you know sweetie, it's about time you realised who I am, wake up and smell the roses - I'm your other half, your partner and, do you know, I'm beginning to realise you aren't so very special." He turned away from her and went over to talk to Dougie, leaving Alice floundering on her own with her mouth gaping.

Leo nudged Hattie in the ribs. "Trouble in paradise," he hissed, nodding his head in Alice's direction, watching Felix stomping off. "Silly tart."

Hattie's heart was hammering. However much she wanted Felix, she hated confrontation and the bereft look on Alice's face upset her. "Poor Alice," she stammered, "things aren't good between them are they?"

"Nope. And the way she speaks to him are you surprised. She's a bitch and she doesn't deserve him. It's only a matter of time."

"Don't say that Leo, that's not kind."

"Hattie you are a right sucker," sniffed Leo exaggeratedly, "you are seriously too nice for your own good. Be careful, I might just puke on your shoes."

"I just don't like people being hurt," defended Hattie. "I truly believe Alice loves him in her own way."

Leo threw his hands up in the air. "Sometimes Hattie you are so gormless I could slap you - grow some balls and fight for him will you."

"Leo!"

"Well I mean it, stop being so fucking nice!"

Max had spotted Alice standing forlorn and on her own. He glanced at Roxy to confirm that she was amusing herself playing to an agog and, adoring audience and picking up a glass of fizz, he sidled away. Icily sober, he'd barely touched a drop of booze all day and his brain was working overtime and there was the sour-faced Alice - like a gift from the Gods. He crept up behind her, mysteriously trailing his fingertips across her bare shoulders. She spun around to face him, her face contorted with anger.

"What the hell!" she spat furiously. "Oh God it's you, I might have known."

"Don't be so abrasive," Max smiled at her, unabashed, "you should try being nicer to your partner's best clients."

"Just fuck off, you slime ball," growled Alice rudely. "I don't have to toady to you or anyone else."

"Ah, but I think you do Alice. I've been talking to some friends about you" threatened Max, his eyes drilling into hers. "I think you can be more than accommodating when you need to be."

"What...?"

"You've turned a little pale - are you okay?" said Max, taking her by the crook of her arm and steering her behind a massive potted palm. "Ernie would be very upset if he knew that you were being so rude to me."

Alice gasped, "You know Ernie?"

"As it happens, very well indeed and, of course he's told me a great deal about you. I was rather surprised I have to say." Max laughed nastily, and gripped her arm hard. "You've quite a chequered past - does Felix know about you I wonder?"

"No, he doesn't know a thing," snapped Alice quickly, "nobody does. Or I thought they didn't."

"You should have been nicer to me Alice, I don't like stuck up little cows like you, they piss me off. Otherwise I wouldn't have given you a second thought, but now I've a feeling in future you'll be more respectful to me and Roxy."

Alice glared at him, hating every second of being forced to capitulate. "Naturally - as they say any friend of Ernie's."

"Ah, that's more polite," said Max dangerously, tracing his finger lingeringly down her breast bone, "so much easier to be nice than nasty."

Alice swotted off his hand. "Don't push your luck buster," she snarled, "that's not on offer."

Max grabbed her wrist. "Don't be so sure sister, I'll decide what's on offer."

Alice squirmed away from him, "Don't touch me."

"Not tonight I won't," Max laughed, "but you're kinda cute in a frosty way - I can save you for another time."

"You two okay?" asked Felix, his eyes heavy with concern as he came up behind them, "what's going on?"

"Nothing at all," smiled Max, dropping his grasp on her hand. "Alice and I are just getting to know each other better."

"Alice?" said Felix dubiously, looking from one to the other, "you alright?"

"Fine darling, we're just chatting," Alice said quickly, edging closer to Felix and taking his hand in hers, "shall we have a dance?"

Felix hid his astonishment after her previous acerbic remarks about the music as she dragged him onto the dance floor with the speed of a formula one car and wrapped her arms tenaciously around his neck. Alice would never cease to amaze him with her rapid about turns of mood. Max watched her go with amusement and took a sip from his drink, a half smile on his face. He had sewn the seed of fear and now it would germinate and grow and then it was only a matter of time. He'd loved creating fear and manipulating people from when he was a boy and tonight was just the beginning with Alice. He licked his lips in anticipation - there was a great deal to play for.

CHAPTER 60

The wedding party rocked on wildly through the night, with more alcohol and dope being consumed than was good for anyone, coupled with a multitude of sexual indiscretions. The following morning, as the autumn sun struggled slowly up the sky casting long, white fingers across the misty showground, Hickstead was littered with horseboxes and tents full of hungover revellers who groaned and rolled over pulling their sleeping bags up over their heads in despair, shocked to see with whom they were sleeping, and vowing they would never abuse their bodies again. It had been a stupendous celebration with the joining of two much loved personalities and, as always in true Hickstead tradition it had been a dynamic carnival of fun and frolicking; great friends, great fun and great laughs, but the following morning was another matter as reality hit home with all the ferocity as the proverbial shit hitting the fan.

At Laundry Cottage the lights snapped on in the wee small hours as Seb and the others arrived back, with Max and Roxy in tow; Alice and Felix having peeled off at the stables when they made their way to their own home. The booze flowed like a running tap as they sat up drinking and talking indiscreetly, lounging on the sofas in the sitting room, cracking open bottles with Hero laying his huge mournful head on Seb's lap desperate for attention. Hattie's eyes drooped unwontedly and eventually she had to admit defeat and crept up the stairs to her room, leaving the hard core to party on. She stumbled into her own lonely bed, pathetically accompanied only with a pint glass of water to assuage the inevitable hangover, as she had to do the yard in the morning. She clutched the duvet between her fingers desperately, the pain of wanting so intense it was as though a knife was driven through her, and big fat tears rolled down her cheeks. The hot stab of jealousy as she remembered Felix and Alice dancing together made her cringe. She had no right to feel as she did but she just couldn't get a grip - it was mortifying. She'd had plenty of offers, it was true, and she just wished her heart was in taking them up, but it was no good. She threw her head back dramatically hard against the pillows in anger and frustration. Why, oh why, couldn't she move on and forget him? Sleep was an elusive stranger as she tossed and turned in frustration waiting for the shriek of her alarm.

Downstairs, as more bottles hit the dust, finally Leo admitted defeat and tumbled into Seb's bed for the remainder of the night and relinquished his own room to Max and Roxy. Leo and Seb cuddled up together, their easy friendship allowed them to spoon with the most perfect fit. Seb's erection was pushing into Leo's lower back and he responded, arching his body inwards and upwards, rubbing like a fawning cat against him.

"God darling, you so turn me on," Leo murmured, "your cock has always been such a draw."

Seb drew himself forward and licked the edge of Leo's ear. "Baby, we are always so good together." He ran his fingers along the edge of Leo's thigh. "You know you love it."

"So terribly true darling," sighed Leo, melting against him, "you are a master of the art"

"I never know why you stray," simpered Seb sadly, "you always come back to me in the end."

"Sweetie, you know not to take anything personally - I never do when you go off the rails. There's nothing like a little bit of variation is there?"

Seb laughed ruefully, "No, but I could never stray to the dark side like you do!"

"Each to our own, nothing wrong with a bit of pussy now and then," laughed Leo, pushing his bum into Seb and rubbing himself against him, " don't whinge - I always come back to you."

"Just one thing," warned Seb, "whatever wicket you're playing, don't fuck with Hattie will you?"

Leo stiffened with pithy outrage and spun around in the bed to face him "How could you say that, of course I wouldn't, she's much too fragile." Then he giggled flirtatiously and sucked Seb's top lip and, releasing him, teased, "Roxy on the other hand!"

"You are incorrigible," sighed Seb, reaching down and searching for Leo's cock" but I do like you."

"Ha ha," laughed Leo sarcastically, diving down the bed evasively and, in retaliation making Seb scream with delight, "let's be having you then!"

Max and Roxy oozed into Leo's unfamiliar bed, suffocating ridiculous, hysterical laughter together as they stumbled across the old sloping floor. The musky smell of Leo's cologne on the cotton sheets was somehow uber sexy. Max held out his arms and Roxy snuggled up against him, warm and comfortable - her naked body fitting his as easily as a jigsaw. Max stroked her arm, his hand straying to her breast and she moaned as his fingertips circled her nipple. She'd telephoned Aiden and told him she was staying under the radar whilst the press were on her tail, and of course, he'd understood, so there was no hassle about her staying here. He didn't know about Max but what he didn't know wouldn't hurt him, and meanwhile, she'd enjoy this respite time and she was pretty certain he'd be enjoying the iceberg Chrissie. She felt safe with Max and she did love him in her way, and she knew he loved her. This coupling was not new, but it was always refreshingly breathtaking, as though they had been waiting for each other for a life time. They fell together with all the familiarity of putting on old slippers, but with the spice of the hottest Vindaloo. As they rolled together and their bodies fell like hungry, feasting vultures, it was, as always, the most natural thing in the world. Later as Roxy curled fast asleep into his arms, Max lay awake festering into the darkness. This was how life should be and, if he had his way, Aiden was toast.

On the far side of the estate Felix and Alice crept into a cold bed. Alice, smashed and not on call, was well pissed; Felix as designated driver, was miserably sober. She tangled herself around him like a clinging vine, sighing ostentatiously and nibbling his ear in a drunken haze trying to blot out the unwelcome visage of Max. She'd do whatever it took to keep the equilibrium - she could manage it, of course she could. Felix lay unyielding, stiff and tense his body brittle against Alice. His life was upside down and he needed to get out of this relationship - but how? He muttered he was tired and rolled onto his side, easing Alice away from him. She tried again, her hands edging around his waist down between his legs, her breath hot on his skin and her tongue making rapid little licks along his back.

"Alice please - I said I'm bushed."

"Don't be like that Felix, you know you don't mean it." Alice mumbled, her voice slightly slurred from the booze. "Come on darling I feel so randy."

Felix rolled over to face her. "Alice I just can't, you must realise that things have been going downhill between us. I can't keep up with your moods. I just can't turn myself on like a tap to appease you when you feel like being a couple again."

Alice's body went rigid and she started to shake. "Felix," she whispered, her voice trembling. "I am so sorry, I know I've been irascible, difficult, irrational even. I've had a few problems at work. I tried to talk to you about them the other day. But I've sorted it now I promise. Please darling forgive me, I really want us to work it out."

"Alice, do you really mean that? Because I'm not altogether certain we shouldn't call it a day. Part whilst we're still friends." Felix gulped, hardly believing that he had been brave enough to say it, "let's be completely honest, we've not been happy for a long time now."

The complete silence seemed to go on for interminable minutes. Felix could hear the pulse of his heart pounding in his head as he waited for her to respond. Alice remained totally still, not moving a muscle, barely breathing and then quite suddenly she started to scream and scream and scream.

"Alice!" Felix hissed, grasping her firmly by the shoulders. "Alice calm down, for Christ's sake calm down." But Alice just screamed and screamed, lamenting at the top of her voice - her pitiful wailing like a wounded animal.

"Felix please, please don't do this, give me another chance, I beg you." Alice pleaded, "you're all I've ever wanted, my life here with you. Please, please."

Felix was shocked, Alice was always so hard, so resilient. This begging, desperate Alice was a person he scarcely knew and above everything, Felix was a softie. He cradled her in his arms, stroking her hair, kissing her head, soothing her like a baby. "Of course we'll try again Alice, you should have told me you were having trouble at work, I would have understood darling."

Alice lay in his arms, her eyes flicking artfully upwards. "Thank you darling for understanding. It's all fine now I promise. I'm sorry for being a bitch, it'll be different now I promise. Just hold me please."

Felix held her close, feeling somehow this was not how things should have worked out and that he'd been duped. "Okay I suppose we could try again," he stammered, "but things have gotta change."

Alice smiled foxily to herself, burying her face in his chest. "Totally understood darling, I promise."

"No more sniping, no more bitching," said Felix doubtfully. "Mutual respect."

"Absolutely. I promise," agreed Alice. "I love you Felix. I don't want to lose you."

Felix cringed. He wasn't at all sure how he felt, other than an innate feeling that this was not right; but he had to be fair, to at least give them a chance. "Alice, I'm willing to give this a go, but only on a month's trial - we both have to make an effort, and if at the end of October things are no better, then we need to reconsider, maybe split up and go our separate ways. Is that understood?"

Alice winced and stiffened, her mind a turmoil of mixed emotions; angry that he had not acquiesced immediately to her; hating him for his obstinacy, yet bizarrely loving him at the same time. She swallowed hard, determined to keep it light and not to lose it with him. "Right my darling, till Halloween then - I guarantee I'll make you as happy as we were at the beginning - starting now."

"I hope so," replied Felix despondently, his voice laden with misgivings, "but tonight I need to get some sleep. I've got to get round a tough track tomorrow and I'm bloody knackered." He turned away, rolling onto his side, wondering if he shouldn't have just grown a pair and ended it with her there and then. But he was ever the softie and reasoned it was only another month to labour through. He eased her trailing fingers away from him and slid himself away from her clutches, wishing that he'd been stronger but thinking he'd wait till after the party at Laundry Cottage and that would be the time. Meanwhile, he'd have to muddle through gradually, extricating himself to make the final break easier.

Alice, determined to win him over, relaxed into the softness of the pillows. Okay, tonight he had rejected her, but she would change his mind. He would not be able to resist her - he never had been able to and nothing would change that.

By the time a hung over Hattie was struggling with the mucking out and packing the truck with all the paraphernalia for the competition, the Sunday papers were already hitting the streets with a leaked photo of Roxy chatting animatedly to a gaggle of dressage superstars. Some bright spark from the wedding had thought it a laugh to sell a photo or two and, sure enough, it had filled a few column inches for the otherwise dull Sunday stories. On the whole, for Roxy to be seen with the divas of the dressage world was no bad thing, and gave her a little more credence in her earnest quest to become a serious rider - rather than a bimbo playing on some tacky hacky scene. The snobbish element of dressage and the money involved gave a curious and upmarket kudos which she had hitherto never achieved - a master stoke as far as Roxy was concerned and the public would definitely love it. She looked lithe and intelligent, soberly dressed for a change and apparently in deep conversation with a dashing and heroic Olympian who'd recently been honoured with an MBE; it was definitely a good look and one to be nurtured. Meanwhile, to the frustration of the paparazzi, who had now jumped on the story, Roxy had gone to ground, but allegedly would be available for comment later.

In reality, Roxy was lounging indolently at the old kitchen table in Laundry Cottage, flipping through the papers and dipping Rich Tea biscuits into a steaming cup of builder's tea. Yesterday morning's catastrophic news may well have been turned around to her advantage developing a whole new persona for her - she *was* a PR genius, she mused - Suzanne would have been proud of her. It was just what was needed - a bit of polish and a swift metamorphosis into a classy new image. She picked idly at her eyelashes, teasing off last night's mascara and sighed contentedly. She may well decide to stay here for a few days, perhaps even give an exclusive to "*Hello*" or "*Okay*" at the yard, although she'd have to send Hattie out for some kit. She could just picture the story - a perfect tableaux with her perching on straw bales looking sheepish and adoringly into Felix's azure blue eyes; him holding her aloft on the glossy Galaxy adjusting her leg position - it would be sexy, yet simple - nice but naughty. This delightful vignette was playing out in her mind when Max stomped in from outside where he'd been trying to get a signal on his mobile.

"Any luck?" asked Roxy, "this must be a bad area, not good for the mill if it is."

"Fuck the mill," snapped Max. "Yeah, I did get a signal as it happens. A car's coming down to pick me up - should be here in a couple of hours. I need to get back - I need to sort out some stuff."

"Chill Max, let me make you a cup of tea," offered Roxy helpfully, getting up from the table and filling up the kettle. "I can't believe how great things have turned out, can you babe?"

"No, lucky you," said Max sarcastically, "you always fall with your bum in the butter somehow don't you?"

"Oi, that's not very nice is it?"

"Take no notice of me. I'm needed in the smoke and agitating."

Roxy moved behind him and started to knead his taut shoulders, her fingers soothing out the tension and she leant forward and kissed the tip of his ear. "Last night was good darling, as always."

Max sighed, easing his head back and resting against her. "As always; why don't you leave Aiden?"

"You know I won't Max, don't start all over again."

Max pushed himself away and turned to face her. "One day Roxy."

"Maybe"

"Forget the tea, I'm going to grab a shower."

"Suit yourself." Roxy shook her head sadly and watched him go, calling after him. "I do love you Max."

"Not enough," murmured Max as he started up the stairs.

Aiden ended the call with Roxy and looked up at Chrissie who was straddled above him.

"Well what did she say?"

"She's going to stay hiding out at the stables for a few days," said Aiden, "she seems in remarkably good form."

"Well, after those pics in this morning's rag, it's not surprising is it," said Chrissie her voice heavy with irony. "All those gold studded stars, she couldn't have engineered it if she tried, could she?"

"Well a bloody good job as it happens. It could have been a fucking disaster!"

"Okay," said Chrissie, "it was lucky, but she's such a stupid cow, I get sick of it," she rolled off Aiden's cock theatrically, "In fact I *am* sick of it. The whole thing's a charade."

"Darling please don't be awkward now," he moaned in frustration, "we can sort this out."

"You bloody bet we will."

"Once this programme is out, the mill restaurant is sorted, I promise I will divorce Roxy and it will be you and me."

"Right, like I believe you."

"I will. I'm sick of it too, but be patient, it's gotta be the right timing for all our sakes. *Rox-Aid* has to go out with a bang not a whimper."

Chrissie rolled over and looked at him. "Do you really mean it Aiden, can I believe you?"

"Definitely you can," said Aiden, looking right back at her. "I promise - but you have to trust me. It will work out and come right for us in the end." Aiden hoped that it would placate her enough to come back to bed.

CHAPTER 61

As she read the papers Kylie's heart was beating irrationally fast, like a bass drum pounding in her angry head. She had never felt so crazily irate. She shook the paper out with irritation and looked at the grainy black and white photograph. It was unbelievable. There was that stupid woman at a flash do at Hickstead, chatting to all those tossers, pretending to be something she wasn't, making herself look good, and in reality she was nothing but an imposter. To say Kylie was angry was an understatement. She had come down to the stables pretending never to have ridden before and now what the fuck was going on? Hobnobbing with the greats? How and why? Something wasn't right, and the lads at Fittlebury Hall Stables knew more about this than they were prepared to admit. But what could she do about it? She was fucked if she was going to go down without a fight. The hate welled up inside her, spilling over into a white hot fury. She kicked hard at the horse she was mucking out - she would get her own back - she definitely would. They would be sorry they'd made a fool of her.

Down at the surgery there was an air of expectancy which was as crisp as crunchy nut cornflakes. The builders were working hard on the conversion at the farm and everyone was in a state of agitated excitement about the move - it was like packing before a holiday. Andrew and Oli were like two kids playing on x-box, it would mean a great deal more room for the team; not just for ancillary staff but for the diagnostic expansion too. X-rays, scanners, endoscopes and the less taxing surgical procedures to begin with. It was hugely exciting for everyone. Alice was strangely on the periphery of all the goings on, and felt a bizarre detachment from them all. Felix had left at the crack of dawn to help Hattie and get ready for his event and she felt totally excluded. The locum, Theo, was a developing into a real sweetie and a great asset proving a total hit with everyone - he had demonstrated himself, beyond all measure, as being more than just an able chauffeur but an intuitive vet too. Oli was impressed with him and he'd relayed this to Andrew. He was lovely to the office staff and had slotted in well with the routine of life at the practice and Oli enjoyed his company, bunking down at the cottage together. Paulene had nastily remarked to

Caitlin that it was a pity that he had not arrived before Alice, as he'd fitted in far more than she ever had, but Caitlin, always the peacemaker, had feebly tried to defend Alice, much to the scoffing of Paulene. The atmosphere when Alice was around was belligerent and hostile, and not enhanced by her erratic attitude towards the others. Andrew was his usual affable self and didn't seem to notice any problems, although Oli seemed to clock the difference but, between them, they were too busy pouring over catalogues for equipment and costings to be overtly concerned about the problems of the staffing personalities.

Alice herself was trying to keep the lid on her pressure cooker of emotions. The meeting with Max had shaken her more than she cared to admit. The black irony that he was one of Ernie's cronies was such incredibly bad luck and sickened her to the pit of her stomach. What would happen now? She couldn't bear to consider. Would he tell Felix, Seb or anyone else, or would he use the knowledge for his own ends? She felt sick with the worry of it. When it had just been Ernie on the outside she could keep him at a far away distance and it had all seemed okay. Now, with Max part of the inner circle infiltrating her friends and her personal life, things had changed and she was now truly frightened. How would she cope? The insidious notion of him looking over her shoulder at every moment was too much to contemplate and she wrung her hands in despair and, in her anxiety bit Paulene's head off once again. Paulene furiously responded and so the atmosphere went from bad to worse, and the downwards spiral of Alice and her gloomy demise deepened, coupled with her worry over Felix. This misty autumn morning life for Alice didn't seem worth living.

Max lounged irritably on the back seat as his swanky car sped back towards London. The driver kept his capped head down and asked no questions. The sultry look on Max's face did not invite small talk. Having left Roxy behind at Laundry Cottage Max was in a weird mood, in a bizarre way glad to be gone. She was so ultimately selfish it rankled with him and yet, conversely, he hated to leave her. Christ - why was she so contrary? Or perhaps it was him? His mind turned to the previous evening, marvelling how, once again, Roxy had turned the debacle of bad publicity into yet another golden opportunity. Her tenacity was staggering. Yet it had given him an opportunity too to have a little dig at Alice - he had put the frighteners on her alright. He wasn't quite sure what he was going to do with the power but it would come in useful, and he was damned sure that sometime in the future there was a bigger cut for him in the racing scam. He just wasn't quite sure how he was going to work it yet. But he was ever patient, and Alice could have a vital part to play. As for Roxy, he'd let her have her little dalliance down in the country. It was obvious she had the hots for pretty boy Felix, but he was fairly certain he wasn't interested, but Max would have to deal with him if he became a problem. It was curious - he put up with Aiden, probably for the sake of Delphinium and Stephanotis, but he was fiercely jealous of anyone else who might make a serious play for her. As usual he'd bide his time, watch and wait - he'd disposed of other problems and he could dispose of this one, should it become necessary. If he couldn't have Roxy, then no-one else would either.

Meanwhile he had other more immediate issues to sort out. All the clubs were now performing well, especially since dear old Ruby had met her maker, and the ambitious scrubber Irene had taken her place. It had been a wake-up call for all the girls; earned him a nice bit of respect and they needed that every now and then. Terry was a trooper, he must bung him handsomely for doing a good job. In fact, he was coining in the money from all his little ventures, the racing included, but for Max it was never enough. He knew that he was only on the periphery of the betting, they used him as a stooge but he wanted the big bucks. He smelt the money and he was determined to have it. The million pound bet had shocked him despite him playing it down, yet it had also fuelled his greed - he wanted that kind of action for himself. No wonder Ronnie had been able to afford that bloody great mansion. Max fancied one of his own - and he needed to be laundering some money somehow. Perhaps it was time he bought a pad like that and he mused Fittlebury might be the perfect choice to be looking.

Another pressing problem was Nigel Brown who'd traced his daughter. It seemed she was in Paris. Brown was going to send him a full report by email, but this was not as straightforward as it seemed. From what he'd said over the phone, apparently she'd started a degree in fashion and design in London two years previously but not completed it. Bizarrely, without any warning, and for no apparent reason, just as she was starting her second year the previous September, she had just upped and gone to Paris and hadn't been heard of since. Brown, as per Max's orders, had not overtly pushed the grandparents for information, and so wanted instructions as to what to do next. Max was eager to settle down and read the report carefully and consider his options. He was so close now and he didn't want to balls it up. His whole life seemed to require infinite patience. He sighed and slumped back in the seat, his head lolling to one side, and he closed his eyes. The luxury of fatigue crept over him. He was tired. Roxy had worn him out last night and, running his tongue over his lips, he remembered their rapturous love making. She was insatiable, like a bitch on heat. There was something animal about her, really carnal in the way they were together. So polar opposite from the way it had been with Jilly. Dear sweet Jilly, his mind ached with those memories, the wound of her loss as keen as if it were yesterday. These two special women, Jilly and then Roxy, as diverse yet complementary as Yin and Yang. Their tangible dualities even in life and death had given a strange balance to his life and he mused how things might have been different if Jilly hadn't left and returned to Oxford. Still, it was no use hypothesising - his road was chosen and he still had paths ahead to take, but this time he was going to take care not to make any mistakes.

It was quiet up at the farm, other than the rooks circling in the sky making a sinister tumult as they flocked together in their dramatic aerial formations. The builders were not working on a Sunday and Colin had brought baby Archie up to see his grandparents in the robust old Trianco pram, allowing Grace a bit of respite time to catch up on a bit of sleep. The builders were doing a good job. The dairy with it's low slung roof and pretty square-paned windows had been sympathetically restored, and very much in keeping with the old Sussex traditional style farm. He wandered through the latch gate, up the bumpy flag stoned path, around the back to the kitchen door. Grace's mum, her silver hair looped up in a bun, with her eyes twinkling behind her spectacles, looked up in delight.

"Colin," she laughed, "what fun. How lovely to see you. Come in."

"Hi Ma," Colin grinned, "thought I'd bring the little man up for a visit whilst Grace has a snooze - lovely morning for a spin in the old pram."

Grace's mother laughed. "It's served a few has that old Trianco."

"Where's Pa?" asked Colin, "the conversion's looking fantastic."

"Isn't it just," said Evelyn. "Let me call George and he can show you what they've been doing. I can give Archie a cuddle."

"Any excuse!" grinned Colin, "although I'd love to see what they've been doing."

"George!" called Evelyn, "Colin's here with Archie. Now come on, give me that baby." She reached into the pram and gently cradled the baby in her arms. "Oh but I love the smell of him," she cooed. " Little mite."

"I know," said Colin, smiling at her, his eyes crinkling, "he's just gorgeous isn't he?"

"Now, now," said George from the doorway, his silver hair slicked back and his dark brown eyes sparkling, "that child 'll be spoilt, mark my words."

"Who cares?" grinned Evelyn. "You don't, that's for sure George."

George laughed. "How are you lad?" He slapped Colin on the back, "and how's our Gracie?"

"She's fine Pa, but tired, so I brought Archie up to see you this morning, and I thought you might show me round the conversion."

"Right you are - it's looking right splendid, so it is. I'm right made up about the whole thing, it was a great idea of our Grace's."

"She's many talents has Grace," agreed Colin, "although to be fair I think it was Caitlin's idea."

"Whatever," smiled George, "it's looking good, very in keeping with the rest of the farm."

"Oh I agree, and for you it's a good offer and a great lease."

"Aye, it is, thanks to you lad."

"You and Evelyn are okay about the extra traffic and people that'll be coming here aren't you?"

"Oh yes - it's not as though they'll be just anyone - all clients of the vets after all. It should be fine," smiled George. "It'd be nicer if no-one came, but needs must and all that."

"Yes, and it's a good rent."

"It is, and will keep the wolf from the door for Evelyn and me let me tell you."

Colin suppressed a smile. Farmers were all the same lamenting their tales of poverty. \h knew that George was far from destitute. "I'm sure, I'm sure," he soothed.

They stepped out into the farm yard. The views across the valley were breathtaking. Far away the bosky downs rolled into the distance, the trees turning into their autumn dance of colour and, already, some of the land had been ploughed in preparation for the winter sowing. Across the way stood the Abbey ruins and, like a little toy doll's house, Colin and Grace's own place at the bottom of the barley fields. This early autumn morning Colin contemplated that life couldn't get much better.

George was clearly delighted with the building work. Being retired now, he was taking a keen interest in the everyday progress. On the outside, the walls had been refreshed with sparkling chalk white paint, and the Horsham slate roof repaired and the rotting windows replaced. Inside the dairy was now a spacious office area, with seating for clients and plenty of room for ancillary staff. Beyond, in what was the old parlour and separately contained, were large store rooms and several large open plan offices, trebling the existing surgery office space. The attached barns were whitewashed, with rubber floors and sides and examination areas complete with slings and stocks which were already installed. Several examination ante-rooms, similarly equipped with rubber sides and floors, were alongside and a knock down box with padded sides and floor. It was coming along a treat.

"What d'ya think lad?" asked George, "pretty fine eh?"

"Indeed it is," admired Colin, "they've got on at quite a lick haven't they?"

"Well there wasn't that much to do really, just a bit of knocking walls about, and painting and the like and putting in a few bits of sheet rubber and some stocks. The machinery will be in soon. The desks and office stuff just needs to be transferred over."

"Amazing," laughed Colin. "What about parking?"

"Got a tarmac machine coming next week - the area's been levelled already - over on the far side of the old beef barn."

"You haven't hung about have you?"

"No, once I got the idea, I thought to hell with it and then it was in for a penny in for a pound - you know what I mean lad."

"Well George - good on you, that's what I say," said Colin, looking into the sparkling eyes of his father in law. His lined face, ravaged with the harsh seasons, was mellow and astute. "I'm sure you know what you're doing, and you know, I think this has given you a new lease of life."

"Bet on it lad, bet on it," grinned George mischievously, "you don't have to worry. It'll be fine, just fine."

Colin looked hard at him and knew that it would.

CHAPTER 62

Nigel Brown considered his options. Cutter was a tricky customer and he couldn't go out on a limb and hassle the grandparents over much, although a cup of tea and a biscuit couldn't hurt. Of course, he'd questioned the others with whom Max's daughter had been at college but they'd been strangely elusive. He'd spoken to her lecturers, whilst imbibing them with booze and he tried to find out more about her, who her friends were, where and with whom she'd lived. But they were cagey and he was sure they were keeping something from him. It would need some serious palm greasing to get them to open up. What was clear was that she hadn't finished her course and left apparently to work in Paris. He couldn't put his finger on it, but there was something not quite right about the story. Okay, she was a fashion and design student, and she had seemingly lived with some low life junkie/dealer, who had died around the same time she had left - it was all a bit too pat. There was more, he knew it, but what? The whole thing stunk of a cover up. She had vanished like an elusive faerie into the night. Where could she be and what had happened last year to make her leave like she had? He needed to look into the news archives, see if he could trace what happened to the boyfriend, but before he did he needed Cutter's permission. Christ knew he was an irascible bad tempered client and there was no way Nigel would incur his wrath before being given the go ahead. This could be a lucrative job and that kind of research could take months, and he might even get a little holiday to France out of it. Nigel didn't have much other work at the moment, so he'd string it out as long as he could. But Cutter was no fool either, so he'd just have to be careful not to take the piss.

Farouk, despite initially being livid at being rumbled in the tawdry tabloid rag, now basked in the positive vibes generated from Roxy at the Hickstead wedding party and was busy maximising on photo opportunities. He'd been on the phone to Roxy who'd affirmed that she could organise some footage with the superstars and he wouldn't be disappointed at the contacts she'd made. By the time she said goodbye, Farouk was as happy as a pig in shit, delighted it would give a great new angle to his programme.

As Roxy ended her call, she considered her options. It was true that she had made a lot of contacts last night. Sycophants the lot of them, so no problem about getting them on film. They'd cut their throats to be there; but more than anything she wanted to cash in and launch the new range of riding wear she'd been thinking about. It would be sensational. Her very own stamp on the stuff, blingy but discreet. She rang Suzanne who, despite it being Sunday, answered her call, listened carefully and promised to get on it first thing in the morning. Roxy sat back in her chair. Next weekend Felix would be out competing and she intended to accompany him. A perfect photo opportunity, coupled with a chance to push the idea of her new range of riding gear, as well as her foxy lingerie, the forthcoming TV programme and the opening of the mill restaurant and spa. She'd get Suzanne to rustle up some reliable press bods; plus Farouk and the cameras - unbelievable press, she could picture it now. Felix would look so good on film, his white blond hair and lean, toned body rippling in snowy white breeches, a moody concentrated look on his beautiful face as he demonstrated his superlative skill on a horse, and then sliding off flushed and exhausted, embracing a concerned Roxy. Wowser! It would be perfection.

Whilst Roxy was musing about Felix, he was struggling on with his top boots. His dressage score from yesterday was surprisingly good and Hattie was ecstatic. He and Picasso were improving all the time, thanks to Seb and their incessant drilling. Now they had to steer around a tough cross country and a big track of show jumps. She, herself, felt pretty seedy if she was honest, but Felix's face was set in grey granite and she wasn't sure if it was after an excess from last night or because he was so determined to do well today. Every time she spoke to him, he bit her head off, and she decided to ignore him. He was being a total arsehole, and luckily for her Brett was here and she was re-igniting her friendship with him. Felix glowered at her, nit-picking at everything she did and Hattie, wounded at every slight he made, kept her head down and didn't bite back. As she bent down and screwed in the studs she could have thrown up, but was determined not to let him see how hungover she was, dashing into the lorry to gulp down a bottle of water, whilst he selfishly screamed at her to fetch his whip.

After Felix had departed for the cross country warm up, Brett took her arm smiling warmly at her. "Take no notice, he's nervous and he's being an arse."

Hattie looked glum. "I'm fed up with him," she looked at Brett sadly,

"I'm wasting my time but I just don't seem to be able to help myself."

"Come on kitten," said Brett, squeezing her arm, "don't you think it's time to move on? I know Ryan would have you on our team like a shot."

"Oh Brett, I don't know. I'm fed up, but I don't know if I'm strong enough to up and go."

"I know .... *you love him,* but Hattie you're crackers you know that? He's a selfish git."

"Don't please ..."

"Oh Hattie, you're a fucking lost cause."

Hattie laughed pathetically, falling into his big strong shoulders. "Thanks for being such a mate. I know I'm daft, I know I've got to get over him, but I just don't seem to be able to - you know?"

Brett stroked her hair fondly. "You are, without doubt, one of the sweetest girls I know - he doesn't deserve you."

"Please don't judge him too harshly Brett," Hattie begged pathetically, "he's so mixed up."

"I don't think he's the only one," laughed Brett, "come on you'd better go and help him work in - show willing and all that."

Hattie pulled back out of his arms, kissing him on the cheek. "Thank you so much, I can't tell you," she gasped, "you've been so brilliant."

"Go on, bugger off to him," muttered Brett, ushering her away reluctantly, "and God help him if he hurts you," he grumbled. "You're too good for him."

At the cross country warm up, Felix was busy concentrating with Picasso. The sparkling black and white machine looked amazing as he soared over the practice fences in the crowded working-in arena. Hattie checked the running order and, as usual, the super-efficient stewards were well on time. She signalled to Felix that he was next to go, and he checked his girth before bounding over to the start box with all the gusto of an express train. Hattie felt strangely detached as she watched him start off. Picasso pulled hard into the first fence and steamed off into the distance until he became a blur on the horizon. She had never felt so miserable. Brett was right, she was wasting her time. He was with Alice who was turning into a prize bitch and it was rubbing off onto him. She'd never known him as grumpy or unpleasant as he had been lately. The wonderful camaraderie they'd always shared seemed to be disapparating as fast as a character in a Harry Potter movie. It was definitely time to move on - if she didn't she knew she'd never get over him and she had to face facts. He didn't feel the same about her. She would ask Brett about a job and no matter how hard it would be, it had to be for the best.

"Wow!" yelled an over-excited Felix, who had galloped over the finishing line without Hattie even noticing he had finished, she had been so wrapped up in making her decision. "He romped round, made every jump look like a cavalletti!" he laughed, fuelled with all the exuberance and explosive excitement of the cross country aftermath. "Awesome, totally awesome!" He threw the reins at her as he leapt off "Fucking amazing!"

"Great." said Hattie, her voice deliberately flat and dull. She was unable to look at him she felt so cross.

Felix noticed nothing he was so wrapped up in himself, his black mood miraculously lifted by the adrenalin rush of the cross country "God yes - unbelievable, the best ride ever!"

"Great," she repeated dryly. "Glad you had fun."

"I *so* did, he was magic. D'ya mind taking him, there's someone over there I wanna see?"

"Go right ahead Felix," sighed Hattie, "leave him to me."

"Thanks babe," he grinned and, without a backward glance, he strode off and left her.

Hattie was furious, but it just reinforced that her decision was the right one. She had become too emotionally involved with him. If she was honest - she loved him. She was jealous when he went off to talk to someone else, resented it when he treated her like a groom, and let's face it, that was all she was to him. She turned away blinking back furious tears and walked determinedly back to the truck.

In that moment, Felix hesitated and turned around to go back with her. She suddenly seemed very small and vulnerable beside the big horse, and he felt guilty and culpable - he knew he took her for granted. No matter how rotten and unhappy he'd felt lately, there was no need to take it out on Hattie, she meant so much to him. He hurried back, scuttling to catch up, but too late he saw Brett put his arm around her shoulders and together they ambled back to the lorry. Suddenly a hand clapped him on the shoulders, the sponsors' voices booming with all the rapidity of a firing squad, stopping him in his tracks, and he watched Hattie disappearing with Brett and felt a pang of loss and despair.

By the time Felix finally returned to the truck, having trotted Picasso up before the show jumping phase, Hattie had negotiated a job with Ryan Clemence. Although the season was drawing to a close, he was more than willing to give her a place as he was planning to stay for another year, at least, in the UK. It would be just be a matter of crossing the *i's* and dotting the *t's* and the position was hers. Good event grooms were invaluable, especially if she might be willing to go back to New Zealand with him in time to come. Now it was just a question of telling Felix and she was not looking forward to it. She'd told Ryan she must stay with him until after Weston in October and asked him not to mention anything to Felix for the time being. He had completely respected and understood this and said he would wait to hear from her. She'd done the right thing, she knew it in her heart - another job. A new start, move on. Just when to tell him? After Weston in October? The season would be over and it would be easier for him. The lads at home would understand and help her - she knew it, and it would be such a terrible wrench, but somehow she would manage. One thing for sure was, she couldn't go on any more like this and, right now, she was angry with him, and that anger was a good thing - making the decision easier somehow.

Felix disappeared with some other riders to watch how the show jumping track was riding and sauntered back later, his head full of advice and tactics, unaware of the turmoil of emotion happening at his own truck. He chatted enthusiastically as Hattie tacked up Picasso until eventually he picked up on her desultory replies.

"You okay?"

"Of course - why wouldn't I be?" griped Hattie, with all the sharpness of a snapping turtle, glaring at him, the hurt spilling out of her eyes, "you'd better get a wiggle on you need to be in the warm up in five minutes."

Felix reeled back as though she slapped him. Hattie had never spoken to him like that. "Right, okay," he said submissively, "give me a leg will you?"

She hurled him up on the horse like she was sending him into orbit and watched him and the skittering Picasso disappear over the showground and then felt like running away. But she had to man up. She picked up her groom's bag and made her way over to the practice arena to do her job.

As it was, Picasso was on pogo springs. He was now becoming quite well known on the circuit, the great black and white jumping machine. Felix negotiated a faultless round, much to the hearty applause from the stands. He threw his hand up in salute to them all and cantered out of the ring, slapping Picasso on his foaming neck to join a waiting Hattie in the collecting ring.

"Well done," she muttered quietly, keeping her eyes downcast and giving Picasso a sly treat.

"Thanks- what a fantastic round, he's bloody amazing isn't he? I'm pretty certain we'll be in the money," gushed Felix, slithering off Picasso and handing her the reins; but then realised he was talking to himself, Hattie had already run up the stirrups and was walking away. "Hats, wait!" he called after her, "don't rush off."

But Hattie didn't turn around. She gritted her teeth, she had to harden herself up, "I'll just get him sorted out Felix," she called back over her shoulder. "See you later."

Felix suddenly felt very lonely, standing alone and isolated, abandoned in the collecting ring. He watched Hattie walking away from him for the second time that day and was overwhelmed with a tumult of emotion. His whole body hissed with deflation and, for a nanosecond, he nearly sank to his knees and wept, but as the sponsors once again surged upon him, overpowering, and insistent, he rallied superlatively, smiling and laughing with them like some programmed robot. Yet all the while, his mind cried with anguish at the memory of Hattie walking into the distance and his irrational feeling of extreme loss.

CHAPTER 63

Max received a terse summons from Ronnie at the beginning of the week for a meet up at his gaff that same night, *'something big'* he said mysteriously and hung up. Usually Max would have been annoyed at being commanded like some lackey to attend but his curiosity overcame his indignation and so, once again, he was heading towards Wallingford. As his car swung into the drive, he was impressed to see a glut of posh motors - there was no riff-raff here tonight. The chauffeur opened his door and he stepped out into the chill of the autumn night.

Inside, Sandra, Ronnie's wife, greeted him rolling her eyes upwards in exasperation at the interruption and directed him to join the others in the study announcing she was going back to watch Eastenders. As Max tentatively opened the door, a fug of cigar smoke hit him like a bonfire, and Ronnie was waving a whisky bottle about and filling glasses with aplomb.

"Come in Max - we're all here now - drink?"

"Please," said Max, eyeballing the others and nodding his head in recognition.

Ernie, the pudgy pouches under his piggy eyes seeming deeper than normal, hailed him like an old mate. "Max - how's tricks?"

"Yeah good thanks - you?" smiled Max, accepting a glass of whisky from Ronnie.

"Definitely on the up," wheezed Ernie, the red veins in his cheeks standing out like roads on a map. "Just like my blood pressure."

"That's doesn't sound good mate - you wanna get a check-up with the quack."

"Oh I have Maxy," rasped Ernie, "gave me some pills, but said I gotta cut out the fags and booze, no greasy food or salt on me chips, just bleeding salads. No fun in that eh?"

"No fun being dead either - you need to take care of yourself," muttered Max, who was terrified of getting ill. "Why not come down to one of my gyms and, I'll get one of my girls to give you a work-out programme and a diet sheet."

Ernie roared with laughter as did Ronnie. "There's only one type of work out with a girl I want!"

Max faked a laugh, "Suit yourself Ernie, offer's there if you change your mind," but thinking *what a stupid fucker*, he was definitely on a shortcut to the cemetery.

Frank the old bruiser looked at his watch pointedly. "As much as we're all keen to know about Ernie and his blood pressure, let's get down to business. I've got other stuff to do tonight."

"You're right - this needs careful planning," chimed in Mick, a small and previously relatively insignificant man sitting at the back in one of Ronnie's vast leather chairs. He rarely said much but Max knew he was one of the serious players and when he said jump the others said *how high*.

"Okay - here's the deal. We're going on a four horse accumulator. First horse is up at Lingfield, then Catterick, then the last two at Kempton. Ernie has been to watch the first horse breeze up and he's looking amazing, but the trainer Frances Spurns is keeping schtum - the horse hasn't been raced for over a year, so he's running as a real outsider and we'll get him on good odds if we go carefully, spread the bets and go early. Word is being put out that Spurns won't be backing him - never a good sign, so the odds will be in our favour. The second horse has had a previous leg injury - it hasn't but that's what everyone thinks. Again the odds will be good and the favourite will definitely be withdrawn at the last minute. The third horse hasn't run for 700 days - so is considered a complete outsider and a no-hoper, but is dynamite let me tell you, and we'll make a killing. The last one is trained by Alfie Butler, a former assistant to Frances Spurns, and doesn't have form but this time will be fitted with a visor and has just been gelded - so he should have more of an attention span."

Everyone looked keenly at Mick, his small ferret face and keen eyes boring into them. This was the first time that Max had been privy to the whole scenario and he was drinking in the information. "Sorry to sound crass," he said, "but is this gilt edged? How do we know they'll win?"

Ronnie sniggered, glancing around the room embarrassed. "It's all sorted mate - you don't have to worry. You just have to put up the money."

Max laughed, "I'm not as green as I'm cabbage looking - how do you *know*?"

Ronnie scoffed derisively, "Don't push it Max, trust us."

"Forgive me if I need just a little more evidence Ronnie, if I'm gonna put up a stack?" laughed Max. "So far I've only been given crumbs."

"Fair comment," agreed Mick, scratching his chin and considering him shrewdly "fair comment."

"I see this could be big, but I need just a bit more credence that it'll come off."

"Quite right," said Mick reasonably, " quite right, so would I, don't blame you."

"Well? What then?"

"You have to believe that each trainer, each vet, each race is engineered. They're all in our pocket. Believe us when we say we *know*. We need people to lay the bet and to play the bet - it makes it kosher. This time instead of laying, you make the bet. It'll be big bucks. You'll love it, you'll cream yourself over the money. Consider it a bonus - a reward, a recognition of your loyalty. You can play with us in the big league now. You're one of us."

Max gulped, this was it. He'd been invited into the big time. "Okay," he said. "I'm in".

"Good, this is scheduled then for next week. Ernie, you've sorted the vets I assume?"

"Oh yeah, no problem." Ernie took a puff on his cigar and let the blue smoke trail through his nostrils "they're completely in my pocket."

"Frank - you've got the lads sorted?" asked Mick, "be generous, we can afford it."

"Yer, don't worry, palms well greased" guffawed Frank lustily, scratching his belly and farting loudly, "they're a fucking greedy lot."

"Ernie, we'll leave you to sort out the finer details of the fix - do what you have to do, whatever it takes. If it involves dogs don't tell Ronnie." Everyone sniggered and Mick continued. "Ronnie, you work out the money angle of who puts on what and when." Mick smiled benignly at them all.

"Next week gentlemen, we will all be a lot richer and now we can drink to that I think."

Max raised his tumbler in a toast with the rest of them looking from face to greedy face as they glowed in the subtle lighting, and realised that now he was to make the serious money, but it did occur to him that if he played his cards right there were even bigger bucks to be made - but he would keep that particular idea close for the time being.

The burden of keeping quiet about leaving followed Hattie around like a gloomy black cloud. She was determined not to tell Felix until after the big event at Weston Park which, after all, was less than two weeks away. Meanwhile she kept wondering if she'd done the right thing. Time and time again she had to remind herself of the reasons behind her decision and how she'd been feeling. It wasn't that she didn't love it with him and the lads at Fittlebury Hall and living at Laundry Cottage. The trouble was, she loved it too much, and in the end it was bound to end in a whole lot of hurting. Ryan would offer her a lot of fun and experience, even the chance to work abroad, and Brett was a laugh, although she had no illusions that he was a player who would probably get bored with her once he got her pants off. No, she couldn't torture herself any longer watching the bloke she loved living with someone else and, what's more, someone who was becoming less and less deserving of him.

"What ya thinking about then Hats," asked Leo, coming up quietly behind her, "you've been leaning on that broom for five minutes."

Hattie flushed with guilt. "Nothing much."

"Sounds like that could be something much," said Leo, his gaydar on full alert. "You've been down in the dumps ever since the wedding."

"Just tired."

"That old chestnut," scoffed Leo intuitively. "Come on, I know you better than that. What's cooking up top?" He tapped his forehead, "Wanna share?"

"No, honestly Leo, I'm fine," mumbled Hattie, keeping her eyes downcast, "just a bit full-on since Kylie left, and what with Roxy, she can be so demanding."

"Hattie, I wasn't born yesterday. All of those things might well be true, but normally you'd cope with it fine. It's Felix isn't it?"

To her horror, Hattie felt big, fat tears sprout in the corner of her eyes. "Please leave it Leo, I really don't want to talk about it."

Leo put his arm around her shoulders, and laid the broom aside with the other hand, "I think you do, come on - let's go back to the cottage for a brew on our own."

"We can't!" Hattie was aghast, "What will Seb and Felix say?"

"I'll say you feel sick and I'm taking you home. Go get in my car and I'll be over in a minute."

Hattie didn't have the strength to argue. The thought of being able to pour it all out to him was like being able to scratch a terrible itch and Leo was so kind. Feeling guilty for the lie, she stumbled over to the car to wait for him. Five minutes later they were heading for the cottage and five minutes after that they were sitting at the kitchen table with a mug of coffee.

"Now what's it all about Hattie?" asked Leo reaching over and taking her hand "Nothing can be that bad."

"Yes it can. I'm leaving, I've got another job. I'm going to tell Felix after Weston, so that it doesn't put him off before the last big run of the season with Picasso."

"Fucking hell Hattie! When did it get this bad?"

Hattie started to sob. "Oh God, I don't know, I suppose the last straw was at the wedding. But I've been feeling I should move on for ages. Let's not delude ourselves - I love Felix, he doesn't feel like that about me. I thought, once upon a time, he might, but he doesn't. Seeing him every day with Alice is like torture, especially when she can be such a Jekyll and Hyde with him; I watched them dancing at the wedding, wrapped around each other, so close, like lovers, which of course they are, and I felt sick, and it brought it on home."

"Oh Hattie, I'm not so sure that's true y' know."

"It is Leo, they say love and hate are often the same thing, and they just have that sort of stormy relationship, and he wouldn't want me, I'm too dull."

"You are so wrong, you are not dull - just the opposite. You're funny, bloody gorgeous to look at, but you don't know it and an amazing horsewoman. You actually are ideally suited."

"Felix doesn't think so. The day after the wedding at the South of England he was a real shit to me, treated me like a skivvy - I'd had enough. Brett, you know the guy I told you about who works for Ryan Clemence was there, he agreed with me and organised this job with Ryan."

"Hattie, don't you think this chap Brett might just have other motives?" said Leo sensibly, "for all of the reasons I've just said. You seriously underestimate yourself you know. Of course Ryan would love to poach you from Felix, any decent yard would, plus every red blooded man fancies you, but you never see it!"

"Felix doesn't," grumbled Hattie, and started to cry again "if only he did."

"I think you're wrong. I think he'll be devastated when you tell him. Whatever the scenario you're dreaming up with him and Alice, let me tell you things in their garden are not rosy, but Felix is a softie about everything. Frankly he needs to grow a pair and sort it out."

Hattie put her head in her hands. "Anyway, I've accepted the job now. I'll give Felix a month's notice after Weston on 13th October, so I'll be gone by November."

"Oh fuck me Hattie, I can't bear it," said Leo. "We are going to miss you so much."

Hattie reached out and grabbed his hands again. "You have absolutely no idea how much I am going to miss you too but I beg you please don't say anything to anyone - not even Seb."

"No - I promise I won't. You've told me in confidence, and it'll stay that way, but I beg you to reconsider Hattie. I think you're doing the wrong thing."

"Leo I've thought of nothing but this for the last few days, churned it over in my mind, and I really can't carry on - it's tearing me apart emotionally."

"Well, you know you can always talk to me. In fact, I want you to, a trouble shared and all that."

"Thanks Leo. Don't think I don't appreciate it, I really do, but my mind's made up." smiled Hattie sadly the tears rolling down her cheeks.

"This is the hardest thing I think I've ever had to do."

Suzanne had set up an exclusive with *Hello* featuring Roxy at the yard. They were wetting themselves over the story, and the good thing about their mag was that they sent their own stylists so Suzanne was relieved of the tedium of setting it up - all she had to do was make sure Roxy was there. It was to be about her taking up riding and also featured the mill restaurant and TV programme, so everyone was happy including Farouk and Aiden. As she had promised Farouk, Roxy rang a few of the dressage supernovas she'd met at the wedding and they'd swarmed like flies on shit to be interviewed in front of the cameras with her and so she was frantically busy and spending more time in Fittlebury than she was in London. It occurred to her whilst she was making the tedious drive down yet again to Fittlebury that it would be a lot easier if she had a place to live down here. The journey itself was not too bad as a one-off and if the M25 played ball, but when you were doing it several times a week it was mind-numbingly boring. At least now she didn't need to be incognito and could drive her Range Rover, which was more comfortable than the Mini, but it was a gas guzzler. Max had remarked that he was thinking of buying somewhere around here as an investment, perhaps she should do the same - ring up that country estate agent who'd organised the sale of the mill. What was his name? Clive or something? She'd get the number from Chrissie. Her mind wandered to the delightful Chrissie who was so kindly entertaining Aiden for her. Their little dalliance had been going on longer than the normal bimbos, and she wondered for a nanosecond if she should be worried, and then decided that she wasn't, she was rather enjoying the free time it was giving her. Max was being very attentive at the moment, plus she did rather enjoy flirting with Felix. On the whole Chrissie was fairly insignificant in the scheme of the things, and if fucking Aiden was part of her job description, so be it. Suzanne was working hard and had set up several meets with manufacturers for the clothing range - ideally she'd like to get that in the shops for Christmas - that was a big ask, but she was always up for a challenge. In reality they had all the blue prints for the breeches and stuff, it was just a matter of putting her stamp on the stuff - a bit of bling here and there and it was done. Marketing, she'd leave to Suzanne. Roxy sighed contentedly as she pulled down the drive to Fittlebury Hall. On the whole things were definitely looking extremely promising.

Seb and Felix nudged each other as the Range Rover swept into the yard. They were way behind this morning and two down with the absence of Hattie and Leo. Roxy was now appearing at random times without warning, popping up out of no-where and taking everyone by surprise and expecting to be treated like a princess. It was all consuming and bloody hard work to flatter her mammoth ego all the time. It was no good they were going to have to get more help, but the disaster of Kylie was still fresh in everyone's minds and neither Seb nor Felix felt much like dipping their toes into another fiasco of nightmare staffing. They both agreed they were unbelievably lucky to have Leo and Hattie and long may it remain so.

"Hi - how are the two most gorgeous men I know?" crooned Roxy, sashaying over in her skin-tight breeches and low-cut shirt, her tits tantalisingly on display. "It's quiet here today, where is everyone?"

"Hattie's not well, so Leo's taken her home to the cottage," explained Seb, "but he should be back any moment." He looked at his watch. "He's been gone ages."

"Oh I don't mind helping if you're short staffed," simpered Roxy, fluttering her falsies, "what can I do?"

"Well if you're sure," muttered Felix doubtfully, "here, grab this."

Despite her offer, Roxy looked taken aback when Felix thrust a broom into her hand, then she threw her head back and laughed. "Umm okay, where do you want me to start?"

"Roxy you star," grinned Seb, "what a trooper."

"Remember you'll have to spell it out baby-cakes, I'm a bloody novice at this kinda thing. And I just hope I don't break a fucking nail! Wish the old cameras were here now!"

Felix laughing spontaneously for the first time in ages, gave her a bear hug. "Ooops sorry, a bit forward of me!"

Roxy laughed and kissed him full on the lips, giving his nuts a quick squeeze, "Bring it on sweetie," she flirted, "bring it on."

By the time Leo returned from his tête a tête with Hattie, the yard was clean, if not actually gleaming, and Roxy was throwing out the double-entendres like she was part of the furniture. Wet stains peppered the back of her tee-shirt and tiny rivulets of sweat ran between her breasts and with her wild hair she was more dishevelled than he'd ever seen her. Yet probably, and ironically, she seemed much nicer and more normal and natural than he'd ever known her.

"Leo!" Roxy exclaimed, wiping a trickle of perspiration from her forehead and sweeping back her hair, "how's poor Hattie, feeling any better?"

"Oh she'll live," he smiled, admiring her tits straining through her shirt, "you've got stuck in I see."

"I so like getting stuck in," she said, artfully hiding a ghost of a wink, "but I'd like to get my leg over now."

"Sorry Roxy," apologised Seb. "Let me saddle up Galaxy and we'll get cracking on a lesson."

"No hurry doll," grinned Roxy, "I thought Leo might like to take me out for a gentle hack today. What do you say Leo?"

"Why not," said Leo, smiling into her eyes, "I'd be delighted, if my boss says it's okay. We could go to your mill and see how the work's progressing."

"Super idea," smiled Roxy craftily. "You don't mind do you Seb?"

"Not a bit, a lovely idea, but just make sure you take great care of her Leo."

"Naturally," smirked Leo. "I'll get the horses tacked up then. Why don't you have a coffee Roxy, I'll give you a shout when we're ready to rock and roll."

"Sweet boy," smiled Roxy, putting aside the broom, arching her back exaggeratedly and pushing her tits out. "Lovely idea. I'll go put the kettle on."

The lads watched her go and Seb gave a lusty sigh and turned to Leo. "Just bloody behave yourself."

"As if I wouldn't."

"Don't give me that sweetheart - I know that look. Just remember she's serious bread and butter money and we don't want it to end in tears 'cos you can't keep your dick in your pants," admonished Seb, a hurt look in his eye, "and remember that one day, I won't take you back."

"Come on Seb," grinned Leo naughtily, "you know you don't care really and you enjoy the tales I bring home."

"Hummmmph - that's all you know," affected Seb, "I do get jealous, one day you'll take it too far."

"Changing the subject you two," interrupted Felix, increasingly tired of their lover's tiffs and not really sure what kind of relationship they had anyway he asked, "How was Hattie?"

"You need to take care of that girl Felix," advised Leo seriously, "she's a real sweetie and you'd be right up shit street if you lost her."

"Why on earth would I lose her you tosser?" said Felix, angry and astonished. "I treat her really well."

"Do you? Think on that eh?"

"Tea's ready," tinkled Roxy, "come and get it!"

"I'll talk to you later," snapped Felix furiously to Leo, "I don't know what you mean."

"Don't talk to me, talk to Hattie," responded Leo airily, "you're a twat sometimes Felix - you don't see what's in front of your nose." He turned on his heel and went to tack up the horses, leaving Felix open mouthed and catching flies.

"Well!" said Seb affectedly, "what's going on?"

"Shut up Seb" said Felix crossly. "I've no idea, but I'd watch your bum chum with Roxy - he's not choosy."

"Wow that's so bitchy," cackled Seb, feigning hurt and then falling about laughing. "Leo's obviously hit a raw nerve with you."

"Oh piss off," spat Felix, and stomped off towards the tack room, "just piss off."

"Temper..." laughed Seb, his eyes twinkling and full of mischief. But once Felix was out of sight his whole face contorted with sadness at the thought of Leo and Roxy hacking out and what they might get up to.

CHAPTER 64

Max watched the last of the accumulator horses romp home and realised that he had won an indecent amount of money. True he had to share some out, but it was a staggering sum. He wiped his brow, the tension as he'd watched the races had been phenomenal; he'd galloped every single stride and snorted every single breath. He leant back against his chair and realised that he had made a total killing and loved every nail-biting second.

His mobile rang - it was Ronnie and he answered as nonchalantly as he could muster. "Hi - good result eh."

"Fucking awesome result mate - big bucks!"

Max laughed softly, "Too right, I love it, I just *so* love it."

"I told you I'd look after you. Mates forever eh?"

"Ah just so, mates forever."

"Party tonight at mine?"

"Love to."

"Bring Anna, it'll be fun."

Max hesitated for a moment. "No, come to mine, I can lay on some babes, a line or two, my turn to entertain."

Ronnie laughed, "Great, love to, I'll invite the others shall I?"

"Do it," said Max, "what a fucking result, I'm over the moon!"

"Too right my son, too right!" laughed Ronnie, "but we need the solid backers like you to make it happen. "Fuck me it's such a buzz though!"

"See ya later - about nine."

As Max disconnected the call he knew why he hadn't wanted to go to

Ronnie's. It was all to do with what had happened before to Anna. What he'd done was cruel and she hadn't deserved it. He dialled her number. She answered straight away - like some mechanical machine programmed to respond on the third ring. He told her to line up some girls for tonight, some coke and some entertainment. He knew she wouldn't let him down. She was his puppet but he no longer wanted her to have to take part in everyone's shared amusement. He sat back in his chair, casting his gaze out of the window and musing about his recent dalliance with Roxy. Since resuming his relationship with her, shagging others had absolutely no significance at all, and indeed if it had been much before was doubtful. Roxy; Jilly; Jilly; Roxy, the only two women of any importance to him, and now he had a daughter, he would trace her and make her the most important thing in his life.

As if on cue the mobile rang, he let it go to voice mail - it was Nigel Brown informing him that he wanted to go to Paris to follow up some leads. Max considered the idea, tapping his pen slowly on the desk. Brown was a tosser, he was slow and had been unreliable in the past. But the dream of finding his daughter had become an obsession. After all, what was a few more quid to him if it meant finding his child? The money meant nothing, he had more than he knew what to do with anyway. Max sat with his mobile cradled in his hand. What was he going to do with his money? Bizarrely, he had never considered his own mortality before, but now he knew he had a child, albeit a young woman he'd never met, it altered things somehow. Even though he had not been there for her childhood, he did have a moral responsibility for her future. He rang Brown back and instructed him that he wanted daily emails on any progress he made in Paris and that, if he found her, she was not to be approached without reference to him first. Once the orders had been given he felt better and then he rang his lawyer - he needed to see them as soon as, he'd procrastinated for long enough.

"The bloke you need to speak to is Colin Allington," said Leo, as they clip-clopped along the estate roads, "he's the local estate agent who deals in that kind of property."

"Yeah that's the guy I was thinking of," said Roxy, suddenly remembering the name, "he sold us the mill. How do I get hold of him."

"He's got a couple of offices I think. The main one's in Horsham, but he lives in Fittlebury, just up the road."

"Really, is it worth my while popping in there today?" said Roxy impulsively, "strike while the old iron's hot."

"Well you could try I suppose," said Leo doubtfully, "but his wife's not long had a baby. There was a bit of an accident and she's housebound with a broken ankle and he's probably not even there on a weekday."

"Perfect," said Roxy selfishly. "Even if he's not there then she'll definitely will be, and she'll be sure to know if there's anything for sale locally."

"I'd get Felix to go with you. He knows them pretty well, they own a leg in Picasso."

Roxy tinkled out little laugh, "What d' y' mean a leg?"

Leo grinned, "Picasso, you know Felix's best horse, the big black and white one, is owned by a syndicate of people. The Parker-Smythes, Colin and Grace Allington, and Sandy and Mark Templeton, he's the Estate Manager at Fittlebury Hall, you met him when you bought the mill, and another couple called Jeremy and Katherine ."

"I know 'em all kidda, even the last two, they did a bit on camera at the pub. But how interesting, so Felix doesn't own all the horses then?"

"Blimey Roxy, of course he doesn't, neither does Seb. Most riders are sponsored in some way or another."

"But what's in it for the syndicate? I don't get it?"

Leo looked at her cynically, "There doesn't always have to be something financial in it does there? They do it for the sport, the pleasure, they all have fun watching their horse compete and Felix is seriously good. They have a real laugh."

"Is that the same with dressage for Seb?"

"Pretty much - we have some good owners and sponsors. Both Seb and Felix are glamorous and successful - so they often feature in *Horse & Hound*, and on the *Horse & Country* TV channel.

"Really," said Roxy, her brain working overtime. "So what - like, you buy them a horse, pay to keep it there and pitch up at the events and cheer 'em on."

"More or less, but you also get caught up in the team spirit of it all - it becomes addictive," laughed Leo, "you ought to come to some competitions and see."

"Now that is kismet Leo," flirted Roxy, batting a false eyelash at him, "as I was intending to do just that. If I like it I might even sponsor one myself."

They trotted off slowly down the drive towards the yard, Roxy's cheeks flushed with exhilaration, not just at the new skill she was acquiring, but at the thought of fresh plans and exciting times ahead. Leo's mind was troubled, he too was thinking of what might lie ahead.

"You're lucky to have found me at home," blustered Colin, who had been completely taken aback when Roxy had knocked on the door. "I only dropped in for a sandwich."

"I'm so sorry to be disturbing you and your family at home," Roxy trilled, turning to Grace and flashing her a beaming smile. "Such a beautiful baby, you must be thrilled to bits with him."

"We are, he's gorgeous, aren't you my poppet," cooed Graced, stroking the baby's silky hair. Roxy's delighted clucking over baby Archie had soothed Grace's initial frosty chagrin at her unannounced arrival. "So you're looking to actually live in Fittlebury then?"

"Well Aiden's bought the mill of course, but it's gonna be a restaurant as ya know, although it'll have a bit of basic staff accommodation, but I've got kinda interested in the riding side of things, even bought a horse now, so it makes sense to have a place to kip in."

"Really!" said Grace astonished. "Where do you keep your horse?"

"With Felix and Seb," grinned Roxy, "I gather you've got one there too."

"Well sort of, but we've also got a couple of hunters here at home as well. My one's in foal at the moment."

"Right, cool, I'm getting more and more into the horse malarkey."

"Now," said Colin, looking up from his laptop, "here's a couple of properties we have on the books now that might suit you. You did say you didn't want anything too big."

"Nah not at the moment, five beds 'll do."

"Crikey! I thought you meant small."

"Babes," laughed Roxy, "that is small."

"Okay," Colin blustered, "hold your horses, let me have a rethink."

"What's it like, this eventing game?" asked Roxy eagerly, "I fancy going to a competition to see what all the fuss is about."

"It's a bit like Marmite, you either love it or you hate it," smiled Grace, flicking out a boob to feed Archie. "For us we meet our friends, make a bit of a social day out. Having a horse run makes it more interesting, but you don't have any of the stress of competing yourself. We love it."

"When's your horse competing next?"

"All being well, 10th October at Weston Park. That's in Shropshire. It's a bit of bugger really, because it clashes with another local event - Pulborough where Felix would probably take some of the novices, but it can't be helped. We don't get that many Internationals like Weston - and the entries have to be made weeks in advance and cost a bloody fortune I might add."

"What do you think of this one Roxy?" Colin pushed the laptop over towards her. "It's a property on the edge of the village. Only four beds, but three baths and several good sized reception rooms. Nice big garden with lovely views."

Roxy studied the details, flicking through the slideshow of photographs and then pushed the laptop away. "It's no good babe, it's nice and all that, but no fucking good for me. Too open, the paps'd be in there like a shot. I need something a bit more secluded where the buggers can't lurk about."

"Oh right," said Colin, disappointed, "what about a barn conversion like ours?"

Roxy looked around her drinking in the vaulted ceiling and galleried floor above "Yeah it's real nice, I like the great big windows too, and down a nice drive like this one, with its own garden around it. Don't suppose you wanna sell do ya?"

Grace laughed, "Definitely not, anyway you don't want land do you?"

"Nah, too much of a commitment. If I have any more horses, I'd keep 'em with Felix."

"Okay I might know of something, but it's not officially on the market yet. I went to give a preliminary valuation the other day. It's quite near to Mark and Sandy's, right on the fringe of the village, a barn conversion and very secluded. You wouldn't actually know it's there hidden behind a high, flint wall on the road side, and thick high hedges and walls around the garden. It's very smart inside "

"Sounds just what I'm looking for," grinned Roxy, "how much?"

"Not cheap," grimaced Colin, screwing up his eyes, "I valued it at £925,000."

"Fuck me, you're not kidding are ya! I thought we paid enough for that old ruin of a mill."

"It's a really nice property," argued Colin, "doesn't need anything doing to it and this is a really sought after area."

"It bloody needs to be," rasped Roxy, running her pink tongue over her teeth. "Well get on the blower to 'em Col and let's have a butchers and see what I think."

"I'll give them a call. Of course, they might not have decided to sell," apologised Colin, "it was only a preliminary valuation."

"Money talks," said Roxy, "especially easy money. Call them and let me know when I can go round."

"I will," said Colin, "I'll need to go back to the office to get the details."

"Sure," said Roxy easily, "Now I'd better get back to the old city, otherwise I'll get caught in the fucking traffic. Thanks for the tea and sorry to disturb ya."

"No trouble at all," smiled Grace, unlatching the dozing Archie from her boob and laying him in his cot beside her and struggling to get up with her plastered leg.

"Don't move please," said Roxy, "stay put, I can see meself out. Now Col sweetie, let me know soonest about this property eh?"

"I will," said Colin, taking her arm and ushering her to the door, "and I'll have a look for some others as well. Don't worry I'll call you."

"Oh, and Col," called Roxy over her shoulder, "don't mention it to

Aiden will ya - no point in concerning him yet."

"No, of course not," assured Colin, as he waved her goodbye, but wondered why on earth she was buying a house down here without letting on to Aiden and the need for a five bedroomed house come to that.

It was no surprise that the weather changed the week that Felix and Hattie were due to go to Weston. It was legendary that the event was plagued with mud and sludge, and Brett who was constantly texting Hattie, urged her to prepare to put in her diving gear. At home, the rain lashed down like a whip, stinging their faces red as they worked the horses and they staggered around with bulging hay nets battling the wind. Needless to say, nothing was seen of Roxy, and the photo shoot with *Hello* was postponed in the hope of better weather, much to the chagrin of Farouk. He doggedly carried on filming in the grunge at the mill, swearing and cursing as he slithered around in the mud.

Hattie started packing the truck with a huge sadness. Her misery like a cancerous growth on her shoulders, seeping insidiously and destructively into her emotions. This would be last time she did this, the last time that she and Felix would go away together. The notorious Weston, always wet, always gloomy, had never felt so poignant. Leo had been true to his word and said nothing to Felix, and Hattie herself had buoyantly and deceitfully kept her spirits up and hid how she was truly feeling, so as to avoid any confrontation. All she wanted was to tell Felix next week she was going, pack her stuff and leave with her tail between her legs, her wounded heart bleeding on her sleeve - not that he would notice, he was so wrapped up in himself.

In reality, Felix was not wrapped up in himself, but in other people. Alice was behaving so strangely, one minute all over him and virtually raping him, the next a wild irrational look in her eye and screaming. He knew he was only putting off their inevitable parting. For him, their relationship was well and truly over, but he'd promised to wait until Halloween, and he was bound to honour what he'd said. He wasn't sure if their parting wouldn't push her over the edge and was worried what she might do - suicide, attack him - who knew? What with Weston coming up he couldn't cope with any more emotional upheaval. To cap it all, Leo had been right, Hattie *was* behaving oddly too, she could hardly look at him and, for the life of him, he didn't know why - they had always been so terribly close. He thought about what Leo had said and tried to probe some more, but the atmosphere between them was as sparky as an electric fence, and Leo refused to elucidate, which was as infuriating as poking a hive of bees. If he had upset Hattie, why didn't she just tell him herself - he would never knowingly upset her; but he was sick of playing games - it was bad enough with Alice and her mega superiority complex. Sitting down in the hay barn, with his head cradled in his hands, his silver white hair flopping over his face, he fondled Fiver's ears and wondered what the hell was going on and how, with this terrible atmosphere, would he cope with all the stress at Weston.

Hattie had hardened and resolved herself to leaving. It was as though she had grown a grotesque horny shell around her. Every time she looked at Felix, she imagined it was some stranger, not him, not even a friend or relative. A distant person who had nothing to do with her. It was the only way she could cope. She was polite and did her job well, because that was her nature, but she had pulled down a black-out blind on her emotions and refused to let in any chink of light. The cold withdrawal slapped Felix like an icy blizzard as he tiptoed around her, and so many times she nearly caved in but with a colossal effort managed to stay focussed. She was leaving and leave she must - only Weston to get through and she'd hand in her notice and be gone.

Everything seemed to hinge around Weston and when, on the amazingly sunny Wednesday morning, with the roads steaming following a heavy downpour, the truck trundled off down the road, the atmosphere was laden with a mixture of emotions. Felix was tense beyond belief, having had a shouting match with Alice half an hour before he left, which ended with her clinging to his leg begging for forgiveness. Hattie felt a gloom like she'd never experienced before. Everything at Weston with Felix was going to be done *for the last time* and then it would be over. It was all so premeditated on her part, and Felix, who'd had to shove his sunglasses on against the glare of the low sun, was so unaware she felt like the worst possible traitor. She should tell him; she was not naturally dishonest, but she knew she mustn't. Their normal camaraderie on these long drives had evaporated. The silence between them felt heavy, laden with tension and, on Hattie's part, guilt and hurt. Felix turned on the radio and shoved in his favourite *Black Eyed Peas* CD. Hattie stuffed in her iPod earphones and closing her eyes before they deteriorated into tears, resignedly turned away from him.

CHAPTER 65

That Thursday, as Nigel Brown stepped onto the Eurostar heading for Paris preparing to eke out his investigations into an elongated holiday at his client's expense, Jennifer and Charles were picking up Sandy and Mark to go to Weston Park. Colin and Grace had decided to give it a miss, bearing in mind Archie was still so tiny and with Grace's broken ankle it was all too much to contemplate. Katherine and Jeremy had decided to join them at Weston at the weekend for the cross country and show jumping phases, as Jeremy was sealing some mega city deal and couldn't get away - much to Katherine's concealed irritation. Jennifer had booked them into The Old Vicarage in Worfield. Chloe had recommended it, saying it was a perfect location and would cater for Charles and his critical tastes and it was only about half an hour from Weston - now all they had to endure was the four hour journey to get there.

The drive the day before had certainly been an endurance test for Hattie and Felix with yawning silences as vast as the grand canyon echoing between them. Felix tried and failed to make idle conversation as he squeezed replies from Hattie in a dull monotone. With her head slumped against the passenger door, she sat staring out of the window and eventually he gave up and the tedious miles rolled by with some curious hidden agenda which Felix simply couldn't fathom and didn't have the courage to pursue for fear of Hattie doing an "*Alice*" and biting his head off.

Ernie was putting more pressure on Alice. The coming week saw races at Kempton, Goodwood, Lingfield and Brighton. As he reeled off the list she felt herself break out in a cold sweat - Ernie and his demands were exacerbating, becoming more insistent and more frequent. Since the menacing incident with Fiver she didn't ask any questions, terrified of the reprisals if she defied him, but it sickened and frightened her at the same time. As he laid his pudgy hands on her arms, allowing his thumbs to stray across her polo shirt over her breasts, she cringed with distaste and he laughed, his rancid breath close to her face. Pushing her away, he winked, said he'd be in touch and giving her one last leer, got in his car and drove off.

Alice struggled into the Toyota and sat in the driving seat for a while before starting the engine. She was glad in a way that Felix was away and had left Fiver with Seb. At least she didn't have to worry about him. She considered refusing to nobble these horses, but Felix would come home, and they would be waiting for him. No, she'd have to just bite the bullet and get on with it. God how she rued the day she'd ever met that little weasel on the race track in Oz all those years ago, and even more when she had been stupid enough to accept that first fat wodge of cash. Her life had never been the same since then. Sighing resignedly she pushed the car into reverse and made her way out on her calls.

Theo and Oli had been nick-named the dynamic duo. The female clients adored them, flirting outrageously and they were in huge demand - being called out for the most random of reasons. The upturn in the nature of their visits meant that Alice was to continue with the trainers whilst Oli and his new pal serviced the ladies and grooms of Fittlebury and surrounding areas. Andrew thought it highly amusing, and the two studs basked in the glory of their popularity. Only Alice seemed disgruntled but this was nothing new. Andrew was pleased with Theo, he was a real breath of fresh air and the staff and clients adored him. His veterinary skills were impressive too - he'd been a good choice for a locum and Andrew would be reluctant to let him go when Oli's wrist had healed. He and Oli had a partners' meeting tonight, perhaps they should think about keeping him on.

The colours of autumn had well and truly set in with a positive riot of colour. Farouk and his team were down at the mill filming with Aiden and Roxy. Celebrations were in order as, at the Planning Meeting held at the beginning of October, permission had been granted for the conversions and rebuilding had begun. Although the site had been largely cleared of rubble, it still had a forlorn and sinister look with a curtain of mist draped over the mill pond and loitering in the woods. Alan was working flat out with the builders and they were fed up with tripping over the cameras and the constant bickering and arguing between Roxy, Aiden and the crew. The barn was looking fabulous. Enormous windows had replaced the wooden clad sides and a tempting turquoise pool had been installed in the smaller of the barns and a paved terrace made outside for the warmer weather. The exercise machines had yet to be installed in the gym area, and upstairs on the galleried mezzanine floor there was still quite a way to go, but it was definitely beginning to take shape. Outside, work on the mill was much slower, hampered by English Heritage who watched proceedings like a slavering Rottweiler protecting a bone. Roxy was now emulating the country set, sporting Dubarry's tucked into jeans as though she had been born in them, and looking every inch what she definitely was not, as she and Aiden scurried around in the mill discussing their future plans and alternately sparring and laughing with each other. Then Roxy was posing in a scanty bikini with a flute of celebratory champagne against the lapping poolside, moaning to all who would listen about being freezing, whilst Aiden was filmed in a garden full of weeds with his glass of fizz postulating how this would be his kitchen garden. As the sun began to crawl up the sky the mist cleared over the pond and Farouk announced that he had enough footage here and suggested they take a trip over to the stables to get some riding shots. Alan heaved a sigh of relief as he watched them pack up and go. He clapped David Bryce on the back and they got back to the serious work.

Seb and Leo were up to their neck in shit and shovels when the crew arrived without warning. With Felix and Hattie away at Weston for almost a week, they were seriously understaffed and grumpy with it and to see that egotistical bunch of wankers arrive was just about the last straw.

"Hi guys!" breezed Roxy, "sorry to pitch up unannounced - we were filming down at the mill and Farouk wanted to do a bit here - hope it's okay?"

"Yes, of course," lied Seb. "It's fine, but we're seriously short-staffed so you might not have our full attention Roxy. Did you want to ride today, only I've just chucked Galaxy in the paddock."

"What's the nag like?" asked Farouk lazily, not bothering to look at Seb, "not dangerous in the field is it?"

"No he's a poppet - why?"

"We could get some takes with Roxy feeding him carrots and stuff in the field, leading him around, that kinda thing. We only need a few minutes and probably use about 30 seconds."

"The horse'll be quiet enough as long as you don't go flapping stuff around and making a lot of sudden noises," remarked Leo. "Use a bit of common sense," he added dryly.

Sam looked at him casually, "Where's Hattie today then?"

Leo looked him up and down dubiously, "She and Felix have gone to a competition, they'll be away till Sunday."

"Ah yeah," smiled Roxy, "Colin and Grace said he'd be away, riding their horse at some fancy event isn't he?"

"Yep, Weston Park, it's a three day event, really high profile show."

"Can we get on," snapped Farouk, "like we're really interested about Felix."

"Actually I am interested in the eventing, I was planning to pop up to see the cross country on Saturday."

Roxy's announcement hit everyone like a bombshell. Their mouths gaped open and they stood there looking at her in astonishment.

"What?" said Seb finally, trying to be diplomatic, "this is a really important competition Roxy, do you think that's wise? He won't want any distractions."

Roxy tinkled her silly flirty laugh, "Oh, I see what you mean, but I won't distract him, he won't even know I'm there."

"Really? With no disrespect Roxy, you cause a bit of a flurry when you arrive anywhere," flattered Leo, "he's hardly likely not to notice is he?"

"Don't fret blossom - I can do discreet," grinned Roxy, "he won't know till after he's finished."

"Can we just get on," grumbled Farouk. "I've got a crew waiting and they cost money."

"Darling," affected Roxy, her voice syrupy as she slipped her arm through his and stroked his hand, "I've got a cracking idea."

"Am I gonna like it?" said Farouk suspiciously, as they walked away from Seb and Leo towards the paddock, "no more fuck ups Roxy, purleease."

Seb couldn't hear her reply but turned to Leo doubtfully. "Oh my fucking God, you don't think she'll go up there really do you? Do you think we should warn him? I can't think of anything worse can you?"

"No," agreed Leo, his face screwed up with angst, "but I'm not sure that telling him will do any good either, he'll only worry all the more, and it's not as though we can stop her going is it?"

"No, you're right, but what a screaming disaster if she does."

"Disaster will be the right word." said Leo despondently. "What shall we do?"

"Dear heart, we'll have to sleep on it. Now get your arse up to the paddock and give the duchess a hand with Galaxy."

Dulcie and Nancy had been hoping to enjoy the brief respite of Jennifer and Charles' absence from Nantes Place. Not that Jennifer was a bad boss, far from it, but Charles could be a scary bugger when his dander was up and he might well be fed up if he knew what was going on. The horses were all sound and well, and the yard was performing like a military tattoo, but a blot had descended on their immediate landscape in the shape of Dulcie's sister who had pitched up on their doorstep. Frankie was a groom, albeit currently a homeless and out of work one. As bonny as her sister, she was funny, bubbly and a great joker. When she'd turned up out of blue with a stuffed holdall and a tear-streaked face, Dulcie had thrown open her arms and said she could stay as long as she liked. Dulcie had asked Jennifer and the rest of the staff knew, but Jennifer had said they would cross the bridge of telling Charles later, and in the meantime for Frankie to keep out of his way. So far this had proved successful, although she'd only arrived the week before. Eventually after several bottles of wine, a packet of fags and a half a kilo of peanuts she spluttered out the sorry tale of her departure from her last job. Nancy listened, her blood pressure surging as Frankie revealed how she'd been working 14 hour days for under the minimum wage, living in an appalling leaky caravan, being verbally abused by an old harridan of an employer. The catalyst had been when the old girl had taken her hunt whip to Frankie instead of her horses and dogs, and Frankie had upped and left in terror, with the virago hurling abuse as she bolted off in her car. Now she was high and dry, taking shelter at her sister's with her tail between her legs, not wanting to go back to mum and dad's.

"This sort of exploitation sickens me," muttered Nancy angrily, her voice slightly slurred with the drink, "I thought it was a thing of the past."

"So did I," said Dulcie, stroking her sister's hair as she told them the story. "It's terrible, what a horrible old woman."

"She truly was," sobbed Frankie dramatically, fat tears rolling down her freckled cheeks. "I did my best I really did, but it was just me for a dozen horses - I was knackered. The horses were on terrible beds and didn't have enough to eat. When I tried to give them more hay, she screamed and shouted at me. Her dogs cowered in the hay barn, and she used to march around with a hunt whip, cracking it all the time. I'm sure she was a drinker too, her breath stank."

"Why on earth did you take the job?"

"Well she seemed so nice at the interview, but of course it was summer and all the horses were out, the yard was tidy, the boxes empty. I didn't ask her about other staff, I just assumed she had some. The caravan looked alright in the sunshine."

"You are clot," sighed Dulcie, "you should have found out more about her "

"Crystal balls," smiled Frankie ruefully, her pretty mouth puckering, "thanks for putting me up sis."

"Of course it's fine, glad we could help, aren't we Nance?"

"Definitely," slurred Nancy, who'd drunk more than her fair share of the wine, "but right now I'm bushed and need to hit the hay, c'mon Dulcie. We'll see you in the morning Frankie."

Frankie snuggled down on the sofa, her head reeling with worry and booze. There was only so long she could stay here before she returned home to face the inevitable parental fireworks. Meanwhile she'd do her best not to be a burden on Dulcie.

In their bedroom, as Nancy snuggled up to Dulcie, the girls whispered worriedly to each other.

"What are we going to do, she can't stay here indefinitely can she?"

"I know but I can hardly throw her out Nancy, she is my sister."

"Of course not, and nobody feels more angry than I do about slave labour grooms. She did the right thing leaving."

"Let's give it a week - time to recover, then she'll have to go back to mum and dad."

"Okay sweetie, we'll act as a refuge, but as much as I'm sorry for her it can't be permanent here - you know that, don't you. We can't jeopardise our own jobs."

Dulcie nestled closer, "I do, Jennifer is brilliant, but Charles might not be so understanding."

"I know, why don't we give a little supper party here on Saturday, to try and cheer her up. We could ask Susie and Beebs from Chloe's and maybe Seb and Leo."

"That's a great idea darling," enthused Dulcie, "you are clever - she'd love it."

"Settled then, I'll call them tomorrow." sighed Nancy. "Now come on we'd better get some sleep."

CHAPTER 66

Friday saw miserable weather. Black, bruised skies heavy with lumbering rain clouds shrouded the whole country in gloom. From Felix and Hattie in Shropshire, to Leo and Seb in West Sussex and Max in London - each and every one of them was busy dodging the heavy showers.

Roxy and Suzanne were meeting with a manufacturing team who assured them the new range would be on the shelves ready for the Christmas market and to coincide with the TV programme and the opening of the mill. In the meantime, the designs were sensational, combining practicality with style. Suzanne had lined up a good marketing team who'd outlined a sales campaign and were awaiting her approval of their promotional brochures and literature. Roxy sat back in her chair sucking the end of her pen considering.

"Fuck me sideways, who'd have thought this would've been my bag six months ago?"

"No true," admitted Suzanne thoughtfully, "this has so much more class."

Roxy laughed ironically, "You could've bloody disagreed with me!"

"Why should I?" said Suzanne snootily, making some notes on the brochure and turning the page, "you need someone to be honest with you."

"I nearly sacked you over the rolling bed incident."

"That just shows what a bitch you can be," retorted Suzanne. "That wasn't my fault nor the poor blighters at *Gallomania* either and it was salvaged."

"I think country life suits me," murmured Roxy, throwing the leaflets down. "I hope this stuff sells."

"Of course it will. It's good quality, and you're playing up market. Internet sales for this kind of product are really excellent, as it will be for the high street store. The marketing company are first rate - leave it to them."

"Life feels very good," sighed Roxy, "and tomorrow it will get even better."

"I just hope you know what you're doing haring up there Roxy, it could end in tears."

"No it won't," giggled Roxy, "it'll be perfect - even Farouk agrees!"

"Be it on your own head," warned Suzanne ominously, "at least this time you can't blame me if it goes wrong."

Hattie's mood was as grey and miserable as the clouds which hung over the beautiful landscape of Weston Park. She'd made herself more than pre-occupied with the setting up for the rigorous few days ahead, and she and Felix skirted around each other like two stiff awkward cats spoiling for a fight. They'd attended the riders' briefing the morning before, with Hattie assiduously taking notes on her own at the back of the marquee, whilst Felix sat apart from her with the other riders. The first official horse inspection was held in number order after lunch and amusingly resembled a competitive fashion show, each riders vying to outdo the others with a variety of striking ensembles. Whether this was to take the Ground Jury's' eye off the horses was a mute point but Felix, looking like something out of an Armani ad and a sparkling Picasso had effortlessly passed the inspection. Hattie led Picasso back to his stable with a Herculean sigh of relief, and looked glumly at his once white legs, now splattered with sticky mud, and groaned at the thought of the clean-up job ahead. Felix watched her go and turned back reluctantly to gossip with the others and watch the first half of the dressage section - he'd been drawn to ride the next day. That night he tried to persuade Hattie to go to the evening entertainment with him, but Hattie, feigning a headache, had refused and annoyed, he'd stomped off to the bar and by the time he got back to the truck she was sound asleep. Early the following morning he'd been glad to escape the sultry atmosphere between them and disappeared with a group of riders to slog around the cross country course and left her to it. They were stabled in long rows of grotty, temporary loose boxes which afforded little shelter against the squally sudden downpours and it was pretty soon a quagmire on the grass outside with the grooms, horses and riders trooping up and down. Rain dripped off the canvas roof and slid down the front of the stable, making it feel cold and damp; Picasso's ears were cold and, worriedly, Hattie rugged him up like it was the middle of winter and gave him a whopping great hay net.

Brett, whose horses were stabled just a few horses along, slipped into the loose box a smattering of raindrops showering off the tilt as he opened the door.

"Christ why is it always so bloody soggy here."

"I've never been before," said Hattie, looking despondently at the grey skies even though there was a temporary respite from the rain. "I'm so glad you told me to bring wet weather gear."

"Weston International is famous for its appalling weather," laughed Brett, "and its appalling showers, and I don't mean rain showers either. You'll see what I mean when you go over to the block later."

"Sounds fabulous," said Hattie sarcastically. "I'm frozen already, I was looking forward to stepping into a steaming hot tub."

"Dream on girl, no such thing here - unless you have a gracious sponsor staying in a local hotel."

"Well ours are staying in some posh hotel, but I can just see them asking me back for a bath," said Hattie ironically, "like in a million years."

"Tough love," laughed Brett, "still you can always shower with me."

"Dream on buster," grinned Hattie, "I think I'll give it a miss."

"Spoilsport."

"Hold his head will you, while I plait his forelock"

"You've done a nice job on him, bloody murder turning out a black and white horse in this weather. Oi, stand still you bugger," grumbled Brett, as Picasso mugged him for a mint, "he's a quality horse for a coloured, they're normally a lot more common."

"Don't listen to him Picasso," crooned Hattie, fondling the horse's ears, "you're not common are you?"

"What time's Felix's dressage?" asked Brett, looking pessimistically out of the stable at the darkening sky, "pity he didn't ride yesterday, it's gonna piss with rain."

"He's on in about an hour and half."

"Rather him than me, better put some heavy old studs in girl - the ground's going to be murder."

"Don't worry I will," snapped Hattie, "I'm not that green."

"I'll give you a hand, where's your stud kit?"

"Really Brett, there's no need honestly."

"Don't be stalky Hattie, I know you're stressed, and the sooner you leave him the better."

"Brett please, I'm having enough trouble coming to terms with it."

"Coming to terms with what?" said a voice from the stable door, as Felix came in accompanied by a cascade of water from the roof. "What are you talking about?"

"Nothing," said Hattie, an ugly, red flush creeping up her neck. "Nothing at all."

Felix looked sadly from her to Brett and back again. "Suit yourself, I was just coming to see if you needed any help but obviously you don't need me." Hattie began to stutter her thanks, but he'd turned his back on her, calling out curtly, "I'll be back in half an hour, if he could be ready by then, thank you."

"Oh no," wailed Hattie, once Felix was out of earshot, "I feel dreadful."

Brett gave her a crippling bear hug and stroked her hair. "It'll be over soon, once you leave you can start getting over him."

Max sat at his desk in the dimly lit back office and rested his chin upon his steepled fingers, preoccupied in his convoluted thinking of how to use his knowledge about Alice. He knew that she was nobbling the horses for Ernie and the odds were big, but supposing they pushed her to do a little more dirty work? The more he thought about how they could use her to even greater advantage, the more attractive the whole idea seemed. Alice was scared, a puppet to be manipulated by anyone who cared to exploit her and he knew all about using people. Max smiled to himself and as the embryo of the idea began to hatch and flourish, he knew there were fantastically big bucks to be made and he was definitely going to be on the receiving end. He would pitch it to the others but he couldn't see how they could fail to win. How long the scam might work remained to be seen, but once Alice became superfluous, then she would be expendable. Max raised and drained his glass and signalled to Anna. Complicated planning always made him sexually voracious and after all that was what he paid her for. The night was young and he wanted someone to assuage his frustrations.

Anna sidled over towards Max, doing as he had bid her, having no idea of what was in his mind. Seductively, she slipped down the shoe-string straps of her dress, her dark brown nipples and large, swinging breasts exposed for him to admire. Anna tossed back her dark curls and threw her head back closing her eyes apparently in ecstasy, but in reality in resignation as Max leant down and took her nipple in his mouth. She steeled herself and jumped through the hoops of sexual desire, gritting her teeth angrily, and vowing it would not always be like this.

The new surgery was nearly finished and it seemed the obvious venue for Oli and Andrew to have their informal partners' meeting that evening as most of their discussion would be centred around the move and installing the new equipment. Andrew had also said there were some things he wanted to talk about which he didn't want overheard and, with Theo being first on call and Alice second, they were both unlikely to be interrupted here. Grace's mum had thoughtfully brought over a jug of coffee and a plate of shortbread and they sat on upended crates like a couple of truanting kids at a midnight feast.

"It's looking great isn't it?" mumbled Oli, his mouth crammed with biscuit "I can't wait to bloody move in, can you?"

"Nope I can't, these last few weeks seem to have gone so slowly," complained Andrew, "it's all the little odds and ends that take the time I suppose."

"Well we've gotta have good electrics and stuff, security systems all that malarkey - takes time."

"I know - but it's frustrating."

"You're frustrated!" He waved his plaster cast in the air. "You wanna try having this beaut buddy - I can't wait to get the bloody thing off."

"Not much longer is it? It's been nearly 4 weeks now."

"No, but it'll be weak after the cast comes off, and I don't know what'll be more aggravating."

"Oli, I've been thinking about Theo. He's fitted in really well hasn't he - I mean been a real hit with the clients, and the staff. You seem pleased with his work - do you think we should offer him an assistant's post?"

"Christ mate, I think it's a marvellous idea, he'd be ideal, but can we afford it? The new equipment's cost an arm and a leg, plus all the extraneous costs of setting up this place. It'd be a big chunk of money."

"I know, but we'll be expanding into bigger premises, so hopefully that'll mean that the clients will expand too. I think we may need to speculate a bit and, if later, we did need to advertise for another vet we might not find one as good as he is."

"True, and I suppose we could take him on a six month probationary contract, explaining that it would depend on how things panned out here - do you think he'd agree to that?"

"He might," said Andrew, picking up another slice of shortbread, "if we were straight with him. What about accommodation?"

"Well, I suppose he could stay with me for a bit longer, but I think he'd want his own place eventually," Oli laughed ruefully. "You never know, I might settle down again one day!"

"Yeah right," grinned Andrew, "seriously, so you think we should talk to him?"

"Definitely, if you think we have the money," said Oli. "Can you get Gary to run up a salary package?"

"I will and then we'll talk to him together - meanwhile we'll keep it to ourselves. Now, come on, let's see where we're going to put everyone here. Paulene would never forgive me if she doesn't get the biggest desk!"

CHAPTER 67

The Saturday at Weston dawned brighter, but the grass in the narrow corridor between the stables was a quagmire following yesterday's rain, and Hattie was weeping with frustration trying to keep Picasso clean whenever she got him out of the box for a leg stretch; although the ridiculous constant announcements over the loudspeakers reminding everyone to be cautious about using too much water made her giggle as she sloshed around in the mud. Felix's dressage the previous day had not been too bad considering the deluge of rain that had tumbled out of the sky. How the judges had marked the test was a mystery with the rain streaming down their windscreens, the wiper blades barely able to cope. Hattie had sheltered as best she could, but her face was so wet, water dripped off her eyelashes and blurred her vision. In the miserable wind, the flapping, canvas tents whipped like crazy semaphore flags from the surrounding trade stands, and forlorn spectators huddled inside to avoid the weather; despite the gloom and distractions Felix and Picasso doggedly went through the movements and managed to pull off an astonishing 47.8 which put them in 7th place. The sponsors, decked out in their Dubarrys, and Barbours did not hang around for the usual congratulations but hot-footed it back to the luxury and comfort of their swanky hotel.

On cross country day there was always a buzz of excitement and expectation in the stables. The riders going off for another course walk, the grooms making sure every bit of tack was as secure as it could be, their valuable steeds having been walked out, and prepared as best they could for the test ahead. Felix was not due to go until later in the afternoon. The CCI1* was to go first, followed by the Juniors CCI1*, which was always a fiercely competitive class, with all the up and coming junior riders snapping at the heels of the golden oldies. Felix's course, itself, was meaty and testing with a fair few questions, but nothing less than you'd expect from a 2*. In a rare moment when they'd had a drink the evening before and been relaxing with the others in the bar, Felix admitted that there was nothing on the course that worried him overtly, but it never paid to be too laid back. So grimly, he walked the course that morning for the fourth time, and would probably do it again if he had time later.

Hattie had started to chill out a bit, slipping into the old familiar eventing routine which she loved. Laughing with the other grooms and lavishing attention on Picasso; roughing it in the tepid showers, and eating too many bacon sarnies. The rain yesterday had been miserable, but when all her peers were in the same boat, they all laughed and made it bearable somehow. She'd made up her mind that there was no point in being dejected around Felix. She loved him, she was leaving for her own sanity, but this one last time away with him she was going to have fun. She would cry afterwards. It wasn't his fault he didn't feel the same way about her.

"Looking forward to tonight?" asked Leo distractedly, as he cleaned tack, "should be a laugh - pity the weather's not better, we could've used the pool as Jennifer and Charles are away."

"Yes and no. I must be getting old sweetie - more often than not I just want to slob about and watch the box with a glass in my hand."

"Give it a rest Seb, you'll be the life and soul when we get there. Anyway, Susie and Beebs from Chloe's are going and Harry the Whip, and few others. It'll be a laugh."

"Probably," said Seb gloomily, rolling his eyes dramatically, "I can't keep up with you young things."

Leo put down his cleaning rag and went over to him, putting his arms around him. "Don't be stupid, you're only a couple of years older than me. What's the matter, you're not yourself lately?"

Seb sighed dramatically, resting his head like a faithful dog on Leo's shoulder, "I don't know, just feeling my age I suppose and, if truth be known, feeling a tad bit insecure."

Leo smiled, stroking his hair with affection, "You've no need to feel insecure, I'm not going anywhere - I'm just a dreadful flirt, you know that. I'd never leave you."

Seb tightened his hold on Leo, "Promise me?"

"I promise. Now stop it, I like women, I always have, but there is only one man I want and that's the one I live with baby - you know that. Look I've an idea - why don't we get make it legal - a civil partnership?"

"What!" gasped Seb, "Do you mean it?"

"Yeah - I do, if it'll stop you behaving like an idiot. Actually - it's a great idea."

Seb unravelled himself, pushing back and looked Leo squarely in the eye to see if he was joking. Leo gave a hoot of laughter and took Seb's hand and flung himself down on one knee, "Seb Locke will you marry me?"

Seb howled with laughter, "Hhmmm, I might, let me think ... oh okay I definitely will!"

Leo leapt up and they locked together in a tight embrace, "How perfect - when shall we do it?"

"I'd like a nice big party," said Seb, clapping his hands together, "and it'd take time to arrange - how about Christmas?"

"Sounds perfect darling," smiled Leo, "and will the bride wear white?"

"Naturally," laughed Seb, "a white Christmas wedding - how perfect will that be! I can't wait to tell everyone."

"Good - I'm pleased and perhaps you'll cheer up a bit eh?"

"I am soooo looking forward to tonight now, I can tell everyone! How simply exciting!"

"And," added Leo decisively, "so we can both celebrate in style I'm gonna book a cab back from Nantes and we can pick up the car in the morning."

Seb flung his arms around him and kissed him passionately, surfacing for air and spluttering, "I do love you!"

Roxy had rung Hattie to find out how Felix was doing and, uber-casually, asked what time he was due to go cross country as it wasn't published on the internet. Innocently, Hattie told her, extolling the good news of his dressage, but grumbling about the mud and the rain. Roxy couldn't wait to finish the call, having gleaned the information she needed, and put the next part of her plan into action, ringing Farouk who in turn alerted the camera crew. She then rang Rachel instructing her to be ready in an hour - there was no way she was pitching up in some muddy field without her stylist. She sat back in her chair just as the nanny brought in the children, both dressed in designer outfits, their little faces pinched with sultry aggression.

"Mummy, this stupid woman won't let me wear mascara," wailed Stephanotis, "like we need to do what she says."

"Don't be a little cow Stephi - be a good girl for Ingrid. She's right, you're too young for mascara."

"I will wear if it I want to," demanded Stephi, stamping her foot and spitting at the nanny, "she's nothing is she, we can soon get another nanny."

"No we can't," snapped Roxy, "do as you're told baby, for Mummy, please."

"Mummy, can I sit on your lap," asked Delphinium sweetly, hanging on Roxy's leg. "I'd love a cuddle."

"Sweetie," said Roxy, pushing Delphinium gently away, "Mummy would love to but I'm busy right now. Ingrid, for Christ's sake, deal with the children please."

"But Madam," spluttered Ingrid, "the children just need a little of your time, if you could just spare them half an hour."

"Perhaps tomorrow my darlings. Mummy may even have a lovely surprise for you," smiled Roxy temptingly, and then turned glaring at the nanny hissing menacingly under her breath, "do your fucking job Ingrid."

Ingrid looked as though she'd been slapped but ushered the complaining children away whilst Roxy popped her mobile into her bag, picked up her car keys and, without looking back disappeared into the underground garage to wait for Farouk to pick her up.

Dulcie and Nancy had finished the yard in record time and Frankie had spruced up the house ready for the guests. From the original, small supper party, it had blossomed into a larger gathering, and Frankie had knocked up a vat of bolognaise sauce and a bowl of green salad. The potatoes were scrubbed, salted and rolled in olive oil ready to chuck in the oven, and Mrs Gupta's shop had been raided for ice-cream and fruit. Ripe Brie was rolling off the plate and, all in all, everything was ready. Frankie plopped down on the sofa, satisfied. She'd gotten over the drama of the debacle of her last job, and realised that it was time to find another. She'd licked her wounds sufficiently and was ready to take on life with gusto and aplomb like she normally did and was looking forward to meeting her sister's friends tonight before scouring the situations vacant.

Up at Weston, Jennifer and Charles were unaware of the preparations for the supper evening planned by their grooms, and were busy enjoying being pampered in the spa of their hotel. A warm shell massage had ensured that they were completely relaxed as they got ready to go to the competition. The weather was showery, one minute sunny, the next the heavens opening and raining down soaking everyone. Jennifer was deliberating about what to wear whilst Charles lay on the bed admiring her naked body.

"What shall I wear?"

"Nothing as far as I'm concerned."

"Stop it," scolded Jennifer, "I think it'll have to be this don't you?" She showed him a smart, long Dubarry skirt."

"Stunning, just don't wear any knickers," drawled Charles wickedly, "gives me a hard on just thinking about it."

"Don't worry I won't," she challenged, "I like to keep you on your toes. Seriously though darling - isn't this just the most dreadful weather?"

"It always is here, my love - shocking place, Weston - always ghastly."

"I hope he goes clear," sighed Jennifer, "wouldn't it be lovely?"

"Darling, of course, but it's tough, he may not, so don't be disappointed - okay?"

Jennifer sunk down on the bed, "I know, I am just so enjoying this whole thing you know?"

Charles reached out and stroked her cheek, "I know, and what makes you happy, makes me happy. You are the best thing that ever happened to me darling."

"Charles, you spoil me."

"I do, and I don't care," smiled Charles, his hand trailing down to her breast, cupping its roundness in his hand, enjoying the plumpness under his fingers, "I love you and I always have."

"I love you too," Jennifer responded, her own fingers trailing along his shoulders and along his back.

"Do we have time?" Charles asked, his fingers exploring further down along her belly "please say yes."

Jennifer murmured under her breath, gasping slightly with the sensation as Charles' fingers explored between her legs, "Yes, yes, yes."

The helicopter circled once and, then again, before it landed. Prior arrangements had been made, and although Roxy was always doubtful and fearful for the outcome, all went smoothly as the whirling bird hovered for a moment and then lurched onto the ground with a dull thump. The gyrating blades gradually ceasing as the miscellany of passengers disgorged onto the damp grass. A welcoming party was on site to meet them and escort them into the main house where arrangements had been made to accommodate the small party before the action began.

Hattie watched the swooping circulating spirals of a helicopter as it came into land but thought no more about it as she tacked up Picasso ready for the cross country. Her back was breaking as she screwed in the mega, heavy studs, two in each hoof, and sloshed on the grease to his legs, so that he could slither over any fences he might catch. The sky was alternatively grey and sunny, but the ground seemed to be holding up well. Felix was as tense as new knicker elastic and needed space. She legged him up and he was off without looking back. Hattie watched him go, keeping everything crossed and dashed off after him, sloshing through the mud on the long walk towards the start with her kit bag slung over her shoulder.

In the main house at Weston, Roxy was being given a right royal welcome, sitting in a fine Queen Anne chair whilst Rachel put the final touches to her make-up, her ensemble laid out on a chaise longue. Farouk was busy with lighting and Sam the camera man, panning in on Roxy's every move. She sipped a glass of water smiling beatifically, whilst everyone rallied around her, delighted that she was here and that Weston was to be featured on her TV show and more than happy to be part of the surprise for Felix at the end of his cross country phase. As the finishing touches were put on Roxy's face and she oozed into her country attire, Farouk was agitating to be gone.

Felix was down at the start of the cross country, popping a couple of practice fences, his face looking grim and pre-occupied. Hattie had arrived and was waiting in the wings and knew better than to interfere. They were running well to time and she signalled to Felix that there were two to go before him. He cantered over to her, and looked down taking the proffered water. Hattie felt a huge surge of stimulation as their fingers touched and looked at him, their eyes locked in a tense moment and he opened his mouth to speak but they were interrupted by the starter calling out his number.

"Good luck," Hattie muttered, "have a good ride then."

"Hattie ..." implored Felix, "Hattie ... I..."

"What?"

"Never mind, see you when I get back, we need to talk."

"Good luck my darling," whispered Hattie after his retreating back, "come home safe," crossing her fingers and toes as she watched the starter counting him down.

Behind her there was a sudden furore, a parting of the waves like Moses parting the Red Sea, a babble of voices, one of which she recognised.

"Hattie darling!"

"What?" Hattie turned astonished to see Roxy coming through the crowd, followed by a camera crew "Have I missed him?"

"Do you mean Felix?"

"Of course I do darling," simpered Roxy, hiding her irritation, "I was hoping to wish him luck."

"Just as well you didn't. He gets awfully tense before he goes cross country," warned Hattie, "you missed him by about twenty seconds."

"I'm devastated darling," sighed Roxy, "still, I'll be here when he finishes."

The cameras homed in on Hattie's face. "I'm sure he'll be thrilled," she said sarcastically.

On the other side of the collecting ring, Jennifer, Charles, Mark and Sandy had been joined by Jeremy and Katherine who had arrived by the skin of their teeth.

"You've just made it," laughed Jennifer, "he's just started."

"Thank God," grimaced Jeremy, "I've broken a dozen speed limits getting here - Katherine would have killed me if I'd missed it."

"Who's that talking to Hattie?" growled Charles. "It's not that tits and teeth woman is it?"

"Come on darling, you know perfectly well who it is," placated Jennifer, "but what she's doing here I've no idea."

"She's been down at the stables," informed Mark, "has a horse with Felix - been learning to ride apparently."

"Saints preserve us, she'll be hunting next," grumbled Charles, not altogether dispiritedly, "what next eh?"

"Shut up, let's listen to the commentary," said Sandy crossly, who couldn't give a fig about Roxy and was more interested in how Felix was doing.

Felix was struggling more than he'd thought. The track was sticky and holding after the previous competitors had gone round during their morning classes - even though they hadn't jumped his jumps, the routes in between were the same. It made for cloying mud and slowed up the time, which was tight enough anyway. Picasso was attacking the fences with his usual enthusiasm but it was taking a huge effort to keep galloping in the heavy going. Two thirds of the way round he was starting to flag dramatically and Felix was kicking like a drowning man. The black and white jumping machine was lumbering into the fences and starting to get clumsy, hitting a substantial, upright timber with careless gusto which nearly toppled him and unseated Felix into orbit. How they both remained upright was a miracle. Whether it was the shock or simply a second wind, it was as though the horse had a charge of adrenalin. He recovered his balance, surging forward after the fence and Felix had a hard time stopping him. Like a mad thing, he took hold of the bridle and charged on wildly with the bit between his teeth as though the very devil possessed him. An already exhausted Felix now had to use all his strength to hold and direct the panicking horse and it was with a huge sigh of relief that he slithered over the last fence and the welcome finishing line beckoned. He kissed the mane of the black and white neck and thanked his lucky stars for the honesty of this divine horse, vowing that next season he would get him fitter.

The watchers were on tenterhooks. The commentary was good, but had emphasised that Felix had hit a fence, and although had righted themselves the horse looked tired. When the huge black and white vision steamed towards the last fence like an express train, it was hard to credit that this was true. He was full of running and looked dynamic. Simultaneously, the sponsors on one side of the finish line, and Hattie and Roxy on the other hugged each other in relief. However good the horse was looking Felix seemed shattered - pale and spattered with mud.

As they hurtled through the finishing line Hattie leapt forward as Felix slithered off. She took immediate charge of Picasso, running up his stirrups and loosening off his girth. She handed Felix a bottle of water and nudged him in the ribs as Roxy came up to him, the cameras in hot pursuit. He was gasping, hardly able to speak, and had his head down between his legs. Hattie patted him gently on the back and said she would take Picasso back to the stables and see to him whilst he dealt with the sponsors and Roxy. By the time he righted himself she was gone.

"Felix darling," gushed Roxy, throwing her arms around him, "I thought I would surprise you."

"Lovely," grunted Felix into her shoulder, "Lovely."

"Did you have a good ride darling," purred Roxy, clearly not knowing what she was talking about "was it fun?"

Felix, who was still barely able to breathe, managed to rasp, "Fabulous, he's a super horse."

"You must be so tired darling?" coaxed Roxy, desperately trying to wheedle some conversation out of him, "are you surprised to see me?"

"Very surprised," agreed Felix, "and yes, really tired. Just give me a minute or two to recover, it was a tough course."

At that moment, Jennifer, Charles and the others arrived. Roxy turned glibly to them. "Hi you guys. You own the horse don't you?"

"Yes we do," snapped Charles. "What are you doing here," he said irritably, "give Felix a chance to recover please."

"I'm planning to buy some horses for Felix myself," smiled Roxy at Charles, "I'm right into this horse lark."

Charles pushed a camera out of his face. "Fuck off you moron."

"Now, now," said Farouk, "don't be nasty."

"You haven't seen me nasty yet," snarled Charles. "Get lost you termites. Come on Felix, let's get you out of here." He put his arm around Felix's shoulder ushering him off and shoving the video camera away.

Roxy simpered, "Don't be like that please."

Charles turned on her, "Look, cheap and nasty tricks might be acceptable where you come from but not here - okay? Find some class, this is just tacky tat."

"Well!" said Roxy angrily, "What a blooming cheek!"

"Perfect," gloated Farouk, as the cameras rolled behind him, "great footage!"

"Don't you dare let this go out," snapped Roxy, "I'll look a total twat."

"Fabulous viewing darling," smiled Farouk, "swallow your pride it'll be amazing - I've never let you down yet!"

CHAPTER 68

The mellifluous sound of Jack Johnson was playing on the stereo when Beebs and Susie arrived at Nantes and, even though it was still quite early the girls were already more than half way down a bottle of fizz. Leo and Seb had rung to say they would be a bit late. Harry should be arriving any time and Oli and Theo would be coming as soon as he could coax Theo out of the bath. A heavenly aroma oozed from the kitchen and the girls lounged on the sofa and armchairs necking down the vino waiting for the others. Frankie struck up an immediate friendship with Beebs and Susie and they were giggling like old mates by the time Leo and Seb arrived struggling with a crate of Prosecco.

"Celebration time my darlings," gushed Seb, "totally wonderful news to tell!"

"Why?" asked Nancy. "What's happened?"

"Leo and I are making it legal - at Christmas!"

"Oh Seb, Leo," crooned Dulcie, her round face crinkling with pleasure, "I am so, like, well totally delighted."

"Thanks," smiled Leo. He put his arm around Seb, "we're pleased aren't we? Time we tied the knot."

"Oh yes," gushed Seb, smiling so hard his face almost cracked, "I couldn't be happier. It's going to be a Christmas celebration - a civil partnership to begin with as, although the new bill has been passed for gay marriages, it doesn't actually become law till next year. So it can't be a proper wedding - we thought we'd celebrate all over again in the spring."

"Lovely," simpered Dulcie, "how completely romantic."

"I know," said Seb, "he only asked me today, and it just seemed - you know sort of right."

"Oh yes," sighed Dulcie, looking sideways at Nancy, "I think it's fantastic, such a commitment, so ... you know."

"Yes I do, makes you feel sort of ... safe," said Seb smugly, "I can't tell you how wonderful I feel."

Nancy glared at Leo, "You know what you've done, don't you?"

"Sorry," said Leo. "Your call I guess. But it was right for me."

Dulcie shot a glance at Nancy, "I wouldn't marry you if you asked me."

"That's lucky then," said Nancy defensively, who'd just been about to suggest a double celebration, "as I plan to stay single."

"Come on you two," rumbled Seb, "you know you don't mean it, stop being so defensive and arsy."

"I am not!" said Nancy, being totally defensive and arsy. "Dulcie and I are fine as we are."

"Definitely," snapped Dulcie.

The atmosphere in the sitting room crackled like lightning ricocheting around black clouds, and a deadly pause embarrassingly halted everyone, into which Oli blundered with all the subtlety of a huge rugby playing half-back.

"Halloo" grinned Oli waving a bottle of wine in his good hand, "we've arrived, with a crate in the car and Theo is dragging it in as I speak!" He paused and looked around him at the stony faces. "What's up?"

"Nothing at all," said Leo breezily, "Seb and I have just announced that we're getting married, so we're celebrating - that's all."

"How amazing," smiled Oli. "Congratulations - to you both!"

Leo's phone rang. It was Hattie. He stood up gesticulating to the others and went outside, bumping into Theo who was humping in a crate of booze. Leo huddled outside listening to Hattie as she talked urgently to him.

"Oh God, you don't want to be up here," she hissed quietly, "the shite has hit the spinning fan."

"Why?" shouted Leo, as the signal was bad. "What's that terrible noise in the background?"

"Don't ask, it's the riders' party, but guess who's arrived and has created a right hullaballoo?"

"Hhmm, I think I might know already," sighed Leo guiltily, "not Roxy by any chance?"

"How did you guess? No don't answer that - it doesn't matter, suffice to say she's created havoc. Charles is livid, Felix is shattered but trying to play devil's advocate, Roxy's playing to the audience like she'd win an BAFTA and everyone is trying to get on camera. It's fucking mayhem. Christ knows how he'll concentrate on the show jumping tomorrow."

"Are you okay baby?" asked Leo, remembering how Hattie had been dreading this last event with Felix.

"I've never felt more sorry for him. Roxy is wrapped round him like a bloody octopus and all he wants to do is get an early night. She's certainly trying to get him in the sack tonight."

"Oh Hattie, that must be hard for you."

"You know Leo, actually it isn't - because he's just pushing her off like she's a nasty virus. He's not interested at all."

"Well that's something I suppose. Have you told him you're leaving?"

"No. I'm dreading it, I thought I'd do it tomorrow in the truck on the way home."

"Well good luck with that - sure it's what you want?"

"No, of course it isn't, but I can't carry on like this mooning after him day after day. A clean break it has to be. Listen, I'd better go, I miss you, I'll call you tomorrow and let you know how the show jumping goes."

"Night then sweetie, take care and good luck tomorrow." Leo ended the call, cradling the mobile in his hand thoughtfully. Why, of why, couldn't Felix just see what was at the end of his nose.

Hattie re-joined the riders' party quietly, standing at the edge of the marquee gazing inside at the revellers. The disco was blaring out some good old 80s tunes and plenty of people were gyrating on the dance floor.

Roxy was centre stage, holding court around a table, her arm curled around Felix's shoulders like a python coiling for the kill. Felix looked unbelievably tired, blue rings shadowed under his eyes and his face was sallow beneath his tan. Roxy urged him to have a drink from the bottles of wine she'd lined up on the table, but Hattie saw him shake his head and take a swig of water. At the same moment, ironically, he looked over and saw Hattie standing alone at the edge of the tent, and their eyes locked, fastened, it seemed, for an age. Hattie felt flustered but couldn't find the strength to look away, all the love, hurt and despair would soon be at an end but, right now, she couldn't stop staring at him. Felix pushed back his chair, grimly throwing off Roxy's arm and pushed his way through the crowds towards her, catching her by the hand and yanking her outside.

"Hattie, where have you been? I've been worried about you?"

"Oh, I just went to ring Leo, check everything's okay at home. Anyway, you've been well entertained it seems," she added sarcastically, "that woman's a piece of work - fancy showing up here like this."

"Forget her, I'm worried about you. Can we go back to the truck? I think we need to talk, I'm not sure what I've done, but you're cross with me about something, and I hate it. Please darling, can't we sort it out, whatever it is?"

Hattie's heart fell into her muddy boots, she hadn't wanted to tell him she was leaving before the competition was over - she didn't want the responsibility of jeopardising the results tomorrow, but she could hardly refuse to talk could she? And had she imagined it or did he just call her *darling*?

"Okay, why not?"

In a curiously intimate and unusual gesture, Felix kept her hand in his and they walked back to the lorry in silence. Hattie rehearsing in her head how she was going to tell him she was leaving to work for Ryan Clemence. They sloshed through the puddles towards the lorry park. The sky was dark and the air damp, many of the trucks had little glows of warm light squeezing out through the curtains, the noise of generators thrummed and the odd radio or TV could be heard through the closed doors. Their own truck stood dark and silent and felt cold when they struggled up the steps, kicking off their dirty boots into the back before padding into the living area and putting on the lights. Hattie pulled the curtains, whilst Felix put on the heater and they sat on the bench seat keeping their coats on until it got warmer.

"Hattie, now come on, what's up? I know there's something, I'm not stupid," said Felix again, "what's going on?"

Hattie swallowed hard, now was the time, no more putting it off. "I'm leaving Felix, I've got another job."

Felix's face fell. "You are joking right?"

"No, I'm not, I'm going to work for Ryan."

"But Hattie, why? Aren't you happy with me? I thought you loved the yard, and the horses, and ... everything," he finished lamely. "I don't understand."

"I do," sobbed Hattie, big fat tears rolling down her cheeks, "I do love it."

"Why are you going then? I can't bear to lose you, I can't imagine my life without you."

"Oh Felix do I have to spell it out for you?" wept Hattie, leaning her elbows on the little table and putting her head in her hands, "are you so stupid that you can't see how I feel about you? I just can't bear it any longer, seeing you with Alice day in, day out. It crucifies me."

"Hattie darling - it's not what you think," stammered Felix, pulling her towards him and trying to cradle her in his arms. "Alice and me, well ..."

Angrily Hattie pushed back from him shouting. "I have to leave Felix. I love you, I've always loved you, and I can't get over you. The only way I can is for me to go away."

"Hattie, will you just shut up and let me finish ..."

"No, I don't want to hear about you and Alice," yelled Hattie, "it's like bloody torture, and I've made enough of a fool of myself already."

"HATTIE!" roared Felix, "Will you just shut up and listen - I don't love Alice, I haven't for ages, not since we were together at Somerford - I love YOU! You silly arse, I've been trying to finish with Alice for ages, but she's terribly unstable and I'm frightened that she'll do something stupid - I promised I'd give her until Halloween, but it's just a date, I know it's over, truly I do."

"What?" whispered Hattie, "say it again."

"All of it?" laughed Felix, taking her by the shoulders and shaking her "or a specific part?"

"Just the bit where you say you love me."

"I love you Hattie, and I have for a long time," repeated Felix, "but I'm not a bastard either, and I'm trying to do the right thing and let Alice down kindly."

"I see," said Hattie seriously. "I'm totally shell-shocked."

"I'm gonna shock you some more then," grinned Felix, and took her face between his hands and, very gently kissed her on the mouth, his lips soft on hers and then suddenly passionate and demanding as she responded like some starved animal.

They tugged off their clothes, hurling the heavy jackets on the floor along with their jeans and hoodies and climbed up onto the Luton, snuggling under the duvet.

"God I've dreamt of this moment ever since you got pissed at Somerford," laughed Felix, as he played with her breasts and kissed her neck. "I don't know how I stopped myself that night."

"I wish you hadn't," said Hattie, "we've wasted an awful lot of time." Her hand wandered down to fondle his erection, "Gosh, you are a seriously big boy Felix."

"You are so beautiful Hattie, I adore you."

"And I adore you right back."

Dulcie and Nancy's party was rocking, the earlier minor contretemps between them seemed forgotten by their guests and everyone was stuffed full and had drunk too much. Theo was a great hit with the ladies, and he and Oli were making the most of not being on call. Seb and Leo were all loved up and no-one really noticed that Dulcie and Nancy were a bit frosty with each other. Frankie was everyone's favourite, she was very much like Dulcie in many ways, with bubbling curling hair and a round merry face with a freckled nose and a sparkling personality to match. Like Dulcie she wasn't tall, but not as plump either, and amazingly she had Dulcie's talent for singing. The two sisters were sparking off each other like Thelma and Louise, jamming and improvising songs while the others joined in. Oli was using his plaster as a mike proving that he couldn't sing, with Theo harmonising in the background.

"Don't suppose Frankie's looking for a job round here is she?" Seb asked Nancy "We could do with some help."

"I'm sure she'd jump at the chance, and it'd be nice for Dulcie to have her close by - but what about accommodation? Charles doesn't actually know she's here and it couldn't be permanent."

"Isn't there a little flat above the stables?" said Leo "I seem to remember Felix saying that was where he lived."

"Yeah, there is, but I'm not sure that Charles would wear it to be honest. Isn't there any room at Laundry Cottage - it's pretty big isn't it?"

"Three bedrooms, but Leo and I have our own rooms" explained Seb "and Hattie has the other."

"Christ what are you two on, you're getting married for Christ's sake, you don't need two rooms!" laughed Nancy, "I've never heard the like."

"We've always had our own space haven't we Seb?" said Leo, "but we do have the little room downstairs, we don't use that much."

"True," pondered Seb, reaching down to top up his glass to conceal his disappointment, "very true."

Leo grinned to himself, vowing he must stop teasing Seb, "But naturally we don't need two rooms now - so she could have my old room, I suppose," *thinking* when Hattie left her room that would be free too.

"Shall we ask her then, we could give it a month's trial on either side - do you think that's fair Nancy?"

"More than fair," said Nancy, relieved that the little problem of Frankie may well have been sorted, the more delicate one, of proving her commitment to Dulcie, would be more tricky.

Frankie, predictably, was astonished and delighted at the same time at Seb's offer of a job, and willingly agreed to the month's trial. Dulcie was absolutely elated, not only had her little sister found a job, but a local one to boot - it couldn't be more perfect. They opened yet another bottle of fizz and made another toast. Seb snuggled down against Leo, things in his world had suddenly become even more perfect.

The weather that early Sunday morning at Weston Park was terrible. The hammering rain on the lorry roof sounded like a herd of thundering elephants, and waterfalls cascaded down the steamed up windows. Hattie, tucked cosily under Felix's arm, couldn't have cared less about the weather, she had never been more happy or content. She rolled over to face him, snuggling her long legs around his body, and he opened his eyes and smiled at her.

"Good morning my beautiful."

"And a good morning to you too." Hattie reached up and kissed him softly, "I can't believe what's happened."

"You'd better believe it," sighed Felix, rolling on top of her and kissing her shoulders, working his way down over her breasts, taking each nipple in his mouth in turn. "Good morning beautiful boobs."

Hattie giggled as he worked his way down her tummy, licking carefully around her tummy button and down towards her thighs. "Oh my," she gasped, "that's a turn on."

"Good, because you turn me on so much," he laughed from between her legs. "Open a little wider my darling and let me play with you."

Obediently Hattie opened her legs, feeling Felix's tongue probing insistently and his mouth gently sucking whilst she wriggled with delight. "So good Felix, so good." As he worked she played with his hair, arching her back upwards and moaning, "Oh darling, I'm coming, it's so good."

"Not yet you don't missus" he laughed, sitting up, and spreading her legs further and pushing his cock up inside her. "Christ, you're so ready for me." He rocked into her, riding her as hard as he'd ridden Picasso the day before, both of them arching and gyrating like a fairground ride.

Hattie felt her breath quicken as her body twitched into a pinnacle of pleasure, her body flexing with each shuddering wave as her orgasm exploded and Felix grabbed her shoulders moaning and arching his back in ecstasy as he too reached his own climax. Afterwards they lay together, their bodies sweaty and sticky, laughing like two naughty children. Outside the rain drummed on the roof and signs of life began stirring on the showground, dogs barked, horses whinnied and voices called. Up on the Luton it was as though they were cocooned in a blissful world of their own.

"We're gonna have to get up," mumbled Hattie, "although, I could stay here all day."

"Me too," said Felix, "and we still need to talk, we didn't get round to doing a lot of that last night did we?"

Hattie laughed. "Nope, not a lot of talking that's true, but sometimes actions can speak louder than words."

"Don't start me off again," said Felix, "otherwise we'll never get up!"

"Come on, loads to do. You've got the show jumping and you've gotta face Roxy and the sponsors."

"They sound like some bizarre rock band," laughed Felix, "but you know Hats, now we're together, I can face anything."

Hattie leant over and kissed him again. "You've no idea how happy that makes me - I still can't believe it."

"Listen darling, I don't think we should say anything to anyone here yet, not until we've had time to decide what we're going to do about Alice. I don't want her to hear anything about us before I tell her. Can you understand that?" Felix looked worried, "she's so fragile and I'm frightened she'd do something stupid."

Hattie took his hand studying his fingers, "You're a good bloke Felix. I want to shout it from the rooftops, but I do understand about Alice. Let's talk about how we're going to handle it on the drive home, meantime we'll keep quiet today - how's that?"

"Hattie, I don't deserve you and I don't know how I'll be able to keep the grin off my face today either."

"Me neither, but come on, we'd better get up - otherwise it might end in tears."

Getting dressed had never taken so long, as no sooner had one of them put on something then the other would tug it off, giggling and cursing as they fell about all over the confined space of the truck, both of them ending up half naked in a heap on the floor shrieking with laughter. A sharp rap on the door brought them to their senses.

"Hattie, you okay?" shouted Brett from outside. "Picasso's banging the door for his grub - do you want me to feed him?"

Hattie stifled a giggle. "Sorry Brett," she called, "I've overslept - don't worry, I'll be out in five minutes - thanks for giving me a knock."

"As long as you're alright, is Felix with you? No-one's seen him either."

Felix looked at Hattie and put his finger to his lips. "No I haven't," Hattie replied, swallowing a laugh, "he probably went back to the hotel with the others."

"Yeah probably," said Brett, "See you back at the stables then."

"Right," shouted Hattie, "be with you in a minute."

Hattie and Felix had to stop themselves guffawing with laughter. They scrambled into their clothes and Hattie snuck out of the truck towards the stables. Felix made himself a cup of tea and waited for half an hour and, peering out of the closed curtains to check the coast was clear, dropped quietly out into the pouring rain and skirted around the back of the lorry park towards the breakfast marquee.

CHAPTER 69

The Sunday passed in a whirl of emotion for Hattie. She floated on a cloud of disbelief and giddy euphoria. She was itching to ring Leo, and even tell Brett, but kept her mouth shut. She and Felix exchanged furtive glances and the briefest of touches when no-one was looking, and it was delicious but mind-blowingly frustrating at the same time.

Roxy had disappeared the previous evening, much to everyone's relief, and was no-where to be seen that morning, although Hattie kept expecting her to pop out of the woodwork at any moment. Charles and Jennifer arrived with the other sponsors at lunch time full of bonhomie and excitement. The weather, if anything, was getting worse, the rain teemed down relentlessly and the show jumping arena was like a swamp. Felix had pulled up to 4th place after the cross country which meant he would be one of the last to jump, and the track would be at its worst, the going as deep as it could possibly be. The one thing in his favour was that Picasso was a horse that could perform in the soft, whereas a lot of horses preferred the top of the ground. Nothing though, it seemed, could dampen Felix's good spirits that day. Brett put it down to Roxy and said as much to Hattie, who just shook her head and tried to look sad. Even Jennifer remarked to Sandy and Katherine that Felix had a glow about him that hadn't been there yesterday.

Hattie fretted over Picasso, putting on an extra rug to make sure he was warm enough in the murky weather, and took ages over his plaits. She cleaned the tack obsessively after its mud bath yesterday, and checked every bit of stitching. She couldn't be bothered with food and kept mentally re-running the events of the previous evening, still unable to credit what had happened. She wondered how on earth it would pan out once they got back home to the reality of Fittlebury. After all, Alice did still live with Felix, and she was not going to relinquish him so easily. They'd have to tell Seb and Leo, of course. They would guess anyway, she was sure. Hattie, herself, would have to tell Ryan and, more awkwardly Brett - who'd been so good to her - that she'd changed her mind and was staying with Felix, although she wouldn't for the time being be able to let on why. Luckily it wasn't common knowledge but she hated messing them around, they'd been kind to her, especially Brett, although she suspected he had ulterior motives. What a mess, of course, they'd work it out, nevertheless it wasn't going to be easy and it was no good pretending it was. They'd just have to deal with each situation as it arose. In the meantime, a great flood of happiness overwhelmed her. When you were in love, nothing was insurmountable.

The final trot up took place in reverse order at 11 am, and it was a tense time for all of the competitors, not least of all Felix. But Picasso was as sprightly as ever and was passed without a backward glance, much to relief of the sponsors. Once it was all over they trooped off for a late lunch with the rain still pelting down in stair rods. Hattie couldn't face any company, all she wanted to do was talk about Felix and couldn't concentrate on what people were saying. She settled Picasso back in his stable, and took shelter in the truck, looking out of the rain streaked window willing the hours away until the time they would be driving home and she had Felix all to herself. She missed Fiver dreadfully. They'd decided not to bring him, knowing the weather forecast was dire and, especially as he needed rest after his kidnapping ordeal they'd decided to leave him with the boys and Hero, but it seemed funny without him. She thought back to that day when they had stolen him from the fat man and his awful girlfriend - it seemed aeons ago and yet it was only in June this year when they'd had a few stolen hours at Hickstead. Such a lot had happened this summer. She hugged herself in her damp clothes and wondered what was to come next. Across the lorry park, scuttling with his head down she saw an altogether too familiar figure and her heart did a double bounce. She thought it was an old wives' tale about that, but it was true, it really did seem to bounce twice as she watched Felix hurtle through the lorry door, shaking off his soaked Barbour.

"Hattie darling, you in here?"

"In here," she called laughing, "drying off."

"Oh come here you, I've been wanting to do this all morning." Felix grabbed Hattie and pulled her into his arms, "I can't keep my hands off you, you witch!"

Hattie laughed, "God, it's so frustrating isn't it. I just want to shout how much I love you from the rooftops!"

"We gotta make plans Hats, I'm not going to be able to keep this up for long."

"Me neither, but there's such a lot to sort out."

"Not really, the main thing is I have to tell Alice. I've been thinking, the lease on the cottage is in my name, it goes with the yard, so I suppose she will have to be the one to move out and it may take her time to find somewhere."

"Okay, I understand that, we can be patient."

"What I don't want is for her to think we're splitting up because of you. Of course you are the catalyst for me, but it's been over with us for ages, months really. She changed towards me, she wasn't the person I thought she was - sometimes it's like living with a stranger. The main thing is, I don't want everyone thinking of you in a bad light because it's just not true and you know what the village can be like."

Hattie looked horrified. "I see what you mean, I hadn't thought about that."

"No darling, you wouldn't - you're too nice by half. You were prepared to leave rather than split up me and Alice. You didn't know that she and I were on the rocks. It doesn't bear thinking about, I nearly lost you Hattie."

"Well you didn't," grinned Hattie, "Damage limitation is what we've gotta do now."

"Blimey, you sound like Charles," laughed Felix, "but you're right. Alice and I gave each other until Halloween, that's only a couple of weeks away. Do you think we could wait until then?"

Hattie's face looked bleak, "That's a huge ask Felix, I'll try but it seems a lifetime."

"For me too. Remember I've got to live with her till then. All I want to do is move on, but I think it'll be easier and kinder and, in the meantime, I can make it clear that after Halloween it's over."

"Okay, but I'll be so worried you're gonna change your mind and stay together."

Felix took her face in his hands and looked into her eyes. "Hattie I promise you, nothing could be further from the truth, you are who I want to be with, who I love - you have to trust me."

"I do trust you Felix," Hattie sighed, "more than anything. Okay we say nothing then till after Halloween."

Seb's head was throbbing, and waves of nausea rose like a relentless sea crashing on the beach every time he moved his head. Fondly, Leo looked down at him. It had been a fabulous night, his voice was hoarse from singing and, although he wasn't hung over like Seb, his throat was as dry as Ghandi's flip flop. He eased out of bed trying not to make too much noise as he dressed, and slipped downstairs to get some tea. Not only had it been a great night, but it seemed they had also found a new groom who'd agreed to start that very morning - Saints be praised, as judging by the state of his Lordship upstairs there would be little work from him that day. Frankie seemed a good laugh and he'd been amazed when she'd said there was no time like the present to get stuck in, especially when she heard that they were short-handed with Felix and Hattie being away. That was a good sign. She was obviously a worker, and they needed that after the snipey Kylie who was always trying to put the boot in. He was positive it was she who had leaked the story of Roxy to the papers, but of course they couldn't prove anything, and what could they do if she had? No, if Frankie worked out she would be a Godsend. He fed Fiver and Hero a can of dog food and made some toast. He wondered how Hattie was getting on, she'd sounded terrible last night, although of course that could have been the mobile signal. He didn't envy her the journey back today with Felix. She was going to find it hard telling him she was leaving. Felix would be devastated. He had no idea, he was so wrapped up in that stupid, abrasive cow Alice, and couldn't see what was under his nose. Leo would miss Hattie dreadfully. She was lovely to work with, and they'd become really good friends. He wondered what she'd say about him and Seb getting hitched. She'd be thrilled - he knew it. He should have suggested it ages ago really. Seb, for all his bravado, campness and flirting was terribly insecure; and as for him, Seb really and truly was the only guy for him. Although he liked flirting with men and women too, the thought of living with anyone else in a relationship wasn't for him, that's for sure - and it was time he settled down. He drained the last of his tea, took Seb up a cup and a bowl, in case he was sick and a jug of water. He planted a big kiss on his forehead and said he'd be back at lunch time to see how he was. Downstairs, the dogs were agitating by the back door to be the first one to the car and plunged out into the dewy garden, scrapping as they went. Leo sniffed the air, autumn was well and truly here. Mist hung across the fields like sad, old net curtains and the apples on the gnarled, ancient apple trees in the garden were laden with fruit, and all the bushes were laced with pearlescent spiders' webs. He felt happy and content. Life was good.

Frankie was nervous. She'd had a shed load to drink the previous night but had consumed copious amounts of water and wasn't in the least bit under the weather this morning. Nancy had given her directions to

Fittlebury Hall, but she knew roughly where it was, as she'd passed it on her way down here, even though her eyes had been blurred by tears at the time. Seb and Leo seemed like really nice guys and Dulcie had endorsed that they were, but also that they expected hard workers. They ran a tight ship and she was not to let her sister down. Even if she decided that it was not for her and she left after the month's trial, she was to work her sock's off for the month she was there. Frankie looked at her sister's unusually serious face and told her not to fret and that she could rely on her. She just hoped she didn't cock up. She worried about meeting Felix and Hattie, and wondered if Hattie would be a bitch and what Felix was like. She hadn't asked about them and Dulcie hadn't said anything so she assumed they were alright, otherwise they would have said something. Frankie was going back to stay with the girls tonight and move in to Laundry Cottage tomorrow, once the boys had told Hattie. She hoped she'd be okay about it and Seb had just laughed in that camp way he had, and assured her Hattie would be fine as long as she was nice to the dogs.

By the time she got to the stables, Leo had already mucked out three boxes and turned out those horses that were going out in the paddocks. As she pulled into the yard in her old car, his face blossomed into the most welcoming smile.

"Am I pleased to see you!"

"That's a nice welcome," smiled Frankie, getting out and walking over, "good morning to you."

"Do you want a coffee?" asked Leo, "then I can show you the ropes?"

"No, ta, I've had a drink, let's get stuck in, shall we?" said Frankie, pulling out a pair of rubber gloves. "Where do you want me to start?"

Leo was impressed. "Right, this way then."

By late morning she'd mucked out, hay nets were filled and feeds made for that afternoon and the following morning whilst Leo got on with the riding. He clattered into the yard, with Casey skittering on the cobbles and Frankie came over and took him.

"I'll just wash him off shall I?" she asked. "He's got a fine coat but he'll need clipping soon."

Leo followed her over to the wash down box, "I know, but it'll have to wait till Hattie comes home."

"I could do him this afternoon if you like."

"Could you?"

"No problem, I like clipping," said Frankie, squirting the hose over the steaming horse. "I'll give him a really good bath now, then he can dry off - it'll make it easier."

"You must be the only person I know who likes clipping," laughed Leo, "so help yourself."

"I'm going to make some tea now. Once you've done him stop for a while and have a cuppa."

"I will," called Frankie, rubbing Casey's coat into a lather as he laid his ears back and snapped his teeth. "Now, now don't be unpleasant" she said mildly, "you'll feel lovely when I've finished."

Leo watched her from the tack room and sighed with relief, they may just have found themselves a diamond. My God they were going to need one when they lost Hattie, he thought ruefully, he could kill Felix for being so fucking stupid.

Roxy had reappeared with Farouk at Weston and was busy signing autographs. She'd sent Rachel out around the trade stands that morning on a shopping spree and she was now suitably togged out in the latest of equestrian wet weather gear. The cameras whirring as excited fans fawned over her with people asking why she was here and she was spouting on about how she was supporting her mentor Felix and how he was teaching her to ride, winking and nodding lasciviously. How she'd bought a horse and was planning to buy more and keep them with him.

Felix himself did not make an appearance until after lunch and he seemed flushed and preoccupied, disengaging himself as fast as he could from Roxy's tentacles. The cameras panned in on the golden boy, who seemed uninterested and distracted, speedily excusing himself when he spotted Mark talking to Jeremy in one of the trade stands.

"Help," he yelped, ducking under the canvas, "get me away from that woman."

Mark laughed, "Lots of men would love to be chased by her."

"Not this one. I'm trying to psych myself up for the bloody show jumping and I don't need her input."

"No indeed," said Jeremy, "although, there is something delightfully tacky about her isn't there?"

"Look, will you excuse me, but I want to watch how the course is riding. The ground's looking terribly cut up."

"It is mate, rather you than me" grinned Mark, "at least these buggers fall down when you hit them though, not like those bloody cross country fences."

"I don't want any of them to fall down" grimaced Felix "although it'll be a bloody miracle in this mud."

"We'd better go and find the ladies" remarked Jeremy "Katherine's on the loose with the credit card in the trade stands."

"Well good luck with that" smiled Felix "see you later."

The show jumping course was causing no end of problems. Fence after fence was falling as the horses slithered around the ring; riders were missing strides, horse's paddling mid-air or refusing to jump out of the deep going. It was mayhem. A few of the bolder gung-ho types steamed round but Felix could see he needed to attack the jumps not pussy foot around if he had a hope in hell of going clear. He sat watching a few more and then covertly skirted around the back of the parkland and headed back to the stables, avoiding the sheltering crowds in the trade stands for fear of meeting up with Roxy and her entourage or his sponsors for that matter. He needed to have his focussing hat on and couldn't be bothered with all the small talk. The only person he could bear to have around him was Hattie. He smiled, his gorgeous Hattie, at last he could be open about his feelings for her, and soon he could open to everyone else. Only a couple more weeks and they could start their lives together.

Hattie was ready and waiting back at the stables. Picasso looked as clean as she could make him under the circumstances, not that it mattered much, by the time they'd made the long trek down to the show jumping the horse would be spattered with mud again. She wouldn't be sorry to kiss goodbye to Weston Park in many ways, she had never been so wet or damp, and yet it was here that she and Felix had finally affirmed their love for each other. A bitter sweet place in so many ways.

Without a word she legged Felix up and he trotted off grim faced down to the last phase of this gruelling event. She knew better than try and chat, and hurried after him skidding and sliding in the mud as she went, her long waterproof flapping in the rain with all the paraphernalia slung in a bag across her shoulder. If anything the rain had got worse and everywhere, forlorn riders and horses were soaked and fed up with the weather and looking miserable as they made their way back to the stabling. Hattie did her best to keep up, but she could hardly stand upright and, all too soon, Felix was a speck in the distance.

Charles was complaining loudly about the weather. "I don't know why we come to this Godforsaken place - it always rains here."

"Stop moaning darling, the hotel has been lovely and we've all had a super time."

"It wouldn't be the same if you didn't moan, would it Charles," admonished Sandy, "none of us take any notice of you."

Charles looked cross and then laughed. "You can't say you're thrilled about the Roxy woman are you?"

"No, of course we're not, but we're not over reacting either," grinned Sandy, "now buy me a drink and shut up."

"Fair enough," responded Charles, and disappeared to the bar.

"Blimey, that put him in his place," said Jennifer, "he does get so worked up about things."

Katherine suddenly clutched Sandy's arm. "Isn't that Felix?" They all peered out through the curtains of rain and, sure enough, the great black and white horse was surging into the ring. "He's going at a hell of a lick."

"Isn't that rather fast?" said Mark, "Not that I know anything."

"It is but I suppose he knows what he's doing," said Sandy ,"the ground is really holding, if he gets a bit of pace on he won't sink so much, I'm guessing."

"Let's hope you're right," winced Jennifer, hardly able to watch, "it looks like he's riding the Grand National."

The judges wasted no time in ringing the bell and Felix pushed Picasso into the first jump. The track was so chewed up it was difficult to find a good line even though the fences had been moved from the morning's class. As always, Weston had done a good job, with lots of innovative ideas for the show jumps; a big parallel featuring a rearing zebra, some rather aptly designed wings which looked like Angel Fish, and others which resembled sail boats. Felix didn't give Picasso a moment to hesitate at anything, kicking him on like a man possessed and, bless him, the horse rose to the occasion and soared over them all, managing to rebalance himself in between with the massive studs that Hattie had screwed into his shoes. The final fence loomed up in the gloom, the rain streaming into his eyes and, with more luck than judgement, Felix managed to wagon the horse over and through the finish to have one of the only eight clears of the section. Back in the collecting ring he slithered off, throwing his arms around Picasso hugging and blessing him for his courage. Hattie dashed over, embracing Felix and for a long moment they clung together, their wet clothes squelching between them. Bringing herself up short, Hattie pulled back quickly, took Picasso's reins and, together, all three of them stumbled back to the stables, for once not a sponsor in sight. Even Roxy and the cameras had been deterred by the rain.

Frankie and Leo had had a really productive day, which was just as well, as Seb did not surface until later in the afternoon and then he looked dreadful, with blood shot eyes looking like red cobwebs. He groaned theatrically and splayed out on the old chair, vowing he was never going to drink again, and that he didn't possibly think he could ride anything today.

"You don't have to, they're all done," smirked Leo. "What wasn't ridden, was lunged."

Seb hauled himself upright, "You are kidding me right?"

"Nope - we have found ourselves a treasure in Frankie - doesn't moan, doesn't take tea-breaks and knows what she's doing and doesn't mind what she does."

"How simply divine," said Seb, slumping back down in the chair again, "kismet darling, it's kismet."

"Whatever it is, it couldn't have been timed better."

"True, how long we could have coped without the delightful Kylie remained to be seen."

"Bugger Kylie, what are we gonna do without Hattie?"

"Hattie?" exclaimed Seb, sitting up abruptly and clutching his head, "what do you mean?"

"Well ... you're gonna know later today anyway - but Hattie's leaving, going to work for Ryan Clemence. She's telling Felix today on the way home in the truck. She's asked me not to say anything, but no point in keeping it to myself now."

"I bloody knew this would happen," spat Seb angrily, holding his head in pain. "Felix can be such a wanker, he doesn't know what's staring him in the face."

"No he doesn't, but for fuck's sake Seb, don't get involved, it's not our place."

"But it will end up being our problem," grumbled Seb. "Thank heavens for Frankie. And what's more, Felix will be in a terrible state once he realises what he's lost, then who's got to pick up the fucking pieces."

"He might be glad, concentrate on making a go of it with Alice."

"Don't be absurd Leo, talk sense."

"I admit that was a stupid thing to say, just trying to see something positive that's all."

Seb leant forward, his head cradled in hands. "I feel really sick now, how the fuck are we going to handle this?"

"We've gotta pretend we don't know anything about it, wait until they tell us themselves," implored Leo, "remember we're not supposed to know."

"Frankly how you can expect me not say anything beggars belief, but I guess I've got no choice. Hattie leaving - I can't stand it, I really can't."

"How do you think I feel?" groaned Leo, "I've known for ages. I've been terribly upset about it all."

"Then how you could have kept it yourself is staggering," rounded Seb, "don't you trust me?"

"Of course I do, but I promised Hattie, and a promise is a promise and I don't break them, just like the promises I make to you." Leo leant down and put his arm around Seb, kissing the top of his head. "Don't make me feel bad baby, it's bad enough as it is."

Seb reached up and touched Leo's hand, "You're right darling, of course you're right."

"We'll just have to try and be supportive to them both, but it's not going to be easy."

"No, but at least we have our celebration to look forward to - I'm terribly excited."

"Me too, it'll be fabulous, we must sit down and talk about it later."

Frankie, who'd been beavering away in the yard with a broom, put her head around the door. "Do you want me to start bringing in Leo? I've skipped out all the beds ready."

"Good idea hun. Wait, I'll give you a hand." He levered himself up from the arm of the chair and ambled out of the door half listening as Seb's mobile rang.

To Seb, the shrill ring tone went straight through his fragile brain and wave of nausea shot through him. He glanced down at the screen flashing *Felix* calling and he steeled himself to answer. "Hi, how's it going buddy?"

"Fantastic," said Felix, his voice tinny and sounding far away on the phone, " we were second, can you bloody believe it! Mind you, the weather up here is shite, we're on our way home."

"Amazing," said Seb cautiously, "great result - how's Hattie?"

"Hattie?" asked Felix, "She's okay, well sort of, pleased with the result of course, but we've got some news for you and Leo; we'll tell you when we get back."

"Oh dear, that sounds ominous."

"Depends which way you look at it. Anyway, we're on our way back, don't worry about waiting in the yard, we'll finish up Picasso and I'll drop Hattie back at the cottage when we're done."

"Okay, safe trip then, keep calm and see you later. Ciao."

When Leo had finished and they were on their way home, Seb told him about the bizarre conversation.

"Extraordinary," said Seb, "he didn't seem to care at all."

"More fool him then."

CHAPTER 70

Max was scheming. He'd devised a way that they might treble their money and the delightful, bad tempered, ice-maiden that was Alice would be part of the key. Ernie was hosting a party at his gaff that night and Max was proposing to outline the plan to the others. To date, he'd been a relatively small but essential stooge to them, nothing but a seemingly insignificant cog in their complicated wheel, a player doing as he was bid, working on the periphery and taking small spoils; hitherto inconsequential he might be, but stupid he wasn't. Besides, he had the mega dosh to put up, and moreover he, unbeknown to them, had a superlative and daring plan. The more he thought about it, the more excited he became. The difference between them and Max was that he had vision.

Anna was ready for him at the required hour. Sophisticated, in an absurdly simple and slinky fitted black dress, clinging to every sinewy curve, her breasts temptingly yet discreetly spilling out, killer heels and musky perfume with dark hair tumbling down her back. Since the awful time when he had given her physically to Ronnie and Tash, his attitude to her had changed. He dangled her on his arm, like a lucky charm and made sure she was always alluringly dressed to kill. He demanded from her his own private sexual gratification and that was becoming less these days but he would never behave like that to her again. Sexually, they did sometimes have other woman involved, but never another man and, as long as she said the right things, kept her ears closed to what she heard in the course of his business ventures and did as she was told, she was safe. He treated her with respect and ensured her education in that she was learning the trade. But it was fragile business, and whilst he was kind to her, she never felt safe; he was always distracted and she never knew what he was thinking.

Ernie's house was ablaze with lights and loud music. Despite the nights drawing in, gaudy lights bobbed in the garden and around the pool, where scantily clad revellers, obviously pissed, were dipping in and out of the water with great whoops of laughter. Music blared out through speakers and discreet waiters trolled through the crowds with trays of glasses and bottles. Waitresses, in short skirts with trays of absurdly inadequate nibbles, whisked through the crowds hoping to soak up the prolific alcohol.

Max, with Anna tottering on his arm sauntered in, and watched from the periphery. Ronnie, his pasty, white belly wobbling in swimming shorts was being propped up by Tash, wearing bikini bottoms, her tits sparkling with gems of water in the fairy lights. The others from the syndicate were equally well greased up, their own floozies on their arms. Max felt Anna's hand tighten with worry on his, and he stroked it absent-mindedly and turned to smile reassuringly at her.

"Hey diamond geezer, glad you could make it." Ernie slurred behind him, grabbing Max by the shoulder and slapping him on the back. "Park your arse and your tart and have some fun."

Max turned and smiled at Ernie, who was well pissed. "Thanks mate - great party, and a great house," he looked around him admiring the décor, "must have cost a bit."

"It did, my son, it did," smirked Ernie, his gold rings flashing on his fingers, the sweat glistening on his face, "but we're winners eh?" he chortled, "no shortage of them where we are!"

"No," smiled Max, "that's for sure. I might have a bit of an idea as it happens."

Ernie's baggy eyes narrowed. "Really, what? We're doing okay aren't we?"

"Could be better, three times what you're doing now?" tempted Max, "Let me tell you?"

Ernie cocked his head to one side, like an absurd cockatoo considering, "I'm all ears, my son, all ears. Let your tart snort a line or two - plenty here, and we can talk turkey with the others before they get too hammered."

"Suits me," said Max. "I promise you, you'll like what I've got to say." He pushed Anna away. "Go and find something to do Anna, I won't be long - no lines though eh?"

Anna's face was cold, her voice colder. "Of course not Max - I'll see you when you've finished."

"I'll round up the others," said Ernie, "they'll be all ears to hear what you've gotta say."

"Rely upon it," smirked Max supremely confident. "We're gonna make a bundle."

As the lorry swung into the yard, the white glare of the security lights popped on illuminating everything like a fairground ride. Hattie and Felix, who'd driven home with their hands super-glued together, only reluctantly separating when Felix had to change gear, took a huge sigh as they hurtled down to earth with a shattering bang. Suddenly, all the barriers of telling Alice and the others loomed ahead like grotesque obstacles to be climbed with all the sensitivity of scaling a monstrous wasps' nest. They turned to each other smiling weakly but confident - they would get through this.

Hattie jumped out, pulling down the ramp and busying herself with settling Picasso after the long journey home. Felix mucked out the truck and begun to unload. From the eerie shadows of the stark lights suddenly Alice loomed out wailing like some demented and tormented creature. She rushed over to Felix and hugged him as tightly as if she hadn't seen him in months. From her own vantage point Hattie watched; Alice was sobbing dramatically, throwing her hands around Felix's shoulders and wildly kissing his neck and chest. To be fair, Felix looked as though he'd been electrocuted, but nonetheless he stroked the top of her head. Hattie felt sick; she stood paralysed watching them whilst Alice wept and cried pathetically and wondered how on earth this was going to work out. Would Felix be strong enough to carry out how he truly felt, or would he change his mind and decide that being with Alice was what he wanted after all? Appalled by the thought - Hattie could watch no more and turned on her heel, stumbling with blinding tears onto the concrete road towards the sanctuary of Laundry Cottage.

Hattie struggled up the path and tumbled in through the kitchen door. Seb and Leo, who had already downed a bottle between them, looked up in alarm. Hattie's face was streaked with dirt and tears as she threw herself down at the table and burst into noisy sobs. The boys looked aghast at each other, before Leo jumped up and put his arm around her and Seb got up to get another bottle and glass.

"Oh God, oh God," Hattie moaned, through great choking gasps, "I've never been so happy or so miserable."

"Oh Hattie, you knew it wasn't going to be easy," consoled Leo reasonably. "I've told Seb now, he knows you're leaving, and he knows why too."

"Oh God, what a fucking mess," groaned Hattie, dramatically heaving herself up from the table and grabbing the glass of wine, tossing it back in one go. "I don't think I'm going now."

"What?" said Leo, his face crinkling up in surprise. "What d'ya mean not going? Why are you crying then?"

Seb sloshed more wine into the glass. "I'm afraid you've lost me, Hattie darling. Look have another glug, calm yourself down, and try and tell us what the fuck's the matter."

Hattie took the glass gratefully, rolling up her eyes with a huge sigh. "Right," she mumbled, "although I don't quite know where to start."

"The beginning's always useful," urged Seb sarcastically, sitting back down and refilling his own glass and then Leo's. "I hope we've got plenty of booze in, I've a feeling we're gonna need it."

Hattie managed a strangled laugh, "You're probably right. Well here goes."

Half an hour later, the whole story had tumbled out, with the boys making the odd interruptions, and Hattie breaking down theatrically, sometimes with laughter and sometimes with tears. She finished up with the scene in the yard the hour before and then looked at them both helplessly, holding out her hands, palms upper-most, in a gesture of desperation.

"Christ," exhaled Seb whistling, "what a fucking tale, not that I'm not delighted for you ducky, but what a shocking mess. Alice is flaky enough, but how she'll take the news, God alone knows."

"Oh Seb don't," wailed Hattie, sobbing again. "Do you think he'll change his mind?"

"No, of course not," reassured Leo, "this has just got to be handled carefully."

"That's what Felix says, we've gotta keep it quiet until he's told her properly and she doesn't think it's all because of me."

"Look Hattie, we all know that it's been on the rocks for weeks, months even, but he's gonna have a helluva job convincing Alice that it's not because of you - even if that's not true."

"That's exactly why our relationship has to be kept quiet until after she's moved out. He says at Halloween, that's only a couple of weeks, we'll just have to manage to keep it under wraps until then. After all, he can always come over here, can't he - he does anyway."

"Hmm, well we've quite a bit of news for you too, darling, as it happens."

"Oh sorry, I'm so selfish, it's all been about me," Hattie looked distraught, "tell me the news."

"We're making it legal darling," said Seb gleefully, "at Christmas."

"Noooo!" squealed Hattie, jumping up and throwing her arms around him. "I am totally thrilled, absolutely delighted - how exciting. You old romantics." She ran over and hugged Leo, "and there's me going on about what I've been doing."

"Well, there is something else too."

"What can be more exciting?" sighed Hattie, smiling dreamily at them both."

"Nothing naturally, but we must tell you this as it does affect us here."

"We've taken on another girl groom," blurted Leo. "She's Dulcie' sister, she's lovely, and you'll really like her. But she needs accommodation."

"Oh fuck," said Hattie deflated. "I don't know what to say, that was right out of the blue."

"It was for us too, but she came and worked a day, and she is such a total, you know, a real grafter. And, of course we thought you were leaving, so said she could have your room, but I will be sharing with Seb now, so actually she could have my room."

"Oh Christ," said Hattie, "it gets more muddled by the second - Felix and I will have to watch ourselves if we don't want the bongo drums to let our secret out of the bag."

"Hopefully it won't be for too long," soothed Seb, "as you said only until Halloween and we're having our party then - you can make an announcement!"

Hattie laughed with glee. "Wouldn't that be fun - but probably not the best time - we'd need to let the dust settle."

"Oh I've never believed in letting dust settle, darling - so much better to watch it fly!"

The mill was looking extraordinarily good. The builders had done a superb job and were romping along with the restoration. Aiden and Farouk were elated, they had some seriously good footage with before and after shots which was going to make excellent TV. Chrissie was well ahead with the New Year's Eve Opening invitations - it was going to be a dynamic bash. Aiden had childishly hoped for a Christmas opening, but pragmatically, the extra few days were proving a bonus. Realistically, the A-list celebs wanted to spend Christmas with their families and, besides, decorations would still be up for New Years Eve and the fireworks could be much more spectacular - what would be better? Outstanding in every way - a really over the top display - the TV coverage, the social mags and rags, the works. Jools Holland eat your heart out.

Chrissie strutted along behind Aiden with a clipboard, admiring his pert buttocks, and when no-one was looking he would push her up against the wall, his hand on her breast kneading roughly until she gasped with pleasure and pain. The laughable irony of believing that they were invisible made Farouk and Alan smirk, but it hardly mattered. Roxy was rarely to be seen herself and, as long as harmony was maintained, that was all that concerned them. The barns were all but finished and although the exercise machines and furnishings were not in place, the construction was complete. The mill was slower but the site had long since been cleared and the skeleton of the new structure was up and was speedily taking shape. The frames for the huge glass windows were in situ and the shutter board was romping up. The roof was complete and part of the mill wheel had been sent away for expert restoration. Aiden was more than satisfied, he'd organised the back of the mill to be tilled and hoed into a kitchen garden. All this careful and thorough work was filmed and recorded for posterity. Aiden wanted his restaurant to be uber-green, desirable and eco-chic. The TV trailer leading up to the opening would ensure maximum publicity and encourage the right kind of people to his place - and those who could afford to pay the most too. Coupled with the spa - it would be a knock out. People were so gullible and so susceptible and he loved it.

The previous week Chrissie was banging on to Aiden how he should be recruiting for his new staff, and Aiden in between banging Chrissie told her to bloody organise it herself. He'd put his head up from between her legs carefully removing a pubic hair, and said that, apart from the chefs, the rest of the hiring was her baby for the restaurant and the spa. Chrissie groaned with lust as he left her on the cusp of orgasm and surrendered, begging him to carry on and finish her off, only to realise later that she had been stitched up ... again. The end of October was nearly upon them and by

Christmas they'd need a dream-team of people from front of house, under dogs, bar staff and the usual works, not mention masseuses, beauty therapists and plethora of other bods, and now she'd let herself in for arranging the whole shebang. Annoyed with herself, she'd picked up the phone and farmed the task out to a couple of agencies instructing them on her stringent requirements. She only wanted to be involved when they had shortlisted candidates and she would attend at the final interview stage. She really didn't see why she should have to hire the staff for Roxy's spa, but that lazy cow wouldn't get involved, that was for sure. This all on top of the publicity campaign - Chrissie was rushed off her feet. Spitefully she thought about sabotaging the spa staff, putting some tarty slags in there to service the posh bitches, but ruefully it would only come back and slap her on the backside, so with regret, she side-lined the idea. She trailed around behind Aiden as he enthused with Farouk on the fabulous future of the mill, and hoped that, once the place was open, he wouldn't forget that he'd promised to ditch Roxy in the New Year. Chrissie was wearing her heart on her sleeve these days and little by little it was bleeding.

Alice clung to Felix that night in bed with all the tenacity of a limpet on a rock. Awkwardly he tried to prise her off, a sweating dread of panic rising in his throat as she circled her tentacle legs around his waist. Even the smell of her made him feel sick, and her touch made him feel sicker. But he couldn't seem to lever her off him without some kind of Herculean force and hurling her across the room. Desperately he tried to control his breathing as it rose in heaving panicky gulps whilst Alice licked his neck, her darting tongue flitting towards his ear-lobe.

"Alice, we have to talk," he gasped, struggling to breathe, and edging away from her, "I ..."

"Darling," Alice giggled, pinning him down forcefully. "I know you've missed me, don't try to pretend, I can tell."

Felix couldn't bear it. He thrust her off him. "No, Alice you're wrong, so terribly wrong." Felix stuttered, his voice almost inaudible. "I can't go on with this anymore."

"Don't be silly sweetie, you don't mean it, you know you don't," Alice soothed, redoubling her efforts, stroking his hair with her hand, and rubbing his thigh with the other, "you love me, you know you do."

"Please Alice, don't I beg you, we have to talk," pleaded Felix, pushing her hand away irritably and sitting upright. "You just don't get it do you? I don't want to be with you any more, it's over between us."

Alice looked at him surprised. "Don't be so stupid Felix," she snapped crossly, trying to shove him back onto the pillows, "pull yourself together, where will you find anyone better for you than me?"

Felix looked aghast, pushing her off again impatiently, this time with more force. "Do you know Alice, none of that matters - I just don't want you, the person you are, that you've become - you have to come to terms with that," he said wearily, "we can't go on pretending."

Alice glared at him, then her tone was condescending, her eyes superior and haughty. "The trouble with you, Felix, is that you are stupid, a moron, you'll never find anyone as lovely as me; so stop being so fucking dim. I will always earn more money than you, be more successful. I'm smarter than you and you need to realise you're lucky to have me."

This time Felix shoved her off with venom, all his resolve of waiting and being patient forgotten. "Do you know Alice, you can just fuck right off," he snarled, "you are so full of shit. I don't give a fuck about you, what you are, or who you are. You can go pack your gear and leave. This is my house, and I don't want you in my life any more. If you're so fucking superior go and live somewhere else."

Alice, initially surprised, looked at Felix like he was shit on her shoe, and then as she registered he was serious, was aghast at his audacity. In fury she began to scream, and scream and scream. In between great heaving selfish, histrionic gulps, she gasped, "how could you, how could you? I'm not going anywhere, I'll kill myself first."

"Don't be so bloody stupid," shouted Felix, pushing her off him as her hands clawed his face, "of course you won't. You don't love me really, you don't love any one. You just want to control and dominate me, make me feel small. You're always crowing about how stupid I am, how smart you are - well good for you - fuck off and live your life with some smart arse and let me live mine."

Alice curled back in the bed like he'd slapped her and, whimpering like a whipped dog, she whispered, "I've never meant to make you feel like that."

"I think you need help Alice, I really do. One minute you're all over me, the next you're a screaming nutter. I don't want it any more. I can't cope with you. You're so smart then go make a life for yourself, but not with me."

Alice began to weep, huge great gulping sobs, "Please Felix, please Felix."

"No Alice, I can't do it anymore. I'm finished I really am. I'm gonna sleep in the spare room tonight and tomorrow when we're less hysterical we can work things out."

Alice reared up on the bed like a demon. "Don't, don't do this! I will ruin you, I will, I promise."

Felix looked at her sadly, "Just stop this Alice, think sensibly for Christ's sake."

"I mean it, I will ruin you if you chuck me out."

"Alice don't be stupid please, you're over-reacting and being daft. Let's try and stay friends, I beg you. We're gonna come across each other, meet socially, let's not be enemies." Felix took her hands in his and gazed at her "Please Alice, don't let us end like this, we could still be friends."

Alice glared at him, "We can never be friends Felix, never. I could have given you so much, but you've thrown it back in my face, after all I've done for you."

"I'm sorry you feel like that Alice, I really am, but you'll find happiness with someone else, just not with me."

"Oh God Felix, you don't know me at all, don't know the half" sobbed Alice "I'm finished."

"Don't be silly," sighed Felix, resisting the urge to weaken, "of course you're not. In six months you'll be amazed how good life is."

"Do you think?" gulped Alice, clutching the sheets between her fingers, the tears rolling down her cheeks. "I find it hard to believe."

"Of course - I'll always be your friend, you know I will be," soothed Felix, having absolutely not the slightest inkling of how wrong he would prove to be. "Come on, let's try and resolve this positively."

"You promised until Halloween, Felix," pleaded Alice desperately, "you know you did - don't break your promise. You can't do anything until then. Anyway, I've got to find somewhere to go, and you may even change your mind."

Felix looked at her sadly, he had promised her until Halloween, but he knew he wouldn't change his mind either. "Alright Alice, but I'm sleeping in the spare room, and by the end of the month, you've got to have moved out."

Alice winced and then shouted at him, "Have you found someone else Felix?"

Felix hesitated, "No I hadn't when I knew it was over between us," he said carefully, "this is not about anyone else Alice. I've just fallen out of love with you. I know that's hard for you to hear, but I think you have to admit you've changed towards me too. You're not the happy-go-lucky person I met a year ago are you? One minute you're a bitch to me, the next you're all over me - I can't keep up with your mood swings and I can't take it anymore and I don't want to live with it anymore."

"You didn't answer the question," said Alice coldly, "have you found someone else?"

"I don't have to answer the question Alice, I've given you the reasons that I want us to part and they're not new, we've been on the skids for months. Most of the time you're pretty awful to me, and I've had enough. End of story."

"You have got someone else," Alice screamed, "you bastard." She battered her fists against him, "you two timing bastard - I hate you."

"For Christ's sake calm down, you're completely nuts you know that," spluttered Felix. "I seriously think you need help."

"You don't know what you're losing," Alice crowed. "I bet she's not a vet, or classy and intelligent like me, just some tarty stable girl I expect that you've picked up."

Felix looked at her in despair, "Alice you are just so pathetic, and so wrong. You lost me a long time ago. All those times when you let me down, treated me badly, made me feel inadequate and a fool. Dismissed my friends, hated my dog and thought I had a second rate job - well this worm has turned, and it's just too late." He picked up his pillow and stalked off into the spare room without a backward glance and swiftly locked the door after him.

CHAPTER 71

Hattie tossed and turned restlessly for what seemed most of the night finally falling into an exhausted sleep in the early hours; waking the next morning with a banging headache, puffy face and eyes that felt like piss holes in the snow. She slunk out of bed, shivering in the damp chill of the morning. The weather was definitely on the turn now, she wiped a clear patch from the condensation on the windows and stared out at the creepy mist laying over the garden and hanging in the trees towards the mill. In the gloom and deathly quiet of the early morning the autumn fog made everything seem ominous and unreal, like it was issuing an eerie warning of sinister things to come. Hattie pulled back sharply, mentally slapping herself and with an effort marched off towards the shower. What would be, would be, and she was just being melodramatic and a good dunking would sort her out.

The boys had already made tea when she got herself downstairs and the kitchen was warm with the Aga and the smell of toast. She slumped down in the chair.

"Now come on chuck," enthused Seb, "no bloody miseries. I won't tolerate them, otherwise you can bugger off and work for that kiwi."

"Sorry," mumbled Hattie, screwing up her nose with the hot tea, "I promise to try and do better."

"Good - we've got a lot on and you've got to meet our Frankie today."

"Should I be worried?"

"Definitely not! She's a real asset - a gem."

"On another note, how should I be with Felix, do you think?" asked Hattie. "I know it seems ridiculous, but I feel kinda awkward."

"Just be yourself," advised Leo sensibly, "be normal."

"Christ," sighed Hattie with all the drama of dying swan, " I'm not sure

I know what normal is any more."

As it happened, Frankie was at the yard before any of them. The horses had all been fed and she had begun on the mucking out. When the Laundry Cottage mob pulled up she was pushing a laden barrow across to the muck heap singing, much the same as her sister Dulcie.

"Good morning to you all," she called, "and hello, you must be Hattie. I'm Frankie, how nice to meet you."

"Hi, nice to meet you too," said Hattie impressed. "You've got a shifty on already."

"Yep, I like to be busy," said Frankie easily, "makes the day go quicker."

"See, I told you she was a breath of fresh air," laughed Leo, "stop a minute now though Frankie, 'cos we need to decide who's doing what today - and we normally do that over a cuppa once the horses have been fed."

Frankie looked surprised. "Well if you're sure, you're the boss, but I'm quite happy to carry on with what I'm doing"

"No, come and meet Hattie properly," said Seb, "we can all muck in together after."

Hattie's phone bleeped a text. She jumped and dragged it out of her pocket, feeling her face flush when she saw it was from Felix. *'Gonna be L8 to the yard. Dramas here - down asap. Check Casso for me. Love you babe xxxx'* Hattie smiled, especially at the last bit, it was okay, well not okay, but okay between them. Quickly she flipped a simple text back. *'Me too. No probs. xxxx'* She guessed they would have to be careful with their texts until their relationship was out in the open.

"Felix is gonna be late," she said simply to the others, who were obviously waiting for a response, "dramas apparently, wants us to check Picasso."

"Right - get the kettle on and we'll sort out the chores then."

That week there were big races on at Windsor, Lingfield, Kempton, and Ascot. Ronnie and the syndicate had listened carefully to Max's idea and decided to give it a try. They were going to go for a permutation of combination, accumulator, single and lay bets. The problems before had all been about how to get a bookie to take such big bet on one accumulator. Now, if they spread out their assets carefully - and really used the betting system in all its forms, they could still coin in and pool the money. True some of the bets would yield more than others, but there had to be honour amongst thieves. Everyone had to put what they made into the pot to be divvied up between them. The races that week all had horses that were running out of yards serviced by the local veterinary practice in Fittlebury. Their vet, Alice, was firmly on the hook and would do as she was told in so far as administering what was necessary. They had others in situ at the race-tracks - so blood testing wouldn't be a problem. It should be a very profitable week and one that was much less suspicious as far as the bookies and Jockey Club were concerned and, in the long run, less risky for the punters. It was a win-win situation.

Max was pleased with himself. He couldn't understand why those dumb arses hadn't thought about it themselves, instead of placing such huge amounts all in one go. None so stupid as rich men, he considered, too much coke up their noses and whisky down their throats. He had never gone down that road himself and was smug about it. Max was restless though, he hadn't heard from his old mate Nigel Brown for over a week, despite his promises to keep in touch, and there he was over in Paris, no doubt living the high life on his expenses and not a fucking thing to show for it. His phone kept going to voice mail, and he hadn't responded to any emails. He was going to get a right tongue lashing when he finally made contact.

Another interesting aspect of his life was Roxy. He was enjoying the rekindling of his relationship with her, even if it was pretty one-sided. She was talking about buying a small place down at Fittlebury, had even asked that chubby bloke, who was always dressed up like a country squire, to find her a place. He needed to offload some money. He'd been to see his lawyer, and his accountant - both a pair of shady buggers, but an investment in property seemed a good idea to them. He had his Docklands flat, other properties in London he let out, many business premises, but a place in the country had its attractions - and it might as well be Fittlebury as anywhere. He could keep the screws on Alice, as well as the odd screw with Roxy if she was going to be there - it had its appeal in many ways. After all, he didn't have to live there. He quite fancied some big fuck-off place like Fittlebury Hall itself, that would give them all something to gossip about; they were such snobs around there. He chuckled to himself, envisaging them all doffing their country tweed caps to him in deference - money talked for sure. He picked up his mobile and called for his car to be ready in an hour. Then as an after-thought - he rang Anna, and told her they were going for a drive in the country. Why not - she deserved a treat and she'd enjoy looking at houses with him and perhaps he may run into Alice which would add a little spice to the outing.

By eleven, Felix had pitched up at the yard. If Hattie thought she looked tired, he looked worse. Violet shadows etched under his eyes and he looked waxy pale under his tan. Fiver was euphoric to see him and leapt about, dancing under his feet, until he picked him up for a cuddle. The yard was looking spic and span, not a wisp of hay out of place, and a girl he didn't recognise was busy filling hay nets in the barn. He smiled at her in obvious surprise and Hattie rolled her eyes gesticulating for him to come into the tack room.

"God, how did it go?" she whispered, "you look knackered."

"Don't ask," he sighed, pulling her into his arms. "Oh Hats, I've missed you."

"I've missed you too, but what happened? I've had to tell Leo and Seb of course, because they thought I was leaving, hence the new girl out there."

"Place looks smart enough - who is she?"

"She's a sweetie, a bloody hard worker, Dulcie's sister - Frankie. She's going to live at Laundry Cottage. But what happened with Alice?"

"She went ape, absolutely ape, begging, screaming and finally accused me of having someone else, which I denied, because although I do have you, it's not the reason for us breaking up. I've had to give her till Halloween to move out as we agreed, so we're going have to keep *us* a secret for a while."

"I know darling, and I understand, we'll just have to be really careful. As I said though I did have to tell Seb and Leo - I hope that was okay?"

"Of course, if you hadn't told them, they'd have guessed anyway. But we'd better not let on to anyone else. That goes for the new girl too."

"Right. Where is Alice now?"

"She rang in saying she was going to be late and has stormed off to work now - but God she's in such a temper, she's frightening when she's like that."

A shadow loomed in the doorway and they sprang apart, but it was

Leo who howled with laughter at their embarrassment.

"You'll have to be a bit more careful than this, you two lovebirds."

"I know," grinned Felix, "for the time being anyway. Are you surprised Leo?"

"Just surprised you didn't get together sooner, you pair of idiots," replied Leo. "Seb and I are thrilled but all four of us need to talk and sooner rather than later."

Hattie piped up, "I haven't had a moment to tell you. Seb and Leo are making it legal!"

"What! Congratulations mate!" Felix rushed over, pumping Leo's hand and hugging him. "Fantastic news - when?"

"A Christmas celebration," said a voice behind them.

"Oh Seb, what lovely news!"

"I'm pleased about you two," said Seb. "At long bloody last!"

"We need to keep the news about Hattie and I quiet for a bit," said Felix, "and I mean quiet. Look let's have supper tonight and we can explain."

"I think we know anyway," said Seb, "but I like the idea of supper - Leo darling can you cook?"

"Fucking cheek," exclaimed Leo, "but yes I can. Now, Felix, come and meet the Fabulous Frankie - every yard should have one like her."

"Can't wait," said Felix, winking at Hattie, "lead on dear heart."

Alice felt as though her world was in smithereens. She stormed along the road not caring who was coming in her path or what was around the corner. She bit the heads off all the clients and snapped at Paulene and the girls in the surgery. She was rough with the horses and careless with diagnoses. Her eyes had a wild look and Paulene remarked to Caitlin that she looked as though she were heading for some kind of break-down.

After lunch, Alice pulled her car into High Ridge Woods and cut the engine, giving herself a moment or two to try and think calmly. She reflected that it had not been so long ago that she had stopped here before, when the nightmare of Ernie was just beginning again. Now Felix didn't want her anymore and what was it all about, what was it all for. She had to try and think logically. Last night she'd said to Felix she'd kill herself, end it all, but she knew she wouldn't - she didn't have it in her. She needed to get out, leave, do a runner like she had in Oz, but she needed funds. Up till now Ernie hadn't paid a thing perhaps it was time he did. The threats he'd made were to ruin Felix and her lifestyle, but if she wasn't with Felix then he had no emotional hold over her. He could try to ruin her professionally, but to do that would be to risk his own discovery and blow their cover and she could of course just deny her own part. He may have tenuous proof from Oz, but there was nothing over here, and she was worth more to him in fixing the races than not. No, she could ask him for money, what had she got to lose? She had lost Felix and her chance of stability here, so why not play some odds herself? She wondered, once again, if Felix had met someone else. If he had, she would find out and, irrationally, she plotted how she would dispose of her. The very thought of making plans for the future made her feel better, more stable. She took deep breaths, she had always believed in having strategies. She was far too intelligent to let a simple man like Ernie take her down.

Max's chauffeur pulled up alongside the Carfax in Horsham. He stopped the car and deferentially opened the rear doors for his passengers to alight. Max and Anna stood looking about them, and Max tucked her arm in spurious affection under his as they walked towards Allington's Estate Agents. The Carfax was the epitome of a quaint paved and pedestrianised country town centre. A farmers' market with gaudy stalls selling everything from home-made pies and chutneys to shabby chic littered the square and a plethora of people were milling around browsing and chattering in the weak sunshine. Just opposite the military bandstand, Allington's the estate agents had a corner plot displaying a large number of properties in the window. Max marched towards it, barely glancing at the market traders and pushed his way through the door into the office.

It was true to say that wherever Max went he made an impression and today was no different. He commanded the attention of the office staff as he breezed in the door and a woman in a smart suit hurried over to him.

"Can I help you sir?" she asked. "Was there anything in particular you're looking for?"

Max was quite used to everyone jumping to his attention and gave his most beguiling smile. He fixed her with his startling eyes, "I hope you can, I want to buy a property, preferably in Fittlebury. I understand Mr Allington lives there and I thought he'd be the person to deal with."

"Of course sir, but I'm afraid Mr Allington is at our other office this morning. I'm Elizabeth Collins, his branch manager here, and am sure I can show you anything we have on our books. Why don't you take a seat? Can I offer you and your wife a cup of tea or coffee?"

Max smiled, not disabusing the woman about his companion, "I'd like a coffee, and Anna, for you?"

"Coffee for me too please," Anna said, in her husky Latino voice, "thank you."

The woman called to a young girl at another desk. "Two coffees please Sarah. Now please sit down Mr ...?"

"Goldsmith," said Max, carefully turning his smile up to full beam.

"Now what sort of property were you looking for Mr Goldsmith? Something detached? How many bedrooms would you need?"

Max looked at Anna, "Well we live in London, so it would be to host parties for friends at the weekend really. But I don't like small houses."

Elizabeth smiled apologetically, "The houses in Fittlebury are very sought after and not often on the market, so they tend to fetch a good price. What was your price range?"

Max was enjoying himself. He looked at Anna again, pretending to seek her opinion. "What do you think darling - say five or six?"

Anna, well used to Max's games, smiled secretively, "sounds perfect."

"So," said Elizabeth doubtfully, "five or six hundred thousand? I'm not sure we'll have anything available within that price range."

Max's laugh rang out around the office and Elizabeth looked up, startled from her computer screen. "My dear," he said condescendingly, "I meant five or six million."

Elizabeth flushed, "Of course," she said flustered, "that's quite a different matter."

Sarah brought over their coffee, placing the cups down carefully, flashing a charming smile, "biscuits?" she said brightly.

"No thank you," said Anna, patting her waistline unnecessarily, "coffee is fine."

"Now we do have one or two properties which might fit the bill," said Elizabeth, swinging the screen around for Max to see, "one is a lovely old eight bed-roomed Georgian property on the outskirts of the village. It's a rare opportunity to buy. It has wonderful old cellars but it is in need of renovation as you can see from the photographs. Set in 11 acres, which isn't too huge if you just wanted it for a second house."

"Hmm," murmured Max, scrolling through the photographs, "what a sad old place and it needs a lot of work. Although it does look empty and that appeals to me. I don't think I said, but I'd want to complete within the month."

Elizabeth could hardly contain herself. "That's awfully quick, Mr Goldsmith, to arrange finances and searches," she spluttered, "do you have a property to sell?"

"No," said Max, enjoying himself immensely. "I'll be paying cash and my team will push the sale through, but I don't want any hold ups with people moving out - you get me?"

"Oh absolutely," said Elizabeth, thinking all her birthdays had come at once and dreaming of the commission. "There is another Victorian property which has very little land now, as it was all sold off, just a large landscaped and attractive garden with a games and pool complex, and it is a seven bed-roomed manor house. Extremely grand with many wonderful features. You can see this has been completely renovated and I just love this art-deco bathroom. What do you think?"

Max was intrigued, it was just what he'd been looking for and the smaller garden suited him just fine. "Vacant possession?" he asked, "it looks empty."

"Yes," said Elizabeth, "and it's a good price considering it's been so well restored - ready to move into immediately."

"Can I see it today?" asked Max. "We'd like that wouldn't we Anna?"

"Definitely," purred Anna, playing her part, "as soon as possible I think."

"I'll get the keys," said Elizabeth. "I can take you in my car."

"We'll take you," said Max, "my chauffeur is outside."

Elizabeth managed to hide her delight. "Fine, let me just get my coat then."

CHAPTER 72

The afternoon saw the veterinary practice moving their paraphernalia up to the spanking new surgery. Paulene and Caitlin were in their element, sorting out the new filing cabinets and revelling in arranging their desks and deciding where they wanted their things. The phone engineer was busy installing and hooking up the new lines and rigging up the broadband for the new computers. As a fail-safe Andrew had bought several new machines and would only bring the others up from the old surgery when he was sure the handover was secure. The girls had laughingly taken the piss, calling him an old woman; defensively he'd retorted he couldn't afford to lose any data in the transfer, and they'd thank him if things went wrong. The vets themselves were still busy that afternoon, out on calls, and it was left to the girls to ferry the boxes of records, the updated stationery headed with the new address, and loads of ancillary gear up to the farm. Karen Rutherford, Gary the accountant's wife, who did the weekly books for the practice was holding the fort in the old office whilst they busied themselves moving out. Only a skeleton of stuff was left behind, with the old computers. The desks had been moved the night before and the only other thing that was left until the last, were the drugs, which were still securely locked up, and the vets themselves would be moving them personally later on.

"Wasn't Alice a cow this morning," grumbled Paulene. "I don't know what gets into her sometimes, she had a face like a slapped arse."

"Probably had another row with Felix," surmised Caitlin logically, stacking headed note-paper onto a shelf. "I don't think they're getting on at all well. Mind you, she can't be easy to live with, to be sure."

"No, she's as moody as a storm and I know you think I'm exaggerating, but I'm sure she's up to no good."

"I know you do hun, but in reality what can she be up to? I don't think she's the type to be having an affair now, do you?"

"Who'd want her," said Paulene spitefully, "she's a ball crusher that one. No, something more sinister - but what I don't know. She's sly."

"Go on with you now," smiled Caitlin, "she's hardly Mata Hari is she!"

Paulene had the grace to laugh and threw a magazine at Caitlin. "It's gonna be fab here isn't it? So much more room for us all and I love the decor, it's all so clean and bright."

"Yep it is for sure, and when the diagnostic equipment arrives next week we won't know ourselves - clients arriving left, right and centre and it'll be so nice to have a decent waiting area for them too."

"Exciting?"

"Yes is it. I know Andrew is thrilled, it's given him a new lease of life."

"Well I think you probably did that," said Paulene generously, "this was just the icing on his cake."

"Ah, you're too kind now Paulene," Caitlin said in her husky Irish lilt, "now let's get this coffee machine set up - I love it that Andrew's bought us one of our own!"

"I know! Aren't we spoilt, but I suspect it's more for the clients than for us! When are they coming up with the drugs?"

"This afternoon, Karen's going to stay until 6pm and, by that time, the phones will be switched over to the emergency line and then she'll close up for us. After that it'll be just be bringing up the last bits of stuff tomorrow, then tidying up the old offices and then they'll be ready to be sold."

"I can't believe it!"

"The bloke'll have finished with the alarms this afternoon. The whole security system is so much more sophisticated than before - infra-reds, video cameras the works."

"Well it needs to be really, the drugs alone are worth so much."

"And all this new equipment, although it would be hard to nick, not the most portable after all."

The BT guy interrupted them. "'Excuse me ladies, sorry to disturb you," he grinned, "just to say your phone lines are in and your broad band's set up and you're ready to rock. I'll need to nip down now to the junction box and *jumper* it over."

"Fantastic - that was quick," said Paulene. "I thought it'd take ages."

"Nope, we're like lightening us BT blokes - well some of us," he laughed, "but your phones, that includes the old line will be out of commission for about half an hour while I switch it all over and then, once I do, they'll only work in this new office - okay?"

"Sounds fine - I'll just ring the boss and let him and Karen know down at the old surgery."

"Right, I'll be back in about half an hour to make sure it goes okay"

"I'll have the kettle on for you," smiled Caitlin, "you've been brilliant."

"Nice chap," remarked Paulene as he left, "here give me a lift with this will you?"

Caitlin and Paulene were heaving the desk into position when the door burst open, crashing back against the wall with a bang. They both looked up in surprise to see Alice, with a face like a bruised peach struggling in with a large cardboard box.

"I've just nearly had a bloody accident, some idiot of a bloke in a van," she spat angrily, "these thickos make me sick." She tossed the box down on the floor, "Still, I suppose that's why they do the jobs they do."

"I think that's a bit high-handed. He's a really nice chap and they're all really skilled engineers," said Paulene defensively, "he probably didn't see you."

"Don't be stupid Paulene, a monkey could do their job, and of course he didn't see me, he wasn't looking. Anyway, get me a coffee will you, I'm bushed."

"So are we, as it happens," replied Paulene, "you'll have to get your own coffee. It's not a skilled job - I'm sure you'll cope," she added sarcastically.

Alice scowled, her mouth contorted with bad temper. "I've got to sort the drugs cupboard out. I've brought loads of stuff up in the car and I need you to help me."

"That's fine Alice, but there are ways of asking, you know, and we're not your skivvies - just remember that eh?"

"Whatever," said Alice dryly, "can you just leave what you're doing and lug some of the boxes in *please*, and then I'll go back and get the next lot."

"I'll do it," said Caitlin accommodatingly, shooting Paulene a warning look. "You start stacking and sorting it in the store room as I bring it in."

Paulene glared with steely dislike at Alice, her eyes narrowing dangerously and then deciding to ignore her, turned to Caitlin smiling, "Great idea, I'll take this first box and make a start." She grabbed the box that Alice had dumped on the floor and stomped off to the store room.

Alice watched her go muttering spitefully under her breath, "stupid bitch," and turned away to make herself a coffee.

Caitlin pretended not to hear and carried on putting away the new stationery. "Let me know when you want a hand," she called over her shoulder indifferently, determined not to rise to the bait.

Paulene beavered away crossly in the store room, checking the drugs carefully as she worked. The new drugs' store was so much bigger than the old one. It was purpose built and had no windows, tall, metal shelves lined two sides with ample room for stacking the medication. On the other side was a decent sized fridge housed under a work top, and a large, metal wall cabinet heavily secured for the scheduled drugs. As she worked, Paulene ruminated, remembering how cagey Alice was that day with the Drugs Register and wondered if this was her Achilles heel. She was going to check and double-check the medication as it came in this time, that was for sure.

Outside, Caitlin and Alice slogged backwards and forward with more boxes, dumping them in the main office, before trolling back for more. It was a tedious task and they studiously ignored each other until the last box had been chucked on the floor and Alice took a phone call and declared that she was off to pick up more from the old surgery.

Caitlin watched her go with increasing intrigue - perhaps Paulene was right, there was definitely something peculiar about the phone call, but she couldn't put her finger on what it was. Alice stalked away, bristling like an irritated cat, so that Caitlin couldn't hear, whispering urgently into the phone, her eyes darting from side to side like a trapped animal and then, just as abruptly, she ended the call and said she had to leave. It was certainly curious.

Hattie rolled over, spooning her naked back into Felix. He gave a deep sigh in his sleep, wrapping his arms around her tighter as she wriggled up against him - she had never felt happier, stroking his arm as he cuddled against her. The difference between them was that she couldn't sleep, snuggled up against him, in this their first time in a double bed, her bed, and he, sexually satiated and replete had fallen into a deep slumber. Their love making had been intense, rapturous, and devouring. As though all those pent up months of denial had come to a head and exploded with them hardly being able to keep their hands from each other. The road ahead may be rocky but it was a road they would travel together, united, as a pair. They were lucky to have Laundry Cottage to escape to that afternoon, but even so, when Frankie moved in they would have to be circumspect. Leo and Seb were being brilliant, the clandestine element had sparked their sense of amusement and they adored being part of the deception. So, as long as Felix and Hattie were careful - no-one should know until they were ready.

Hattie moved again, rolling this time face to face and feeling Felix's sweet breath on her face. Her tongue darted out and licked his lips tentatively, then more ardently. He began to stir and responded by pulling her into his arms and kissing her hard, rolling her breast under his hand. Her nipple sprang to attention, hardening under his touch. Hattie moaned, as Felix pushed his tongue between her lips searching and pushing harder. He pulled her head back, kissing her neck, sucking at her ear lobes and moving down towards her breasts. Arching her back, she pushed her boobs forwards forcing them towards his mouth and pushed her body towards his, groping for his cock with her hands.

"God you're gorgeous. Turn over baby," groaned Felix, "on all fours."

Obediently Hattie rolled over, her pert bum perched enticingly in the air. Felix stood above her, his hands exploring her from behind, as she dropped her head down, pushing her bottom up higher. "I'm so ready for you," she pleaded, "so wet and waiting."

"Be patient little one," he laughed, "we've loads of time."

"Purleese don't make me wait, I've waited for so long darling," pleaded Hattie, "now, now, now."

Felix eased himself inside, rocking backwards and forwards, gently at first, then more forcibly, gripping her shoulders with intensity as the passion grew. Hattie tensed and shrieked with excitement, as the hot beating pulse intensified between her legs, finally throbbing into one huge, shuddering orgasm. Felix, barely able to contain himself with excitement, gasped a moment later, floundering on top of her, spent and satiated. They lay together, moulded as one, with love, sweat and pleasure and, this time Hattie did fall asleep; until much later when the boys came home crashing into the cottage and shouting for them to get up.

That night they all sat at the kitchen table stuffing pasta and drinking wine. Hattie and Felix could barely keep their hands, let alone their eyes, from each other, and Leo and Seb looked on with sweet indulgence.

"Now we thought we should have a Christmas Eve do," said Seb, "what do you think?"

"I think it sounds amazing," said Hattie, "where will you have the reception?"

"Here naturally," squealed Leo, who was pissed, "we've loads of room and it'll be whacky!"

"Yeah, but if you have it on Christmas Eve, lots of people won't be able to come," remarked Felix sensibly. "What about the day before, or even Boxing Day? People are funny about Christmas Day and Eve."

"Possibly," agreed Seb, "and of course if we had it on Christmas eve people wouldn't feel they could stay would they?"

"No true," agreed Leo. "What do you think Seb?"

"Bloody Christians," said Seb, "No of course I don't mean it, but it would have been nice, okay then how about Boxing day?"

"Good call, in fact, much better I think," observed Leo, "we'll need to get invitations out as soon as. People get terribly booked up you know, sweetie."

"I would so hate it to be a damp squib," sighed Seb, "can you imagine?"

Leo took his hand affectionately, "How could it be?"

"Listen, I know this is all hearts and flowers, but what am I going to do about Alice?" asked Felix, "She was crazy last night. Mad as."

"She's always been crazy," droned Leo, downing another glug of wine unsympathetically, "she'll just have to deal with it."

"I'm worried she'll do something stupid."

"Of course she won't," assured Seb, stroking Leo's hand, "she's much too switched on and sensible. Hard nosed too, if you don't mind my saying so."

"I just feel so guilty."

"So do I," chimed in Hattie pathetically, " after all, if it hadn't been for me ..."

"Oh for God's, sake shut up the pair of you," said Seb crossly, "before I puke up."

"I don't want to go home tonight," said Felix morosely, "the thought of it makes me feel ill."

"Well don't then," said Seb, "to be honest, I don't understand why you are."

"He has to - for the time being at least," moaned Hattie, "not for long though, just until Halloween. Felix has promised her he'll wait until then."

"You are a tosser Felix, why on earth?"

"Can we not go there?" grumbled Felix, "just suffice it to say it has to be then."

"Well we're supposed to be having a bloody party! We can make it an engagement party now."

"Go right ahead, it'll be a celebration in more ways than one for us all."

"You sure? It could be a fucking disaster, why not just come clean now?"

"Can you just let me do this my way?" asked Felix. "She isn't stable, it gives her more time to come round to the idea."

"Oh have it your own way" expostulated Seb dramatically, "the party goes on, and fabulous it will be, with or without you."

Felix laughed, the old magic sparkling in his eyes as he put his arm around Hattie. "Don't be such a drama queen, it'll be a great party. In fact, we all have so much to celebrate."

"Whatever, you old bugger, just don't fuck my little beauty around anymore," said Seb, beaming fondly at Hattie, "I don't want to wish my life away or be unkind either, but roll on November and bye-bye Alice."

"Hear, hear - I'll drink to that," laughed Leo, "and I don't know about you two but it's time we were going up the stairs to Bedfordshire."

"You old love birds," smiled Hattie, "see you in the morning."

"Night," called Felix as they disappeared, "Sleep well."

"What are you going to do? Are you going back home?" asked Hattie despondently, as she watched them go, knowing what his answer would be but asking anyway.

Felix took both her hands in his and looked her squarely in the eye, "I have to baby, it's not for long. I'm kipping in the spare room and it's just another couple of weeks that's all."

"I know," sighed Hattie wearily, "but it seems like a bloody lifetime."

"Tell me about it, I can't bear it either, but we have to take just one step at a time, and I'm seriously worried that she's going to go off the rails. You should have heard her last night. It was tragic and I felt so dreadful."

"Oh sweetie, I know, it must be awful for you and for Alice. I'm just being selfish, I can't imagine how dreadful it must be for you to have to go back tonight."

"The trouble is, for two pins, I'd stay here, but the cottage is mine, leased in my name and she needs to find her own place. If I move out, that just won't happen. I need to stand my ground."

"Well you know best, darling," said Hattie, "you have to do what is right for you."

"What's right for us," responded Felix firmly, "is that she moves out, it is my house after all. Alice earns much more money than I do, she can easily afford a place of her own. She moved in with me," he explained, "she should be the one to move out."

"Darling, please I don't want to do this," pleaded Hattie, leaning back against him, "you have to do what you think it right and I will back you with whatever you decide."

Felix leant down and kissed her long and hard, his tongue edging between her lips, searching tenderly for hers. Hattie kissed him back hungrily, sexily stiffening her body against him, arching her back and pushing into his thigh. Felix's hand roamed over to her breast, rolling and squeezing. Their kiss became more urgent, their tongues exploring, Hattie raking his hair with her hands, whilst Felix's strayed down over her belly. Gently he pushed her backwards onto the table, the empty glasses rolling dangerously to the edge. Moaning with desire, and pulling off her pyjama bottoms he gazed down at her naked thighs splayed apart before him.

"You are so beautiful Hattie."

In answer, Hattie reached out for him, but very slowly, he bent his head and licked her belly, his tongue working slithering round and round her tummy button, taking little nips with his teeth, until eventually he moved his way down towards her pubic arch and dived down between her legs. Hooking her legs under his shoulders his mouth fastened on her clitoris and began licking and sucking. Hattie squealed with delight as she clutched his hair. Bringing her over and over again to the breaking point, he finally undid his jeans and thrust himself inside her. Madly they rocked on the table top, the glasses smashing unnoticed onto the floor. Oblivious and wrapped up in their crazy passion, they devoured each other like things possessed until their sweating bodies peaked to a shuddering climax, all thoughts of the moral issues crashing as easily as the smashed glasses on the floor.

Alice had moved most of the drugs in relays that afternoon, cleverly sidelining a batch from each consignment until she had a stash of contraband. Barely considering that Paulene might be suspicious. Her distress of the previous evening had hardened into a bizarre and steely resolve. With clouded thinking, Alice had determined that she would maximise the opportunity to filch the drugs and turn the tables on Ernie. As she schemed it gave her a degree of satisfaction; she had a plan, a target and she would get one over on him and it no longer mattered about the outcome or the cost. As she stashed the drugs in the shed at the cottage, carefully hiding the boxes she smiled to herself. Felix may have callously dispensed with her, but she was still a force to be reckoned with, a professional in her own right and, fuck it, she would show him, show them all. This coming week, until she was sorted, she would do as she was bid, but thereafter, watch out Ernie, he could go fuck himself. The thought delighted her - bitterly she knew she had lost Felix but, in the end what did it matter, Ernie had no trump cards without him, nothing to hold over her and she could make serious money - the big bucks like he was making, she would take her share. The tables had turned and the notion was amusing to say the least. Her convoluted thinking spinning in a muddy whirl as she made clumsy irrational plans. She'd decided to be gracious to Felix, let him realise what he was missing, not cling on like some needy puppy; no she would make him see the fabulous woman he was throwing away. Shrugging her shoulders with vigour and resolve, she put her nose in the air and made her way home.

    The cottage was empty and nippy when she arrived. The sweeping chill of autumn crept through the house like the freezer door had been left open. Keeping her coat on she lit and banked up the fire, switching on the electric heaters to alleviate the immediate cold. The Rayburn was slumbering and she bent down to riddle it with gusto, the coals falling through and, dispiritedly, she went outside to fill up the scuttle. There was no sign of Felix, but after all why should she worry, he clearly didn't care about her anymore, and she had to resolve herself to that, but it still hurt nonetheless. She was waiting for the call. The orders from Ernie - and they would surely come. This time she would be ready for him, would blast him a warning shot and see what he said. Her lips curled in a smile. If she couldn't have Felix and the happiness of his security and this cottage, she would have money, and lots of it and to hell with the consequences. She was almost willing Ernie to press her more, she was looking forward to it. To hear the shock in his voice when, for a change, she laid down her terms. Irrationally, she hurled the coke into the scuttle and wondered where the hell Felix had got to, not that she would pretend to care, she had steeled herself to over-ride her emotions but somewhere a little spring of hope still trickled, after all, it wasn't officially over until the fat lady sang and he could bloody well tow the line until Halloween - when their contract was over. She glanced up as a car bumped along the drive, he was home. Tonight she would try another tactic, after all no-one likes to be a loser, but it really didn't seem that important any more.

    Max finished his call with Nigel Brown. He maintained he was closing in and Max could barely contain his excitement that he may at last be on the cusp of finding his daughter. Brown was a tosser, and Max was fairly certain that he was stringing things out as much as he could, but in the scheme of things if he found her, then it would be worth it. Max drew in a lungful of breath and forced himself to be calm. The dream of his daughter was worth waiting for, and wait he would. He leant back in his chair, throwing his head back and spreading his fingers tautly on the desk, watching the screens of the punters in the club. Anna sat quietly filing her nails beside him. He leant over and whispered in her ear, gesticulating at the monitor. She moved off quietly to deal with the situation, a girl not quite performing as he would like, and he took a long slug of the amber nectar on his desk thinking about the house they had been to view that very afternoon. It was perfect. Ostentatious, outrageous and delightful. He loved it. Not too much of a garden, but a decent pool house, with a Jacuzzi and games room with vignettes of tasteful fountains and ponds and big enough to put up a marquee if he needed it. The reception rooms were all oak panelled with massive medieval fireplaces, and large enough to have a grand piano and a billiard table. There was the obligatory status symbol four oven Aga in the kitchen that every country gaff had but this one was not some tired old relic but almost brand new and came with a traditional matching stove - not that he did much cooking. The bedrooms themselves were something else and the master suite had the most ostentatious art deco bathroom he had ever seen. The house was perfect. Perfect as H. E Bates would have described and he'd put in a cash offer much to the obvious and lascivious glee of Elizabeth Collins.

The one thing, though, was that he hadn't told Roxy. Normally he'd have been on the blower and spilled the beans straight away but for some reason he held back - let the whole thing go through and be a surprise. The property sat on the edge of Fittlebury. It was ridiculously expensive in the scheme of things, and yet he liked it and he had to lose the money, so why not? He wanted to bathe in that art deco bath, entertain in that house. Roxy'd be miffed but she'd love the place and moreover he fancied getting her in that tub. Deep down though there was another reason - he wanted a proper house, an established base, not the cold clinical flat in Docklands, somewhere with character and warmth where you could sling your boots in the corner, put your feet on the sofa and watch a movie, ready for the day when he brought his daughter home.

Meditatively, he took a sip of his whisky, his eyes roaming to the monitors and watched Anna with interest as she sashayed over to the gaming table and gently laid her hand on the offending girl's shoulder. The girl turned around, surprised, and looked questioningly into Anna's serious face mesmerised by those dark and beautiful eyes. She leant forward and whispered in the girl's ear, all the time patting her arm and smiling coquettishly at the punter. Max watched the girl quail visibly. Anna straightened up, signalling for a drink to be brought over to client and moved quietly away. Max nodded his head in approval. Anna was becoming a great asset to him. He must make sure he took care of her.

CHAPTER 73

Despite the tension at his cottage with Alice, where the atmosphere rocked with more highs and lows than a ship on high seas, Felix had never been happier. He had never been one to will his life away, but the couple of weeks leading up to Halloween couldn't come quicker as far as he was concerned. At least he was away for four days with Hattie when they were off to Aldon International doing a CIC*, and he couldn't wait. By contrast, the atmosphere on the yard was sparkling. Frankie was a diamond, worked liked a steam train, never moaned, and had fitted in like the last piece in a jigsaw. Leo and Seb were like a pair of gloves - perfectly matched and went everywhere together. They'd been on the phone to all and sundry asking them to the engagement party at the end of the month and what was going to be a small Halloween do, was turning into a mammoth, masked fancy dress bash and planning the costumes was a constant talking point. Leo, with his dark hair, was a perfect candidate for a gothic vampire, and Seb was debating between a man eating shark costume or an enormous inflatable pumpkin. Hattie and Felix were leaning towards a Harry Potter theme - Hattie as Bellatrix Lestrange and Felix as Severus Snape, which Seb immediately declared was *so last year*. Frankie was coming as a sexy mummy scantily wrapped in gory bandages, and Dulcie and Nancy hadn't yet made up their minds. Naturally Roxy had wangled an invitation for herself and Max. Farouk seeing another possible angle for the storyline, convinced Seb to invite the cameras, temptingly saying the production company would pay for the booze, but in truth Seb, ever the star fucker didn't need much persuasion. The guest list was growing like a weed, from the dressage fraternity, to the eventers, to darling Dougie and the Hickstead crew, and, of course, all of the locals - it was going to be one messy party.

It was only Alice whose behaviour became stranger and more erratic as the end of the month approached. Her moods swung between clinging onto Felix, begging him to change his mind, to disparaging and humiliating him, from screaming hysterically, to coldness which would freeze a leg of lamb at twenty paces. Fiver cowered every time she came near him and slunk off to his bed, shrinking onto his belly in submission. Felix felt much the same. She was terrifying when she was in full angry flow, hurling physically and verbally whatever was in her path, and then breaking down pathetically the next. Felix tried to reason with her, but she was beyond reason and rationale and he wondered how on earth she managed to hold down her job. But her mood swings and bad temper carried her though at work and it was evident that it was only with him that she wheedled and broke down and even more he longed for it to be over. He continued to say that, after Halloween, she must move out and it was over between them. Alice said she was making plans, but refused to say what they were and Felix, afraid of pushing her too far for fear of sparking her off into more dangerous histrionics, kept his counsel and backed off.

For Alice, she'd fulfilled the last instructions from Ernie down to the letter. No doubt he and his cronies were now coining in the money, but she'd told him that she would no longer play ball without being paid off. She'd made it clear she was leaving Felix at the end of the month. Ernie would no longer have a hold over her, it made no difference what he did or said, she had no fear of exposing him and that snake Max. The hysteria in her voice was unapparent to her, but had rung alarm bells for Ernie and he'd placated her smoothly, soothing her and saying, of course, they would cut her in on the deal - after all, why not, she had been a good contact for them. Alice was satisfied. From now on, she'd be paid a proper amount for her services - if not - she'd bubble the lot of them. She'd felt empowered, in charge and superior to them all - low lives the lot of them.

Ernie was concerned. He rang Ronnie, who in turn rang Max. Max made an impromptu visit to the yard with Roxy, hoping he might see Alice. But she was nowhere to be seen and he pumped Felix for information. He was curiously reticent and reserved about her which had Max's antennae bristling. On the alert, he decided to drop into the cottage whilst Roxy was having her lesson. Alice's Toyota was parked skew-whiff outside. The back door was open and he stepped quietly into the kitchen - there was no sign of her and he stood for a moment, tempted to call out but decided on the element of surprise. Softly creeping through the sitting room and, taking the stairs quietly he came upon her in the bedroom.

"Hello Alice," he said gently, his voice barely audible.

She spun around angrily, her eyes flashing madly, "What the fucking hell!"

"Just thought I'd pop in and say hello," Max said easily, "I hear you've been talking to my pal Ernie."

"What the fuck's it got to do with you?" spat Alice furiously, her eyes mad "I'm finished with that shit Felix and I'm moving out of here - so I don't care what happens to your lot and you can play my game now or I blow the whistle on the lot of you."

"I see," said Max dryly, his eyes glinting dangerously, "are you sure that's what you want?"

Alice laughed manically, her voice high pitched and taut, running her hands through her hair she screamed, "I've so had it with you;" picking up a clock and hurling it at him, "you'll play my game now, you stupid fucking wanker, and do as I say."

Ducking the hurling missile and stepping backwards, Max considered her coldly for a moment. "Alice, do you think you are quite well? You seem a bit ... deranged to me."

"How fucking dare you," Alice yelled, picking up everything within her grasp and lobbing it at him, "get out and get out now. Go back to your cronies and tell them I'm calling the shots."

"Okay, okay," Max said calmly, "have it your own way. Whatever you say."

He moved backwards carefully one step at a time out of the room as she threw things haphazardly after him, screaming and yelling at him as he went.

As Max beat his retreat and left the cottage, Alice slumped on the bed crying. She tore her hands wretchedly through her hair, determined to get herself back together before she had to go back to work. Max walked regretfully back to the yard, poor Alice had, without a doubt, lost the plot, that much was clear. Such a pity in one so young, clever and beautiful. She was a loose cannon, that was for sure.

At the mill, work was continuing splendidly. The spa barn was almost finished now and Alan was impressed that he had cobbled it all together in record time. Even the pool was finished, sparkling in turquoise delight and surrounded by ancient timbers and shabby chic. The mill too was romping along. The shell was complete which was a Godsend before the onset of the winter really set in, as the innards could be finished in the dry and even English Heritage were impressed. It was amazing how much money talked. The driveway was very smart, the old cinder track had been replaced with tarmac and widened too to provide more car parking. The mill wheel was returned after vast expense and was being re-erected alongside the pond and its vast glass windows gave surreal views outside. Inside was still rough, the old floors being renovated, but the blue print was clear - it was going to be startling in its conception. Aiden was thrilled and his dreams were all coming to fruition - Farouk captured every moment on film, alongside with Roxy and her endeavours - it would make marvellous television. Aiden was preparing a superlative menu for his opening night which was to be New Year's Eve and Chrissie had invited more celebs than a night in Cannes. Staffing was coming along nicely and had been farmed out to a local agency. Chrissie would be in on the final interviews at the beginning of December and they allegedly had a plethora of candidates.

Aiden was determined that, once the new place was up and running, he and Roxy would split - amicably, of course, for the sake of Delphinium and Stephanotis, but they couldn't carry on as they were. Chrissie was putting on more pressure although he was beginning to wonder if she wasn't as much of a ball breaker as Roxy was. Did it really matter about Roxy, he thought, at least he knew where he stood with her? Once again, his little dalliances seemed to fizzle out to a damp squib and he would realise the grass was not really greener on the other side. Oh well, time would tell, nothing like putting your head in the sand. Meanwhile he decided to push on to the New Year and Chrissie was a superlative organiser - he would be stupid to let her go now.

Roxy was content. Max was constantly such a delightful distraction, as he had been on so many previous occasions. She did love him, of course she did, but live with him, no definitely not. Aiden was with Chrissie pro temps - but it was a phase - it would pass. It always did. Take each day as it came and enjoy the day, that was her motto.

Max was closeted with Ronnie, Ernie and the others. The hour was late and the air was thick with smoke. Anna whisked discreetly around them with enormous drinks, whilst luscious girls were waiting in the back wings to service their needs. Max reported back on what he had found. The others were studiously serious, shaking their heads sadly.

"I'm afraid she's lost the plot - crackers," Max said, with an edge to his voice, "it's a pity but there it is. No reasoning with her."

"Christ," moaned Ernie, "she was always highly strung, whatya think? Back off or what?"

Ronnie cradled his glass. "What a fuck up, just when we had other plans. But in my experience we are best to cut our losses. These crazy chicks never come right, she'll always be nuts, and we'll never be able to trust her."

"I tend to agree," said Ernie, swigging back his drink. "She's flaky."

"She might just be going through a tough time and come right," suggested Max sensibly, "worth giving it a shot?"

"Nope, she's gotta be dumped," grumbled Ronnie ,signalling to Anna to refill his glass, "she's a fruitcake, we can't risk it."

"I agree," sighed Ernie reluctantly, "a pity, as she's a pretty thing, but if she's lost the plot we can't afford for her drop us in the shite can we?"

"No, of course not," agreed Max, "What then?"

Ronnie grinned at him, "Your baby I think Max - you do this best don't ya?"

Ernie laughed, "Anyway Maxie - you need to prove your worth, you sort it out. Now that's decided I don't want to think about it any more - where's the sport?"

Max sighed and glanced at Anna who was hovering on the periphery and immediately moved to bring in the girls. He felt sad, he never liked this side of his business although it had to be done - there were no options. "No problem, just leave it to me, but probably the end of this month."

"Cool - I'll not contact her again," agreed Ernie, "she can sweat until then."

"I'm glad that's sorted," said Ronnie, "we've plenty of others in our pocket. We don't need some crazy bimbo rocking our boat, do we? Max, you're so good at dealing with this stuff."

"My pleasure," preened Max conceitedly, "now come on, let's forget it, leave the problem to me and you enjoy the rest of the evening. Ah well done Anna." He stood up as Anna ushered the ladies in and he made a move outside to telephone Terry, he might as well make the arrangements for Alice's demise now, before he had second thoughts.

CHAPTER 74

The surgery had now fully moved over to the new premises and Andrew and Oli had offered Theo a permanent position as an assistant with them. He was delighted as were the other members of staff - all that was except Alice, who was miffed to say the least and saw it as a personal slur on her that they had taken on another vet. Both Oli and Andrew were beginning to agree with Paulene and think that Alice definitely had some inter-personal difficulties which she managed to hide most of the time, but of late were bubbling more and more to the surface. Theo made no comment but it was fairly certain that he had noticed as had the others. The clients no longer requested Alice to call, preferring one of the other vets, and that was never good news. The partners knew that they would have to deal with it, but they were both reluctant, as Alice could be so aggressive when she was challenged. It was not a happy situation. Paulene had gone to Andrew with her suspicions about the missing drugs, but she had no proof and there was no paper trail and so he was impotent. They had no idea that her relationship with Felix was over and had all been invited and were looking forward to the fancy dress Halloween party. Alice herself was hysterically elaborating on her own outfit and it was the only light moment together when discussing what they would all be wearing. Theo had nobly offered to be first on call and the veterinary hospital as second, so they could all have a wild uninhibited time. None of them intended not to be going large at such a splendid local occasion.

At Aplington's two very favourable sales were going through. Max Goldsmith was happily purchasing his pretentious residence and Roxy Le Feuvre was buying her barn conversion, each unbeknown to the other. Colin was delighted - big fat commissions on either side and apparently with no hitches to boot. He liked cash sales, with no chains. smooth transactions and no hassle. The day that Max and Roxy came into his life gave him a nice little packet of commission. The ostentatious place that Max had bought was not everyone's cup of tea but he had bought it without a backward glance, and had only been to see it once. It would be done and dusted before Christmas and that was just the kind of conveyance that

Colin liked. As for Roxy the barn had hardly hit the market before she'd snapped it up. The vendors hadn't wanted to move, but Colin had persuaded them it was in their best interests to vacate quickly and pocket the money in the dodgy economic climate. It should prove to be a healthy Yule tide.

Meanwhile Grace's ankle was mending quickly considering, and little Archie was not so little, putting on the weight in leaps. They had even coerced Grace's mum to baby sit for the grand party, with an agitated Grace feeling guilty but excited in equal measure. She'd made simple yet effective costumes and even Colin had to admit it was fun dressing up. They were looking forward to the evening - it seemed ages since they'd been out.

Roxy was in two minds what to wear. She didn't have the imagination to design or choose something herself, so dispatched Suzanne to find a suitable outfit for the party. She came back with several and laid them out for Roxy to inspect. Considering them all, Roxy chose the Sultry Witch Outfit, a combination of a short rah-rah skirt and a bra top with fish net sleeves and a flamboyant witch's hat both trimmed with masses of ostrich feathers. Suzanne said it just needed long black leather boots and fish net tights. Roxy preened in front of her huge mirror - it did look good - leaving a good expanse of bare thigh, midriff and bosom on show. Just how she liked it. The costume even had a witch's broom trimmed with ostrich feathers - it was sumptuous.

"Perfect Suzanne" Roxy murmured appreciatively, licking her pink tongue over her lips "just right for the occasion."

"Good" said Suzanne sycophantically, laboriously gathering up the other costumes to take back "I thought this would be the one." Thinking to herself how supremely tarty it was and how very well it suited Roxy.

"What's this?" asked a voice from the door "You look amazing."

"Aiden!" cried Roxy "What are you doing home?"

"Obviously you weren't expecting me" said Aiden "Why are you all dressed up?"

"Don't be thick" snapped Roxy "this is my outfit for the Halloween party."

"Right, very nice" approved Aiden "a bit different to mine" he laughed "just wait till you see it!"

"You're not invited" shrieked Roxy hurling the witch's hat at him "you don't even know the boys."

"Farouk wants me to come" smiled Aiden "so come I will, and Chrissie too. What d'ya think about that my angel?"

"Bastard" hissed Roxy glaring at him "I hate you sometimes."

"No you don't" grinned Aiden "love and hate are close bed mates my darling don't you think?"

"Just piss off Aiden."

"Don't you want to know what I'm coming as?"

"No, I fucking don't" snarled Roxy "Like I care."

"Fair enough" laughed Aiden "It is a masked ball after all, do you think you'll recognise me?"

"I won't be looking. So dream on."

"Well" he grinned looking her up and down "I'll know exactly what you look like darling eh?"

"GET THE FUCK OUT!" screamed Roxy tearing off the costume and hurling it onto the floor, with Suzanne sighing resignedly and picking up the debris.

Max too was wondering about his costume. He was not taking Anna but asked her to organise his ensemble. He gave her absolute instructions about what he wanted and as always she obliged him in every detail. For Max this would be a difficult night and he had chosen to be the Plague Doctor; the *dottore della peste* wearing the hideous mask and blighted beak associated with the ancient profession. His cold heart was prepared and he was shielded behind the repugnant mask. He might accompany the most sexy woman on the night, but he himself was intent upon an evil task.

Aiden had chosen for himself the guise of the Grim Reaper and for Chrissie she would be a red devil, a hot demon to hang on his arm to mingle amongst the ghouls and ghosts. If Roxy's costume was anything to go by, they should all compliment each other perfectly. Farouk was ironically to be a white faced zombie streaked with blood - all good clean fun and ready for the camera. Aiden was chuffed, Roxy had looked damned sexy in that outfit - it would make startling TV, and a nice slant on village life. He himself felt empowered in the Grim Reaper costume, it was a potent feeling and one he liked. He knew that Max was coming and wanted to get one over on him and thought that no outfit he sported could possibly as commanding as his own.

Oli and Theo were coming as zombies. Theo was on call, so no alcohol could be consumed but it didn't detract from the fun, he was high on life. They'd gotten plastic axes slicing through their heads and realistic shadowy stage make up which was hugely lifelike and coupled with tee shirts squirted with stage blood they looked amazing. It was a real boys outing and they were leaving women behind hoping to pull big time on the night and Theo hoped for zero crisis on the night to spoil his fun.

Dougie had rung Seb to find out what he should wear. Seb as usual was hopeless and had no idea at all and suggested he rang Felix. Conversely Felix had no idea either, but did offer Dougie a bed for the night which he'd readily accepted. Afterwards Felix wondered where he would put him, his cottage or Laundry? Where was Alice going to be, the subject was tender and still not sorted. Every time he tried to talk to her, she waved him away either loftily or tearfully depending on her mood. She refused to discuss anything with him further saying that he had promised to wait until the end of the month. It was as if she was in complete denial, and the more he pressed her for her plans, the more she closed up. They'd slept in separate rooms since Weston and they hardly spoke unless it was to argue.

Come 23rd October Hattie and Felix disappeared to Aldon International in relief, gladly leaving behind them the awful situation with Alice and a furore of preparation for the party. Alice was becoming stranger and stranger and Seb and Leo were whizzing about organising catering, apple bobbing, Mummy wrap and all the usual rubbish of Halloween. At Aldon they spent time in between Felix competing, in bed in the Luton luxuriating in each other, marvelling anew in each other's bodies and not wanting to go home to reality on 27th. The rain spattered on the lorry roof and the windows steamed up, loved up and happy they spent four days in a hazy cocoon of euphoria and Felix brought home a 4th for his sponsors and a several firsts for his lover.

Back home plans were escalating for the party - Seb had gone totally over the top with the decorations and ordered a truck load of pumpkins from Mrs Gupta in the village shop and sourced masses of spooky ideas from the internet - all of which were to be a closely guarded secret until the evening. He was like a kid, squirreling away packages as they arrived from E-bay and Amazon in the garden shed and tapping the side of his nose irritatingly when anyone asked him what he was up to. A mammoth delivery of food and booze was expected from Tesco and Leo and Seb had agreed that they would not come to the yard on the day of the party but would stay at the cottage and get everything ready. Hattie and Felix would come over when they had finished up at the stables and help with the last minute stuff and change into their outfits there.

"What are you going to do about Alice?" asked Leo "is she coming to the party?"

"Christ no" exclaimed Felix "at least I don't think so. We hardly speak, so why would she?"

"Look buddy, not my business, but don't you think it would be a good idea to get the showdown over and done with before the night?"

"I've seriously tried" moaned Felix "but she just keeps repeating *not until Halloween* what else can I do?"

"I think you should have it out with her before the party, find out when she's actually planning to move out. Stop shoving your head in the bloody sand Felix."

"I know, but she's really crazy at times you've no idea. It's impossible she simply clams up on the subject."

"Well it's only the day after tomorrow, so you'd better do something mate - we don't want her fucking up our evening do we?"

"No, of course not. I'll definitely speak to her tomorrow."

"Make sure you do" warned Leo "otherwise it could end in disaster."

Roxy was in her element, she loved parties, especially ones where you could dress outrageously. It was going to be an interesting evening with Max and Aiden there and little mistress Chrissie, plus the cameras. Farouk had booked all of the rooms in an exclusive, small and, the proprietors had assured him, discreet hotel, although how they could all be discreet dressed as they were was an understatement, but at least they would be masked; although that was about the only bit of her that would be unrevealed Roxy thought carelessly. Anyway she suspected that Farouk wanted the publicity and no doubt would tip off the press, and if he didn't she would ensure Suzanne did. The sleeping arrangements would be interesting too, who would be sleeping with whom by the end of the evening she wondered.

Max was pre-occupied. His sinister costume hung in his office like a ghoul, the grotesque mask with the huge pointed beak and glass eyes leering at him from the hanger. He shuddered, it gave him the creeps. Everything was prepared, Terry was primed and ready for his instructions and now it was a waiting game. The cover of the party provided excellent camouflage whilst he could oversee the job. A necessary evil, he glanced up at the costume and thought how fitting it was for him, he couldn't have asked for better.

Alice was at home early, she had the serious jitters. Ernie had agreed to her terms and said Max would be in touch shortly about handing over her dosh although so far she'd heard nothing from him. She couldn't believe her luck, it had been that simple; if she had to be involved in their filthy game, she would at least be rich. Felix was agitating to have her gone, but she was planning one last ditch attempt at reconciliation. She'd chosen her outfit with great care and she would go with him to the party, hanging it out to the very last with him, and then make her play. He'd been away for the last few days, so she hadn't seen him and last night he'd come home very late and she'd missed him. This evening she must try and talk to him, rationally, calmly and without losing her temper. She sat on the edge of the bed wringing her hands together rocking gently. Once she had met Max and he'd handed over the money she would feel better, feel that she had the upper hand again. Now she felt like a fragile china ornament, as though she could break at any moment. The more she willed herself to be nice to Felix the nastier she was with him, as though some inner demon spurred her on to be spiteful. It was no wonder they had grown apart. She stood up and looked in the wardrobe, hidden at the back was her costume for the party. It was quite beautiful and it really suited her, the woman in the shop had said so and it was so appropriate. Sighing, she touched the beautiful white flowing satin and the exquisite lace bodice, the shimmering fabric seemingly opalescent in the changing light - it was the perfect wedding dress. How could he resist her in it - she was certain he would fall at her feet. She placed the delicate lace veil with its wreath of white roses around her head and admired herself in the mirror, her shining eyes blinded with delusion.

CHAPTER 75

Max picked up his phone and asked Terry to pop into see him. He needed to finalise plans for tomorrow evening, he didn't want any slip ups. Things happened differently down in the country and more questions would be asked about the demise of a lady vet, than some old slapper from the smoke who ended up in the drink. The foul curled beak and leather mask of the *dottore della peste* smirked at him from the back of the door like some dreadful omen.

Anna popped her head around the door and asked if there was anything he needed.

"Give my shoulders a massage will you, I feel really tense."

"Of course" she said moving behind him and stroking his hair and knowing better than to ask the reason why "there, just relax" her hands began to knead his knotted muscles "that better?"

"Hmm, yes" sighed Max rotating his head "I need to know I can trust you Anna."

"You know you can Max."

"Can I?" He reached up and grasped her hand "You do mean that don't you?"

Anna kissed the top of his head "Always Max" she murmured, trying not to wince "of course you can." She felt his body relax underneath her free hand "let me pleasure you."

"No, just rub my shoulders, that's all I want."

A sharp rap and the door opened, Anna jumped and Max looked up, Terry strode in "You wanted me boss?"

"Terry, yes, sit down, I just need to make sure you're sorted for tomorrow night."

"Do you want me to go" asked Anna "is it business?"

"No need, just keep massaging" said Max, his eyes closing with pleasure

"I've got a couple of good blokes on the job boss. We've got our costumes and we'll be fine. No-one will suspect a thing. Easy as and let's face it we've done plenty before."

"I'm sure Terry but just be careful, it's gotta look like an accident."

Terry laughed a full bellied throaty twenty a day snort "Can you just leave it to me boss - me and the boys, we're hardly amateurs."

"Okay - tell me I'm an old woman" laughed Max shrugging Anna off "go on and do it well Terry and don't tell me any more. Enough now Anna eh?"

Anna and Terry bowed out simultaneously - each with a different mindset, whilst Max rocked back on his chair feeling somewhat mollified and more determined to enjoy his evening than he had five minutes before.

Hattie was sick of cutting up pumpkins. Sick of the smell of them and sick of the slimy seeds inside which stuck to her hands like a sticky mess. Leo on the other hand was having a fantastic time and had obviously lost his vocation in life. His creativity with *how to carve a pumpkin in as many ways as possible* was beyond belief, and he could have made his own Youtube video or presented Blue Peter he was becoming so adept at saying and *here's one I made earlier*. Hattie had to admit they were brilliant, he'd done the normal traditional grinning teeth type but others had hats and glasses, hair and some he'd drawn spooky images on, so that when they were lit inside they gave out ghostly silhouettes - it was all really clever.

"You've done brilliantly with these Leo, they're amazing!"

"You've not seen the half yet"

"Oh God, don't say there are more pumpkins, we must have done fifty already" groaned Hattie rolling her eyes "how many more ways can you do a pumpkin?"

"I'm not going to spoil it for Seb, he's worked so hard designing it all but the house and the garden are going to look pretty awesome let me tell you - he's terribly creative you know."

"Well judging by these pumpkins you both are."

"Not half as much as him, I just do as I'm told and work from the templates, he's the really artistic one. He's gone well over the top this time."

"Blimey, brought out the drag queen in him has it?"

Leo laughed "and the rest, but it is our engagement party, so let him eat cake, that's fine with me."

"Me too, 'cos it's a celebration for me and Felix as well. I don't know how he's lived with Alice these last few weeks. I think she's gone off her rocker."

"I think he's nuts to have pandered to her. He should have stuck to his guns and finished with her when you came back from Weston - all this bloody waiting until Halloween crap."

"I know, but he's such an old softie and I think she frightens him a bit, she can be really aggressive when she goes into one. Apparently he's made it clear that it's over but she's insisting they wait until tomorrow - why I don't know. He hasn't even be able to find out if she's got anywhere to go."

"I said he'd got to have it out with her before the party." said Leo firmly "I'm not cutting up all these fucking pumpkins for there to be any bad vibes tomorrow."

Hattie laughed "Well I'll drink to that, he'll be back in a minute, he's just at a sponsors' meeting at the Parker-Smythes' gaff. Charles wants to a pow-wow apparently."

"Sounds ominous" said Leo "not trouble?"

"No, I don't think so, they just want a résumé of the season - an excuse to have a get together for drinkies probably, although they are all coming tomorrow."

"I don't know anyone who isn't coming" laughed Leo "everyone I've spoken to is, I just hope we've got enough food and booze."

"I thought the production company was paying for the booze?"

"It is, but you know what Seb's like - we've got a whole load more in. People always bring booze too don't they?"

"What is Seb wearing - has he decided?"

"He has, it's amazing" Leo stifled a laugh "he looks absolutely ... ridiculous!"

"You'll have to tell me now" said Hattie "I can't wait to find out."

"It's a huge grey shark costume which goes over all of him like a massive johnny, very life like, and it's got legs hanging out of it's mouth like it's just swallowed someone. Seb can only just see out! His arms go where the fins are - he looks a right knob! But it is hilarious!"

Hattie laughed, "Well it'll be different that's for sure. You still going as a vampire then?"

"One of us has to be sensible, and moreover be able to see what we're doing." grinned Leo "personally I can't see Seb staying in that suit for long - he'll boil."

"Oh yea of little faith" said a voice behind them "just you wait and see."

"Right master, we've cut up all the bloody pumpkins, what do you want us to do now?" asked Hattie "what other little gems have you got lined up."

"It's so exciting" squealed Seb like a toddler at playgroup "I've got all the usual bats and spider webs and stuff for indoors, but I've made some ghosts and ghouls as well - it's amazing what you can get off E-bay!"

"The mind boggles" said Leo "when are these decorations going up?"

"Not till tomorrow, I want some in the garden, but if it pisses with rain, they'll have to come indoors."

"The forecast is okay."

"I don't trust the weather forecasters - take that Michael Fish." said Seb waving his hand expansively in the air and looking up at the sky.

"That poor bloke - he'll never live it down will he and you probably weren't even born then."

"Makes no difference - he still got it wrong and he went down in history."

"Oh for heaven's sake" exploded Leo "you are becoming more eccentric as time goes on."

"I know duckie and that's why you love me!" grinned Seb plonking a sloppy kiss on Leo's cheek "and we're getting married!"

"Saints preserve me - what have I done - I've unleashed a monster!"

"Definitely all ready for Halloween!"

Felix had stopped off from his meeting at Nantes Place. He needed to talk to Alice. Her Toyota was in the driveway when he pulled in. Bracing himself, he went in, this was not going to be pleasant but he definitely had to man up now and sort it out once and for all.

Opening the kitchen door he was surprised to hear soft music playing and the smell of home cooking. The house was warm and welcoming, something which it hadn't been in months. Suspicious that Alice was entertaining he crept into the sitting room.

"Hi" he called "Alice?"

"I'm upstairs" she called back "in the bath."

"Okay"

There was no way he was going upstairs, he'd just have to wait for her to come down. He went back into the kitchen and made a coffee, glanced into the oven and saw a casserole bubbling nicely. She must be expecting someone. He was pleased, perhaps she was moving on, and in that case their conversation wouldn't last long. He took the coffee back into the sitting room and settled down to wait. The minutes ticked by, half an hour came and went, still no sign of her.

Growing impatient he called "Alice?" No answer this time. "Alice?"

A sudden chill of fear that she might have done something stupid washed over him, he ran up the crooked stairs, two at a time and burst into the bathroom - it was empty. He pushed into their old bedroom afraid of what he might find.

Alice was lying naked on the bed, her arms and legs sprawled open, her bush shaved and her body oiled to perfection. She had put on make-up and looked like a painted doll splayed out on the quilt.

"You took your time," she purred, "I've been waiting for you."

"Alice, oh my God," spluttered Felix, "for Christ's sake get dressed, what are you doing?"

"Waiting for you lover. What's the matter don't you fancy me any more?"

"Alice, I've told you, time and again, it's over between us. There is no going back for me, not like this, not like any way."

"Don't be a silly boy Felix, you don't mean it, of course you don't. You've just been playing games, and of course I forgive you."

Felix couldn't speak, it was as though all the previous conversations they'd ever had had never taken place. Her painted face was like a mask, he shook his head sadly. His instinct told him to leave, but he had to make it clear, had to tell her there would never be any going back, no matter what she did or said.

He sat gently on the bed and drew the duvet over her "Alice you have to listen to me, as hard as it is, I don't love you, I haven't for a long time now. I am sorry but there it is. I can't make it any plainer. I've gone along with this idea of yours that we wait until after Halloween but it makes no difference how long we wait, I don't want to be with you. I want you to be strong and find yourself a place to live. You have a good job and career, you are young and beautiful and you will find someone else, but not me. I am trying to be totally honest with you."

Alice mouth twitched into a little smile "You are of course just saying that, you don't mean a word of it. I know I've been unkind to you at times but I promise that will change now, and we are going to be very rich - there's something you don't know."

Felix sighed "I don't know what you're talking about being rich, but it's not about money, or you being unkind to me. How many times do I have to tell you, I am not in love with you any more, I simply don't want to be with you. I know that's brutal but that's how I feel - I can't be any plainer than that."

Alice rocked back and forth in the bed "I know you don't mean it Felix. You'll change your mind come tomorrow night - just wait and see."

Felix groaned in exasperation "Alice I won't, in fact, I'm gonna pack some stuff and move into Laundry Cottage for a while until you've found somewhere to go. You won't be able to stay here. I saw Mark Templeton tonight, the tenancy for this cottage is tied up with the stable yard, and that's in my name. It's actually not down to me, the estate won't let you live here."

Alice smiled simply at him "See you tomorrow" she said and continued her slow rocking.

Felix sighed and threw some stuff into a holdall, glad that he had left Fiver in the car. He hurried downstairs, turned off the oven before he left and put down the lock on the door. What else could he do or say? He couldn't have been more blatant, but she was in complete denial.

Alice swayed gently on the bed upstairs humming quietly to herself. She was confident that when she rocked up at the party tomorrow night in her beautiful wedding dress, he would change his mind and sweep her off her feet just like he had in the old days.

CHAPTER 76

The day of the party was sunny and crisp, with a startlingly bright blue sky. In contrast the darkened bare branches of the trees stood trees starkly etched with just a few straggling leaves like ragged crows' wings left hanging on for grim death before they finally tumbled for the winter.

Laundry Cottage was a positive whirl of activity. Hattie and Felix had long since gone to work and left Seb and Leo in charge of the preparations. A white van had arrived early that morning stacked high with crates of booze, compliments of Farouk. He certainly hadn't stinted and they would have to go some to drink this lot dry, and coupled with what Seb had already bought they certainly would not go short in the alcohol department. They lugged it into the kitchen and began to set it out. The food was being delivered after lunch, and only needed to be pre-heated. The fun bit was finishing the decorations. Seb trundled off into the shed and came back armed with boxes, piling them onto the kitchen table.

"Fuck me" said Leo aghast "what's all this lot?"

"Just wait and see" said Seb "we are just gonna have the spookiest stuff ever!"

"Right" grinned Leo "let's open the box then shall we?"

Seb rummaged in the boxes tossing skulls, fabric, bones, bats, spiders, polystyrene blocks and all sorts on the table "Let's get cracking" he declared "just watch these babies come to life!"

Three hours later and Leo was amazed. Seb had created the most ethereal spectres from tattered net fabric floating with frightening skull faces from the ceiling in the sitting room and hallway. In the garden a small trail of pumpkins led to the woodland where another set of eerie figures were wedged in the trees, their hollowed out faces ghostly and sinister. He painted the polystyrene slabs to resemble tombstones with spooky epitaphs and planted then haphazardly in the garden alongside the path, tossing skulls and bones and more pumpkin faces. Tonight Seb explained they would put tea-lights in the pumpkins and the skulls to bring them to life, so it would look like you were arriving in a graveyard. Black plastic bats swung from the trees and the ceilings inside with plastic cobwebs sprayed everywhere. Laundry Cottage looked sensational - Seb was bursting with pride.

"Darling" said Leo proudly "you have missed your vocation, you should have been an undertaker."

"Piss taker" said Seb indignantly "doesn't it look marvellous?"

Leo put his arm around him "You've done a fantastic job, it looks A M A Z I N G ! You are a real artist."

Seb flushed "Thank you Leo, I do try, I know you all take the piss, but it does look good doesn't it."

Leo kissed him gently "It so does, it so does."

"Hello, Alice Cavaghan speaking" snapped Alice on the hands free "who is this please?"

"Hi Alice, it's Max, Max Goldsmith."

"Who?" said Alice rudely "Are you a client?"

"You know exactly who I am Alice, and I have something for you, but if you don't want it, I'll leave you be" said Max nonchalantly "your choice of course."

"Wait ..."

"That's more like it. Don't fuck with me girly or you'll regret it. You either want the package or you don't. Make your mind up, I'm not as sweet as Ernie."

"Of course I want it, and don't fuck with me" snarled Alice "where and when shall I meet you?"

"That's more like it. You going to this bash tonight? I could meet you beforehand?"

"Yes, as it happens I am, although I've not made it common knowledge to Felix."

"What you do in your private life is nothing to do with me - I don't give a fuck. Just behind the woods at Laundry Cottage is the Old Mill. I'll meet you there at 8.30 pm. Don't be late."

"I'll be there" said Alice "Don't let me down."

"Don't be stupid, you've one chance. If you're late I'll go. Understand?"

Alice was just about to make a sharp reply, but realised he'd disconnected. Her heart was beating fast, money and lots of it. She could change into her gown, meet him there and then drive off to the party. It would work perfectly, she could sweep Felix off his feet and have a bundle of money in her pocket too - a flawless situation. She just had to keep her head down now and work her socks off today and not enter into the inane conversation at the new surgery. They were all full of chatter about their outfits and the party. She was stalling about what she was wearing although she had said she was definitely going. She'd feel a whole lot better when she'd picked up the money.

Felix and Hattie had talked all day about Alice. He'd told her what'd happened the night before and neither one of them could think of a solution. Felix thought it all hinged on this one evening, and once it was over possibly Alice would be able to see reason. In the meantime he would stay at Laundry Cottage if she and the boys didn't mind. Hattie had smiled indulgently, all she wanted was for Felix to be free.

The day had passed well enough, with Roxy coming for a lesson on Galaxy. She was progressing incredibly. Sam was behind the camera and picked up a few golden shots whilst making eyes at Hattie much to Felix's chagrin. Max was determined to keep up with Roxy although they hadn't found him his own horse yet, but Seb was working on it, his head full of the commission. A strange tension of expectation crackled in the air and Hattie put it down to the anticipation of the party. Frankie was whistling and singing, just like her sister, and Roxy was in high spirits. Max was tense, and so was Felix but it was more than that, a sort of edge to the day that Hattie couldn't put her finger on. She kept glancing into the parkland wondering if she saw the glance of a camera lens, or a stranger lurking in the bushes. In her mind she still thought about Kylie and how she had dubbed them all in to the papers, and she was pretty certain that her malice abounded still; she was so spiteful and hell hath no fury and all that stuff. She shrugged her shoulders, what a pile of crap, she had to stop being so silly, she had Felix now, and they had moved on from the Kylie days and soon Alice would be out of his life too. Although she felt awful about her, to lose Felix must be more than anyone could bear. She had almost lost him herself and she knew how she had felt. Alice though was a cold fish and she wasn't sure that she was quite all there sometimes, the way she looked at her, or responded to people. Not quite normal, but who was she to query how she behaved, she felt very sorry for her, and wouldn't have hurt or wounded her for the world. The guilt Hattie felt weighed her down like a stone, but it made no difference, she couldn't help herself, she was intrinsically linked to Felix no matter what the cost.

Frankie had asked to go early if possible and naturally Felix had said yes, she was such a good girl. These days he and Hattie were so loved up and time spent together, even if it was finishing up the yard proved to be nectar to their souls. They bade her good night and said they would see her later, watching her skip off to get ready for the party. Felix dragged Hattie by the hand into the tack room planting a smacking kiss on her lips.

"God I love you baby" he sighed kissing her hair and rubbing his body against hers "you make me so happy."

"Hmm, I know the feeling" mumbled Hattie, "but darling I feel very uneasy about Alice, it'll be so much better when tonight's over."

"Bugger tonight" said Felix "let's have some fun now, we're on our own, only the dogs and us. Plenty of time."

"Dream on lover, it'll have to be a quickie, we need to get back to the cottage to help Leo and Seb, otherwise they'll have our guts for garters literally and metaphorically and I don't fancy being part of the Halloween decorations!"

"Spoilsport, but I can do quick"

"How quick?"

"Watch me?"

"You're on" laughed Hattie tumbling onto the old armchair.

At Laundry Cottage final preparations were almost finished and the effect was startling and extremely creepy. The cottage itself was like a little gingerbread house in an ideal setting, but dressed up like something out of Sleepy Hollow with its faux tomb stones and garden ghouls it was ultra sinister. The back drop of the woods and the house in the clearing was perfect and once the tea-lights were lit in the pumpkin heads it would be amazing.

Seb and Leo sat back and admired their handiwork, it had been a slog of a day and they hadn't stopped, all the food had been cooked and just needed warming through and all that remained was for the candles to be lit and Hattie and Felix could do that, now they both deserved a well earned drink or two.

"Fuck me, I hope it's a bloody success after all this hard work" grumbled Leo "I'm worn out already."

"Oh it will be" laughed a thoroughly over-excited Seb "everyone loves dressing up, and as long as there's plenty of booze - it'll be faberooney!"

"I just hope that fucking Alice doesn't pitch up and give everyone a headache."

"I think she's lost her marbles you know" said Seb "we should try and be sympathetic."

"It's not easy when she's such a hard nosed cow. She doesn't exactly endear herself to anyone does she? She's been awful to Felix ever since we've known her, it's no surprise is it that he's finally woken up and realised what a bitch she is?"

"No, you're right she's an unpleasant person at the best of times. Remember how awful she used to be when we had to borrow their bathroom?"

"God yes, she made me feel like we'd give her a disease."

"Ah well, hopefully it'll be sorted soon, and it's not as though we see much of her now anyway."

"No true and Felix is so much happier isn't he?"

"Who wouldn't be - Hattie is so lovely, they're a perfect couple, just like us! Now we've got Frankie in the yard too, things are on the up baby!"

The following morning Seb and Leo would remember this conversation and realise how wrong they could be.

By eight pm the music throbbed and pulsated in the dark night air and the first of the guests had begun to arrive. Everyone had gone to town with their costumes and soon the cottage was filling fast with masked witches, wizards, zombies and ghouls with yells and shrieks as people tried to guess who was behind the sinister masks.

Farouk and his camera crew recorded Roxy and her entourage arriving in spectacular fashion. Roxy her tits spilling out of her sultry witch outfit and looking very sexy with a small cat like mask, Max on the other hand looked hideous as the infamous plague doctor with the grotesque mask, Aiden totally hooded was equally menacing as the grim reaper with his red hot devil Chrissie on his arm. They did look sensational swooping up the garden path like they possessed the place.

Seb greeted his guests in his ridiculous man-eating shark costume, whilst Leo was suave as the Vampire. Dulcie and Nancy arrived in the most outrageous and enormous gothic dress, in which they had been sewn together which made them look like a woman with two masked heads; Dulcie was the right arm and Nancy was the left, it was seriously weird, made weirder as they could hardly walk and kept falling over; with Frankie in her sexy mummy costume desperately trying to prop them up. Most of the guests were reasonably recognisable, Charles and Jennifer especially, even though they were masked, it would have been difficult to disguise themselves. Grace of course was still on crutches and Colin who had quite a gut these days still couldn't quite manage to hide it under his mad monk outfit. Dougie or at least everyone thought it was him, owing to his amazing dark brown voice was a Voodoo Witch Doctor, but the costume was amazing, a full length black velvet coat, covering a skeleton jumpsuit and mask, with a top hat and a crazy grey wig. Mark and Sandy came as Frankenstein and his bride, Jeremy and Katherine as Beetlejuice and a skeleton. But beyond the obvious ones, there were so many guests who could have been anybody at all. If there were any gatecrashers no-one would have known and nobody cared either.

Alice had prepared herself methodically. She made up her face, lashing on mascara to her eyes and applying smoky kohl underneath the lids. Daubing some colour on her cheeks and lipstick she sat back to look at the effect. In the mirror she looked good, her silvery blonde hair falling gently over her shoulders. Yes, she was pleased. Wriggling into the slippery satin dress she felt empowered. She wasn't afraid, and she felt strong. Placing the veil with its rose wreath onto her head and clamping it down with clips she was ready to go. She would knock him dead. But first the tiresome but necessary meeting at the mill - she glanced at the clock it was 8.00pm. She had plenty of time, one quick drink before she went. She swished down the stairs the dress swirling fabulously around her ankles and poured herself a large gin. She shivered, the house felt a bit cold, or it could be that she was excited. Knocking back the drink in a gulp she grabbed her silver clutch bag and made her way to the car.

At the cottage more guests had arrived and by this time Seb and Leo had given up greeting people and newcomers were just filtering in and helping themselves to booze and food. The music was pounding and bodies were gyrating wildly, those that weren't dancing had taken refuge in the kitchen so they could hear themselves speak. Farouk and his crew had abandoned filming and were joining in with the silly games Seb had organised. In the garden small groups of masked and hooded figures stood smoking by the pumpkin lights, the butts of the cigarettes glowing in the dark.

"Enjoying yourself?" shouted Hattie to Felix above the din "some amazing costumes eh?"

"Fabulous, people are so clever, I can't believe Dulcie and Nancy, how do they move in that thing?"

"Short answer - I don't think they can."

"Do you know everyone, there are so many people here and I've no idea who they are."

"Me too, but of course that's the fun of it I suppose."

"I hate to say this, but do you think Alice is here?"

"No, believe me we'd know if she was."

"I'm a bit worried she'll turn up Felix."

"Look darling, there's no point in worrying, there's nothing we can do if she does. I've tried to be straight with her, now let's just enjoy ourselves tonight, it's an amazing party."

"It's spoilt it a bit for me though, thinking she might pitch up."

"Let's have a dance, take your mind of it."

They drifted onto the crowded dance floor, edging to get a space amongst the revellers. Surprised to see Jennifer stunning as a black and evil Maleficent with Charles as Dracula rocking and rolling like a pair of teenagers.

"Fantastic party" Jennifer mouthed "enormous fun!"

Felix grinned "they're enjoying themselves, now let's do the same."

In the kitchen Grace had taken refuge on a chair, bandaged up like a mummy to disguise the plaster on her leg she was still easy to identify, Colin had pulled down his hood, his face red and hot under the thick woollen cloth. They were chatting to Mark and Sandy, Mark scratching wildly at the bolt which was stage-glued to his neck.

"This thing is driving me nuts."

"Well pull it off then and stop complaining" laughed Sandy "I think we've all seen the effect now."

"It's all right for you" grumbled Mark pulling off the offending prop "this mask is so hot, yours is only make up."

"I've taken mine off, you do the same" suggested Colin "we've had our bit of fun now, anyway, how can you have a drink with it on, that's what I'd like to know?"

Mark ripped the mask off "That's better, now I can see properly too."

"Blimey what's going on over there?" said Grace craning her neck round to see "who is that?"

"Can't tell from the dim lighting" said Sandy "but looks like its a three cornered snog to me!"

"I think I'm getting old" said Colin "did I do this sort of thing?"

"No" said Grace lightly "you never did darling. It was always the others but you always enjoyed watching!"

"Watch out here comes Roxy and her companion" moaned Sandy "the *dottore della peste* is such a hideous costume isn't it? Do we know who it is? I'm assuming either Aiden or that ghastly man she hangs about with."

"No idea which of them it is" said Grace "not keen on either to be truthful."

"Well there's no escape - they're coming over. Oh hang on - slight reprieve, the Plague Doctor's gone out the back door, for a smoke I suppose - that's a relief."

Roxy tottered over to join them "Hi - having a good time - what a fun idea this is."

"Hi Roxy" Colin said awkwardly "do you know everyone here?"

Roxy glanced around the little group "I think I do, and of course Colin will have told you, soon we'll all be proper neighbours" Roxy looked expectantly round at everyone clapping her hands together "I'm buying the lovely old barn conversion just outside the village, so we won't just be running the restaurant and spa but living here too. You must all be so excited."

Sandy's jaw almost hit the floor in disbelief, and Mark managed to mutter "How ... incredible."

"Yes, isn't it" purred Roxy oblivious to her bombshell "so I'll actually be living locally to you some of the time, in between the London house of course. I knew you'd just love it. So you'll be seeing a lot more of me."

"Astonishing news" mumbled Sandy stifling a giggle "naturally we are delighted."

"Of course I'll be asking you all over to dinner at my gaff, but Aiden's planning the big opening bash first on New year's eve so make sure you keep the date free won't ya?"

"Oh most definitely, I know Katherine and Jeremy are coming" said Grace sweetly, "I'll have to make sure Mum's free to babysit of course."

"Oh Mums love all that shite" laughed Roxy "never can resist an opportunity to look after the little blighters."

"Well, we must keep the date free" lied Sandy "we wouldn't want to miss the opportunity to be there on the opening night."

"Of course you wouldn't" laughed Roxy adjusting her tits "be nothing like you've ever been to before."

"I'm sure it wouldn't" remarked Sandy, her sarcasm completely lost on Roxy "a veritable spectacle I'm sure."

Roxy looked over her shoulder suddenly bored with their conversation, "Gotta go babes, find that fucking *dottore*, he's a sly one you know!" She blew them a kiss and staggered off towards the dancing.

"Thank God she's gone" grumbled Mark "she really is the most dreadful woman."

"I think she's quite sad in a way" said Grace "can she really not see that behaving and wearing clothes like she does makes her look like a complete idiot?"

"Nope I don't think she does" said Sandy "she's a lost cause, don't waste any sympathy on her Gracie."

Alice pulled her car along the new tarmac road towards the mill. She cut the lights and waited, reluctant to get out of the car in her sparklingly clean dress. There were no artificial lights, and no sign of anyone. In the eerie half light of the moon and the clear sky, the builders' paraphernalia cast spooky shadows across the pond, the builders' protective barriers seemed sinister and unnecessary. Alice checked her watch - it was 8.25pm. The boom, boom, thump, thump from the party matched her heartbeat as it beat across the woods and echoed over the pond and she could see the soft glow of the orange pumpkin lights from the garden and longed to be there and facing Felix. From the shadows a hooded dark figure stole out, seeming to glide across the drive towards her car. She felt a moment of fear, and then remembered that he would be in the fancy dress for the Halloween party and forced herself to relax. The figure stood in the centre of the drive and crooked a beckoning finger to her. Slipping out of the car, she lifted her skirts and walked over, the shape turned away and indicated for her to follow. Stifling a moment of suspicion she tagged after it into the security of the ruins to collect her well earned money.

At Laundry Cottage the party roared on. Apple bobbing was going great guns in the garden with more water being spilled and hurled than apples being eaten. Wet ghouls and ghosties ran amok around the garden and screamed around the house casting garments asunder with a lot of laughing and debauchery. Onlookers egged them on, and then they played the mummy wrapping game on the naked ones with a plethora of flour, lavatory paper, and cling film ending extraordinarily messily. Mark Templeton's head fell in his hands wondering what Lady V would say if she found out. Luckily Farouk's cameras has long since been stowed away and Roxy herself was astonished at how the horsey brigade knew how to party. Even the staid brigade were in fits of laughter and the night rocked on with Seb producing a Ouija board at around midnight, but everyone was too drunk to take it seriously and kept knocking the letters over and falling off their chairs.

Hattie and Felix were only drunk with each other. They had long since slipped upstairs to Hattie's room, forgetting that Alice may well arrive at any time and spent some time pleasuring each other. The notion of so many people downstairs fuelling their ardour. As they lay naked listening to the revellers shouting and screaming they snuggled up together and thought how lucky they were. As they got dressed, Hattie craned out of the window, looking out at the garden towards the mill, all was quiet and she wondered how things would change when the restaurant opened, would it affect them? She glanced at her watch - it was nearly ten, they should go downstairs and be sociable. Felix was sleepy, tired after a long day and didn't want to get up, but she prodded him, hissing that he must and eventually they sauntered down the stairs. No-one had noticed they had been missing and they mingled in once again joining in with the dancing. The plague doctor and Roxy dancing close, with the red hot devil and the grim reaper in a close embrace, Charles and Jennifer were gossiping now to the other syndicate members, and Dulcie and Nancy had discarded their outfit and were in their bra and pants. Oli was suckling on a witch's nipple whilst Theo was dancing close with a wood nymph. Dougie had found two willing zombies for a threesome. On the whole it was an average party and Hattie discovering she was starving wolfed down a load of sausage rolls and prawn toasts. She and Felix smiled at each other deciding life couldn't get much better than this.

Terry smiled, smacked his hands together and pushed his hood back. Job done. He nodded to his boys. They emptied Alice's bag, took out and pocketed her mobile and chucked the bag in the mill pond and watched it sink. Her body was face down spread-eagled and floating out into the centre of the pond, the voluminous wedding dress splayed out in the water like the sails of a galleon. They'd been very careful with her physically, wrapping her in a blanket and once the Ketamine had taken effect and she'd become drowsy it was easy to hold her down in the water, and see her life force bubble away and then to launch her out into the pond. The last part of the job now was a quick visit to her cottage, drop off some vials of Ketamine into her bedside drawer and Bob's your uncle. Suicide verdict, unsound mind. Cosy. Max would be pleased. He and the lads had done a good job - real pros.

CHAPTER 77

The morning of 1st November arrived in a frosty sparkle, heralding the inauguration of the winter months to come. The grass stood stiffly to attention on the lawn, and the rime on the trees was slight but evident and a thin film of ice coated the windscreens of the abandoned cars slewn across the drive and down the lane.

Laundry Cottage was awash with unwashed inebriates, sleeping on the floor, the stairs and the sofas. Many people had managed to struggle home, but plenty hadn't made it that far. Roxy and her mob had staggered back to their discreet hotel in the early hours and luckily for many a lot of filming had been done earlier before the naughtier and more incriminating antics had taken place. Hattie and Felix woke early, they'd not over-drunk considering, having paced themselves and picked their way downstairs over the precariously fallen bodies, and then, surveying the wreckage in the kitchen decided to go to the yard for their morning coffee. Frankie was meeting them there, she'd not been drinking the night before being the designated driver, and praise the lord had sweetly offered to work. Seb and Leo hadn't surfaced and Felix seriously doubted whether anyone would see them today. Dougie had found solace with a couple of gay guys in the snug and was comatose curled around them both when Felix popped his head around the door to say goodbye.

When he and Hattie arrived at the yard, they slurped down a couple of hair-raisingly strong coffees and got down to mucking out with a sickenly fresh faced and singing Frankie. She was bright and breezy and full of the joys of spring, or should she say winter - whatever - Felix pulled up his hoodie and got on with his job. Hattie did the same. Neither of them felt able to talk or sing along; leaving Frankie to it they donned their crash hats and after schooling a couple in the arena schlepped out for a hack passing Felix's cottage as they went. They could barely glance over for fear of seeing Alice but when they did steal a surreptitious glance saw her car wasn't there and Felix muttered that he would try and call her later and find out what she was planning now the deadline had passed.

Back at Laundry no-one stirred, the clock ticked and the phone rang intermittently. No-body answered. Hero and Fiver dozed beside the Aga and the candles had long since guttered out. In the garden the debris from the night before littered the lawn. Toothy cigarette butts were ground out on the grass, plastic glasses, empty bottle and the remnants of the apples were strewn far and wide. The tattered robes of the ghosts fluttered in the light breeze of the morning and the birds pecked at the eyes of the pumpkins.

Down at the surgery an angry Paulene repeatedly rang Alice's number but it kept going to voicemail; she hadn't shown up for work and there were a number of calls stacking up. Everyone was feeling fragile, all suffering from the exploits of the previous night, except for Theo, who hadn't indulged and was irritatingly unaffected despite going spectacularly large in the shenanigans with Oli. When Alice hadn't turned up at the party, without exception they'd all been relieved, but not truly surprised either judging by her strangely erratic behaviour of late. Still, she should be answering her phone this morning which made Paulene even crosser, it was just another example of how high-handed Alice had become recently. Andrew and Oli looked concerned and gave each other a side-ways look, telling Paulene they would cover for her. Andrew nudged Oli whispering quietly that he'd pop around to the cottage to see if she was okay.

At the mill, the builders being paid exorbitant overtime rates pitched up to start work for the day. They donned their hard hats, ducked behind the safety barriers and dismissed the fact that there was a strange car parked outside. Still theirs was not to reason why. Making a brew before they started, and lighting up a fag, collecting their instructions from the gaffer they climbed up into the ribs of the mill to begin work. Moments later an horrific shout went up, as in the morning light appeared a ghastly apparition of shimmering white silk spread out like a gigantic jellyfish across the pond. The monstrous folds of fabric cradling the upturned corpse ballooning out in the water as the body swayed gently in the ebb and flow of the water like a gothic horror movie.

The wheels of justice move exceeding small and exceeding well. The emergency services once called dealt swiftly and deftly with the situation. The police surveyed the area taking in the scene of the car with the keys left in the ignition, the handbag, and the retrieval of the body for post mortem. The nature of the corpse gave no immediate or overt reason to suspect anyone else or foul play. It seemed that Alice had simply fallen in the mill pond and the weight of the wedding dress had dragged her down and she had drowned. This could have been accidental or deliberate on her part.

The abandoned vehicle clearly belonged to the dead woman and had the Vets' Logo on the side. A phone call to them immediately identified Alice as being missing, and the police winged their way to the surgery to speak to Andrew. It was a sad and painful interview. Andrew told them about Felix being Alice's partner, but that their relationship was on the rocks. Also of Alice's unstable and erratic behaviour of late and how he had suspected her of stealing drugs. The police asked if he would be prepared to identify the body and he affirmed that he would.

Felix collapsed in total shock when he was told about finding a body in the mill pond believe to be that of Alice Cavaghan, his former partner, and he was then swamped by a seismic wave of guilt, sorrow, love and despair. Following the interview with Andrew, the police seemed to be leaning toward the conclusion that Alice had committed suicide. In an unhappy and unbalanced state of mind, possibly taking illicit drugs she had driven to the mill. Left her car unlocked and waded into the water. There was no evidence of another car, or another person. The question was, if she was on her way to the party why did she go via the mill? When the police spoke to Felix he was compelled to confirm that they had split up but Alice was in denial. Initially he totally refused to consider she would kill herself even if at times he thought her behaviour was irrational and bizarre. He shouted he knew her more than anyone else and she just wasn't the suicidal type, no matter what the provocation, and then to steal drugs, it just went so totally against what she stood for and who she was that he simply wouldn't believe it. Alice would never take Ketamine in any shape or form - no matter how bad she felt. It was bollocks. Something must have happened to her, but he was buggered if he knew what - perhaps she was meeting a lover, and had slipped and fallen.

Further investigations were made for the inquest. The body was taken to the mortuary for an autopsy where death by drowning was pronounced. The DS took statements from Paulene and Alice's other work colleagues, all of whom stated her state of mind was fragile. On examination at her home, Ketamine was discovered in her bedside drawer and Diazepam in the bathroom cabinet, which was known to be used on occasions in cases of depression, and possibly in this case was being self-administered. Her finger prints were found on the syringe in the drawer and suspicion of theft of drugs from the surgery was confirmed in writing by the Practice Manager and the Senior Partner, although they had no proof that the missing drugs had been taken by Alice and no other drugs were found in the cottage. Statements were also taken that she had been having problems with her boyfriend and was in denial about the end of their relationship. Her behaviour had been odd and bizarre of late. All of these facts were presented at the inquest. Medical evidence and toxin reports following post mortem indicated that she had taken alcohol with Diazepam, coupled with Ketamine and that she had gone to the Mill for reasons unknown. On the body there was no evidence of physical force, bruising or a fall. There was the possibility of parking there to attend the party at Laundry Cottage as there was a shortage of space at the cottage itself, but equally possibly for other reasons. It may be that she had planned to commit suicide whilst the balance of her mind was disturbed. She was attired in a wedding dress and had just been spurned by her boyfriend and as an act of desperation had committed suicide. Felix was also called to give evidence and he said that he had never seen Alice take drugs at any time and to his knowledge she had always abhorred those that did. He had never seen the Ketamine in her bedside drawer or Diazepam in the bathroom before. Nonetheless, considering all the evidence the coroner gave a ruling of death by suicide and that Alice had killed herself whilst the balance of her mind was disturbed.

Outside the coroner's court Felix was in complete shock, propped up by Seb and Leo, with Hattie feeling totally helpless and shrinking in the background like she'd been hit by a ten ton truck. Andrew and Oli came over and they put their arms around her helping her into their car, glancing at the boys who were dealing with Felix. Hattie felt sick. How could Alice have done this, planned such a terrible revenge on him and she wondered if he would ever get over the guilty feeling that it was his fault that she'd died. She felt impotent and no matter what she said nothing seemed to reach him. The boys had been brilliant and although in her heart all she wanted to do was comfort him they seemed to be the best ones to help him at the moment. Andrew and Oli were being so kind. They both knew how unbalanced Alice had been and this wasn't just down to Felix, although Hattie believed there was more to it than met the eye and in his heart she knew that Felix thought so too. But right now he was wrapped in a mental chaos of guilt and blame and no-one and nothing could reach him.

The whole village was in a state of shocked albeit delighted tittle-tattle. Most of the talk was about Alice and the party and elaborated on how the mill was a doomed place. The tales of the murders from the previous year were gleefully resurrected, and speculation that one of the kidnappers had never been caught was once more gleefully elaborated. The gossips had a field day but those that were close to the tragedy prayed that soon they would move on and poor Felix would be left alone to grieve and lick his wounds.

Alone, Felix limped back to his cottage in a state of shock and disbelief. Alice's parents traumatised and devastated by their daughter's death had not come to England for the inquest, requesting that her valuables be returned to them in New Zealand and what seemed of no consequence be sent to the charity shop. Alice's body was being flown home to them for burial. Leo helped Felix sort everything out and the police, once the verdict had been given, had allowed them free rein. It was a tragic task. The cottage seemed frozen in time. The clothes she'd been wearing lay discarded on the bedroom floor, her make-up strewn on the dressing table; the last bath she'd taken hadn't been cleaned; the coffee cup she'd used was still left on the kitchen table; the gin from her last drink out on the coffee table. It was eerie and sad. Felix kept repeatedly collapsing in state of remorse, falling to the floor moaning and clutching his knees. Leo stalwartly helped him up and urged him on. Hattie felt powerless and ostracised, but Felix insisted she must not be involved for her own protection. It was something he had and must do himself. In a way of course Hattie understood and in another her heart screamed out that she didn't. But Felix had to come to terms with his grief, and Hattie had to allow him liberty to do just that, but nonetheless it was like torture not to hold his hand and support him in his hour of need. Leo urged her to be patient, to be there when he needed her and not force the situation. So whilst Felix grieved, Hattie waited.

When Roxy had heard the news she was ghoulishly thrilled. They'd all shoved off back to London pretty smartish the day after the party, arrogantly pushing past the cameras with secretive smiles plastered on their hung-over faces and slipping into the limos blissfully unaware of anything untoward floating in the mill pond. She'd hardly known Alice, but the fact that she had chosen to chuck herself into her pond was terribly enthralling. More to the point - there was clearly more to Felix than she thought -how fabulously fascinating she thought idiotically. Farouk and Aiden considered the outcome, publicity of course was always good, but in this case it could be negative. They needed to downplay the notion of suicide that was for sure. Fuel the idea of intrigue and suspense, that would bring the punters in for the opening. In a way Alice chucking herself into the pond could be a super bit of exposure. They were disappointed with the verdict of suicide and decided to downplay the whole nasty business. What was a surprise to them, and which surfaced as neatly as Alice's bloated body in the wedding dress was the news of the murders the previous year. Farouk racked his brains for a good publicity angle and decided that there was nowt so ghoulish as folk.

Max watched with interest how things panned out in the press. Terry had done a good job it seemed. He'd reported back that things had gone without a hitch. She'd not put up a fight, and actually had been a little bit drunk and deranged. She'd been completely unsuspecting as they'd shoved in the Ketamine intravenously so fast she hadn't known what had hit her, cautiously wrapping her in blankets so as not to bruise her body whilst she pathetically struggled against them. Terry himself had held head under the mill race and watched as she flapped weakly until the bubbles ceased to trickle out of her nose and mouth, whilst she'd drowned in the muddy water. The lads had teased her body out into the middle of the pond, the heavy dress and veil spreading out like an ethereal stain on the top of the water. Afterwards they had sped to the cottage, planting the Ketamine in the bedside drawer and the Diazepam in the bathroom cabinet. Terry said it was as easy as pissing. Max felt no remorse, it was a strange feeling this total lack of emotion, it had been a job well done and for that he was prepared to reward Terry. He drew open the desk and bunged him a huge bundle of money, and more besides, dismissing him with a nod. Anna sitting in the chair opposite came over and rubbed his shoulders and he threw back his head revelling in the touch, although frankly it could have been anyone massaging him at that point. His cold callousness sickened him yet he could find no genuine sorrow, it was dog eat dog. Shoving Anna smoothly to one side he picked up the phone and dialled Ernie's number and laughingly informed him that the deed had been done.

    The shock of Alice's demise was heartfelt at the surgery. Paulene felt shaken, guilty and dazed. Whatever she had thought of her Paulene had never wanted Alice to commit suicide. The result of the inquest caused much speculation between them all. Alice had been unstable, her behaviour had been unbalanced, and drugs had gone missing there was no doubt, Ketamine had been found, but killing herself -no it didn't ring quite true. That sounded crazy but Alice was too hard-nosed, too blatant and just too ...calculated. Andrew came down on them all with a heavy hand quelling all speculation saying they should all try and move on and none of them knew what went on in another person's mind and the verdict had been passed - Alice must have been very disturbed and it was very sad, but enough was enough. Their thoughts and love should be with Felix who needed their support to get through this. Guiltily, like naughty children caught nicking sweets they all murmured their assent and said they would.

    Seb and Leo tried to pick up the pieces. Felix was one thing but Hattie was quite another. She was in a terrible state, envisaging that Alice had killed herself as a statement against her and Felix, knowing that they had been together. No matter what the boys said, Hattie still felt blame, eaten up that she had been responsible for so much. If she hadn't been with Felix, Alice wouldn't have taken her own life especially in such a dramatic and spectacular way. Even though Hattie hadn't seen the body floating in the pond, she could only imagine how it looked and the swollen and distended features of her face harangued her imagination constantly. Her mind and body felt sick with it all. Most of all she felt helpless. Felix seemed to have slipped beyond her, like some elusive dream that she had in her grasp and then was suddenly and frustratingly gone. She felt bereft and lonely. He tried to be close to her, but his mind was else where and any closeness they had made them feel cheap even though this was ridiculous.

For Felix he rocked like a pendulum clock between being extremely angry and extremely sad. He had no guilt about his feelings for Hattie - he had not loved Alice like she wanted, and he refused to deny his love for Hattie. There was no going back from that. But that he cared about Alice was a given, of course it was. He could not believe she had taken her own life, he knew her better than that. She was on the edge it was true, but it must have been a bizarre accident, but what could she have been doing at the mill and in a wedding dress? It was all so strange. That Ketamine was found in the bedroom was odd too, it went against the grain. Alice would never have taken it - she was anti that sort of stuff to the absolute degree - that much he did know. The police took no notice of him whatsoever and he was tired of telling them so. He just had to recognize the verdict of the Coroner and move on but it just didn't seem right and, it was going to take a long time to accept.

CHAPTER 78

Max was pleased. The purchase of his house was finishing faster than a serviced bitch on heat. He hadn't mentioned a thing to Roxy, and he'd told that tosser of an agent that if anyone heard about him buying the place, he'd pull out faster than the bishop from mother superior. So far so good. He couldn't wait and in the scheme of things he could be moving in by Christmas. Anna was in the know, and was in charge of furnishings and decorations. They were half way through November now and he was confident the place would be up and running by the time the festivities started. When the mill opened he wanted to be able to entertain his cronies here. He was planning to book a table for Ronnie and Ernie on party night and then for them to come back to him afterwards. Perfect - he'd show them he could entertain like them.

Anna was stressed, busy looking at curtains, carpets and furniture. Max's taste was elaborate and extravagant, over the top, vulgar and obscene. Fine in the scheme of things but it needed time to arrange. She hoped that by flashing the cash she could pull it off. After watching the way he worked, ruthless and without remorse she didn't want to end up in the Thames if she didn't come up with a four poster and other ostentatious clutter, and so cajoling and threatening was becoming second nature. By exchange of contracts she more or less had it all in hand. Money had a joyous language which Anna was happy to use. It should all come together but it would be her head on the platter like the proverbial John the Baptist if things went tits up. Max himself was pre-occupied, if it wasn't the gambling, it was the tarts, and the clubs. but more than that he was involved in the racing scam up to his neck, loving the thrill of laying and playing the bets. She knew he was coining in the money and in a way it was what to do with it all. He kept throwing money at her to do up the new house and she spent it, but not as fast as it came in. She questioned him on his taste in bed linen, furnishings, crockery asking if it suited him, and he brushed her away in irritation, telling her to get on with it and not fuss. He said keep it simple, and she did but expensively so, with the odd flourish now and then which he thought he would like. The money ran through her fingers like sand in a sieve. The house would be ready in time and he didn't care how much it cost.

Gradually Felix began to surface, the initial whammy of shock had subsided into a muddy pool of emotion, whirling between grief, guilt and disbelief. Seb fluttered hopelessly like a trapped moth whilst Leo in his stalwart way had doggedly bundled up Alice's clothes and packed them off to the charity shop. He and Felix had sorted through her personal stuff and shipped it off to her parents. The cottage was now devoid of anything overt that had been hers, other than those poignant reminders that only Felix knew of and no-one else could remove other than him. Felix leaned heavily on his friends for support and quashing those nagging feelings of guilt had welcomed Hattie into his nucleus and they had talked endlessly into the night. Neither of them believed that Alice had killed herself, thinking that she had fallen bizarrely, tragically drowning and this notion helped them both to come to terms with what had happened. The cottage itself was now strictly Felix's domain, and whilst Hattie longed to move in, they both realised this wasn't feasible for a few weeks at least. Hopefully before Christmas but they could wait, there was no hurry, it all seemed stupidly academic now. Frankie had moved into Leo's old room and Hattie remained in her old room, tossing and turning alone and forlorn in her bed. Felix lay sleepless and sad in the spare room at his cottage, not able to bring himself to sleep in Alice's double bed. Together yet apart, separate yet as one, it was a huge mess.

The work on the mill was progressing extremely well. The external part looked authentically fantastic and the builders were going like maniacs inside. Alan was enthralled and driven. Roxy and Aiden had to be impressed, he certainly was. In his wildest dreams he had never dreamt that it would be this far ahead and there was no doubt that they would get the launch off the ground for New Year's Eve. The outside of the mill was restored back to its original state. Inside dramatic and state of the art kitchens were designed with good storage. The back gardens had been tilled and the ground prepared, impressive kitchen produce would appear to supply the food, but in reality, most of it would be bought in. Simple dormitory accommodation for the staff was planned above the kitchen and storage area. The ribs and structure of the mill were complete, now safe and sound with the floors in situ as were the windows. Now it was a question of the fixtures and fittings, electrics and the like. Dotting the *i's* and crossing the *t's*. It was all the tiresome snagging that took the time, the actual structure seemed to zoom up, but it was the God of small things that was frustrating and tiresome in the extreme. Alan had, as per his instructions from Aiden, enlisted the help of an interior designer and ordered all the chairs, tables and peripherals. Aiden had ordered the kitchen essentials; Chrissie was holding the final staffing interviews at the end of the month. It was all coming together. Chrissie had issued invitations to the New Year's Eve party and was waiting for the replies. No-one expected these in for a while. These A listers waited to see who'd invited them where, before they replied. But Aiden was confident of David and Victoria, and his old friend Jeremy Clarkson would definitely come, which would be a serious draw. All in all it should be an intriguing and *'place to be seen'* invitation.

Aiden was experimenting with the menu and it was to be a gastronomic furore worthy of the very best and most serious of gastronome critics. A frenzy of food, tantalisingly fragranced with the most subtle of seasonings bursting on the palate like a firework display of flavours. He worked tirelessly in the trial kitchen rigorously testing dishes with more voracity and greed than Emelda Marcos'd had for shoes. He decided on simplicity without diversity and, rather than a huge variety of main choice menus, it would be a series of small dishes of exquisite experience. Thus he worked tirelessly to perfect the overall dining outcome. A bit Heston and the *Fat Duck* but with a definite and original Aiden Hamilton stamp.

Chrissie was in awe of him and, his passion for food was mind blowing, but equally she was sick of him too. She had her work cut out with hiring the fucking staff, let alone playing mega interested with the notion of taste experiences. For fuck's sake - let's live in the real world here - she was as content to go to Maccie D's in the long run, yet she dare not say this to Aiden. So intensely was he wrapped up in his work at times he could be frightening. His eyes blazed manically with the concept of the mood, the perception and the ultimate perfection. On the upside tickets for the gala night were blazing. Based on a myriad of factors from star gazing, ghoulish curiosity about the history of the mill, actually wanting to sample the food and something different to do on New Year's Eve, people were busting a gut to get themselves a place. Although it was the end of November there were only a few tickets left. Chrissie was smug, at least it was a sell out, despite the extortionate price and she couldn't be blamed for a damp squib, even if the food was far from finalised. She just had to make sure she had enough lackeys to serve the grub on the night.

Kylie was sorely disgruntled. She'd hoped the money from the leather jacketed reporter would have led to so much more. But once she coughed the dirt he didn't want to know her. Now she was left back where she started shovelling barrow loads of shit and the weather was getting colder and the arseholes at Fittlebury Hall hadn't really come out of it any the worse. That stupid Roxy was swanning round like she owned the place and had got Kylie sacked to boot. Since the exposé in the papers they were all much more careful, especially that fucking Hattie. She was always on the look out for the hacks, the other day Kylie even thought she'd spotted her spying at them out in the woods. But what a result it had been when stupid Alice had topped herself - the dozy tart. Kylie had been watching her, seen how off the wall she was and seen her stashing stuff in the shed that day. Alice had looked so suspicious, the way her eyes darted frantically around her, sneaking backwards and forwards from her car stashing boxes, and then driving off in a tearing hurry. Kylie hadn't wasted her opportunity and couldn't resist taking a gander at what she'd been up to and had rifled through the shed. Boy, what a result. She must be on the mega-take was our Alice. Kylie wasn't stupid , she knew what the drugs were straight away. She'd been around horses long enough to know. Pocketing as much as she could carry, her coat laden with contraband, Kylie 'd raced off, skulking in the woodland long enough to make sure she was unobserved. Her heart racing she'd leant heavily against a tree deciding what she should do next. Thinking quickly, and dashing back to the shed, within half and hour she'd nicked the lot and was driving away in her car. Within 24 hours Alice had topped herself and Kylie was left with a stash of drug evidence and no-one to blackmail, plus the possibility that she could be implicated in Alice's death. Suddenly the cottage was swarming with pigs. Furiously she ruminated, praying that she hadn't been seen taking the stuff, and guiltily knowing that she had to keep quiet about it, even though it might shed a different light on Alice's death. If she'd been up to no good, could someone have bumped her off? Kylie decided not to think about it, let the dust settle and she would sell the stuff off bit by bit. Horsey people would always buy it on the cheap and not ask questions. The more Kylie thought about life, the more hard done by she felt. That lot at Fittlebury Hall had a lot to answer for and one day she'd get them back. What was that old saying - Revenge is a dish best served cold, well she could wait, she was good at that. In the meantime, she planned to apply for a job as evening staff at the mill. Waitressing had to be better than shit shovelling any day of the week, and she considered that the risk of Roxy remembering her was remote in the scheme of things, and they were paying good money for the right staff.

CHAPTER 79

"**My God, do you realise it's only four weeks till Christmas!**" wailed Sandy, scooping up her briefcase and planting a kiss on her husband's head. "I must schedule some time off."

"Come here you," said Mark, grabbing her hand, "can I have a proper kiss please?"

"Sorry darling," smiled Sandy, "it's just been a bitch of a week already, this case has gone on longer than I thought. There are just never enough hours in the day and the traffic into town at this time of year is awful." She stopped talking suddenly and plonked herself down on a chair giggling. "Do you know you're right! Just listen to me! I'm gonna stop and have another coffee with my husband."

"That's my girl," laughed Mark pouring out another cup, "life's too short."

"I know, when you think about Alice. Stupid girl."

"I still can't quite believe it."

"Me neither, you never know what goes on in people's minds though do you?"

"No, and she did behave oddly at times and I suppose splitting up with Felix was the last straw," said Mark. "I know I go on about it, but how bizarre - to drown yourself in a wedding dress."

"Gives me the creeps," agreed Sandy. "How is Felix?"

"Well put it this way, I'm glad he's got Hattie and the boys to prop him up."

"He and Hattie are definitely an item then?" asked Sandy, "that can't be easy."

"Not officially, but you've only got to be around them to know to be honest. I feel sorry for the pair of them - Alice killing herself was a selfish shitty thing to do. If she couldn't have him, she was determined to make him feel guilty for the rest of his life."

"Suicide - the ultimate selfish act. What about the boys - are they still going ahead with their civil partnership? It's planned for around Christmas isn't it?"

"No, they've decided to postpone it, the Alice business has rather marred things and also too if they wait till the spring when the bill becomes law they can get married properly which will be much nicer than a civil partnership."

"Good idea, something for everyone to look forward to and they certainly know how to throw a party."

"Yes, that Halloween bash was a rip-roaring affair just a pity for everybody it was spoiled by the Alice aftermath."

"Darling can we change the subject? I'm sick of talking about her. How's the shoot going?"

"Yes really well. Young Will Fry is doing a great job, I'm really pleased. We've got plenty of birds and his organisation of the first couple of days has been excellent."

"Lady V must be pleased."

"Yes, she is, you know how important the shoot is to her. Will is handling himself and the guns well, he's making an excellent keeper."

"Well, it's in the blood isn't it," said Sandy, "his old dad and his dad before him."

"Definitely," laughed Mark ,"although Will's not as awkward as his old dad was."

"There's a relief," smiled Sandy, slurping her coffee and glancing at the clock, "crikey darling, I'd better get a wiggle on, otherwise I really will be late."

"Okay sweetie, have a good day - hope you win."

"I will - don't fret."

Max picked Roxy up from a small side street at the back of her London gaff. For once he was driving himself in the Aston. Roxy scooted into the passenger seat with all the skill of a limbo dancer and they were off before the long lens of a paparazzi could take focus. Threading out of London towards Fittlebury Roxy settled back into the luxurious leather seats and closed her eyes.

"I get sick of this journey," she murmured adding guiltily, "and babe there's something I've been meaning to tell you."

"Really tiger - what's that?" said Max concentrating on the road and giving a passing cyclist the finger.

"I'm in the final stages of buying a house in the village," Roxy blurted sheepishly, "I don't know why I didn't say before really, just in case something went wrong I suppose."

"How interesting, you did say you might buy down there," said Max indicating right and pulling out, "whereabouts?"

"It's a cute barn conversion on the Cuckfield Road," said Roxy, "we'll drive right past it, I'll show you on the way down."

"I'm really pleased for you darling, this drive is tedious I agree, and what with the riding, the new restaurant and everything, you do need a base down here."

"Yes, and it'll be nice for the kids too in the summer to get out of London." Roxy eyed him sideways under her lashes. "I don't envisage Aiden staying here much, once the restaurant is up and running he'll only pop down now and then to check it's running okay, like he does with the other places."

"Not really a country bird is our Aiden," said Max spitefully, "might get shit on his loafers."

"Now, now, don't be nasty, I thought he was in good form at the Halloween Party"

"Yes, the grim reaper suited him with his red hot devil at his side."

"Our Chrissie might be getting a little hot for him to handle. She was a real cling-on wasn't she?"

"Not jealous tiger?" asked Max glancing over at her "think this one might be serious?"

Roxy shut her eyes again. "Possibly," she confessed, "and no, not jealous. *Rox-Aid* is a good product, he'd have to think carefully before he gave it up - so would I come to that."

"Ah," said Max thoughtfully, "it all comes down to money doesn't it?"

"It is what makes the world go round," laughed Roxy, "and you love the fucking stuff! Look at this car!"

"True," agreed Max, "I do like money and I like spending it too. Whilst we're confessing. You might as well know, I've bought a house too."

"No!" squealed Roxy, sitting up and spinning round to look at him. "Where?"

"Fittlebury. How funny is that - we've both bought a place there."

"Fuck me sideways! I don't believe it - you sly old sod, you kept that quiet," said Roxy testily, "you could have said."

"Why? You didn't." replied Max reasonably. "Anyway, I'm enjoying the riding too, I'm hoping the boys will find me a horse and I need to offload some cash and what better investment than property."

"You old bugger, how long before you complete?"

"Next week, we've exchanged already, and it was empty so it's been dead straightforward."

"Can we see it?" asked Roxy, "I'd love to have a poke around."

"I was planning on showing you today, that's why I drove down. Elizabeth the agent is meeting us there after lunch."

"Brilliant - now doll put your foot down on this baby, so we've got enough time to ride and see both houses."

Max grinned, accelerating hard as the G force pushed them both back in their seats, and swept down the fast lane as Roxy's manicured hand crept onto his crotch, he felt himself grow erect but as always he was mindful of the speed limit.

To say that things had resumed normality in the yard would be an exaggeration. It was over four weeks since Alice had allegedly killed herself. The initial shock and overwhelming crushing guilt was passing for Felix. Now he'd reached the angry stage, loudly berating to anyone who would listen as to how Alice could have been such a bitch. The others kept their heads down, determined not to stir the pudding any more than necessary, often leaving him mouthing off to himself. Hattie had bitten her nails to the quick and the weight had dropped off, her face was gaunt, with hollowed cheeks and haunted eyes. To anyone but Roxy this would be a sign of extreme sadness but she saw it as the perfect look for modelling her new equestrian range. Whipping Hattie away from the yard she had her posing sexily in her new breeches in a bland studio against searing lights, her huge grey eyes accentuated with subtle kohl makeup. Changing sets Hattie was arranged sitting slightly forward astride hay bales, in an edgy, low-cut sparkly, logoed top with her breasts dangling, a far away look in her eyes. Roxy was delighted, Hattie's lean body, her boyish hips jutting out in the breeches was perfect, her angular cheekbones and huge grey eyes were gorgeous. To boot so much cheaper than a hiring a model. Hattie was posed and arranged as though she were a rag doll, the photographer moving her arms and legs about like she was a toy, tilting her head this way and that, all the time in her mind, Hattie was believing that she was doing it for the good of the yard, for the boys, and ultimately for Felix. As for Felix, anger coursed through his blood, he boiled with it, fried with it, spat with it. When he watched Hattie posing for the cameras he berated her, flaying her with his tongue like a whipped animal. Leo grumbled in disapproval and walked away shaking his head sadly. Felix immediately was sorry and asked Hattie to forgive him and naturally she did. In the end they did the shoot together, making a stunning connection with their extraordinary good looks and love sparking between them like two touching wires. Roxy smirked delightedly in the background.

Seb had found the most perfect horse for Max. Dougie phoned giving him the heads up on a suitable nag and last week the horse had come on trial. So far so good. Simeon was a gent, an old fashioned sort even though he was only eight, big boned, but quality with a beautiful head. Despite his size at 17hh he was nimble on his feet and well schooled, although he was never going to be Valegro. A charmer in the stable with a good brain and didn't pull or hot up. Seb though he'd be perfect for Max and all being well they could ask plenty of money and make a tidy commission. Max had ridden him a few times and definitely been impressed, but so far had no idea he was up for sale. Seb knew what he was doing, let him fall in love with the horse first and then when he felt safe as houses on him, he'd sell him, then everyone would be happy.

Max and Roxy had slipped into the habit of coming down to the yard together, either in her car or chauffeur driven in his, as he so rarely drove himself. They were due today and Seb had decided to make his move about selling Simeon - Max was more than ready to buy and Simeon had to be sold soon or go back to his owner - Seb couldn't afford to wait any longer. Felix and Hattie were sick of them - last time Roxy had been down, she'd hinted heavily about committing them to their next photo shoot and they didn't want to engage with her any longer than they possibly had to, but Seb was supremely adamant, and stressed if they wanted to land the commission then they all had to play ball and Felix and Hattie had to stop being so prissy. Today was going to be the big push and if it meant slathering on the butter and jam then so be it. Only Frankie seemed immune from the tension as she swept and sang and stuffed haynets and when Max's Aston finally crunched onto the gravel, nerves were jangling as loud as the Rotary Club's sleigh bells in the Carfax.

"Hi darlings" trilled Roxy, slithering out from the passenger seat, her long legs encased in her now supple leather boots "how's you all this morning?"

"Hi" called Seb "great to see you dear heart. How was the traffic?"

"Not bad for a change " said Max crisply getting out of the car and stretching "can we crack on today Seb, I've got a lot to do."

"Of course" replied Seb marginally taken aback as he'd hoped to have an opportunity to chat him up "Simeon is all groomed, just needs tacking up. I'll give Frankie a shout - a coffee first?"

"Love one I'm parched" said Roxy "we can ride together Max, that'll work, then we can get on eh?" she winked sweetly at him and turned to Seb "that okay with you babe?"

"Whatever you say Roxy" assured Seb "you go ahead and put the kettle on and I'll marshal the troops with the tack."

"Fine doll but don't be too long Max is itching to show me something" smiled Roxy intriguingly "and I want to talk to you about my dressage debut."

"Fabulous darling" said Seb masking his astonishment "definitely. Back in a mo'."

Roxy and Max sauntered over to the tack room heartily hailing Felix and commandeering him to join them as Seb hissed to a loitering Frankie to tack up the nags PDQ. When he walked into the tack room, Roxy was centre stage, sprawled on the old arm chair, one leg dangling over the edge her chest heaving spectacularly as she laughed dramatically to Felix. Max lounged in the corner, his lizard eyes flicking from one to the other with amused interest.

"Listen babe, you and Hats make a cool couple, just right for the range, I've even thought we could make a bit of a serial thing about the two of you, ya know, sort of like the Oxo ad?"

"You're not really serious Roxy?" grumbled Felix "I'm sorry, I just don't see it."

"Don't be such a pussy, I'm telling ya, you've got summat you two. Love's young fucking dream. Ya make the camera fizz let me tell ya!" Roxy laughed crossing her legs and sitting up "don't ya think so Max baby?"

Max levered himself upright smiling indulgently "Absolutely Felix, Roxy's right, you and Hattie, a perfect combination."

Felix looked uncomfortable "Right, yeah well we are good together" his words tumbled out like a torrent "but what with Alice ... you know ...?"

"For goodness sake, can you change the record - just forget Alice can't you?" snapped Max irritably "I'm sick of talking about her. She was a selfish bitch. You aren't responsible for her or what she did in the end. So stop being such a dork."

Felix looked as though he'd been struck by a truck. A warning look from Seb shut him up "We were all affected by what Alice did" Seb said pointedly "it'll be a long time before we get over it and most of all Felix. He and Hattie want to keep their relationship low key for the time being and I can't say I blame them."

Roxy laughed "Of course, what Alice did was her fault, not yours, you and Hattie are good together, and life's for living. You could make yourselves famous with my campaign."

"Not everything is about publicity and being famous" smiled Seb pragmatically "now let's change the subject. Max - the people who own Simeon have asked me to find a buyer for him. I wondered if you'd be interested?"

Max slid off his chair slapped his leg and threw back his head back in laughter "Hmm, Simeon well there's a surprise. You are nothing less than predictable Seb. However, I could be tempted, he's a nice chap and I like him. Do I get to ride him today?"

"You do indeed" grinned Seb "see what you think."

"Don't think I am completely wet behind the ears Seb" warned Max "you've been lining this up all along haven't you?"

"Not at all" blustered Seb "as if I would."

"Have it your own way" smirked Max "but as it happens I do quite like the horse, so give me a figure, and we'll see if we can meet somewhere in the middle."

"Max" whined Roxy "stop teasing Seb "you know you like the horse, and you were only saying you wanted to buy one."

"All true Roxy, but I'm no mug Seb" Max stared at him, his eyes glinting dangerously don't make the mistake of treating me like one."

"Of course not, I wouldn't ...I mean ..."

"Forget it" reassured Max "I am interested in the horse, let me ride him today and I'll decide."

"That's better" purred Roxy, blowing on her coffee "you know it makes sense" she laughed stupidly.

In a trance Felix watched the game of verbal ping-pong and felt sick. Max and Roxy were dreadful people, they meant nothing to him, yet he had to go along with them when all he wanted to do was tell them to piss off. How could they be so flippant about what had happened with Alice? He looked from Seb to Max, and Roxy to Max. Their avaricious sly faces were incongruous in the sharp beautiful purity of the frosty morning. Shaking he stood up, excusing himself and stumbled outside into the sparkling crystal air, leaving behind him the stench of greed. Hattie who'd been on her way to find him, took one look at him and grabbed his hand and they gazed sadly at each other, words unnecessary. and they moved away heading stealthily towards the cottage, hands knotted together.

Sighing, Leo watched them go as the pair trod stealthily towards the cottage their hands entwined, Felix's blond head drooping with despair and Hattie listening intently. He marched into the tack room to face the others; as usual he would hold the fort; he was buggered if he would let the commission slip through his fingers from that bastard Max.

Hattie and Felix reached the cottage with Fiver scampering lightly after them, and ironically despite their distress their footsteps still fell together in perfect synchrony. Felix was a bundle of jittering agitated nerves, befuddled with anger and despair; Hattie's face was pinched with worry as he ranted and complained, furiously spitting out the gist of the scene in the tack room.

"Darling, it's okay, they are crass, stupid people, take no notice" she whispered kindly as they stumbled into the kitchen, taking him in her arms and cradling his head "they don't know what they're talking about."

"I know" Felix snapped shoving her off rudely, turning away in anger shouting, "they didn't even know Alice, but they make me sick the way they think they can stand in judgement over her."

Hattie reeled with hurtful shock as he thrust her away, and at the venom and hatred in his voice. Like a bolt from the blue, she suddenly snapped all the emotion of the last month erupting in a nanosecond. She glared angrily at him "No, you're right but what I do know Felix is that you need to start living in the here and now. What Alice did, she did, you can't change that, neither can I. So just get on with it, deal with it, and stop punishing yourself, me, and everyone else. It's time to start picking up the pieces and start living again and stop being a self centred arse."

Felix was defiant, replying testily "I'm so not."

"Yes you are" blurted Hattie boldly, her eyes blazing with anger, "you're full of shit and self pity, and everyone is tip-toeing around you and your feelings, and when Max comes out with the truth you don't like it. Alice wasn't some hallowed saint, immortalised now because she had the temerity to kill herself. Most of the time she was a bitch to you, and made your life a misery. Her life mistakes were completely hers, not yours; stop taking responsibility for them."

"Have you finished?" screamed Felix furiously "she wasn't all bad."

"No, of course she wasn't but stop this stupid blame game " snapped Hattie angrily "there was a lot in her life that she didn't tell you or any of us, and stuff we'll never know, that drove her to do what she did. But for fuck's sake don't let it affect your life now, or the life you have to come. If you have any feelings for me at all can you please stop wallowing in shite and think reasonably."

Felix sank onto the kitchen chair, his head in his hands anger oozing out of him like a deflated balloon, "I know, I will try and rationalise it all darling, I do, I truly do."

"Well stop blaming yourself, everyone else and not the wonderful fucking Alice. She wasn't a fucking saint; she was nasty and supercilious, often to you, especially over the last few months. Stop trying to wrap it up in something it wasn't. Okay you feel like shit, we all do, but it is not our fault. And I am sick of you thinking like this and making us all feel like it."

Felix stared at her "Hattie please, I'm sorry."

It was too late, Hattie had lost it, "I'm tired of things Felix, the amazing Alice. She kills herself and is bloody wonderful. It's simply not true. The rest of us are left to pick up the pieces and you spend the rest of your life thinking it's your fault. Christ what an epitaph. She must be laughing all the way to the pearly gates."

"Please don't say that" implored Felix "I admit that there's a lot of truth in what you say."

"Yeah right," sneered Hattie, wearily shaking her head and making a move towards the door. Fiver was shaking, whimpering and cowering in his bed. "I don't want to live in Alice's shadow Felix, apologising for being her substitute every few minutes, tiptoe around her memory. I want a proper life. Someone to love me, for who I am."

"But I do Hattie, I've always loved you. It's like Alice played the trump card. I don't want to feel like this, but she has made me feel guilty and I shouldn't. I can't explain it, but I do."

Hattie looked at Felix, his shock of dishevelled blond hair and startling blue eyes and she crumpled emotionally. He looked like a little boy sitting at the kitchen table, forlorn, sad and lonely. She moved over and wrapped her arms around him kissing the top of his hair. They swayed and rocked together clasped in the moment, and Felix looked up at her, pulling her towards him. Her soft plump lips searching for his and they locked together. Their embrace was so tender, so sweet; his hand reached up and stroked her hair, her ears, her face and traced along the side of her neck. He felt her body relax as he pulled her onto his lap. Their kiss became more intense, his tongue searching for hers; her hands massaging his head and down towards his shoulders. Surfacing for air Felix got to his feet and took her hand leading her into the sitting room, and they both dropped cross legged onto the floor. Both hands over her head he pulled off Hattie's clothes until her pert breasts were exposed, the tight brown nipples standing erect. Felix dropped his head down, licking and sucking, pushing Hattie backwards, her body arching upwards, as he took each nipple in turn in his mouth whilst she groaned in pleasure. Snatching a cushion from the sofa he pushed it under her head and proceeded to remove her breeches, easing her long legs out one by one. Felix sat above her, his gleaming torso exposed and he admired her nakedness, enjoying her stunning body, and traced his fingers lingeringly up and down along her stomach. Hattie marginally embarrassed cast her gaze down, his cock was huge bulging out through his breeches, and gently she opened the zip and out it sprang out like a demon waiting to devour her.

"Darling, he's up and ready and so am I" whispered Hattie opening her mouth "it's so huge."

Felix reared up above her, "So ready. Where would you like him first sweetie, in your mouth?"

Max had had an expensive day. He'd bought Simeon and had completed on his property for the following week. Roxy had been impressed with both of his purchases. That the house was amazing was a given, how could anyone not like it? He'd paid over the top, but in the scheme of things he didn't care. Both the horse and the house were perfect for him and he had no doubt the boys had taken a juicy back hander, but again, that was the way of the world and for the first time in his life he felt reckless. He had money to burn and it saved him doing the looking and worrying. They'd earned their commission. He thought of Elizabeth Collins and the evening he had planned ahead. She'd definitely earned her commission. She had a nice body had dear Elizabeth - for an older woman that was - and he had enjoyed every orifice and tiny part of it - several times over in fact. He smiled to himself, it never failed to astonish him what people would do for money. Elizabeth like the greedy avaricious woman she was had come across with the goods faster than an Olympic sprinter. That first day with Anna had been spectacular. Dear Anna, she always homed into what turned him on. When Elizabeth had taken them to view the house it had been very erotic. Elizabeth's hunger for her commission had been blatant. Normally Max wouldn't have given her second glance, but he'd been intrigued by her overt behaviour. Her coquettish innuendoes fascinated him. Anna wearily recognised the signs but said nothing, nevertheless preparing herself to go ahead with anything Max wanted. By the end of that afternoon Elizabeth had been blatantly stripped, splayed naked on the floor, toyed with and enjoyed sexually between the two of them, and then returned, flustered and flushed to her office in the Carfax. Since then Max had enjoyed several afternoons with the delightful Elizabeth Collins, sometimes combining his pleasure with Anna, sometimes without, and each time he had discovered that dear Elizabeth was becoming delightfully submissive and more embracing of the S&M culture. Her bottom last time was quite rare meat by the time he had finished with his antics, and he wondered how she would explain it away to her husband, but shrugging his shoulders dismissed the worry. Let her deal with it and he'd sent Anna out to find new toys to play with for their next adventure. He did love these middle class tarts. In truth he did feel a smidgeon of pity for Anna, who was of course owned by him and would do whatever she was told, and God forbid if she disobeyed, but Elizabeth, was entirely different. It gave a whole new meaning to power when she succumbed to him. This evening, once Roxy had been safely returned to the smoke, he had planned for Elizabeth to be screaming with desire having invited her to *'measure up'* the new house with him. Anna had organised for a four poster to be delivered the previous week, and later this afternoon would be arriving in the car with his chauffeur, to set up video cameras, bringing along the necessary toys; shackles, whips, nipple clamps, and other little fripperies and he knew she could be relied upon to have sourced the latest interesting gadgets. Dear Elizabeth, such a slave now to his desires would have the time of her life. Meanwhile they showed a cooing Roxy around his new home, and Max cast Elizabeth small meaningful and dangerously erotic glances. Excusing himself sincerely and profusely to a blissfully unaware Roxy of the antics that were about to take place, he instructed his chauffeur to take her back to London without delay, saying he had tedious things to organise with his move, which albeit were boring, had to be done prior to completion. He stood in the driveway with Elizabeth and waved her goodbye, whilst upstairs, Anna was already unpacking the cases she had brought with her. Once the tail lights had disappeared, Max took Elizabeth's little hand, clasping her tightly and ushering her into the house, and once inside within moments he'd forced her whimpering and submissive onto the floor and had her crawling like a dog towards the bedroom.

Kylie was frustrated and cross. She'd stolen the drugs, but had no idea what do with them now especially since she no longer had the promise of a cash cow in Alice. She'd off-loaded a batch of the stuff onto a dodgy local yard for a pittance but at least they'd asked no questions about the provenance. But she still had a shed load of Ketamine, if she knew how to get rid of it on the black market she surely would. In the meantime, work was a tad sparse. A couple of places she'd been freelancing at had said they didn't need her any more and she was convinced that Hattie and Felix had been bad mouthing her. She'd seen the advert in the local paper for work as a waitress at the mill when it opened. A local job agency were doing the hiring and she had an interview next week, when someone from London was coming down. For a nanosecond, Kylie considered that it could possibly be her old nemesis Roxy, but then on rationalising thought it probably wouldn't be. She wouldn't get involved in such small fry. Kylie quite fancied the comfort of a warm restaurant whizzing about with a few posh platefuls of dinner; it had to be an improvement on shoving a cartful of shit about an icy yard, and more to the point the money was really good. Anyway if by some small miracle it came off she could keep her head down and Roxy wouldn't ever know she was there. It didn't solve the problem of how to off load the drugs. She could chuck them away, but it stuck in her craw to ditch what could potentially be worth a load of dosh. Nope, she'd sit tight and bide her time, these things had a funny way of sorting themselves out. If she got the job at the restaurant she might make some useful contacts there.

"Look I'm bloody sorry - okay?" said Felix "I really mean it. I buggered off and left you to it, but what those awful people said about Alice upset me. Hattie had a real go at me and sorted me out."

"Oh Felix" sighed Seb "I can understand how you felt, they were crass and stupid. In hindsight you probably did the right thing just buggering off. But on the bright side darling Leo and I persuaded Max to get Simeon vetted and if it goes well, then we all stand to get a hefty commission."

"Mate, that's amazing news, you've done a brilliant job, what a coup! He's such a tricky sod that bloke and I feel I've let you down not helping, but I'm gonna change, starting now, and I've some news, Hattie has agreed to move into the cottage with me."

"Wow! That's the icing on the cake for the day" hallooed Leo "bloody fantastic news and about time too."

"I'm so glad you feel like that" said Felix sheepishly inspecting his hands "I thought you might disapprove."

"Disapprove? You've gotta be fucking joking. It's about bloody time."

"Oh guys, that's marvellous. Hattie 'll be thrilled, we both are. We need to lay the ghost of Alice and start living."

"Thank fuck for that - you do indeed" laughed Seb "you are *so* made for each other it makes me vomit."

"Glad to hear that Seb" grinned Felix slapping him on his back "I'm never so happy as when I'm making you vomit or come to that when I'm with Hattie either."

Frankie popped her curly head around the door "Hattie says is it ok if we feed now?"

"Definitely" they all chorused "we'll be out in a minute to give you a hand."

"Corks popping tonight methinks" said Seb marching to the door "just wait till I get hold of that Hattie the little minx."

"Any excuse for a booze up, you really are an old soak Seb" shouted Leo after his retreating back and turning to Felix smiled "but you know he's my old soak and one in a million."

"You're right there" agreed Felix "and so are you mate."

Whilst Roxy was being chauffeured driven back to London, luxuriating in the plush leather seats of Max's car she wondered what on earth possessed him to want to stay on at the house and *'measure up'* as he put it with Anna and that agent woman. What exactly were they measuring up that he couldn't have left Anna to do it - or the woman herself come to that? He must be paying a shed load of money for the place after all and she must be on a hefty commission. She felt a bit put out that he preferred to stay with them and not accompany her home. That was another thorn in her side - home. What was there for her when she returned? The children were on a sleep over and she had no doubt that Aiden wouldn't be there. He was spending more time out of the place lately than in it, pleading business, but Roxy knew that wasn't true. She wasn't stupid, he was with Chrissie, and whilst she claimed she wasn't jealous or worried, this little dalliance had more staying power than a Duracell battery and Chrissie was not the normal yellow haired bimbo. She had all the tenacious grasping tentacles Roxy associated with a man-eating squid. She may well have to deal with her soon if Aiden didn't sort himself out. Pity as she wasn't a bad PA in the scheme of things. Perhaps she should wait till after the New Year launch, which was not so far away after all and Chrissie was doing a fair job on the arrangements, and then get shot of her, and they didn't need any scandal to rock the boat for the finale of the TV programme. No, she considered it would be best to keep quiet until the new year, then she would have to go. As the miles rolled past and the countryside turned to concrete she thought about what her life had become, she really didn't want to come back into London any more. She leant forward, tempted to ask the driver to take her back to Fittlebury, and then slumped back again. Max was probably finished at the house by now and was having dinner somewhere with Anna. She reluctantly resigned herself to a quiet evening on her own and pondered on where her life was going - she needed more publicity, a swankier image and she had to find a way to get it.

Max watched dispassionately from his chair as casually he instructed Elizabeth to strip off her clothes. Standing pathetically and obediently in the centre of the large room she undressed, timidly holding her hands over her body when she had finished and was completely naked. Anna was waiting by the bed already prepared, in stockings and a suspender belt, her shaved pubic mound and bare breasts glistening with oil. Max took his time staring at Elizabeth, as though she were an interesting specimen in a jar, enjoying every moment of her discomfiture and then gave the nod to Anna, who took Elizabeth's trembling hand and led her to the bed.

Max was fascinated to watch Anna at work. Elizabeth's eyes were terrified yet excited, as she was submissively prepared for Max's pleasure. As instructed Anna had gone for some more hard line equipment this time, and she had not disappointed. Instead of the usual shackles and handcuffs, she was busy encasing Elizabeth around the ankles and just below the knees and wrists with jute ropes strapping her arms and legs onto a clever v shaped pole device; in a trice, with the use of a pulley she had suspended her above the four poster, her limbs splayed apart at the widest angle with her breasts, clitoris and anus completely exposed, her bottom hanging vulnerable and available. Elizabeth's neck was in the crook of the two poles and in itself the weight of her suspended hanging body must have been alarmingly painful. She groaned pitifully but Anna ignored her.

"Would you like her gagged?" Anna asked "before I start?"

Max considered, walking over and stroking Elizabeth's hair and face "You know you need to be punished don't you and you do so love it my stinking dirty old tart. I won't have Anna gag you yet, in a while maybe - when I have you pleading for mercy."

He nodded to Anna to begin. Elizabeth eyes glinted with fear and excitement as she watched Anna open her instrument case and pull out the nipple clamps.

The next half hour found Max becoming very aroused, his erection was throbbing. Elizabeth, despite the pain was loving every minute he could tell, she was squirming and moaning and pretty soon he knew he would have to join in. He was not so sure about Anna - to her it was just a job. Elizabeth by now, had her nipples severely clamped, pegged and bound, her breasts were going red and swollen under ropes. Anna had applied spiteful pegs to her rib cage and upper arms.

Max walked over to Elizabeth stroking her hair again "Are you okay?"

"Yes" she whispered "I need more."

"Then you shall have it my dear."

Max nodded to Anna. Without a word Anna sank down fastening her mouth onto Elizabeth's clitoris, sucking hard. Elizabeth's suspended body bucked madly in the air, and Anna came up for breath, twisting the nipple clamp wickedly and ordering her to be still, before diving back down again. Elizabeth screamed and Max sighed, tutting sadly he reluctantly forced the ball gag into her mouth. Anna took a breath, and taking a huge screw-in vibrator from her case, she showed it to Elizabeth, lovingly teasing it around her cheeks and face. Elizabeth's eyes widened in anticipation as Anna smiled sweetly at her and without hesitation wound it into her waiting anus as Elizabeth's eyes bulged with shock and pain. Anna switched on the vibrator, as together, she and Max watched their captor buck and plunge in her ropes. Anna took another vibrator plunging it with aplomb into Elizabeth's vagina and tightened the nipple clamps. Elizabeth's face was contorted with a mixture of emotions as she gazed on her tormentors. Max looked on, stroking himself and considering his options.

Anna looked up seductively through her lashes at Max, who nodded and she stopped, leaving Elizabeth frustratingly swinging on her ropes the vibrators buzzing whipping her into a frenzy of pain and ecstasy.

"A gimp mask I think" instructed Max "do we have one?"

"Of course," replied Anna, rummaging in the box and producing a particularly vicious black number, "wait, I'll put it on." She wrenched Elizabeth's head back brutally, pulling out the gag and forcing on the mask as she struggled and swayed in the slings - all the time her body twitching and jerking with the buzzing vibrators.

"Can she hear us?"

"No, this one makes you deaf, blind and mute," said Anna, "she's in a world of her own now."

"Perfect. Let's leave her in her world of never ending vaginal and anal punishment. Come here Anna," he reached over and took her by the shoulders, "you look very tempting tonight with your little shaved fanny peeping out under those suspenders, and you excite me when you are disciplining the snobby Elizabeth. You do know how I love to fuck your arse my dear, it's always turned me on more than your cunt. Elizabeth can swing in her bondage and wait a little longer for us to play with her."

"Your pleasure will be my pleasure Max" Anna lied, coyly reaching for the oil and smothering it lavishly between her bum cheeks "shall I bend over and spread my legs?"

CHAPTER 80

As the weeks to Christmas rattled away, like the stops on the tube, suddenly it was only a week to go. The mill looked amazing, completely finished all bar the finishing touches to the decorations, no-one could have recognised it for the blackened old shell that it had been nine months previously. The kitchens were equipped, the larders stocked; the restaurant furnishings had arrived with high backed leather dining chairs and round or square glass topped tables. The distinctive crockery and cutlery symbolic of Aiden's restaurants had arrived, and behind the bar rows of bottles with every concoction of alcohol were stacked alongside sparkling new glasses. Farouk's cameras had been recording the metamorphosis tirelessly, including the cataclysmic rows between Aiden and Roxy with the odd sneaky shot of a smug Chrissie for good measure. Farouk was a tosser but he was not totally stupid, he could see which way the wind was blowing and wanted to catch the action on celluloid for posterity and use it whichever way he could, even if it wasn't for this particular production. The TV show was rolling out weekly, made up of tantalisingly short clips of the sparring *Rox-Aid* duo and their adventurous new project, complete with all the little intrigues of Roxy and her unbelievable and natural talent for riding, and fascinating new range of equestrian gear, which had hit the shops in time for Christmas. The relentless Aiden perfecting his menu and the lustful hovering Chrissie; Alice's suicide and the dramatic deaths of the previous year had been played to an enormous proportion and the mill now had a veil of dark mystery which couldn't fail to fascinate anyone, from the totally ghoulish to the utterly terrified. A fantastic example of PR marketing at it finest. The New Year's Eve party was a complete sell out, with a host of celebs and wannabes. The new staff had been hired and being trained in groups by a Maître D from his London restaurant including an incognito Kylie. Aiden had decided on the menu, which he considered a triumph and he was bringing down his favoured chefs from his most popular restaurants in London, whilst the new boys were trained up. The spa had been finished weeks before and was looking at its most glamorous. The equipment was all in situ, the massage rooms, the therapy areas and like a wonderful jewel, the turquoise pool sparkled under a glass atrium. Fully trained staffed were straining in their pristine white uniforms raring

BIG BUCKS

to get started on the punters when they opened for business after the New Year's eve bash.

Roxy was trying to finalise on her house before Christmas and seemed to be frustrated with idiots at every turn, and it was increasingly unlikely to reach a conclusion no matter how much she shouted and threatened. Whilst Max was well ensconced already in his monstrous house, already furnished by the ever ready Anna and was spending quite a lot of time there. He'd booked big table at the mill for New Year's Eve for a bunch of his racing cronies and was putting them all up at his new house. Roxy was in a strange way jealous and scathing, all at the same time. Max seemed to be slightly edging beyond her grasp which was frustrating. True, she still slept with him occasionally, but somehow he seemed to have a whole life outside her, and she didn't like it one bit.

Hattie had moved in with Felix and apart from a few rocky moments they were certainly love's young dream. A few people had made snide remarks about it being a bit soon after Alice had died, but they'd doggedly ignored them and got on with their lives. Hattie was actually blossoming and Felix was too in his own way, gradually getting over the guilt thing and starting to live his life again, but always there remained a nagging doubt that Alice hadn't committed suicide, even if most of the time he did manage to shove it to the back of his mind.

Seb was increasingly histrionic that he couldn't have his big celebration at Christmas and played the drama queen card to the maximum, alternating between tossing his hair back theatrically and holding his head in his hands, but it did seem sensible to wait until the bill actually became law and they could actually '*marry*' rather than just have a civil partnership. But Leo held firm, telling him not to be silly and to be patient and trust him. On the upside, to everyone's collective relief Simeon the horse had passed the vetting. Theo had been despatched to do the job and was thorough, demanding and unbiased but the horse hadn't faltered and he was pronounced fit and sound. The commission, even taking Dougie into the equation was substantial and their bank balances were all looking extremely buoyant going into Christmas and the New Year. The big bucks stacking up had luckily made Seb a great deal more joyful which was just as well, as if he hadn't cheered up Leo could easily have murdered him as Christmas approached.

Hattie strung up baubles and festive lights on the Christmas tree in the sitting room with evergreen garlands along the wooden beam of the inglenook. Stuffing red tinsel in for a bit of colour she stood back and looked at her labours. It really did look very jolly. Her first Christmas with Felix. The old cottage was a perfect place to decorate, it looked like a Christmas card, all they needed was the snow, but luckily there had been none so far, just a few sharp frosts. She was in charge of dinner on the big day and they'd naturally invited the boys over, plus Dulcie, Nancy, and Frankie, and Oli and Theo for the day, although poor old Theo was on call - the perils of being the junior assistant. Hattie was having a few moments of despair about the menu but Felix eased them away as smoothly as massaging the tension in her shoulders; shove the Turkey in, he'd do the veg and they'd buy the puds. Ask the others to bring nibbles and starters and they were sorted - don't make a drama out of crisis. Hattie wished it would be that easy. She'd been into Horsham to buy presents struggling to park amidst the hordes of shoppers in the inadequate car parks, finally ending up squeezing into the narrow slots in Piries Place. It was a minefield, shouldering alongside the crowds, jostling each other in the hustle and bustle of the Swan Centre and then the main drag of the high street. In the end she settled for some boring scarves and mittens in the Edinburgh Woollen Mill for immediate relatives, but still was at a loss to buy something whacky and original for Felix and the others. In truth she wanted to shower Felix with presents, give him a stocking, place it at the end of their bed, so they could unwrap each little trifle and laugh stupidly together and then dive back under the covers for a marathon session. But it seemed a bit intimately presumptuous, he was still so fragile in many ways. She hesitated outside Anne Summers and then decided a few presents under the tree would be better. But those presents had to be more than just run of the Edinburgh Woollen Mill. Where should she go?

If Hattie had but know it, Felix was having the same quandary. He hesitated about what he should do. He so wanted to spoil her beyond belief, but was held back by invisible tentacles. The shadow of Alice lurked in his background and no matter how much he shoved her out, she loomed like some pernicious influence. He snuck into Anne Summers rummaging about for stupid knick-knacks, chocolate willies, body lube and some saucy knickers, but then wondered if it a might be a bit risqué, and was just on the point of leaving empty handed when Dulcie came in.

"Hi Felix!" she yelled across the shop "good to see you - Happy Crimble!"

"Hi" mumbled Felix embarrassedly diving behind a display of crotch-less body stockings "fancy seeing you here."

Dulcie hooted with laughter "God I always shop for Nancy's stocking fillers in here - great place. What're you buying for Hattie?"

"Keep your voice down Dulcie" hissed Felix glancing over at the shop assistants who were watching them in amusement "I've no idea what she'd like, I've never been in here before."

"I'll give you a hand if you want, I know what turns us girls on. But if you don't trust me, ask Edwina" she pointed at one of the girls behind the counter "they're always happy to give advice."

Felix groaned, what he'd hoped would be a discreet expedition was turning into an Ealing farce "thanks, but perhaps I'll leave it, get her something from Equitogs."

"Don't be daft Felix, she's your lover, not your mother. Look this is a great section to get you started" Dulcie took Felix by the hand and led him past the saucy underwear and over to the back of the shop "lots of sex toys here and erotic stuff. What sort of vibrator are you using at the moment?"

"Dulcie, for Christ's sake, I don't need a vibrator, I have a cock, if you haven't noticed."

"Oh that old thing" laughed Dulcie "that's great, but a girl loves a vibrator too and so will you, you'll get a right horn on when you use it on her."

"I don't believe this" sighed Felix "I only came in to Horsham to do a quiet bit of shopping."

Dulcie ignored him pulling down a matching cock ring "What about this then? Crikey it's got three speeds and four pulse settings, imagine the pleasure."

Despite his awkwardness Felix surreptitiously picked up the box and read the label "Christ, what a gadget."

"It's only £25 too, you could get the Rampant Rabbit as well" said Dulcie turning her attention to some fur lined hand cuffs "what about these?"

"No, absolutely and definitely not, we are *not* into that sort of stuff."

"Don't know what you're missing" teased Dulcie "you might get around to it one of these days. Let's have a look at the lubes."

By the time she'd finished, Felix had left the shop with a red face and a small stash of toys and to go with them, swearing Dulcie to total secrecy saying he was on his way to Equitogs now for Hattie's *'proper'* present.

Dulcie and the girls in the shop watched him disappear and then fell about with peals of laughter "Blimey he's so gorgeous" Edwina exclaimed "but so terribly naive, I wouldn't mind enlightening him!"

"Wasting your time babe, he's head over heels in love" laughed Dulcie "but I'm pretty sure his education is only just beginning!"

Christmas Day heralded a sharp frost and icy patterns on the unheated cottage windows. Hattie and Felix who'd struggled out of a warm love nest donned Santa bobble hats and scarves and stomped off, hugging each other in a tight embrace matching their steps along the track to the stables their steamy breath ballooning out in great plumes. They'd made a pact, that no matter what the temptation to stay in bed, they'd do the horses before putting their feet up in the cottage and exchanging their presents whilst waiting for their guests to arrive for lunch. Hattie had stoked up the Rayburn and shoved in the Turkey and it was toasting away merrily, heating the water nicely for a steaming bath when they returned. The eventers at this time of year were on furlough until the new year, having a break after their hard season, roughed off and out in the paddocks with a couple who didn't cope with being out 24/7 in their boxes. By contrast Seb's were still tucked up in their stables and still in normal work, but today was a simple muck and chuck job. Hattie and Felix whisked their way around the diminished yard, filling haynets, making feeds for the evening, changing rugs and turning the remaining horses out, mucking out their boxes and emptying barrows. Within the hour they had finished and were returning home, Fiver scampering around them shoving his nose into the freezing grass every few strides."

"Looking forward to our first Christmas together darling" asked Felix his arm firmly wrapped around Hattie "I'm so happy."

"Me too" sighed Hattie hugging him back "I just hope I don't muck up the dinner!"

"Don't be daft, course you won't, what's to muck up anyway? Ready made starters and pud, and a Turkey - come on!"

"It's all right for you!"

"I'm gonna help" laughed Felix gently "don't let's make it a big deal, I just want to have a lovely relaxed day."

"Me too, when shall we open our presents?"

"Let's have a bath when we get back and do it straight after" suggested Felix "I hope you like yours."

"I hope you like yours!" laughed Hattie "It's a bit different."

"Intriguing, but actually so is mine."

"Can't we open them when we get in - I can't wait." Hattie turned her face up to his, her eyes shining brilliantly "we can have a bath afterwards!"

Felix kissed her, a deep searching and lingering kiss "why not Hattie, let's do it."

Laundry Cottage stunk of fags, booze and sweaty feet. Seb and Leo had been down to the Fox in the village the night before and had a sinful skinful. Dougie and his friend Roberto had come over to join them and had been too pissed to drive home. Frankie, who rarely drunk much had come to the rescue and driven the inebriates home, and the party had carried on into the wee small hours with Dougie and his mate crashing in Leo's old room. Christmas morning was no respecter of a hang over and now looking around the breakfast table at the haggard faces, the collective fumes exuding from their pores would have been enough to stop a rampaging stallion in its tracks. Frankie who was whisking about the kitchen humming to herself screwed up her nose in distaste as she approached the table with a steaming pot of coffee.

"Time to sober up you piss artists" she smirked "hot, strong coffee, and I'm making dry toast, and scrambled eggs with tomatoes."

"Oh for fuck's sake don't" pleaded Dougie theatrically throwing his head in his hands "I can't bear it."

"Well you will matey - 'cos it's a good hangover cure, and you're gonna have some Alka Seltzer and plenty of fruit juice too" grinned Frankie unsympathetically "and by the way you reek, so after the coffee, go grab a shower."

"Who is this woman?" grumbled Dougie histrionically, appealing to Roberto "save me - why does she hate me?"

Seb managed a feeble grin "she doesn't hate us buddy, she's doing it for our own good and we've gotta sober up, we're going up to Felix and Hattie's gaff for lunch."

Roberto looked up "Dougie" he drawled, his Italian accent heavily spicing his dialogue "no-body hates you. We all love you, but she's right, we need to sober up and we do stink."

Dougie slumped onto the table groaning "I am going to die" he drawled feebly.

"No you're not, get this inside you" laughed Frankie, "tomatoes are good for a hangover and so are eggs."

"I'm going to ring Hattie and tell her we have two more for Christmas lunch" announced Leo sensibly "there's no way you're gonna wagon your way anywhere today."

"We can't" grumbled Dougie almost incoherently "we're supposed to be at Carl's."

"Face facts, neither of you are sober enough to drive. Text him, he'll understand, he's got a houseful anyway."

"Oh dear, my street creds just gone right out the bloody front door" whined Dougie frantically "why did I drink so much?"

"Because you're a tosser?" laughed Leo heartily scooping up his eggs, "this is delicious Frankie."

Roberto smiled lasciviously at Frankie "Darling you have hidden talents, rather nice tits to be frank, as well as good cooking."

"Is your cock as big as your mouth?" asked Frankie calmly pouring herself a coffee "or is it tiny and your mouth works overtime to make up for the shortfall?"

Roberto choked on a mouthful of egg "I really like you."

"You don't even know me, and I haven't even started on you yet" threatened Frankie sweetly "now big boy, eat your eggs and belt up."

Seb choked affectedly "Well said darling, these boys need putting in their place."

"Just a load of piss heads" remarked Frankie mildly sprinkling salt on her tomatoes "if you're coming to eat Christmas lunch with us, smarten up will you and don't fuck up our day, because you smell like blocked drains and look like tramps."

"Fuck me" gushed Dougie to no-one in particular "she doesn't pull her punches does she?"

"No I don't sweetie" smiled Frankie "shape up or ship out."

"*Sieg heil mein Fuhrer*!" exploded Roberto imitating a Hitler moustache with his forefinger "we will obey."

"Good" said Frankie unruffled and marginally satisfied "just make sure you behave yourselves."

Dulcie and Nancy were up with the lark and had the yard done and shipshape before the sun had risen. The horses' beds were as usual snowy white and banked up, hay nets filled and feeds made ready for them to be brought in for the evening. It was just another day for them, although underlying the normality of the frozen fingers was the anticipation of a big roast dinner cooked by someone else, complete with presents and silly games. Charles and Jennifer invited all of the Nantes Staff in on Christmas morning for drinks and nibbles before they began their own celebrations and it was a tradition that they finished off the yard themselves in the evening. Nancy had offered to come back but Jennifer would hear none of it, saying they must have their Christmas off and she was happy to pop out and bring the horses in.

At first they stood stiffly in the drawing room whilst Charles dispensed drinks and Jennifer whisked about with canapés. Mrs Fuller hopped from toe to toe with Doris and Fred, she hated being waited upon, it felt so alien. In Celia's, the first Mrs Parker-Smythe's day, she would have been doing the cooking and waiting with Doris helping and Celia orchestrating and complaining, but since Jennifer had married Charles, the order of things had changed. None of that now. The staff were invited in on Christmas morning and were given their presents and waited on by Jennifer and Charles. Ivy, Jennifer's mother had come down to stay and luckily served to put Mrs Fuller at ease, she and Freda had become firm friends and today Freda Fuller was to join the family at Christmas lunch - hitherto unheard of previously. Times were changing. Jennifer's somewhat outrageous sister Susan and her partner Wayne were also here together with Susan's children from several alliances. Considering they were all East End born and bred and proud of it, Charles was adapting well, although rather than staying in the house itself with Ivy, Susan and her mob were in the old gardener's cottage, which was probably just as well. Charles was a total snob, but to give him credit, he'd embraced his second wife's family and seemed to tolerate them well, even if he did have to hide his surprise at their behaviour at times. His own children were denied him on Christmas day by his ex wife but were coming for the New Year along with own his parents who were coming up from Devon to stay and so this Christmas belonged to Jennifer and her family.

The staff loosened up once their presents were opened with many delighted exclamations and thanks. Jennifer put on cheesy Christmas music and soon toes were tapping and Ivy began humming enthusiastically . Dulcie couldn't resist joining in and was soon leading a full blown sing song, carols blaring out at full blast and Wayne and Susan started dancing exaggeratedly. Christmas morning at Nantes had never been so jolly. Ivy wiped the tears away from her eyes and laughingly clutched Jennifer's arm. They smiled at each other happily and Jennifer went over and took Charles' hand and they rocked off in a rumba. Freda and Ivy slipped away into the kitchen, clutching their sherries and checked the lunch, content to share the chores, it was to be a real family affair. A get-together of the upstairs and the downstairs. Dulcie and Nancy took their leave, with Jennifer saying they were definitely not to come back to put the horses to bed and she would do it. As the girls ambled back arm in arm they marvelled again at what a great boss they had.

Oli woke up to the sound of the Church bells rattling the cottage windows and light breathing beside him. For a nanosecond he struggled to remember where he was and then smiling reached over to stroke Sarah's naked back. She rolled over, sighing and wrapped her long legs around him and he felt himself getting aroused, the old dawn horn shifting into overdrive as his erection pushed against her.

"Blimey, you're up with the lark" she murmured sleepily "still want more after last night?"

"You can't keep a good vet down" mumbled Oli nibbling the side of her neck and allowing his hand to stray over her breast "don't mind do you?"

"Nope, but I could do with brushing my teeth."

"I don't care, if you don't."

Sarah rolled over, straddling herself on top of him, her splendid tits dangling in his face "I'm so glad I had to call you out last night."

"So glad I was on call" agreed Oli looking up at her "you made my evening."

"Never shagged in a stable before?"

"Christ when you rang Sarah I never expected ..."

"I've always fancied you Oli."

"Really?" said Oli surprised "I had no idea! You've never even given me a hint!"

"Good old Nimrod, he chose a good evening to get a touch of colic" Sarah laughed "there's nothing more sexy than a man stripping off to the waist to do a rectal examination."

Oli grinned up at her "Well I certainly did plenty of those last night!"

"I've always been partial" agreed Sarah "It was fun darling. My poor Nimrod though, he did need you, we were lucky it wasn't worse, but on the upside the waiting did give us time to get to know each other rather better." She smiled coyly at Oli "Since Justin and I split up, I've missed sex dreadfully."

"Oh baby, I hope I can help you out in that department" smiled Oli, taking her breast in his mouth and licking the nipple.

"Darling I certainly hope so" sighed Sarah "I've a feeling you and I are going to have a lot of late night calls."

Oli relinquished her tit and held her by the shoulders looking into her eyes "I certainly hope so sweetie."

Theo was also woken by the bells, but on the other side of the village. The house was eerily quiet and moreover bloody freezing. He shoved his head back under the duvet and then put his nose out again remembering it was Christmas morning. He'd only had a couple in the pub last night and today he was on call; Oli had been on take last night, with Andrew second. Judging by the silence in the house, Oli had either had a long night and was now fast akip or he was still out. He dragged himself out of bed and shoved his head around Oli's door, seeing his bed hadn't been slept in he immediately felt guilty. Struggling down the stairs to make coffee and toast he pondered whether he should ring him and see if he could take over but then decided to wait an hour or two. He was looking forward to today, he liked the Fittlebury Hall crew, they were a good laugh and it should be relatively quiet on the work front with any luck. A surge of guilt swept over him, he really ought to ring Oli and find out if he needed any help.

The phone rang and then went to voice mail. Theo tried again and this time it was answered by a panting Oli "Hi Theo mate, what's up, you okay?"

"I'm fine Oli, just ringing to see if you are and if you need me to take over? You sound breathless - you alright?"

"Yep, fine, been out on a colic call. Just doing an internal."

"Sorry do you need me?" asked Theo "give you a break?"

"Nah, don't worry, I've got this covered now. Anything new is yours. I'll see you down at Felix's when I've finished."

"Okay Oli, if you're sure?"

"Yes definitely, I'd like to finish this off myself - you know how it is."

"Sure, ciao then." said Theo relieved, but it was funny because he was sure he could hear someone giggling in the background.

Hattie and Felix had exchanged their presents. She'd bought him a onesie and a range of sensual oils for massaging, together with a little massage machine laughing that she would get the pleasure from them too. Felix was nervous and fascinated as he watched Hattie open her gifts from him. He'd wrapped the sex toys inside a new fleece from Equitogs and they tumbled out onto the floor. Far from any embarrassment Hattie had laughed with glee as she examined them, claiming they were the best Christmas presents she'd ever had. Tugging at his hand and insisting they must try them out straight away they'd galloped up the stairs like things demented. Now they were terribly late getting the spuds peeled having spent a good hour playing with the toys. Felix was seriously aroused as he'd the inserted the big pink vibrator and switched it on. He watched fascinated as she'd squirmed and wriggled, the little rabbit ears going hell for leather on her clitoris as he turned up the speed. Hattie bucking like a rodeo horse gasped with pleasure, a red flush creeping over her neck as she convulsed with sensual gratification. As Hattie fell back on the pillows gasping and exhausted, Felix rocked back and pulled on the cock ring to his throbbing erection, switching it on he pushed into her slippery wetness. As she took the real thing he thought her erotic groaning would never stop; spinning her over onto all fours and taking her from behind, he managed a few more minutes before he exploded himself. The toys had been a great hit, Dulcie was right it was such a turn on.

The phone rang whilst they were desperately trying to catch up with preparing the veg. It was Leo asking if it was okay to bring Dougie and Roberto for Christmas lunch and they'd bring plenty of booze and grub, so no need to panic about food. Hattie still on a blissful sexual high just said the more the merrier and went back to the potato peeling.

When the phone rang again Felix answered this time. It was Oli begging to bring a friend with him for lunch, Felix who was also still on a high from his sexual marathon also agreed immediately, but as an afterthought asked if he could bring some extra chairs, as otherwise they'd be sitting on the floor. When he replaced the receiver it occurred to him he hadn't even thought to ask who it was that Oli was bringing.

As he and Hattie continued in their sexual and domestic bliss in the kitchen gossiping like an old married couple they remarked how their intimate first Christmas had now turned into a total houseful and just hoped there was enough grub to go round; neither of them could have been happier and neither of them knew what complications the New Year would bring.

CHAPTER 81

The excesses of Christmas Day were, for many in Fittlebury, expunged by following country pursuits, in particular going hunting on Boxing Day. Charles and Jennifer always made a striking cameo appearance at the meet, posing like Posh and Becks. They rarely stayed out for long but enjoyed coffee-housing at the meet with Colin and Sandy and Katherine, and some of the other nobs and this meant that the girls were on duty, driving the truck and keeping sober throughout the day. Felix and Hattie went on foot, as did Leo and Seb, and this year, Roxy had inveigled an invitation to go with them, dragging along with her the reluctant Stephanotis and Delphinium and Ingrid, their nanny, leaving Aiden in London to sort out last minute menu decisions for New Year. Max, who'd spent a lonely Christmas Day in town at his clubs, had rung Seb to inform him he was coming down to ride his horse, and once informed they were all going hunting, by default, had gone along with them instead.

The meet was held at a quaint pub called The Devil's Jump, about ten miles west of Fittlebury. Steeped in local folklore, allegedly the Devil, in order to amuse himself, was said to jump from a series of Bronze Age barrows on the down land, severely angering the God Thor, who in turn, threw stones to keep him at bay. The pub, typical of the West Sussex long house, stood isolated aloft the side of the downs, with a large car park and plenty of space for the mounted field and foot followers, which was just as well, for the Boxing Day Meet always brought out a massive crowd, and today was no exception.

The sensible ones had got there early to make sure of a good parking space. The meet was officially midday, but generally people started arriving at about eleven, ostensibly to see the tradition of horse and hound but, more often than not, to have a social hobnob and to get pissed if they didn't have to drive. The pub provided a stirrup cup for the mounted followers and did a roaring trade for those on foot. By midday the car park was thronging with horses, their steamy breath blowing out in great plumes in the icy air, their riders laughing and knocking back the mulled wine with gusto. Waiters whisked nimbly amongst them with sausage rolls and cheese straws, avoiding the piles of droppings steaming on the tarmac. The foot followers bellowed to friends, cat calling, laughing and joking, and toiled backwards and forwards inside the pub to replenish their drinks.

Roxy was spellbound, excitedly declaring, above the whingeing and moaning of the children, "I desperately wanna do this," she said, her eyes gleaming, "When can I go out on Galaxy?"

"Well, you are doing really well, but you'd have to come out on a quiet day," said Felix diplomatically, "as it can be very dangerous and seriously fast once they get going, it's not all posing about with a drink in your hand. Wait and see what you think once the first line's over."

"I quite fancy having a go," stated Max firmly, "doesn't look that difficult to me."

"You've both got good, quiet horses," chimed in Seb, "I don't see why you couldn't take them out on a week day soon, Felix. Hattie could go with you, we'd cover the yard."

Felix glared at Seb. "It'd have to be on a non-jumping day."

"Why?" asked Roxy, "I've done a bit of jumping now."

"Yes, I know," Felix tried to explain, "but this isn't the same as jumping in a controlled environment. The horses get very excited, no matter how quiet they are normally, and you never know what you're going to be jumping next, or what the ground's like - there are a lot of variables"

"If I didn't know differently," said Max shrewdly, "I'd say you were stalling Felix. I think if we're asking, you should take us. We're very good clients."

"Of course, but I do have to think of your safety. Take note that Seb isn't offering to take you either and there is a reason for that."

Seb flushed and started to bluster, "I don't do jumping darlings, everyone knows that. I get brown breeches."

"What?" asked Roxy, bewildered.

Leo laughed, "He means he's shit scared and I would take Felix's advice if I were you Roxy, hunting to hounds isn't for the faint hearted."

Seb sighed, clutching his hands together apologetically, "'Fraid so, terrifies the life out of me, but hats off to you doll for wanting to do it."

"I've always been a fucking speed junky," declared Roxy brazenly, "bring it on I say."

"In more ways than one," remarked Max dryly, looking at her sideways, "but yeah, I'm up for it too - make sure you arrange it early in the New Year, Felix."

Felix glared at them, stifling his anger. "Whatever," he managed to spit militantly, "I'll see what I can do."

"Good lad," said Max condescendingly, "get on to it eh?"

Felix was just about to fire off a scathing response when Stephanotis grabbed her mother around the legs and cried out, "Do the dogs rip up the pretty foxes Mummy?" she shrieked wildly, "do they honestly? Bastards!"

"That'll do Stephi baby," sighed Roxy, picking the clutching hand from her jeans in distaste, "course they don't - 'gainst the law, aint it Felix?"

"Yes it is, they follow a false trail, you'll see in a minute."

"I don't believe you," shouted Stephanotis, "you're a bloody liar."

In his mood Felix could have slapped the kid, but Roxy just ignored her, signalling to the nanny to take the child away. Then Delphinium started to cry pitifully, mewing like an animal in distress. "Mummy please - do they kill the foxes?"

"Oh for fuck's sake, take the children away, can you Ingrid," Roxy spluttered angrily. "I am trying to watch. Buck up and do your bleeding job."

Hattie felt sorry for the kids. They didn't have much of a life, no wonder they were so stressed out and obnoxious. She was sure that Stephanotis wouldn't be quite so ghastly if she had more attention and, as for little Delphinium, you could see she was desperate for a cuddle. She moved over to talk to them, taking them by the hand and offered to show them the hounds.

"Hattie's good with the kids," remarked Roxy sarcastically, "you'd better watch it Felix, she'll want to be knocked up before you know it."

"I think it's rather sweet," said Leo butting in, "the children are loving the attention."

Roxy looked at him nastily, "you gays are all the same, soft as shit."

"Now girls," said Felix easily, defusing the tension, but determined not to let Roxy get away with her snide remarks. "Hattie doesn't have a mean streak in her Roxy, you know that, you should be pleased she's so nice to your kids."

"I am, as it happens," said Roxy guiltily, "I wish I was more maternal in many ways."

Max laughed sarcastically. "Don't make me laugh, there's not a maternal bone in your silicone body Roxy, never has been and you never wanted there to be. Always too busy shoving coke up your nose or getting your tits out."

"Max, how dare you," hissed Roxy furiously, "I changed that way of life a long time ago, as you well know. That's a fucking outrageous thing to say. I'd like to spend more time with the kids."

Max laughed in his most patronising *Michael Winner* voice, "Calm down dear, only teasing."

"Perhaps when you all move to the country it'll be easier," intervened Leo, "much nicer for them than living in the smoke."

"Yeah possibly," said Roxy doubtfully, as she had no intention of moving the kids down during term time and would leave them with the nanny in London most of the time.

A loud melancholy note from the hunting horn shut them up and everyone's attention was drawn to the Master, Ian Grant; a tall, lanky chap in a red coat standing up in his stirrups on a fine, grey horse who was addressing them all.

"I'd like to welcome everyone here today to the Fittlebury and Cosham Boxing day meet and our very grateful thanks to our generous hosts, Shelia and Pete, the landlords of the Devil's Jump, for their hospitality. We are delighted to have the support of a big, mounted field out today. As always, please be aware of horses with ribbons on their tails, and avoid crashing into them if you can. Don't want any accidents." He brayed loudly at his feeble joke and continued. "When we start on the lines, those of you who are non-jumpers, please follow Giles, our other Field Master, out today," he indicated to a portly man in a red coat with a matching red face seated on an equally portly cob, who jovially waved his whip in the air. Everyone cheered and waved at the popular, rotund Giles and Ian raised his hand imperiously for quiet, "those of who are jumping today please follow me; we have some splendid hedges and gates for you and we should have an excellent day." He smiled benevolently to one and all, and the crowd cheered, whooping and clapping loudly, sending highly strung horses skittering into the foot followers, and mulled wine splashing onto breeches.

Giles continued, "A reminder to everyone, mounted and on foot, to respect our landowners and farmers, without whose permission we could not enjoy our sport. Please shut gates after you, respect the stock and ensure any breakages or damage be reported to the secretary without delay. Speaking of the secretaries, they will be coming round to collect the cap, and to remind you that today the monies collected go to the hunt staff for their Christmas box, so dig deep everyone please!" He laughed heartily, "One last thing - no doubt we'll encompass some antis - please don't let them antagonise you into retaliating to their jibes. Remember, we are hunting within the law. Now, ladies and gentleman I hope you all have a very good day." He signalled to the huntsman, "Hounds please."

"Fucking hell," said Roxy impressed, "that was quite a speech."

"Important man is the Master," agreed Leo, "everyone bows and curtseys to him."

"Yeah I've always respected a masterful geezer with a whip," flirted Roxy, her eyes flashing a challenge to Felix. "Get this hunting trip organised babe."

Charles nodded to Jennifer at the signal to move off from the master. He'd knocked back a whole tea service of stirrup cups and was a trifle pissed; Jennifer had been a tad more careful, being the less experienced rider and needed her wits about her especially as the first line had a notoriously large, unseating hedge where the foot followers waited, hoping for some spectacular and entertaining falls. Neither Jennifer nor Charles had to worry about driving home as Nancy was at the wheel of the truck and, as they clattered off after the huntsman, Jennifer was beginning to wish she'd had one more for the road, because her tummy was spinning round like a fairground ride at the thought of the infamously, wicked opening line and she could do with some Dutch courage. Behind them trotted Sandy and Katherine, seemingly totally unconcerned and gossiping madly; Colin waving wildly at Grace, and baby Archie, hoisted aloft by his grandpa grinning inanely as they trotted passed. Jennifer was looking particularly glamorous, her beautiful, blonde hair scooped up under her crash hat only served to emphasise her high cheekbones and smoky eyes. Charles, even though mildly inebriated, was fiercely protective and continually laid his hand upon her breeched thigh. Every woman was envious of Jennifer, drooling over the haughty handsome, doting and wealthy Charles; and every man was envious of Charles with the stunning and beautiful Jennifer looking adoringly into his eyes. It was hard to believe the trials and tribulations of the previous years between them, but now things had settled and on an idyllic Boxing Day they trotted off after hounds in apparent marital bliss.

From the throbbing crowd of onlookers, Dulcie and Nancy watched them ride off, sneakily grasping hands and hoping not too many people would notice. Gay they may be, advertise it they would not. Leo and Seb nudged each other knowingly and carried on chatting up Roxy, who was so wrapped up in herself she wouldn't have spotted anything unless she'd broken a nail. Max, on the other hand, was more observant, smiling slyly at the girls who studiously ignored him.

Hattie crossed the car park with a little girl in each hand, followed by a miserably cold and inappropriately dressed nanny. "Right come on Felix, we'd better crack on to the first line if we are gonna get a good place to see them jumping," she called, veering off towards the parked vehicles. "Come on my little lovelies," she crooned to the kids, "this'll be fun, you wait and see."

The kids were beaming, their designer clothes all covered in slobber from the hounds and looking adoringly at Hattie. "Will they really jump hedges?" asked Stephanotis. "Will the horses be alright?"

"Yes, they'll love it, but some of the riders will fall off," laughed Hattie wickedly, "everyone cheers when they do. If you ask Felix nicely, he'll put you on his shoulders so you can get a good view."

"Hooray!" shouted Delphinium, "this is fun!"

The others raced over to join them at the cars, piling into the seats and careering off down the road followed by a hordes of other 4 x 4s. The field of horses could be seen way over the downs cantering around the headlands, hounds streaming ahead of the red coats stark and brilliant against the dark green of the holly bushes and scrub. The masters gave the horses a good settling canter before the first line of fences and it allowed the foot followers plenty of time to get themselves into position for a good view of the jumps. The old hands knew exactly where to go, and gradually the line of vehicles threaded into a large farmyard, slewing haphazardly as they pulled up. There were plenty of open barns where the hunt supporters had set up coffee urns, with soup and refreshments but no-one was much interested and trooped out into open fields to wait for the hunt to arrive. The viewing was good - with at least six hedges in all and, right in front of them, the notorious big bugger with the massive drop on the landing side.

For the faint-hearted a smaller version had been etched out beside it and, for the non-jumpers, a gate had been opened to gallop through. In the good old days, this would have been unheard of, but nowadays the hunt was much more accessible for the lily-livered and invited everyone, and all abilities were generously catered for. However, if you did jump and you fell off, your name went into the Tumbler's Club, where you paid a fine. At the end of the season a prize was given to the rider who'd fallen off the most - it had taken on a bizarre form of prestige to win the award.

Whilst they waited, they clapped their hands around their bodies to keep warm, their breath coming in great curls in the cold air. The little girls shrieked with delight, when Felix and Leo hoisted them aloft their shoulders for a better view, whilst the nanny glowered in the background with a miserable, bad-tempered face, blue lips and glowering expression.

"I'm gonna sack that fucking witch," snapped Roxy, throwing the girl the evils, "that's her bleeding job."

"Chill Roxy," soothed Seb, who felt sorry for the girl in her short skirt and designer heels, "she must be bloody freezing in that gear."

"Serves her fucking right," muttered Roxy unkindly, "she's useless."

"Whatever babe," growled Max, "just shut the fuck up can't you, we're all sick of it. Go home and sack her, but just stop moaning will you."

"Do you think the children would like to ride?" asked Hattie innocently, "they seem to love the horses."

"For Christ's sake Hattie, don't go there," grumbled Roxy, "just 'cos you like playing fucking Mary Poppins - I don't."

"Oh okay, sorry," muttered Hattie, "I just thought they'd enjoy it."

"Well I wouldn't," snapped Roxy, "listen - what's that?"

Felix laughed up at Stephanotis. "Look little sweetie, here they come!" He pointed out across the fields and, heading towards them at a crashing lick, came a stream of hounds, red coats, black coats, sweating horses of every colour, straining against their mud splattered riders and the melodious sound of the hunting horn.

The foot followers craned to look. The area had been cordoned off with rope to keep the riders separate and avoid any accidents. The first hedge had been negotiated - much to the excitement of the crowd, who were yelling and calling out, then the second with a few fallers, horses refusing and some near misses, and then the next fence was the big one. The first rider, the huntsman, approached, kicked his horse on and sailed over with gusto, as did the whips. Next came the master and an enormous cheer went up as he leapt over, pecked on landing, but his horse righted itself and he managed to stay on. Tipping his hat to the crowd and with an enormous yell he cantered on. Bunched up behind him, several horses took the hedge together and, to the glee of the crowd the hedge claimed two fallers. They rolled into the old turf unhurt as their horses galloped on, and the embarrassed riders righted themselves holding their hands on theirs knees in humiliation, much to the cat calling of the onlookers. They quickly exited the line, as further riders were hurtling over the hedge, some more stylish than the others. Charles took the fence with all the style that would have been expected - effortlessly and with aplomb. Next came Jennifer, who opted for the smaller alternative and, she too, made an elegant attempt and galloped on after Charles, but the relief on her face was evident. Colin came next, kicking on like mad, and hurtled over with absolutely no finesse but a clear round nonetheless. Katherine and Sandy cleared the hedge with all the assurance that would be expected from them and galloped on. Thereafter it seemed to be carnage, as by this time the ground was beginning to be cut up and the going getting deeper. More and more tumblers and loose horses and the crowd was loving it.

"Fuck me," said Roxy disparagingly, "what tossers! I can ride better than they can."

"Don't be so scathing," advised Felix, "it's not so easy when you're out there and everyone is clamouring to get over, the best of us can fall off."

"Whatever," dismissed Roxy, "I wanna have a go, and so does Max, don't cha baby?"

Max, who'd been devouring the entertainment said, "Definitely - I love a challenge."

Felix gave up, acknowledging he was beaten, he'd have to take them. He'd give Giles a ring and find an easy day for them after the New Year - a couple of muddy falls and they'd soon change their tune.

After the second line, Dulcie and Nancy cadged a lift back to their truck, as Jennifer and Charles decided to go home. Felix was desperate to join them, but Roxy was insistent they stayed to the bitter end. The children were loving it. They were filthy and muddy, much to the chagrin of the nanny who would have to clean them up, but it was probably the only real fresh air the poor kids had had all year. Max, on the other hand, was thoughtful, pumping Felix for information about the point to point races, and who trained the local horses, how they qualified for the races. Felix admitted he didn't know much but he could introduce him to some people who did, if he was really that interested. Max merely smiled infuriatingly and inclined his head, tapping the side of his nose, which irritated the hell out of Felix who decided to ignore him. He'd never been more relieved at the end of the last line when they made their way home managing to steer Roxy away from the pub.

CHAPTER 82

The days following Boxing Day were quiet. The mill was in a state of huge preparation. Last minute finishing touches were being applied to the outside; Winter wonderland had arrived - thousands of tiny, sparkling white lights festooned like cobwebs from the trees along the drive. The mill, itself, had the same tiny lights draped around the windows and outside were two huge Christmas Trees on either side of the entrance, swathed in crystal and white decorations. Inside followed a similar theme, the tiny, white lights twinkling all around the beams trailing with ivy; the tables with their ice white linen had a centre piece of white Christmas roses or cyclamen with shiny, green ivy and discreet little fairy lights. It looked sensational.

Chrissie was working flat out and had hardly seen Aiden other than for a quick fuck in the store cupboard, but it hardly mattered - she was so busy. The outfitting of the staff was paramount - they were all dressed uniformly in black tee shirts embroidered with the mill logo and black trousers, pristine white half aprons, and all long hair was tied back. Three chefs had been brought down from the London restaurants and Aiden himself, of course, was there to supervise. The new chefs they'd employed were still being trained up but Aiden couldn't afford any mistakes tonight. Both the Maître D, Victor, and the Sommelier, Philip, had worked together in London for a long time and were a perfect team. A fine selection of wines had been selected and Victor had his eagle eye on the waiting staff. Philip had interviewed and chosen his bar staff, and the chefs their kitchen porters. The undertaking had been colossal and expensive. Still, on the upside, they had a full house for New Year's Eve and were booked solid for evening meals until the end of January. Lunchtimes were quieter, but hopefully once people started using the spa this would change.

Roxy flitted decorously into the spa, poking her oar into everything. Chrissie, through the agency, had hired Kirstie - a first rate manager and she had the place looking amazing. She'd decorated it in a similar way to the Mill and the staff were both charming and efficient - they were all set to go for their first booked appointments on New Year's Day, and ready and waiting to do guided tours the evening before if anyone wanted a look around. Kirstie had Roxy's measure straight away; in a soft Scottish accent she brushed away her snide remarks and suggested she have a massage. A bad tempered Roxy left the spa soothed and relaxed with Kirstie scoring the first points.

It was the day before New Year's Eve. Anna was struggling to get Max's ivory castle ready for the influx of his guests and had enlisted the assistance of a couple of village girls, identical twins, who were looking for work whilst on their Christmas break from Uni. They were nice girls, both reading Drama at Plymouth, and had been glad of the money. Anna soon had them making up the vast beds and cleaning the bathrooms. The guests were arriving tomorrow and leaving two days later, and the girls had agreed to stay in the staff flat above the garages to help out for the duration. Anna had organised for caterers to come in on New Year's Day to do a hot lunch and set out a buffet meal for the evening, and again the next day. The wine cellar was stocked to gunnels, and the girls would be handy to serve and tidy up, clean the bathrooms and make the beds. Max, himself, was coming down from London today. She glanced around the house. It wouldn't have been her taste, she would have liked something more homely - the rooms were huge with those big ostentatious fireplaces, and that intimidating, huge dining table, laden with candelabra and silver. The billiard room was no cosier, the table taking up most of the room, with enormous Victorian stuffed bears holding the cues which loomed out of the shadows, their prosthetic eyes fixed and staring. The room gave her the creeps. The other reception rooms were not much better. Upstairs, the bedrooms, although sumptuous were full of playthings, for doling out pain and pleasure alike and the en-suites merely receptacles for further antics. No, it wasn't a home in the true sense of the word and, once again, she longed for her family back in Romania, the warmth of her mum and dad's house and the love that had surrounded her. She still sent them money, of course, but she could never let on what she did here or how the money was earned.

She heard the throaty sound and the crunch of gravel as a car pulled into the drive. The Aston purred up beside the front door and Max oozed out. She watched him from the window as he sprang up the steps. He had lost none of his mesmerizing good looks, but to her he was like a snake and she marvelled at how someone so beautiful could be so cruel and callous. Yet there were times when he was incredibly kind - she would never understand him.

"Anna! Where are you?"

Anna jumped and ran out of the bedroom, down the stairs and into the grandiose hallway with its stuffed stag's head and mahogany side tables laden with the sickly smell of white lilies. Max was flinging off his coat and scarf and passing them to her.

"How are you getting on?" he asked, "all organised for tomorrow?"

"Yes Max, more or less, just a few last minute things."

"Got the caterers sorted, booze, taxis for tomorrow evening?"

"Yes, all done, just making up the bedrooms."

"I'll want my usual room with you in it." Max said carelessly, not looking at her. "Give Ronnie the south facer, he's bringing Tash, she's such a raunchy bitch. Make sure they've got plenty of toys - let me see what you've got up there to entertain them."

"Of course," said Anna quietly, "It's all in hand though - you really don't need to look."

"Yeah right, actually baby but I fancy a good look at you." He reached over and slipped his hand up her skirt and put a finger inside her pants, "a nice long clinical examination."

Anna held her breath, she knew only too well what he was like in this mood. "Great, why don't we go downstairs to the playroom? We could do doctors and patients."

Max pulled his hand out, he wasn't stupid. "The playroom eh? You're keen all of a sudden, you normally quake when I make you go down there?"

"No, no," Anna gasped, "It'll be fun, you can put my legs in the stirrups. You know you love it."

"Anna," said Max emphatically, shoving her away, "who or what is upstairs that you don't want me to see?"

He marched out of the hall and up the stairs, with Anna flying behind him, bursting into each bedroom in turn, until he saw Cheryl and Naomi who were chattering and busy making up one of the beds.

"Well, well, hello sweet ladies," Max whispered excitedly. "Twins, how delightful and who are you two and what are you doing in my house?"

Both girls turned in astonishment at the tall, extraordinarily handsome, man sizing them up from the doorway. Breathlessly Anna tumbled in behind Max.

"Let me make the introductions, Cheryl, Naomi, this is your boss - Max. He's just arrived."

"What beautiful girls you are," purred Max wickedly, moving over and stroking Cheryl's arm. "You didn't tell me you had hired such gorgeous creatures Anna. Now, my dears, you must tell me all about yourselves. Anna, I want you to run into Horsham for me and buy me a new dress shirt and, whilst you are there, get more food in - I think we may have more guests staying after all."

"But Max ..." stammered Anna, "we have plenty of food in the house and you do have several new shirts."

Max turned to Anna and glared dangerously at her. "Don't question me Anna and do as I ask you and don't hurry back. Leave me to find out more about our new staff."

Anna had no alternative but to leave. Max licked his lips at the notion of identical twins and, in their innocence, Cheryl and Naomi smiled prettily at him. It had been different with Elizabeth Collins - she was an old hand and knew what she liked and wanted - these two were just kids. Dear God, thought Anna, Max scared her - the man had no scruples at all.

Kylie was kitted out in her black uniform and, whilst she detested taking orders from the jumped up poof Victor, with his waxed back hair and handlebar moustache, at least it had to better than struggling outside in the muck. They were on the final dress rehearsal before the big night and Victor had been on all their backs today, demanding it all had to run like clockwork and emphasised, in no uncertain terms - one fuck up and you're out. Normally Kylie would have told him where to shove the job, but the money was too good to pass up, plus at the end of the evening they all got to pool the tips. Victor had said that some big names would be coming, and the gratuities were bound to be fantastic if they went the extra mile. He winked knowingly at them all, work hard and do the job and they would be well rewarded. Philip, the sommelier joined them, reminding everyone that Aiden would not tolerate poor attitudes, that nothing was too much for the customer and remember you always had a smile on your face. Kylie listened with one ear, and nudged the girl next, to her rolling her eyes. Philip shot her a deeply, withering look which would have stopped a rhino at a hundred paces; Kylie flushed and had the grace to look awkwardly down at her shoes. Victor clapped his hands and dismissed them.

"That girl's got attitude," remarked Philip, nodding his head at Kylie, "you'll have to watch her."

"Don't worry sweetie," agreed Victor. "I've noticed, but we need the staff for tomorrow, if she doesn't shape up I'll get rid of her."

"I just hope she doesn't fuck up tomorrow," said Philip, "where have you put her?"

"Table ten. That hood Max Goldsmith - he wouldn't notice good service if it bit him on the arse. He's bringing a load of East Enders and their tarts. They'll be so pissed up, if she's off with them they won't notice and, frankly, it won't matter if they do."

"Hmm, I thought he was a great friend of Roxy's?"

"Exactly, but definitely *not* a friend of Aiden's, so it hardly matters. She'll do well there I think."

"Well take a tip from me, keep an eye on her, she's trouble that one."

"Don't fret sweetie, I'm on it."

"I'd feel an awful lot better if the bloody cameras weren't going to be here tomorrow," grumbled Philip, "supposing there's an incident?"

"There won't be, you are such a glass half empty man - which is not good news for a sommelier." Victor laughed loudly at his little joke. "Come on, it'll be fine!"

"This bloody place hasn't exactly got a great reputation for good luck has it though," observed Philip, "there have been some terrible goings on here in the past."

"Well, time we turned the luck around then," laughed Victor, his eyes twinkling. "What can possibly go wrong?"

Despite wanting to run and desperately keep on running, away from Max and her life with him, Anna had to return - she had nowhere to go and, besides, he would never let her leave him now and would definitely seek her out - she knew too much. Tentatively, she ventured back to the house three hours after her hesitant departure. She eased open the front door quietly and stood listening, wondering what they were doing. She could hear voices coming from the billiard room, and a lot of muffled giggling. Undecided, she hopped from foot to foot and eventually tip-toed into the kitchen with the grocery bags, plonking them down on the counter with a hefty sigh. She flicked on the kettle and considered her options, go and join them or sit and have a cuppa. The cuppa won, although she was as agitated as junkie waiting for his next fix, as she sat and drank it. Finally, knowing her options had run out, she made her way out into the hall and down the corridor where the shrieks of laughter were getting louder, and knocked on the door to the billiard room, and braced herself for the inevitable ordeal ahead.

"Come," called Max's voice.

Anna pushed the door open. God alone knew what she was about to see. The twins were playing billiards - badly by the looks of things, but remarkably, they were fully dressed and so was Max, who was leaning against one of the stuffed bears, watching in amusement, as they fluffed one shot after another. The girls had obviously been drinking, several bottles of champagne had been opened on a small, side table, and they were both pretty drunk. Max winked at Anna, he'd clearly not touched a drop.

"Anna, so glad you're back, the girls were just telling me all about their drama course - sounds fascinating. I was saying I have some good contacts in the business, I could introduce them to plenty of influential people."

Anna didn't know whether to be relieved or afraid, so far nothing untoward had gone on, other than a lot of drinking, but she knew Max and how his mind worked. He would delight in leading them on, saying he would promote them, but in return the girls would have to do a few favours for him. Mind you, looking at the pair of them, they didn't seem at all concerned and Anna wondered why she was bothered, what did it matter to her, after all? They were over eighteen and could make their own life choices. She knew though he would expect her to play her part and do as she was told.

Max moved over to one of the studded, wing chairs and motioned for Anna to join him. He pulled her onto his lap and kissed her on the lips, his hand roaming into the front of her blouse and exposing her breast and nipple. Anna willed herself not to stiffen, and to relax; she could see the girls watching with curiosity as Max pulled off her blouse and undid her bra, her wonderful tits spilling out into his hands. He fondled them between his thumb and forefinger, pushing Anna back so that her throat and neck were exposed, her long dark hair trailing over the edge of the chair. Cheryl and Naomi had, by now, stopped playing completely and turned to watch, both tipsily holding onto the billiard table for support. Max looked up and smiled at them, pulling up Anna's skirt to reveal her panties.

"Would you like to play," he asked huskily, "or just watch?"

Cheryl was the first to slur, "I dunno, we've never done anything like this before."

"Don't be shy," soothed Max, "you can just watch if you prefer, nobody's forcing you. Help yourselves to more champagne."

"I'm pretty drunk already," said Naomi, "I can hardly stand up."

In one swift movement Max stood up, lifted Anna like a rag doll and placed her on top of the billiard table, pulling off her knickers exposing her shaven bush. He yanked her legs apart, the pink lips of her labia spread open to reveal her deep rosebud clitoris. Anna moaned, her skirt rucked up about her waist and her breasts falling to each side as she lay on the table.

Thus positioned, Max turned away from her, leaving her callously exposed and she knew better than to wriggle or move for fear of angering him. He motioned to Cheryl and Naomi, "Come and look - isn't Anna beautiful?" he smiled at them, "bring some champagne over my dears."

The girls hesitated and, finally, Naomi tottered over with a bottle and whispered, "What are you going to do?"

"Watch and enjoy, or of course you could assist me. You don't have to take your clothes off."

"Okay ..." said Cheryl tentatively, "what do you want us to do?"

"I am going to give Anna some champagne, but not in the place that she expects." Max grinned wickedly, "she likes it in her cunt and then I'm going to drink it."

The girls gasped - not just at the notion but at the language, "Oh my God, you've gotta be joking."

"No, you love it - don't you Anna?"

Anna nodded her head lamely - she knew what was coming and it was better to agree than try and struggle.

Cheryl and Naomi were fascinated - they couldn't stop staring at Anna's naked body.

"Feel free to touch her anywhere you like - while I get things ready," laughed Max, "she won't move." He walked over to a concealed cupboard and, out of the corner of his eye, glimpsed Naomi inquisitively stroking Anna's breast, and then Cheryl joined in. By the time he'd returned they were blatantly playing with her.

"We've never had lesbian tendencies before," whispered Cheryl awkwardly, "we didn't know we had."

"You haven't now sweet thing," crooned Max, "this is just a bit of fun sex that's turning us all on. Now let's start giving Anna some pleasure shall we?" He produced a funnel from his pocket and several vials of Amyl Nitrite. "We're gonna have a ball."

CHAPTER 83

New Year's Eve day arrived. Hattie and Felix lay in bed, their limbs wrapped around each other, and welcomed in the early morning of the last day of the year.

"You know, I won't be sorry to say goodbye to this year," mumbled Felix, his lips nuzzled into Hattie's neck, "we've had some shit times."

"Oi you," snapped Hattie, poking him in the ribs. "Thanks for that, you and I have hooked up together, that's good isn't it?"

"Sorry babe, yeah, course, but I meant with Alice and everything, and the pressure of toadying around Roxy and now bloody Max."

Hattie cuddled up to him "I know what you meant; let's hope the New Year brings some really good times and lots of successes. Time to wipe out all the bad memories."

Felix felt himself getting horny as she nestled into him. "Any chance of a last shag for 2013?"

"I thought you'd never ask," laughed Hattie, rolling over on top of him and pinning him down, her breasts swinging in his face, "although you never know, we might make time for another one before the party tonight."

As Felix and Hattie were tangled in the throes of passion, Seb and Leo were also rousing themselves. Leo's black, curly hair looked like a blow dried poodle as he swung his long legs over the side of the bed. He glanced down at the comatose Seb who was feigning sleep under the duvet.

"Come on, get up you lazy bugger," grumbled Leo, stretching and yawning and reaching down for his socks. "Christ your trainers stink Seb, can we shove them in the washing machine?"

"Do what you like, but just don't wake me," muttered Seb irascibly in a sleepy haze, "what time is it?"

"Seven o'clock babycakes and time to come out of dreamland."

"Please darling, just five more minutes."

Leo flung off the duvet in exasperation, exposing Seb who looked like a plucked chicken, in all his naked glory. "Get up!"

"Oh you beast - I don't know why I love you."

Leo jumped on top of him kissing him hard on the lips. "Yes you do, you smelly old soak."

"You didn't give me time to brush my teeth sweetie," grumbled Seb, clamping his teeth together.

"And you think I care," said Leo kissing him again, "now come on, get up."

Frankie was already in the bathroom and couldn't help but overhear their banter. She smiled to herself. She liked living here, the boys were outrageous, and you never knew who was going to be sleeping in the spare room but she liked her job and life was good. Unexpectedly, Roxy had invited her tonight along with the rest of the crew at the yard and she was really flattered, she'd never have been able to afford a ticket otherwise. She didn't often go to these sort of dos and was the envy of Dulcie and Nancy who weren't going. She and Hattie had done the rounds of charity shops in Horsham and in the Cancer Research she'd bought a classy vintage frock from the designer rail. Hattie, finding nothing in the thrift shops finally pushed the boat out and went to *La Vida* and bought a sassy cocktail number in the sale. It had been a real girly session and they'd loved it. Men were so lucky, all they had to do was put on a tuxedo and a bow tie and they were sorted. They'd all agreed that they'd work like smoke today to get finished early, and the lads said the girls could go and spruce up before them, as long as Frankie did the early stint in the morning. Frankie didn't care, she rarely drank much and was more than happy to get up. She sighed happily as she dried her face and slapped on some face cream - what a fabulous party it was going to be.

Jennifer was in a chipper mood this morning, laughing and joking with the girls in the yard as she tacked up Polly. She was sad they weren't coming to the party but it just wasn't appropriate really. Jennifer and

Charles were making up a table with Grace and Colin, Sandy and Mark, Katherine and Jeremy and Chloe and John. Charles wasn't pleased when she'd organised it, saying that after her terrible ordeal in the Mill Cottage it was the last place he thought she'd have wanted to go. Jennifer was nothing if not tenacious and laughed - saying there was no better way to exorcise what had happened to her than go and celebrate the coming of the New Year with their closest friends. The venue was immaterial. As always, where his wife was concerned, Charles capitulated - albeit reluctantly. He would be taking great care of her tonight and woe betide anyone who stepped out of line. This morning he'd stomped off to London in a shocking temper, furious at being called in to avert some minor crisis which had flared up in the office, but promising he would be back after lunch to ride and asking if the girls could have Beano ready for him. Jennifer had rolled her eyes as he hurtled up the drive in the Range Rover, it was no good telling him to slow down, he was turbo-charged in this mood. She'd make sure they had a very special evening - she knew exactly how to please him.

Roxy was still in London and to say she was tense as a small nun at a penguin cull didn't cut it; fuelled predominantly by the petulant children who were giving her more aggro than a dirty reggae band and the gloomy nanny who was on the verge of taking an overdose; coupled with a petulant Aiden and a superior Chrissie, she was seriously about to implode. That girl was definitely on her way out, but until the New Year there was well and truly little she could do about replacing her and she would have to put up with her sultry moods. Aiden was being impossible, but she could understand the pressure, tonight was important for both of them. The cameras would be there of course - it was the culmination of all the shows that had been building up to this huge finale, although Farouk said that there may well be a follow up show - whatever - tonight was still a big deal for *Rox-Aid*.

She'd chosen her outfit with care. Since she'd taken on a her new persona with the shiny, shaggy, chocolate brown bob and the boob reduction, it was still a skimpy sexy number - in fact, barely covering the essentials but with the previously obscene tits reduced and the proxy loxy hair gone - it did have a little more finesse than it might have before. Nonetheless made of the clingiest fine jersey, with an asymmetrical one shoulder, the side spliced dress skimmed across the curve of her silicone breasts, back across her pelvis and barely covered anything else. It was the height of extreme tartiness, with a touch of the glamour model. In deep blood red, it suited her perfectly. She hadn't showed the dress to Aiden, he would have disapproved but she didn't care. What did it matter if she tantalised Joe Public and the cameras with the goods, they could drool all they liked. *Hello* mag had bought the exclusive feature for the opening night, and their stylist would have a fit, but she could scream the place down as far as Roxy was concerned.

What the hell, she felt like a kettle on the boil, snapping at everyone and anything that got in her way. Chrissie was a real thorn in her side, she had a sneaky feeling that she was going to be more difficult to get rid of than she'd envisaged, like a persistent blackhead always lurking under the surface waiting to make an appearance. Somehow Aiden was a little more intense with this tart, and of course she wasn't such a tart was she? Chrissie was classy, and had proved herself indispensable, running along behind him with her clipboard, checking and rechecking every fucking detail. Aiden's little helper, in more ways than one. It was time she moved on and, come what may and no matter how, Chrissie would be part of Roxy's detox for the New Year. A good toxic flush-out was needed and there was nothing like a colonic lavage to bring out the shit.

Aiden was himself taking relief from the other side of the pavilion, bumming one of the new waiters, who was all too happy to oblige. He occasionally liked to alleviate himself without the complications of women, the screaming protestations of Roxy and the increasing demands of Chrissie. There was nothing like a bit of uncomplicated bum foolery in the bog, and as he held onto Manuel's head, ramming his cock into his delectable chocolate starfish he oozed all the tension of the last few weeks out with a great gasp. Aiden didn't consider himself gay, just enjoyed assuaging himself with the lack of complications that accompanied the women in his life. He pushed back from Manuel, wiped his cock and patted his back, thanking him and handed him fifty quid; he zipped up his flies and left. It was the end of the matter. No questions asked. He smiled to himself, if Roxy or Chrissie knew they'd have a nervous breakdown, but he didn't care, needs must as the devil drove.

Whilst Aiden was having his way with the greasy Manuel, Chrissie was motoring down along the crisp, frosty lanes towards the mill. She felt as buoyant as her buxom, natural tits. By the end of this year Aiden had promised he would finish with Roxy and they could start their new lives together. She would orchestrate the sensational New Year's Eve party, delighted to work her butt off - because ultimately it was to be for them - not bloody *Rox-Aid*. She didn't care what the cameras portrayed. She knew that Roxy would arrive in some tarty, tactless outfit, and she, Chrissie, would be the belle of the ball in hers. She had blown a whole month's salary at the delightful and fairly unknown Hackney Shop which harboured some of the most edgy designers, and had come away delighted with the most chic of chic catwalk numbers. She'd knock Roxy into the outer cosmos and smile all along the Milky Way. It couldn't come faster as far as she was concerned.

In their quaint cottage just outside the village, Sandy and Mark were soaking in their enormous bath. She was assiduously soaping Mark's toes and he was wriggling with delight. Sandy hadn't worked since before Christmas and was enjoying her long break; she certainly needed it after a troublesome and tricky lead up to the yuletide festivities. Next week would see her back at her desk, her nose to the proverbial grindstone, but right now, Mark's toes needed her full attention. They too were looking forward to the evening ahead, although Mark's head was stuffed with details of tomorrow's shoot when Lady V was hosting a number of guns, all great friends of her late husband, and for her it was a very important day. Will Fry was more than up to the job and assured him of many decent birds on the drives, but Mark wouldn't be Mark if he didn't take every aspect of his job too seriously. Sandy sternly told him to let Will get on with his job and he could worry about it tomorrow and please to enjoy his day and evening with her. As Sandy sucked Mark's big toe, he sighed with ecstasy and slipped down under the water, content to forget about the shoot, concentrating entirely on her sexual ministrations.

The fragrant steam billowed up from Jennifer's bath, misting the gilt encrusted mirrors and flushing her face. She wriggled her body down in the silky, scented water, rolling her shoulders and arching her back. After the icy cold of the day the water felt glorious. Poking out a moist hand, she groped for her book and oozed down to read another sizzling chapter of P J King's latest best seller. For two pins she would stay at home tonight, but she couldn't let everyone down; it was New Year's Eve and, after all, she'd been the one to organise this bloody evening out- talk about laying ghosts - all she fancied right now was laying Charles and an early night with a bottle of fizz. As she read on, her eyes becoming heavier than a *Weight Watchers* clinic, she realised that the water had grown quite tepid and, shaking like a Labrador, made a Herculean effort to haul herself out. Shivering, and wrapping herself in a huge, fluffy bath towel, she padded out into her bedroom plonking herself on the edge of the bed, extending her legs out and studying her toes. Tonight could be difficult for her but she was determined to get through it, to put to sleep the nightmare of the kidnapping and the ordeal of those forty eight hours she had been held prisoner. She hadn't been up to the mill since the fire, hadn't wanted to.

Charles had protected her like a precious jewel from the place and quelled, with the most sinister look, anyone who dared mention it. But the time had come, with a New Year coming in to close the chapter and move on. She felt good in herself, with her marriage and her life and she was going to kick out those bad memories once and for all, and what better way, than with good, loyal friends who'd supported her through those dark months.

She was still deep in thought and pondering her toes when the door burst open. Charles, tall, rugged and handsome strode in, his face glowing from the cold and his hair wild from riding.

"Darling, you okay? You look a bit miserable?" He knelt down beside her, putting his arms around her waist and holding her close, "is it about tonight, we don't have to go you know."

Jennifer stroked his hair and pressed him close, he smelt of horses and lemony aftershave, a lethal combination, "No, I'm determined, and what's more I'm fine about it."

"Sure sweetie?" said Charles, looking up at her and stroking her cheek, "I won't have you upset."

"Sure," Jennifer leant down and kissed him, letting the towel slip off as she did so to reveal her curvy breasts and rosebud nipples. The kiss lingered on as their tongues entwined; finally coming up for breath she added, "I love you."

"And I love you," Charles sighed, standing up and tugging off his clothes, leaving them in an unruly heap on the floor. He lifted her up under her arms and pushed her back onto the bed, his huge cock erect and ready and levered himself astride her, "Now I am going to show you just how much."

Grace was excited. Since having baby Archie and breaking her bloody ankle, life had definitely been quite tricky. She was lucky to have such an adoring husband as Colin, especially as he was his own boss and was pretty much able to take time off when he was needed, and of course, she had her mum and dad just around the corner. It was the damned incapacitation that had been the worst part. But at long last things were looking up, she was riding Col's horse again whilst her own was in foal, and was feeling much more like her old self. She and Colin were both looking forward to tonight, although when Jennifer had suggested it they'd both had misgivings especially after what had happened, but they were in the company of good friends, although they had some snobbish reservations about Roxy and Aiden. Colin also felt professionally obliged to support the opening, as he had made such superlative commission on its sale, as indirectly had Mark. Jennifer, herself, was a plucky girl and was not in the least concerned, or so it seemed, and their loyalties luckily had not been divided. Baby Archie was to spend the night with his grandparents and Grace, who had lost her baby tummy, had treated herself to a new dress. Her ankle was strong now and she planned to dance the night away with Colin and see the New Year in with style.

At the mill, preparations were going smoothly. The diners were to be seated on the upper two floors, whilst the dancing would be later on the ground floor, where the bar was situated and the decking which overlooked the mill pond. The musicians were busy setting up their gear, testing the sound and their lighting. As the area was quite small and couldn't take a big band, Chrissie had organised a couple of guys who she'd seen herself several times and had been impressed. Theirs was clever act; with strong voices, they sang along to background synthesised music and beefed up their performance by playing the sax and the guitar alongside - it was like being in on an intimate jamming session. They could pick up more or less any tune, sang any request and were good entertainers. Plus when they needed a break, they had a plethora of disco tracks back to back which meant the music was non-stop. The piped music was discreet low key, Elton John, Dire Straits, Eagles and all the other classics destined to get people in the party mood.

In the kitchen, Aiden was ruling supreme, screaming and yelling at the quaking underlings and throwing more histrionics than pre-menstrual prima donna. The old handers brought down from London, ignored him and doggedly carried on, but the newbies cowered as he wreaked havoc, criticising everything from the wild mushroom veloute to the egg and bacon ice cream. Nothing was good enough. Five hours to go and counting and Aiden was steaming nicely.

Victor had the tables laid with their pristine, starched white cloths, the glasses polished to a shiny, pearlescent sheen and the cutlery sparkling like a Colgate advert. He surveyed the scene, the ambience was perfect, fairytale, yet sultry. He spun the disc on the CD player and the smooth tones of Elton enveloped the space of the dining areas. When the light faded, the massive, swagged windows would give the most perfect view over the mill pond, its surreal ethereal light enhanced by the twinkle of the fairy lights strewn around the perimeter. Victor sighed happily. Totally prepared, he sank down into a chair and enjoyed a glass of sherry with Philip. They both glanced at each other. Judging from the shrill screams issuing from the kitchen, which sounded more like a slaughtered animal than a place of culinary genius, they knew that tonight would be one to be remembered.

Hattie was getting ready. She slipped the silver cocktail dress over her glistening, naked body, its opalescent hues subtly changing as she moved. The simplicity of the dress suited her perfectly - it was sensational, loose fitting and just above the knee with a round simple neckline, but dramatised by a deep and daring cutaway back. Hattie had dressed her reddish brown hair swept up and fixed with a silver clasp. She was now an expert with the kohl eyeliner and smoky eye look which Leo had slavishly taught her to apply to such effect and with her height ,and cheek bones you could cut bread, on she could pass for any super model.

Felix came out of the bathroom wrapped in a towel and whistled, "Oh my fucking God Hats, you look amazing."

"Do you really think it's all right?" she said nervously, "don't think I've got too much make-up on do you?"

"Nope, you look like that Georgie Wass, the one that models for Mulberry and the White Company."

"Don't take the piss Felix," admonished Hattie crossly, studying herself in the mirror. "Seriously? I'm okay?"

"Seriously! You do look like her and, yes you look amazing - come here!"

Hattie squeaked as he dropped his towel and made a lunge for her. "Don't you bloody dare! It's taken me ages to put this make up on."

"Oh, all right, but wait till I get you in bed later!"

"You blokes don't know how lucky you are not having to think of what to wear or put make up on."

"Well, unless you're Seb and Leo of course," laughed Felix, "I haven't forgotten who showed you how to use make up, I bet they're preening over the mirror as we speak."

"Now, now, that's not very kind is it? Don't be horrid."

"I'm only joking sweet pea, I love them as much as you do!"

"You'd better hurry up and get dressed - Frankie'll be here in a minute to pick us up and she doesn't want to see you cock aloft!"

Felix considered his member. "Nope this baby's staying put in my pants until we get home."

"Good," said Hattie. "I'm sure Roxy wouldn't mind getting her hands or her teeth into it come to that."

"Bob Hope and no hope babe," grinned Felix, "only one woman for me - you sure we haven't got time for a quickie?"

At Laundry Cottage the bathroom looked as though a tsunami had hit it without warning and come back for a second go. Towels were heaped like sodden mountains on the floor and thrown outside in the corridor. The floor was awash with water and the windows and mirror were so steamed up it was more like a sauna than a bathroom. Frankie was pleased she'd insisted on first dibs and had left the boys to fight over who went next. The immersion had been boosted more times than a space shuttle and poor Leo had to fill his bath with hot kettles from the Aga. Dougie and Roberto were coming with them to the party and were arriving at any minute, so at least they hadn't had to cope with their ablutions as well. Frankie was pleased with the effect of her vintage dress from the charity shop. Black was always flattering, especially as she was not the tallest and, with her bouncy, curly hair and freckled face, she could look dumpy - so she'd added a jewelled headband with a red and black feather and strappy heels to give her height, sporting a mocked-up cigarette holder with long lace gloves. The effect was cheeky, flapper-esque and stunning. Asphyxiating herself with perfume, she gave herself one last look and tottered off, unaccustomed to the heels, down the stairs to wait for the others.

Leo and Seb were putting the finishing touches to their hair. Seb had gelled his to a racy James Dean lookalike, whilst Leo had opted for the bed head look which, despite its name, took a meticulous effort to achieve. Satisfied, he stepped back from the mirror and they surveyed each other critically.

"I think we'll do," laughed Leo admiringly, reaching out his hand and giving Seb a high five. "God we're gorgeous."

"Aren't we just doll - you look so debonair in that dicky bow. If I wasn't already engaged to you, I'd ask you to marry me."

"Actually sweetie, it was me who asked you," reminded Leo playfully, "so you can ask me if you like."

Dramatically, Seb flung himself down on one knee, grabbing Leo's hand with gusto, "Darling, will you marry me?"

"Get up you dummy," muttered Leo embarrassed, "you know I will and want to."

Seb struggled up, brushing fluff off his trousers. "Come on then grumble bunny, let's go."

CHAPTER 84

The car park at the mill was beginning to fill up. Fabulous cars lined up side by side. Ferraris, Astons, Porsches and Rollers, with the odd personalised mini tucked in between. The crew from *Sunrise Productions* couldn't get enough footage, and the *Hello* magazine cameras were snapping faster than an aquarium full of starving crocodiles. Like exotic birds of paradise, elegant women hanging on the arms of tuxedoed men swept towards the mill's magical entrance. The two enormous Christmas trees festooned with white lights stood sentry on either side of the door and the warm glow from inside oozed from the windows. Couples were posing on the steps against the mystical backdrop, before disappearing inside to be greeted with a glass of ice cold Cristal.

Roxy and Aiden were holding court inside like royalty, standing in line as they personally greeted their guests. Roxy air kissing everyone madly and exclaiming over-loudly how fabulous the women looked, and winking lasciviously at the men, as she spilled out of the outrageous red dress. Aiden masking his exasperation was more conservative, shaking hands seriously as he handed guests over to the hovering staff to take coats, and accept glasses of chilled champagne.

Three chauffeur driven ostentatious stretch mercs pulled up simultaneously outside, with the drivers dashing obsequiously to open the rear doors. The cameras went wild, hovering around the doors, clamouring to get shots of the newcomers. A long, shapely leg stretched out, showing a great deal of thigh. The chauffeur offered Anna his hand, her long, tumbling curls falling around her shoulders and her dark eyes flashing as the cameras went into overdrive. The startling, sleek, long, red dress hugging her body, totally understated in its simplicity, was oozing sex appeal on her long legs which were visible only by the long slits on either side. Anna was followed by Max, Ron and Tash, Ernie and his current floozy Cynthia. Max tucked Anna's arm in the crook of his elbow and posed for the cameras, cradling her gently around the shoulders as they made their way inside. Max's other cronies followed them, slipping out of the cars which slipped quietly away into the night.

Roxy's eyes narrowed to dangerous little slits when she saw them. Anna's stylish red dress, so sophisticated yet so sexy, made her own look like she'd come out of a bordello. Air kissing Anna through spitefully gritted teeth, when in truth she could have spat in her ear, but managing to pull herself together, she turned to Max and turned her smile up and gave him her most intimate greeting. Aiden gladly ignored them all, snapping his fingers at Kylie to take their coats.

Max was furious at the distinct snub from Aiden and, equally ignoring him in return, ushered the rest of his party over to the bar promising himself that Aiden would be sorry for giving him the cold shoulder. He liked revenge and he liked it stone cold.

There was a hubbub of excitement as Lisa and Mike arrived. Lisa in a white Grecian number, impossibly even tartier than Roxy's own, her breasts surely glued to the fabric to keep them in place. Roxy made a great show of welcoming them, gushing unnecessarily with half an eye on the cameras, whilst Aiden pumped Mike's hand as though he were drilling for oil. Behind them a furore of interest as the Beckhams pitched up, and the whole charade was repeated. Victoria, beautiful and unreachable, her face devoid of any interest whatsoever, followed her husband like the original Stepford wife. At the signal from Aiden they were ushered away to a discreet booth in the corner overlooking the mill pond.

"Did you see who that was?" hissed Tash, adjusting her tits. "Posh and Becks! She's so fucking thin and she's always looks like she sucked a bleedin' lemon!"

"Behave will ya?" spat Ronnie, barely looking at her, "there's gonna be a lot of celebs here tonight, so keep ya gob shut."

"Pardon me for breathing," said Tash sulkily, fluffing back her hair indignantly, "just saying."

"Well don't fucking say," snapped Ronnie nastily, "don't make me regret bringing ya."

Anna was silent, she glanced across at Max. He was talking anxiously to Ernie, his head bowed and his fingers weaving tensely in and out like he was knitting a sweater. Business, it was, always business, and often dirty business. She shifted uneasily on her spiky heels, her own position was becoming more fragile, the more embroiled she became. He would never let her go or move on, she knew too much. She thought about Ruby and how she had ended up in the drink when she'd crossed him, and one thing was sure, she wasn't going to end up like her.

Tash threw her a knowing glance. "Penny for 'em love?"

"Nothing," smiled Anna, "I was miles away, sorry, you having a nice time?"

"Yeah lovely," Tash glanced at Ronnie who had his back to her. She whispered back, "loads of fucking snobs."

Anna grinned, "Still, makes a change. It's a nice setting, beautiful place. Aiden's certainly made it look lovely."

"Santa's fucking grotto if you ask me," dismissed Tash, "hold on, here come the cameras, look up and smile. The girls posed, clinking their champagne flutes together and plastered fake smiles on their faces until the snapper had moved on. "What a bleeding farce."

The mill was beginning to fill up. Most of the tables were occupied, although the Fittlebury Hall mob were still missing. Roxy was agitated - they were her guests and were sitting on her table. She'd have egg on her face if they didn't show. Aiden, of course, would be behind the scenes supervising with the delectable Chrissie, who was as cool as an ice statue. Pity she didn't look like one, thought Roxy spitefully, in that white chiffon meringue concoction; Chrissie looked more Eton mess than Greek goddess. She had to laugh, talk about *all the gear and no idea*, so far it was the only amusing thing about the whole evening.

A virtual explosion of flash lights erupted outside from the press and a lot of shouting and appeals to whoever had arrived to stop and pose for the cameras. Jeremy Clarkson's voice boomed out in his indomitable way, demanding attention. Arriving with his entourage the press were going wild, as in his usual exuberant style, he wore his trade mark jeans with a sparkling white shirt and bow tie. The press were lapping it up as his party made their way inside and were greeted by an enthusiastic Roxy and Aiden, flapping around him like dumb moths to a naked flame. Jeremy's huge bulk diminished the others as a smiling waitress led them upstairs to their table.

There was still no sign of Felix and Hattie, nor Seb and Leo. Roxy had honoured them by seating them on a prominent table beside her, personally anxious to be seen with the beautifully young but relatively anonymous people and perfectly situated alongside the A-listers. She would be livid if they let her down. She'd deliberately placed Max and his riff-raff in a dark corner where they could do the least possible harm. She knew these gangland hoods he knocked around with. The Crooked Road in San-Fran had less deviations than they did, and she'd warned him on pain of death against any trouble tonight.

Chrissie, who when she'd tried on her dress had felt invincible, now felt like an overstuffed clown against the other women who seemed sleek and sylph-like. She pulled down the frills distractedly and checked her notes, tapping her pen on her nose. She gesticulated to Aiden who was busy supervising the waiting staff whirling about with the starters. Aiden ignored her with irritation, and threw his hands up in exasperation at the furore outside the door when once again the press went wild with the flashlights.

A stunning, willowy, auburn-haired, high-cheek boned girl in a silver slither of a dress was posing with a silver-haired, delicious lad. Together, they were like an Armani ad, and yet no-one had any idea who they were. Behind them came a tall, honey-voiced man, surely related to the famous Fox family - he was so like a younger version of Edward or James and with him a dashing Italian man, and three equally beautifully people. The press had no idea who they were, other than that they were the most unusual, interesting and delectable people they'd seen all night. As the group filtered like spectres into the restaurant, the reporters were scribbling like mad, and googling crazily into their phones.

Hattie clutched Felix's arm as they stepped inside, their eyes adjusting to the subtle lighting. Aiden tutted exaggeratedly as other diners turned to stare at the newcomers, whilst Roxy gushed like a geezer, more with relief than pleasure. She ushered them upstairs personally, with all the others punters craning to get a look at the late comers.

Kylie whisked the starters deftly onto Max's table, sliding the entrees into place just as she had been taught. The male diners barely acknowledged her, but a couple of the women managed to utter a muted conciliatorily *thank you*. Kylie glared at them, stuck up bunch of wankers she thought, as she doled out the plates, and the women were nothing more than a tribe of upper class courtesans. It was if she were invisible, not a person at all. She felt enraged at the rudeness of them all. Victor snapped his fingers at her to be gone, smiling obsequiously at the diners making sure all was well, and politely ignoring Ronnie's fingers sneaking inside Tash's bodice and rolling her nipple between his fingers. Max rocked back in his chair, challenging Victor to remark, but ever discreet, Victor simply walked away and signalled for Philip that it was time to bring over their wine.

Upstairs, Jeremy Clarkson and his party were going large. Noisy and loud were enjoying themselves hugely. In their discreet booth, the footballers were less ostentatious, although clearly enjoying the Clarkson floor show. Roxy was hanging on every word falling from Felix's lips and the cameras could not stop snapping Hattie from every tantalising angle.

The marauding film crew were insidiously everywhere. The celebs lapped up every shot as naturally as cats lapping cream, and Seb and Leo were not far behind them, posing delightedly and hamming up every moment. Dougie, with his dark brown voice and the handsome Roberto were busy being chatted up by an agent friend of Roxy's. Frankie, stone-cold sober, was feeling a little de trop. Amidst all these flashy buggers she felt a bit out of her depth and sadly inadequate.

Anna was feeling decidedly edgy. Max had a weird glint in his eye. He was drinking heavily and talking closely with Ronnie. Tash was stoned. She'd been out to the toilets several times and had a little tell-tale line of white powder under her nose. Christ, Anna couldn't believe how stupid she was. She knocked back another glass of wine, working on the premise if she drank enough she could forget what she knew. But in reality, she had to ask herself, what was the difference really, between her and Tash, except her own form of escapism was legal. Anna sighed, and wished she didn't know so much, it would be so much easier. She knew that tonight they would go back to the house and Max would expect her to be in full, party expansive mode and, of course, she would be expected to perform. But how long could she go on like this, it was nothing short of abuse and how much did she value herself?

Upstairs, the main course had been served with a cacophony of ooos and aahs! Aiden had surpassed himself and it was truly delicious, even if Leo could have done with three times the amount - grumpily declaring it would make a fool of his mouth, as Seb kicked him, none too diplomatically under the table, hissing to behave himself. Felix forked up the grub in a couple of mouthfuls and clattered down his cutlery hoping that Hattie might leave a soupcon of her own meal for him, but Hattie was in reality ravenous, and the silly little sprigs had hardly touched the sides of her starving appetite. Felix looked at her appealingly and she ignored him, stuffing the last scrap down with desperation. Leo and Seb tried to behave with more aplomb, but the tantalising flavours forced them to cram the food into their mouths like famished men and, like some form of exquisite torture, the plate was all too soon bland, white and empty. This was no food for working men - just a lot of frippery for dandies who dipped their wick into food and were never really genuinely hungry.

Felix sighed and looked longingly at Roxy's untouched plate. His long, tapering fingers snuck over and dipped his finger into the sauce decorating the edge. "Gorgeous," he sighed to Roxy, smiling beseechingly at her.

Roxy, sufficiently conceited to believe he was talking about her, offered him a forkful of food from her plate. Felix didn't hesitate, gobbling it up, he took her finger in his mouth and licked the end, sighing with desire and thought he could eat the whole of her. Luckily Hattie knew better and smiled as Felix extricated and excused himself for a pee.

At their table, Anna watched as Ronnie, Ernie and the others grew drunker. Tash's head lolled slightly, and the other tarts looked equally smashed. Max was cool, rocking back on his chair, eyeing the others with a cool detachment. He smiled sweetly at Anna and she returned his gaze as steadily as she could, although he always frightened her. Unexpectedly he stood up, gesticulating mildly for her to follow him, and as always, without question, she did. He eased out through the tables, taking her hand in his, slipping through the people smiling sweetly at everyone, until they were outside, stepping down the few steps by the twinkling Christmas trees at the entrance. Her hand still in his, they stepped across to the edge of the mill pond, the thousands of tiny, white lights casting cobwebs of silver threads across the water.

Max cupped her chin and stared hard at her, "Are you scared Anna?"

Anna returned his gaze, her fine eyes and face not wavering. "No Max, why would I be?"

"A few people have died here," he smiled, looking deep into her eyes her dilating pupils betraying her fear, "doesn't that worry you?"

Anna studied his face carefully, taking in his beautiful face, his long lashes, and the ethereal blond hair glinting in the glowing light. She thought in that moment, if she died here and now it wouldn't matter. Her life had become a sham, a nothingness, a farce. "No - I'm not afraid of you Max. This is where you killed her Max - Alice. This is where she was murdered wasn't it?"

Max's expression changed, his eyes narrowed. He pushed her back a tiny step, "Ah Anna, what makes you say that? Of course, you know it is. Where the sad little Alice took her own life, but me ... it was nothing to do with me."

Anna's gaze didn't falter, it was neither hard nor scared. "Of course it was Max, what do you think I am ...stupid? It was here wasn't it? The night of All Hallow's Eve - you and Terry. I heard you. You met her here that night and wore the costume, the *dottore della peste,* so you wouldn't be recognised. You and Terry did the job didn't you? She drowned - was it you or Terry who held her down in the water?"

In the ethereal light Max's face visibly hardened, his features crystallising into a sinister mask. A little pulse throbbing near his temple. "Oh my dear, that's such a pity. I was hoping you wouldn't be silly Anna, your loyalty to me was so paramount. What exactly are you saying to me now?"

Anna, realising that she had gone too far back-tracked wildly. Stuttering and stumbling her voice full of fear, "Nothing at all, just thinking that's all. You know I'd never say anything about it. I am totally yours."

Max smiled. He slowly lit the cigar, his features illuminated in that moment and Anna could see the smile did not reach his eyes. "Fine my darling, as long as that's clear, remember loyalty is everything. As long as you understand that you'll be fine."

Anna felt her insides go to liquid, and wanted to crumple at his knees and beg him to forget what she'd said. She was far from fine, she was suddenly terribly afraid of this ruthless man. Max looked out pensively across the pond, the waxy lights dancing innocently in their virgin white and the sinister silence yawned menacingly between them both. Anna knew it was not to end there and was fearful of the outcome.

Max took her hand gently and escorted her back inside. Anna's feet dragged reluctantly as he towed her behind him. She was desperately fearful, his eyes were blazing and almost manic when they returned to the others. As they resumed their seats, Max became the life and soul of their little party, whipping everyone into action, laughing, telling jokes and every now and then sending a poke of white-hot discomfort into her increasing uneasiness.

Unbeknown to Max and Anna, a tedious queue outside the gents had forced Felix outside for an urgent pee in the bushes. Staggering outside, slightly tipsy he'd reverently pulled out his cock, stroking the stem and aimed a stream of steaming piss into the freezing earth. Sighing blissfully as he'd relieved himself, he stepped back, zipping up his flies and stopped short. Voices - two distinct yet ghostly tones echoing across the water, a man and a woman. Talking insistently, urgently. Unbelievably, he realised he was listening to Max and Anna by the pond, and stood transmogrified, eavesdropping keenly on their disclosure, seemingly about Alice. He stood like an idiot with his prick in his hand, as he absorbed what they were saying - surely this couldn't be true? His fuddled brain struggled to compute the awful truth of their information, unable to move, anaesthetised and rooted to the spot, his heart beating like a sickening death knell. Anna and Max must have moved away, and an eerie silence crept through his veins like a drug hit to an addict. Mythical aeons passed before he could get his wits about him, finally mustering the strength to stumble back to the mill. White and clearly disturbed as he reached their table, Hattie knew immediately something was terribly wrong, although no-one else twigged anything was amiss as she ushered him to one side. Gasping and barely coherent, Felix blurted out what he'd overheard. She grabbed his arms forcing him to look at her and calm down. Babbling and angry, Felix was all for hell-raising, but Hattie, struggling to make him see reason, forced him to stop and think. There was no proof, only a rambling overheard conversation, and one which Max would just simply deny. Felix slumped down in a chair groaning, as he realised that Hattie was right, but it was what he had always believed - Alice hadn't killed herself, she'd been murdered - but why?

Roxy who'd been watching the little charade between Felix and Hattie was delightfully amused and intrigued - what the hell was going on with those two? She eased herself up from the table, expertly flipping a boob back inside the skimpy frock and shimmied over to Felix who looked as though he was about to throw up.

"What is it babe? You not well?"

Hattie glanced up at her, her incredible grey eyes full of concern. "Oh Roxy, I'm sorry" she improvised, "Felix is feeling dreadfully ill, I think we'll have to go home. Do you think you could ask one of the staff to call us a cab?"

Roxy's eyes narrowed, he didn't look sick, just terribly shocked, like he'd seen a ghost. Perhaps the old place was haunted after all. Nonetheless, she smiled at Hattie, "Hold on love," she flicked her fingers imperiously at Chrissie. "Hey you! Call a cab will ya?"

An indignant Chrissie strutted crossly over to them, "You'll never get a cab on New Year's eve."

Roxy barely acknowledged her. "Then get my driver to bring my car round, and take this lad home, he's not well. Probably ate something that disagreed with him," she added nastily, "so unless you want the press to get hold of that dearie, be discreet."

Chrissie stomped off to moan to Aiden and then thought the better of it and rang Roxy's driver. Roxy took Felix's hand, "Sure that's all it is love, no-one's upset ya have they?"

"No, no, of course not," said Hattie quickly, "Felix has been over-doing it lately, I think he's had too much to drink and then ate too much."

"Honestly Roxy, I'll be fine," stammered Felix, avoiding eye contact and gulping for air, "but I need to get home to my bed, and I don't want to spoil the evening for the others."

"You two wait downstairs for the car," said Roxy, "I'll come down with you."

"There's really no need," implored Hattie, "we'll be fine."

Roxy looked dubious and gestured to Chrissie. "You! Go down with these two and organise their coats dearie while they wait for my car." She turned to Felix and Hattie who'd already started to stagger down the stairs and bade them a curious farewell.

Chrissie was livid at being treated like a lackey, and once she was out of earshot of Roxy clapped her hands at a waitress. "You," she commanded, as imperiously as Roxy, "bring these guests their coats." She handed over the cloakroom ticket, "and be quick about it." Chrissie turned to Felix and Hattie and inclined her head, disappearing back up the stairs in a flurry of white chiffon to the upper restaurant.

The waitress brought back their coats, shoving them unceremoniously and rudely into their hands.

"Thanks so much," smiled Hattie, doing a double take as she recognised her old adversary. "Kylie what are you doing here?"

"What does it look like?" spat Kylie spitefully, "doing my new, fucking job and not having to bow and scrape to you, you lazy bitch."

"God you're poisonous Kylie," said Hattie sweetly, concealing her annoyance, "nothing's changed about you. You have chips the size of a rain forest on your shoulders - I'd hate to be as obnoxious as you."

Howling with anger, Kylie lunged forward in uncontrolled temper trying to claw Hattie's face, but Victor, who'd been keenly watching the interaction ,stepped in smartly, grabbing Kylie's wrist. "I'm so sorry madam, I think my waitress is out of order here, please accept our sincere apologies. Let me help you with your coat." He picked up Hattie's coat and turned to Kylie with anger, "You - to the kitchen now please."

Kylie narrowed her eyes dangerously, spitting venomously into Hattie's face, squaring her shoulders for a fight. Phillip joined Victor, who'd stepped nimbly between them, glaring hard at Kylie who backed off, spun around and stomped off. Luckily, at that moment Roxy's driver arrived at the entrance to take them home and the ugly situation was swiftly diffused, but later it was to prove to be the catalyst for the catastrophic events that were to follow.

As a shell-shocked Hattie and Felix were swept home in style in the long sleek limo, upstairs in the mill, Roxy was holding court, expanding forth on the gastronomic delights of the culinary genius that was Aiden. The Beckhams were enjoying much hilarity with Mike and Lisa, along with a couple more footie couples, whilst Jeremy Clarkson was giving it large about the fabulous decor of the vamped up mill and the new Range Rover that was due to be unveiled. On the lower floor, the live band opened with a brilliant rendition of Dave Brubeck's *Take Five*, which was simultaneously piped onto all three floors. Everyone went wild, the infectious music coursing its contagious beat into the limbs of the most modest diner. People were dancing everywhere, bodies entwined and pulsing with the rhythm and, without a respite, the band then swung into Al Green's *Lets Stay Together*. The whole mill was rocking and from the outside looking in, it was a swirl of writhing bodies. As the seeping music resonated out across the mirror of still water, the crisp, icy stems of the reeds were like stiff, ghostly bodies standing to attention as they waited for the year end to approach.

Hattie and Felix arrived home, falling out of the car and tumbling up the path to the cottage. Fiver, demented with pleasure at seeing them, as though they had been gone for years, whirled round them jumping up and down at their legs and demanding attention. Hattie picked him up stroking his silky little ears and gave him a dog chew, settling him down on his bed and followed Felix into the sitting room where he was slumped in the arm chair, his head in his hands. Chucking a log onto the slumbering embers of the fire she stoked it up, coaxing some life and warmth into the chill of the room.

"Felix darling, now tell me exactly what you heard," she asked tentatively, "first of all - who was it you overheard?"

"That fucker Max," snapped Felix, "he was talking to the Latino bird in the red dress. She said she knew it was him who'd killed Alice."

"Christ!"

"Now you know why I was so upset," snarled Felix, "Now you know why I wanted to punch his lights out."

"But did he admit it?"

"Not in so many words, but she knew he had, on the night of the Halloween party, he was dressed in that outfit and he and some thugs did it."

Hattie knelt down beside him, taking his hands in hers. "But Felix darling, we can't prove anything, can we? And moreover - why would he do it? What's the reason? He hardly knew her did he?"

"It's to do with those drugs - I'm sure of it. Andrew said he thought Alice was stealing from the surgery - although they never found anything. I'm sure she was into something illegal. That Max is a thug, gambling, racing. Alice might have crossed him in some way. She behaved so strangely towards the end - you know she did."

"I know, but we've no proof of what she was up to, and at the end of the day, it was just a scrap of a conversation you heard. It could have all been bravado on Max's part. He's such a prick, he could have just been showing off to his girlfriend."

"I don't think so," growled Felix, "you didn't hear it Hats, he was menacing. I didn't like it one bit, he's a nasty piece of work."

"Well, I agree with you there, but if we go to the police what can we say? Let's sleep on it darling and think rationally in the morning. It's a new year tomorrow and a new chapter."

Felix pushed her away, "I know he did it Hats, I just fucking know it. I never believed she killed herself and after tonight ... well."

Hattie sat up crossly. "Well whatever Felix, this conversation does us no good does it? You seem obsessed with Alice. Perhaps you're still in love with her? You make me feel totally fucking useless and frankly I'm getting tired of it."

Felix sat up quickly taking Hattie's hands in his. "Hats, I am so sorry, I am being selfish and stupid, of course I'm not in love with Alice. I wasn't for months before she died. You are my life. I just want to know the truth about what happened to her, surely you can see that."

Hattie, the old softie that she was, immediately backed down. "Okay love, but can we just give it a rest, our evening's ruined and I'm tired."

"Course we can, let's go to bed. I'm sorry, but all the things I feared tonight came to a head. I just don't know what to think or do."

"How about an earlier night than we planned?" smiled Hattie, taking his hand, "it's a new year tomorrow and a new start - let's make it the best ever."

"Okay darling - the best ever."

CHAPTER 85

Jennifer, Charles and their guests noticed Hattie and Felix making their hasty departure. Whilst most of them dismissed the incident, Jennifer, as ever, worried about them. Felix had looked white and ill, and Hattie totally distraught. Jennifer was a kind woman and a sensitive one. She looked at Roxy, who'd been solicitous in the extreme and decided to put it down to a tummy bug - although she thought it was odd. Charles, demanding a dance with his wife, put all thoughts of Felix out of her mind as she bopped away and their guests whooped and laughed their way towards the bewitching hour.

Seb and Leo were having a great time, dancing frenziedly to the music, alongside Dougie and Roberto who had moves no-one could have made-up in a million years. Frankie had paired up with Theo and was outside busily engaged in a snogathon, whilst her erect nipples stood to attention more with the cold, than his drunken ministrations. He was a good kisser though, and she wouldn't have minded trying him out with a blow job but it was too cold to strip off and get naked. Inside, Oli was wrapped around Sarah, his hands caressing her bum and bare back whilst getting stuck into nuzzling her earlobe, and to be fair she was reciprocating with equal ardour, much to evident enjoyment of Jennifer and Charles' table. Despite their sniggering and nudging, they were pleased to see Oli so enamoured, he needed someone special since his wife has buggered off and left him.

Andrew and Caitlin smooched on the dance floor. She oblivious to the goings on with the junior staff. Their love was totally affirmed and they had no eyes for anyone other than themselves. Andrew though, did cast half an eye on Oli and Sarah and gave his seal of approval, whilst the naughty lad Theo and the even naughtier Frankie, who'd disappeared outside, seemed a perfect match pro temps. Caitlin snuggled into him resting her cheek in his neck and Andrew lost himself into the very essence of her. His love so deep that everyone else seemed unimportant. Just last year they had come through major upheaval and now they were here - survivors and lovers. Nothing else mattered.

Roxy surveyed the triumph. The evening was a total success. She glanced over to Aiden, he'd changed into jeans and a jacket and moved easily, sexily gyrating his hips and smiling towards her. She reached out her hand invitingly. Between them, they knew how to throw a party. *Rox-Aid* was in max-thrust and the mill was on its way to being a sell-out total success. Aiden took her proffered hand leading out onto the dance floor and once again Roxy felt the thrill of his arms around her. He was a git, no doubt about it, but together they were an invincible team, and as the cameras snapped and flashed, immortalising their intimate moment, they both knew that, whatever the odds they were stronger together than apart.

Max slipped unobtrusively outside. Ronnie, Tash, Ernie and the others were boogying outrageously to the pulsating music, getting more shockingly disarrayed as they danced. Anna was grasped in a sweaty, tight embrace by Ernie and felt his hand edging up to touch her tits and flinched, wishing she could be a million miles away. The smell of his sour breath so close to her face made her feel sick.

Standing by the mill pond, the crisp, freezing air hitting him like a sledge hammer, Max called Terry. Speaking urgently into his phone, he issued his curt instructions and ended the call abruptly before he changed his mind. Checking his watch unnecessarily, he reasoned he'd had no choice. Terry would deal with the problem and, as sad as it was, it truly wasn't his fault. Anna had made her own bed and she must lie or die in it. But for tonight she would give him one last fuck, and then it would be over. They could not risk another accident here. Plans made, he trod a weary path back inside and joined in the festivities, as the clock made its way towards midnight.

As the countdown began and the revellers joined hands for Auld Lang Syne, a myriad of feelings swung between everyone. Chrissie glowered as Roxy and Aiden glowed, swearing to herself that she would drive them asunder. Max swung Anna into his chest drilling into her eyes, his own, regretful but hard, and she returned his gaze with deep-rooted fear. Ronnie, pissed and coarse, touched Tash's tits overtly looking forward to a night of wanton debauchery far removed from Sandra's cold clutches. Jennifer held Charles and they smiled into each other's eyes - their proximity and love exuding from every pore. Leo and Seb whooping and whirling like mad things, stopped suddenly and held each, other thrilled with the novelty of their closeness, whilst Roberto and Dougie played downright dirty and naughty. Theo and Frankie looked into each other's eyes and got serious, and Oli realised that Sarah was more than a one-off shag. Andrew, who already knew that Caitlin was more special to him than a precious jewel, cradled her carefully and kissed her with tender care. As the final strokes of midnight boomed out and everyone joined hands for Auld Lang Syne, Roxy signalled for the fireworks to begin . Ushering everyone outside, the ladies cradled their hands around their bare, goose-bumped arms and the gentlemen huddled against them. Over the dull glint of the mill pond, shards of glittering illuminations exploded into the night sky lighting it up like the blitz. The collective appreciation from the watchers began to subside as the cold seeped into their bones and gradually the audience crept back towards the warmth of the mill; the die-hard locals to carry on dancing, but many to collect their coats and bid goodbye to a jubilant Roxy and Aiden who, arm in arm, inordinately satisfied with a triumphant first night, performed a theatrical and royal farewell as people left. Chrissie smouldered angrily at the sight of them, it was her hard work that had made the evening such a success and it should be her standing with Aiden, not that bitch Roxy.

Max and his noisy party were preparing to depart. Their cars had arrived to take them back home and the women were teetering on their stilettos as they tottered down the entrance steps and over the gravel. Max shook Aiden's unenthusiastic hand and kissed Roxy's cheek reverently, thanking them for a splendid evening. Aiden could barely conceal his dislike for Max, and Roxy hers for Anna, although to be fair the poor cow looked white and drawn as she stepped into the waiting car. Roxy thought how ill Felix had looked earlier in the evening and wondered if it was something they'd eaten - Christ that would be the last thing they needed fucking food poisoning. She mentally shook herself - no, she was being stupid, something else was wrong. although she had no idea what, nor frankly did she care.

In the staff room, Victor and Philip were sorting out the tips - it had been a good night and the punters had been supremely generous. The waiting staff were tired and weary dragging on their coats and getting ready to go home. They'd all gone the extra mile tonight but they'd enjoyed it, pulling together and working hard. Aiden, despite his histrionics, paid well and had even laid on a mini-bus to take them back home.

As Philip shared out the gratuities to the others, Victor took Kylie to one side. His face was unsmiling. "I think you know what I'm going to say don't you?"

"No," snapped Kylie sulkily, although of course she knew he was going to sack her but she wasn't going to make it easy for him. "What?"

"I don't think you're suited to this job Kylie, your behaviour towards those customers tonight was inexcusable. You have an attitude problem and that doesn't work here. So I won't be wanting you back to work. Here's your wages up to date."

Kylie howled with rage and all the others turned to stare at her, "You tight arsed queer," she screamed, "that fucking bitch tonight has always hated me, I should have smacked her in the gob - that would have given the fucking cameras something to look at."

"Kylie," said Victor, his tone dangerously quiet, "calm down, you *were* and *are* way, out of order. Take your money, go get in the mini bus with everyone else and let's call it quits."

"I'll take my fucking money - you owe me that at least, but you can stuff your ride home," she screamed, picking up her coat and thrusting it on glaring at everyone, "and what are you fuckers staring at?"

"What's going on?" said Aiden, stalking into the staff room, "I can hear you from outside."

"Kylie won't be returning to work here Aiden," informed Victor coldly, "she's unsuitable and there was an ugly incident tonight with a client."

"And you can fuck off," yelled Kylie, turning on Aiden, "with your pissy bits of crappy food - don't worry I'm going." She barged out through the door, colliding with Roxy who was coming in to see what the shouting was about.

"YOU!" snarled Roxy, recognising her immediately. "What are YOU doing here? You're a fucking menace, ya bring havoc wherever ya go."

In reply Kylie gave her a hefty sock in the mouth, flooring Roxy and cutting her lip. "Piss off the lot of you," she shouted, and pushed her way past the whirring camera men from *Sunrise Productions* who'd captured the whole exciting scene.

Chrissie, who'd been loving the drama, in particular the assault on Roxy, was livid when Aiden bent down and tenderly helped Roxy up, wiping the blood from her mouth with his pristine, white handkerchief, kissing the corner of her mouth affectionately.

Kylie stormed off - her coat flying behind her like an escaping highway man. Irrational, full of anger and with malice aforethought, she eschewed the main driveway and stumbled her way across the estate, taking the concrete road towards the Fittlebury Hall stable yard.

CHAPTER 86

Drunk and deliriously happy, propping each other up like bean sticks in a gale, Seb and Leo lurched out of the mill, closely followed by Dougie and Roberto, who were singing their lungs out. Theo and Frankie, desperate to get naked, followed with inordinate haste, laughing immoderately like punters at a second rate floor show.

"What's that?" squealed Seb theatrically, clutching Leo's arm as he caught a glimpse of Kylie's long coat disappearing in the moonlight as she scuttled along the estate drive, "it's a fucking ghost!"

Leo squinted into the gloom, the moonlight picking up the hint of a shadow as the image of Kylie ebbed out of his sight, "It's nothing sweetie, you're imagining it."

"I simply wasn't," said Seb affronted, "who was that?"

"I saw them," affirmed Frankie, who although she was pissed still had the youth and delight of twenty-twenty vision, "someone hurrying down the track towards the stables - in a long coat."

"Noooo!" howled Dougie, "A ghost?"

"Don't be bloody stupid," growled Leo, sobering up, "of course not."

"Let's go hunt it," suggested Roberto with drunken bravado. "Come on." He grabbed Dougie by the hand dragging him off down the concrete road.

"For fuck's sake," grumbled Leo, "can't we just go home - I'm knackered," as he tried to steer Seb through the trees behind the mill towards the cottage.

"Don't be a spoilsport," laughed Theo, running after Dougie and dragging Frankie with him, "it'll be a laugh."

They started to jog down the road towards the stables. Reluctantly Leo joined them, feeling as though his meagre meal was about to come up all over his shoes. Laughing and joking they egged each other on, their eyes glued to the road for the figure ahead.

Kylie heard the voices behind her and stopped for a heartbeat, spinning round and listening keenly. The sounds were clear on the still, night air as she realised she was being pursued. Still incredibly angry, but not as blindly irrational, she slid into the cover of the trees, there was nothing she could do with these drunkards hell-raising after her. Using the woods as shelter, she carefully backtracked, skirting away from them, until, she reached the track to the main road, determined that revenge would have to wait for another day.

"I told you you'd imagined it," grumbled Leo, after they'd gone half a mile down the farm road, "there's no-one here, and I'm frozen." He stopped walking and turned round. "I'm going home."

Seb smiled pathetically at him, "Okay babycakes, I'm cold too. Let's call it a day, it's not fun anymore."

Dougie and Roberto were whooping like silly kids and making ghostly noises ahead of them, whilst Frankie and Theo had long since abandoned the ghost hunt to discover their own secret proclivities and were getting naked on the frosty verge side.

Barely noticing their state of undress, they scooped up the sexual deviants, shouted to the ghost busters that the comfort of hot chocolate was calling from Laundry Cottage and made their way home - little realising of the shadowy disaster, in the shape of Kylie, that they had headed off at the proverbial Khyber pass.

Max and his entourage arrived back at his gaff with all the aplomb of a gaudy fairground pulling into town. The ladies, in their multi coloured plumes and extravagant costumes, sashayed out of the cars, whilst the men, resplendent in garish cummerbunds and matching bow ties, followed them. The twins met them at the door with flutes of champagne and had laid on a finger buffet in the drawing room. Dulcet tones of music drifted through the house and it looked as though the party would carry on until the small hours. Max took Anna's hand lightly and led her indoors. His fingers felt icy cold as they grasped her own and she shivered involuntarily, when, instead of following the others, Max ushered her upstairs to his bedroom. Below them, the strong beat of the music pulsated and shouts of laughter floated up the stair-well, as Max slid off Anna's dress, and she stood naked except for her strappy shoes in front of him. Ordering her to stay still, he walked around her, appraising her body, touching her lightly, on the shoulders, her breasts, her buttocks, admiring her neat shaven bush. Anna felt her cheeks flush, like a horse for sale in the market, she was being scrutinised before purchase. Very gently he moved his lips over to hers and kissed her like he had never kissed her before. A loving tender kiss. Anna shut her eyes pretending that theirs was a normal relationship and melted into him, kissing him back. It was all she'd ever dreamed of, to be loved and to love in return and, for a while, she could just pretend. Max made love to Anna that night like never before. Courteously and kindly, warmly and sweetly, lovingly and with great dexterity. She blossomed under his touch, lapping up the tenderness in a way she'd never thought possible. Afterwards, she snuggled up to him and, whilst the mad sounds of the party continued downstairs, he wrapped her safe, cocooning her in his arms until she drifted off into a happy, untroubled sleep.

As the silver morning broke, with slim cold fingers of light slithering over the stiff, cold stems of grass, Felix woke as though shards of glass were glued to his eyes. He felt he'd hardly slept at all, and the chill of the night seeped through his bones, despite Hattie wrapping herself around him. His thoughts churned repetitively about what he'd overheard. That bastard Max. He'd been responsible, but how had Alice been involved with him? She could barely have known him surely? Struggling to escape Hattie's tentacle legs, he fidgeted free, edging out of the bed, and dragged on his jeans desperately trying not to wake her. The awful part of this whole thing was that none of this was Hattie's fault. He had not loved Alice, but had felt a sense of responsibility for her. She was so isolated in her death, and he felt he was her only ally - her only friend. He was sure now that she'd been into something bent, but of what, he'd no idea. Max was a dodgy bastard and now he knew he was involved and had brought about her demise. But what could he do? He was helpless. He had no proof, nothing on Max, other than an overheard conversation. The police would laugh at him. But avenge Alice he would. He wouldn't let that bastard Max get away with it.

Hattie stirred, reaching out in the bed to find that Felix was already up.

"You okay?"

"Yeah - just a bit restless. Sorry I didn't mean to wake you."

"Don't be daft, do you wanna talk?"

"I'm all talked out babe," Felix reached out and stroked her hair, "you mean everything to me Hats. You know that don't you?"

Hattie struggled up in the bed and looked at him seriously. "You mean everything to me. I know what you heard, and I know it's hard, but you've got to try and let it go, otherwise it'll eat you up and drive us apart."

Felix flopped back on the bed taking her face in his hands. "I'll never let anyone or anything drive us apart. It's okay, all okay. Let's forget it baby. It's a new year, a new start."

Hattie gazed at him, her great doe eyes assessing him. "I wish I could believe that."

Roxy and Aiden had stayed in the crude staff accommodation at the mill. Sex had been a given, but ironically it was tender and loving, something that had been missing from their marriage for years. Aiden had packed a venomous Chrissie, as poisonous as a pit of vipers, into one of the mini buses destined for a local hotel with instructions to return the next morning and, without a backward glance, had returned to spend the remainder of the night with his wife.

The nesting pair woke to the call of moor hens on the pond and the eerie screech of pheasants from the neighbouring fields. Roxy draped herself around Aiden in the inadequate little bed; neither wanted to get up, content to lay snuggled up together. They heard stirrings from the neighbouring staff rooms. Victor and Phillip had stayed overnight and a couple of the chefs. There were bookings for lunch today and the evening too. Aiden had organised the menus well ahead and he could leave them to get on with the prepping. The cleaners would be coming in first thing and the waiting staff were due back at eleven. There was no rush for him and Roxy to show their faces. Aiden allowed his hand to stray between her legs, his thumb and forefinger finding the nub of her clitoris easily and gently he massaged until he felt her becoming wet and slippery. Roxy sighed with pleasure, opening her legs further as Aiden slipped his fingers up inside her, moving rhythmically and upwards towards her pubic arch. He watched her face as he played, her eyes were closed but the changing expressions as he experimented with his ministrations were fascinating. Suddenly she snapped her eyes open, and in a swift movement, had pushed away his hand and made a dive under the covers for his cock. Taking it in her mouth, she looked up at him from under her lashes and enjoyed turning the tables to watch his expression change as she worked it backwards and forwards. Deftly spinning her round, his cock still in her mouth, Aiden's tongue found its own mark, licking and sucking her fanny until Roxy felt she would explode with lust. Bucking and rearing in mutual orgasm they fell exhausted, half on, half off the little bed, and laughed like they hadn't in years. It was a great start to the New Year.

It was still early and Max lay with a sleeping and contented Anna, stroking her shining dark hair. It was regrettable but he considered it totally necessary to instruct Terry. He'd be here very soon. Anna was becoming a loose cannon and, whilst he had become fond of her, and she was a perfect foil for his games, she was also beginning to have a conscience and that would never do. She knew far too much and like most of the people in his life she was totally dispensable. The last fuck had been nice, simple and normal and surprisingly he'd actually enjoyed it. No perversions, no anal, no threesomes - just Anna and him. He often wondered if he'd ever be really *normal*. Or would his depravities always float to the top like bloated corpses. He thought about that silly tart Alice, floating in the mill pond, and Ruby floating in the Thames. He'd told Terry he didn't want Anna to suffer - make it quick and clean. Anna sighed beside him and snuggled closer. Max lay waiting, his senses on high alert, although he didn't hear the car slip into the drive, or the turn of the key in the back door, but he did hear a quiet tread on the stairs - Terry and his guys had arrived.

CHAPTER 87

Nigel Brown was living the life in Paris, and had been for the last few weeks at the expense of his gullible patron. Bonne Année in the City of Light was colourful in the extreme and, the best part was, Cutter was paying for it. He headed for the Champs-Elysées, secreting a bottle of fizzy wine and a plastic glass in his capacious pockets - although you weren't supposed to bring your own, it seemed most people did and he wasn't going to see in the New Year sober. The crowds were something else, and if you were claustrophobic this wasn't the place to be, but the atmosphere was buzzing and he drank in every moment, literally and metaphorically. Cutter hadn't bothered him much of late and he guessed he had other fish to fry, but Nigel had located the girl and he was just spinning out his trip now, more for the craic and the hell of it. Once he passed on the information he'd be out of a job and he had no other work offers. The girl - was a funny thing. He hadn't made contact yet but knew where she lived and watched her on a daily basis. She worked for one of the fashion houses. She had few friends seemingly and kept herself to herself, living in the bo-ho area of the city. He couldn't quite understand why. She was very attractive, beautiful even, but barely went out, and lived like a virtual hermit. Still, why should he care if she was a misfit. He'd report back this week and then take the slow train home. Meanwhile, he would enjoy the celebrations in Paris, courtesy of Cutter and his endless supply of cash.

With the New Year festivities well and truly over, life outwardly to all intents and purposes had settled down at the stables. Only Hattie knew differently that Felix was brooding horrifically about what he'd overheard, although he managed to conceal his feelings pretty well. Seb breezed on in his usual flamboyant way, riding rough shod and insensitively over everyone, seemingly unable to pick up on any negative vibes floating like elephants in the room. Leo, on the other hand, was more astute, picking up on Felix's distracted behaviour. He tried to pump Hattie, but she was keeping schtum, ever loyal, but he was certain something was up and they weren't saying.

Roxy, was keeping them all on their toes, being her usual demanding self, insisting that she wanted to do more jumping and putting the pressure on Felix to organise a day's hunting. The sale of her house had gone through, and she'd set up camp locally and was far more on the scene than ever before. Seb flattered her outrageously and Felix managed to keep his distance, whilst Hattie took the middle road. As for Max, for the first few days after the New Year, they saw little of him. He'd disappeared off to London and only to reappear the following week. He breezed into the yard slapping his whip against his breeches looking outrageously debonair. Directly he'd arrived, without a word to anyone, Felix had slapped tack on Woody and headed off for a hack and hadn't been seen since. Normally Felix would have sorted out Simeon, but it was as though Max and his horse were red hot and Felix couldn't bear to touch them, which Leo thought was odd. So he did the honours and gave him a jumping lesson. He was surprisingly good, took risks like a man possessed, angry and indefatigable. Leo was impressed, but it was more than that, it was as though Max was exorcising his own demons as he took on the fences with no natural fear or thought of the danger. Roxy stood by the arena watching and was seriously impressed. Max was a natural, a real natural, not a fake like her. When he finally slid to a halt, the session finished, she gave a long slow hand clap, whistling her approval. He nodded over at her, but his face was as hard and cold as steel. Roxy was disturbed, she knew him well, something had happened. Max was pre-occupied and this exhibition of bravado was covering something up. Moreover where the fuck was Felix? He was supposed to be organising this day's hunting - and he kept prevaricating. She was going to ask him one more time, and if he didn't sort it, she would do it herself.

Felix was cantering across the downs on Woody, the wind in his face was cathartic - cleansing. He needed to sort out in his mind what he could do about Max. Legal means would be no good, he had no proof, but he had to pay him back for what he'd done. But how? What could he do? He couldn't talk to Hattie about it, and he wouldn't implicate her in anything he did, but what could he do, and how? The dilemma tumbled round and round in his head like a washing machine on a 1600 revolution spin until he could barely think straight. Frustrated he brought Woody down to a walk, stroking his mane and neck. Then it came to him - hunting - they wanted to go hunting and he could take him - manufacture an accident. No-one would suspect anything - a novice rider falling at speed - he might not kill him but he could be badly hurt, or shaken up, and that would do - anything would do. He turned Woody for home - the embryo plan nurturing in his mind.

Charles was reading the paper in the morning room and Jennifer had her head in Horse & Hound. Mrs Fuller had brought in their breakfast and they were planning to ride together later that morning.

"Darling, there's a good meet coming up, do you fancy taking a day off and we'll go together?" asked Jennifer. "It'd be great if you could. I much prefer it when I go out with you."

Charles looked at her from over his paper. "Where is it?"

"Brigstock Farm - that's supposed to be a good jumping day, isn't it?"

"Hmm it is. But some easy ways round too. When?"

"Tuesday week. Do you think I'd manage it?"

"Definitely, it's a big old day, but you can go through the gateways if you can't do the hedges," smiled Charles, shaking out the paper. "The children are away with Celia skiing so we won't have to worry about them - it's a great idea."

"Nancy and Dulcie might like to come too," suggested Jennifer, "be nice for them to have a day out."

"You are an old softie darling," laughed Charles, who wasn't as benign about the staff as Jennifer, "if you like."

"They don't often get the chance - it'd be a treat for them, they deserve it, they work hard."

"Jen, I don't think they work that hard, but you ask them if you like, now let me finish off the paper!"

Max was tetchy. Stupidly he missed Anna, although Terry had despatched her quietly and, as promised, without overt stress. She'd been found in her bath in her rooms above the club, her wrists slashed, having taken a massive overdose, coupled with a hefty dose of vodka. It hadn't even been reported in the press and the verdict would be suicide; the inquest was scheduled for later in the month. He'd enjoyed the recklessness of jumping Simeon, the risk taking, the dicing with fate. He hadn't told Roxy about Anna' death. She hadn't liked her but, regardless, it would serve no purpose. He carried the burden of guilt with him like a hard stone, and for Max, this was an uncomfortable first.

Roxy herself, sensed a change in Max. His reckless behaviour was out of character, he was normally totally in control of his feelings and actions. She didn't press him, considering that he would tell her when he was ready. But it was almost as though he were on some kind of death-wish as she watched him pushing himself to extremes.

The phone call from Nigel Brown, when he finally contacted Max, came as an overwhelming sense of shock. The long awaited news of his daughter, coming tight on the heels of Anna's death, left him reeling. He listened to Brown, taking in all the information and told him to email the details immediately, making an urgent appointment with his solicitor. He would make sure that all his wealth, everything he owned, was left to her. He'd done nothing for her in his lifetime, but if he died the whole shebang would go to her.

Roxy had kindled a new and meaningful relationship with Aiden. Their successful coupling on New Year's Eve had brought them close and they were busy bonking each other's brains out. The new house had made a difference. The children, still in the London house with the petulant nanny, had given them free rein to shag without encumbrance and they had made the most of it. The mill restaurant was superlatively successful with evening bookings stacked out and lunch times filled up daily as the spa became more popular. Aiden couldn't have been more delighted, but Chrissie couldn't have been more sour-faced. He did continue to shag her when he grabbed the opportunity, but this was little, rather than often, and she was disgruntled and stroppy. Roxy cast a blind eye, enjoying Chrissie's catastrophic fall from favour, and Aiden, realising that he had to extricate himself, but not wanting to lose a good PA, serviced her enough to keep her on the hook, but kept her at a subtle distance.

A few days after the party Dougie and Roberto had disappeared. Dougie being called away to Ocala in Florida to commentate, and the dishy Roberto to hold the fort at their yard whilst he was away. Theo and Frankie were well loved up and spending every given moment together in Laundry Cottage, much to the amusement and ribbing of Leo and Seb. Theo was enamoured with the lively, bubbly Frankie and she with him. As for Theo's peers, Oli was loved up himself with the delectable Sarah, and Andrew, who'd already found his soul mate in Caitlin was pleased that his colleagues were happy and prayed that they stayed that way.

Felix put his plans into action carefully. The Brigstock Farm meet would be perfect. In just a week's time he and Hattie would take out Roxy and Max. There was enough big jumping to challenge Max, and for Hattie to take Roxy round the easy routes. It would be perfect. Felix would spur Max on to take the hedges with him. It would be a bravado challenge, and as they went over, Felix would push him off. Felix, the far superior rider, would have no trouble unseating the novice, and at full lick, the consequences would be humiliating and with any luck bring about the odd broken bone or two. He wasn't going to tell Hattie, he wasn't going to tell anyone. It would be a tragic accident - just like Alice.

Kylie was struggling for work. She'd touted around the yards for a bit of casual mucking out, but her odious reputation had already preceded her. Naturally, she blamed it on Hattie and Felix. They were responsible for bad-mouthing her, adamantly refusing to believe it was anything to do with her, and her irrational and bizarre thinking became more and more confused. The stash of drugs she'd pinched from Alice's shed was burning a hole in her pocket, but what could she do? No-one trusted her farther than they could throw her. She exhausted everyone she knew who might take them off her hands. Angrily, she pondered how she could off-load them, knowing their street value must be vast.

Down at the Fox, Nancy and Dulcie were enjoying a frothy pint with Patrick the farrier who was demonstrating some of his latest dance moves - whirling them with gusto around the tiny snug, bumping into tables and chairs, until Janice called for them to behave themselves. Theo and Frankie had joined them and by now they'd all downed far more than was good for them. Colin and Grace, who'd left baby Archie with Grace's mum, were on a night out and were meeting Sandy and Mark, so the pub was throbbing with stalwart hunting folk in the tiny bar.

"Who's going to the Brigstock Farm meet?" yelled Sandy over the din, "should be a grand day - plenty of fuck-off hedges!"

"We are," shouted back Grace, "Mum's having Archie. I love that meet, Chloe's lending me a pony - it's one of the best of the season."

"Frightens the pants off me," brayed Colin, who'd drunk too much and whose nose was throbbing red, "I shut my eyes over those bloody hedges!"

"They've made a way round the really big buggers though, haven't they?" said Dulcie, who wasn't as brave as the others. "Jennifer has said Nancy and I can go out this time, but I don't fancy it if it's a really big day."

"You'll be fine," said Grace kindly, "these days you don't have to do the big ones if you don't want to, there's nearly always a gateway or a smaller option if you don't fancy it, and there'll be two field masters, one for the jumpers and one for those who aren't so keen."

Dulcie smiled gratefully at Grace. "That's a relief, although I expect once my blood's up, I'll be okay."

"Sure you will," agreed Nancy, who loved the cut and thrust of taking on the drops and ditches, "we'll have a lovely day, and it'll be nice not to have to be babysitting the little ones for a change."

"Anyway sis," smiled Frankie, "I'm sure Jennifer won't do all the big lines, she sometimes misses out the hedges, doesn't she?"

"Yeah, that's true, but she's getting braver every time out," grinned Sandy, "we'll have to get you out Mark!"

"No thanks - it is definitely not for me. I'll keep both my feet firmly on the ground darling, if it's all the same to you. I'm very happy to support but that's as far as it goes! I married you, not the bloody horse!"

"Don't blame you mate," agreed Patrick, "we'll go to the meet and watch you nutters instead and catch your ponies when you fall off in the mud!"

"Actually I think the going should be good, we've not had as much rain, and Brigstock land is fabulously springy old turf," said Colin seriously, "I hate it when it's like a damned quagmire and you're jumping out of a foot of mud before you start to leave the ground."

"Absolutely," agreed Sandy, "let's hope we don't have too much rain between now and then."

"Right - whose round is it then?" asked Patrick, knocking his glass on the bar. "Janice - when you're ready love."

"Any of your lot going Frankie?" asked Grace, "Felix must have some of the horses fit enough by now."

"Dunno, he might. Roxy and Max are desperate to go out, but by the sounds of it, it might be too big a day for them."

"Trouble is, with novices they've no idea really," said Sandy. "They go and watch and think it looks easy."

"Yeah - case of all the gear and no idea," laughed Nancy cynically, "they'll learn the hard way."

"Don't be unkind Nancy," remonstrated Dulcie crossly, "everyone has to learn sometime."

Nancy smiled down at her, ruffling her hair, "Sorry. You're right, that was unkind, we don't want any accidents - do we?"

Felix began to orchestrate his plan. Max was staying at his house, as was Roxy in hers and that meant they were riding most days. Instead of avoiding them, he now courted their company, taking them both under his wing for jumping lessons. Praising them to the hilt, although it was clear that Roxy was not so proficient, and Max was just purely gung-ho. Luckily Galaxy was a tolerant horse, and although not a natural jumper forgave, Roxy her constant loss of balance and caught her every time, as she lurched over the fences. Simeon was much more proficient and, once Max kicked him into the fence, the horse simply took over, adjusting his stride perfectly, jumping cleanly and economically, so that Max was lulled into a false sense of his own abilities. *Perfect,* thought Felix, as he coached him into jumping bigger and bigger and the grand horse adjusted accordingly. By the end of a few days of concentrated work Max believed he was invincible. Roxy felt less so.

Later, over steaming mugs of coffee in the tack room, Felix planted the seed of the Brigstock Farm meet which was to take place in a couple of days, saying that he and Hattie were taking a couple of the eventers out for a jolly and how much he was looking forward to it.

"Don't you think it's about time we went out?" demanded Max, "you said you'd arrange it."

"I know I did, but this meet is quite fast and some of the fences are quite big," said Felix trying to remain casual, "you might not be ready for it yet."

"I definitely am," declared Max determinedly, "anyway, it's up to me to decide."

Felix felt his heart skip a beat, this was just the response he was hoping for. He saw Hattie give him a hard look, she knew there was no way Max would cope, let alone Roxy. "No, not this meet Max, really start with something more modest. Come and watch by all means, but some of those hedges are really mean."

"You and Hattie are going are you?" asked Max, "and it's true you don't always have to jump if you don't want to, isn't it?"

"Well yes, I suppose," stammered Felix, desperately hiding his delight at the fish taking the bait, "but honestly Max it could be quite dangerous."

"I'm definitely up for it. What about you Roxy?"

Roxy looked a little white, but not to be outdone, "Definitely I am, as you say I don't have to jump if I don't want to - do I?"

Hattie looked at her imploringly, "Really Roxy, it isn't the best day for you, why not come and spectate, then choose an easy day."

Roxy glared at her. "No, if Max is going, I'm going. What the fuck have we been doing all this jumping for if it isn't to try hunting?"

Hattie looked at Felix shrugging her shoulders, "Felix please - do you think this is wise?"

"It's not up to Felix," snarled Roxy. "Max and I are going, that's an end to it - now what gear do we have to wear?"

Hattie's heart sunk as she realised they were serious - Christ it was a recipe for disaster, and she and Felix would have to pick up the slack when it all went tits up. She looked at Felix, whose sapphire blue eyes were glittering and she suddenly felt very confused. What was he up to?

Kylie stopped in at Penfolds in Cuckfield. A good sale had lured her in, even though she was short of dosh, there might be a bargain to be had and she loved just nosing around. She'd made out a card to put in the window offering her services for clipping, mucking out and house sitting. You never know she might get some much needed work. Penfolds was a great shop, a veritable treasure trove of goodies, and everyone who was anyone in the equestrian world breezed in there to stock up or browse. The shop was on two levels. On the lower floor were racks of fleeces, jackets, and breeches; shelves of riding hats and boots were crammed into every available space. Suspended from the ceiling were body protectors, fluorescent coats, bush hats and other paraphernalia - it was a veritable Aladdin's cave of riding gear. At the back six wooden steps led to the next level. The smell of leather filtered pungently down from the stacks and stacks of saddles, along with bridles, headcollars, martingales and a surfeit of other tack. You could lose yourself in Penfolds for hours. Kylie was sifting through the bargain trug on the upper level when the old-fashioned bell clanked and she heard new customers coming in. Immediately her hackles shot up when she heard them speaking, and dashed to hide behind a rack of saddles piled eight high and listened intently.

"Hi," the assistant greeted the shoppers warmly - she knew Hattie well, "How are you?"

"Great thanks - I've brought along a couple of our liveries today, they're coming out hunting for the first time next week, and we need some kit PDQ."

"Of course! I recognise you from the TV and we're stocking some of your breeches as it happens!"

Roxy preened visibly. "Cool, but I need the right kit for this hunting lark - can ya help me and my friend?"

Hattie intervened, "We need a hunt jacket, shirt and stock, with some buff breeches, oh and a crash hat with a velvet cover. Oh yeah, we'd better have a plain stock pin if you have one."

"And boots?" enquired the assistant, moving away from behind the counter to look out some jackets.

"No, we got some plain black ones which'll do the job."

"Right, try this on for size," she passed Roxy a smart black wool jacket. "What size do you think you are sir?"

Max smiled, he liked the deferential tone this girl used, "About a 42 chest."

Kylie's ears were on stalks. Both of her arch-rivals were here downstairs, and here she was, privy to their plans to go hunting. She wondered where and when they were going. It must be with the local hunt.

"When are you going out?" asked the assistant, handing Roxy some breeches into the changing room.

"We're hoping to do the Brigstock Farm meet," said Hattie hesitantly, "or maybe another smaller day."

"We *are* doing the Brigstock Farm meet. I'm getting sick of people trying to put us off" emphasised Max, "and we're looking forward to it too I might add."

"I'm sure you'll have great fun," remarked the assistant, looking sideways at Hattie and wondering if she was out of her mind taking two novices there out for their first time.

Kylie, from her hiding place, couldn't believe her luck. Brigstock Farm - that was a bloody huge day. She'd definitely turn up at the meet and watch them make fools of themselves. Then it occurred to her that she could assist in bringing them down to earth and eat dirt in more ways than one. Smiling delightedly, she remained in hiding - dreaming of Roxy in her smart new gear covered in mud.

CHAPTER 88

They were lucky with the weather and the day of the meet was fine. A slight frost soon lifted as the sun rose and, by 11am it promised to be a perfect day for hunting. Seb and Leo had turned the horses out to perfection, with tiny, neat plaits in uniform rows along the crest of their necks, the coats glossy and polished. Every bit of tack was gleaming and the stitching checked. Hattie was riding the dependable Rambler and, to her surprise, Felix had elected to take the headstrong Woody.

"Why on earth are you taking him, Felix?" she asked seriously. "Don't get me wrong he's a great horse, but not easy is he? You can hardly babysit anyone on him."

"I think the outing will do him good," said Felix, not able to meet her eye, "and he'll eat up those hedges."

"Felix, stop right now, you know, and I know, Max and Roxy will never be able to do them - in fact it would downright dangerous to try."

"Well you can take them round the easy routes and I can pop a few difficult fences to settle him, then I'll join you - that okay?"

"It'll have to be, won't it," snapped Hattie crossly. She didn't want the lone responsibility of looking after the two newcomers, "just don't leave me on my own with them for long."

"I won't, I promise," smiled Felix, "anyway Woody's not that fit yet, so I won't be over doing him."

"Just remember that when your blood's up," said Hattie sarcastically, "and don't drop me in it with them."

"Calm down Hattie - it'll be fine."

Brigstock Farm was about ten miles as the crow flew but about fifteen miles by road. Leo was driving the horses there in the truck, with Hattie and Felix following behind in his car. Roxy and Max would travel under their own steam and join them at the lorry. As was traditional, Leo planned to park a couple of miles away from the actual meet, so that he could help everyone mount up and they could settle the horses down with a gentle hack to the Farm itself. He'd follow behind them in Felix's car to be on hand if they needed any extra help at the meet or if Max or Roxy got themselves into trouble. Seb and Frankie were to be left at home to do the yard. It was all timed and planned like a military operation.

Leo planned to park in a lay-by, large enough to hold the truck and the other vehicles, and far enough off the road to be safe. He just hoped that no-one else had the same idea. They'd left in plenty of time and he was relieved to find the pull-in was empty as he waggoned the truck smoothly to a halt. Felix nipped in behind him, leaving enough room for the ramp to come down. The rich aroma of shit exuding from the back of the lorry was testament to the excited horses stamping and clattering around in the back whilst they waited impatiently for the off. The minutes ticked agonisingly past whilst the truck rocked back and forth, and still there was no sign or Roxy and Max. Felix looked at his watch, they'd already been hanging around for fifteen minutes. He glanced anxiously up the road, other lorries and vehicles had passed them, the occupants waving madly, but no sign of the black Range Rover.

"They're late," Felix grumbled to Leo, "I don't want to be rushing, it'll be bad enough as it is, the horses'll be too excited."

"Shall we get them off?" asked Hattie, "Or leave them on board till they get here?"

"Better wait I suppose," said Leo dubiously, "although they're getting mighty fired up inside."

A clattering of hooves sounded from down the lane. In the distance, a group of riders hacking to the meet were trotting towards them. As they approached, they slowed down to a walk, calling hello and then, once past, picked up a smart trot again. The lorry began to sway wildly as Woody became more agitated waiting for the off. Even the normally quiet Galaxy was looking anxious.

"They'd better fucking hurry up, otherwise we'll have to leave them behind," moaned Felix, "Woody's not going to stay in there for long."

A beaten-up old car chugged down the road and pulled over. Hattie groaned recognising Kylie's car. "What the fuck does she want?" she grumbled to Felix, and felt her hand tighten on her hunt whip.

Kylie parked the car and got out and walked over, putting both hands up in a gesture of surrender. "Before you say anything - I've come to apologise. I was way out of order and I'm sorry - okay?"

Hattie, completely deflated by the abrupt turn around in Kylie's attitude and just stared at her. "Okay," was all she could muster.

"I really mean it," affirmed Kylie sincerely, "I'm bloody sorry. Look, can I help at all? I'm on my way to the meet, but you look as though you've got your hands full."

Felix, who was now desperate to get the horses off and, would have taken any offer of a port in a storm, "If you don't mind, helping get this lot unloaded before they come through the bloody living."

"Okay. How about I jump in the back of the truck and hand each one down to Leo?" She turned to him, "then you can help them mount Leo, whilst I keep an eye on the others."

"Good idea," agreed Leo, "save you two getting filthy, before you've even started."

"Leave the back of the ramp up," advised Kylie, walking over to the truck, "until I'm inside and have got hold of them. Judging by the rumpus, the fuckers will jump straight out, directly you open up, otherwise." She pulled down the steps to the living and struggled inside.

Hattie, Felix and Leo waited patiently outside. They could hear her talking to the horses, and the crazy rocking of the lorry began to subside. "You all right in there Kylie?" called Felix, "what are you doing?"

"Just calming them down," called Kylie's muffled voice from inside the truck, "they'll squash me otherwise."

"Oh, sorry. I hadn't thought. Just be careful."

"I will, don't worry. Just be ready to get the ramp down when I say."

"We will," said Leo, turning to the others, "if Kylie hands them down to me, one by one, Woody will come off first, so Felix, you jump on. Then I'll get you on Hats, while she waits with Galaxy and Simeon. Those two are much quieter."

"Ready!" called Kylie, "Take care though, Woody's in a right fucking state!"

Leo lowered the ramp, the electric motor whirring down gently, and it was all he could do to open the back partition doors before Kylie and Woody exploded out with a furious clatter. Felix grabbed the horse's bridle, gritted his teeth and, in one fell swoop, vaulted on top. Woody, bucking madly, almost unseated him, as Kylie was bringing Rambler out of the truck, but Felix hung on with more determination than a tick on a dog.

Five minutes later, the other two horses were all unloaded and both Hattie and Felix were on board. Leo had taken the more placid Galaxy and Simeon from Kylie, and tied them up to the lorry.

"Thanks Kylie," said Leo smiling at her, "good job you came along, we're really grateful."

"Definitely," grimaced Felix, who was desperately trying to stay on the skittering Woody and wondering if it had been such a great idea to bring him after all, "you've been a great help."

"Yes, thanks Kylie," called Hattie, although she didn't trust her or her motives one bit, but she had helped when they needed her, "see you at the meet."

"Okay if you're sure you don't want any more help?"

"No, no," said Leo, terrified that Roxy would arrive at any moment and be less forgiving than Hattie had been, "we're fine now thanks."

They watched Kylie get back in her old banger and chug off down the road, all heaving a sigh of relief that Roxy hadn't seen her, as moments later the black Range Rover swooped like an angry bird into the lay-by.

"Good they're all ready, I see," she said imperiously, looking every inch the part in her new hunting togs, "give me a leg up will you Leo?"

Max strutted out looking very handsome and suave, slapping his new hunt whip against his leg. "Right, let's get this show on the road and no hanging around."

Felix looked at him with loathing, he was the epitome of everything he hated and that was without the knowledge of what he had done to Alice. Today, Felix was going to give him the ride of his life and teach him a lesson or two - how the mighty are fallen, he thought grimly.

Hattie watched Felix and felt a cold chill of fear. She knew that today Felix was hunting Max and would not rest until he was brought to task for what he'd done.

Kylie drove off down the road. She was laughing out loud in her car like a demented witch, shoving a fag in her mouth and lighting it up. That had gone more perfectly than she could have possibly imagined. When she'd thought of the plan, she didn't really envisage how she could pull it off, and then suddenly it had all just fallen in her lap like a gift from God. Her hollow apology, helping when they badly needed her; slipping into the horsebox to pass down the nags to them. No-one saw her, or suspected her of slipping the gel under the horses' tongues - the beauty was they didn't even have to swallow it. She knew those damned drugs would come in useful and now she was going to enjoy watching the outcome. She checked her watch. *Dormosedan* Gel took about 40 minutes minimum to take effect and would last anything up to two hours or so. She'd given each horse the maximum dose, so by the time they got to the first line, they'd start to feel below par - try jumping a hedge when your horse is doped and you'll hit the deck and she was going to laugh like a drain when they did. She pulled into the farmyard, parking with all the other foot followers, and unobtrusively dropped the empty tubes of *Dormosedan* into a skip as she passed to join the throng of horses and people milling around the yard.

Instead of the leisurely walk to the meet, Felix and the others had to trot most of the way, which at least settled Woody, who would probably have been in orbit if he'd had to take it steady. At least it had taken a bit of the edge off him, although he was still dancing around when they joined the field, most of whom had arrived by now. People were still whisking around with the hot stirrup cup, steaming in plastic glasses and Felix knocked back a couple straight off, with Hattie giving him the evils. Roxy was enjoying a lot of attention, people were clamouring around her, asking for her autograph and asking about her horse, and how long she had been riding. Max, who sat glowering in the background, had several drinks too, determined to keep up with Felix. As they'd arrived late, most of the food had gone, but the drink was plentiful and it swiftly went to their heads. Hattie declined a second glass, and took a lemonade, but Felix had more and so did Max. Roxy was too busy with her adoring audience to be drinking anything other than the attention. The Master, Giles Pillsworthy, who had seen their arrival and immediately recognised Roxy, made his way over and was busy engaging her in conversation too, followed hastily by his wife Rachael, seated on a flashy, bay sports horse with a white blaze and four white socks.

"Great to have you out Ms L Feuvre," bellowed Giles, who was slightly deaf, "good looking horse you've got there."

"Yes, he's a beaut," smiled Roxy, sucking up madly, "please Master I insist you call me Roxy."

"Ah Roxy, charmed m'dear I'm sure," Giles beamed, his round face going even pinker, "Now let me introduce me wife - Rachael, she's a Master too - and will be taking care of the jumpers today. I take the non-jumpers, as my little cob," he patted his horse affectionately, "doesn't jump the big stuff. You stay with me, we can do the smaller fences and go round the ones with the bloody great drops and ditches."

"Good idea," said Roxy, relieved that she'd been personally invited by this charming man to stay with him. "Hattie is going to accompany me as it's my first time out too - don't want any accidents!" Her voice tinkled with silly laughter, and Giles lapped it up, whilst Rachael rolled her eyes upwards.

They were marginally delayed in moving off and it was about 30 minutes before Rachael called to the huntsman, "*Hounds please*."

Everyone trotted off down the road. Hattie and Roxy riding quietly side by side and Felix, on the excited Woody, cantering sideways with Max behind him. Felix called out to him

"Stay with Hattie and Roxy for the first line, until you get used to it, then try a few jumps."

As much as Max wanted to show off his new skills, he decided the first line would be best spent doing small jumps and getting the feel of things. From what Rachael had said when she made her opening speech, there would be four lines, so he had plenty of time to show his prowess later over the meatier stuff.

Kylie hugged herself with glee as she watched the riders move off, although none of the horses looked particularly dopey, she guessed it would be a while for the drug to take effect. Not wanting to cadge a lift with any of the other foot followers and have to make small talk, she jumped in her car and followed the long procession of four wheel drives making their way to the beginning of the first line. Following the other drivers, she pulled up on the side of the verge alongside a patchwork of fields separated with thick hedges.

The *pah pah pa* of the hunting horn could be heard way across the fields and suddenly streaming out of a small copse, came a wonderful sight. A torrent of hounds, hard on a scent, their noses to the turf, covering the ground with massive speed and behind them the huntsman blowing his horn and the whip, both dressed in hunting pink. The hounds were in full cry not deviating from the trail laid and tore over and through the first hedge. The huntsman followed, his legs shooting forward as he leant back with his arm raised and hunting whip aloft. The drop on the other side of the hedge was about three feet and the horse landed and carried on following the hounds at a gallop. The whip followed suit and then came the field, one by one they took the hedge with grim looks on their faces. A few fallers scrabbled out of the way for the oncomers who weren't able to stop, and the foot followers raced out to catch the loose horses. Felix appeared on the amazing Woody, his chestnut coat in a lather and took the hedge with all the grace and beauty of a professional and galloped onwards to the next. Charles Parker Smyth was next; he was nearly unseated on the landing side as his horse pecked but he managed to rebalance and looked behind him to make sure Jennifer was over safely. The solid little Polly, taking care of her mistress at all times, made an economic jump and she caught Charles up, and they were off across the field. Grace, who'd borrowed an experienced hunter from Chloe, as her mare was now heavy with foal, and Colin, both seasoned pros that they were, made effortless jumps, as did Sandy and Katherine. Nancy, riding Charles' other horse, made a fantastic effort and whooped as she went over and the crowd cheered like mad. From the back of the copse came the non-jumpers, amongst them Hattie, Roxy, Max and Dulcie, they were cantering at a fair lick around the headland with Giles in the lead. There were some optional jumps which his little cob loved, and he led some of the braver ones over them. Max was in his stride now, the delightful Simeon taking over and doing his own thing, Galaxy jumping despite what Roxy did to him, and Hattie bringing up the rear with Dulcie who was enjoying the smaller fences.

All too soon the first line was over. They'd checked in another farmyard on the far side of Brigstock where the horses were recovering their wind. The gleaming mounts that had started out were now sweaty and muddy, as were their riders. Fallers were being reunited with their horses and hip flasks were being handed round and great gulps of Whisky Macs and Sours were fortifying and energy stoking. Hattie pulled out a bar of Kit Kat and offered a finger to Roxy, who snootily declined, but Dulcie gratefully took a piece. Felix was standing apart from them and was stroking Woody's neck thoughtfully. He'd been bit lack lustre at the end there, although possibly the brave horse had just tired himself out with all the nervous energy beforehand. He looked at his flanks, he was breathing quite heavily, he'd keep an eye on him and not over push him. Max had sidled up to Felix declaring that he would be joining him and the jumpers this time. Felix didn't deter him, he was looking forward to this moment.

In the end they had to check for about ten minutes whilst a couple of stray hounds were rounded up, before they began the hack to the next line. Max went ahead side by side with Felix. Hattie hanging at the back with Roxy to let the jumpers go first. Hattie was beginning to feel a bit concerned about Rambler, he was really dead to her leg and seemed to be stumbling, she gave him a sharp crack with her whip and he lashed out and rocked on his feet. Screwing up her face in concern, this was not like him at all, he was a really game horse, and if she didn't know better she'd think he was ill. Roxy who was trying to trot beside her was complaining about Galaxy.

"He's so fucking lazy," she moaned, taking out her whip and lashing him to urge him forward, "he wasn't like this to start with."

"No, he wasn't," said Hattie, as Rambler stumbled again. It was like riding something that'd had too much to drink.

Roxy raised her whip again and Galaxy wobbled and went down on one knee, almost collapsing. Hattie shrieked at her to stop and leapt off Rambler, pulling Roxy off before the horse came over. Leo, who'd been following on foot realised there was a problem and fought his way over through the crowd.

"What's up Hats?"

"I dunno?" she exclaimed, "they've just lost all their energy, wobbling and stumbling all over the place. Galaxy nearly came over then with Roxy. I don't know what's the matter with them."

"This horse is a fucking dud," shouted Roxy, "it nearly had me off. I could sue you for this!"

"Just shut the fuck up," snarled Leo, "the horses are sick, something's happened to them you stupid tart."

Roxy, who looked as though she'd been slapped, stepped back in surprise. "Whatdya mean sick?"

Leo looked inside Galaxy's mouth, the horse's head was now visibly drooping, and a small trickle of mucus from his nose, his penis was drooping out. "Hattie, I think he's been doped. Let me take a look at Rambler."

"Doped! How?" said Hattie incredulously, as she watched Leo examining Rambler, who was exhibiting similar symptoms.

Leo wrenched his mobile out of his pocket and rang Andrew's direct line. Speaking urgently into the phone he told him what he'd suspected, and Andrew said one or other the vets would get there as soon as they could, but not to get on the horses again, untack them and keep them quiet.

Roxy was livid. "You've totally spoiled my day out," she grumbled, "why on earth have you doped the horses?"

"Don't be fucking stupid - we didn't dope them - someone else did, and I've got a pretty good idea who that someone is," snapped Leo, "but what I'm worried about is, did she dope Woody and Simeon too?"

Hattie looked worried. "Christ they've gone to jump that huge line. Supposing the horses come down with them? I'll try and ring Felix." She speed dialled his number. It rang and rang and then finally went to voice mail. "Oh God Leo, I think we're too late, they must have already started."

Actually Felix had seen Hattie's call but decided to ignore it. He was looking forward to this, he was going to give that fucking Max a run for his money he'd never forget. Woody was still breathing heavily but appeared to have plenty of running. He ran on adrenalin that horse, he thought fondly, and today, more than ever, he was supremely grateful.

Max was excited, he was longing to do this. He was the ultimate thrill seeker and he'd make that smug Felix look like a pussy cat. He set his jaw into a hard determined line when he watched him, he knew that Felix wanted him to fail and he wasn't going to give him the satisfaction.

Felix sidled up to him on the dancing Woody, "Nervous?" he asked Max, "some hefty old hedges out there."

"Nope," said Max coldly, "I can do it - can you?"

"You make me laugh. You think you're invincible don't you, untouchable? That you can do what you like, hurt who you please and get away with it. Well dream on - you've just met your nemesis."

"I don't know what you're talking about boy," said Max dismissively, although a cold chill feeling was running through his body. "Grow up."

"Oh I've grown up, and I've woken up and smelt the roses and I've got your number. I know about Alice."

The *pah pah pa* of the horn interrupted them as the hounds gave cry and sped off with the red coats flying after them. Rachael gave the signal and the rest of the field followed at a respectable distance.

Woody got a second wind and shot off, with Simeon racing after him. Felix held Woody back until they were cantering side by side. "Did you hear what I said? I know about Alice," he shouted above the wind in their ears, "I know about you."

Max, who was doing all he could to concentrate on staying on board the thundering horse, didn't have the breath to reply. He hung on board as they galloped towards the first line of hedges. Felix edged Woody ahead kicked on and sat back for the landing, executing a perfect jump. He turned around and saw Simeon lumbering over with Max clinging on for grim death. The next jump was a field away, the horses blundered on and Felix began to feel Woody once again losing power, in fact he'd go so far as to say he was running on fumes. He'd have to pull him up if he didn't buck up. Simeon struggled to gain ascendency, the brave horse being egged on by a maniacal Max determined to outdo Felix. The next hedge was approaching - a big bugger, wide with a heavy rail through its centre and a colossal drop and ditch on the landing side. Woody was now flagging badly, his breath coming in great rasps and gulps, they were less than 50 metres from the jump and Felix knew he couldn't ask any more of the horse and he started to pull up. Max was selfishly and wickedly whipping Simeon on, but the brave giant horse was fading too, gasping to get his breath, his limbs failing to co-ordinate. With Max beating him mercilessly, Simeon launched himself at the hedge, plunging with the last of his strength to take the mammoth hedge but his feet just didn't take off. He hit the middle rail so hard it splintered and broke. The impact somersaulted horse and rider high into the air, rotating round and coming down on the landing side with an enormous thud and crack. Felix had, by this time, pulled up the panting Woody, and gasped with horror as he witnessed the awful spectre of Simeon cart-wheeling out of sight. Leaping off Woody and casting his reins aside, he tore across to look over the hedge, but the carnage that lay on the far side made him want to weep. The brave Simeon was lying flat out and dead still on the grass, and of Max there was no sight at all.

CHAPTER 89

Desperately, Felix flew back to his horse, which was now standing in a weird, seemingly confused state; he tossed the reins to Libby Newsome, who'd sensibly pulled up alongside, screaming at her to divert any following horses around the headland with Giles. Forcing himself to be calm, he ran back to see if he could move the great hulk of Simeon, and prayed that Max, by some miracle might have survived the fall.

His breath coming in great gasps and his legs like lead, he scrambled through the hedge fighting with the briars and thorns and took a gigantic leapt over the ditch, squidging into the holding mud on the other side. In front of him, the huge prone mass of horse was twitching slightly, its legs stuck out rigidly, its head flung back in the mire, the eyes rolling in pain. It was as much as he could do to look at the mangled mess. In the rotational fall, Simeon's huge bulk had totally crushed Max, and all that was evident of him was a leg stuck out at a strange angle from underneath the body of the horse. In fact, Simeon wasn't dead as Felix had first thought, but dreadfully winded, and something else was wrong too it seemed, as despite his best efforts, Felix couldn't get him up. Simeon's limbs were flailing about uselessly, and he didn't seem to have the strength or energy to get on his feet. The brave horse thrashed uselessly, pummelling Max's mangled body like some bizarre marionette, as he jerked from side to side, repeatedly pounded underneath the massive bulk of the horse. Felix, no matter how he hard he thumped and cajoled at Simeon's flanks, he was powerless to induce the gigantic horse to stand.

Bewildered, frustrated and helpless, Felix sank to his knees weeping in frustration, struggling to keep his wits about him until he realised his phone was ringing. Looking down he saw, with absolute relief, that it was Hattie. He answered in incoherent wailing sobs and tried to tell her what had happened.

"Felix, Felix pull yourself together," Hattie snapped crossly, taking immediate control. "Our horses have all been doped, luckily Roxy and I managed to get off before any damage was done. Andrew is on his way to us, but I'm gonna divert him over to you. Have you called an ambulance for

Max?"

"No, he's dead Hattie, he must be. He's trapped right under the horse, totally squashed," wept Felix, "and Simeon's in a terrible state. I managed to pull up Woody - he's okay, I knew there was something wrong. Oh God, oh God, I can't get him up. Max is dead - what am I gonna do?"

"Felix, for fuck's sake calm down. Now you listen to me. I need to know exactly where you are, so I can get the ambulance and Andrew to you."

"Christ," wailed Felix stupidly, "I don't fucking know, I'm in the middle of a fucking field. It's the second jump of the second line. We went out through Willow Bank and hung right for the first fence, so in that direction."

"Right, just try and hold yourself together. I'll get one of the foot followers to bring me over in a 4x4. Just keep yourself in one piece until I get there. I'll bring help, try and keep calm. I'll get there as soon as I can. Leo can cope with these horses. Roxy can stay with him."

"For fuck's sake - don't tell her yet, until we know for sure about Max, but I'm sure he's dead. He couldn't have survived - he totally mangled. Oh Hats, you should see it."

"Keep calm Felix. I'll be there as soon as, try and get Simeon up if you can. Sounds as though there's nothing you can do for Max, but now get off the phone and let me get that ambulance and Andrew to you asap."

By the time Andrew arrived, a number of foot followers had struggled over the fields and Giles had summoned help from the hunt Kennels, fully armed and prepared to shoot the horse and drag him off with a winch.

"No need for that I think," said Andrew pragmatically, as he examined Simeon, "we'll get this chap up no problem. He's been doped, my best guess is *Dormosedan*, so it's not long lasting. Right now everyone, I'm gonna need you mob-handed here." Andrew slapped Simeon hard again and again on the back, like he was herding dumb cattle. The shock of the slap and the noise worse than the actual pain, as the horse responded sharply to Andrew shouting, "Come on, up you get now, Come on!" The rest of the helpers shouted too. Suddenly with a supreme effort the horse levered itself up and wobbled unsteadily to one side.

Andrew immediately made way for the waiting ambulance crew who pounced on their patient, but in truth there was no need for haste. You could see straight away that Max was dead. His handsome head twisted in an ugly unnatural wrench to one side, his once beautiful face contorted in an ugly death smirk with a trickle of blood coming from his nostril; his neck broken on impact. His legs and arms too, lay buckled at bizarre and obscure angles underneath him and he looked like a grotesque, broken puppet discarded on the floor. The crew went through all the necessary checks but announced that there was no more they could do for him, and asked everyone to step back and leave them to do their job.

Felix watched as they put the, hitherto handsome, body of Max into a black, body bag and struggled with it in the quagmire of mud into the back of the ambulance, which they had ridiculously argued about driving over the field, claiming they might get stuck, and he wondered about the stupid trivialities of life. Hours before he had been so angry, so sure that he'd wanted revenge and now, watching that lifeless crooked body zipped into the bag with no more reverence than a boil in the bag fish dinner, he felt how transitory life truly was and could have wept. For Max, however callous and cruel he'd been and for Alice, and for himself. Did Max really deserve that terrible end or was it kismet, his fate for all the awful things he'd done in the past. Felix couldn't even begin to deal or compute the situation. Hattie came over and slipped her hand in his, stroking his face, and brought him back to the here and now and, right now, they had to break the news to Roxy, and sort out their horses and be strong over the nightmare that was to follow in the days to come.

Roxy had been so distraught when she was told about Max that she'd had to be sedated and Aiden was called to take her home. It was probably the first real and genuine emotion she'd had in years. Her distress brought out the cavalry in her husband, who treated her like a virgin queen, much to the mortification of Chrissie, who'd personally thought Roxy was milking the situation. But Roxy was genuinely bereft; Max had meant a great deal to her, they had been close friends and occasional lovers and he would leave a gaping void in her life. He'd rescued her at her lowest ebb and dragged her up from the gutter - yes she would miss Max. Aiden was only too pleased to be able to offer succour and loved the new needy Roxy who clung to him weeping, like a lost soul in the night.

Of course, as with any sudden death the police had been involved, and blood samples from the horses had been taken by Andrew to discover that all four had been doped with Detomidine Hydrochloride otherwise know as

Dormosedan. Leo, Hattie and Felix had all been interviewed individually, as had Frankie and Seb. None of them could shed any light as to how the horses could have had access to the drugs and invited the police to search for any evidence of discarded plastic syringes in the truck or at the yard. Hattie though, expounded that she was completely convinced that Kylie was at the bottom of the mystery. Her previous vicious behaviour when she had been so irrational and venomous towards them all, and then on the day of the meet how, totally out of character, she had assisted them in unloading the horses with her hollow and spurious apology. Andrew confirmed that it would have only taken a second to put the gel under the horses' tongues and it was feasible for it to have been done then and would have fitted the time frame for the drug to have taken effect. The police officers listened with interest but, however easily this theory fitted, they could do nothing. Hattie's dramatic hypothesis was, after all, merely speculation and there was actually no proof that Kylie had doped the horses. To all intents and purposes she had merely randomly stopped to help them out. Out of a sense of obligation to follow all leads, they did however follow up the idea and interview Kylie, who testily denied any involvement, becoming insolent and angry, shouting that they were trying to frame her. With her vehement denial, and their lack of evidence, there was little that the officers could do but leave her be.

At the inquest Leo, Hattie and Felix were called to give evidence, as was Roxy amidst a massive press presence. She arrived with Aiden, and he tucked her arm protectively in his as they made their way up the steps; her face pale and wan as she brushed away the microphones stuffed in her face and the eager, persistently clamouring and sweaty faces of the reporters. In court, the medical evidence given was clear and concise. Max had died initially as a result of a broken neck, coupled with multiple injuries as a result of his horse falling at the fence. Andrew gave evidence that all four horses were confirmed to have been doped with a fast acting drug which would have been easy to administer under their tongues. Hattie, Leo and Felix's evidence was short and to the point, as was Roxy's. Hattie and Roxy confirmed that Max and Felix had gone on without them, and it was only after they had left that they had pulled up, realising something was amiss with their horses. The coroner listened carefully to all of the evidence, asking Andrew to return to the stand for more information as to how the drug could affect horses of different temperaments. Andrew confirmed that quieter horses would react to the drug more quickly, and the more highly strung horses, such as Felix's and Max's, would take longer to react and succumb to the sedation, which could explain why they had gone on ahead. On due balance the Coroner ruled that, as the horse was known to have been doped by person or persons unknown, and that this doping would have directly caused the horse to fail to jump the hedge, hence causing risk of death, a verdict of death of unlawful killing must be ruled.

The verdict held a huge black cloud the size of Wales over the yard. They were all so certain it was that bitch Kylie, but they couldn't prove any of it, and until they could, they were all under a cloak of suspicion. Everyone sat gloomily in Felix and Hattie's cottage drinking whisky in maudlin mood. The death of Max had been a huge shock to them all. None of them had liked him, he was a sinister figure, and there was something about him that was threatening and ominous. Before the inquest, Felix had come clean and told them all what he'd heard at the New Year's Eve party and, ironically, they'd been startlingly unsurprised, declaring that they'd put nothing past him, but agreed once again there was no proof. The law seemed an ass. Felix couldn't pretend that he was sorry he was dead, but despite his own bravado that doomed day, he'd just wanted to give him a fright, killing him wasn't on the agenda, even though he'd felt like it. Max was a bastard, but he didn't want to feel responsible for his death, because he simply wasn't. None of them had seen Roxy since the dreadful day of the inquest and would be surprised if they did again, and the knock-on effect, if they didn't discover who'd done the drugging would be awful. Who would want to be a livery or an owner with them again? Sheena had been fine, realising it wasn't their fault, but she was a client in a million - Abbey and Peter Marchant, who owned Rambler were a little more diffident, but luckily Charles, with his arm twisted by Jennifer, had smoothed the waters and they had settled down and they had left Rambler with them.

"There must be a way we can nail fucking Kylie, if we don't, our reputation's in shreds." said Seb, knocking back his fourth Whisky Sour. "Where did she get the stuff from in the first place?"

"No idea," said Hattie, who was feeling sick, "it's only available from vets, so she must have either nicked it or had a contact."

"She's got such a shocking reputation no-one would have given it to her," said Leo logically, "so she's nicked it from somewhere."

"Who keeps that stuff? First of all it's so bloody expensive to have lying around and you'd only have it if you really needed it in the first aid cupboard. After all we don't keep it - do we?"

"No, we don't, if we did use it for clipping and stuff, I usually asked Alice for some," said Felix, and then suddenly jumped up. "You don't suppose that it was part of the stash that Alice was supposed to have hidden away do you?"

"No - that was never found or substantiated was it? Why would Kylie have it anyway?" asked Seb reasonably, "She hardly knew Alice. I think we're grasping at straws here."

"What did Andrew say had gone missing from the surgery?"

"Oh I can't remember, all sorts - Ketamine mainly I think."

"Don't you see it all fits!" exclaimed Felix excitedly, putting down his drink and slopping it on the carpet, "if Kylie found Alice's stash even by chance, she'd have access to the drugs wouldn't she and I bet she's got the rest too!"

"You'd have to have a reason to search her gaff," said Leo doubtfully, "and I'm pretty certain that a hunch isn't good enough for a search warrant."

Felix felt as deflated as a sunken soufflé, he'd been certain he was onto something. "Right, yeah, okay."

Leo thought for a moment, scratching his eyebrow. "When she left the horsebox, she beat a hasty retreat didn't she? Left in her car and went straight to the meet. I just wonder if she ditched the syringes at Brigstock Farm?"

"Possible, possible," muttered Seb, in his best Dr Watson voice, "we could go tomorrow and look."

"No you silly arse, we have to take the law with us," said Leo, laughing at him, leaning over and ruffling his hair, "otherwise we could be accused of planting the stuff. I'll ring that DC in the morning and see what he thinks."

"Good idea, now can we change the bloody record, I'm sick of it all. When are you two getting married?" asked Hattie, "I fancy buying an outrageous hat!"

The following day, a determined Leo and a reluctant DC traipsed up to Brigstock Farm, pulling into the yard and looking about them.

"It's like looking for a needle in a haystack," grumbled the policeman, looking irritably at his smart shoes and the muddy yard, "I don't think there's a case."

"Gotta be worth a try surely," said Leo keenly. "Right we parked here, and the horses were over there. So we walked this way." They strode past a couple of skips vomiting out rubbish. "This looks possible," said Leo enthusiastically, jumping into the skip, "come on, don your Marigolds."

Grumbling and fed up, the DC pulled on his gloves, but within fifteen minutes he was smiling and four white syringes were tucked neatly into an evidence bag and he was pretty sure he would have an arrest within the day. "We'll process these for finger prints straight away," he grinned at Leo, "you're not just a pretty face are you?"

"Steady on," grinned Leo, "I'm getting married in the spring!"

Kylie was arrested when her fingerprints were found on the syringes and had come up as a match on the national data base. A search of her home discovered the rest of the drugs, all of which were traced as ones which had originally come from Napier and Travers where Alice had worked. Copious amounts of Ketamine, Dormosedan, Diazepam, Acepromazine and others were found hidden under her bed.

After interview, Kylie was charged with involuntary manslaughter. She swore, fought and kicked her way into the courtroom, declaring that they had it in for her and she was only having a bit of a laugh to teach everyone a lesson. The magistrate looked at her severely as he routinely ordered her case to be tried at the Crown Court. Bail was refused, owing to her irrational and dangerous behaviour, but Legal Aid was granted and her brief declared a defence that she had acted whilst temporarily insane. Hattie and Felix sat in the court whilst she hurled abuse at them and they wondered if she had ever really been sane.

On the way home in the car, Felix confessed to Hattie that he had wanted to confront Max, and more that day. He'd even told him he knew about Alice and what had happened to her. Hattie said she'd suspected as much, but that he wasn't to blame for Max's death, it was a miracle he hadn't met his maker earlier, given the life he'd led. The ultimate irony was that he'd lived as he died, taking ridiculous risks with a stupid bravado that he couldn't possibly justify. But Felix realised that, in reality none of them knew Max, or his business, or anything about the man he was, and perhaps that was just as well. Let the man die in peace as some kind of super hero on the hunting field as opposed to a gang land villain, who was in reality, a ruthless killer. Roxy knew more about him than anyone else and she was keeping that sacred information to herself, like she was locked in some divine confessional. What would happen to his horse, his house, his car remained yet to be seen. Perhaps Anna would know, but none of them had seen her either since the New Year's Eve bash and, no doubt, the executors of his estate would be in touch with them to sort out paying for the livery.

CHAPTER 90

The spring rolled into Fittlebury with all the freshness of Febreze eliminating odours from every crevice. The cataclysmic catastrophes of the previous six months had been laid to rest, even if some of the questions may never be truly answered. Felix felt as though Alice's death, although never truly punished, was at least avenged in Max's spectacular and awful demise. Kylie was still waiting to go to trial - these things took time, but it was likely that she would plead *guilty*, so that at least the matter would be put to bed.

Roxy and Aiden were enjoying the triumphant success of the mill. It was a huge hit, with the spa packed to the gunnels on a daily basis, with leotard clad beauties, sweating in their headbands in the trendy atmosphere. Dance classes gave way to massage parlours, facials and the like, with the decorous ladies trooping off to have their Caesar salads, coupled with goat's cheese and olives in the mill restaurant. *Rox-Aid* revelled in the solid bookings. To get a reservation now you'd have to book weeks in advance. Their new house suited them well, although Roxy was complaining that it was too small and wanted something bigger and more ostentatious, wondering to herself what had happened to Max's house, as it would suit them perfectly. They were still commuting backwards and forwards to London and now, she'd decided, she wanted the children to come down to the country, as the "*vibes*" were so much more positive. A new dimension to *Rox-Aid* had been born and Farouk and the cameras were devouring it. They lapped up every frame as they filmed Chrissie, as mad as a wet hen, packing up her clip board and leaving in total fury, hurling a few choice words to Aiden as she went. Roxy delighted in ignoring her with a superior Siberian blast, but Aiden looked hotly embarrassed as she stormed out of the door. It was always the same, Roxy thought delightedly, as she watched her go from the window, these little tarts came and went, some with dignity and some without. She was busy interviewing for a new PA - the only criteria being they had to be ugly, gay or male - whatever - Roxy had her finger on pulse this time round. Personally, she'd barely recovered about Max. It had been a colossal shock; he'd been in her life for aeons, but theirs had always been a rather strange relationship and perhaps a dangerous one, and she'd never really known what happened to Pete, her first husband.

Max had always been so cagey about it, brushing away his overdose, repeating that the man was a loser, but Roxy had never really believed that he'd had nothing to do with it. It seemed odd too, that Anna had disappeared so suddenly. She'd not seen her after New Year's eve and, when she'd enquired at the club, was told she'd tragically committed suicide. Now Roxy wasn't daft, and she knew Max and how he operated, and suspected that Anna had definitely stepped over Max's line. What a silly cow, thought Roxy, although there was no love lost between them and certainly it was not her business. Anna should have hung on tight and, kept her trap shut and now, she was dead. Anyway, Roxy must concentrate on her own affairs, whatever form they took, from promoting her wares and changing her image again, to indulging in the fantasy of her riding. Lisa was planning to bring her horses down to livery with Felix and Seb, so she had company again and that would be more fun. Roxy was sure she would outshine her, and perhaps they could persuade a few more of their WAG friends -who knew what the future would bring? She would love to get Hattie to do a bit more modelling for her, the girl was a siren, wasted as a rider. Felix was besotted with her, and actually Roxy would quite like a shot at Felix, so perhaps she could muscle in there - food for thought perhaps?

Aiden watched Roxy as she sat in her study characteristically chewing her pencil, ostensibly working, but knew, in reality, she was scheming - they were a good team on the whole. He'd been sorry to see Chrissie go, but luckily Roxy didn't know he was now picking up the tab for her flat in Chelsea. She was too good a fuck and too good a soul mate for the time being, and he knew Roxy of old. She would wander soon enough, and good luck to her; a man needed a bit of distraction after all. Manuel the waiter didn't quite cut it as nicely as a tasty bit of fanny. He was pleased with the restaurant and was already looking at another country site - no sitting on his laurels or greens for him.

The huge news of the spring was the double wedding celebration of Seb and Leo and Felix and Hattie. Deciding upon two quiet simultaneous Registry Office ceremonies where they would each stand witness for the other, their actual nuptials would be celebrated a few days later with a joint blessing at Laundry Cottage. They poured over the burgeoning invitation list, adding up the cost of it all. In truth, there was as much hope as a fart in a thunderstorm, that it was likely to be a small bash; the friends, families, and sponsors of the two couples ran into sizeable numbers. Hattie just wanted a simple affair, very casual and low key, but Seb, who was like an over-enthusiastic Labrador puppy with a new roll of Andrex, had wheedled and cajoled until, finally, she'd had caved in and agreed to a posh do, not quite top hat and tails, but certainly not jeans and tee shirts either.

For the lads, their attire was easy-peasy, but for Hattie, with everyone else dressed to kill and trying to outdo each other, she secretly dreaded the notion of being the centre of attention and making a Horlicks of her own outfit. She, Frankie, Dulcie and Nancy made a sortie into town to buy a dress. Initially she was gawkily embarrassed and hesitant fingering the beautiful materials and outrageous dresses, gingerly saying it was all a bit over the top for her; but once she'd accepted that this was *it*, and to stop being the reluctant bride, she'd thrown herself into the event with whole-hearted gusto. The girls had spent a wonderful day enthralling themselves with lace and frills, coupled with champagne and delights pressed on them by over-enthusiastic shop assistants. As it transpired, just when Hattie thought she was all *dressed* out she knew directly she spotted *the one*. Far removed from a meringue, it was sleek, simple and close fitting to her lithe body, embracing every lovely curve. The enticing silky, pearlescent fabric slithering around her body like a gossamer sheath, slashed at the back to the deepest sexy swirl across her buttocks, whilst the front was demure with a cowl neckline draped softly and studded with thousands of seed pearls into a sweep of shimmering fabric across her pert breasts. Nancy insisted that she have a simple pearl and flower circlet woven into her hair which gave her an elfin, almost gamine, look. Hattie considered herself in the flattering mirror and was impressed, the look was sensational, she felt so sexy, yet feminine, even she was impressed. Baulking at the price tag, but egged on by the girls, the dress and accessories were packed into smart, glossy bags and Hattie walked out of the shop feeling giddy with excitement.

As there was no hope of being able to fit the number of invited guests into the cottage, they'd borrowed an outsize marquee used by the local village scouts for their jamborees, which was like stepping back in time to the 1940s with its old creamy, canvas sides and huge, heavy, wooden centre poles. Grace and Jennifer had bravely offered to take charge of decorating the inside, and Freda Fuller, who'd always had a soft spot for Felix, had borrowed trestle tables and table cloths from the WI, complete with delightful matching vintage chairs. Fred Windrush, Doris' husband, agreed to erect a make-shift dais at the far end of the tent as a stage, firstly for the formal blessing and then later for the band. The vicar, apologising that he was unable to marry Seb and Leo in church, had agreed to do a simple blessing ceremony. As an extravagant wedding gift, Roxy had coerced Aiden into doing the catering, saying there'd be a lot of influential people there and it would be great publicity. Naturally, Suzanne had been instructed to tip off the press and *Hello* magazine said they'd make an appearance, as well as Farouk and his team. Thus, steam-rollered into putting on a good show since the press were going to be present, Aiden had pushed out the proverbial boat and would make sure the food would be sensational.

On the morning of their official mutual Registry Office weddings, Seb was as nervous and agitated as a dog with a plague of fleas. Running around in circles, dashing to the bog every five minutes, he kept changing his trousers and gelling his hair. Leo, much calmer, sighed to Dougie in resigned exasperation, rolling his eyes and shaking his head. Dougie, who'd offered to drive them into Horsham and play official photographer, was now beginning to regret he'd offered, he'd never seen Seb in such a state. Finally bundling a babbling Seb into the car, they trundled down the concrete road to pick up Hattie and Felix. They were already waiting outside their cottage, Felix holding her hand protectively whilst Hattie jumped anxiously from foot to foot. They had both dressed simply, Felix in chinos and a striped shirt and jacket, and Hattie in a cream linen shift with matching bolero piped in navy, tiny cream flowers in her shining hair, but not a button hole or bouquet in sight. Squashing into the car, Hattie grasped Felix's hand even tighter, her grey eyes anxious and worried. Felix turned and kissed her firmly, slipping his arm around her shoulders until she felt herself relax. Within the hour she would be his wife, how brilliant would that be? Leo looked radiant, smiling and happy, but Seb was white; ever the joker, he clutched onto Leo's hand for support, desperate for reassurance, he couldn't believe that, at last, the day had arrived.

Dougie pulled into the Registry Office and parked in the designated spot for their bridal car. Park House, a grand old Grade II listed building right in the heart of Horsham, was magnificent, with impressive entrance steps and huge sash windows. As theirs was such a small wedding party they'd opted to have their ceremonies in the smaller marriage room rather than the larger imposing Drawing Room, and it was much cosier, with squashy pink sofas and seemed much less formal. Dougie opened the door reverently for Hattie, helping her out and, to the astonishment of them all, produced from the boot, carnations for the men and a posy of freesias and roses for Hattie.

"If you think you're getting married without bloody flowers, you've got another think coming," he grumbled to cover his embarrassment, "come on, let's do it."

Hattie threw her arms around him, "You are a love Dougie, thanks, they are just gorgeous."

"Thanks mate," agreed Felix, pinning his carnation onto his lapel, "great idea."

To everyone's astonishment Seb started to cry. "I just don't know what to say," he blubbed pathetically, pulling out a hanky and blowing his nose loudly, "it's all too much."

"Give it a rest Seb," laughed Leo, reaching over and attaching his carnation, "otherwise I'll stick this blood pin in you, then you'll have something to cry about."

The Registrar, a smiley, older, grey-haired lady, whose dress reminded Felix of a contemporary Virginia Woolf, performed the simple, legally-binding ceremony. Each couple witnessed the other's wedding, whilst Dougie recorded it all for posterity on video and camera. But it was all over in the flash of a lecher's wink. Some vows, and declarations, a signature or two, and it was done, they stood smiling and marginally bewildered. But all too soon the next wedding party clamoured outside and they were ushered out to the back of Park House where the stunning garden was teeming with spring flowers which made a great backdrop for Dougie's artistic camera skills. The photographs were taken with much hilarity - from artificially rigid Victorian poses with poker straight faces, to them fooling around like clowns, whooping and laughing hysterically. Falling back to the car, out of breath with giggling, they tumbled into their seats, and the dutiful Dougie chauffeured them home whilst they guzzled fizz and ate Pringles, hardly able to believe that their whole lives had changed within the last hour.

A true spring day welcomed them for the occasion of the wedding blessings when all their friends would congregate to celebrate. The sweet breath of warm air was like a delicate kiss. The leaves were bursting with a tangy, nubile freshness as they sprang into life, and the spring flowers and early blossom etched like a Japanese painting against the pale blue sky.

Mr and Mrs Stephenson, aka Hattie and Felix, were already basking in the delightful bliss of being married. Somehow it had subtly changed things between them. Adding a delightful seal of purity to their relationship which had deepened like a massive embalming flush. Seb too, had discovered a new found calm - no more jealousy, and a security which shrouded him in a fabulous ethereal glow. Only Leo seemed immune to the civil ceremony and was as sensible as he was before, maintaining that he didn't need a certificate to be faithful to Seb.

The celebrations were due to start at two in the afternoon, and from early that morning, Jennifer and Grace, along with Sandy and Katherine, and the faithful Mrs Fuller and Doris had been ferreting about in the garden. An army of WI ladies had also arrived and none of the wedding party were allowed inside the marquee - the interior was to be a surprise. Aiden and his team were superlatively well organised, and extra staff had been hired for the day. Catering wagons came and went, setting up the temporary kitchen in an adjacent catering tent. Hattie and Felix planned to get ready at Laundry Cottage along with Seb and Leo and were forbidden by Dougie and Roberto, who by now seemed to have moved in, to look out of the window at the preparations. Frankie was holding the fort at the yard, and Nancy and Dulcie were giving her hand - the horses were having double rations of hay and could wait until the evening before they checked them again.

The wedding four were in fine fettle. This time Seb had no nuptial nerves, he was a married man now after all, and this was just a party at which he could *shine, shine, shine*. Relaxed and happy, they'd opened a bottle of pop, although Dougie would only permit them to have one glass each. Like a latter day Napoleon, he was orchestrating the proceedings with military precision, despatching Roberto out to give Jennifer the seating plan and place cards which he'd painstakingly written by hand. Putting on the immersion to boost the hot water he sent them at allotted times for their baths and gave them a meticulous timetable to follow. Giggling like kids at boarding school, they'd obeyed him dutifully, rolling their eyes behind his back and sneaking another drink when he wasn't looking.

At one o'clock the vicar appeared and set himself up on the little stage, and by half past one, the guests began to arrive. Cars swept up the drive, parking in the adjacent field which fortunately, for this time of year, was dry enough not to need tractors to tow them out. The ladies in an array of stunning, multi-hued outfits were hanging onto their partners' arms, their hats and fascinators marginally in danger, as their stiletto heels sunk into the grass unbalancing them, as they struggled like bizarre moon walkers to remain upright. Inside the marquee, Dougie and Roberto, resplendent in matching grey, pinstriped tailcoats greeted the guests, handing them to Frankie, Dulcie or Nancy, who ushered them to their tables. Jennifer and Grace had done a brilliant job. Inside, the old tent looked spectacular, the hefty wooden posts entwined with ivy and delicate spring flowers - freesias, daffodils and early roses from the local florist, their elusive sweet scent seeping out and filling the air. The creaky old trestle tables were now covered in bleached and snowy linen and laid with sparkling cutlery, crockery and glasses, all compliments of Aiden. Each table had a simple centre piece of spring flowers, daffodils, tulips and freesias in a cream enamel jug, with scatterings of rose petals on the cloth, complete with a shabby chic lantern ready to be lit for later on. It was very French boudoir and vintage. At the side, on a small table of its own, was the wedding cake - quite the most inspirational piece of confectionary to behold. A large based two-tiered cake, unusually of black and white. The bottom tier was simple with flat, matt black icing, upon which had been elaborately etched in white, a mural of horses in various poses, dressage and jumping, so real it was like looking at a painting. Supporting the smaller identical upper tier, a stunning pillar in silver, interlaced with white icing roses. The crowning glory was the intricately moulded chocolate horses heads entwined on the top - so lifelike in detail, their flowing fairy-tale manes entwined with icing roses. It was quite breathtaking.

The oohs and aahs chorused around the marquee as the guests took in the ambience of the setting, each chatting excitedly to their neighbour. The vicar began to look at his watch and fiddle suspiciously with his vestments. Waiters were whizzing around the tables with bottles of champagne filling up glasses and in the back ground soft light classical music played.

At two o'clock, the last stragglers had taken their seats, and Dulcie and Nancy had been dispensed to fetch the wedding party, whilst Frankie stood by to change the music. Dougie strode to the front of the stage.

"Welcome everyone on this fine spring day to this beautiful marquee," he began in his best *Mr Kipling cakes* voice, "we are here to celebrate and bless the weddings of two of my most favourite couples - Hattie and Felix Stephenson, and Seb Locke and Leo Cooper, although we're not sure if Seb will become Mrs Cooper yet."

A mild swell of laughter rippled through the gathering. "Before we begin I would just like to thank everyone for coming and to say we are going to change the music and it'll make you all laugh as the words are just so appropriate - a good old golden oldie from the 1960s - *"I got you babe"*!"

On queue Frankie switched on the music and the crackly recording of Sony and Cher echoed around the tent.

"They say we're young and we don't know, We won't find out until we're grown, Well I don't know if that's true, ' Cause you got me and baby I got you, Babe," crooned the duo, *"I got you babe, I got you babe."*

Felix and Hattie stepped into the marquee, hands clasped tightly together, smiling at each other, all the sea of faces turned towards them. Hattie waved and blew kisses as she spotted her mum and dad. Felix returning the laughs as people mini-cheered as they walked past, blowing

Mrs Fuller a kiss when he saw her, and grinned as he watched her go pink with pleasure.

"They say our love won't pay the rent, Before it's earned, Our money's all been spent, I guess that's so, so we don't have a pot, but at least I'm sure of all the things we got, Babe, I got you babe, I got you babe," trilled Cher, *"I got flowers in the spring, I got you to wear my ring, and when I'm sad, you're a clown and if I get scared, you're always around"*

Hattie gripped Felix's hand tighter, her eyes shining, as she heard the audience applaud madly when Leo and Seb pranced in. Seb was wearing the most outrageous white tails with a canary yellow, spotted cravat. More camp than the caravan club, he was loving every second of the attention. Leo was more sober and traditional but indulging him outrageously as they held their entwined hands aloft and he brought Seb's hand softly to his lips for everyone to witness. Seb, fairly skipping and whooping along beside him was waving to everyone with his free hand.

"Don't let them say your hair's too long, 'cause I don't care, with you I can't go wrong, then put your little hand in mine, there aint no hill or mountain we can't climb, babe. I got you babe"

The happy couples stood together at the make shift altar as Sony and Cher came to their last verse. *"I got you to hold my hand, I got you to understand, I got you to walk with me, I got you to talk with me, I got you to kiss good night, I got you to hold me tight, I got I won't let go, I got you to love me so. I got you babe."*

The vicar harrumphed and cleared his throat, welcoming everyone in much the same way as Dougie, barring his voice was soulful, and began the serious business of the blessing. The room fell appropriately silent whilst the abridged ceremony took place, shortened and adjusted as it was not taking place in the sanctity of church, but inviting the congregation to make appropriate responses and finishing with the Lord's Prayer.

The newly-weds turned and faced their friends and family, linking hands and smiling, and simultaneously gave a deep bow, much to the huge applause of the audience.

Dougie called for their attention, clapping his hands, and everyone fell silent again. "I am sure Hattie, Felix, Seb and Leo," he turned seriously to face the newly-weds, "all of your friends offer you their heartfelt congratulations, and," he turned to the congregation, "I ask you all to raise your glasses to the happy couples!"

"The happy couples!" shouted a plethora of voices, "congratulations!" A cacophony of shouts reverberated around the marquee, accompanied by whoops of delight and cat calling.

Dougie put his hand up once more for silence. "And my dear children, to play you to your table, Dulcie and Frankie are going to serenade you." With a wild theatrical gesture, he threw his hands to one side to reveal the two sisters, who like two peas in a pod, stood nervously with mikes in their hands. Nancy queued in the music and struck up the chords of the old familiar Shania Twain song "*You're still the one.*" The girls nodded, smiling to each other, tapping their toes and swinging their hips.

Dulcie began, speaking at first rather than singing, "*When I first saw you, I saw love, and the first time you touched me I felt love, and after all this time, you're still the one I love.*"

The music tempo changed and Frankie swung into song, her beautiful, clear voice ringing out around the marquee, "*looks like we made, look how far we've come my baby, we might have took the long way, we knew we'd get here someday, they said, "I bet they'll never make it", but just look at us holding on, we're still together still going strong.*"

Dougie, Nancy, and Theo, in various parts of the marquee, held up massive prompt cards with the words, whilst Dulcie roused the audience to join in the chorus and soon everyone was singing along "*You're still the one I run to, the one that I belong to, you're still the one I want for life, still the one. You're still the one that I love, the only one I dream of, you're still the one I kiss good night.*"

Frankie continued alone in her sultry, solo voice, "*aint nothing better, we beat the odds together, I'm glad we didn't listen, look at what we would be missin', They said "I bet they'll never make it", but just look at us holding on, together still going strong.*"

The final chorus, with everyone singing madly was uproarious and the applause deafening as the fab four made their way through the crowds to their table. They stopped to speak to people en-route, the men pumping hands; Seb theatrically air kissing everyone like a thing demented, until Leo laughingly dragged him on. Felix grasped Hattie's hand, his eyes blistering into hers. The smiles on their faces said it all. It was true, against all the odds, they had made it and they had so much more fun to come.

EPILOGUE

Max's solicitor, Caleb Akkerman, was toiling through the enormity of his estate. The house in Fittlebury, his docklands flat, several other residences he owned but had never lived in, both in this country and abroad, the clubs, the brothels, the casinos, the massive investments, the offshore accounts. It amounted to millions. The funeral still had not been sorted out as Caleb searched for his next of kin. Just before his death, Max had informed him about his daughter, living in Paris and had altered his will, as, other than some substantial gratuities to his loyal friends, he had left his entire estate to her. When he'd tried to contact the girl at the address Max had given to them, it seemed she'd moved on and they were having trouble locating her, as she'd left no forwarding address. After copious searching through Max's personal belongings, a paper trail had led Caleb to Nigel Brown. It was monotonous and time consuming, and the legal wheels moved tediously slowly. Meanwhile Max lay waxy white on ice in the funeral parlour awaiting the instructions of his daughter and his last resting place. Although the assets were as frozen as Max, the clubs and businesses continued to work, as did the rest of his empire, in the vice like grip of his second-in command Terry, whom he had wisely named should take control, if anything happen to him. It was a shaky limbo as his shady solicitor took control to conserve his assets and find the girl.

Nigel Brown was shocked to find that the short-tempered man whom he'd only known as Mr Cutter was, in reality, Max Goldsmith, infamously one of the most dangerous men in London. He reasoned he was lucky to have got away with as much as he had, without having his legs broken. At first, when the East End solicitor had contacted him, he'd had no idea what he was talking about, but then it had clicked and he realised that, of course, Max had used Cutter as an alias. The girl he'd found in Paris would be heir to that fucking huge fortune, even if it was made by ill gotten gains, and if he, Nigel, was lucky he could still have a portion of it. He strung the solicitor along, feigning that he'd have to consult his notes and that he'd ring him the next day with more information. In truth, Nigel knew exactly where the girl was.

As Brown beat a far too hasty retreat with a greedy gleam in his eye,

Caleb shook his head sadly and picked up the phone. Terry answered on the first ring. "Our man is stalling, he knows where she is. Can I leave it to you my boy? I'm too old for this sort of thing."

"Fucking bastard," grumbled Terry angrily, "are there no values left in this world, Max is dead for fuck's sake. Is there no honour?"

Caleb smiled at the irony of the remark, this from a man who had no moral values at all. "I know my son, I know. But we do need to find her, so tread carefully eh?"

"Yeah right, I will. I'll do the job meself."

"Don't take any risks, I can't afford to lose *you*," warned Caleb, wearily scratching his bald pate, "there's enough of a muddle as it is, and plenty'd move in if anything happened to you."

"Don't worry about me, plenty 've tried and failed," laughed Terry ruefully, "I'm not ready for me box yet."

"I don't suppose Max was either. Dreadful business, dreadful. I'm still in shock about it."

"Don't worry Caleb, once the bint that did for Max gets put away, and she will, her life won't be worth living, I swear to you. She'll beg to be dead - I promise you."

"Oh Terry, you never let it rest do you? I'd hate to get on the wrong side of you," Caleb sighed, "you're a ruthless fucker when you're roused"

"Yeah I am Caleb, Max's killer will be punished the old fashioned way. Pity I can't do it meself."

"Well go find his kid, and sort out this Brown character and let's lay Max to rest - poor bugger."

Nigel knew exactly where she would be. It was as easy as pissing. He'd found her with no trouble in the first place, by chatting up the grandparents, even though Cutter had warned him off them. He'd got her address though, tracing her to an old apartment in one of the crooked streets that ran like gnarled veins in the bohemian part of Paris. He'd lingered outside and, then surreptitiously bumped into her in the Boulangerie just around the corner. Pretending to have difficulty speaking French, she'd kindly helped by translating what he'd wanted and they'd struck up a conversation. After that, he'd offered to buy her an espresso to say thank you. It has just progressed from there, with him pretending to know Oxford and the area where her grandparents lived. She said she'd been working in one of the fashion houses, literally as a tea girl, hoping to make her way into the design suites, but it was a hard industry to crack and she was sick of being the English dog's body. She'd been really excited as now she'd landed a really good job in the Pierre Cardin Museum, which moved from St-Ouen to the north side of the Seine the previous November. The only downside was it meant that she'd had to move herself from the trendy part of Paris, which she adored, nearer to work, but she considered it was worth it for the career move. Nigel had thanked her for her help and they'd said goodbye. Nigel had reported back to Cutter, with a photograph, her name and where she lived. He got paid and that was that. Now, with Cutter dead, and the old Jewish solicitor anxious to trace the girl, it must be worth his while to find her first, and then ask for a hefty finder's fee and he knew exactly where she'd be. He fairly ran back to his flat, packed an overnight bag - just in case, and made his way to St Pancras. He was so intent on what he was doing he didn't spot the huge man and his mate in their short leather coats watching his every move.

    The Eurostar pulled into Paris Gare Du Nord spot on time, just two and a quarter hours after leaving London. Nigel pulled down his overnight bag and checked his wallet. He just wanted to make sure that the girl was working where she said she was, that was all he needed to do. He had no idea where she lived now, but if he could trace her to the Pierre Cardin Museum that would be enough. He could report back to the solicitor, get his money and bow out all the richer. He checked his watch. If he hurried he could be across to *Rambuteau* on Metro Line 11 in about 20 minutes and walk to the museum. The Pierre Cardin wasn't that large, and if she was there, he was bound to spot her.

    Terry pushed up his glasses, nodded to his accomplice Sam, who had become Terry's own second-in command, and they followed, keeping a safe distance behind the pudgy figure of Nigel. They needn't have worried about him spotting them, Brown was hell bent on his mission and had no idea they were behind him. The other passengers surged onto the skinny, blue and white metro train as it pitched into the station, lurching to a stop with a jolt, taking Nigel and his stalkers with it, pell-mell towards *Rambuteau*. The stations rattled past disgorging passengers, with Nigel glancing at his watch in agitation at every stop.

    At *Rambuteau*, Nigel got off and looked uncertainly around him for signposts to the museum. Terry stopped too, turning his back for a moment, pretending to be on the phone, in reality watching Nigel in the mirrored screen. When he moved off, they followed at a discreet distance, stopping in doorways, and lighting multitudes of fags to dally behind him but kept Nigel under close observation, becoming keenly interested as he turned into the Pierre Cardin Museum.

Nigel paid his admission, but barely paid any attention to the exhibits, his eyes scanning the assistants for any sign of the girl - but he couldn't see her. He trailed dispiritedly under the enormous, glass-domed roof of the museum, where innate mannequins displayed iconic and emblematic selections of the couturier's designs, but it was all lost on Nigel as he searched for Max's daughter. Terry and Sam too had no eye for design as they paid their entrance fee, although they pretended to be engrossed, but in reality, they only had eyes for Nigel. An English voice rang out from a group of students, a girl's voice, and Nigel spun around, it was her, definitely her. His face creased into smiles of elation. He stared again; yes, he was certain, it was definitely her. Terry caught his animated look and glanced over at the girl speaking in English and then, he too, started to grin. There was no doubt that it was her, he plucked out the photograph the old solicitor had given him, but he was certain. She was talking to a group, vivaciously discussing the merits of the design, laughing and joking. Terry could see shades of Max in her, his gestures, his eyes, his hair, everything about her smacked of Max. There could be no doubt, even without the photograph. He turned to Sam and smiled, nodding his head in satisfaction. Nigel Brown, too, was satisfied. He turned on his tail and walked out of the museum heading for the metro and the Eurotunnel for home and the big bucks coming his way when he divulged to the old solicitor the whereabouts of Max's daughter.

At the Gard du Nord, the trains were coming in thick and fast. The Paris rush hour was hot and furious. The chic Parisians, their noses skyward and attitudes flying higher than any kites, were struggling to gain ascendency on the platforms. Elbows digging with gusto in the mêlée, Nigel struggled off his train. Close behind him came Terry and Sam, sunglasses and caps pulled down. With lightning speed, they lifted the stumpy, little man by his elbows clean off his feet and hoisted him towards the opposite platform, just as another train rattled towards the platform. They hurled Nigel with relish under the approaching train wheels, as a wave of thrusting passengers surged forwards to force themselves aboard the train. Nigel, hardly comprehending what was happening, gave a strangled cry as he fell, the train pummelled over the top of his jerking body. Terry and Sam, smiled to each other and melted anonymously into the crowd, dispensing with the glasses and caps. Regretfully shoving their leather jackets into a nearby bin and donning sweat shirts from their rucksacks, they ruffled their hair, and made their way back towards the Eurostar. Job done.

Two weeks later, Caleb Akkerman had written to Max's daughter, informing her that she may possibly be the beneficiary of a large estate and inviting her to come to London to meet him. Now he was anxiously waiting to meet her for a scheduled ten o'clock appointment. As the clock struck the hour, he considered what this would mean to the girl. She would inherit a vast fortune from a father she had never known. As far as he could tell, she had never known what it was to have money either, not seriously real money. For her, life was to change in a big way. He wondered if she would take his advice on how to proceed. Only time would tell. Terry, in the meantime, continued to manage the business interests, but even without those, she would be a very wealthy woman. The old grandfather clock ticked the minutes away as he waited for her to arrive.

His secretary appraised the attractive, young woman who had arrived for the appointment with her boss. She knew how important she was and how long they had been looking for her. As the girl came into the office, her long, blonde hair swinging dramatically like a Pantene advertisement, she was reminded of a wood nymph, she was elusive and not altogether real. Her off the shoulder shirt revealed a small tattoo which the secretary found slightly distasteful, but she supposed was the norm these days. The secretary buzzed Mr Akkerman to say his client had arrived and he came out himself to welcome her.

"Now Miss .... or shall I just call you Laura?" he began searching her face.

"Laura will do just fine," she smiled at him, her face hardly betraying any emotion at all. "What's this all about?"

"Ah Laura, fine, just fine. Come in please and do sit down." Caleb waited until she had settled herself in the worn, leather chair opposite him, "I trust you had a pleasant journey."

"I did, but I'm at a loss to know what all this is about Mr Akkerman," smiled Laura, titling her head to one side and meeting the old man's gaze with a direct inquisitive look. "I understand you've discovered the identity of my father and all I know is that he has died."

Caleb sighed, he didn't quite know where to start. "Now Laura, your father - Max Goldsmith, as you correctly say, died recently in an accident. I'm sure you will have many questions, and hopefully I may be able to answer some of those for you, but not all I fear, because it was only a few days before his death, that Max found out where you were, and until that time, he did not know he had a daughter."

"You mean to say that my mother didn't tell him she was pregnant?"

"I gather not, so he had no idea until very recently about you, and when he did, he employed a private detective to track you down in France, fully intending to get to know you. Also, he immediately changed his will, and more or less, left his entire estate to you. It was a lucky thing he did, as he died a week later, the tragedy being that he never got to meet you."

"How awful," stammered Laura, "I knew nothing about him, of course. My grandparents never mentioned anything about my father. My mother never told them who he was."

Caleb sighed, trying to find a way to tell her about the enormity of the estate and decided to start simply, rather than bamboozle her with too much information at their first meeting. "Your father was an extremely wealthy man. He had a large house in a tiny village called Fittlebury in West Sussex, which he recently purchased, and that has been left to you," began Caleb, "it's a sizeable property by all accounts," he said, looking down and shuffling through a plethora of documents on his desk. "Let me see ... yes, here are the particulars."

Whilst the old man was occupied with his paper work, Laura's face drained of colour as though someone had pulled a plug. She quaked inwardly at the mention of Fittlebury, the very mention of the fated place that she had tried so desperately to obliterate from her memory. An icy prickle of dread made her feel sickenly faint; her clammy hands clutched anxiously at the fabric of her skirt; her eyes darted desperately from side to side as those terrible recollections skittered frantically in her mind, like a loose horse in the Grand National, tumbling her back to the catastrophic events of the previous year. A nauseous fear seeped through her body, as she recalled her rollercoaster relationship with the maniacal Jonty and how she'd jumped ship just in time, managing to catch the Eurostar and run away to France, terrified of being caught and being implicated in what'd had happened in the kidnap of Jennifer Parker-Smythe and her step-daughter at the old mill. Jonty, who had played such a manipulative, controlling part in her life whilst she was at college, and whom she now realised had been a calculating sociopath. Her mind rocketed back to the humiliating memories of how he had subjected her to sexual deviations which, at the time, she'd found exciting yet increasingly bizarre and disturbing. Of course, all along, she'd know he was into all sorts, drugs mainly, but she'd kept out of it. When after her one-off encounter with Charles Parker-Smythe, and furiously she'd naively been so intent on seeking revenge, Jonty had become particularly interested. He'd used her, encouraged her *'to get her own back'*. Even persuading her to inveigle fanatical hunt saboteurs to use in his plan. She had been his pawn. All along Jonty had been scheming to kidnap Charles' wife, Jennifer and step children, and would stop at nothing, including multiple murder. The tragedy was, she - Laura, had never known the whole story; he had kept her in the dark. Under his controlling spell, she had gone along with it all. Only later finding out that he had murdered so many people in his greed and thirst for money. She had been lucky to make her own escape. He would probably have killed her too, if he'd had the chance.

"Laura, my dear? Are you alright?" asked Caleb concernedly, believing her reaction was about Max, "you look unwell. I am so dreadfully sorry about your father, this has obviously been a terrible shock for you. Would you like a glass of water?"

"No," replied Laura, swallowing hard, marginally managing to recover herself. She forced herself to rally, her voice clear and determined. "I'm fine honestly," she faltered momentarily. "A house in Fittlebury, how perfectly lovely. I've heard that's a beautiful part of the world, I'll look forward to living there," she said, without betraying the salad of mixed emotions churning relentlessly inside her. She struggled frantically to collect her thoughts, determined not to allow the disruptive feelings to erupt like some timeless volcano and spill out in an incoherent mess before this benign old man. Laura summoned a sweet smile for Caleb, she knew that for her, the story certainly hadn't ended yet.

The End... or maybe not...

ABOUT THE AUTHOR

P J King was brought up in the country, on a small farm. Her father was a horse dealer and she could ride before she could walk! Despite her rural upbringing and love of horses, she decided to pursue a career on the front line of an acute psychiatric hospital with a multi-disciplinary medical team. After some years, the innate draw and passion for horses lured her back, and she is now a dressage trainer, judge and sports psychologist, living on her own stud farm in the South East of England. She is married with three grown-up children, and has a host of horses and dogs, together with the inevitable uniform of Hunter wellies and Barbours, and the most long suffering and tolerant husband! Drawing upon her own life experiences in the medical and equine industry, she decided to write about what she knew best, and to recreate some of the wonderful (or otherwise!) characters that she has met and, weave them into a series of stories centred around the fictional village of Fittlebury. **Big Bucks,** is the second book in this series. The first, **Rough Ride,** published in 2013 is available on Amazon.co.uk in ebook format, paperback and audio book.

Find out more about P.J King

http://www.pjkingauthor.co.uk/

https://twitter.compjking.author

https://www.facebook.com/rough.pjking

Printed in Great Britain
by Amazon